TEVYE
IN THE PROMISED LAND

"The Jews of Anatevka have three days to clear out of the area."

Thus begins Tevye's unforgettable journey to the Promised Land. Tzvi Fishman's stirring family saga of the continuing adventures of Sholom Aleichem's beloved character, Tevye the Milkman, immortalized in "Fiddler in the Roof," takes up where the original stories left off.

At a crossroads at the outskirts of their Anatevka village, Tevye and his daughters meet up with a troupe of Zionists headed for Palestine. Just then, as if the Almighty is pointing the way, the Anatevka mailman comes running with a letter from Tevye's long-lost daughter, Hodel. Her communist husband, Perchik, has been exiled from Russia, and they are living in the Holy Land on a non-religious kibbutz!

Clinging to the Bible and the tradition he loves, Tevye has to defend his daughters, not only against the modern lifestyle of the Zionist pioneers, but against malaria-infested swamps, deadly plagues, swarms of locusts, Turkish prisons, and Arab marauders. With steadfast determination and faith, Tevye perseveres through trials and hardships in rebuilding the Jewish homeland. While trying to do his best as a father in marrying off his daughter's to suitable husbands, Tevye himself finds a new bride to take the place of his deeply-missed Golda. Finally, as World War One threatens to destroy the Jewish settlements in Palestine, Tevye joins the first Jewish fighting brigade since the days of Bar Kochba and Rabbi Akiva. In a daring secret mission, he helps the British rout the Turks.

Filled with laughter, heartbreak, and joy, **"Tevye in the Promised Land"** is the compelling story of a people's rebirth, and a triumph of inspiration and faith.

TEVYE
IN THE
PROMISED LAND

SUGGESTED BY THE
SHOLOM ALEICHEM CHARACTERS
TEVYE THE MILKMAN AND HIS DAUGHTERS

Tzvi Fishman

Shorashim • Jerusalem

Computer typesetting and layout: Moshe Kaplan

Shorashim
19 Shoshana St.
Jerusalem, Israel 96149

For my wife
Yaffa
and my children
Yehuda, David, Noam, Sarah, Benyamin,
Amichai, and Matanel
and for so many more…
the millions of Jews who perished
without ever seeing the Holy Land,
and for all those who died in the
struggle to rebuild it.

With heartfelt thanks to the Almighty for enabling me to write this book; to my wife for her patience and love; to my parents for their unending support; to Uncle Al for his encouragement and faith; and to Rabbi Moshe Kaplan and David Fein for their dedicated work in getting the book ready for printing.

Author's Preface

The stories of Sholom Aleichem stand as masterpieces of Yiddish literature. Like a gifted artist, he painted his characters with a rich palette of colors. His Tevye lives on in the imagination, defying all duplication. Therefore, before beginning, the reader will have to excuse the present writer's inadequacies and make do with the miniature Tevye which he has fashioned. However, if even a small part of this saga survives in the memory, then we are certain that Sholom Aleichem himself would be pleased and would forgive the liberties which the writer has taken with the lives he has created. Different times and different challenges bring out different qualities in people. Just as the Jewish People have undergone a transformation in the last hundred years, so too has Tevye. From being oppressed and downtrodden wanderers, without a permanent home of their own, the Jewish People, and Tevye with them, have struggled to achieve a new hope, stature, and independence in the Promised Land.

Many of the events in this novel were created around historical events which make up the background canvas for this saga. While inspired by the characters in the Sholom Aleichem stories, "Tevye the Milkman," all of the characters are the invention of the author, and are entirely fictional. Exceptions are the public figures, such as Rabbi Kook and Baron Rothschild, who lived at the time, and whose portraits in the novel, while embellished with fiction, have been made a part of the story. To aid the reader, a glossary of Yiddish and Hebrew terms can be found at the end of the book.

Contents

Contents

Now the Lord said to Abraham, get thee out of thy country, and away from thy place of birth, and away from thy father's house, to the Land that I will show thee; and I will make of thee a great nation, and I will bless thee, and make thy name great.

Genesis, 12:1-2

If thy outcasts be scattered at the upmost parts of heaven, from there will the Lord your God gather thee, and from there will he fetch thee; and the Lord thy God will bring thee into the Land which thy fathers possessed, and thou shall possess it.

Deuteronomy, 30:4-5

TEVYE
IN THE
PROMISED LAND

Chapter One

ANATEVKA

Nemerov, the district Police Commissioner, reared his horse in the air.

"Three days," he warned. "The Jews of Anatevka have three days to clear out of the area."

Tevye spat in disgust at the ground. "Three days," he brooded. Three days were all the authorities were giving the Jews to sell their belongings and evacuate the village they loved.

It didn't matter that the Jews had lived in Anatevka long before the Russians. The Police Commissioner didn't care that Tevye's great-grandfather, may his memory be a blessing, had cleared the forest by the lake and built the first house in the region. It didn't matter to the Czar and his soldiers that for as long as anyone could remember, the Jews had dutifully paid the taxes which had laden the Czar's table with food, while the pantries of the Jews remained bare. Nor did it matter to them that the Jews had cleaned out the stables of the Russian landowners, chopped their wood, sewed their garments, and delivered their milk. It didn't matter that a Jew would bow in respect when a Russian passed by, just to keep peace. Nor did it matter to them that the decent folk of Anatevka had no other place to call home. They were Jews, and that was that. The Czar, may he and his loved ones be cursed, had made his decision in the interests of the motherland. His order was final. The Jews had three days to get out. The butchers, bakers, and candlestick makers of Anatevka had been declared enemies of the state.

The usually goodhearted milkman spat in anger as the Police Commissioner and his soldiers rode out of the village. Then he looked up at the heavens and prayed.

"My Father and King, Whose ways are perfect and just, and Who does only good to His people – even if we can't understand Your kindness in throwing us out of our homes – after the Jews of Anatevka have journeyed to some faraway land, may the Czar and his Cossacks be swallowed up into the earth."

Not that all Russians were as wicked as the Czar and his soldiers. After all, the same God had created all people, Jews and Russians alike. Loving God meant loving all of His creation. But sometimes, it wasn't so easy. When someone kicks you out of your home, and treats you like dirt, it's hard for a man to be grateful.

Where would they go? Tevye didn't know. To Broditchov, in a distant part of Russia, where the pogroms had not yet struck? To America? To Poland? To the Land of Israel? To England? Or France? Tevye didn't have time to think up a plan. He would simply go along with everyone else in his village, wherever the Almighty led them. After all, had Abraham known his destination when God told him to leave his birthplace for some faraway land? As the Torah says, "And Abraham believed!" He trusted in God. Without complaining, he packed up his belongings and went.

Tevye's head kept spinning like it did when he drank too much vodka on Purim. There were so many things to arrange. How do you pack a lifetime into three days? Maybe he should have pulled the Police Commissioner off of his horse and given him a good thrashing. Maybe he should have rallied the Jews to rebellion. But what would that have accomplished? Reports of pogroms had reached them from all over Russia. Burnings, lootings, evacuations, the slaughter of innocent women and children. Just because they were Jews. How could they rebel? Did the Jews have an army? Did they have weapons with which they could fight? Was Tevye Judah the Maccabee, that he could rally people to follow him? What kind of resistance could the lowly Jews muster?

Tevye trudged back to his tiny castle, the home he had built long ago with more youthful hands. Was a house merely pieces of wood that a man could so easily sell it? What about all of the years, the memories, the joys, and the sorrows? True, Tevye thought, he could have survived just as well without all of the sorrows, but that was the life of a Jew. There were good times and bad. A house could be sold, but what about all of the memories engraved in the planks of the walls? Well, he supposed he could take his memories with him.

His daughters, Tzeitl, Bat Sheva, and Ruchel, stared at him as he sank into his chair. They had witnessed the degrading spectacle from the doorway of the house. They had watched the Commissioner rear his horse and almost knock their father down when Tevye had grabbed the stallion's reins in an effort to plead for his people.

"Where will we go?" Tzeitl asked.

"Where the Almighty leads us," Tevye answered.

"What will we do when we get there?" Bat Sheva, the youngest, inquired.

"What the Almighty decrees."

"Who will buy our house?" Tzeitl continued. Her two small children, Moishe and Hannie, ran over to hug her. They gazed up at their grandfather with big, searching eyes.

Tevye didn't have an answer.

"Is it true, *Tata*," Ruchel said. "Do we really have to leave Anatevka?"

Their questions were giving him a headache.

"Am I the Almighty?" he asked, slamming a hand on the table. "Do I decide what will be in the world? Do I stand in the place of the Creator that I know His secret plans?"

Tevye stood up from his chair. In painful situations, a father had to appear confident. When the ship was sinking, the captain had to keep firm command. In times of crisis, children needed the example of a father's unwavering faith.

"Enough pointless chatter," he said. "Haven't our Sages warned us that a man who talks at length with women brings calamity down on his head? The Almighty will provide for us, just as he has for the last four-thousand years. Pack up what you need for a journey. The rest I will sell in the city. In the meantime, your father has important business which he needs to transact."

In the barn, Tevye saddled his horse. He didn't have the heart to tell the creature the news. They had been companions through rainstorms and blizzards, through famine and blight. Together, they had shared life's burdens for thousands of miles. The old mare had been as faithful to him as his wife.

"*Oy* Golda," Tevye said, sighing at her memory. "May your soul rest in peace."

Finally, he understood why God, in His kindness, had taken Golda away from him while she was still in the prime of her life. To spare her the humiliation of being chased out of her house by the soldiers of the Czar.

In his crestfallen state, the journey into Yehupetz seemed to take longer than usual. Tevye's horse must have thought it strange to travel such a long distance in silence, but Tevye was not in the mood for conversation. His thoughts were so jumbled, his usual erudition escaped him. A lone verse of King David's Psalms echoed in his thoughts: "Some with chariots, and some with horses, but we in the name of the Lord our God call out." There was some consolation in that. Even if the authorities took away his house, his wagon, and even his horse, Tevye would still have his God.

Luckily, the milkman's *mazel* was with him. The tax collector agreed to buy Tevye's house. Out of all the Russians Tevye knew, the tax collector, Karamozky, was the man he most trusted. Like clockwork, every three months, on the first day of the week, the punctual civil servant would arrive in Anatevka. After paying his village taxes, Tevye would invite him for a drink in his house. The tax collector seemed to enjoy Tevye's discourses on the Bible, and Tevye cherished nothing more than drinking with someone who was willing to listen. Golda was less enthused.

"It's not your wisdom he likes," she said. "It's your vodka."

Like the experienced salesman he was, Tevye set forth the advantages of buying the house as if it were a splendid estate. The tax collector himself could testify to its sturdy construction. Hadn't he sat there himself, a guest of the family, year after year, through winter snowstorms and the summer's scorching sun? Tevye even advised Karamozky to buy six or seven houses in Anatevka. That way he would become a principle investor in the village, like a baron with properties all over town. Finally, Tevye begged him.

"If not for me, your devoted milkman, then for my daughters."

What was left of his daughters, Tevye mused. On the road back to Anatevka, waves of pent-up sorrow poured out of Tevye's heart. The milkman, had been known for his beautiful daughters. Seven more radiant creations could not be found. Their graces were praised all over the Pale. "Vanity of vanity, says Tevye, all is vanity." What did their beauty bring except endless trouble? Did not the wise Solomon teach, "Grace is deceptive, and beauty is vain – a woman who fears the Lord is the one to be praised?" It would have been better if his daughters had all looked like him, with his big *shnoz* of a nose, and not like his beautiful Golda. Not that Tevye was complaining. After all, who is a man to complain? Doesn't everything he have belong to his Maker? As it says, "The Lord giveth, and the Lord takes away."

What could a father do? He had tried to raise his seven daughters in the traditions of his people. Like the four legs which hold up a table, there were four pillars to every good Jewish home. The honor due the father and mother; the honor due the Sabbath; the honor of Torah; and the honor of God.

But modern times had crept in, and newfangled notions, like termites, had begun to eat away the foundations of the past. First, Tzeitl wanted to pick her own husband. The match her father had arranged with Lazar Wolf, the butcher, wasn't to her fancy! She was in love with the poor tailor, Motel! In love! What did his daughter know about love? Living with a woman for twenty-five years – that was love. When you worked all day like a slave, and came home smelling like your horse, and your wife opened her arms to you and clung to you in the night, even though you didn't know if there would be food to feed another child – that was love. Not the beating of the heart that comes from a walk through the woods.

"But I love him!" Tzeitl had pleaded, with tears in her eyes.

What was Tevye to do? Was his heart made out of stone? Besides, Motel was a good boy. A bumbling *shlemiel* of the highest order, that was for sure, but he could read from a prayerbook, and it was certain from the way he looked at Tzeitl that he would burn their candles down to the wick, sewing garments all through the night to provide a decent life for Tevye's daughter.

But as the saying goes – when the milk begins to go sour, it soon begins to stink. His second daughter, Hodel, was even more of a beauty. Her features were stately, like the portrait of a queen hanging on an aristocrat's wall. Her flight from the nest had been Tevye's own fault. He himself had brought the free-thinking Perchik into their home to teach her to read. While the father was in the barn, milking his cows, the young revolutionist was in the house, milking his daughter's dreams.

"A new Russia! A classless society! A worker's state! Equality for all!" the young communist preached.

Tevye got headaches listening to his speeches, but to Hodel, he was a prince on a gleaming white steed. And his stock only went up with the girl when he was arrested. The memory haunted Tevye even now – the picture of Hodel standing at the railroad station, waiting for the train which would take her away to her Perchik in exile on the other side of the Pale. What a long wagon-ride home it had been for Tevye, not knowing if he would ever see his beautiful daughter again!

But at least Perchik had been a Jew. Tevye and Golda could thank God for that. A Jew with his head screwed on backwards, but a circumcised member of Abraham's faith. Their third daughter, Hava, hadn't been so lucky. In Tevye's mind, she was dead. His third daughter had ceased to exist. When she ran off with the poet, Hevedke Galagan, that was the end. Here the line had to be drawn. Hodel's sister's marriage to the heretic Perchik was a tragedy which had to be mourned, but there was always the chance that the Almighty would hear Tevye's prayers and open the misguided youth's heart to the Torah. But that a heathen poet should marry his daughter? To allow such a breach would mark the doom of his people. It was a rejection of Tevye's whole life, of everything he had ever believed. A gentile was a gentile, and a Jew was a Jew. The two shall not come together in marriage. When a priest informed Tevye of the secret elopement, Tevye ripped his shirt in anguish, the sign of mourning, as if his daughter were dead. He tore her memory out of his heart. The name, Hava, was never, ever, to be mentioned in his house!

You would think that a milkman had been punished enough for his sins. But the Almighty was only beginning. Oy, Shprintza, Shprintza, my pretty little bird, thought Tevye, as his horse automatically stopped by the lake. Tevye recalled the scene as if it were yesterday. The crowd of people. The running. The screams. With a voice of doom in his heart, Tevye had jumped down from his wagon. The crowd made way as he bent down by the girl's body. Shprintza, drowned! Heartbroken over the suitor whom Tevye had brought to the house. The wealthy Aaronchik had stolen the tender girl's heart, and then disappeared like a thief, may both he and his mother be drowned!

The shock proved too much for Golda. A more valorous woman never existed, but after Shprintza died, a part of Golda went with her. The light in Golda's eyes seemed to flicker and fade. Tevye brought her flowers and a new dress from the best boutique in Yehupetz, but nothing could lessen her pain.

"Why did you squander our money?" she asked. "Couldn't I have sewn a dress just as pretty?"

That was his Golda. That was why he loved her. Tevye spoke soothing words, sang happy songs, and even romanced her with a dance around the table, but nothing could bring her out of her mourning. One tragedy after another proved too much for her heart. Hodel had left home to follow her Communist into exile. Hava had run away with a sweet-talking Chekhov. And now Shprintza had drowned. The strong Golda simply shattered like crystal. Late one evening, Tevye came home from work and found his wife sprawled dead on the floor.

Why had King David composed his Psalms if not to help mortal man find strength in trying times like these? As the Rabbis teach, God's ways are not our ways. Who is a milkman to understand the mysteries of heaven and earth? With every tragedy, the sun still rises in the morning, the rooster crows, the Jew has his prayers, the cows must be milked. In short, life must go on.

And where was Baylke, the most beautiful rose of Tevye's bouquet? Already in America, with her good-for-nothing Pedhotzer. Who could have foretold it? Before her wedding, Baylke was certain she had found the key to the Garden of Eden on earth. And so, to be truthful, had Tevye. Wasn't Pedhotzer fantastically wealthy? A builder of houses, bridges, and roads. His house was a castle. His yard an estate. He had two silver carriages, with a team of Arabian horses for each. People said there was a servant in every room in his mansion. Even his ashtrays were gold. Tevye knew. He saw them himself, on the day Pedhotzer summoned him to appear at his home.

The extraordinary invitation came several months after the wedding. Tevye had not seen his little girl since the happy, regal affair. Finally, a messenger arrived with a call from her king. Pedhotzer wanted to see him. Finally, Tevye thought, his fortune was changing. His daughter had not forgotten her poor, aging father. Surely she had secured him a job of prestige and authority, with a servant, a driver, elegant new clothes, and summer vacations at Boiberik Lake with all of the other rich Jews from the city.

"Tevye," he said. "I know I can talk straightforwardly with you, because I know you are an honest man. You know I am wealthy, and I intend to give your daughter all of the treasures on earth. I have been informed from very private sources that the great Baron Edmond de Rothschild is interested in doing business with me. In fact, I expect him to come for a visit to our house very soon."

Tevye was anxiously waiting to hear the fantastic job offer.

"Tell me," his new son-in-law continued, "how do you think the Baron would react if he heard that my wife's father is a milkman?"

He said the word milkman as if it were something disgusting. Baylke stood by his side, looking like royalty in a dress the likes of which Tevye's poor Golda had never even seen in her dreams.

"That is why I think it would be better for everyone if you were to take a long trip to *Eretz Yisrael*. I'll pay all of your travel expenses, of course, and even help get you started in a business if you decide you want to stay there."

Tevye felt as if a demon had snuck up behind him and stuck a knife in his back. Pedhotzer wanted to send him away to the Land of Israel! And Baylke, his warmhearted Baylke, stood silently at her rich husband's side, staring at her father with a gaze as cold as a winter day. What had happened to her? What had transformed his sweet, loving princess into such a statue-like queen?

As Tevye's friend, Sholom Aleichem, would say, to make a long story short, money is not always a blessing. Carrying his wounded pride as nobly as he could, Tevye made his way to the door of the mansion. As things turned out, that was the closest he had gotten to Jerusalem. The winds of revolution in Russia changed the future for everyone. Suddenly, Pedhotzer's government contracts were canceled. His fortunes plunged. His building empire collapsed. Baron Rothschild found a different partner. Almost overnight, Pedhotzer was penniless. Baylke had to sell her silk dresses and furs to help buy them passage to America. Her husband was humiliated, just as he had humiliated Tevye. Measure for measure, the wise Rabbis teach. The doings of man do not go unnoticed. An Eye sees, and a Hand records. Not that Tevye felt any great satisfaction. True, his insult had been repaid, but at the expense of his daughter. Who knew if he would ever see his Baylke again?

At least Tevye still had his babies, Bat Sheva and Ruchel, to comfort him in his solitude. Both were as pretty as their sisters. They had not yet found husbands, though their turn under the wedding canopy had come. No doubt they had postponed their own happiness to look after their poor, widowed father. Not that Tevye needed any special attention. After all, he was a man, not a horse. But that was the nature of his daughters. They were kindhearted, just like their mother had been.

Not only were Bat Sheva and Ruchel still with him, but Tzeitl, the eldest, had returned to Tevye's house after her poor tailor of a husband dropped dead. Motel was taken from the world by the croup, his reward for mending clothes night and day in his damp basement workroom, in order to buy a decent piece of meat to honor the Sabbath.

Tevye laughed. Joke of all jokes. All of a sudden, with Motel's untimely departure, grandfather Tevye, the "*Zaida*" became Tevye the "*Tata*" the substitute father for Tzeitl's two little demons, Moishe and Hannie. Just when the old stud had been whipped and broken, when his legs barely could walk, and his heart could no longer pull the load of the wagon, when his horse had a nail in its shoe, just when he longed to be put out to pasture, Tevye became a father for Tzeitl's two wild little *kinderlach*!

"Not so fast, Tevye," God seemed to be saying. "You think I have no more surprises in store? You think your mission on earth is completed? No, no, my precious Tevye – your adventure is only beginning!"

After all, wasn't Rabbi Akiva forty years old when he started learning Torah? And wasn't Moses eighty years old when God first spoke to him in the wilderness? And wasn't Abraham 100 years old when Sarah gave birth to Isaac? For the Jews, the people of miracles, life was always just beginning. Who knew what tomorrow would bring? Tevye was not even allowed to feel sorry for himself, which was the only real luxury a poor man had. The Almighty had many more tricks up His sleeve!

He was at home, making last preparations for their departure from Anatevka when Tzeitl told him she had a surprise.

"A surprise," he asked? "What kind of surprise?"

"Please, *Tata*," she said, "Give her a chance."

Give who a chance, Tevye wondered? Tzeitl opened the door to the bedroom and who was standing there? A dybbuk? A ghost? No. It was Tevye's dead daughter, Hava! His beloved Hava who had run off with the Russian poet, Hevedke.

"*Tata*," she cried. "*Tata*!"

Before Tevye could react, his daughter rushed forward and threw herself in his lap. "*Tata*, forgive me," she tearfully pleaded. "Forgive me!"

"Who am I to forgive?" Tevye answered. "Do I sit on God's throne? Is a milkman in charge up in Heaven? It is written in the

Torah, `A daughter of the children of Israel shall not take a husband from among the foreign nations.' I didn't make the rules. Why do you come weeping to me now?"

But in the very next moment he thought, "Is it not also written in our prayers, `Lord, Lord, God, compassionate and gracious, slow to anger and abundant in kindness and truth. Preserver of kindness for thousands of generations, forgiver of iniquity and error...?'"

Tevye stared down at his naive, errant daughter as she sobbed at his feet.

"Tevye," he asked himself. "In all fairness, are you not commanded to imitate the ways of your Creator? Just as He forgives, aren't you commanded to forgive also?"

Yet another voice asked:

"But what about Golda? What about my Golda who died of a broken heart? Can her death be forgiven? Oh, Golda, who deserved to be buried in the Tomb of the Patriarchs, in the sacred cave in Hevron next to Sarah, Rebecca, and Leah. Oh, Golda, the saint of a woman who suffered with her poor husband, the incompetent *shlimazl* of a milkman, for so many years – would she herself forgive this weeping, penitent daughter?

"She wants to come back, Tevye," he heard Golda say, as if she were standing with them in the house. "She's ashamed she didn't listen to us. She's ashamed of what the Russians are doing to the Jews. She's a good girl, Tevye. She just was confused."

Tevye glanced down at his daughter. The way she said *"Tata"* shattered Tevye's doubts. Her tears on his hands melted his long frozen heart.

"Hava," he answered. A sob shook his body. Not just any ordinary sob, but a sob of a lifetime, a sob of generations, not just the pain of Tevye the milkman, but the anguish of Jewish fathers and Anatevkas all over the world.

"Hava, my daughter," he said.

"Father," she answered, her cheeks shining with tears. Tzeitl was weeping along with little Moishe and Hannie. Bat Sheva and Ruchel were crying too. Even Tevye's horse was moved by the reunion. Hearing their sobs, he stuck his head in the window to

see what new misfortune had befallen his master. The whole
house was in tears. Only Golda was smiling. For a moment, Tevye
saw her, standing like an angel in the kitchen, gazing happily upon
her brood.

"Golda," he mumbled.

"Enough crying, my husband," she scolded. "Act like a man!"

True, Tevye thought. There was work to be done. Packing,
selling, deciding what treasures to take. But all of that tumult could
wait for the morrow. Now was the time for a hearty *L'Chaim*! A
wandering daughter had found her way home! This was no private
simcha. This was the joy of the community! The victory of
tradition! The homecoming of everyone's child, reaffirming the
ancient covenant between God and the Jews.

Tevye stood up, grabbed a bottle of vodka, and strode out to
the porch.

"My Hava's come home!" he shouted. "My Hava's come home!"

His daughters tried to stop him, but their father's happiness
was not to be bottled. He strode down the main street of the
village, yelling out the good news. People came out of their houses
to bless him with *mazal tovs* and congratulatory kisses. Tevye's joy
was infectious. The news spread through the village like the smell
of hot soup. As the Purim verse says, "The Jews had light, and
gladness, and joy!" Soon, Jews were dancing with joy in the street.
A fiddler stood on a porch, head tilted over his fiddle, filling
Anatevka with music. For the moment, Tevye and his friends
forgot the Czar's decree. A daughter had returned to the fold. Even
in an hour of danger, there was reason to give thanks. The God
of Israel was with them!

Chapter Two

GOLDA

All of that night, Tevye was unable to sleep. He rose from his bed, paced around the tiny room where his family had shared their modest meals, said a prayer over his sleeping children, and walked outside, holding his aching head from the after-effects of the vodka he had imbibed earlier in the day. The winter was ending, and the night was cold and black. Rays of moonlight shone now and again from behind a thick quilt of clouds. A thin layer of snow remained on the ground like manna, the wafers of food which God provided six days a week to the Jews in the wilderness. Tevye glanced up at the clouds.

"My God, and God of my forefathers," he said, as if speaking to someone close by. "I know you are Master of everything. I know that a blade of grass does not grow unless you give it an order. I know we are like sheep in Your hand. I know that Tevye, Your servant, is a worm and not even a man. But what great sin did I transgress that You, in Your very great kindness, are throwing me out of my house? Haven't I tried to please you all of my miserable life? Haven't I woken up before dawn to milk the cows You gave me? Haven't I trudged off to work day after day, pausing only at sunrise to don my *tefillin* and say morning prayers – just as You have commanded us in Your Torah? And though I could not always pray in a *minyan* with nine other men, and though I do not study Talmud as much as I might, haven't I always tried to be a good Jew? And for my reward, I am given three days to abandon my house and my village. Yes, I know, Tevye is not the world's biggest saint and *tzaddik*, and sometimes my neighbor's horse looks a lot healthier than mine. But what, may I ask, do You want from us here in tiny Anatevka? Instead of uprooting us from our homes, don't You have something more important to do in some other part of the world?"

Tevye walked through a familiar path in the forest. The night was as dark as the exile of the Jews from their land, but Tevye knew the path's windings by heart. How many thousands of miles had he traveled back and forth through the forest, bringing his milk products to the neighboring villages, and to Boiberik and Yehupetz, where the aristocrats lived? Usually, he would lead his horse and wagon along the main road, but when the four-legged creature was sick, Tevye would drag the cart behind him in order to delivery his fresh milk and cheeses on time. And that meant taking the less traveled path through the forest.

Now in the moonlight, he could see the Jewish cemetery. A glow seemed to shine off Golda's small tombstone. Careful not to step on Lazar Wolf, the butcher; nor Mendel, the cantor; or Shendel, the wife of the sandal maker; nor on the grave of the poor tailor, Motel, his son-in-law, Tevye walked to the only resting place his Golda had ever enjoyed.

He sighed a loud, weary sigh, a sigh of centuries, the sigh of a gypsy who has to wander on to yet another temporary home. A sob shook his body. He was not a man to break down like a woman and cry, but if he could not share his feelings with Golda, if she was not at his side to listen to his complainings, *kvetchings*, and moments of despair, where would he find the strength to carry on for the children? Hadn't she been his helpmate since the day their fathers had brought them together under the canopy of the marital *chuppah*? True, she always moaned that she had been a fool to agree to the match, yet, dutifully, she had borne the pain of seven childbirths, and raised up seven daughters. As it is written in the Holiest of Books, "And they became one flesh." She was his wife. Even in death. How could he leave her? How did he dare?

He bent down and placed a small stone on her grave, a sign that someone had visited.

"Oy, Golda, my Golda," he groaned. "Forgive me for bothering you in the middle of the night, but the whole world has turned upside down. Your Tevye does not know whether he is coming or going. Sometimes, I say to myself, Tevye, enough. You've been punished enough. Give some other milkman a chance to be chosen. It's time to join your wife, Golda. But, of course, you are right – who will look after our children?"

Tevye heard footsteps. In a graveyard, in the middle of the night, who could it be? From a distance he wasn't certain, but as the figure came closer, the bearded face became clear. It was Hershel, the sandal maker, with a shovel in his hand.

"Greetings, *Reb Yid*," he called to the milkman. "May the *Mashiach* come soon so that we may be finished with grave yards."

"Amen," Tevye answered.

"You also could not sleep?" the little Jew asked. Not that the sandal maker was short of stature, but his back was bent over from a lifetime of hammering heels.

As was his custom, whenever he could, Tevye answered with a verse of Scripture. "Like it is written, `And Achashverus, the King, could not sleep,' may his name be erased. But tell me, my friend, why are you carrying that shovel? Has somebody died, God forbid?"

"Millions of people have died, but, thank God, not anyone I know of today," came the philosopher's reply.

"*Nu?*" Tevye asked, "Why are you here?"

"What do I look like to you, some kind of animal that I would leave my beloved Shendel behind? Who knows what the Russians will make out of her bones? Perhaps a church will be built here, or a pub for their drinking."

Tevye had not thought of that possibility. What about his Golda? Did he love her less than the sandal maker loved his wife? Perish the notion.

"Where's your shovel?" Hershel asked.

For a change, Tevye was speechless.

"No matter," Hershel said. "There should be another one in the undertaker's shed. You help me, and I'll help you. That way the work will go faster."

"You plan to take her with you?" Tevye asked.

"That's right," the sandal maker answered. "Don't you?"

"Well...." Tevye stuttered.

"After all, our wives are already crated. All we have to do is load them on our wagons."

"Where are you going, if you don't mind my asking?"

"Wherever God takes me. Is it a problem for the King Who created the world to find another six feet of earth for my Shendel? Besides, haven't our Sages told us, `Change of residence, change of luck?' Maybe our *mazel* will improve. Take my shovel. I'll find another in the undertaker's shed. And hurry. The faster we work, the less we wake up the dead."

Tevye took the shovel and started to dig. The earth was hard from the winter, but after breaking through the frozen topsoil, the ground became looser below. Whoever would have dreamed of Tevye digging up his Golda, may her soul rest in peace?

"Forgive me, my queen," he beseeched, "Our good friend, *Reb* Hershel, is right. Who can tell what our friends, the Russians, might build here? How would you feel with a beer hall over your head? As it says about Laban, `And Jacob beheld the face of Laban, and behold, it was not the same towards him as before.'"

Tevye dug with all of his strength. The exhausting work helped take his mind off of his problems. Soon he reached Golda's coffin. Lovingly now, he scraped the dirt away from the wood. Then he began to dig a wide pit so he could get in the grave to lift the heavy crate out. He wasn't quite sure what he would do with her, but he was certain that *Hashem*, the Almighty, would help out. Wasn't it a *mitzvah* to prevent the desecration of the dead? And when a Jew does a good deed, the Almighty always stands ready to help.

After an hour, Tevye was finished. A short distance away, Hershel continued to stab at the earth. Tevye called him to come over. Hunchbacked, he climbed into the grave to help lift Golda's coffin. Bracing his feet in the dirt, Tevye gave a push and the box slid out of the pit. Then Tevye helped the sandal maker rescue his Shendel. After catching their breaths, they agreed that Hershel would stand guard in the cemetery while Tevye fetched his wagon. Before the morning sun had risen over the village, Tevye had picked up his precious cargo and driven it back to his barn. To make the crate seem like any other piece they were taking, he spread a large blanket over its sides to disguise its distinctly rectangular shape.

"Don't you go anywhere, my Golda," he said, patting his secret treasure. "Before you know it, we will be on our way."

Outside the barn, the sun was beginning to shine in the treetops. Tevye hurried to the house to see if his Hava had truly come home. She lay sleeping with Tzeitl's children, her blanket characteristically thrown at her feet. Tenderly, Tevye pulled the patchwork quilt up to her chin, just as he had done when she was a girl. Then, letting all of his angels sleep a little longer, he went off to the synagogue to say his morning prayers.

All of that day, Tevye ran around in circles like a slaughtered, headless chicken, selling the belongings they were leaving behind. It was no easy task to squeeze a whole lifetime into a wagon. The girls worked all day in the house. By the following morning, the packing was finished. Tevye took down the *mezuzahs* from the doorposts of his house, hoisted their last crates of memories onto his wagon, fastened the heap with a rope, and climbed aboard alongside Tzeitl and the children. Hava, Bat Sheva, and Ruchel sat in the rear with their mother's coffin. Where were they going? Only God knew. Once again, the wandering Jews were heading off to an unknown destination.

Tevye coaxed his horse into the procession of wagons. On the third day of the decree of expulsion, the caravan set off, leaving the village of Anatevka behind. Other Jews had sold their wagons and horses and were beginning the exodus on foot. Villagers bent over, carrying heavy satchels and bundles on their backs. Expressions were downcast and grim except for Tevye's smile. On that blackest of days, Tevye at least had the solace that his long-lost daughter, Hava, and his cherished Golda were traveling with him. As the great Rabbi Nachman had taught, it was a *mitzvah* to always be happy, in good times and bad. So to cheer up his family and friends, Tevye put on a smile and looked bravely out toward the future.

Chapter Three

OFF TO THE PROMISED LAND

Tevye saw him when they reached the outskirts of the village. At first he wasn't sure, but when he saw Hava keep turning her head, his suspicions proved true. It was Hevedke Galagan, the Russian who had stolen his daughter, the gentile she was supposed to have left – he was following the procession of Jews as they made their way down the bumpy dirt road.

"What's this?" he said, tugging on the reins of his horse. The wagon stopped. Tevye turned a fierce eye on his daughter.

"What?" Hava asked.

"Don't what me," Tevye roared. He started to stand up in the wagon. His hand rose threateningly up in the air.

"I swear, *Tata*," she said. "I've left him, I have. I told him I can't be his wife. But he wants to come with us. He's ashamed of his people. I told him no, it can't be, but he wants to be a Jew."

"A Jew!" Tevye roared. "A Jew! Is our life such a picnic that he wants to be a Jew!?" Tevye stared up to Heaven. "I ask you, good Lord. Isn't exile enough of a punishment? Or is Tevye to suffer this disgrace as well?"

"It doesn't have to be a disgrace," Tzeitl said.

"Silence!" Tevye shouted. "The answer is no!" He sat down in his seat and whipped the reins of the horse.

The procession moved on through the dust. Wagons rattled under their loads. Golda's coffin bounced over the rocks in the road. Glancing over his shoulder, Tevye could still see the tall Hevedke, following at the end of the long march of Jews. His fleece of blond hair shone in the sun under his brown student's cap.

"No, I don't want to know what is written," Tevye brooded to himself, fighting to keep control of his thoughts. No, no, no. Hevedke could walk. He could crawl. He could die from hunger and thirst before Tevye would let him into his wagon.

Tevye, the guardian of tradition, refused to look at his daughter. He refuse to speak. For miles, they road in silence. Yet as they turned every bend, he could still see the lone figure of Hevedke Galagan walking determinedly after the Jews.

Suddenly, the procession came to a halt. Tevye's horse snorted. "What's the matter?" Moishe asked. "Why have we stopped?"

"Are we there already?" Hannie questioned.

"I'll go and see what the problem is," Tevye said, getting down from the wagon. He trudged off toward the head of the line. The caravan had stopped at a crossroads. One road led north to a stretch of Russian wasteland where pogroms had not yet erupted. Another road led to Europe, the Atlantic Ocean, and America beyond. And the third path led to Odessa and *Eretz Yisrael* and Jerusalem.

Naturally, a lively debate was in progress. Everyone had an opinion on which direction to take. All of a sudden, Jews who had never ventured beyond the boundaries of Anatevka became experts in international travel. Yitzik, the woodcutter, advised journeying on to Broditchov, a distant part of Russia, where at least people spoke the same language. Leb, the ritual slaughterer, argued that Jews speak the same language wherever they live. Tzvi Hirsh, the tanner, had an uncle in America who wrote that all the Jews had houses as big as hotels and rode in fancy carriages just like the gentiles. But Shammai, the scribe, warned that ocean travel after the winter rains was a dangerous affair.

"Is that so?" Tzvi Hirsh retorted. "And since when did you become a Columbus? How many times has our village scribe sailed around the world?"

"Here's Tevye," Shammai said. "You can ask him."

Everyone turned to the milkman. Tevye looked up at the sign at the crossroad and gazed down each path, as if he could see the future at the end of the road.

"What do you say, Tevye? Which way should we go?"

Before the milkman could answer, Elijah, the town herald said, "The Midrash teaches that every road leads to Jerusalem."

"Well, the Midrash must have been wrong," the tanner responded. "Only one of these roads leads to Jerusalem."

"The meaning is that wherever a Jew wanders, sooner or later he is going to get beaten over the head until he ends up back in Jerusalem," Elijah explained.

"I have an idea," Tevye said. "Let's ask the Rabbi."

That was a suggestion that everyone agreed to. It was always wise to ask the Rabbi. It was even wiser to listen to him, but nowadays, less and less people did. Still, everyone agreed it was proper to ask, so the crowd walked back to the elderly sage, who was sitting in his wagon alongside his married son.

"Rabbi, where should we go?" Yitzik, the tanner, inquired.

The Rabbi squinted his eyes and peered down the road. "Where the Almighty takes us," he said.

"Yes, of course, but in which direction?"

"In which direction?" the Rabbi asked.

"Yes, there is a crossroad, and we have to decide which direction to take."

The Rabbi nodded his head. "Go in the direction... which will take us as far away from the Czar as possible, may his name be erased from the earth."

Just then, a loud burst of singing turned everyone's head. A group of twelve beardless Jews, knapsacks on their backs, were marching down the road, singing a spirited Zionist song, "Zion, Zion, Zion, won't you ask how your exiled people are faring?" A few wore small caps on their heads after the manner of students and peasants, but the majority had no head covering at all.

The Jews from Anatevka stared at the Zionist contingent in wonder. They marched down the road like soldiers on parade, their arms swaying in time with their steps. There was a feeling of boldness and zest in their singing, and brazenness in their upright gaits, as if there weren't a King in the heavens to whom every head had to bend.

"Shalom," their leader called, holding up his hand.

He was handsome with a rapier-thin moustache that made him look like a swashbuckling pirate. The group came to a halt behind him.

"Greetings, fellow Jews," he continued in Russian. "Permit me to introduce myself. Though I was born to the family Poprinchkov, my name today is Ben Zion, and my companions and I are off to reclaim our ancient homeland. Where, may we ask, are our comrades heading?"

"Fellow Jews, yes. Comrades, that's a topic for a debate," Hershel, the sandal maker, answered.

"Are we not comrades in having been uprooted from our once beloved Russia?"

"That only makes us brothers in our shared misfortune, not in our beliefs," Elijah called back.

"I see that we have come upon the guardians of tradition. By all means come with us. Join us on our journey. You are welcome to share in the modest provisions we have. Come with us to Zion, the land of our past, and the land of our future – to live as free Jews in our own Jewish land."

"Jews go to the Land of Israel to die," the woodcutter said.

"Not anymore," the spirited youth responded. "Look at us for example. We are going to the Land of Israel to live!"

Tevye noticed that his daughters had joined the crowd, with other curious women. The milkman frowned. Wasn't curiosity the very trait that had led Jacob's daughter, Dina, to disaster? As the Torah says, she went out to see the daughters of the land. By the time her father, Jacob, realized she was missing, an uncircumcised heathen had raped her.

"Naftali," Ben Zion called. "Sing us the song you composed."

A thin, moustachioed minstrel stepped aside from the group. His first notes wavered, and his voice seemed to crack, but then he found his range and sang out the words from deep within his heart. Everyone stood in silence and listened, spellbound by the gentle, haunting tune. Even the little children stopped playing to hear the beautiful song.

"As long as in the inner heart,

The soul of a Jew beats,
Forward
To the ends of the east,
The eye gazes toward Zion.
Our hope has not been abandoned,
The hope of two-thousand years.
To be a free people in our Land,
The Land of Zion
And *Yerushalayim*."

All of Tevye's daughters had tears in their eyes when he finished the anthem. Even their father, who never cried in public, had to wipe a bit of moistness away. The Jews of Anatevka were speechless. The words and the melody had struck a deep-seated chord in them all. Almost in unison, they turned to the Rabbi. His eyes, weary from a lifetime of candlelight study, were also filled with a nostalgic sparkle.

"Why don't we join them?" Shammai asked.

"Where are their skullcaps?" the Rabbi responded.

"God looks on what's in the heart, not what's on the outside," their leader, Ben Zion said.

"Has God spoken to you that you know what He judges important?" the white-bearded scholar retorted.

"God doesn't have to speak to us in words for us to understand His message. How many times must the Russians chase us out of our villages until we realize that we don't belong in their land? Haven't we been exiled enough? God wants us to have our own country."

"God wants us to live by the Torah," the Rabbi said.

"We have a new Torah," one of the other Zionists called out. "The Torah of freedom, and the will in our hearts to work the soil of our own Jewish land."

Tevye looked from the young heretics with their uncovered heads to the old, wizened face of the Rabbi.

"We will return to our land when the *Mashiach* takes us there," he said, pronouncing his final decision. As if to emphasize his resolve, the Rabbi took the reins out of the hands of his son and gave their horse a flick. The wagon jerked forward. The tanner yelled out "*Mashiach*!" Others echoed his cry. Soon, the Jews of Anatevka were singing a song of their own, a lively Hasidic ballad filled with longing for the *Mashiach*, the Jewish messiah and king:

"*Mashiach, Mashiach, Mashiach*, la, la, la, la, la.

Mashiach, Mashiach, Mashiach, la, la, la, la, la.

Even though his coming may be delayed,

We will wait for him every day

With the hope that he will come, la, la, la, la, la."

The tanner, the woodcutter, the scribe, and the slaughterer all returned to their families and wagons, and the procession once again moved onward, on the road to other lands and other foreign rulers. Only Tevye stood in his place, dust on his shoes, deep in ponderous thought.

"What about you, old man?" Ben Zion asked him. "Do you have the courage to stand tall and be a proud Jew in our own Promised Land?"

There was something in the words of the young Zionist pioneer that tugged at Tevye's heart. True, his daughter, Baylke, was in America, and everyone knew that even an incompetent *shlimazl* of a milkman could become a millionaire in New York overnight, but how long would it be before persecutions began even there? At least in the Land of Israel, a Jew could feel like a Jew! After all, three times a day in his prayers, a Jew faced Jerusalem, not New York.

The words of the Rabbi echoed in Tevye's mind as if in rebuttal. "Where are their skullcaps?" he had pointedly inquired, meaning that everyone enjoyed a nice Zionist song, but where was their tradition; where was their love and reverence for God? Hadn't Tevye suffered enough from free-thinkers when Perchik had stolen away his daughter? Perchik too was brimming with slogans and highfalutin ideals, and where had it led but to prison? Who knew if Tevye would ever see his wonderful Hodel again? Did he want to take the same chance with another one of his daughters? Tevye wasn't blind. He had seen the look in their eyes when the cocky, young "Herzl" had exchanged passionate words with the Rabbi.

Tevye stared after the Zionists as they marched in formation along the road to Odessa. There was a confidence, a pride, a spirit, and a purpose to their movements that Tevye recalled from his youth. They held their backs straight, actualizing the prayer which a Jew said everyday of his life, beseeching the Almighty "to shatter the yoke of foreign rulers and return us upright to our Land." It was happening in front of Tevye's eyes! The Zionists marched upright, their heads held high, envisioning a more hopeful future. What a different picture from the Jews of Anatevka who trudged along on their journey, bent over from the burdens of exile, dragging their tired feet in the dust, heads bowed like cattle, not knowing what lay ahead, where they were going, nor what they would do when they got there.

Tevye reached down for his *tzitzit*. The thin strings hanging down from his ritual undergarment were like lifelines, reminding the dreamer in him that he was a simple milkman, and not a young pioneer. "Thou shall not wander after pulling of your heart, nor after the sight of your eyes," the commandment instructed. His daughters were staring at him. Tzeitl, Hava, Ruchel, and Bat Sheva. Little Moishe and Hannie gazed up at their grandfather too, as if to say, "*Nu?* What are we waiting here for?"

Tevye glanced up to the Heavens. "What now?" he asked. "How can Your servant, Tevye, please his Master and King? Haven't our Sages taught us that even a man with good eyesight is blind before his future. You are my shepherd. Send me a sign. Tell us, dear Lord, which way should we go?"

Hershel, the sandal maker, drove by in his wagon.

"Waiting for *Mashiach*?" he asked.

"May his coming be soon," Tevye said. "And what about you? Where are you off to?"

"I have a distant cousin in London. They say there are more than a million people there. That's two million feet for my shoes. I am going to be a multi-millionaire. What about you?"

"I am a millionaire already. Look at my daughters. Can a man be wealthier than that?"

"That's what they say: 'Tevye is known for his beautiful daughters,' but they also say, 'Happy is the man who does not walk in the council of the wicked' – meaning the Zionists."

"Wasn't God a Zionist?" Tevye asked. "Didn't He tell Abraham and Moses to go and dwell in Israel?"

"God is God, and Abraham and Moses are Abraham and Moses. What do Hershel, the sandal maker, and Tevye, the milkman, have to do with them?"

"What about your Shendel and my Golda?" Tevye asked. "Are you going to bring her to London when you could bring her to the holy soil of *Eretz Yisrael*?"

"My Shendel, may her soul rest in peace, always talked about going to London to visit her cousin. Now she will have her chance."

"My Golda, may her memory be for a blessing, wouldn't have know where London was even if you had shown it to her on a map. Such a pure soul never existed. She lived only for her poor beast of a husband and her seven daughters. Doesn't a woman like this deserve to be buried in the Tomb of our Forefathers? In the Cave of Hevron? Or on the way to Efrata, in Bet-Lechem, beside our mother, Rachel?"

"Think of your daughters, Tevye. Who will they find there to marry? The Zionists? The blasphemers of our holy Torah? It can only come to no good."

Tevye nodded his head. His friend, *Reb* Hershel was right. All his life he had struggled to build a protective wall around his daughters, so that the evil of modern times would not lead them astray. And now, in a weak moment, he was thinking of following the Zionists on their journey, like a shepherd who abandons his lambs to packs of roving wolves. The sandal maker's warning was filled with common sense. Tevye had to think of his children. It would be better to take them to their sister, Baylke, in New York. Hadn't she written that she wanted them to come to America to help her pick the gold off the streets? And if it meant stomaching

her good-for-nothing husband, so be it. Tevye was ready to
swallow his pride for the sake of his family. In America, he could
get a matchmaker to find kosher husbands for Bat Sheva and
Ruchel, and two kosher suitors for Tzeitl and Hava too.

"Onward, Reb Hershel," Tevye said. "You lead the way, and we
shall follow."

As Tevye mounted the wagon, he could see the poet, Galagan
in the distance, waiting to see which direction their wagon would
take. Behind him, a lone figure came running along the road,
waving a hand in the air and shouting something which was lost
in the wind. When his family was secure in the wagon, Tevye
urged on his horse. With a tug, the four-legged creature inched the
heavy load forward. The wagon squeaked. Grudgingly, the wheels
started to roll. "What was the hurry?" the horse seemed to say.
Though he wasn't a Jew, the beast had been listening to Tevye's
soliloquies for years, and he had learned the difference between
the Sabbath and an ordinary day of the week. With an animal's
sense, he knew it would be a long journey. So he took his time
catching up to the wagons ahead of them.

It wasn't long before Tevye heard someone calling his name.
He glanced around to see Borsky, the Russian mailman, running
after the wagon, out of breath, a letter held aloft in his hand. Once
again, Tevye pulled on the reins. The mailman collapsed by the
seat of the wagon. He handed Tevye the letter. Compassionately,
Tzeitl handed him some water to drink.

"This letter arrived just after you left," he said between pants.
"I figured it was the decent thing to do, to bring it to you, after
you've been delivering our milk for so many years."

"My appreciation," Tevye said. He handed the letter to Hava,
his reader of books.

"It's from Hodel!" she exclaimed. "From Palestine!"

"From Palestine?" Tevye mumbled, unable to believe what he
heard.

Quickly, she opened the envelope. Her lips silently read
through the letter. Impatiently, Tevye grabbed it and held it up
to his eyes to see for himself. It was truly from Hodel. He

recognized her handwriting. Unable to decipher her swirls, he handed the letter back to his daughter. Her eyes raced over the feminine script.

"Well?" Tzeitl asked. "What does it say?"

"Perchik was let out of prison on the condition that he leave Russia and never return. They've been in *Eretz Yisrael* since the beginning of the winter. Perchik is busy working the land and organizing a worker's committee which he says will be the beginning of the new Jewish State."

"Skip all of his crazy *meshugenneh* slogans," her father impatiently said.

"We are living in a new settlement called Shoshana with another thirty families," she read. "We have heard of the pogroms in Russia and want you to come. The Land of Israel is beautiful, and the skies are like out of a dream. And there are several religious settlements for you, father, that the Baron Rothschild has built."

"Religious settlements?" Tevye inquired.

"That's what she writes," Hava answered.

"Is that all?" Tevye asked.

"No. There's one other thing," Hava said with a smile. "Hodel is pregnant."

A big grin lit Tevye's face. "*Mazal tov!*" he said. "*Baruch Hashem*, thank the good Lord."

"Mazal tov," the Russian mailman said. The two men shook hands. They had been good friends for years until the Czar and the dark clouds of history had declared the Jews traitors.

"Tzeitl, get me the vodka from out of the crate," Tevye commanded.

A pregnant daughter was reason to celebrate. A grandchild meant that Tevye would survive on in the generations to come. But that wasn't all. A grandchild born in the Promised Land was something much greater. It was a fulfillment of prophecy. It was the hope of new life not only for Tevye's family, but for the Jewish people as a whole. How many Jewish fathers in the last thousand years could boast of an achievement like that?

Tzeitl dutifully opened the chest and handed a bottle to her father. Tevye pulled out the cork. With a hearty "*L'Chaim*! To life!" he took a deep slug. Then he handed the bottle to the mailman.

"You have brought us this happiness," Tevye said. "May the Almighty reward you with healthy children of your own."

The mailman drank a "*L'Chaim*" and handed the bottle back to the Jew.

"Are we going to Palestine?" Bat Sheva asked. "I want to see Hodel."

"So do I," Ruchel said.

"We all do," Tzeitl agreed.

Everyone waited for an answer from Tevye. He looked to his right, and he looked to his left, as if judging his options. What was more important? Money, or the promise of milk and honey? On one side of the world, there was Hodel. Only a Jacob, who had lost his son Joseph, could know how much Tevye had missed her. Since the day she had left Anatevka, not an evening had passed without her memory flashing before him as he fell off to sleep. Then again, on the other side of the ocean were Baylke, and the gold of America's streets. But the thought of her husband, Pedhotzer, turned Tevye's stomach. True, Hodel's heretic was no bargain either – the young revolutionary could make a listener dizzy with his *mishegoss* notions about saving the world. But though his head was stuffed with goose feathers, he had a good heart. A few children of his own would teach him that before a man can save the world, he has to be sure that there is bread on the table at home. And finally, Tevye knew that if he wanted to keep the chain of tradition and Torah intact in his family, he himself would have to be on hand in the Land of Israel to teach his grandchild the beauty of the "*Shema Yisrael*" prayer.

"*Tata*," Tzeitl said. "You asked for a sign from the Almighty. Isn't Hodel's letter enough, or do you want a burning bush too?"

The girl had a point. Tevye took another drink and wiped his mouth with his hand. If Golda were present, she would have pointed toward Zion. To see her Hodel again, she would have given the world. But had Tevye forgotten? Golda was with them, in the coffin in the back of the wagon. Could he give his wife a more precious gift than to bury her in the Holy Land? And if it demanded strenuous labor to rebuild their ancient land, when was Tevye ever afraid of hard work? With the help of God, he had some productive years left, and when his time came to retire, he would sit in the shade of the Western Wall in Jerusalem, and spend his days learning the holy books. Hodel had written that there were religious Jews in the land. The Rabbi, may he live a long, healthy life, must have had the wrong information. And if the Baron Rothschild were financing the Zionist endeavor, no doubt Tevye could move his family into one of the villas that the billionaire surely had built for the new pioneers.

Tevye held up the bottle. "To the Land of Israel!" he proclaimed. His daughters and grandchildren cheered. The mailman, Borsky, smiled. Even Tevye's horse felt the excitement when it heard about their new destination. It didn't have to wait for Tevye's command. With an enthusiasm it hadn't shown for years, the beast swung the wagon around in a half circle and galloped off after the parade of pioneers.

"My Nachson!" Tevye called to the steed as the wagon thundered toward Zion. "As the Lord led the Jews through the wilderness, may He lead Tevye and his children to Israel!"

Up ahead, the poet Hevedke Galagan stood in the path of the gallopping horse and wagon. He stared at Tevye, and Tevye stared back at him. Fired by the vodka and joy of his decision, the thought flashed across Tevye's mind, "What a good chance to teach him a lesson!" What a fitting last memory of Russia on their way to the Holy Land – to trample the devil himself under the wheels of the wagon!

"Yaahaaa!" Tevye shouted, whipping the reins of the horse. Hava cried out. The blond-headed Hevedke stood frozen, as if his long legs were stuck in his boots. "Yaahaaa!" Tevye yelled.

"Father!" Hava screamed.

Tevye's eyes were aflame with revenge. At the very last minute, the youth showed enough sense to leap out of the way of destruction. The wagon sped by. Tzeitl clutched onto her children. Golda's coffin bounced in the air as if it were bursting with life.

"*Am Yisrael Chai*!" Tevye shouted at the sight of Hevedke sprawled in the dust. "The nation of Israel lives on!"

Chapter Four

"THOU SHALL NOT MURDER"

The Zionists were happy to have Tevye and his family join them. Feeling no pain from the vodka, Tevye invited their young leader to sit alongside him in the wagon. In a feeling of brotherhood, he even offered him a drink. Ben Zion refused. Alcohol, he said, was a drug which the wealthy class used to keep the peasants content in their religious stupor. He and his friends were drunk with the spirit of freedom, so who needed vodka? But if their distinguished traveling companion needed a drink, then by all means, he should imbibe – it was a day of emancipation, a time of independence, a cause for celebration.

"Emancipation from what?" Tevye asked.

"From the yoke of the Czar."

"Amen," Tevye said, taking another hearty drink.

Tzeitl reached out to take the bottle away from her father.

"Honor thy father," Tevye warned, holding the vodka out of her reach. "Didn't the angels inquire of Abraham, `Where is your wife?' A woman's place is out of sight, a queen in her palace, not with the men in the front seat of the wagon."

"We believe that women should be liberated too," Ben Zion said.

"You believe in a lot of foolish nonsense," Tevye answered. "But you have an excuse – you're still a young whelp."

"Wasn't Elazar ben Azariah even younger than I am when he was chosen to head the Sanhedrin?"

"Oh, I see I have the privilege of sharing my seat with a scholar of Torah. I truly am honored," Tevye said.

"Just because I go with my head uncovered, don't think that I haven't learned. My father sent me to *heder*, and I was quite a good student until I discovered that the world had entered new times."

"Hasn't King Solomon taught us that there is nothing new under the sun?" Tevye asked.

"I can quote Scripture too, but don't you see that it's all an old-fashioned fable which doesn't apply anymore?"

Tevye pulled on the reins until his horse came to a halt. "There will be no words of heresy in this wagon. While it may lack a roof, this is, for the time being, our humble abode, and Tevye, the son of Schneur Zalman, will not tolerate blasphemy in the presence of his family. So if you cannot control your speech, please step down from my wagon."

Ben Zion smiled. "No problem, old man," he said. "While I am unable to agree with your beliefs, I respect both you and your beautiful daughters. Besides, evening is approaching, and you probably would like to pray to your God. In the meantime, my comrades and I will look for a suitable camp site."

"My beautiful daughters," Tevye mumbled when the insolent scoundrel climbed down from the wagon. He would have felt safer if he were traveling with thieves. This free-thinking Herzl was cut from the very same cloth as his son-in-law Perchik. Why, Tevye wondered, had he turned a deaf ear to the Rabbi?

They camped in the woods by the roadside. Tevye unhitched his horse and fed him a bucket of oats. Then he spread out blankets and mats for his daughters under the wagon. The father intended to keep guard under the stars, where he could keep an eye on the Zionists. The family enjoyed a modest meal of black bread and potatoes which Tevye baked in the campfire. A swig of vodka helped to wash down the food. While they ate, Tevye's eye kept wandering to the flickering light of a campfire on the other side of the road.

"He's following us like a dog," Tevye said.

"Please, *Tata*," Hava appealed. "Don't talk about Hevedke like that."

"I see the devil still has you under his spell."

"I'm not under a spell. If I were, I wouldn't be here. But

Hevedke is a good man. It isn't his fault that he was born one of them."

Tevye took a big bite out of his potato. Grumbling, he tilted his head back and poured some more vodka into his belly.

She's right, he thought. It wasn't the youth's fault that he had been created that way, just as it wasn't Tevye's fault that he had been born a Jew. But just as Tevye had to suffer his fate, then let this Galagan suffer his fate too. How long was he planning on following them? Till he drove Tevye out of his mind?

"If our father, Abraham, were here," Ben Zion said pointedly from his seat by the campfire, "I bet he would invite a fellow traveler over to join in his meal."

"He is not one of us," Tevye answered.

"That never stopped Abraham," Ben Zion responded. "Didn't he bring everyone he met under the roof of his tent to spread the knowledge of God? After all, are not all men created in God's image?"

"There are men, and there are men who look like men, but behave like wild beasts."

"Oh, *Tata*," Tzeitl said. "You know there are lots of exceptions."

"Like our wonderful Russian friends who threw us out of our village."

"Which one of your daughters is he in love with?" Ben Zion asked.

Tevye stood up. "What business is it of yours?" he demanded.

It was Naftali, the singer, who answered. "He just wants to know which of your roses are still up for grabs."

His comrades all laughed. Tevye growled. One of the group, a *mamzer* named Peter, jumped to his feet and said he was going to invite Hevedke to join them. With a laugh, he started to walk toward the road, but Tevye grabbed him. With a powerful grasp, he spun him around and shoved him into the fire. The Zionist landed on the burning branches with a yelp. Quickly, his comrades pulled him out of the flames.

Tevye stood glaring.

"That's the last time anyone mentions either that uncircumcised Philistine or my daughters! Is that understood?"

Even the usually garrulous Ben Zion was silent. Tevye walked back to his wagon. It was a pity, he thought, that the brunt of his anger had to fall on a Jew. How much better it would have been if he had pulled the Russian Police Commissioner off of his horse and broken his bones instead. Or if he were to set Hevedke on fire and wish him a final good riddance.

His daughters didn't dare open their mouths when their father returned to their side. Tevye sat down and leaned back against a wheel of the wagon. He was tired from the vodka and from the strains of the day. The fire across the road had waned in brightness, but the silhouette of the Russian poet could still be seen against the trees of the forest. Tevye's eyes closed in the darkness. Exhaustion swept through his body. Before long, he was snoring. Ben Zion called over in a discreet, polite voice, asking him to be quiet, but the milkman didn't hear. Hodel gave her father a nudge, but he was deep in some other world, dreaming of a carriage pulled by a team of white horses.

Tevye only awoke after everyone else had fallen asleep. His daughters were huddled in blankets under the wagon. The Zionists dozed in the warmth of the campfire's embers. When Tevye was certain that everyone was sleeping, he quietly stood up, opened the chest in the wagon, and pulled out his slaughterer's knife. Careful not to step on branches or twigs, he walked across the road toward the wisps of smoke rising amongst the pine trees. Hevedke was sleeping. His features were serene and innocently youthful. A small smile, like a baby's, was curled on his lips. A stubble of blondish red hair covered his cheeks, as if he were growing a beard. And a hand-sewn *yarmulka* had fallen off his head to the ground. Bending down to lift it, Tevye recognized Hava's skilled stitch in the traditional Jewish skullcap.

When Tevye let out a roar, Hevedke jerked upright, still half asleep. Tevye grasped him around his chest and lay the blade of the knife gently on his throat.

"This is a slaughterer's knife," he said. "Its blade is kept extra sharp in order to kill the animal quickly so it won't have to suffer needless pain."

"Thou shall not murder," Hevedke whispered in terror.

"That's as much as you know," Tevye said. "It is also written that if a thief enters your house to kidnap your daughter, then you are allowed to kill him."

Tevye scraped the steel of the knife along his prisoner's neck.

"I want to be a Jew," the young Russian vowed in a hush.

"And I want to be Baron Rothschild with a carriage pulled by four fancy zebras," the milkman responded.

"Give me a chance," Hevedke pleaded.

"Just like the chance which your Czar has given to us. The chance to flee and never return. My daughter is finished with you and never wants to see you again. Tomorrow, when I look back down the road, I don't want to see you following us. Is that understood?"

"Yes," Hevedke whispered as the blade pressed into his skin.

Tevye let the youth go. The Russian fell to his side and gasped. The milkman stood up in satisfaction and started to walk back toward the road. But now it was Hevedke's turn. His voice pierced Tevye's back as if he were holding a knife of his own.

"Wherever thou goest, I will go; and where thou lodgest, I will lodge; thy people shall be my people, and thy God, my God."

"Oy vay," Tevye thought. Another Bible scholar! It was maddening enough that the Zionist, Ben Zion, could spout verses like water. Now this blond-headed Gorky was quoting the Book of Ruth. Soon Tevye's horse would be talking!

"I love Hava," Hevedke said. "And I always will. Where she diest, I will die, and there I will be buried."

"*Gevalt,*" Tevye thought. "Do I have a problem."

Without turning, he walked back to the road. Stars sparkled high over the trees. What future did the constellations hold in store for him? After all, he reasoned, trying to see the good side, a gentile could convert. It said so in the Torah. Wasn't Ruth, the Moabite, the great grandmother of King David? And if you want to talk about converts, Rabbi Akiva, the son of a convert, became the greatest Torah scholar in history. On the other hand, being in love with a pretty Jewish girl did not make someone a Jew. There were rules when it came to converting, like with everything else. If Hevedke Galagan really wanted to enter the Covenant of Abraham, he would have to pass the test. And the first proof of a Jew was suffering. He would have to prove himself beyond any shadow of a doubt before Tevye would let him speak to his daughter.

Chapter Five

A HUSBAND FOR RUCHEL

The next morning, Hevedke was waiting out on the road when Tevye and his Zionist entourage took up their journey. The two men stared at one another in silence.

"He has more guts than I thought," Tevye brooded, giving the reins of the wagon a whip.

Hava was hoping that her father would give Hevedke a chance to prove his sincerity, but there was no sign of conciliation in her father's angry expression. Hava herself was confused. Her heart was torn between a man she still loved, and the realization that the bond between them could never be sanctified as long as he belonged to the tormentors of her people. It wasn't enough that Hevedke was ashamed of the evil decrees of the Czar. Unless he tore up all ties to his religion and his past, he would always remain one of them. Even if he were to fast a hundred days to prove his love for Hava, that would not be enough. Hava knew that he loved her. He had to prove he loved God by taking on the yoke of her people. Though Hava felt compassion and pity for Hevedke, she didn't plead with her father to accept him into the fold. If she had listened to her parents in the first place, the whole painful situation would never have occurred. Now she wanted to make amends for the breach she had rent in the family. She wanted to be faithful to her father. She wanted to show her mother in Heaven that she was sorry for the pain she had caused. So sitting beside her father as their wagon drove down the road, Hava fought off her desire to gaze at the man she had lived with only a short time before. She stared forward at the future as if Hevedke did not exist, as if they had never crossed paths, trusting that one way or the other, God would restore peace to her torn, aching heart.

That evening they reached the Jewish *shtetl* of Branosk. The ultra-religious community was smaller than the Jewish community of Anatevka, but the sights, sounds, and smells were the same. The same wooden porches, tiled roofs, and shutters. The same sagging, weathered barns which stood erect by a miracle. The same aroma of horses, chickens, and soups. The same beards and black skullcaps on the men, and kerchiefs and shawls on the women. Even the fiery red sunset had been stolen from Anatevka and pasted over the Branosk forest.

The villagers rushed out of their houses when they heard that pioneers on the way to the Promised Land had arrived in the *shtetl*. Children and teenagers crowded around Tevye's wagon. They all wore the caps and long curling *peyes* sidelocks which distinguished the Branosk community. Apparently, they had seen other Zionists, but the sight of Tevye, a bearded, God fearing Jew among them, was a novelty to be sure. Ben Zion jumped up on a porch and tried to deliver a spirited harangue, inviting the townspeople to throw off the yoke of the Russians and join them in rebuilding the ancient Jewish homeland, but he only drew heckles and a rotten tomato. Tevye and his daughters attracted a far larger crowd.

Where was he going, they wanted to know? To *Eretz Yisrael*, he answered, the Land of Israel. With the heretics, they asked? Tevye said that by accident they were traveling together, for safety along the way. But, Tevye assured them, his family was headed for a settlement more religious than the city of Vilna – in God's Chosen Land. What could be better than that? For hadn't they heard? The great Baron Rothschild, may he live several lifetimes, was building "*frum*," God fearing communities throughout the Holy Land. Everyone who came got a villa and acres of orchards bursting with olives, pomegranates, fig trees, and dates.

People bombarded Tevye with questions. He answered with authority, as if he truly knew, as if he were the Baron's agent, auctioning off parcels of land. When a question came his way for which he did not have an answer, he responded with a verse or two of Torah. One thing was clear – the expulsion which had hit Anatevka was sure to reach Branosk. Surely they had heard that the Czar's Cossacks had been thundering throughout Russia, slaughtering thousands of Jews. Now was the time to flee for their lives. Now was the time to stop praying for God to take them to Zion, and let their feet do the talking instead.

"*APIKORSUS!*" roared the Rabbi when he heard Tevye's words. "Heresy! Slander! Blasphemy and falsehood!" he cried. "Throw the Zionist sinner out of this holy house!"

Before the milkman knew it, he was lifted off his feet and whisked out of the synagogue, where he had been taken to join in the afternoon prayer. Tevye heard the *minchah* service begin as he tumbled down the stairs: "Fortunate are those who dwell in Your house," the worshippers declared. Outside, Tevye sat on the ground and brushed off the dust. What had he said to so anger the Rabbi? What had he done wrong? Against whom had he sinned?

When Tevye walked back to his wagon, Ruchel was missing. Tzeitl reported that a young man from the village had unharnessed Tevye's horse and taken it to the barn for a feeding. Apparently, he had taken Ruchel with him. Tevye's eyebrows rose in surprise. Of all of his daughters, Ruchel most resembled his Golda. Not only in looks, but in her practicality and down-to-earth wisdom. The girl's heart was firmly attached to the ground, not adrift in the clouds. Unlike his other daughters, Ruchel followed her head and not her emotions. If she went off with a strange man to a barn, it wasn't just to feed Tevye's old horse some oats.

In truth, the moment Nachman had appeared at the wagon and offered to feed their road-weary nag, Ruchel had seen something special. The youth spoke with his head slightly angled, looking modestly toward the ground, so he wouldn't gaze at the women. His tone was quiet, almost timid, and he blushed when Ruchel addressed him. And while his features weren't classically handsome, his eyes were the most beautiful blue that Ruchel had ever seen in her life.

"The horse gets a little nervous with strangers," Ruchel had said. "I had better come with you."

Tzeitl and Hava had stared at each other without saying a word. For one thing, in all of God's creation, there didn't exist a more docile animal than their father's faithful horse, and even more wondrous, they had never seen their sister converse with a member of the masculine sex.

The young man was clearly embarrassed to enter the barn alone with the girl. Sensing his discomfort, Ruchel kept a distance, standing in the open barn door. Without speaking, he filled up a trough with oats and started to rub down the horse with a brush.

"My name is Ruchel," she said. The bashful young man continued caring for the animal without glancing up at the girl.

"What's your name?" Ruchel asked.

"Nachman," he answered.

"Aren't you going to *daven* with the others in the *shul*?"

"I have already prayed in the yeshiva," he answered.

"We are journeying to Palestine," she said.

"Yes. I heard. I would very much like to go to the Holy Land too."

"Why don't you?" the girl asked.

The shy scholar didn't answer. "With God's help," he said softly.

"God helps those who help themselves," she retorted. "When we are sick, God forbid, we pray for God to heal us, but we also go to the doctor. We pray for God to provide us with food, but we go out and work for a living. It isn't enough to pray for God to take us back home to our own Land, we have to make the effort ourselves."

The youth looked up in surprise upon hearing her passionate words.

"You sound like one of the Zionists," he said.

"What's wrong with the Zionists? I like them."

Nachman didn't answer. Suddenly, his blue eyes sparkled like the heavens, as if he could see the borders of the Promised Land beyond the walls of the barn.

"Did you know that all of our prayers first travel to Jerusalem before they go up to Heaven?" he asked. "And that everyone who takes four steps in the Holy Land is guaranteed life in the World to Come."

"Then why don't you go and live there yourself?"

Embarrassed by the pointed question, the young man blushed and lowered his head. "My father won't let me," he said.

"Aren't you old enough to do what you want?"

Before Nachman could try to explain, a dark silhouette appeared in the door of the barn. It was Tevye. He stared at his daughter and nodded for her to go back to the wagon. Then with long, purposeful steps, he strode into the barn. He nodded at the young lad and patted his horse on the rump.

"I am grateful for your kindness," Tevye said.

"May your coming be a blessing," the pious youth said.

"May our going also be a blessing," Tevye answered. "I have been a Jew all of my life, but until today, I have never had a rabbi throw me out of a synagogue dedicated to the worship of God."

The young man blushed. He hung his head toward the ground. "My father probably mistook you for a Zionist."

"Your father!" Tevye said in surprise. The boy didn't answer. He bent down to lift the empty bucket of oats and replace it with a bucket of water. A rabbi's son, Tevye thought. A Torah scholar, no doubt. And a e *mench* to boot, who went out of his way to perform acts of kindness toward strangers. Tevye approved. It was a suitable match for his Ruchela. If the lad cared for his daughter half as much as he had cared for Tevye's horse, then the girl had found an excellent husband.

"Since when is loving the Land of Israel a sin?" Tevye asked.

"It isn't a sin if you love Torah too," the boy answered. "My father isn't against Zion. He is against those who throw off the yoke of the Torah and go there. He is afraid of their influence on the minds of our youth."

Just then, Ben Zion appeared in the entrance.

"Greetings fellow comrades," the flamboyant Zionist exclaimed.

"Greetings," Tevye said. "Were your ears just burning? We were just now speaking of you."

"In a complimentary fashion, I trust. Though there are those who say that it is better to have bad things spoken about you, than to have nothing said about you at all. I understand we have been invited to leave this holy conclave of Branosk," the capless adventurer quipped.

"We have a journey to continue," Tevye said.

"Then we should start out before dark," Ben Zion suggested.

"Tell the others I'm coming," Tevye answered.

Sensing that he was interrupting the discussion in the barn, Ben Zion dramatically bowed and departed. Tevye slipped the reins of his horse over the animal's head.

"You are invited to join us," he told the Rabbi's son. "I am a widower with unmarried daughters, and the companionship of a Torah scholar like you will help shorten the journey. As our Rabbis teach, when two men discuss matters of Torah, the Divine Presence is with them."

The youth did not answer.

"In addition, the Baron Rothschild has extended an open invitation to all Jews to join his religious *yishuvim*-settlements in the Holy Land, and as his representative on this journey, I hereby extend his kind offer to you."

"I thank you," the lad said. "I will think about it. But now I have to go home."

"We will be camped down the road," Tevye said.

"May your camp be guarded by angels, just as they guarded our forefather Jacob as he journeyed back to the Land of his fathers."

Tevye's horse snorted as if to answer "Amen." The men parted ways, and Tevye returned to the wagon. As he hitched up the horse, he glanced up at Ruchel who was anxiously waiting to learn what had transpired between them.

"I invited your new friend to join us," Tevye said.

"And?" Ruchel asked.

"As our Rabbis say, `Many are the thoughts in a man's heart, but it is the counsel of the Lord which will stand.'"

"What does that mean?" Bat Sheva asked.

"It means I left my crystal ball back in Anatevka. In the meantime, like in the story of Abraham and Lot, we are parting ways with our brethren in this village."

With his rump still hurting from his fall down the synagogue stairs, Tevye flicked the reins of the wagon and the pioneers once again took up their journey.

"If the hospitality in this village is an example of religious behavior, I'm glad I'm a heretic," Ben Zion said.

"They believe they are doing the right thing," Tevye sorrowfully answered.

"So does the Czar," Naftali quipped.

"That's awful," Tzeitl exclaimed. "How can you dare compare them?"

"What's the difference?" Peter answered. "A Russian boot in the rear, or a Jewish boot in the rear, it hurts the same, eh, Tevye?"

The milkman didn't answer. He gazed forward into the darkening evening. Only Ruchel stared back down the road hoping that Nachman would come running after their wagon. But no one appeared. They turned a bend, leaving the *shtetl* behind. A ditch in the road jolted the wagon and Ruchel's dreams of a husband. She sighed and faced forward, but then, out of a corner of her eye, she saw a figure materialize out of the shadows of the forest. A beat of excitement rushed through her heart, but for naught. The tall, upright figure wasn't Nachman, but the indefatigable Hevedke.

"Don't worry," Hava said, sensing her sister's thoughts. "Your turn under the marriage *chuppah* will come."

When Tevye spotted the Russian poet, he growled.

"It is a sin to murder," he said, glancing up to the treetops, "So why must You send this devil to tempt me?"

Before long, they came to a clearing by the side of the road and agreed to make camp for the night. The men gathered wood while the women arranged a frugal meal, and once again two fires were lit, one for the Zionists, and one for Tevye and his family, a modest distance away. Everyone huddled around the warming blazes to ward off the evening chill, but the Almighty had other plans for the night. A burst of lightening flashed in the sky. Thunder rumbled in the treetops. Rain poured down from the heavens like brimstone. Within moments, the campfires were quenched. Tevye gathered his brood under the wagon, while their companions scattered for the shelter of trees. The rain pounded on the canvas stretched over Golda's coffin. A bolt of lightening lit up the forest. A tree cracked in half and toppled to the ground with a crash. Little Moishe and Hannie started to cry.

"Fear not my treasures," their grandfather said. "Hasn't the Almighty promised not to destroy the world again with a flood? And things could be worse. We could be standing outside in the rain like our companions."

"Or like Hevedke," Hava added.

"A torrent should wash him away," Tevye said.

"Why do you want him to drown, *Zaida?*" Moishe asked. "He's married to Hava."

"He is married to Hava like my horse is married to a fish," Tevye answered.

"How can a horse marry a fish?" the young child asked.

"It can't," Tevye answered. "Horses marry horses, and fish marry fish."

Just then, someone came running toward the clearing.

"*Shalom, shalom,*" he called out.

It was Nachman. He was carrying a bulging handbag in one hand and a suitcase in the other. He bent down under the wagon, said a hasty hello, and left his belongings with Ruchel.

"Take care of my books," he said and hurried off toward the trees where Ben Zion was waiting to greet him.

"Welcome, welcome, son of Israel!" the speechmaker exclaimed. "I trust you have come to enlist in our lofty mission."

"With the help of the Almighty," Nachman responded.

"Whether He helps or He doesn't, it's all the same to us. Just let Him not interfere."

Tevye crawled out from under his wagon. He threw the cover off of their chest of belongings and held up a bottle of vodka. "To Zion!" he shouted.

Like the *meshugennehs* they were, the crazy Zionists joined hands and started to dance in the rain. "Zion, Zion, Zion," they sang in the black Russian woods. Ben Zion dragged Nachman into their whirl. With a healthy slug of vodka warming his belly, Tevye joined them. He grasped Nachman's hand, and with the joyous *simcha* of a wedding, they swirled round and round in the mud. Ben Zion held the bottle of vodka to the young rabbi's lips. The bottle changed hands until it was finished. The ground spun. Trees and clouds swirled around and around as they danced.

"With your permission," Nachman said to Tevye. "I would like to marry your daughter."

"Permission granted," Tevye agreed.

With a cheer, the dancing continued. The women were all giggles under the wagon. Everyone congratulated Ruchel and showered her with *mazal tovs* and kisses. Discreetly, they joined in with the traditional wedding song, "Let soon be heard in the cities of Judah and the streets of Jerusalem, the sound of joy and the sound of gladness, the call of the groom, and the song of the bride...."

"Thank the good Lord," Tevye said when he finally crawled back under the wagon. His rain-drenched clothing clung to his flesh. "Tonight, a miracle has transpired. The son of a rabbi wants to marry Tevye's daughter."

Ruchel kissed him. "I am so happy, *Tata.*"

Suddenly, Tevye raised himself up with a jerk and whacked his head on the planks of the wagon. "I forgot to tell your mother," he said. Quickly, he scrambled back outside in the downpour. He bent over the coffin and whispered the good news to his wife, Golda.

"Our Ruchela has found herself the son of a rabbi," he whispered. "You can rest in peace, my Golda. Our luck is finally changing."

But then again, a man can never be sure. As the Talmud advises, a man should keep good fortune a secret lest the evil eye glance his way. Suddenly, galloping horses thundered by in the night, a stone throw away from the Jews. Tevye recognized the sword-wielding figures of Cossacks. His family sat frozen, holding their breaths until the rumbling cavalcade passed. The darkness of the forest had saved them.

Within minutes, Tevye was asleep, snuggled between his

daughters. Nachman fell asleep in the arms of the Zionists. Only Ruchel remained awake with her thoughts of a wedding in Israel, and of the gown she would soon need to sew.

The first time that she heard their horse sneeze, she thought it was from the rain and the chill. The animal neighed restlessly. Its ears straightened, and it started to beat the ground with its hooves. Then a smell of smoke filled Ruchel's nostrils, causing her to sneeze also. Yells came from the forest. It was Hevedke.

"Fire!" he shouted. "Fire! Branosk is burnt to the ground!"

"*Tata*," Ruchel called, shaking her father. "*Tata*."

Tevye woke up and scrambled to his feet. Quickly, he ran to the road. In the distance, he could see clouds of smoke. The rain had ceased, and a towering fire reached up to the treetops. Ben Zion and his comrades ran past him. Tevye hurried back to the campsite, threw the reins on his horse, and swung onto its back. Nachman ran over and Tevye extended a hand, lifting him up alongside him. They rode off, galloping back down the road. Within minutes, they were back in the village. Pillars of fire blazed all around them. Houses were burnt to the ground. People in their nightgowns lay slaughtered in the street. Others ran in helter-skelter confusion, trying to douse out flames with buckets of water. Crying children searched for their parents. Nachman jumped down from the horse and ran toward his house. Tevye bent down by a man who was pierced through with a saber.

"Cossacks," the Jew whispered and died.

Down the main road of the *shtetl*, the barn where Tevye had met Nachman caved in and collapsed. A man staggered out of the burning synagogue, clutching a *Sefer Torah*. Lungs choking with smoke, he handed the sacred scroll to Tevye. Hevedke appeared by his side. The fire's reflection flashed over his face. He tried to speak, but couldn't find words. Ben Zion ran up alongside them.

"They didn't want to come with us to Palestine," he said, and he ran off to help with the wounded.

Tevye shuddered and embraced the Torah scroll in his arms. By a twist of fortune, his family had escaped the massacre. If they had spent the night in the village, they too would have been victims. And if the rain hadn't extinguished their campfire, the Czar's soldiers would have set upon them. Why had the Almighty protected them, Tevye wondered? Because they were headed for the Promised Land?

Clutching the holy Torah, he headed for the house that Nachman had entered. He climbed the porch stairs and pushed open the door. Dozens of books were scattered on the floor. Bookcases had been toppled. A menorah lay shattered. Tevye set the Torah down on a table. Nachman appeared in the door of the bedroom, his face as white as the *kittel* worn by the cantor on Yom Kippor.

"Blessed art Thou our Lord, King of the universe, the true Judge," the young man whispered.

Tevye stepped to the door of the bedroom and peered inside. The boy's father lay sprawled on the floor, his white beard reddened with blood.

"Fear not, my son," a woman's voice said.

It was only then that Tevye noticed the old woman standing in a corner. She clutched a shawl tightly around her thin figure and gazed across the room with an open-eyed stare. Tevye could tell she was blind.

"Before your father died, he gave you his blessing," she said. Her eyes seemed to shine as if she were gazing at an apparition which they could not see. "And he asked that you pray for his soul at the holy Wall in Jerusalem."

Nachman stared at his mother in silence. One of his brothers ran in the house.

"Your father died with the *Shema* on his lips," the old woman said. "The house filled with light, and an angel escorted his soul up to Heaven. The prophet Elijah was waiting with a chariot of fire. Your father glanced down at me and said not to worry. Then, with a serene smile, he disappeared into a gateway of light. May his memory be for a blessing."

Chapter Six

A WAGON OF WORRIES

Overnight, it became clear to the Jews of Branosk that there was no future for them in their village *shtetl*. Who could predict when the Czar's soldiers would return to continue their wanton destruction? Nonetheless, with the optimism which eternally beats in the hearts of the Jews, there were villagers who wanted to stay and rebuild their razed homes. Others decided to pack up their belongings and seek their fortunes elsewhere, some to western Russia where the pogroms had not as yet reached, others to Germany and Poland. Only a handful of Nachman's companions volunteered to join the Zionists on their journey to *Eretz Yisrael*.

One had the nickname Goliath. A woodcutter by trade, he towered several heads above Tevye. His real name was Alexander, and while he certainly wasn't a scholar, he was fiercely devoted to Nachman. He even called the young Torah prodigy his rabbi. Another friend, Shmuelik, was like a brother to Nachman. They had grown up together, studied *Gemara* together, and dreamed of going to the Land of Israel together. When they were just children in *heder*, Shmuelik would collect sticks in the forest, hand them out to his companions like rifles, and lead them on make-believe attacks, as if they were Maccabee soldiers fighting for the freedom and honor of Israel. Always keeping an eye out for husbands, Tevye reasoned that Shmuelik might prove to be the right man for Bat Sheva, who with every passing day was becoming more enamored with the gallant Ben Zion and his bombastic speeches.

Their other new traveling companion was Hillel, an accordion player by trade. He was older than the others, with streaks of gray hair in his short scraggly beard. He walked with a limp, as if from the weight of his accordion which he lugged with him wherever he went. "Be happy today," was his motto, "Because tomorrow you could be food for the worms." It was a philosophy which Tevye shared. Hillel was a man he could talk to. Though he didn't have a lucrative profession, Tevye thought that the musician might be a match for his Tzeitl. After all, with two children, she wasn't exactly a new cow in the market.

But a greater *mitzvah* than marriage lay before them at the moment – the *mitzvah* of burying the dead. Tevye took a shovel from his wagon and helped in the work of digging graves for the corpses. His daughters helped with the wounded. Ruchel volunteered to assist Nachman's mother and sisters in the kitchen of Nachman's house, where with his brothers and sisters, he had to sit *shiva*, the traditional week of Jewish mourning. People came to offer their condolences all through the day and the evening, and Ruchel kept busy baking cakes for the guests. Though she rarely exchanged a word with Nachman, a deep bond was building between them. She felt that they communicated even without speaking, and he felt it too. When the elders of the community urged him to stay on and inherit his father's position, the young scholar was uncertain where his greater obligation lay, as a guardian of the Torah in the exile, or as a builder of the Promised Land. Ruchel vowed to stand by him whatever he decided, even if it meant saying good-bye to her family. The dutiful son had qualms about leaving his mother, but his older brother and sisters promised to watch over her. After several days, he arrived at an answer.

"Our future is in the Land of Israel," he said.

To pass the time while Nachman was observing the week of mourning, Tevye and the Zionists pitched in with the work of repair. One afternoon, as Ben Zion and Peter were out strolling through the woods to get away from the pious *shtetl*, they came across Hevedke, who had kept out of sight in the forest ever since the night the Cossacks had raided the village.

"Well, look what we have here," Peter whispered to his friend.

"Hiding out in the woods like a spy," Ben Zion answered.

"You think he's like all the rest of the anti-Semites?" Peter asked.

"I don't know, but for Tevye's sake, let's teach him a lesson."

Ben Zion raised his hand in salutation and called out with a smile. "Hey, Hevedke! Over here!"

The Russian waved in a good-natured greeting. He was happy to see them. He hadn't spoken to a soul in two days. He was running low on food, and he was beginning to feel profoundly unhappy walking around in endless circles to fight off the boredom and chill.

Smiling, Ben Zion walked up to him and reached out to shake his hand. Only he didn't let go. He twisted Hevedke's arm behind his back and held on to him tightly as Peter punched him hard in the stomach. When the Russian doubled over in pain, Ben Zion released him and added a shove of his own. Hevedke stumbled, but he didn't fall down.

"Let's see you fight!" Ben Zion shouted.

The poet refused to raise up his fists.

"Fight!" Peter yelled, hitting him again. Hevedke collapsed to his knees.

"Make sure we never see you again," Ben Zion told him, leaving him on his knees in the forest, as if he were praying in church.

When the week of mourning was ended, Nachman packed his father's *Chumash* and *Siddur* into his sack along with a few other books, kissed his blind mother good-bye, and joined Tevye's family and the Zionists as they set off down the road.

"Don't you worry about me," his mother told him, as if reading his thoughts. "The Lord will be gracious. In His kindness, He has stricken me with blindness to spare me from seeing the horrors which are befalling our people, and in His kindness, He will send the *Mashiach* to bring all of us back to *Eretz Yisrael*."

"May it be soon," Nachman said. He kissed his mother one last time on the forehead and ran tearfully off to catch up with the others.

The voyage took almost three months. After having hurled fire and rain in their path, the Almighty dispatched a late winter snowstorm which covered their boots up to their knees and made traveling treacherous and slow. With heads lowered to escape the biting wind, the group trudged eastward toward the port of Odessa. For miles on end, blinded by the snow, they could barely make out the road. Only the instincts of the horse kept them on course. During the height of the blizzard, the wagon had to be pushed, and finally, as the wheels became buried in drifts, it refused to budge at all.

A feeling of despair fell over their endeavor. Hillel tried to cheer them up with a tune on his accordion, but his fingers were too frozen to manipulate the keys. Then, as if to dash their hopes completely, a group of Zionists coming from another evacuated region told them that a roadblock of soldiers a mile up the road was preventing Jews from entering the province which led to the port of Odessa. When the leader of their group had tried to break through the roadblock, the soldiers had shot him dead on the spot. His comrades were carrying his body to a proper Jewish cemetery and postponing their journey until more favorable conditions prevailed.

"What are we going to do now, *Tata?*" Bat Sheva asked.

"Haven't our Rabbis told us that three things are obtained through suffering?" he philosophically answered.

"I suppose they did," Bat Sheva responded. "They had something to say about everything."

"What three things?" Hava inquired.

"Tell them, Nachman," Tevye called, wanting to show off the wisdom of his learned groom, his daughter Hodel's *chassan.*

"The Torah, the World to Come, and the Land of Israel," the scholar responded. "They are the most precious things a man can attain, and to achieve them, he has to be willing to suffer."

"In what tractate of Talmud can the teaching be found?" Tevye asked.

"The tractate *Berachot.*"

"On what page?"

Nachman blushed. He wasn't a braggart, and it embarrassed him to be put on display. "Page five," he responded.

"What's the use of memorizing a lot of ancient history?" Ben Zion asked. "If you want to read a truly important book, you should read 'The Jewish State,' by Theodor Herzl. He was a prophet who spoke to the Jews of today."

"The Lord has many messengers," Nachman answered. "In our time, God chose Herzl to bring the message of Zion to our exiled people. But it wasn't Herzl who invented the Zionist movement. It comes from our holy Torah and the Jews who have been following its call for thousands of years."

"But how can we continue?" Bat Sheva asked. "The road is blocked by soldiers."

"We'll go through the woods and over the mountain," Ben Zion answered. "Though my version of Jewish history differs from the young rabbi's, our destination is admittedly the same."

All eyes turned to the snow-covered mountains which loomed up on both sides of the road. "What about the wagon?" Tzeitl asked.

"The girl has a point," Tevye said. "We can't take the wagon over the mountain."

"Hevedke can drive the wagon," Hava said. "There is no reason for the soldiers to stop him."

Everyone stared at Tevye, who sat in the wagon perplexed. Hevedke, as usual, was trailing behind them. Every few miles, he would appear like an apparition out of the snow. If Tevye gave in, it would be a victory for the Russian and arouse Hava's hopes. But if he said no, they would either have to turn back, or abandon the wagon out on the road. What would become of his Golda? He couldn't *shlep* her coffin over the mountain. Nor could he bury her in the snow. He turned to stare back along the tracks of the wagon. Down the road, a snowman stood rigid in the winter landscape. Tevye had to give the Galagani some credit. For a gentile, he was as stubborn as a Jew.

With a grumble, Tevye lay down the reins and climbed off the wagon.

"You go talk to him," he said to Ben Zion. "But I want everyone to know - it's only for the success of the journey."

"This is insane," Naftali argued. "We can't be climbing mountains in this weather. I say we find shelter and wait for the storm to subside."

"He Who formed the mountains and causes the winds to blow will give us the strength to succeed on our journey," Shmuelik said.

"If you people are on such good terms with Him, why doesn't He make the mountain disappear altogether and save us the effort?" Peter asked.

"According to the effort is the reward," Shmuelik answered.

Like Nachson ben Amminadav, the first Jew to brave the mighty waters of the Red Sea when the children of Israel stood frightfully on its banks pursued by the chariots of Egypt, the faith-filled youth from the village of Branosk started out up the snowbound ascent. It was agreed that Hevedke would meet the group on the other side of the mountain. Wrapping the children in blankets, they set out on the arduous trek. The climb took most of the day. When the children tired, the men took turns carrying them up the rugged incline. Tevye's beard turned white with snow. Several times, they had to pause and wait up for Tzeitl. Her feet were frozen, her legs felt like stones, her teeth chattered, and sneezes racked her thin body. By sunset, she was so weak Tevye had to lift her and carry her in his arms. He staggered forward beneath his precious load. Her eyes were feverish, and through her heavy clothing, Tevye could feel her body shivering with each raspy breath. Several times, she inquired after the children, then fell into a deep sleep in his arms. Gradually, the winds and snow stopped. At nightfall, they reached the summit. Clouds drifted apart over their heads, revealing patches of stars. Ben Zion wanted to camp for the evening and make the descent at dawn, when they would have a better idea of their bearings. But Tevye kept walking. He wanted to get Tzeitl to a lower altitude, where it would be warmer, and even try to meet up with the wagon that night. The girl needed a doctor. With a prayer on his lips, he hoisted his bundle over his shoulder. His legs carried him forward down the slope of the mountain. Shmuelik walked at his side. Nachman followed with Ruchel. Soon, everyone fell into line. After an hour, Tevye's muscles were depleted of strength. With a groan, he sank to his knees in the snow. Gently, Goliath reached down and lifted Tzeitl into his arms. Nachman and Shmuelik helped Tevye to his feet, and the weary hikers continued on down the mountain.

When they reached the road, the wagon was nowhere in sight. Tevye gazed up to Heaven. A man was not supposed to rely on miracles, but the gates of prayer were always open to pleas from he heart.

"My dear and gracious King, have You brought us this far just to turn us into pillars of ice in this tundra?" he called. "Save us. If not for the sake of this miserable wretch of a milkman, then for the sake of his saintly wife, Golda."

Tevye took his unconscious daughter from the arms of the giant, and once again the group started off in the darkness. Then, to everyone's joy, around the first bend in the road, Tevye's prayer was answered. Hevedke sat waiting in the wagon.

With shouts of triumph, the hikers ran forward. Tevye quickly lifted Tzeitl into the back of the wagon. The rest of his daughters climbed aboard. Goliath sat up front beside Hevedke who continued to drive. The others were to meet them in the next town along the road. The Russian whipped the reins and urged the horse onward into the night. Everyone's thoughts were on finding a doctor for Tzeitl. Within a short time, the houses of a village appeared in the distance. Hevedke pounded on the first door they came to. The doorpost, Tevye noticed, lacked a *mezuzah*. The Russian peasant who answered pointed the way to the house of the local doctor. Tevye asked him if there was a Jewish doctor in town. The man shook his head, no. There weren't any Jews in the village at all.

Once again, at the doctor's, Hevedke did all of the talking. He said that his sister was sick. Reluctantly, the sleepy, night-gowned physician invited him into his house. Soon the small salon was crowded with Tevye's snow-covered family. Like a guard, Goliath waited outside with the wagon.

Tevye set Tzeitl gently down on a bed in the doctor's examining room. The physician quickly dressed, put on his eyeglasses and glanced from the dark, bearded Jew to the tall, blond Hevedke.

"I have to charge more for night visits," he said.

Hevedke nodded, reached his hand in his pocket, and showed the doctor some rubles. Hava stood watching as the doctor examined her sister. Little Hannie cried for her mommy until Bat Sheva rocked her to sleep. Hevedke spoke to the doctor's wife in the kitchen and convinced her to warm up a large samovar of tea. After a short while, the doctor reappeared. Tevye's worries proved accurate. The girl had pneumonia and the doctor had given her some medicine which would bring down her fever. Hava was toweling her down. The patient would have to stay in bed for a few days and drink lots of hot tea. Tevye knew the rest of the story. What would be, would be. Tevye had known of people who had recovered from pneumonia, and others who had died, God forbid. Like Tzeitl's poor husband, Motel, who had coughed himself into the grave.

Tevye prayed and followed the doctor's orders. In the meantime, their journey was postponed. The Zionists arrived and went straight to the town inn to rest. Hevedke rented a room for Tzeitl and her family in the house of an old widow. Every day, he escorted Nachman and Ruchel to the market to buy fresh vegetables for soup. For the sake of his sick daughter, Tevye relied on the poet's help, but he was careful to keep him a safe distance from Hava. Since there was no kosher meat in the town, Tevye bought a chicken and slaughtered it himself. If the doctor's medicine couldn't cure his daughter, certainly some chicken soup would.

It was agreed that Ben Zion would continue on to Odessa, another three days away, to arrange for ocean passage to Palestine. Tevye handed him a sizable share of the money he had received from the sale of his house, so that Ben Zion could buy them tickets. Before their departure, the Zionists returned to the inn for one last, hearty non-kosher repast.

Goliath said he was staying behind to travel with Tevye. Though the giant wouldn't admit it, he had fallen in love with Tzeitl. Carrying the sick woman in his arms through the snow had stirred his big heart. Though he had barely exchanged a word with her, he felt like her guardian angel, duty bound to protect her. He played with her children and took them on rides through the woods on his back. At night, instead of sleeping in the warm corner which Shmuelik, Hillel, and Nachman had found in a barn, he slept on the porch of the old widow's house, just to be closer to Tzeitl.

Although in principle Ben Zion shunned alcohol as the brew which kept the Russian peasantry content in their servitude and squalor, before setting out on the next leg of their journey, he allowed himself several glasses of wine during lunch. His head was happily spinning when his comrades led him out of the inn. Bat Sheva stood across the road, waiting to wish him good-bye. Catching a glimpse of her, he told his friends that he would rendezvous with them at the outskirts of town. Then with a wink, he walked off toward the girl.

"I came to say farewell and to wish you good luck," she said.

"Don't tell me farewell," he said. "Tell me *L'Hitraot.* It's Hebrew for `Until we see each other again.'"

"Do you really want to see me again?" she asked.

"What kind of question is that?" he answered. "Listen. I have something to tell you. But wait, we can't talk here on the street. Come with me now."

Quickly, he led her away from the houses and into the woods. When they were out of sight of the village, he took her hand and pushed her against the trunk of a tree. He looked into her eyes with a gaze so bold that it made her gasp for breath.

"I have a confession to make," he told her.

Bat Sheva stood paralyzed, waiting for him to continue.

"I have the feeling that... I am falling in love with you."

"I feel the same way," Bat Sheva answered.

"Our beliefs are so different," he said.

"They are not so different as you think," she replied, blushing under his gaze.

"If you mean that, then show me. Let me give you a kiss."

Bat Sheva trembled. A kiss was sacred. A kiss was a gesture of love. Just being alone with a man was forbidden. Her heart pounded so loudly, she felt certain that the whole village would hear. Before she could say no, Ben Zion bent his head down and he kissed her. When their lips touched, she tasted the pungent sweetness of wine.

"You've been drinking," she accused, pushing him away.

"Since when is drinking a sin?" he retorted, grabbing her and kissing her again.

"Do you really love me?" she asked.

"Yes, yes, I love you madly," he vowed.

"Will you marry me?" she asked

"Yes, yes," he promised. "I will marry you a thousand times over."

"You swear?" she asked.

"On the Holy Bible," he told her.

"Oh, Ben Zion, I'm so happy," she said.

"Well I'm not," a deep, husky voice interrupted. It was the voice of her Father.

"*Tata!*" she cried.

Tevye seemed to tower above them, clutching a stick in his hand. When Ben Zion looked up, all he saw was a shadow standing in front of the sun. The stick slammed into his back. Whack! Whack! Whack! Crying out, the Zionist raised his hands to block the blows to his head. Bat Sheva cried out and wept.

"I'll kill you!" Tevye bellowed. "I'll kill you if I ever catch you with my daughter again!"

Tevye landed a kick to Ben Zion's butt, and the Rasputin ran off like a thief. When Tevye turned to his daughter, his eyes were ablaze.

"Is the Almighty blind that He doesn't see what goes on in the forest?" he shouted. "Your dead mother is shamed!"

Red in the face, the girl couldn't look at her father.

Tevye growled. The Zionists be damned. Maybe he was making a dreadful mistake in following them so blindly. A cloud of worry filled his head. What would become of his daughters?

Chapter Seven

"GET THEE FORTH TO THE LAND"

Because of her treatment, or in spite of it, Tzeitl seemed to improve. She sat up in bed, color returned to her cheeks, and her fever subsided. But Tevye still worried about the rattling cough deep in her chest. The doctor said he could offer no more assistance. Fresh air and the approaching summer sun were the best things for her now. He didn't know if a voyage to the Land of Israel would harm her. In fact, the ocean breeze might do her good. And Palestine's mild, Mediterranean climate was certainly a healthier environment than Russia's drastically changing seasons, he said.

When ten days passed and no word arrived from Odessa, they decided to continue their journey, as it says, "You have dwelt long enough in this mountain, turn away and take up your journey." Tevye chided himself with having trusted Ben Zion with a large chunk of his savings. Fortunately, Hillel and Shmuelik had agreed to journey on with the Zionists to make sure that the money didn't get lost. Tzeitl was still too weak to walk on her own, so her sisters helped her into the wagon. Nachman sat alongside Tevye, and the giant, Alexander Goliath, walked behind on the road, as if to make sure that the children didn't fall out on the way.

"What about Hevedke?" asked Hava.

"What about him?" Tevye said.

"Aren't we going to wait for him to come back from the market?"

"Why should we? It is a blessing to be rid of him."

"How can you say that after all he did for Tzeitl?" Ruchela asked.

"He isn't a part of this enterprise," Tevye said. "My horse has done a great deal for me too, but I am going to part from him in Odessa. As Solomon says, There is a time to find, and a time to lose."

"I think he has proven himself," Tzeitl said. "I think you should give him a chance."

Tevye was happy to see his daughter's spirit returning, but his answer was no.

"Tell him, Nachman," Ruchela said. "Tell my stubborn old Father that a gentile can convert."

Nachman didn't want to enter the family quarrel. "Halachically," he said, "Jewish law makes it possible, but it isn't a simple matter. Besides a *brit milah*, and immersion in a ritual *mikvah*, a long period of learning is required."

"How long?" Hava asked.

"At least a year," the young rabbi said. "And during that time, the prospective convert certainly isn't allowed to be in the company of a Jewish woman with whom he has been intimate in the past."

Hava blushed and fell silent.

"There!" Tevye said. "The rabbi has decided. You heard it from his mouth yourselves."

"I'll wait a year," Hava said. "I'll wait ten years."

"Agreed," Tevye answered. "After ten years, I will reconsider my decision. In the meantime, it's final, and I don't want to hear anymore."

"I don't blame Hava for loving Hevedke," Bat Sheva said. "Jewish men are awful."

They were the first words she had spoken for days. When word hadn't arrived from Ben Zion, she had fallen into a lovesick depression. He had seduced her, betrayed her, and made her feel like a fool. All of his promises had been nothing but lies. He had wounded her heart, tarnished her purity, and worse than all, damaged her feminine pride. Though she had only succumbed to two kisses, she felt compromised beyond all repair.

The days turned beautiful, as if God had answered Tevye's prayers for good weather. The sun melted all of the snow on the ground, and the Russian landscape seemed to sparkle with the promise of renewal which comes with the spring. Tzeitl's spirits were characteristically cheerful. She seemed to feel better each day, but her cough clung to her like a shroud. Each time Tevye heard it, he felt a dagger pierce through his heart. Then, when they were only a half day's journey from Odessa, a different kind of danger appeared on their path. Two highwaymen on horseback galloped out of the woods in front of the wagon and ordered them to halt. They both brandished rifles and their faces were covered with masks.

"Hand over your money and no one needs to get hurt," one of them said.

"Have pity," Tevye pleaded. "It's all the money we have."

"If we had pity, we would be priests, not robbers. Now get down from the wagon and hand over your rubles."

Tevye had no choice. He didn't have a gun, and even if he had, he didn't know how to use one. Slowly, he stepped down from the wagon. His daughters huddled together, shielding the children. Just then, the protecting angel whom Tevye had prayed for appeared. As Tevye opened the wooden chest containing their valuables, he heard a loud roar like the sound of a bear. It was Goliath. With a terrifying bellow, he charged at one of the highwaymen. The startled bandit swung around in his saddle and fired his weapon. Miraculously, the shot missed its mark. The giant rammed into the horse and its rider, toppling them both to the ground. Before the other highwayman could steady his own horse and fire, Goliath grabbed his leg and dragged him out of the saddle. A wild shot went off in the air. The robber's head hit the ground with a thud. His partner scrambled for his gun which had fallen to the road, but Goliath leaped over and crunched a foot on his hand, cracking his bones. Yelping in pain, he scurried off into the forest. Goliath picked up the rifles and broke them in half, as if they were twigs. Tevye grabbed the reins of the riderless horses.

"It looks like we have two new horses," he grinned.

Goliath hurried back to the wagon. "Are you all right, Tzeitl?" he asked.

Tzeitl nodded.

"And the children?"

Breathless, Tzeitl nodded again. Tevye checked through the pockets of the unconscious robber sprawled on the ground. He found close to two hundred rubles.

"Booty from the battle," he said, holding the money in the air. "As the Good Book says....."

When Tevye couldn't think of a verse, Nachman came to his aid.

"'Thou has smitten all of my enemies on the cheek; Thou has broken the teeth of the wicked,'" he quoted a Psalm by heart.

To Tevye, it was a sign that their *mazel* was changing. At the first farm they came to, he was able to sell the two horses at a respectable price. When they arrived, exhausted but cheerful in Odessa, they headed straight for the port. Odessa was the biggest city Tevye's daughters had ever seen. The stores, the boulevards, the carriages, and the smartly dressed women looked like they were part of a dream. Yet the wonder which made everyone stand up in the wagon was the sight of a motorized carriage that rode along the street without being pulled by a horse! Nachman said it was a miracle. Tevye called it an automobile. He had seen them before in his travels. For the moment, he was more concerned with the soldiers who stood idle at every corner, as if waiting for some menacing order. Though the wagon load of Jews looked out of place in the bustling city, no one ordered them to stop. Nevertheless, the milkman from Anatevka was reluctant to ask directions. He relied on his instincts and his sense of smell to lead them to the port. Though they may not have found the shortest route, before long the odor of fish and seawater filled everyone's nostrils.

To the simple milkman's family, the giant steamships and freighters which towered over their wagon as they road along the dock were symbols of the great new world which lay waiting over the ocean. Even a man as worldly as Tevye had never seen anything close to their size. The yachts belonging to the aristocrats in Boiberik were like tiny rowboats compared to these motorized whales. Workers, cargo men, porters, and passengers scurried over the dock, but Ben Zion, Naftali, Peter, and their friends were nowhere to be found. Tevye and Nachman ventured into a few shipping offices to inquire about boats leaving for Palestine, but they only received discouraging shakes of the head. There were ships taking vodka to France, potatoes to Hong Kong, coal to Spain, and lumber to Portugal, but none seemed to be taking Jewish pilgrims to Palestine.

With fallen spirits, Tevye and Nachman returned to the wagon. To their surprise, a little *pitseleh* of a man with a beard and a cap was standing by Goliath, barely reaching up to his waist.

"I understand you are looking for a boat to the Holy Land," he said to them in Yiddish.

"*Du bist a Yid?*" Tevye asked. "You're a Jew?"

"Through the kindness of God," he answered. "Ever since I was born, or more officially, eight days later, when my father brought me into the Covenant of Abraham and gave me the name Eliahu."

"Can you help us?" Tevye asked.

"To the extent that God allows," their new acquaintance answered. "Isn't it a *mitzvah* to help a fellow Jew? Of course it is. But it is also a *mitzvah* that a man support his family, and since my work is helping Jews, I will have to be paid a small, modest fee for my services."

"Of course," Tevye answered. "Never let it be said that Tevye, the milkman, failed to reimburse a man for his labor."

"In advance," the man said.

Tevye nodded. He turned his back, reached in his pocket, and peeled a small note from his stack. He handed the money to diminutive Jew, who glanced at it and made a small face. Tevye gave him another.

Satisfied, Eliahu led Tevye to the same shipping office where he had taken Ben Zion two weeks before. The Zionists had been lucky to arrive in Odessa the very day a boat was setting sail for Palestine. Not wanting to miss the opportunity, they had boarded at once. Bat Sheva turned red when she heard the report. She could picture the scoundrel, Ben Zion, laughing with his friends

on the boat as he told them how he had seduced the milkman's
innocent daughter. Tevye was no less enraged, thinking of the
money he had given the thieving *gonif* to purchase tickets for his
family. Hadn't his friend, the sandal maker, warned him back at
the crossroads about the Zionist scoundrels? "Fortunate is the man
who does not walk in the counsel of the wicked." Of course the
heretic had run off with the money. But then again, Tevye
reasoned, to be fair, if they had not encountered Ben Zion, they
would never have reached Odessa at all. How could Tevye
complain? He was now only a boat ride away from his Hodel.

The miniature Jew, Eliahu, brought them to the shipping office
and introduced them to an agent. Then he took their leave, giving
them an address in the Jewish ghetto where they could find
lodging and food. Swatting a fly away from the crackers and tea
on his desk, the agent leafed through a thick heavy ledger and said
he had a boat leaving for Constantinople in another fourteen days.
From there, they could buy passage to Italy, which, he said, was
only a short boat ride to Palestine. Or, if they preferred, he could
sell them one ticket for all three sections of the journey, which
would cost them considerably less in the end. The only problem
was that the freighter leaving Odessa was already sold out, and the
next scheduled departure was six weeks away.

"Six weeks away?" Tevye exclaimed.

"That's the situation," the shipping agent curtly replied.

"Isn't there something you can do?" Tevye asked.

"The boat is overcrowded already," the Russian replied.

"I am willing to pay a higher price," Tevye offered.

"I'm sorry, but we have company rules."

"I have to get to Palestine. I have a sick daughter."

"I understand," the man said.

Tevye waited as the agent opened a file and glanced through
some papers, shaking his head. "I'll be taking a big risk," he
declared.

Tevye pulled out his cache of newly found rubles. The agent
stared at the money.

"It will cost you double the normal fare," he said. "But in light of your sick daughter, I can try to arrange it."

Tevye might have been a simple milkman from the country, but he had enough business experience to know when someone was playing him for a fool. But what could he do? He didn't have a steamship of his own to sail the seven seas. So if he had to pay a little extra money, what else was new? Being a Jew was a blessing which came with a price.

The agent wrote up an agreement of sale for the tickets. Then, as if suddenly remembering, he handed Tevye an envelope which Ben Zion had left in the office. The envelope, addressed to "Reb Tevye from Anatevka," looked as if it had already been opened. The letter inside was written in Ben Zion's floundering Yiddish, apparently to prevent the shipping clerk from understanding its contents. "My dear and respected *Reb* Tevye," it read. "Upon arriving in Odessa, we have been informed that a ship is sailing for Turkey today. Since the zealous are careful to perform the *mitzvot* as quickly as possible, we are boarding and continuing on our way. We will meet you in kibbutz Shoshana, in the land of our future. In the meantime, I am enclosing your money in this envelope. I have a feeling that it will be safer in the care of the shipping company than in the hands of the little Jew who brought us here. *L'Hitraot.* Ben Zion."

Then, scribbled at the bottom of the page was a brief explanation, "I am writing in my childhood Yiddish because I don't trust the shipping clerk either."

Except for the letter, the envelope was empty. Tevye looked up at the bookish shipping agent who had returned to his work and his papers. A feeling of shame swept over Tevye for having judged the young Zionist in too hasty a fashion, thinking he had run off with his money. But he felt even worse knowing that the money had ended up in the pocket of the clean-shaven Laban before him.

"Excuse me," Tevye said. "There was supposed to be money along with this letter, but the envelope is empty."

The agent looked up with an innocent glance.

"Maybe your friend forget to put the money inside. I seem to remember that he was in a big hurry."

"No," Tevye answered. "He writes that he put it inside with the letter."

The shipping agent shrugged.

"Somebody stole my money," Tevye said.

"I'm afraid I can't help you. Since I received the letter, it has been right here, locked up in my drawer. And I am the only one with a key."

"That sort of limits the possibilities," Tevye said.

"I resent the implication," the clerk answered. He stood up with a look of great indignation. "If you would like to cancel your contract, I will be happy to oblige. I certainly won't stand here and be insulted by a Jew. If you have a complaint, go tell the police."

"Don't you worry, I will," Tevye threatened.

He strode out of the office. Wouldn't you know it? A policeman was walking alongside the dock, eyeing the women in the wagon. Tevye decided to approach him. He was so enraged, he didn't seem to notice that Hevedke was standing near the wagon talking to Hava.

Seeing Tevye and Nachman stride over to the policeman, Goliath walked over to find out what was the matter.

"A good day to you, officer, and to all upholders of the law" Tevye said. "I have reason to believe that the shipping agent in that office has stolen a considerable sum of money from me."

"Who are you?" the policeman asked, staring at the thickly bearded Jew.

"Tevye, the milkman, from Anatevka."

"It's a long way from Anatevka for a milkman," the policeman said. "What brings you to Odessa?"

"We are on our way to Palestine."

"Have a good voyage. When Russia is free of all you stinking parasites, it will be a better country."

"What did you say?" another voice asked. It was Goliath. He towered beside Tevye.

"Look what we have here," the policeman said, staring up at the giant. "A whole mountain of filth."

Nachman's "No!" came too late. Goliath reached out and grabbed the policeman by his collar. With one hand, he lifted him off his feet into the air. With three giant strides, Goliath reached the edge of the dock. Grunting, he hurled the startled policeman through the air, down into the water below.

"*Gevalt,*" Tevye moaned, leading the race back to the wagon. When all of the Jews were aboard, he whipped the reins of the horse and the wagon sped off. Hevedke held his hand in the air and hollered out, "Wait!" but Tevye urged his steed onward as if he were in the midst of a chariot race. As the wagon thundered down the cobblestones of the dock, the women held fast to their mother's galloping coffin. Porters rushed out of their way. Passersby cursed them. Though no one was chasing them, Tevye didn't relax until they reached the neighborhood of the Jews at the outskirts of the city. "Refuge," Tevye thought. Store signs were written in Yiddish. Shops sold pickles in barrels, dried fruit, chickens, and fish. Rolls of fabric stood in the doorway of one store, dresses in the window of another. If there was a problem of anti-Semitism in Russia, you wouldn't have known it from the busy life of the Odessa ghetto.

Tevye found the address which Eliahu had given him. He lived in a small basement apartment, cramped with relatives and children. Like a king entertaining royal guests, the diminutive Jew sat them around a table and ordered his wife to bring rugelach cakes and tea. When Tevye told him what had happened at the dock, an aghast expression spread over his face.

"Your friend did what with the policeman?" he asked incredulously. Tevye, Nachman, and the oversized Alexander Goliath all started laughing. Their host failed to see anything humorous.

"Something like this can bring a pogrom on all of the Jews of Odessa," he said.

"What should we do?" Tevye asked.

"You'll have to set off on your voyage tonight."

"But how? Our ship doesn't leave for two weeks."

"You can't go back to the dock. The police will be waiting for you," Eliahu warned them. "There are small boats for hire that can be secured for a price. The crossing is dangerous, but others have made it. With God's help, I can arrange for one of the captains to sail tonight."

"In a sailboat?" Nachman asked.

"That's your only other choice. Unless you want to walk across Russia and Turkey, and that can take a year."

"How dangerous is dangerous?" Tevye asked.

"I haven't made the crossing myself," the little Jew confided. "But there are Russians who do it for a living, and even a gentile doesn't want to get killed. But I'd be lying if I told you that there haven't been shipwrecks and drownings. The Black Sea isn't a duck pond. It's as big as an ocean and the winds can be treacherous."

"God will answer our prayers for a safe journey," Nachman said with his unflinching faith.

"What about the money I paid to that thief at the dock?" Tevye asked.

The Jew held up his hands. "*Kaporas*," he said. "It is lost. May it be considered an atonement for your sins."

The little Jew was right, Tevye decided. Why cry over spilled milk? Right now, the important thing was escaping from Odessa without going to prison. And besides, in the turn of events, there was one big consolation which Tevye didn't dare mention. By sneaking off on a boat in the middle of the night, they would be rid of the tenacious Hevedke forever!

The Jews got down to business. The voyage would cost them three hundred rubles. It was almost half of the money that Tevye had left. And there were still two more sea journeys to follow. Which meant that they would be landing in the Holy Land with an empty purse and a prayer. As if sensing his thoughts, Goliath offered to pay the cost of the passage for everyone.

"It's my fault that we have fallen into this mess," he declared.

"You meant well," Tevye retorted. "Besides, you upheld the

honor of the people of God, and no man should be penalized for that."

Finally, when it was agreed that each man would put up his own share of the fare, their host hurried off to arrange for a boat. In the meantime, Nachman wandered off to find an evening prayer *minyan* where he could say the mourner's *Kaddish* for his father. Having spent the greater part of his life voyaging through Talmudic texts in the study hall of the yeshiva, it was his father's dying blessing which gave Nachman the confidence to set out on such a hazardous voyage. As the Talmud states, a man who undertakes to do a good deed will be Divinely protected from the dangers of travel. And could there be a greater deed than going to live in the Land of Israel, a precept which was equal in weight to all of the commandments in the Torah? Especially when it had been his father's last wish that Nachman pray at the sacred Wall in Jerusalem, at the site where their ancient Temple had stood. Surely, in the merit of his father, the Almighty would protect them on the way.

In a matter of hours, the Constantinople-bound Jews rendezvoused with Eliahu under the cover of nightfall. Sneaking out of the city like fugitives, Tevye's daughters were frightened with the great rush and mystery. The boat was waiting for them at a dock at the edge of the forest. From the bow to the stern, the vessel was several wagons long, but it was tiny compared with the great freighters they had seen at the port. Eliahu introduced the captain as Leo. He wore what looked like an admiral's jacket and cap, but Tevye eyed him with doubts. The captain's breath reeked of cheap liquor. Not that Tevye blamed him for drinking. The roar of the waves, and the blackness of the sea in the distance invited the thought of a strong vodka or two, but it wasn't something that inspired confidence at the start of a voyage. Especially since Tevye had never learned how to swim. And neither, of course, had his daughters.

The seaman greeted his passengers gruffly and shouted commands to his crew of three sailors, who helped carry their belongings aboard. It was Hava who voiced everyone's worries.

"This is crazy!" she said.

No one expressed disagreement, yet no one could offer an alternative plan. As the captain and crew hurried to get the ship ready, Tevye and Goliath slid Golda's coffin out of the wagon and carried it toward the boat. Suddenly, with an arm upraised, the captain told them to stop. Crossing himself, he said that corpses were bad luck on a voyage. He wasn't about to set sail with an evil omen on board.

"An evil omen?" Tevye said, offended to hear his wife spoken about in such a crude manner.

"It's enough of a curse that I'm carrying Jews."

The ungrateful dog, Tevye thought. But before he could get into an argument, Nachman stepped between them and persuaded the captain to set aside his religious objections for another twenty-five rubles.

Tevye was impressed. The lad wasn't only a scholar. Like Jacob, he knew how to get along in the world. Satisfied, the superstitious sailor put the money in his pocket and went on with the work of hoisting the sails. Then, when everything was ready, it was Hava who balked. Like a borscht which has been left boiling too long on the fire, her emotions spilled out from the pot.

"I am not leaving Russia without Hevedke," she declared.

"We made an agreement," her father said. "Let this be his test."

"But how will he find us? And he doesn't have any money. How will he get to Palestine?"

"That's his problem, not ours," Tevye answered.

Hava glared at her Father.

"Don't worry," Tzeitl told her. "He'll find his way to Israel. And this will be proof to everyone that he really is serious about being a Jew."

Soothed by her sister's assurance, Hava let Tzeitl take her hand and lead her across the small wooden plank leading on to the ship.

Then came the most difficult part of the journey for Tevye. After all of their belongings were fastened on board in a compartment under the deck, he walked with heavy footsteps back onto shore to say a tearful good-bye to his horse.

To Tevye, departing from his wagon wasn't the end of the world. A wagon was merely wood planks. Selling it to Eliahu was like any transaction. It was true that in the darkness of the forest, at this late hour by the sea, there were no other bidders to insure a good price, but the wagon had seen its best days, and anything at all which the milkman received was like extra money in his pocket. His horse, however, was a part of the family, a part of his history, like a brother and companion in life. Tevye couldn't bring himself to sell him. He told Eliahu to look after him and to find him a kind owner, who wouldn't work him too hard. Inhaling a last whiff of the horse's musky aroma, Tevye stroked the animal's mane and gave him a kiss on the cheek.

"Take care my good friend," he said softly. "May the Almighty Who created us both, bless you and keep you. If there is a Heaven for workhorses and mules, if you get there before me, put in a good word for Tevye."

Soon their boat was sailing away from the dock. Eliahu disappeared into the blackness. As the crew busied with the sails, the voyagers sat close together in an apprehensive huddle. As it turned out, their trepidations proved groundless. All week long, the Lord heard their prayers and kept the ocean winds calm. The captain said he had never seen anything like it. Tevye didn't have to look far to discover the cause. Nachman sat all day on the bow, studying a tractate of Talmud. Obviously, the Almighty didn't want to interrupt the scholar's learning with the splash of a wave, so the sea remained as tranquil as milk in a bucket. And yet, over their heads a breeze billowed their sails and sped them on their journey.

Though Tevye was by no means a scholar, he enjoyed having a *hevruta* on board with whom he could argue the fine points of the law. While his mind worked at a much slower pace than Nachman's, Tevye relished their Mishnaic exchanges. For the milkman, the time on the boat was like a vacation. When had he been able to sit all day in the sun and study the Torah? For as long as he could remember, his work day had started at four in the morning, before the rooster's first crow, and finished late at night, after the children had fallen asleep. As it says in the Bible, "By the

sweat of thy brow, thou shall eat bread." So if Tevye had ever
envied Baron Rothschild and his yachts, now he could tell
everyone that he had been out yachting too.

Because of the clear skies and the gently rocking sea, the
captain and his crew had little to do. They spent most of the day
playing cards and drinking liquor. There were drunken arguments,
and an occasional fight, plus a steady stream of bawdy songs and
jokes that made the women blush. Goliath sat protectively near
Tevye's daughters and whittled stick-figure dolls to pass the time.
If the crewmen entertained any non-kosher thoughts, the sight of
the giant guarding the ladies was a convincing deterrent.

The gently rolling waves had a soothing effect on Hava also.
The lullaby of the sea and the steady wind in the masts calmed
her restless spirits and restored her belief that everything would
work out in the end. To pass the time, she read the book of
Psalms. The songs and prayers of King David lifted her out of her
worries and transported her to a world where goodness and justice
would triumph. For her, the boat ride was exactly what the
Psalmist had penned, "He makes me lie down in green pastures;
He leads me beside the still waters. He restores my soul."

Only the downcast Bat Sheva remained obsessed with stormy
ruminations. Tevye's youngest daughter tried to push Ben Zion
out of her mind by organizing meals for the crew, but her thoughts
were possessed with schemes of revenge. Like rolling waves, her
passions swayed back and forth. Chopping potatoes, she would
dream of cutting off the hands that had held her; while peeling
onions, she would cry at the thought that the gallant Zionist
already had found some other woman to wed.

To make a long story short, everyone but Bat Sheva was in
jubilant spirits when they reached Constantinople. Stepping onto
dry land, Nachman said a blessing of thanks for God's faithful
providence, and everyone answered Amen! The dock of the port
was bustling with action. Turks garbed in an assortment of caftans,
turbans, and robes, scurried in every direction. Porters carried
enormous loads on their backs: piles of silk, carpets, bananas, and
ivory – bounty from all over the world. A red flag decorated with

a yellow crescent moon flew over the roof of a limestone building which was guarded by red-turbanned policemen. Sweet, exotic smells filled the air. The new arrivals from Anatevka gazed around in a daze. Dressed in their winter clothing, the Jews looked out of place in the bright Mediterranean setting. Tevye and Goliath stood holding Golda's coffin, not knowing in which direction to turn.

Just then, a small apparition, dressed like an Arab, rushed up to greet them in Yiddish. With his black moustache and beard, he could have been Eliahu's double. It was as if the little Jew from Odessa had sped ahead to Constantinople to continue his work assisting fellow *landsmen* as they arrived in the strange, foreign port. Excitedly, he led them to a shipping office filled with flies, a broken overhead fan, and the stench of Turkish tobacco. For a small fee, he helped them book passage to Italy, where they would switch boats for the last leg of their journey.

Once again, after waiting ten days in Constantinople, the Lord blessed their trip. This time, their ship was a ship! The travelers even had cabins, and though the airless quarters made their stomachs rise up in their throats during the long nights of unending swells, come morning, the fresh air on deck brought color back to their cheeks. For the children, the ocean voyage was an exciting adventure, but their poor mother couldn't bear the suffocating nights. She coughed and she coughed, as if gasping for breath, so Tevye slept up on deck with Tzeitl. With his daughter bundled in blankets in his arms, Tevye stared up at the stars and beseeched the Creator of heaven and earth to heal his ailing, firstborn girl.

Disembarking from the ship in Trieste, Tevye half-expected to meet an Italian version of Eliahu. Instead, he was greeted by an even bigger surprise. The tall, blond figure of Hevedke was waiting for them on the dock! Seeing him, Tevye almost dropped Golda's coffin. Hava waved and called out his name. Her whole face was a radiant smile. She looked at her father and grinned.

"An agreement is an agreement," she triumphantly said.

"He still has to study the Torah," Tevye answered, clinging to the hope that time would extinguish the stubborn flame in their hearts.

But the bonds which had already formed were not to be broken so easily. Hava was in love with Hevedke, and her faith in him made her certain that he would overcome every obstacle which her father placed in his path. If he had to study the Torah to complete his trial, Hevedke was no stranger to books. It was his keen, open mind that had attracted Hava to him in the first place. Back in Anatevka, his discourses on Aristotle, Shakespeare, and Dostoyevsky had captured her heart. On their walks through the country, he filled her head with a new vision of the world, where all men were equal to share in God's blessing. It was a world without boundaries and prejudices, based on brotherhood and universal love, far more inspiring than the ghetto of Anatevka with its superstitious mistrust of anything and anyone new. At least, it had seemed that way to Hava when she ran away from her family to marry her poet and to embrace his modern, enlightened world. But the pogroms and expulsions had shattered her dream, teaching her and Hevedke alike that behind the beautiful speeches of Tolstoy lay a festering darkness which sought to wipe out the true light of God in the world.

The first chance she had, when her father went off to arrange passage to Palestine, Hava rushed off with Hevedke, filled with a burning desire to be alone with the man she had sworn not to see. He reached out for her hand and whisked her down an alley to the back of a warehouse. They stood there, holding hands, without saying a word. For Hava, just being near him again was enough.

"Oh my valiant, faithful Hevedke," she said.

"Did your father see you run off?" he asked.

"No," she replied, wanting him to kiss her.

"He will kill me if he finds us together."

"It's all right," she assured him.

"When he finds you gone, he will surely come looking."

"Stop worrying," she told him. "Kiss me before I drop dead."

"I can't. I made a promise to your father, and I intend to keep it."

At first, Hava was offended. She was dumbfounded by his words. She gazed at the light of honesty which shone in his eyes and realized that was the reason she loved him. His soul was pure and inspired by a passion for truth.

"I want to do everything I must in order to truly make you my wife," he avowed.

"I am willing to wait if I have to," she promised.

"Oh, Hava, I love you," he said. "More than the oceans and more than the seas. Nothing can come between us."

She stared in his eyes. "I worry about you," she said.

"I'm fine," he assured her. "Your God is looking after me now. You see, He brought me here even before you arrived."

"How?" she asked.

"I boarded the same freighter that you were scheduled to take."

"What happened to the policeman?"

"He got wet, that's all. And his pride was insulted. But the Jews of Odessa fared a lot worse. The day after you left, there was a terrible pogrom. People were killed. The little Jew who helped you was arrested."

"How awful," Hava said.

"We will have a better life in Palestine," Hevedke promised. "And once we set up a house of our own, we will work to bring all the Jews in Russia home to the Promised Land."

Hava smiled with happiness.

"You had better hurry back," he said. "I don't want to give your father a chance to renege on his end of the bargain."

Hava longed for a parting kiss, but Hevedke held her away and made her settle with a smile.

"Can't you kiss me just once?" she asked him.

"Your father may not be watching, but God is," he said. "I have to be true to Him, too."

Reluctantly, he took a few steps backwards, smiled goodbye, and ran off down the alley.

Two weeks later, Tevye and his family boarded an overcrowded steamship heading for Jaffa. Along with the throng of Jews who had gathered from all over Russia, religious Jews and

secular Zionists, Litvaks and Galitzianers, there were a family of
Jews from France, German merchants on the way to Damascus and
Cairo, Christians on their way to Jerusalem, Spanish Moslems
journeying to Mecca, Turkish businessmen, and Hevedke. As the
ship set sail, the Jews burst into a chorus of spirited songs, but a
day out of port, the weather changed for the worse. Towering black
clouds darkened the sky. As if stirred by some heavenly turmoil,
the sea rose threateningly over the bow of the ship, splashing angry
waves on board. The Jews had to huddle on deck under a
tarpaulin, which they pulled over their heads to shelter them from
the fierce, driving rain. Almost everyone grew seasick. Children
cried at the crashing of thunder. Again and again, the bow rose in
the air and plummeted into the depths of the ocean as if the
steamship were sinking. Water splashed over the railing, soaking
the Jews and their clothing. A chill shook Tzeitl's body. Tevye and
Goliath hurried her down below to warm her in the blast of the
boiler.

The ocean's fury lasted all through the night. The sun didn't
appear throughout the next day. Without any sign of letup or
mercy, the hurricane raged unabated. Even the crew became
nauseous and sick. Everyone prayed.

"Why doesn't God stop it?" Ruchela asked in despair.

"We are getting closer to Israel," Nachman explained. "Stepping
foot in the Holy Land is the greatest blessing in the world. The
reward only falls on the bravest, on those who are willing to
sacrifice everything to reach the palace of the King."

"Is it God's will that we all die in the midst of the ocean?" Bat
Sheva asked.

"No. He wants us to pray for His help."

"Then what's taking so long?" the girl asked. "We've been
praying day and night."

"If God doesn't answer at first, it doesn't mean He isn't
listening. He simply wants us to pray harder, with all of our hearts."

Nachman's faith was an inspiration to everyone. He closed his
eyes and bobbed back and forth in deep prayer. With his heart
directed to Heaven, he shut out the howl of the wind and the

splash of the sea. His lips opened in a softly sung prayer, the prayer of the High Priest in the Holy of Holies on *Yom Kippur*, the holiest day of the year.

"May Your kindness prevail
Over Your wrath,
May Your kindness prevail
Over Your wrath.
Have mercy on Your children,
Have mercy on Your children."

Over and over, Nachman sang the refrain until he stood on his feet in a trance, pouring out his heart to the thundering clouds. Little Moishe stood up and joined him. His young, high-pitched wail pierced everyone's heart. Soon, it was impossible to tell if the ship was swaying from the waves of the storm, or from the turbulent prayers of the Jews.

The next morning, one of the merchants was discovered dead in his cabin. Two crew members wrapped him in a sheet and threw him overboard, as if they were offering a sacrifice to a vengeful god. A few hours later another corpse was found. Rumors spread quickly that a plague had broken out aboard ship. Before long, the captain and four crew members stood in front of Tevye.

"Get your coffin and dump it overboard," the captain ordered.

Tevye was stunned. His coffin. Golda. Overboard?

"I protest," he mumbled when he found words to speak.

"I am not asking you. I am ordering you," the captain repeated. "If you don't, my men will. That coffin is endangering everyone on the ship."

"My Golda? Endangering the ship? It's preposterous," Tevye replied.

"The plague is coming from somewhere," the captain answered. "And I am certain it's from that coffin. In fact, I wouldn't be surprised if this storm has been inflicted upon us because I am carrying a stinking dead Jew on my ship."

Hearing his wife cursed, Tevye shuddered. With a growl, he lunged at the captain. A crew member held out a club and pushed him away. Tevye's feet slipped out from under him, and he crashed down on the deck. Goliath started forward, but three drawn pistols stopped him in his tracks.

"It is only another day to Palestine," Tevye pleaded, raising himself to his knees.

"The coffin goes overboard now," the captain said.

"Please," Tevye begged, grabbing onto the captain's leg. "I beg of you, please."

"Either you do it now," the captain threatened, "or my men will do it for you."

Tevye felt the barrel of a pistol press into his back. He let go of his grip on the captain, not because he was afraid for his own life, but because of his daughters. What would they do if he gave the captain a reason to shoot him? How would they survive all alone? The uncircumcised scoundrels would throw Golda into the ocean whether he helped them or not, so what was the use of resisting?

With his head bowed in anguish and submission, he slowly made his way to the cargo deck of the ship.

"Oy Golda, Oy Golda," he moaned. "Is this to be your reward? To be thrown to the fish? To have your bones scattered to the ends of the seas? Without any dry earth to warm you, or a flower to grow over your head? Is this to be your reward for being Tevye's wife for twenty-eight years and for raising his seven daughters?"

Goliath helped him carry the coffin onto the deck. The pistols were still pointed their way. Passengers cursed Tevye as he made his way to the rail. Several tattered umbrellas hit Tevye on the head. Jews crowded around to protect him and keep the crazed, superstitious heathens at bay. His daughters stood at his side, eyes filled with tears. A Hasid with a long beard pushed forward.

"Say *Kaddish*," he said.

Tevye closed his eyes. He would rather have jumped into the ocean himself than obey the captain's orders.

"Don't cry," he heard Golda say. "Be strong for the children."

Catching a sob in his throat, Tevye choked out the words of the mourner's prayer. "*Yisgadal v'yiskadash shemay rabboh...* May His Great Name be sanctified and magnified forever."

The Jews on deck responded, "Amen."

"Good-bye my love, Golda, good-bye," Tevye whispered. He balanced the coffin on the rail of the ship and then gave it a push. A chill seized his body upon the sound of the splash. He felt he was going to faint. A hand kept him from falling.

"Be strong, my husband, be strong," he heard his wife call.

The storm winds howled. A wave towered up over the coffin and snatched it away. A bolt of lighting lit up the sky. The coffin vanished from view. Long after it was gone, Golda's voice echoed over the ocean.

"Be strong, my Tevye, be strong!"

Chapter Eight

THE HOLY LAND

Tevye stood alone on the rain and windswept deck and stared at the merciless sea long after everyone else had retreated to whatever shelter they could find. His head hung down in surrender, and he clutched at the railing as the ship rose and fell. Stricken with pain, he raised a fist to the sky and cried out to the heavens, "I'll show you what Tevye is made of!" But the howl of the wind muted his shout of defiance, breaking his last vestige of pride.

He knew he was being tested, yet he didn't know why. He had sins like any man, but this final punishment was more than a creature of flesh and blood could endure. True, the Rabbis taught that the Lord does not test a man's powers, but without his wife, Golda, Tevye felt crushed. Let God choose some other poor fool to suffer for all of the world. Tevye had already borne enough of the burden.

Not that he was complaining. The Almighty had created him, and He was free to do with him as He wished. But if it were all a part of some Divine, cosmic purpose, then Tevye wanted to be informed. What was the plan? Why did the simple Jew suffer, while the wicked lived like kings? Nachman said that God punished the righteous for their sins in this world so that He could give them everlasting life in the World to Come. And the wicked were rewarded in this world for whatever good deeds they performed, so that God could cut them off from Heaven forever. In theory, it sounded fine. Like everything else in the Bible, Tevye readily believed it. But what good did it do him as he stood soaking wet in the rain? And what good had it done Golda? Once again, when he was on the verge of despair, Tevye heard the sound of her voice in his brain, "Be strong, my Tevye, be strong."

The rocking of the ship put Tevye into a trance. His eyes stared tearfully out at the sea, as if searching for Golda's coffin. He didn't respond when Hava tugged at his arm and urged him to abandon his watch. He didn't budge when Bat Sheva begged him. He didn't listen to Ruchel and Nachman. At some point, the afternoon slipped into night. Finally, the storm abated. The ocean calmed as if it had been appeased by the treasure it had stolen from Tevye. Exhausted, Tevye fell asleep on his feet. All through the night, Goliath sat on the deck beside him, holding Tevye's legs so that he wouldn't fall into the deep alongside his Golda. With the first morning light, the giant stood up and peered out at the horizon. A shimmer of gold, like a faraway outline, appeared between the sky and the ocean.

"Tevye," Goliath whispered. "Tevye, wake up. Look! The Land of Israel!"

The milkman opened his eyes. Was it a vision? Was it a dream? A shudder swept through his body. His flesh tingled. He squinted to get a better glimpse of the Land, of the legend, of the longing of Jews for thousands of years. As if by itself, the words of a blessing rose up from his soul, a blessing for himself, for all of his family, and for all of the Jews who would come after him to these sacred shores:

"Blessed art Thou, Lord my God, King of the universe, Who has granted us life, and sustained us, and enabled us to reach this moment!"

The good news spread quickly. Soon, all of the Jews were crowded on deck, waving, cheering, hugging each other and singing. Men grabbed hands and danced, whirling around faster and faster until their feet seemed to hover over the deck. The women formed their own festive circle a modest distance away from the men. When the boys and girls of a Zionist group grabbed hands and started dancing together, a group of Hasidim rushed over, yelling, "*Shanda*! The scandal! The shame! This is the Holy Land!"

By the time morning prayers were completed, the ship had narrowed the distance to shore. A golden tiara of sunbeams shone down on the Promised Land. The sun-baked buildings of Jaffa stood on a hillside ringing the harbor. Here and there, a minaret protruded over the sun-bleached roofs. Beyond a cove of rocks guarding the bay, rays of sunlight sparkled over tranquil green water. Masted schooners rested alongside the dock. Long, flat rowboats were anchored in colorful bunches. The new immigrants stood gazing at the land of their forefathers. As they neared the harbor, an official-looking launch pulled up to the side of the steamship, and a Turkish officer climbed up the ladder, followed by several soldiers. Out of earshot of the passengers, the red-turbanned officer and the boat's captain conferred.

As a Jew says in his prayers every morning, "Many are the plans in a man's heart, but it is the counsel of God which prevails." The captain turned to the excited crowd of passengers on deck and told them that everyone could prepare to disembark except for the Jews. The Turkish authorities were refusing to issue the Jews permits to land. They would have to travel on with the boat to the port of Alexandria, in Egypt.

Tevye was stunned. After all they had gone through! To be turned away when they could almost reach out and touch a dream of ages. Who were these heathen scoundrels to deny the children of Abraham the right to step foot on their very own soil?

It was one of the Zionists who cried out, "This is our land! The land of the Jews!"

He rushed forward as if to charge the captain and the Turkish official. Without waiting for an order, a soldier raised his rifle and fired. The bullet struck the Jew in his chest. Clutching his heart, he fell to the deck. Goliath took a step forward but Tevye held him back. Rifles remained poised in alert. Instantly, the rebellion was quelled. The Jews lifted their dead and retreated to the aft of the ship.

"Who are they?" Ruchel asked. "Why do they act like Palestine belongs to them?"

"They're Turks," her father answered. "They rule here. We've escaped one Czar and found ourselves another."

"We outnumber them," Goliath said. "We all should have charged."

"And what would we have done when we finally reached shore?" Tevye asked. "Gone to war with the entire Turkish army?"

The big lumberjack looked confused. No one had ever bothered to explain to him the political situation in Palestine. In truth, he had never thought to ask. In his mind, the Land of Israel belonged to the Jews. God had given it to them. He had promised it to Abraham as an everlasting gift. The oversized Jew wasn't a rabbi, but he had heard the Torah read aloud on the Sabbath every week of his life, and he knew almost all of the Five Books of Moses by heart. The land of Canaan was the inheritance of Abraham, Isaac, and Jacob. In Russia, a Jew could expect to be thrown out of his village – he was a stranger in someone else's country. But in *Eretz Yisrael* – forbidding a Jew to land on its shores was like trying to keep a man out of his very own home!

The Jews fell into a restless depression. They stood whispering in groups as rowboat after rowboat arrived to carry the other passengers ashore. Zionists and Hasidim alike paced nervously back and forth like caged lions. Tevye's daughters were heartbroken. Tzeitl's coughing shook her whole body. Her eyes had lost their light, and her face was drained of color.

"Where are they going to take us?" Hannie wanted to know.

"To Egypt," Tevye answered. "To see the pyramids our grandfathers built."

Once again, it was Nachman who offered a glimmer of hope.

"Remember, *Reb* Tevye, I have heard you say it yourself, 'Everything that God does is for the best.' Maybe He wants to give us reward for walking from Egypt to Israel, just like our forefathers did long ago."

"I can hardly wait," Bat Sheva said cynically.

"What about the poor soul who was shot?" Hava asked. "Did things work out good for him too?"

As the last passengers were leaving the ship. Hevedke made a point of walking over to be with the Jews. He took a place toward the back of the ship-bound ghetto and stood tall and determined as if he were making a statement. When the soldiers climbed down the ship's ladder and returned to their launch, Tevye strode up to the captain. Goliath stuck to his side like a shield.

"We bought passage to Palestine and we expect to be set ashore here," Tevye said.

"You heard what the Turkish lieutenant ordered," the captain responded.

"If not in this port than in some other," Tevye demanded.

"There is no other port in the direction we're heading."

"Then you'll just have to set us ashore on a beach."

The captain laughed. "You think it's so easy? Plenty of vessels have gone aground in these waters."

"We will make it worth your while," Tevye said.

The captain paused. He looked at the Jew. "And just how do you propose to make it worth my while?" he asked.

"With a gift to the captain of two hundred rubles."

The captain smiled. "Five hundred," he said. "I have to share it with my crew."

Tevye nodded. "You'll get it when the last one of us is safely ashore."

"Half before the landing. Half afterward," the captain said.

Tevye reached into his pocket and pulled out all the money he had. It came to a little less than two hundred rubles. Goliath handed him a pile of notes, and Tevye counted out the difference. Greedily, the captain took it from his hand.

"Throwing your wife overboard was nothing personal, you understand. I did it for the welfare of the ship."

Tevye wanted to spit in his face. A pool of saliva welled up in his mouth. But once again, like he had done all of his life, he swallowed his pride and his anger.

The ship pulled up anchor and continued its way south along the sandy coastline. Tevye related the agreement to the other Jews on board and collected the remainder of the bribe money in a hat which Goliath held out in his hand. Within a short time, Jaffa could no longer be seen. Jews lined the railing to view the desolate shoreline. Undulating sand dunes extended inland as far as the eye could see. Only an occasional palm tree interrupted the desert-like landscape. Nachman said they were date trees. The honey of the Land of Israel wasn't the honey of bees, but the honey of dates, a fruit which none of the Russian Jews had ever tasted. For an hour they saw nothing but desert, rolling dunes, and endless mountains of sand. Up on the bridge of the ship, the captain held up a hand. The crew once again lowered the anchor, and the captain waved Tevye over.

"Get your people ready," he said.

"Can't you bring the ship closer to shore?" Tevye asked.

"Not without endangering the vessel," the captain responded. "If I get too close to the beach, the current could sweep me aground."

They were still at least two-hundred meters from land. Foam-capped waves raced toward the coastline. The small rowboats that were lowered from the ship rocked forebodingly in the ocean between the powerful swells.

"You agreed to take us to shore," Tevye said.

"The rowboats will take your people as close to the beach as possible."

"But most of these people can't swim!"

"Take it or leave it," the captain replied.

Once again, Tevye had no choice. But when the captain demanded the rest of the money, Tevye insisted that he would pay only when all of the Jews had reached the beach safely. Tevye wasn't a seaman, but he realized the undertaking would be no easy matter. The waves crashing onto the beach, and the powerful undertow they caused, prevented the rowboats from reaching the shore. The small crafts had to stop a considerable swim from the beach. A crew member swam into shore with the end of a rope which he fastened to a trunk of a palm tree. From the rowboats, the Jews would have to hang onto the rope and battle the waves and the undertow the rest of the way to the Holy Land.

"What about everyone's belongings?" Tevye asked. "How will people manage if they have to hold on to a rope?"

The captain shrugged. "You can always change your mind and sail the rest of the way to Alexandria," he said.

Who knew what new disasters would arise on the way to Alexandria, Tevye thought? *Eretz Yisrael* was so close, they could almost reach out and touch it. Jews were already pushing and shoving to climb down the ladder of the ship. They jumped into the small rowboats as if the chance might never come again.

"At least take the belongings ashore," Tevye pleaded. "It's everything these people have in the world."

"I can try," the captain said. "But it has to be worth risking a boat and its crew."

Reluctantly, Tevye agreed on another one-hundred rubles.

If God were testing the resolve of the Jews, He tested them to the very end of their journey. With one hand clutching the lifeline which stretched to the beach, and their other hand clutching their children close to their breasts, Jews fought their way through the pounding waves to collapse on the cherished shore. Goliath and Hevedke carried Moishe and Hannie to safety, then splashed back into the undertow to help others make the punishing journey from the rowboats to the white, pristine sand. A mother cried out in anguish when a wave swept her child out of her arms. Goliath dove underwater. Waves crashed over his head. Finally, the whale of a man emerged clutching the terrified girl.

Tevye waited with Tzeitl on the deck of the ship until all of the others had disembarked for the shore. When a rowboat filled with suitcases and boxes coasted on a wave to the beach, Tevye handed the captain the rest of the money. Then he and Tzeitl climbed down the ship's ladder into the tiny rowboat which was to ferry them toward shore. Tevye sat holding his shivering daughter as the crew battled the waves with their oars. Seawater splashed over their heads. The spray of the sea filled their nostrils and eyes. Finally, it was their turn to grab onto the rope which stretched the last thirty meters to shore. Tzeitl set out ahead of her father. Weakened by her sickness, the exertion demanded all of her strength. A wave crashed over their heads, drowning them with water. Tevye latched onto his daughter. But when the next wave hit them, Tevye's grip slackened. When he emerged and glanced around him, Tzeitl was nowhere to be seen.

"Tzeitl!" he screamed.

A wave swept him up in the air, and he glimpsed what looked like her dress.

"Tzeitl!" he roared, letting go off the rope to dive into the sea. A wave splattered him. His mouth filled with water. Choking, he flailed wildly out with his hands, hoping to rescue his daughter. But another wave swept over him, rolling him head over heels underwater. Everything turned into darkness. Suddenly, a hand grabbed him and raised his head back into the light. It was Hevedke. He dragged Tevye back to the rope and half pushed him, half carried him to shore.

"Tzeitl," Tevye moaned, collapsing onto the sand.

"She's all right," Hevedke answered. "Goliath pulled her out of the water."

"Thank God," Tevye said in exhaustion.

The milkman turned his head to the side and pressed his cheek into the warm, soothing sand. His hands clutched at the soil. The realization that he was in the Holy Land swept over him like another huge wave. He rose up on his knees, glanced at the water-soaked Jews on the beach, and let out an exuberant scream. Cheering, he raised his hands up to Heaven. Ruchela rushed into his arms.

"We're in Israel!" he shouted. "The good Lord has brought us to Israel!"

Nachman shouted the *Shehecheyanu* blessing out loud for everyone to hear. He and Tevye embraced. Then Tevye hugged all of his daughters. Even the shivering Tzeitl managed a broad, happy smile. All of the Jews on the beach felt the same sense of joy and relief. Everyone hugged one another. Goliath embraced Tevye, lifted him in the air, and spun him around in a circle. When Tevye landed, ready for the next hug, he stood face to face with

Hevedke. For a moment, he froze. When he moved away to the right, Hevedke moved with him. When he moved to the left, Hevedke followed. Once again, they moved back and forth like two Russian dancers. Then Tevye held up his arms and snapped his fingers. Hevedke smiled and mimicked the gesture. Then to a silent tune, the two danced a traditional Hasidic dance on the beach. People watched them and clapped. Hava shed tears of joy. Other Jews joined in the dance. It no longer bothered anyone that they were all tired and wet, nor that they didn't have any food or fresh water. They were in the Promised Land! Their long journey was over. God would take care of the rest.

A call echoed over the beach. High on a towering sand dune, one of the young Zionists stood waving his cap and calling people to follow. The men stopped their dancing and made a charge for the mountain. Shoes sank into the soft, sandy slope as they scrambled hands and feet up the hill. Tevye joined them, crawling on his knees when the trek proved too steep. A young pioneer let out a scream and jumped off the summit. The *meshugenneh* toppled into the sand and rolled over and over down the long slope of the mountain. Like children, the other Jews followed. Tevye panted as he stood at the summit. To the north, he could see the long coastline. To the east lay endless stretches of swampland and desert. To the south, sand dunes filled the landscape as far as the eye could see.

"Are you coming?" Nachman asked.

The young rabbi jumped off the hill like a boy in summer camp. With a prayer in his heart, Tevye followed. Laughing, he rolled down the sand dune. He rolled and rolled, covered with sand, blanketed in the holy soil. When he stood up, his face was a mask. Sand filled his beard, his hair, his mouth and his eyes.

"Isn't is written, 'Your descendants will be like the dust of the earth,'" Nachman exclaimed, reciting God's promise to Jacob.

Once again, the young Zionists set off in a race up the mountain. Nachman grabbed Tevye's hand.

"*Gevalt,*" Tevye said. "Not again."

"*Reb* Tevye, my father to be, I love you," the ecstatic youth said.

Nachman theatrically raised up a hand and called out as if he were making a speech. "Go up the mountain, the Lord said to Abraham, and every place that you see, I will give to you and to your offspring forever."

Nachman's happiness and spirit gave Tevye the strength to brave the ascent once again. Struggling and gasping for breath, Tevye was the last climber to reach the summit. Down below, sand-covered Jews were jumping into the sparkling blue water. Tevye turned around in a small circle, feasting his eyes once again on his Land, the Land God had promised to give to the Jews, and here Tevye, the milkman from Anatevka was standing like Abraham on the top of the towering sand dune, surveying God's priceless gift.

Down below, he watched Goliath playfully pick up Hevedke and hurl him into the water. Beyond them, out to sea, he glimpsed something floating on the top of a wave. In the glare of the sunlight, it looked like an oar from a rowboat, or the plank of a ship. But as it bobbed into view on the very next crest, Tevye could make out its sides. It was a crate of some sort, long and shallow in depth, like the shape of a . . . coffin.

Like the shape of a coffin!

Goose-pimples broke out all over Tevye's flesh.

"Golda," he whispered. "Golda!"

"GOLDA!" he screamed, hurling himself down the descent, running as fast as he could until he tripped in the sand and rolled the rest of the way down the mountain. Covered with sand, and white as a ghost, he staggered to his feet and ran along the beach yelling, "GOLDA!"

Tevye ran and he ran to catch up with his wife as the tide swept her coffin further south. His heart pounded so loudly, he felt it was sure to explode. Then, like a hand returning a precious jewel to its owner, a wave lifted the coffin and whisked it onto the beach. Like a lost treasure chest, it slid up to Tevye's feet. Tevye collapsed to his knees. Seaweed stuck to the wood like a wreath.

Tevye fell over the coffin and cried. He sobbed like a baby until the others arrived. His daughters huddled around him. Everyone stood in stunned silence.

Hevedke was the first one to speak. "It's a miracle," he said, expressing the word on everyone's lips.

Tevye gazed up to Heaven as if to say thanks. It truly was the Holy Land. Bending down, he put his head on the coffin and spoke to his beloved wife.

"Forgive me, Golda, for all that I've put you through. But you can rest now, my princess, we're home."

Chapter Nine

MAZAL TOV!

"Didn't I tell you that everything God does works out for the best?" Tevye said to Nachman as everyone gathered excitedly around the coffin on the beach. "If the Turks had let us disembark in Jaffa, I would never have seen my Golda wash up on shore."

It didn't matter that, in fact, Nachman had been the one who had reminded a crestfallen Tevye that God's loving, invisible hand never stops guiding life's twists and turns. If Tevye, in a moment of despair, had forgotten this teaching of the Talmud, God would certainly forgive him. Now, with Golda once again at his side, Tevye's faith was stronger than ever.

But Tevye's reunion with Golda was not the only miracle which had transpired. Since stepping foot in the Land of Israel, Tevye had imperceptibly changed. He couldn't say why. He couldn't explain the sensation, but somehow, his mind, his soul, and his heart underwent a rejuvenation, as if the clock of his life had turned backwards, making him feel twenty years younger. Yes, he felt more confident now that his beloved Golda was back at his side. Yes, he felt comforted that the Almighty had returned her to him. But even more than these blessings, the realization that he had reached the Land of Israel overwhelmed all of his thoughts. The prayers, the prophecies, the dreams, the yearnings of two-thousand years, all had come true. Wasn't it written in the Book of Psalms, "When God will return the exiles of Zion, we will be like those who dream. Then our mouth will be filled with laughter and our tongue with glad song?"

Tevye the milkman, the son of Reb Schneur Zalman, was in Israel! He was in the Land which God had promised to give to Abraham, to Isaac, and to Jacob. It was the Land of Joshua and the prophet Samuel. The Land of King David and his son, Solomon, the wisest of men. It was the home of the Jerusalem Temple, of the Maccabees, and Rabbi Akiva. While Tevye's faith in the Biblical stories which his father had taught him had always been steadfast, now he was standing on the very soil where Jewish history had unfolded in all of its glory and pain. Suddenly, the ancient stories had a down-to-earth setting. Suddenly, the Land of Israel was real, not just a faraway dream. It was like hearing about a famous person, and then suddenly meeting him, like when Tevye had met the great writer, Sholom Aleichem. What a thrill!

Nachman experienced the same indescribable sensation. Feeling the secret power of the Land surge into his body, he burst into song. Everyone had the same feeling. Everyone sang. They were in the Land of Israel! They were home!

Their singing gave way to exhaustion. It was time to learn their next lesson. Life in the Land of Israel, like its sand dunes, had its ups and its downs. Everyone was astounded at the landscape as they started the trek north back toward Jaffa. Dunes and desert stretched around them as far as the eye could see. Occasionally, they had to make a long detour around a foul-smelling swamp. The land was barren and desolate, as if still suffering from the Divine curse which had fallen upon the soil since the Jews had been exiled from their home. Gone were the lush gardens, the fruit trees, the fertile green valleys, and overflowing rivers of Biblical days. If there had once been milk and honey in the Land, the ferocious sun had long ago turned them to sand. Miles passed without the sight of a single tree or bush. Beside their motley-looking caravan, there was no sign of human life. Eyes searched the horizon for Jaffa, but all they could see was an ocean of heat waves rising off a desert wilderness.

Before long, their enthusiasm started to wane. It was as if they had returned three-thousand years through history to their ancestors' wanderings through Sinai. Their footsteps became heavier. The fierce sun beat down on their heads. More and more frequently, the men had to set down Golda's coffin and rest. Tzeitl fainted. Once again, Tevye had to carry her in his arms. Within an hour, their supply of fresh water was finished. Children cried. Grown-ups collapsed in the sand. Complaints could be heard in every corner of the camp.

"Why did we come on this journey? We could have died just as easily in Russia."

"At least there we had water."

"The Spies that Moses sent to scout out the Land were right," another voice moaned in despair. "This is a land that devours its settlers."

Tevye began to feel gloomy. Was this to be their destiny after months on the road – to drop dead from thirst on the promised shores of Zion? To be roasted alive by the sun? To be swallowed up by a wasteland still angry for the sins of the past?

"*Rachmonus*," Tevye begged, looking up at the sky. "Is it too much to ask for some mercy? After all, is this any way for a Father to act towards children who have come home seeking shelter? Are we to perish on Your doorstep without food or drink?"

Once again, as if God merely wanted to hear Tevye's prayer, salvation was wrought from the depths of despair. Just when the heat overcame the new immigrants, and the strongest among them collapsed in exhaustion at the peak of a sandy incline, their eyes were feasted to an oasis of greenery and life. Spread out in the valley before them were shade trees and orchards, fields of barley and corn, and a sparkling blue pond. Houses were clustered along the road running through the center of the colony. But the thing that made Tevye believe he was dreaming was the sight of the settlers who rushed forward to greet them. They were all bearded Jews like himself, with *yarmulkahs* on their heads, *tzitzit* dangling out of their breaches, and farmers' tools in their hands. Their faces were the color of gold, and their handshakes were like the grip of a blacksmith. Could these really be Jews, Tevye thought?

The moshav was called Rishon LeZion, one of the first Jewish colonies which the Baron Rothschild had established in the Land. When the news spread that immigrants had arrived from the old country, work in the village stopped. Settlers flocked to greet them, each one dressed in a different style, depending on where he had come from in Russia. Others wore articles of clothing they had picked up on their journeys. Some men sported vests and brown derbies, others Russian military shirts with high collars, while others wore khaki jackets and the broad-rimmed hats of hunters, as if they had just returned from an African safari. Field workers strode forward in boots. They wore caps on their heads and dirt-stained aprons over their clothes. Young boys out from *heder* and *Talmud Torah* schools wore caps like their fathers, jackets and knee-length knickers. Many went barefoot. Women wearing aprons and bonnets brought food and drink in abundance, as if the new arrivals were kings. Everyone had questions. Everyone spoke out at once. Where were the newcomers from? Had they heard what had happened in this place and that? Did they have letters? Did they want to join the Rishon community? Were they under contract to the Baron, or free to strike out on their own? When they reached the colony, someone named Aharon stood on the steps of a porch and waved his cap, inviting them to stop all of the chatter and *kibbetzing* and come into the mess hall to get something substantial to eat.

Tevye was more concerned with finding a doctor for Tzeitl. She was taken into a house and fed sips of water until she opened her eyes and smiled. Only when the doctor told him not to worry did Tevye think to quench his own thirst. Along with the fresh fruits spread out on the meeting-hall table, there were bottles and bottles of wine brewed from the grapes of the Land of Israel, from the vines of Rishon LeZion! The sweet, pungent beverage made the heads of the newcomers spin and made their hearts burst with song. It made Tevye's tired feet dance and his parched lips forget the punishing sun. "How good and how pleasant it is for brothers to sit together!" everyone sang in an outburst of spontaneous *simcha.* The Jews of Rishon were equally jubilant upon the arrival of a new group of pioneers. As the name of the colony implied, these first settlers of Zion were encouraged by the reinforcements. More Jews meant more workers and more helpers in their dream of rebuilding the Land. But in the ecstasy of their dancing, in their closed eyes, clasped hands, and fervent expressions, there was something much more. The whirling circle of men seemed to spin around and around with a spiritual force beyond the strength of their legs. There was a messianic fervor to their singing, and the feeling that the *Mashiach* was just around the bend.

Even Hevedke felt an exaltation he had never known in his life. Until then, his desire to become a part of Hava's people had stemmed from his love for her. But now, seeing God's promise to the Jews materializing before his eyes, to bring His people home, he was moved by an overwhelming love for the God of the Children of Israel. Dramatically, he stood up on a chair, and, like the poet he was, he read aloud from his wet, sandy Bible. Hearing the baritone, Russian translation, the Yiddish-speaking Jews stopped dancing and stared up in wonder at the blond, blue-eyed orator.

"I will take you from the nations," Hevedke read with a flourish, *"and gather you out of all countries, and will bring you into your own Land, and you shall dwell in the Land that I gave to your fathers; and you shall be My people, and I will be your God."*

Everyone cheered. Goliath lifted Hevedke on his shoulders and swung him around in the middle of the dancing. Tevye danced and drank *"L'Chaims"* until his eyes wearied with sleep. But as his head fell onto his plate in exhaustion, he suddenly bolted up from the table. How could he think of resting when his Golda was outside in her coffin? How could he think of his own peace and comfort when Golda had not found her final rest? Wasn't burying the dead the most pressing *mitzvah* of all? Without further delay, he rushed out of the hall. Now that they were in the Land of Israel, it didn't matter where she was buried. As the Sages taught, burial in the Holy Land atoned for sins, just like the altar in the Holy Temple.

"Not that my angel of a wife needs atonement," Tevye said to his new friend, Aharon, who led the way to a treeless plot at the colony's border. Tevye was surprised to see rows upon rows of gravestones in the cemetery of the young village, which Aharon called a *yishuv*. So many deaths in the short years of its history could be seen as an ominous sign. But philosophical speculation could wait. The time had arrived to put Golda to rest in the sacred ground of *Eretz HaKodesh*, the Holy Land. With the farmers of Rishon sharing in the work, a grave was dug out in no time.

When they were finished, Tevye got down on his knees. "Rest in peace, dear Golda," he whispered, gently patting down the soil covering her final abode. "You don't have to worry any more, my princess. Though, of course, I know that you will. What other pleasure does a Jewish woman have? Please forgive me for having disturbed your sweet sleep, and for *shlepping* you all over the world, but, you see, it has all turned out for the best. Put in a good word for our daughters, that they may find husbands who will honor them like queens, and give regards to my father and mother. With God's help, your Tevye will take care of the rest."

The funeral assembly made its way back to the colony along a path bordered by tall eucalyptus trees. The sweet smells of the Rishon winery hung in the air. Vegetables of all sizes, colors, and shapes filled the gardens beside every house. When they arrived at the mess hall, everyone wanted to continue the party, but a short, clean-shaven man stood on the steps of the porch blocking their way. He wore a Fedora hat and a tailored suit incongruous to the hot, rustic locale. As if to accentuate his aristocratic image, he gripped a riding crop in leather-gloved hands.

"The party is over," he shouted. He spoke in a rudimentary Yiddish, but his accent was unmistakably French. "Everyone is to return to their work. The Baron isn't subsidizing this enterprise to have you squander his wine and engage in extravagant parties in the middle of the afternoon. There are rules to this colony, and it is my job to enforce them. As for the newcomers, let it be known that Rishon LeZion is not interested in absorbing any new workers. The Jewish Colonization Association has several young settlements to the north which are accepting new candidates. Inquiries can be made at company headquarters in Zichron Yaacov. Under the authority invested in me as Manager of this *yishuv*, I hereby order all new arrivals to immediately evacuate the colony confines."

Shouts of protest rang out from the crowd.

"Who is he?" Tevye asked Aharon.

"Dupont - the '*Yaka*' manager. The watchdog of the Baron."

"What is *Yaka?*" Nachman inquired.

"It's the Hebrew abbreviation for the Jewish Colonization Association," Aharon answered.

"Is he a Jew?" Tevye asked.

"He claims he is. But a lot of the Company managers aren't."

Dupont started to walk down the porch stairs, but a horde of new immigrants rushed forward, surrounding him, cursing him, even reaching out to bat him on the head. Not accustomed to such uncivilized treatment, the miniature baron quickly retreated to the safety of the porch. Not being indentured to anyone, the new arrivals had nothing to lose. They were all exhausted from the long journey, thankful to be alive, and here this little *knocker* of a Frenchman was ordering them to get lost!

"One minute, one minute," he called. "You don't seem to under-stand."

A few of the newcomers followed him threateningly up the stairs.

"Who put you in charge?" an angry Hasid yelled.

"He deserves to be lashed and hung from a tree," another asserted.

The mob cheered and pushed toward the porch. Aharon shoved his way through the crowd to come to Dupont's rescue.

"These newcomers are liable to act on their threats," he warned the little Napoleon. "They don't understand the rules of the Company. Let them stay here for the night, and tomorrow I will make the necessary arrangements to help them on their way."

Dupont's confidence seemed shaken. He squared his hat on his head. The uprising was a threat to his rule. But any objections he had were quelled by the jeers of the crowd and the formidable figure of Goliath who strode up the porch steps looking like a walking eucalyptus. Four company workers arrived on the scene carrying rifles. They halted as Aharon raised up his hand.

"Very well," Dupont conceded. "You speak with them. But they can only stay here one evening."

Aharon nodded. He turned to the crowd.

"The manager has asked me to explain that everyone is welcome to stay for the night, and that tomorrow, arrangements will be made for everyone's placement at another Company colony."

The crowd of Jews applauded. Aharon hurried Dupont into the mess hall, and led him to the rear door, where a getaway carriage was waiting to meet him.

"Put them all in the barn for the night and make sure they are back on their way in the morning," the colony manager ordered.

"Yes, sir," Aharon answered.

"What *chutzpah!*" Tevye said after the carriage had sped away. "Does he think this is Russia?"

"Even in the Holy Land, it isn't always easy being a Jew," Aharon answered.

"Why do you let him pretend he's the Czar? You outnumber them ten to one."

Aharon nodded. "That is true, but we need them to survive. Turning sand dunes and swamps into farmland takes time. The Baron sends us a lot of assistance. In return, he has his rules, his managers, and his J.C.A. company policy. As they say, you can't bite the hand that feeds you."

"I don't understand," Tevye said.

"I'll explain it to you later," Aharon assured him. "But first I want to get everyone settled."

Aharon returned to the indignant new immigrants, and after a brief explanation, herded them off to the barn where everyone was to bed down with the horses and cows. Many of the Jews had a list of complaints, but most of the travelers were so tired, they soon fell fast asleep. For modesty's sake, because of the women, the devoutly religious slept outside under the stars. Once things were organized, Aharon invited the more vocal Jews to his house for a cup of black Turkish coffee and a lengthy discussion. Tevye went with them. Nachman and Ruchel decided to seek out the local rabbi to inform him of their decision to marry. Goliath and Hevedke bedded down near the barn door to watch over the children, and Hava and Bat Sheva sat by Tzeitl's side in the infirmary where she was fitfully sleeping.

Aharon lived in a tiny, cramped cottage whose yard was planted with tomatoes plants, melons, and a strange looking gourd he called *dlatt*. A vine laden with grapes hung from the veranda at the entrance to the house. Inside, the men crowded around a table and savored the rich, aromatic coffee which Aharon's wife served them. An evening sea breeze blew through the open shutters. Patiently, for more than an hour, Aharon explained the intricacies of the Jewish Colonization Association. Behind him, on a small wooden shelf, was a small blue metal box of the Jewish National Fund, filled with Megidas, Napoleons, and whatever other small coins the family could spare to help purchase land in the country.

The benefactor of the ambitious Jewish resettlement project was the famous Baron Edmond Rothschild. The fabulously wealthy Rothschilds of Europe were banking and railroad magnates, backers of governments and wars. Edmond was the maverick of the family, whose philanthropic scheme to build a Jewish economic enterprise in Palestine siphoned off millions and millions of dollars each year from the family fortune. Because of the costly investment, he was careful to oversee the development of the colonies through a rigid system of management and monetary control. Being a private person himself, his style of land acquisition was patient and pragmatic, avoiding the aggressive imperialistic policy fostered by other Zionist leaders. He preferred to gradually establish a foundation of settlements which would one day be self-supporting. Accordingly, he maintained cordial relations with the ruling Turkish authorities, who were wary of mass Jewish immigration to Palestine. While the Baron had not founded Rishon LeZion, he had bailed the swamp-infested colony out of the grips of malaria and bankruptcy, and kept it afloat with the monies he channeled into its coffers through the *Yaka* organization each year.

Aharon told them that while many of the Jewish settlers had gripes against the Baron, he himself respected "The Benefactor" greatly. The colonies, he declared, could not survive without the Company's assistance. Furthermore, while the Baron was not strictly religious himself, he insisted that every JCA settlement have a synagogue, *heder* for grade-school children, *mikvah* for ritual immersion, slaughterer-*shochet* to supply kosher meat, and rabbi. On the negative side, Aharon confessed, the life of the colonies was controlled by the *"Pakidut HaBaron,"* the managers whom the Company appointed to oversee the development of each settlement. The managers, gentiles among them, tended to be small-minded bureaucrats, more interested in their positions of authority and financial reward than in the idealistic goal of resettling the Jewish nation in its ancient homeland. Basically, Aharon explained, the pioneer settlers were indentured farmers, at the mercy of the tyrannical managers, and beholden to the JCA for their salaries and badly-needed loans. Although the Baron lived in a palace himself, he was against bourgeois standards of living, insisting that his workers live in Arab-style huts, or large barn-like dorms. Settlers were told what crops to grow and where. There were long lines to receive animal fodder, and their meager ten-francs per-month salary could be withheld at the first sign of rebellion against the JCA management. The settlers could be evicted at any time, and even their personal life was restricted. There had even been cases where managers had forbidden workers to marry or to invite guests to their homes. Once, when Aharon took the initiative to write the Baron a letter complaining against the Company's frugal policy toward the settlers, the Baron personally wrote back, saying that Aharon should more productively dirty his hands in the fields, and send his wife and children to work, instead of complaining.

Aharon showed his guests the letter.

"We were better off in Russia," one of his listeners said.

"A lot of pioneers end up going back," Aharon admitted.

"Why don't you tell the Company managers to go to hell?" another new immigrant asked.

"We would all die of starvation," Aharon answered. "The price of land is so high, we could never afford it ourselves."

His listeners sat in glum silence.

"We'll manage," Tevye said. "The Almighty will help. Anything is better than being a slave to the Czar."

Aharon told them not to despair. In the morning, he would take down all of their names and travel to Jaffa with their documents to bribe a Turkish official into issuing immigrant permits to the group. That way, they would be free to travel throughout the country without fear of arrest and possible deportation.

Outside the house, Nachman was waiting. He wanted to see Tevye alone.

"We have good news, Reb Tevye," he said. "Ruchel and I have decided to get married tomorrow. We have been to the Rabbi, and he agrees that it is halachically possible. Ruchel spoke with his wife, and all of the proper ritual arrangements can be made. With your permission, of course."

Happily, Tevye embraced the young man. "My permission is granted, my son. But what about the Company manager?"

"The Rabbi said he would talk to him. He thinks Dupont can be persuaded, because the wedding will provide revenue to the colony, since we will be paying for the food. He said he would also talk to him about letting us live in Rishon LeZion. The *Talmud Torah* needs a new teacher, and he wants me to take the job."

"*Mazal tov, mazal tov,*" Tevye said. "The kindness of God never ceases."

And so it was. In the morning, Aharon collected documents and bribe money from the new pioneers, or *chalutzim*, as they were called in Hebrew. When he had finished making a list, Tevye took him aside and gave him money to buy a wedding ring for Ruchel. Dupont, in a gesture of public relations to soften the bad feelings he had created the day before, gave his permission to hold the wedding celebration in Rishon. As if he had arranged the marriage himself, he returned to the porch of the dining room to magnanimously announce that the wedding would be held after nightfall in the courtyard of the colony. While Tevye tried to love every man, Jew and gentile alike, and to judge all of God's children in a favorable light, he didn't always succeed. The pompous Dupont was a perfect example. Tevye knew it was wrong, but he felt an urge to wipe the insincere grin off the manager's face. But being a peace-loving man, and for the sake of his daughter, Tevye smiled and thanked Mr. Dupont for his kindness.

The women of the community worked in their kitchens all day to prepare a proper feast. A *chuppah* wedding canopy was erected by tying a prayer shawl to four poles. The Rabbi's wife found Ruchel a white gown that fit her exactly. Nachman borrowed a shiny white *kittel* robe, and Tevye's eyes moistened as he escorted his new son-in-law to the marriage canopy to wed his beaming daughter. The wedding guests, dressed in their most elegant Sabbath bowlers and bonnets, held up lanterns to light the way.

"Every wedding is special," the Rabbi declared before pronouncing the nuptial blessings. "But this wedding is even more distinctive because it is the joining of two lives in the Land of Israel after a long, two-thousand-year exile."

All of the wedding guests were silent as they listened to the words of the Rabbi. A glow shone in all of their eyes. Even Dupont felt a shiver of destiny in the cool evening breeze. Bat Sheva, Hava, and Tzeitl stood beside Ruchel, the bride, the beautiful *kallah*, overjoyed with their sister's happiness, and filled with dreams of their own. Little Hannie and Moishe sat perched on Goliath's broad shoulders, watching the wedding over the heads of the crowd. The big-hearted giant shed tears of joy as he watched the beaming countenance of his dearest friend, Nachman.

"Two-thousand years ago, the Romans invaded the Land of Israel, destroyed Jerusalem, and expelled the Jews from the land. To what is this like? To robbers who come and throw a man out of his house. The injustice can only be righted when the rightful owner returns to live in his home once again. So too with the return of the Jewish people to *Eretz Yisrael*.

"Nachman and Ruchel, the happiness of this occasion is not only your own private joy," the Rabbi continued. "It is the happiness of all of the Jewish people all over the world. You are pioneers, leading the way for the rest of the nation, preparing the foundation for the great waves of *aliyah*-immigration which will follow. Our Sages tell us that every new home in the Land of Israel, and every new family, is a new stone in the building of Jerusalem. For two-thousand years at Jewish weddings all over the world, men and women have been saying the words of King David's psalm, *'If I forget you O Jerusalem,'* to remind them that their own private joy cannot be complete until our ancient city is rebuilt. This great love for our land and for Jerusalem is our secret. This is our strength. May the Lord bless you and keep you, may He shine His countenance upon you and grant you peace."

The Rabbi recited the wedding blessings, and Nachman and Ruchel became man and wife. Raising his foot with a smile, Nachman shattered the traditional glass. A clarinet started to play. Tevye gazed teary-eyed at his family under the wedding *chuppah*. Could it be, he asked himself? Were his eyes truly seeing what they saw? Standing beside his Ruchela was the living apparition of Golda, crying a mother's proud tears! Yes, yes, it was Golda. How could it be otherwise? There was no way she was going to miss this great joyous *simcha*. She had returned from her rest in *Gan Eden* to be with her loved ones on this special glorious day.

"Golda!" Tevye whispered in surprise.

The white-gowned apparition looked at Tevye with a mother's satisfied glance.

"*Mazal tov*, my husband, *mazal tov*," she said. "Finally, you have done something right."

Chapter Ten

RABBI KOOK

Good to his word, Aharon succeeded in securing the red immigration cards that the Jews needed to become foreign residents of Turkish Palestine. Theoretically, the permits allowed them to live and work in the country without fear of expulsion, but the permits could be revoked at the whim of a nasty official. When their one day of welcome at Rishon LeZion expired, the pioneers once again gathered their belong- ings and set off like gypsies on the road to Jaffa. Like a make-believe emperor, Dupont stood in his carriage at the entrance to the colony, making sure that all of the newcomers vacated his vassal state. The religious Jews headed for Zichron Yaakov to arrange for absorption in one of the *"frum"* religious JCA settlements, while the Zionists went off to find work in secular kibbutzim.

Tevye and his family set off for the historic reunion with Hodel. Ruchel and Nachman had been granted a two day vacation before they had to report back to Rishon, so they were traveling with Tevye to Jaffa. They had rented a Company wagon, and everyone crowded inside.

The morning after the wedding, it was impossible to tell what shone more brightly, Nachman's face or the sparkling sun of the Holy Land. As the Rabbis of the Talmud had said, "When a man finds a wife, he finds a blessing." Yesterday, Nachman was a youth. Today, he was a man. Ruchel too was all smiles. Now that she was married, she had to cover her hair with a kerchief, which gave her a special "grown up" status. All the morning, she kept her head lowered to hide her continuous blush.

Tevye sat between the bride and groom, at the helm of the wagon. He was in a jubilant mood. Not only had his Ruchela married a scholar, a real *Talmid Chacham*, but he himself had undergone a miraculous transformation. It seemed liked a dream, but here he was, holding a pair of reins in his hands, driving a horse and wagon, not in Czarist Russia, but in God's chosen land! And who could tell what other wonders were in store? According to the great Bible commentator, Rashi, God's promise to Abraham included not only the Land of Israel, but children, affluence, and fame. Though an aging widower like Tevye could not expect any more children, he certainly was not loathe to the prospect of receiving a modest fortune and world renown. Nonetheless, he was happy with what he had. With hardly a ruble in his pocket, Tevye felt like a very rich man.

So high were Tevye's spirits, he didn't seem to notice the desolation around him. All of the landscape was scorched. There were more rocks on the road than on the bordering hillsides. A shade tree could barely be found. The scant vegetation which managed to grow in the wasteland was shrouded in dust, like old furniture stored in an attic. Besides an occasional bedouin, not a human being could be seen along the entire stretch of their journey.

Nachman also felt joyously happy. With an unrestrained enthusiasm, he didn't stop talking. He didn't speak about his new wife. Nor did he chatter about his wedding. Nor about being in Israel. He spoke on and on about Rabbi Kook. With a look of mystical rapture, he confessed that meeting Rabbi Kook was the dream of his life. Any other woman besides Ruchel might have been jealous, but she was happy that his dream was about to come true. Tevye was more anxious to get on to the reunion with Hodel, but Nachman would not be dissuaded. Nachman insisted that they meet Rabbi Kook. First, he wanted to receive the exalted Rabbi's blessing. Second, he wanted to hear everything he could from the respected sage. To understand the great spiritual adventure they were living, Nachman insisted, they had to meet the mentor of their generation, the rabbi of rabbis, HaRav Avraham Yitzhak HaCohen Kook.

Tevye was skeptical. He had met lots of rabbis in his lifetime, and though he respected them all, he didn't see a big difference between one Torah scholar and the next.

"What great spiritual adventure?" Bat Sheva asked.

"The redemption of our people," Nachman answered.

"Being kicked out of your village, murdered, and exiled from country to country is not what I call redemption," the willful girl responded.

"She has a point," Tevye agreed.

"You'll understand when Rabbi Kook explains it to you," Nachman assured.

"Why must I understand? Aren't the pains in my back and the aches in my feet enough learning for a lifetime?"

"That's just the physical side of our life. There is a whole spiritual reality as well."

Tevye didn't see anything spiritual in milking a cow at four in the morning, but he didn't want to get into a mystical argument with his new son-in-law. The milkman from Anatevka was a simple Jew, not a Kabbalist. It was enough for him to serve the Lord with gladness and a peasant's simple faith, believing that everything was in the hands of His Creator. Life was a never-ending series of trials, with joyous occasions scattered like bread crumbs along the road, to give a man hope and the strength to continue. A Jew had to stick to the Torah and thank the Almighty for both the good and the bad. As King Solomon had said, "Fear God and keep His commandments, for this is the sum of man." Anything more, like Nachman's talk of redemption and the Kingdom of Heaven on earth, only gave Tevye a headache.

After several long hours of travel, they reached the port city of Jaffa. In contrast to the barren desert landscapes which they had left behind, the noisy congestion of Jaffa came as a welcomed sight. Narrow streets and alleyways were infested with man and beast. Arab porters scurried in every direction, laden with fleeces of wool, copper vessels, and Persians rugs. Caravan drivers led their camels toward the market. The aroma of oriental spices and teas perfumed the air. Vendors cried out, selling their wares from booths on the street. Turkish soldiers with bayonetted rifles strutted through the crowds, keeping order. Crippled beggars stuck out their hands for money, and dark-faced Africans and Moslems offered juice drinks from jugs strapped over their backs. The cobblestone pavement was soiled with sheep dung and donkey droppings. Flies swarmed everywhere. They stuck to Tevye's beard, unfazed by his swats and his curses. Only when the Jews made their way through the teeming city toward the harbor did an ocean breeze rescue them from their furious attackers.

The roadway along the port was congested with carts loading and unloading merchandise. Dozens of sun-bleached rowboats were tied to the wharf, while schooners and four-chimneyed freighters lay anchored further out to sea. Tevye pulled alongside a wagon laden with wine barrels and driven by Jews. Nachman greeted them and asked the way to Rabbi Kook's house. They answered in Russian and pointed down the roadway to a cluster of houses at the outskirts of the port.

Soon, more and more Jews could be seen as they approached the white-cottaged neighborhood. Many of the faces were so dark and oriental that Tevye wondered if they were Jewish. Some wore the same caftans and turbans of the Arabs. Other Jews, paler in complexion and recognizably Ashkenazim, were dressed like Russian workers with vests, caps, and bushy beards. Everyone they asked seemed to know where the Rabbi of Jaffa lived. In his excitement, Nachman jumped down from the wagon and ran on ahead. The Rabbi's wife showed them into the house. She said that the Rabbi was resting, but he appeared in a doorway at the far end of the parlor, eager to greet his guests as if he had been expecting their arrival.

Nachman rushed forward and bowed, grasping the Rabbi's outstretched hand. Rabbi Kook was dressed formally in a long black frock. A black fur-lined *shtreimel* covered his head like a crown. What astonished Tevye were his eyes. In the depths of their piercing blackness, a light shone with a mystical radiance. When he glanced at Tevye, the humble milkman felt that his secrets lay open before him like playing cards spread out on a table. The great Torah scholar smiled at the newcomers and wished them a pleasant *shalom*. His eyes glowed with kindness, but at the same time, they were incredibly serious. The Rabbi's glance seemed to say, "My friend, Tevye, I love you like a brother, but we both know that being a Jew isn't so simple."

The holy sage invited the men into his book-filled study. Tevye suggested to Hevedke that he stay outside to guard the wagon. Rabbi Kook said it wasn't necessary, the neighborhood was safe, but Tevye insisted. He wanted to discuss the delicate matter of Hevedke and Hava in privacy. With a glance at the fair Russian poet, Rabbi Kook understood. Ushering Tevye, Nachman, and Goliath into his study, he asked his wife to kindly prepare them some tea.

Tevye guessed that he was several years older than the Chief Rabbi of Jaffa, but he felt like a young man in his presence. The Rabbi's aura of wisdom and piety commanded unquestioned respect. Tevye had the feeling that he was in the presence of a king. Whether it was the Rabbi himself, the library of holy books, or something more mystical, Tevye didn't know, but the awe of the High Holy Days pervaded the room.

With genuine interest, the Rabbi asked where they had lived before their arrival in Israel. He had of course heard about the terrible pogroms sweeping through Russia, and he was visibly chagrined to hear about the murder of Nachman's father, may the Almighty revenge his spilled blood. He himself had studied in the Yeshiva of Volozin, and he dreaded that the great Torah center would also fall prey to the ever-spreading attacks.

"We have to understand that the time has come for the Jewish people to return home to Zion," he said. "God has decreed. The ingathering of the exiles is at hand. We can choose to hear the shofar of freedom calling us back to Zion on our own, or we can be compelled to hear it by the Czars and Cossacks of the world. I fear in my innermost being that if we don't hear the call of our prophets; if we don't actualize the words of our prayers to return to the Land of our forefathers and rebuild our ancient cities; if we close our eyes to the expulsions and murders which come upon us every day in the exile; if we cling to foreign lands and foreign rulers and foreign ways, then a wave of horrible violence will come upon us, more devastating than anything we have experienced before."

The Rabbi's eyes blazed as if envisioning some unspeakable horror beyond the walls of his study. Tevye trembled. Nachman sat breathlessly listening to every word.

"The spirit of Israel is awakening," the Rabbi continued. "The soul of our nation is demanding its own Land. Zion is to become a beacon of light to the world, and we who are fortunate to hear the voice of our forefathers calling to us from the past, it is our job to teach others to hear the call too."

"I am only a simple milkman," Tevye confided. "I came to *Eretz Yisrael* because my daughter is here with her husband on some communist kibbutz in the north."

"You have come home to Zion for much more than that," the Rabbi answered with a smile in his eyes. "The Almighty has chosen you, Reb Tevye, to be one of the builders, one of the pioneers. In this generation, in this monumental time of our national rebirth on our holy, ancient soil, there can be no simple milkmen, no simple Jews. Each one of us is called upon to be like a thousand until all of our scattered brethren flock here to join us."

"Even if I understood all of the things which your honor is saying, I don't think my atheist son-in-law would listen."

"No Jew is an atheist," Rabbi Kook answered. "No matter how confused our young people are with foreign ideas and creeds, the Jewish soul is always pure. Sometimes our eyes are blind and our ears are deaf, but our inner souls long for our God and our Torah. We carry the flame of our heritage eternally within our hearts. Nothing can extinguish it, not even two-thousand years of darkness and exile. If your son-in-law doesn't listen, then his children, or his children's children will. The repentance of our nation is promised. *`For from Zion shall go forth the Torah, and the word of God from Jerusalem.'* In the light of this great beacon shining out from Jerusalem, all of mankind will come to recognize the Kingship of God over the earth.

What could Tevye do but nod his head and agree? He had

never heard a rabbi speak before in such an exalted manner. Usually, you went to the rabbi to ask him how to slaughter a chicken, not for a philosophical discourse on the salvation of the whole human race. In a way, Rabbi Kook spoke in the visionary style of Perchik and Ben Zion, but where they were full of senseless babble, the Rabbi was unquestionably graced with the word and spirit of God.

"With the honorable Rabbi's permission," Tevye ventured to ask. "It is true that in Russia, we common Jews never thought much further than making a living and getting to sleep at the end of the day. We were content to receive whatever crumbs we could from the Czar, and observe the Sabbath in peace. I was blessed with seven wonderful daughters, but to put bread on the table, I spent more time with my horse and my cow. When I looked up from my milking, modern times had set in, and my daughters had been seduced by its charms. One girl is in America. Another, may God shelter her, has drowned. My poor Tzeitl's husband dropped dead. My Hodel ran off with a Marxist free thinker. And Bat Sheva, I am afraid, has fallen in love with a Zionist Rasputin. Only Ruchel, who has just married Nachman, has merited a life filled with Torah. The girl you saw outside, my Havala, ran off with the Russian you saw in your salon, breaking my heart and the heart of my tortured wife, Golda, may her memory be for a blessing. Now, against all of my wishes and threats, this very same Galagan has followed us here, at the risk of his life several times over. All he talks about is properly marrying my daughter and becoming a Jew. I ask your advice. What is a father to do?"

The Rabbi glanced over at Nachman.

"His heart is set on converting," Nachman answered. "Not only because of the girl. The pogroms in Russia seemed to have affected him deeply. Even when some of our traveling companions gave him a beating, he still insisted on following us. I told him he would have to study, and he agrees, even if it means being separated from Hava."

"We can find him a place in Jaffa if he is truly willing to learn for a year," the Rabbi said, turning toward Tevye. "The heart must be filled with a love for all people. Feelings of hatred must be directed against wickedness only, not against people. We must always remember that there is a spark of godliness in everyone."

Tevye was not certain that the Rabbi's answer was the solution he wanted to hear. But at least a year in some yeshiva would keep Hevedke away from his daughter. Before they left Rabbi Kook's study, the Rabbi gave Tevye his special blessing as a *Kohen*, a member of the ancient priestly class.

"Perhaps, your honor, the Rabbi, could give a poor milkman a blessing that I find suitable husbands for the rest of my daughters?"

Once again, the Rabbi's eyes glimmered when he gave Tevye the blessing he asked for. Nachman lingered for a few extra minutes to tell the Rabbi about his teacher's position in Rishon LeZion. The sage seemed especially pleased with this news. It meant that the light of Torah in the Holy Land was growing along with the orchards and vineyards. As Rabbi Kook led Nachman out of the room, he invited the young scholar to visit him on the holidays so that they could learn Torah together. More than anything else in the world, this was what Nachman wanted to hear.

Rabbi Kook escorted them to the porch, said good-bye, and called for Hevedke to enter. With a look of surprise on his face, the tall Russian walked up the stairs, glancing back for a last look at Hava. When the door closed behind him, Tevye told his daughters to climb back into the wagon.

"What about Hevedke?" Hava asked.

"Hevedke is becoming a yeshiva *bocher*," her father said.

"What do you mean?" Hava demanded.

"He's starting his studies today."

"Isn't he coming with us?"

"No. He'll be staying here in Jaffa, in the yeshiva of Rabbi Kook."

"For how long?" Hava asked.

"At least for a year. Isn't that what we agreed?"

"Will I be able to visit?"

"No, not while he's learning. The *halacha*-law forbids it."

"Is Jewish law everything?" the girl protested.

"Yes," her father replied.

"What about emotions? Aren't they important?"

"They certainly are. In the right place, in the right time, and with the right person."

"Can't I even say good-bye?"

"No," Tevye said. "Until Hevedke becomes a Jew, being together is out of the question."

It hurt Tevye's heart to say it, but he kept his face frozen in a stern, disapproving expression. It was best for the girl. After all, the experiment could fail. In the end, it might turn out that Hevedke's love for Hava outweighed his love for the Torah. Until he proved himself in the purifying crucible of a yeshiva, where the Torah was learned day and night, all of his proclamations had as much substance as wind.

Hava stared at her father. She bit down on her lip. If this was the way it had to be, so be it. If this was a test, she was ready. If this was the way she could atone for the mistakes of her past, she would wait two years if she had to. Once, she had recklessly rushed off to be with Hevedke, and now, to make amends, she would have to wait a long time. With her heart pounding inside her, she turned away from the house of the Rabbi and stared out at the road. She wanted to be strong. For Hevedke's sake. To give him a genuine chance to earn her father's blessing.

Chapter Eleven

MADE IN HEAVEN

When Tevye's entourage reached the port of Jaffa, hoping to discover something about their fellow travelers who had set sail to Palestine ahead of them, the first thing he saw gave him the shivers. Hadn't he just asked Rabbi Kook for a blessing to find husbands for his daughters? Who was sitting at a dockside cafe but Nachman's two friends, Shmuelik and Hillel! For weeks, they had been waiting for Tevye and Nachman to arrive in the Holy Land. Like long lost relatives, everyone rushed to embrace.

"*Shalom aleichem!*" they called.

"*Aleichem shalom!*" Tevye answered.

"May your coming be blessed and your prayers all be answered," Shmuelik joyfully wished.

"Amen," Tevye answered. "Amen."

Nachman's friends grabbed his hands and swung him around in a dance. Tevye turned toward his daughters who were watching from the wagon.

"Tzeitl, Hava, Bat Sheva, come quickly!" he called. "Look who fell out from the sky! Our old friends Shmuelik and Hillel!"

It was a match made in Heaven, Tevye thought. Several matches at once! With a father's imagination, Tevye dreamed that Shmuelik would marry Bat Sheva, Goliath would marry Tzeitl, and after Hevedke failed in his studies, please God, Hillel would make Hava his wife. Satisfied with the happy futures awaiting his daughters, Tevye seized the hands of his companions and joined the festive circle of singing. Ignoring the ominous glances of Turkish soldiers who were looking their way, the Jews threw their heads back and sang up to Heaven a traditional wedding tune.

"Soon we will hear
The singing of the *chatan* and *kallah*,
The joy of the groom and the bride,
On the hills of Judea and Jerusalem."

Chapter Twelve

HODEL

It was impossible to tell which thought gave Tevye more happiness. The thought of stepping foot in Jerusalem, or the thought of seeing his Hodel again. True, Hodel was his own flesh and blood. She was like a little piece of his Golda. Hadn't he listened to his wife's painful groans through eight excruciating hours of childbirth? Hadn't he cradled the girl in his arms when nightmares disturbed her sleep? With pride and with great fatherly joy, he had watched her grow from a tot into a woman. And how empty and heartbroken he had felt when she rode off on a train to follow her Perchik into exile. But Jerusalem – Jerusalem was more than a child. Jerusalem was more than a man's family. Jerusalem was a dream. It was more than a dream. Who ever thought that the dream of Jerusalem could ever come true?

How could it be, you ask? How could it be that a city which Tevye had never seen could occupy such a powerful place in his heart? For a Jew, the answer was simple. For two-thousand years, three times a day, Jews prayed to return to their city. After every meal, after every piece of bread, and every piece of cake, they prayed for Jerusalem's welfare. No matter where a Jew lived, the city of Jerusalem was to be the center of his life. It was the place where the Pascal lamb was to be eaten on the Passover holiday, and where first fruits were brought on *Shavuos*. There, by the pool of Shiloach, joyous water celebrations were held on *Sukkos*. It was the site of the ancient Temple, the *Beis HaMikdash*, may it soon be rebuilt. It was the place where the Sanhedrin declared the new months, and where the High Priest atoned for the nation on Yom Kippur. There, the miracle of Hanukah had occurred when the Maccabees had won their great victory over the Greeks. For Jews all over the world, each day started with the hope – perhaps this was the day that God would rescue them from their exile in foreign lands and bring them back to Jerusalem.

But the dream of his father, and his grandfather, and his great-grandfather before them, and all of his grandfathers all the way back to Abraham wasn't to come true for the moment. They only had use of the JCA wagon for a week, so the ascent up the mountains leading to Jerusalem would have to be postponed so that they could make the three-day journey up north to the kibbutz where Hodel was living.

With tears in her eyes, Ruchel kissed her sister Tzeitl goodbye. Tzeitl seemed so frail and so thin, Ruchel feared that she might never see her big sister again, God forbid. For weeks now, Tzeitl hardly touched any food, and the weight she lost had hollowed her cheeks. Her cough clung to her like a menacing shadow, and her always hopeful smile seemed more to comfort others, so as not to cause her family anguish. The sisters hugged without looking too deeply into each other's eyes. Ruchel kissed Hava, Bat Sheva, and gave the children big squeezes. Then she turned toward her father. The time had come to return to Rishon so that Nachman could assume his new position as *melamed*, teaching in the *Talmud Torah*. Tevye wore a big happy grin. If he had done one good thing in his life, it was bringing Ruchel to the *chuppah* to marry Nachman. Not that the match had been so much his doing, but it showed that he had succeeded in educating his daughter along the right path. Married to Nachman, she would always live a life of tradition. So even if they were setting off on their own for Rishon LeZion, away from the rest of the family, Tevye felt happy and confident that he was entrusting his girl to a God-fearing man who loved her with all of his heart.

"Remember, *Abba*," she called from the wagon, using the Hebrew expression for father. "Tell Hodel and Perchik that we are expecting them to come visit us soon."

Though Shmuelik and Hillel wanted to accompany their childhood friend, Nachman, he advised them to wait until he could arrange permission for them to join the already established *yishuv*.

Though he was skeptical about his chances of persuading Dupont, he felt the resourceful Aharon might be able to help. In the meantime, they agreed to travel with Tevye. The decision required no forceful persuasion – both of them nurtured a secret attraction for Bat Sheva, Tevye's fiery, plum-cheeked daughter. Though she hardly glanced at them, each had high hopes.

Tevye was nobody's fool. Being as good a judge of men as he was of horses and cows, (except in the case of the crook Menachem Mendel, his wife's fast-talking, second cousin, who persuaded him to squander his life's savings in worthless stocks) he realized that both men were on the lookout for wives. In Tevye's mind, Shmuelik was just the right man to tame his youngest daughter. True, the scholar was quiet, and Bat Sheva liked spice and adventure, but Tevye was hoping that the lesson she had received from Ben Zion would teach her that a sincere, God-fearing husband was better than a swaggering Machiavelli she never could trust.

As for Tzeitl's future, her father could only sigh. Goliath was ready to make her his wife, and sweet-natured Tzeitl probably would have consented, if not out of love, then for the sake of her children. But in her present condition, there was no sense in pursuing the match. Tevye wanted to hospitalize her in Jaffa, where she could rest and recover from the hardships of their journey, but she stubbornly refused. She even defied her father's wishes on the doorstep of the hospital where Tevye had deviously brought her.

"I am ordering you," he commanded.

"No," she protested.

"Remember, I am your father," he said.

"I don't need a hospital," she answered. "I want to see Hodel, that's all."

"What you want isn't important," he said. "What your father wants is what counts. Since Motel, the poor creature, went to his Maker, you have returned to my care, and I am commanding you to do what I say."

"I am going to the kibbutz to see Hodel, and that's final,"

Tzeitl argued. "The last thing I need is to be cooped up in a hospital with other sick people."

There was something to be said for her argument. After all, more people died in hospitals than lived. But, still, in her condition, she was too weak to travel. To convince her, Tevye resorted to a verse from the Torah.

"Isn't it written in the Ten Commandments, `Thou shalt honor thy father and thy mother that thy days may be long in the Land which I gave to your forefathers'? Here we are in the Land, and I am commanding you to obey my wishes, whether you want to or not."

"Oh, Abba," Tzeitl said. "Haven't you learned by now that your eldest daughter has a mind of her own."

"Yes," he admitted. "When I arranged for you to marry Anatevka's wealthiest man, the butcher Lazar Wolf, and you fell in love with your tailor. Who ever heard of a girl falling in love before her wedding?"

"You can't set the clock backward. Young people have changed."

"Well, if you won't listen to me, then for the sake of your children, please let the doctors try to help you."

"All right," she agreed. "To please you. But only after I see my sister Hodel."

She stared at him defiantly. Tevye remembered that look, when her eyes turned to ice. There was no use in arguing. When Tzeitl made up her mind that was that. Hell could freeze over before she would give in. A battle would only weaken her strength. So, with a shrug, Tevye turned away from the hospital.

With the last rubles he had, Tevye purchased a horse and a wagon, and the wanderers headed north along the Damascus road to join their Hodel in Shoshana.

Once again, Tevye was amazed at the desolation they encountered as they traveled along the coastal plain, then ascended the range of hills that made up the backbone of the country. Boulders covered the landscapes. The topsoil was nothing but rock. Hardly a shrub could be seen. Here and there, an olive tree grew like a reminder of the country's once glorious past. "Some *metsia*," Tevye thought. A land filled with rocks wasn't such a big bargain. But at least it was theirs. Occasionally, a lone bedouin rode by on a donkey, carrying produce to the Jerusalem market. Now and then, a few Turkish soldiers would salute them as they galloped by on their horses, but otherwise, the countryside was deserted, with hardly a town or a village to welcome them on their way. Miles and miles of hillsides and valleys lay barren, having staunchly resisted cultivation for two-thousand years, turning away foreign conqueror after conqueror, as if waiting for the Land's true children to come home.

To help shorten their journey, Hillel sat in the rear of the wagon, playing his accordion and singing. Hadn't musicians accompanied the Jews when Ezra led them back to the Holy Land to build the Second Temple? And didn't the Psalm promise, "When the Lord will return the exiles to Zion, our mouths will be filled with glad song?" Hillel had a merry, soothing voice, and the children loved to listen. You might have thought he was a minstrel trying to win Bat Sheva's heart, the way he kept smiling at her, hoping for a look of approval. But his intentions were the furthest thing from her mind, possessed as it was with thoughts of Ben Zion and the approaching moment when she would see him again.

Tevye's spirits remained boisterous, not only with the prospect of soon seeing Hodel, but with the wise transaction he had made for the horse. Like a learned and experienced veterinarian, he had given the animal a careful examination, checking its teeth for decay, its legs for spastic twitches, and its feces for worms. The Jew who had sold it to Tevye was a carpenter. Unable to make a decent living, he was leaving the country to seek better luck in America. He said he was disillusioned with the Jewish Colony Association and with the Baron's dictatorial clerks. They were the reason he had moved to Jerusalem. In the city, he couldn't compete with the cheap Arab labor, so, to feed his family, he was forced to move on. Instead of fixing tables and chairs in Palestine, he would build mansions for the Jews in America. Tevye didn't try to dissuade him. At the price he was asking, the horse was a steal. And, thank God, the beast passed the test in the field. It pulled the wagon with ease and didn't seem to tire in the unrelenting sun. And to Tevye's great pleasure, the animal responded to its new master's cues as if they had been partners for years.

To entertain the children when Hillel wasn't singing, Tevye pointed out the sites of famous Biblical battles and stories, as if he really knew the locations where they had occurred. On the hill over there, King Saul was born, he declared with great authority. And over there, by the very same olive tree, the prophet Samuel would receive pilgrims seeking the word of the Lord. Here, of course, in Gilgal, Joshua had commanded the sun to stand still. And here, on what was definitely Mount Tabor, the valiant Deborah had led an inspired Israeli army on a rout of Sisera's forces. Shmuelik knew the Biblical stories with a great deal more textual accuracy, but since he wasn't familiar with the geography of the Holy Land, he abstained from correcting Tevye and embarrassing him in front of his family.

Reaching the city of Shechem, which Jacob had captured with his bow and his sword, the travelers stopped to pray at the tomb of the saintly Joseph. Then, journeying over the mountains, they reached the Jordan Valley, north of the desert plains north of Jericho, where the Children of Israel had come into the Land of Israel after their forty years of wilderness wandering. The road wasn't so much of a road as a trail of old wagon tracks. Sand-covered mountains rose up around them. Goliath suggested they rest during the fierce noon hours, but there was hardly a shade tree that could provide them with shelter all along the desolate way. To the east, an oasis of green date palms, cypress trees, and willows lined the serpentine path of the Jordan River, but the steep sand dunes and treacherous chasms in the valley prevented the wagon from reaching its banks.

To help pass the time, Shmuelik opened the Book of Books and read aloud, as if he were teaching children in *heder*.

The words of the Torah and the stark ancient landscape had a magical, inspiring effect. Tevye had traveled through many of the forests and mountains of Russia, but he had never experienced anything spiritual in the air. But here, in the Holy Land, everything was steeped with Biblical wonder. Tevye didn't even complain about sleeping outdoors on a burlap sack which he spread out over the rocky, back-breaking earth. Had Jacob complained when he had slept on a pillow of rocks and dreamed of angels ascending and descending a ladder which reached up to Heaven? Imagine what would Moses have given to be in Tevye's place! Moses, the faithful shepherd of the Children of Israel, who devoted his whole life to leading the Jews, had only one wish for himself – to enter the Promised Land, a blessing that was ultimately denied him. Lying on his back, staring up at the twinkling heavens, Tevye understood why Moses was so heartbroken after his entreaties failed. Even a simple milkman could feel the spirit of God in the Land. A canopy of constellations glimmered like gold dust in every corner of the sky, a witness to the promise which God had made to Abraham to make his offspring as illustrious as the stars in the heavens.

Finally, after a sweltering, week-long journey, a shimmering blue hallucination materialized out of the haze in the distance. They had reached Lake Kinneret, also called the Sea of Galilee, shining in the sun like a jewel. With a cheer, Tevye urged the horse forward. Goliath ran to keep pace with the wagon. Further north along the winding hillside road was the holy city of Tiberias, where they would spend the Sabbath. Fully dressed, everyone rushed to jump in the lake to cool off in its sparkling fresh waters. Tevye knelt on his hands and knees alongside his horse and lapped up the fresh, life-giving liquid. Then, like a king in a royal bath, he rolled over on his back in the shallows and let the gentle waves of the lake massage his weary bones.

Refreshed, the pioneers continued toward the city of Tiberias, burial site of the great Jewish sages, Rabbi Akiva, Rabbi Yochanan, the Rambam, the Ramchal, and Rabbi Meir Baal HaNess. But a blockade on the road prevented them from reaching the ancient lakeside city. Turkish soldiers ordered the wagon to halt. Shmuelik, who knew Aramaic and Hebrew, and who had picked up rudiments of the Arabic language and Turkish during his month in Jaffa, acted as interpreter. Apparently a plague of cholera had broken out in the city, and dozens of people had died.

"Among the Jews?" Shmuelik asked.

"Why shouldn't the Jews be stricken along with everyone else?" the soldier answered. "We all drink the same water. People drop dead every day."

Tevye spit up a few drops of the mouthfuls of water he had swallowed in the lake. The news of the plague dampened everyone spirits. Perhaps invisible bacteria were already invading their blood. One of the red-caftanned Turks asked what business they had in Tiberias. When Shmuelik told him where they were headed, the soldier said that the village of Shoshana was only a two hour ascent up the mountain. Tevye wanted to know if the kibbutz had also been hit by the plague, God forbid. The soldier shrugged. He hadn't heard anything. He acted like he really didn't care. Obediently, Tevye swung the wagon around in the road. Hoping they had found the right trail, the group set off into the mountains.

There were wagon-wheel tracks along the primitive path, some drying horse dung, and signs that a sheep herd had recently passed. Suddenly, up ahead of the wagon, an Arab tent topped by a red Turkish flag was stationed at a bend in the road. Two nasty-looking Arabs clutching rifles stepped out onto the trail, blocking the path of the wagon. Tevye tugged on the reins. Goliath protectively walked forward alongside Tevye's horse. The taller of the two Arabs barked out angry orders. At first, Shmuelik didn't understand what he wanted. Frustrated, the Arab began yelling. Goliath stood tensely, waiting to pounce. Finally, the Arab shouted the word, "Tobacco." Shmuelik told him they didn't have any. Angrily, the Arab shouted the word tobacco again. Ominously, he raised the rifle which he held cradled in his arms. Once again, Shmuelik began to explain, but Hillel interrupted before he could finish.

"I have some tobacco," he said.

He opened his traveling bag and fished out a pouch of tobacco.

"They told me it makes a good bribe with the Arabs," he explained to the others in Yiddish. "Under Turkish law, tobacco is outlawed. This must be some kind of checking station. You can be sure our two friends are going to keep the booty for themselves."

He flipped the pouch to the Arab, who snatched it from the air with a smile. Grinning, the unsavory couple returned to the shade of their tent. When the roadway was clear, Tevye whipped the reins of the wagon and hurried the wagon on down the trail.

"I wonder what they would have done to us if we didn't have any tobacco to give them," Bat Sheva said.

"They probably would have cut off our hands," Hillel answered.

The girl looked at him seriously. "Maybe we should invest in a rifle," she said.

Tevye laughed. The idea was amusing. "Who ever heard of a Jew with a rifle?" he asked.

"Why not?" Hava said. "This isn't Russia. Certainly in our own Land, a Jew has the right to bear arms."

"Spoken like a true Zionist," her father said.

"Well, at least now we know the best crop to grow when we have our own farms," Hillel said.

"What's that?" Moishe asked.

"Tobacco."

Hillel strapped his accordion over his shoulders and began to bang out a tune. In what seemed a short time, they came to an open valley and a patchwork of neatly plowed fields tended by industrious farmers. A worker walked along, scattering seeds from a bag slung over his back. Another carried a sheaf toward a wagon already overflowing with a mountain of hay.

Seeing them, Shmuelik stood up in the wagon and sang out the words of the Psalm which they all knew by heart, a prayer of longing for the Land of Israel recited at the end of every Sabbath meal.

"Those who sow in tears
Will reap with joyous song.
Though he walks along weeping,
Carrying his bag of seed,

He will return with joyous song,
Carrying his sheaves."

Hillel accompanied him on his accordion. Hearing the melody,
the worker closest to the wagon looked up. It was Perchik, Hodel's
husband, the Russian revolutionary turned Zionist farmer. Tevye
stood up in the wagon. How incredibly happy he was to see the
young dreamer. Perchik too felt a shiver of joy as he recognized
the bearded face from the past. He cast off the bag of seeds from
his shoulder and came running toward the wagon to greet them.

"Tevye!" he yelled in heartfelt surprise. "Hodel come quickly!
Your father and sisters are here!"

Tevye leaped off the wagon. The two men embraced. Long
ago, the first time Tevye had delivered milk to the summer house
where Perchik was vacationing with his parents, the milkman had
been attracted to the lad's cheerful eloquence. Tevye had liked
him, the way he naturally liked people, and that had caused all of
the *tzuris* and pain. Tevye had treated the youth like the son he
had always longed for, inviting him into his house to tutor his
daughters. Instead of teaching, the dreamer lectured for hours on
end about all of the world's wonders. He carried on as if he were
a professor of philosophy, history, and international affairs. And
what upside-down chatter! Everything with Perchik was reversed
from the normal way of the world. Money, he claimed, was the
root of all evil. To his way of thinking, Tevye should be thrilled
to be poor! The peasant worker, Perchik insisted, was the "cream
of the milk," while Tevye knew from firsthand experience that a
working man was no better than dung. The university student
glorified physical labor, but all he did was talk. Then, for weeks
on end, he would suddenly disappear on some secret revolutionary
mission. And to repay Tevye for his hospitality, this
self-proclaimed champion of universal justice stole the poor
milkman's daughter away like a thief who breaks into a house on
Rosh HaShana while the family is praying in *shul*.

For a moment, Tevye remembered the day he had said
good-bye to Hodel at the railway station, and the heartache which
her free-thinking husband had caused. But that was then, and this

was now. Every man made mistakes. And every man could change for the better. Didn't it say in the Torah, "Thou shall not hold a grudge in your heart?" It was time, Tevye realized, to put the past behind them and opt for a new beginning. So Tevye kissed his smiling son-in-law and made room in his heart to welcome him into the family.

Out of the corner of his eye, he saw Hodel come running. Her sisters ran to greet her. Who would have recognized her, so suntanned and as pregnant and round as a cow! Who ever heard of a woman working in a field in her condition? But then again, who ever heard of Jewish farmers? In Russia, a Jew wasn't allowed to own farmland at all.

"Tzeitl, Hava, Bat Sheva!" she called.

Ecstatic, Hodel hugged one after the other. Finally, she pulled herself free and turned to her father.

"*Abba*," she sobbed, using the Hebrew expression for father. Happily, she fell into his outstretched arms. "How much I have missed you. How I've missed you all."

A sob shook Tevye's body as he embraced the little girl he had held in his arms, bathed, and taught how to milk a cow.

"Ah, Golda," he thought. "Ah, Golda. If only you could be here now."

But when he looked at Hodel, his heart was relieved. She was a picture of his wife in her youth, with the same sparkling smile and eyes. In a way, Tevye's wife, Golda, was with them.

"I can't believe it!" Hodel said. "Finally, finally, you've come!"

"Thanks to God," Tevye said.

"And the Czar," Bat Sheva added.

"May his name and memory be cursed," Hillel said.

"Where is Ruchel?" Hodel asked.

"Married!" Hava answered. "To a handsome young *talmid chacham*."

Hodel giggled in happiness. "Tell me, tell me. I want to hear everything!"

"They are living in Rishon LeZion, and they insist you come visit as soon as you can," Tzeitl said.

"And Baylke?" Hodel asked.

"Off to America with her bankrupted millionaire," Tevye answered.

"It's disgusting," Perchik said. "Here we are struggling to rebuild our homeland, and there are Jews living the life of capitalist kings in New York."

Moishe and Hannie shyly came forward and embraced Hodel's skirt. She bent down and gave them a hug. "How big they have grown," she marveled.

"How big you have grown," Tevye joked.

Everyone chuckled. "Can you believe it, Reb Tevye?" Perchik asked, giving his father-in-law a slap on the back. "Soon you will have a grandchild born in *Eretz Yisrael*!"

Tevye smiled. Loudly, he said the words of the *Shehecheyanu* prayer, thanking God for having kept him alive to experience this great reunion with his daughter. Other kibbutz workers began to gather around them. The deeply suntanned men were dressed in white blouses, dark pants, and boots. Some were bareheaded and others wore caps. The women wore white kerchiefs, simple, hand-knitted dresses and aprons. Others let their tresses hang down freely in the sun.

Hugging her sisters again, Hodel noticed Tzeitl's pale smile.

"What's the matter?" she asked. "Are you weak from the journey?"

"Don't worry. I'll be fine," Tzeitl said.

"Let me get you some water to drink."

"I'm a little tired, that's all," Tzeitl insisted.

"We had better hurry," Shmuelik said to Tevye. "Soon it will be *Shabbos*."

Tevye glanced at the sky. The sun was beginning to set in the west.

"*Shabbos*?" Perchik asked. "Who worries about the Sabbath? One day is the same as the rest when you are a worker rebuilding the Land."

Tevye eyed his loudmouthed son-in-law. "Here he goes with

his heretical babble," he thought. But before he could think of a fitting response, a loud greeting sounded behind them.

"*Shalom aleichem*!" the hearty voice shouted.

Everyone turned. Bat Sheva's poor heart nearly jumped out of her body. It was Ben Zion. When she saw him, she felt she was going to faint. The sun sparkled around him, blinding her eyes. He sat straight and tall on a horse, clutching a rifle in his hand. Swathed in an Arab *kefiah*, and wearing two belts of bullets crisscrossed over his chest, he looked like a picture-book hero.

"Greetings, greetings, my friends!" he exclaimed, swinging down from his steed. He slapped Shmuelik and Hillel hard on their backs. For a moment, he gave Bat Sheva a gaze so unholy and brazen, she nearly collapsed. Then he offered his free hand to Tevye.

"*Shalom aleichem*," he said.

"*Aleichem shalom*," Tevye solemnly answered without extending a hand in return.

Ben Zion grinned, undaunted by Tevye's unenthusiastic reception.

"No doubt the journey has exhausted our visitors," he announced to the crowd. "And knowing my honored friend, Tevye, I am sure he would like to get ready for the approaching Sabbath day. So why don't we all call it a day in the fields to prepare the kind of homecoming celebration that Hodel's family rightly deserves!"

His proposal was answered with a common assent from the workers.

"Let me take your accordion," Ben Zion said to Hillel.

Good-naturedly, Hillel swung the cumbersome instrument off his back and handed it to Ben Zion.

"Take this instead," Ben Zion told him, handing him his rifle.

"What do I need this for?" Hillel asked, bewildered. "I'm a musician."

"You were a musician," Ben Zion answered. "Now you're a full-fledged *shomer*, with the duty of guarding the collective like everyone else."

"But I don't know how to use a rifle," Hillel protested, knowing that *shomer* in Hebrew meant guard.

The field workers laughed.

"Don't worry," Ben Zion assured him. "You'll learn. And if you prove to be a good watchman, then God willing, your son will have the chance to grow up to be a musician without any need for a gun. That's the sacrifice this generation has to make in building our new State."

Unable to overcome her emotions, Bat Sheva swooned and fell in a faint to the ground. The women rushed to her aid. Hodel slapped her face. A hand held out a gourd of water. Ben Zion stepped forward and bent down to lift her.

"Let's get her into the wagon," he said.

Tevye stretched out his hand, halting the rogue's valiant gesture. They stared into each other's eyes, like two roosters ready for a fight. The women lifted Bat Sheva and carried her off to the wagon. The sun continued to set in the west. It was time to get ready for *Shabbos*.

Chapter Thirteen

TZEITL'S LAST WISH

"What are we going to eat?" Shmuelik asked Tevye as they changed into their Sabbath clothing.

Tevye did not understand the question. "What do you mean?" he asked.

Before Shmuelik could answer, Hillel spoke up in a bard's satirical manner. "He means that though you may be overjoyed to be reunited with your daughter, the Lord has commanded the Jewish people to observe certain dietary laws like eating properly slaughtered meat. And while we have only been here a short time, I have not seen the likes of a God-fearing butcher."

"So we won't eat meat tonight," Tevye responded. "There is no sin in that."

"Not eat meat on *Shabbos*?" Hillel asked. "Even when my mother, God bless her, didn't have a *kopeck* to buy a new pair of shoes for me or my brother, we still had meat on *Shabbos*."

"That's the way it goes," Tevye answered. "The Almighty is in charge of the menu. Whatever He gives us is more than we deserve."

"The meat is not the only problem," Shmuelik observed. This is the Holy Land. There are laws of priestly dues and tithes. Before we can eat vegetables and fruits which Jews have grown in the Land, the proper portions must be set aside as commanded in the Torah."

Tevye sighed. Whoever said it was easy to be a good Jew? Your thoughts had to be holy. Your deeds had to be holy. Your food had to be holy. Your day of rest had to be holy. Even your Land had special religious laws of its own which no one ever thought about in Russia.

"This is one of the reasons why Moses begged the Almighty to let him enter *Eretz Yisrael*" Shmuelik informed them. "So he could fulfill the *mitzvos* which we can only perform in the Holy Land."

"If it was important to Moses, our teacher, than it certainly is important to us," Tevye agreed. "But how does one take these tithes?"

Because sundown was almost upon them, and a detailed explanation would take much too long, Shmuelik volunteered to hurry to the kitchen to prepare the food as required. Dressed in his Sabbath finery, he ran off across the kibbutz grounds in search of the dining hall. Kibbutzniks pointed the way, their eyes wide with wonder as they stared at the ultra-Orthodox Jew in his white stockings and knickers. Embarrassed, he tapped on the kitchen doorway, noticing that it lacked a *mezuzah*. The young women inside stopped their work to gape at the bearded, black-coated apparition with a fur *shtreimel* hat on his head.

"We are visiting Hodel," Shmuelik explained. "That is, her father and sisters have arrived, and there are certain matters of *kashrut* which need to be performed."

The girls stared at him brazenly, directly into his eyes, the way men look at each other. Shmuelik had never encountered females like this. Embarrassed, he looked away.

"Do whatever you have to," one said. "You are a guest."

Quickly, Shmuelik entered the kitchen and set aside small portions of the vegetables which the women had prepared. When he finished separating the *trumah* and *maaser* tithes as the Torah prescribed, he began washing leaves of lettuce in a bucket of water.

"We already rinsed them," one of the young women said.

"Hold a leaf up to the light," he answered.

The girl inspected one of leaves which had already been washed. The green stalks were speckled with insects.

"Yeech," the girl said in disgust.

"A Jew isn't supposed to eat crawling creatures," Shmuelik explained.

He asked for some vinegar. Soaking the leaves in the bitter

liquid was the best way to make them bug free. "After soaking the leaves in the vinegar, they have to be washed again so that the taste isn't spoiled," he taught.

"Oh, nonsense," said a girl with long braided hair. "Bugs are so small, what harm can they do?"

Once again, with the Sabbath only minutes away, Shmuelik didn't have time to answer the question. "Did you bake any loaves of bread?" he asked.

"Certainly we did," the girl named Sonia answered. "What do you take us for?"

Shmuelik broke off some pieces from the bread which the women had baked and said a blessing over the special *challah* portion. As it turned out, kosher meat wasn't a problem at all. The evening's main course was fish. Meat was a luxury which the kibbutz could not afford even on the Sabbath.

"Tevye arrived in the dining hall clutching a small bag in his hands. Lovingly, he withdrew two silver candlesticks and a white Sabbath tablecloth which his Golda had sewn. They were Tevye's most cherished possessions. He had brought them from Anatevka just for a moment like this, though in his wildest dreams, he never thought he would be setting up the candles for his Hodel to light in the Land of Israel.

"Thank you God," he said. "Thank you for bringing me to Hodel, and for giving us the blessed Sabbath day."

More than the Jews had kept the Sabbath, the Sabbath had kept the Jews. Like a beacon in the night, the Sabbath came to remind a man that God, not the Czar, was the Ruler of the world. A Jew rested on the Sabbath, not because he was tired from the labors of the week, but because God had commanded him to make it a holy day. It was a day when every Jew, even the most downtrodden and humble, could feel like a Rothschild.

Spreading the tablecloth, Tevye recalled the Sabbath feasts which his Golda had prepared. Her *challahs* were baked with so much love, they seemed to drip with honey. And her Sabbath soup was so rich, a guest at their table would have thought that Tevye was really a millionaire! Even if it meant starting out the coming week without a ruble in the house, Tevye didn't care – to honor the Sabbath, he would bring home the finest piece of meat he could find. And to top everything off, his Golda's freshly baked cakes were more delicious than the desserts in the fanciest Boiberik hotels. The feast she prepared was her way of saying she loved him. It did not matter that come Sunday, she would curse him for being a hopeless bumbler and *shlemeil* - on *Shabbos*, he was her king.

Hodel appeared in the doorway clutching a set of candlesticks of her own. Her father remembered them. They too had been a gift from Golda. When Hodel had set off to join Perchik in exile after his arrest for subversive activities, her mother had handed her the candlesticks with the admonition to always remember the Sabbath. Though Hodel had chosen a path far different from the life of her parents, she always lit the Sabbath candles and preserved their message in her heart. Even though her husband, Perchik, was not religious in the sense of observing the rituals of Jewish law, he was an earnestly principled man with a love for all of humanity, and a dream of universal brotherhood and peace. For Hodel, that was the essence of religious belief. Though her husband disapproved of "meaningless customs," Hodel continued to light the Sabbath candles out of respect for her parents and the tradition they cherished.

She set down her candlesticks on the familiar white tablecloth next to the candlesticks she remembered from Anatevka.

"You brought them with you," she said.

"Certainly," Tevye answered.

"Do you remember these candlesticks?" she asked.

"How could I forget? They were your grandmother's."

"I have lit the Sabbath candles ever since I left Anatevka," she said.

Closing her eyes in deep concentration, and gently waving her hands, Hodel beckoned the holiness of the Sabbath to descend over the kibbutz, just like her mother had done when reciting the Sabbath blessing. Tevye watched her light the candles which had brought blessing to Jewish homes for thousands of years. Then he placed his hands on her head and pronounced the traditional paternal prayer, "May the Lord make you like Sarah, Rebecca, Rachel, and Leah.... may the Lord bless you and grant you peace."

Hodel felt the warmth of her father's love radiating out of his fingers as he sang the words of the blessing. A sob welled up within her, reminding her how much she had missed his fatherly caring and his monumental faith. There was an aroma of history to her father, like the smell of dusty old books. True, the books which her father valued were different from the books her husband loved, but she felt an inner bond with her father which nothing could weaken, like her love for God Himself. She wanted to tell her father that the chasm wasn't as deep as he thought. She wanted to tell him that she still believed in the things he had taught her. But as he closed his eyes in a reverent Sabbath melody, she couldn't find the words to express the emotions she felt in her heart.

In retrospect, looking back at her marriage, she understood it was the exciting novelty of Perchik's personality which had swept her heart away, and not his revolutionary speeches. Because she loved him, she followed after him like a dutiful wife. What he thought, she thought. What he believed, she believed. The Torah that she had inherited from her father and mother, she had hidden away in her heart.

Just as the candle-lighting ceremony was finished, Shmuelik appeared and told Tevye that everything was ready in the kitchen. There was no synagogue on the non-religious kibbutz, so the newcomers prayed in the spacious dining hall before the kibbutzniks arrived for the meal. As Herzl gazed down upon them from a picture framed on the wall, Tevye and his friends chanted out the time-honored tunes which accompanied the arrival of the seventh day of the week. Tevye was particularly joyous this Sabbath Eve in the Holy Land. With a proud, soaring spirit, he sang the *"Adon Olam"* at the end of their prayers. Soon, every bench in the dining hall was filled with hungry settlers. Everyone in the kibbutz ate together, in accord with their goal of building a classless society, free from the evils of private ownership and capitalist gain. Surprisingly, the kibbutzniks came formally dressed for the meal, the men in high-collared shirts and ties, the women in floor-length dresses with ribbons tied in bows at the neck. In his deepest baritone, Tevye held up his cherished goblet and chanted the traditional *Kiddush*. Out of respect, many of the men covered their heads with their caps or their hands as Tevye sang out the blessing. One striking figure with a great white beard and balding countenance turned his chair to the side as if in disdain for the ceremony. Tevye remembered the words of Rabbi Kook that with time these Zionists would return in joy to the Torah after their secular enterprises and idealistic experiments failed to provide food for their souls.

After finishing a bottle of Rothschild wine, Tevye felt so spirited, he imagined seeing a group of Sabbath angels enter the dining hall to join them for the repast. In keeping with the local custom, the minstrel, Naftali, stood up and led the kibbutzniks in a romantic Zionist song, which exalted the work on the Land.

> "Here I built a house
> In *Eretz Yisrael*.
> Here I planted trees
> In *Eretz Yisrael*.
> Here I built a road
> In *Eretz Yisrael*.
> Here I sang a song
> In *Eretz Yisrael*."

Then, with eyes shining brightly with love, the women sang in a chorus. Their mellifluous voices, together with the Torah prohibition of hearing a woman sing, caused Shmuelik to blush and turn to sit facing the wall.

> "*Eretz Yisrael*, my land
> *Eretz Yisrael*, my love
> *Eretz Yisrael*, my dream
> *Eretz Yisrael*, my world
> Forever."

Before the women could continue their singing, Hillel stood up and sang a haunting solo which received an appreciative applause, and not a knife or fork moved in the hall when little Moishe stood up to accompany him in a stirring Sabbath duet. When the kibbutzniks called for an encore, Hillel began singing a spirited Hasidic melody. He grabbed Tevye by the hand and dragged him up from his bench. Soon they were dancing with Goliath in the middle of the hall. Not to be upstaged, Ben Zion grabbed the hand of the pretty young girl whom Shmuelik had met in the kitchen. With his usual flair, he started to swing her around. Swirling the girl past Bat Sheva's table, Ben Zion winked, and the milkman's high-strung daughter nearly fell off of her bench in a faint once again. Then with Perchik's encouragement, the kibbutzniks got up from their tables to dance a spirited *hora*. This was too much for Shmuelik. The sight of the young men and women holding hands and dancing soured the food in his stomach. He stood up and hurried out of the hall, as if someone had set it on fire. Tevye too was distraught. If a man and wife wanted to dance in the privacy of their own home that was one thing, but mixed dancing in public was strictly forbidden!

"*Oy*, the Jew who does not listen to his Rabbi," he thought, remembering the scene at the Anatevka crossroads and the Rabbi's stern warning against linking up with those who had defiantly thrown off the yoke of the Torah. In the Holy Land, this brazen behavior could only be a portent of evil, leading to even worse breaches. When the *hora* continued, he gathered his family and led them outside. Besides the dancing, Bat Sheva's dizzy spells had Tevye worried. He kept thinking about the plague in Tiberias, God forbid. But when the girl recovered immediately in the fresh air outside of the dining room, and a reddish glow returned to her cheeks, Tevye guessed the real cause of her distress. He did not have a degree in psychology, but he was a father to seven daughters, and he recognized the pangs of young love.

"Forget the scoundrel," he told her. "He will give you nothing but heartache."

"It's none of your business," she said.

Tevye stiffened. "It is true that I am a milkman by trade, but I am also a father, and that makes my daughter my business."

"I am not a cow that I don't have a will of my own," Bat Sheva answered.

"In a woman, that can be a very dangerous thing."

"Don't preach to me, father."

"Very well, my princess. If I have learned anything in my life, it is that one doesn't argue with Tevye's daughters. However, advice is something that a father is required to give, as it says, `Do not turn aside from your father's advice.' Between a husband and a wife, there has to be trust. Trust in each other, and trust in God. In a marriage, that is the most basic foundation."

"Hodel and Perchik are happy," Bat Sheva retorted.

"True happiness is in doing God's will."

"That's what you believe. Hodel and Perchik believe something else."

"It isn't only what I believe. It is what my father believed, and what my father's father believed, and what his father believed for four-thousand years, ever since God first spoke to Abraham."

"Maybe they were all wrong."

"God forbid," Tevye said. He backed away from his daughter. "I see you only want to anger me, as if I were to blame for your wounded pride."

"Why should my pride be wounded?" the young girl responded. "I am just as pretty as the girl he danced with. If I had some nice, modern clothes like she has, I am sure I would be even prettier."

Tevye sighed. He had expected more from his daughter than the jealousies which her immature outburst revealed. Were pretty clothes and a pretty smile the most important things in life? Certainly, the girl had not learned this shallow *narrishkeit* from her mother, may her soul rest in peace, and certainly not from him. As the Sabbath song taught, "Charm is deceiving, and beauty is vain; only a God-fearing woman is to be praised." How had such dangerous foreign notions found their way into her head?

While Tevye was still pondering this question, the answer suddenly appeared. Perchik, the university student whom Tevye had brought into his home to tutor his daughters, came running up to them in great haste. It was the stories he had read them, the literature of the "enlightened" free thinkers, which had poisoned their minds. Bat Sheva, the youngest and most vulnerable of his daughters, had not had the defenses to guard herself against such head-spinning tales. And Tevye himself was to blame.

"Tevye, come quickly!" Perchik said out of breath. "Tzeitl is ill."

A feeling of hollowness gripped Tevye's soul.

"Please, God," he prayed, hurrying after Perchik. "Please save my daughter."

Hodel was holding Tzeitl in her arms. At the start of the Sabbath, Tzeitl had felt too weak to leave the house. After lighting the candles in the dining room, Hodel had returned to sit with her. As if compelled by a deep inner need, Tzeitl had spoken on and on about Motel's tragic illness, about the shock of Shprintza's drowning, about Hodel's leaving home to follow after Perchik, about the elopement of Hava and Hevedke, and about their mother's subsequent death. Then the down-to-earth Tzeitl, in a strange flight of fancy, confided that in her fevers, their mother had appeared to her from Heaven, urging her to warn Hodel to alter her ways and return to a life filled with Torah.

Tzeitl had spoken with an urgency which seemed to have weakened her. Hodel tried to take her sister's mind off of the past by talking about her pregnancy and asking her sister's advice on how to take care of the baby. But before Tzeitl could answer, a sweat had broken out on her forehead, and she was engulfed by a burning fever. By the time Tevye arrived, she was struggling for breath.

"Don't worry, *Tata*," she said. "Mama and Motel are waiting for me."

"Nonsense," Tevye answered. "You just need to rest from the journey."

Tzeitl smiled. "A long rest," she said. Then she told her father to kiss Moishe and Hannie for her. "Take them to Ruchel and Nachman so they will grow up believing in God."

That was Tzeitl's last wish. She passed away in Hodel's arms. This was the reason she had fought death away for such a long time on the journey. Before she left this world for the next, Tzeitl wanted to accomplish one final mission – to bring a message of faith to her sister. Her eyes closed in relief, with a smile on her lips, content that she had succeeded. With a last peaceful breath, Tzeitl's soul returned to its Maker.

"Blessed be the true Judge," Tevye said.

Gently, he helped Hodel lay Tzeitl down on the bed.

"She said that Mama and Motel appeared to her in her dreams," Hodel told him.

"I believe her," Tevye answered. "I have seen your mother myself, several times. May they be reunited up in Heaven."

Tevye led Hodel out of the room. Perchik, Bat Sheva, and Hava were all standing in the doorway.

"What will become of the children," Bat Sheva asked.

"For the present, they'll stay with me," Tevye said. "Later, I will bring them to Ruchel. That was Tzeitl's dying request."

"They can stay here with us on the kibbutz," Perchik offered.

"We'll see," Tevye answered without further elaboration. This wasn't the time to enter into an ideological debate about the education of children.

Tevye said he was going to look for Shmuelik. It was forbidden to bury a corpse on the Sabbath, and he wanted to make sure of the laws. Though a painful remorse filled his whole being, Tevye was determined not show his emotions. The Almighty had loaned him a jewel of a daughter for thirty blessed years, and now He was taking her back.

"The Lord giveth, and the Lord taketh away. Blessed be the Name of the Lord."

Chapter Fourteen

THE DYBBUK

Strangely, the person who seemed most affected by Tzeitl's death was Goliath. Upon hearing the news, he surrounded himself with an impenetrable wall. He even found it hard to play with the children. Shmuelik said the body had to remain wrapped in a sheet on the floor of Hodel's house until the Sabbath was over. During the Sabbath, mourning was forbidden, and Tevye did his best to remain strong. But come *Motzei Shabbos*, when the day ended, the children's sobs at the funeral made everyone feel the very great weight of the loss. Little Moishe and Hannie clung to their grandfather as if he were father and mother in one. For their sake, Tevye kept his face locked in an optimistic expression. When the *Mashiach* came, he told them, their mother would return. With God's help, they wouldn't have long to wait. If they prayed hard enough, the *Mashiach* could come any day. All things considered, he reasoned, the situation of the dead was a lot better than that of the living. That is, if there were cows which had to be milked, and wagons which broke down in the World to Come, Tevye had never heard about it.

Tevye's hope-filled posture paid off. After a few days, with the resilience of children, Moishe and Hannie ventured away from Tevye's shadow to play outside with the youngsters of the kibbutz. Tevye and his daughters sat out the seven-day mourning period in Hodel and Perchik's tiny, mud hut of a home. Goliath joined them as if he were a part of the family. He kept to a corner, trying to be as unobtrusive as possible, but owing to his size, he filled up a substantial part of the room. He was gladdened when the children mustered enough courage to venture outside on their own. It gave him an excuse to sit outside the house, where he could keep an eye on their activities. That way, he could keep out of the way, yet still be a part of the mourning.

Because her family had to eat in her home while they were sitting *shiva*, Hodel had to be more stringent in the kitchen. While she never mixed milk products and meat, she had become less mindful of some of the other kosher laws. Since she and Perchik normally ate in the dining hall with the other members of the kibbutz, she had to make use of the communal kitchen in preparing the meals for her family. Shmuelik boiled the utensils which needed to be purified, and he *kashered* the pans in a blazing fire. Perchik called the procedure a primitive voodoo, but he controlled his disapproval as long as Tevye was in the house. However, he warned that when the week of mourning concluded, the foolishness would stop.

"It may seem like foolishness to you," Hodel answered. "But to me it is important."

"Has your father been brainwashing you again?"

"Don't you dare to speak out against my father," she said in a temper.

Perchik stared at his gentle wife in surprise. She stood glaring at him in defiance, as if she were seeking a fight. Since Tzeitl's death, something in Hodel had changed. As strange as it sounded, she felt that Tzeitl's spirit had entered her body. Everyone knew that stories of dybbuks were true. Souls of the dead could enter a person on earth until they found rest. In Anatevka, the Rabbi had exorcised more than a few. After all, Hodel reasoned, God had not brought Tzeitl all of the way to Israel to die in her arms for no reason at all. It was enough that Tzeitl wanted her children to grow up with Ruchel and the young rabbi, Nachman, to make Hodel realize the shortcomings of her present lifestyle. She had experienced a sense of rejection in her sister's last wish, a condemnation of the path she had chosen, but in her heart, she knew that her sister's decision was sound. After all, what sort of Jewish tradition could Hodel pass on to the children if the basics of Torah observance, like *kashrus*, *Shabbos*, and prayer were not to be found in her house? Soon, she realized, she would be a mother herself, and she wanted to bequeath to the next generation the things which had been important to her. Not only the aroma of freshly baked *challahs*, but the reverence for religion which had filled her house in Anatevka with a blessing from one Sabbath to the next. After all, it was the faithfulness to tradition which made a people last. Who said that modern ideas were necessarily better than the beliefs of the past?

"You are my wife, and you will do what I say," Perchik commanded when Hodel refused to give in.

"Who says that a wife has to do whatever her husband demands?" Hodel retorted. "That's just some foolish old-fashioned nonsense."

Perchik understood the barb in her message. After all, he could not preach the equality of all people, and treat his wife like a slave in the privacy of their home.

"Anyway," Hodel continued. "I am not just your wife. Soon I will be a mother, and I have an obligation to my children. Being with my family again has made me realize that I have a responsibility to educate them as Jews."

"I will decide what we will teach our children," Perchik answered.

"Is that so?"

"Yes, that is so."

Hodel heard her husband's answers, and wondered why he sounded so differently now. She realized that this was the way he always spoke, authoritatively, dogmatically, egotistically, imposing his worldview on their marriage. It had been that way from the start, when as a young sheltered girl, she had been swept away with his certainty and knowledge, as if he possessed all of the truths of existence. On their long walks through the woods of Anatevka, he had transported her out of the tiny village to new and breathtaking worlds. Like a child, she had gone along for the ride, trusting in his confidence and wisdom. But now she was no longer a child. She was about to have a baby of her own, and Tzeitl's death had reminded her that life did not last forever.

"Do you know why Tzeitl wanted her children raised by

Ruchel and Nachman, and not by us?" she asked. "Because she wanted them to grow up in a good kosher home."

"That's fine with me," Perchik answered.

"Well it isn't with me. I'm ashamed."

"Hodel stop it. Don't you see what has happened? Your father has been here a week, and already we are fighting. When was the last time we had a quarrel before that? I can't even remember."

"That was because I always listened to you. I always accepted your way. But I have a mind of my own."

Perchik nodded, remembering how strong-willed his Hodel had been with her parents when they had opposed their marriage.

"Isn't that one of your sacred principles?" she asked. "Freedom of thought and expression? The liberation of the workers from the oppressive ruling class?"

"Are you implying that you are being oppressed in this house?"

Hodel didn't answer. For a moment, they faced one another in silence.

"Shouldn't women have rights? Aren't we allowed freedom too?"

"You are my wife," he said, flustered.

"Now you sound like my father," she said. "Before anything else I am a person. Soon, with God's help, I will be a mother. And along with everything else, I am a Jew."

"All right," he said, not wishing to continue the argument until he had formulated a clear line of reasoning and proofs. "You set up the kitchen the way that you want."

"Back to the kitchen, is that it? Now you really sound like my father. What about all of your modern ideas? Do they apply to everyone in the world except for your wife?"

"What more do you want?" he asked.

"A real Jewish *Shabbos*."

"You know I can't agree. I came to Israel to work the land, not to sleep and eat *chulent*."

"The Sabbath is only one day a week."

"You do what you believe is right, and I will do what is important to me."

"What kind of marriage is that?" Hodel asked.

"I don't know," he answered. "All I know is that until today we had no problems, and now that your father has come, it is as if we were back in Anatevka."

Angrily, he strode out of the house. The door slammed shut. Hodel shuddered. Their fight had exhausted her. Standing up to her husband was no easy matter. It was true, their life together had been a united endeavor until her family arrived. What had happened? What change had taken place? Standing alone in the room, Hodel could only pray, as her father always did, that everything would work out for the best.

Chapter Fifteen

GUARDIAN OF ISRAEL

As a sign of his grief over Tzeitl, Tevye tore his shirt and sat on a low stool in Hodel's house in the traditional custom of mourners. He maintained a stalwart expression to disguise the hole he felt in his heart. His strength came from Golda. She appeared to him in a dream and told him not to worry.

"Don't be so sad, my husband. Our Tzeitl is fine. She is back with her Motel, and she visits me all the time."

When Bat Sheva blamed God for being unfair, Tevye reprimanded her for her bitterness. Who was man to complain, he asked her? God was in Heaven, and they were on earth. A mortal had to accept the Almighty's decrees in humility and believe that all of His doings were just.

The traditional period of *shiva* allowed a mourner to express his grief in the comforting presence of family and friends. All during the week, the pioneers of the kibbutz arrived at Hodel's house to share their condolences with the family. Though none of the members of the kibbutz were religious, the men agreed to make up a prayer *minyan* so that Tevye could say the mourner's *Kaddish*. Since they did not have prayerbooks for everyone, Shmuelik wrote out handwritten copies of the prayers. He also convinced the community that they should all have *mezuzahs* on their houses. It was decided that Ben Zion's friend, Peter, would accompany Shmuelik to Tiberias, where he would buy kosher parchment. The quarantine in the city had ended, and Shmuelik was happy to find a thriving religious community in the ancient lakeside enclave. Throughout the rest of the week, the young scholar sat hunched over a table, quill in hand, carefully forming the letters of the *Shema Yisrael* prayer on the small *clafs* of parchment which he rolled up into the wooden *mezuzah* cases that Goliath whittled while watching the children. Though the kibbutzniks had made a religion of denying religion, they all willingly nailed the *mezuzahs* to their doorways as an expression of their Jewishness, in the same way that they all circumcised and bar-mitzvahed their sons.

Bolstered by his faith that man's brief existence in this world was but a doorway to an eternal World to Come, and that Tzeitl was truly happy in Heaven, Tevye was able to enjoy the long and often heated discussions which filled Hodel's house throughout the week. After all, as much as a Jew liked a good sour pickle, he savored a juicy debate. Most often, Perchik or Ben Zion represented the Zionist platform, while Tevye defended the sacred path of the Torah. The striking, white-bearded Gordon also had plenty to say. The philosopher and writer was the oldest member of the kibbutz, and the younger people, including Perchik and Ben Zion, showed him a great deal of respect. In a play on the life of Moses, Gordon would have been chosen to play the lead role. His high, balding forehead glowed red from his work in the sun, his eyes shone with intelligence, and his long, untrimmed beard gave him a prophet's charisma. But, without a *yarmulkah* to cover his head, he looked more like a Jewish Tolstoy than the lawgiver of the Jews.

Surprisingly, the kibbutz women were as outspoken in their opinions as the men. In Tevye's eyes, this breach of modesty was shocking. Ever since the time of Abraham and Sarah, the place of a Jewish woman was in the inner sanctums of the home. In the home itself, a woman could express her opinions from morning to night, but in public, when strange men were present, speaking out like a man was strictly taboo. The young, long-braided girl, Sonia, whom Ben Zion had danced with, was particularly loose with her tongue. Her free-thinking outbursts caused Shmuelik to redden with embarrassment and seek pretenses to withdraw from the room. The girl's *chutzpah* particularly annoyed Bat Sheva. Tevye's daughter would argue with her fiercely, even when she agreed with the things that Sonia was saying. Ben Zion greatly enjoyed their jousts, knowing they were meant to win his attention. Recalling

Tevye's warning in the snow-covered forest on the road to Odessa, the Zionist kept a respectable distance away from the milkman's daughter, but now and again, he cast her passionate glances which made her believe he still cared.

For Perchik, the gatherings in his house were opportunities to expound his philosophies. Not that Tevye wanted to hear, but having to sit out the seven days of *shiva* in his son-in-law's domain, he was Perchik's captive. Perchik felt equally trapped by his father-in-law's presence, and, like the collegian fencer he was, he used the discussions to score as many barbs as he could in Tevye's ancient armor.

Since his arrival in Shoshana, Tevye had decided to bury the wounds of the past. And certainly now, in the wake of Tzeitl's death, family quarrels were forbidden. Furthermore, Tevye was a guest in Perchik's house. And finally, though Tevye and Perchik were as far apart as the sun and the moon, they had one thing in common. Hodel.

"*Nu*, Reb Tevye," Perchik inquired as he returned home from work toward the end of a discussion between Tevye and group of visiting kibbutzniks. "Becoming a Zionist?"

"Isn't God Himself a Zionist?" Tevye answered.

"I suppose that He is, but for all of your prayers about returning to Zion, I don't see many devout religious Jews flocking to join us."

Tevye nodded his head. It was an argument for which he had no rebuttal. Now that he had seen the stark beauty of *Eretz Yisrael*, and felt its holiness saturate all of his being, Tevye could only wonder himself why all of his exiled brothers delayed coming home. Already, like a man crazily in love with a woman, he couldn't think of being anywhere else.

"On behalf of the kibbutz, I would like to extend a permanent welcome," Ben Zion magnanimously said. "We want you to know that you have a place with us here in Shoshana if you would like to join our community."

Perchik flashed his loud-mouthed compatriot an unenthusiastic expression. Having Hodel's father in Shoshana would finish his marriage completely.

"That's right," he said cynically. "Shave off your beard, throw away your *tzitzit*, and become a part of the Palestine of today."

"You don't have to shave off your beard," Gordon said. "But your fringes and skullcap are relics of the past. Today, a Jew has to make himself over completely. Jewish self-fulfillment will only come through physical labor and contact with the soil. The kibbutznik, not the rabbi, will be the future image of a Jew."

Tevye grumbled a response. He had grown weary of the orations on the Jew of the future and the ideal society which the new pioneers were building in Palestine. The name Palestine had been coined by the Romans two thousand years before. Conquering the country, the Romans renamed the *Eretz Yisrael* of the Bible after the Philistines who had dwelt in the land. Similarly, to erase all signs of the land's Jewish history, they renamed the city of Jerusalem, *Aelia Capitolina*, after the Roman emperor. A parade of conquerors followed, spoiling the land and drenching its borders in blood. They ruled over the country from afar, making its Jewish citizens pay tribute to foreign treasuries. Though Jerusalem was forced to house idols and wear the garb of an adulterous culture, the Jews remained true to their Heavenly city. No other nation made her its capitol. Coliseums, churches, and mosques were built over the remnants of the Jewish Temple, but through all the waves of oppression, Jews stubbornly clung to the one remaining Wall. Throughout the centuries, Jews continued to dwell on their sacred soil, though the majority of the nation had been exiled and scattered to the four corners of the globe. Conquerors raised their banners over the ramparts of the city, blasted their trumpets for a passing fortnight or two, then disappeared from the stage of world history. The mighty kingdoms of Babylon, Persia, Greece, and Rome all turned to rubble and ruin. Only the Jews lived on, maintaining an unbroken presence in the Land, in defiance of the nations who sought to sever the Jewish people's bond to their eternally cherished home.

While Ben Zion was an adamant champion of the Jews'

exclusive right to their homeland, Perchik was less extreme in his views. A universalist by nature, he believed that other people could live in the Land as well. He agreed that the rule of the Turks had to cease one day, but the Arabs, for instance, could stay. They were a small and scattered community, comprised of Bedouin tribes who had never ruled over the country, and who had no nationalistic ambitions. They called themselves "Southern Syrians." To Perchik's way of thinking, they added a Mediterranean charm to the region. In his literary moods, he spoke of them as "sons of the desert."

From both a military and Zionist point of view, Ben Zion rejected Perchik's conception completely. If the Jewish people were to rebuild their nation in Israel, Jewish sovereignty, and Jewish sovereignty alone, would have to be imposed throughout all off its borders. If a foreigner wanted to live in Israel, he would first have to sign a document recognizing that *Eretz Yisrael* was the Land of the Jews.

"Our friend, Don Quixote, proposes to do battle with all of our neighbors," Perchik quipped.

"When all of the Jews in the world return to populate our borders, we will have the strength to overcome all of our enemies," Ben Zion declared.

"Why fight when we can live side-by-side with our cousins in peace?" Perchik rebutted.

"Your cousins don't want peace. They want the whole land. To their way of thinking, it's theirs."

"All the people who have been living here have a justified claim. Whatever parcels of land we can buy and reclaim, we shall. As for the rest, agreements can be made, respecting each other's rights."

"The Turks and the Arabs are scoundrels from birth," Ben Zion insisted. "Their agreements are not worth the paper on which they are written."

"That remains to be seen," Perchik argued. "Besides, who made you such an expert on this part of the world?"

"I've dealt with them enough. Their whole culture is founded on falsehood and theft."

"That is a racist remark," Perchik exclaimed.

It was difficult for Tevye to remain silent in such a fervent debate. He made a noise in his throat, as if to attract their attention.

"By all means," Ben Zion said. "Let's hear from our learned friend, Tevye."

"A learned man, I am not," Tevye responded. "But it is written in the Torah that the children of Ishmael are highwaymen and scoundrels who live by the sword."

"There, you have it – straight from the Bible," Ben Zion said, as if to prove his point.

"Since when do you believe in the Bible?" Perchik asked.

"The question seems to be a straightforward matter of law," Tevye continued, remembering the parable of the rabbi at Ruchel's wedding. "If a man owns a house and thieves come and force him to move, and then other thieves come along and chase out the first robbers, and then more robbers follow, one after the other, each one taking the house from the next – when the original owner returns, it is still his house, is it not? The others simply stole it from him, one after the other, but they cannot legally claim it is theirs."

Ben Zion nodded. In this instance the laws of the Torah were in accord with his way of thinking.

"The Arabs believe in squatter's rights," Perchik said.

"The Bible is our deed to this Land," Tevye argued. "It is recorded there time and again that God gave this Land to the Jews."

"That's what you say," the girl, Sonia, injected.

Tevye looked over at her in surprise. Quarrels were known to occur in the best of families, but for a strange girl to publicly challenge the words of a man twice her age, that was unheard of.

"It is not what I say, but what the Bible teaches," Tevye answered patiently.

"Who says that the Bible is right?" the girl challenged. "If you ask me, it is all a big fairytale."

Tevye felt it improper to enter into a religious debate with the bad-mannered creature, but her impudence had to be put in its place.

"No doubt your father, and his father before him, and his father before him, and all of your ancestors for over four-thousand years were fools until you came along with your superior wisdom," Tevye said mockingly.

The girl blushed. Ben Zion laughed.

"I suppose you believe that Jonah was eaten by a whale!" the girl quipped.

"Of course," Tevye answered.

"And that Bilaam's ass opened his mouth and talked?"

"Yes," Tevye said. "Is that so surprising? You yourself are a living example that a dumb, brainless creature can speak."

Ben Zion slapped his hands on his knees and roared with laughter. Flustered, the girl stood up and glared at him.

"You'll be sorry," she warned.

That only made Ben Zion laugh even more. Red in the face, the girl hurried out of the house.

"Good for you, Reb Tevye," Ben Zion said.

Bat Sheva felt like giving her father a kiss. She sat as sweetly and modestly as possible, a well-behaved contrast to the outspoken girl.

"I agree with Sonia," Perchik said. "You can't use the Bible as a deed."

"Why can't you?" Ben Zion asked. "The book is the chronicle of our history. With or without God, you can't claim that the Jews didn't live here before the Arabs and Turks."

"The heathens chased us out of the country, did they not?" Hillel remarked. "We should do the same thing to them."

"We are supposed to be more enlightened than the other nations," Perchik answered. "Because we were uprooted is no reason for us to uproot others."

"Nobody is being uprooted," Ben Zion protested. "All of the

land which the Jews are reclaiming in Palestine is being purchased for large sums of money. There is no uprooting in that."

The argument wasn't mere philosophical speculation alone. The day after Tevye's family had concluded the week of mourning, the clamorous ringing of the dining-hall bell brought all of the workers hurrying back from the fields. Ben Zion's friend, Peter, and another kibbutznik named Ari had taken a wagon to one of the settlement's wells to fill barrels with water. While they were working, six Arabs on horseback appeared and ordered the Jews to vacate the site. The well, they claimed, was theirs. Peter had protested. He himself had dug out the well. But the Arabs still insisted that the well belonged to them. The entire region, they claimed, was a part of their pasture land. Their tribe had lived in the area for decades, they said, wandering from place to place, and all of the land and the underground springs were their ancestral inheritance.

When Peter refused to flee in face of their threats, an Arab had fired a rifle and wounded the kibbutznik in the shoulder. The shot, Ari said, seemed to have startled the Arabs as much as the Jews. As Peter lay bleeding on the ground, the Arabs galloped off in a panic.

Everyone in the kibbutz gathered outside of the dining hall. While Ari was recounting the story, comrades lifted Peter out of the wagon and carried him into a house. His shirt was stained crimson, and he was unconscious from the blood he had lost. Fortunately, the bullet had passed through his shoulder without causing more damage. By evening, he was back on his feet, but the incident caused outrage throughout the kibbutz, and the Jewish settlers were calling for a speedy reprisal.

Perchik, the pacifist, made a plea for restraint and negotiation, but Ben Zion took the lead in rounding up a troop to strike back at once.

"You know how to ride a horse," he said to Tevye. "You come with us."

A mount was brought over to Tevye and reins were placed in his hand. True, Tevye knew how to ride a horse, but he couldn't remember the last time he had sat in a saddle. When he and his horse had been young, he had enjoyed a good gallop, but once he was married and had to make a living to take care of his family, he had exchanged his saddle for a wagon. After thousands of journeys between Anatevka and Yehupetz, the horse had forgotten how to gallop completely. Occasionally, in a snowstorm, or when the horse hurt its leg and was too weak to haul the wagon itself, Tevye would pull the horse and the wagon together. As the Good Book said, "There is a time for everything under the Heavens – a time to be a man, and a time to be a horse."

Ben Zion quickly ran to a hut and emerged with a few extra rifles. He handed one to the milkman.

"What is this for?" Tevye asked.

"To shoot with," Ben Zion answered.

"I don't know how. In Anatevka, where I come from, the Czar did not make it a habit to hand out rifles to Jews."

"You are no longer in Anatevka, Reb Tevye," Ben Zion responded. "Don't worry. I'll teach you. Rifles are really quite simple contraptions."

"But I am going to be a grandfather soon."

"Wasn't Moses ninety years old when he went to war against Midian?" the Zionist asked.

"I suppose that he was," Tevye answered.

"And Joshua was seventy when he led the Jews into battle against the seven Canaanite nations."

"Joshua wasn't a broken-down milkman like me."

"Isn't it written, `In a place where there are no men, be a man?'"

When did you become such a Biblical scholar?" Tevye asked.

"I studied in *heder*, remember?"

"Why did you stop?"

"The *rebbe* would tweak my ear when I wasn't paying attention."

"Is a pinch in the ear a reason to abandon the Torah? Our forefathers had more mettle than that."

"I'll show you what mettle we have," Ben Zion answered. He

called to his friends to mount up. Then he swung a bullet belt over Tevye's shoulder, and with a smile, helped him into his saddle. Bat Sheva and Hava watched from the doorway of Hodel's house as their father rode off with the rifled *shomrim*.

"I don't believe it," Hava said. "It's *Tata*!"

After a few nervous moments, Tevye brought his steed to a gallop alongside the others. He remembered, of course, how to ride, but the jolts to his spine were painfully new. With each bounce in the air, he felt another disc slide out of place. Nevertheless, Tevye found himself enjoying the ride. Blood rushed through his veins. The wind swirled around him. The hooves of the horses thundered over the earth. If Ben Zion had yelled out a war cry, Tevye would have yelled out too. In the adventure, he forgot about his mourning for Tzeitl. Suddenly, for the first time in ages, he felt like a young man with his whole life just beginning anew.

Like soldiers of fortune, the Jews rode along hillsides and streaked across valleys. The horses were just beginning to work up a sweat when they reached the well at the southern border of the kibbutz. The area around it was completely deserted. Sitting tall in his saddle, Ben Zion scanned all of the hillsides.

"It may be an ambush," he said.

Everyone gazed over the mountainous terrain. Rifles were pointed in every direction. Tevye mimicked the others, not knowing if his rifle was loaded. Ben Zion slid gracefully down from his horse and told Tevye to follow. With far less elegance, Tevye let his boots plunge back down to the earth.

"You load a rifle like this," Ben Zion said, taking Tevye's rifle and sliding a bullet into its chamber. "To shoot, you cock the hammer, aim with one eye, and fire."

Ben Zion pulled the trigger. The rifle roared. The bullet splintered the trunk of a tree a short distance away. "You try," he said, handing the rifle to Tevye.

Tevye took the rifle, slid a bullet into the chamber, cocked the hammer, aimed, and squeezed the trigger. His shoulder jerked with the explosion. The crackle of the rifle echoed in his ears like the bark of an angry dog. This time, the tree stood unscathed.

"You shut both of your eyes," Ben Zion said. "Try again."

Once again, Tevye took aim. Slowly he squeezed the trigger. This time, he was braced for the recoil. To his surprise, a chunk of bark flew off of the tree.

"*Mazal tov!*" Ben Zion said. "You stay here and guard the well, while we scout the area."

"Alone?" Tevye asked.

"You have the rifle. If the Arabs come back, fire a shot in the air to alert us. We will be within earshot."

"What if they shoot at me?" Tevye asked.

"Shoot back. Most Arabs are cowards. Usually, at the sound of gunfire, they flee."

Tevye did not feel reassured. With his *mazal,* if there were only one brave Arab in the world, he would be the one who returned to the well.

Ben Zion swung up to his saddle. *"Yalla!"* he called. He spurred his horse, and everyone rode off, leaving Tevye alone. Clutching his rifle, the milkman scanned the surrounding hills.

"Vayzmeer," he mumbled aloud. The Yiddish expression of worry sounded strangely foreign in the Biblical hills of the Galilee. Tevye realized that to become a real part of the Land, he would have to learn everyday conversation in Hebrew. Once again, Tevye made sure the rifle was loaded. His eyes roamed over the countryside for signs of the enemy.

"I raise my eyes unto the hills," he said, reciting the comforting Psalm. *"From where shall my help come? My help cometh from the Lord Who made heaven and earth. The Guardian of Israel will neither slumber nor sleep."*

The "Guardian of Israel," Tevye thought. *Shomer Yisrael.* That's where the expression *shomer* came from. Like the Almighty Himself, Tevye had become a *shomer,* a guardian of the Jewish people. No doubt, the Master of the World, the *Riboyno Shel Olam,* could aim His bullets with far greater accuracy than the milkman from Anatevka, but with practice, Tevye felt he could learn. In the meantime, he kept his ears open, his eyes on the hills, and his finger tight on the trigger.

Chapter Sixteen

A VOTE IS TAKEN

Ben Zion's troop returned empty-handed to the well. They found Tevye hiding behind a tree, sunburned and poised to shoot. Back at Shoshana, a community meeting was once again summoned by clanging the dining-hall bell. Everyone in the kibbutz gathered to express an opinion. Perchik and Ben Zion sat at the head table, representatives of the two leading camps. Within minutes a fiery debate erupted over the best course of action to follow – whether to negotiate with the Arabs, or to declare outright war. Shouts in Russian and Hebrew were heard from all corners. Tevye did not understand every word, but he gathered that Perchik led the pacifists, while Ben Zion championed a more militant posture. As far as Tevye could tell, the settlers were divided in half. Even the women participated, shouting out opinions as vituperatively as the men. The milkman had never seen anything like it. In fact, all of his life, he had never attended at a gathering where men and women sat mixed together. Even at a wedding, the sexes were kept discreetly apart.

During the week-long conversations in Perchik's home, Tevye had learned enough history to grasp the roots of the problem. Rome's long conquest over *Eretz Yisrael* had been brought to an end by the Persians. Omayyad Moslems chased out the Persians, overcoming the last Roman strongholds. Then came the Crusades, as the Christians set out to conquer the Holy Land by slaughtering all of the Moslems and Jews in the country. Then Mongul hordes swept through the region, leaving behind a devastating trail of destruction. Cities were razed, landscapes burned, fields uprooted, and the population terrorized. Two-hundred years of savagery followed as warring Moslem tribes battled for control. They had names which Tevye could scarcely pronounce – Abbasids, Fatamids, Seljuks, and the barbarous Mamluks. Throughout the rampage of history, Jewish life in the Holy Land always continued, like a candle that never burns out. Finally, for the last four-hundred years, the Ottoman Turks had ruled over Palestine. Presently, the country was a hodge-podge of Ottoman districts, ruled over by Turkish *Muktars* who took orders from Constantinople and Damascus. The Bedouin and Arab tribes who roamed through the country never had ruled over Palestine. Some sheiks possessed legal deeds, but more often than not, they lived far away in other districts. Roaming Arab tribes ignored Turkish law and squatted on lands to which they had no legal right. Thus their claims of land ownership brought them into conflict with the new wave of Jewish settlers who were purchasing tracts of land. These transactions were officially recorded in the Ottoman Land Office in Constantinople, which people were now calling Istanbul. The tiny community of Shoshana was not the first Jewish settlement to find itself at odds with the largely unfounded claims of these nomadic Arab tribes. Further complicating the matter was the lackluster way which the Turks had made surveys and maps. Property boundaries were forever in dispute and detailed deeds were a rarity, if they could be located at all in the bureaucratic labyrinth of the disorganized Istanbul archives.

When the tall, stately figure of Gordon rose in the hall, the noisy, raucous debate momentarily quieted to give the respected visionary a chance to speak.

"Herzl proposed that the benefits of economic advancement would outweigh Arab nationalism," he said. "We have to let our hard work and economic endeavor convince the people of Palestine that our presence here is a boon to the area and not a threat."

Following his lead, another intellectual rose to his feet.

"Sokolov wrote that cultural rapprochement would bring a new Palestine civilization. We should invite our Arab neighbors to Shoshana for a social encounter."

A statesman for Ben Zion's camp rose in rebuttal.

"Arthur Ruppin asserted that a policy of transfer is the only solution. The Arabs need to be chased out of the Land."

A roar of approval from the militants sounded throughout the room. With a gavel, Perchik banged on the table.

"You all know how I feel," he said. "Marxists believe that peace and world unity can only be achieved through a cooperative society – through a pan-worker state without nationalist factions. As Herzl said, if we will it, this region can be a model for the world."

Ben Zion stood up beside him.

"While we all hope for an ideal future, when it comes to these Bedouin marauders, the only solution is war."

A woman stood up to express her opinion.

"The Arabs are not the problem," she shouted. "The Turks are. They are the ones who rule here. They have to be overthrown."

"Overthrown with what?" Perchik asked. "We barely have rifles for a half dozen men."

"Overthrown with the truth of our cause," Peter's friend, Ari, declared. "We must build a new Jewish state in Palestine."

Applause broke out in the hall.

"Enough speeches," another woman yelled. "What are we going to do about the disputed well?"

"The Arabs have no legal claim to the site," Ben Zion asserted.

"That may be true," Perchik responded. "But they believe it's their land."

"Land ownership is not based on illusions, but on a legal proof of sale. And we have a copy of the deed in our possession."

"Yes, yes, we all are aware of the legality of our settlement here," Perchik said. "But these Bedouins have their own customs and beliefs."

"Are you proposing we pick up and move?" Ben Zion asked.

"No, of course not. I propose that there is enough land and water for everyone. We should meet with them and reach an agreement."

Once again, there was loud applause in the dining hall.

After a two-hour discussion, a vote was taken. Even the women were allowed to raise hands. Shmuelik stared down at his shoes when all of the bare arms rose up in the air. When the counting of hands was concluded, the outcome was an absolute deadlock.

"I propose that we let the new arrivals take part in the vote," Ben Zion called out, certain that the religious Jews would share his view that the Land of Israel was the rightful homeland of the Jews.

Immediately, Sonia protested. They were visitors, she said, and not official members of the kibbutz. Renewed shouting erupted. A vote on Ben Zion's proposal was taken. Again, both sides were even. Perchik banged his gavel on the table. The meeting was declared adjourned. For the moment, no action would be initiated. Instead, they would wait to see how the matter developed. That seemed like a sensible solution to Tevye. As the Talmud taught, if a man doesn't know what course of action to take, he should just sit and wait.

Chapter Seventeen

THE MILKMAN'S DAUGHTER

Tevye decided to stay in Shoshana until the birth of Hodel's baby, which was only a month away. He forbade Bat Sheva to speak to Ben Zion, and asked Goliath to keep his eyes open to make sure there were no rendezvous. Tevye, by nature, had a trusting, good-natured soul, and in the past, it had led him to be too lax with his daughters. This time, he was determined to keep a tight rein on his youngest, lest her impetuousness lead her astray.

Hava went to work in the kitchen. For all of her openness to modern ideas, Hava felt ill at ease with the notion of women's rights. To her way of thinking, a man had his duties, and a woman had hers. The theory that a woman could do the work of a man seemed foolish to her. As far as she was concerned, it was better to work in the kitchen, feeding people, than to work in a stable, feeding horses and cows.

Everyone in the commune ate together in the dining hall, so there was always plenty of work to occupy Hava, and to keep her from thinking about Hevedke's new life in a faraway Jaffa yeshiva. The kibbutz diet consisted of sour cereals, vegetables, olives, goat's cheese, black bread, eggs, and sardines. Meat was a luxury which the treasury of the kibbutz could rarely afford. The unrefined olive oil they used for cooking was purchased from Arabs in goatskin bags which gave the oil a bitter taste. There were not enough knives and forks for everyone, and settlers had to sometimes eat their main course with spoons. Though many of life's staples were lacking, a spirit of thankfulness and singing accompanied the meals. Even Tevye was impressed. He had been in the luxurious homes of the rich people of Yehupetz and had never experienced such genuine happiness and joy. Inspired by their mission of working the land, the kibbutzniks were happy with the little they had. Hava tried to do what she could to improve their conditions, but when she put flowers and tablecloths on the tables for the Friday night meal, she was criticized for being bourgeoise.

For all of his devotion to Torah, Tevye was not a fanatic. Though the lifestyle in Shoshana irked him, he was able to restrain his chagrin over the secular character of the kibbutz. He remembered the words of the wise Rabbi Kook who said that the very act of settling the Land of Israel was a religious act in itself. Hadn't the Sages of the Midrash taught that living in the Land of Israel was equal to all of the commandments in the Torah? Perhaps it was his age, or because Hodel was his daughter, or because Tzeitl's death had left him too tired to fight – whatever the reason, Tevye accepted the lapses of *Yiddishkeit* as a situation which was not in his power to change.

Shmuelik's reaction was different. The fervent scholar was horrified by the kibbutzniks and by their disdain for Jewish tradition. While Tevye had traveled far from Anatevka with his wagonful of cheeses, rubbing elbows with the rich and meeting free-thinkers in Boiberik and St. Petersburg, the young Shmuelik had never left the sheltered confines of his *shtetl*. To him, the kibbutznikim were heretical *apikorsim* who were to be avoided as much as the plague. "Gentiles who speak Hebrew," he called them. Their desecration of the Sabbath, of the dietary laws, and the laws of family purity, were offenses that cried out to Heaven. That their heretical behavior should occur in the Holy Land was even more of an outrage in his eyes. When he learned that an animal pen under construction was intended for the breeding of pigs, that was the end. Though Shmuelik had come to love Tevye as a father, he found the situation unbearable. After ten days, he decided to set off for Zichron Yaacov, where the central office of the Jewish Colony Association was located. Just as Jacob's son, Yehuda, had journeyed to Egypt to prepare the way for his family, Shmuelik would scout out new settlements and send word to Tevye regarding the opportunities he found. That way, Tevye would have a kosher, religious community waiting for him when he left the kibbutz. Alexander Goliath, the oversized Jew with the oversized heart, decided to stay by Tevye's side. At Tzeitl's gravesite, he had made a solemn promise to look after her children. Her last wish had been that Moishe and Hannie would grow up with Ruchel and Nachman, and Goliath felt it was his duty to carry out her request.

Hillel faced a much harder decision. While he had long ago made peace with his bachelor's existence, an awakened yearning stirred the blood in his veins. Tevye's daughter, Bat Sheva, aroused dreams in his head which pushed out all other thoughts. It wasn't just her beauty which attracted his fancy. Her unrestrained spirit which yearned to break boundaries appealed to the artist in him. While his music provided him with horizons of freedom in which he could roam, balancing the constraints of a life bordered with religious restrictions, her wanderlust was impulsive and untamed. He knew that he couldn't compete with the swaggering Ben Zion, but he had a minstrel's hope that she would come to hear the song in his heart.

One afternoon before sunset, when the kibbutzniks gathered outside the dining hall, awaiting their dinner, Hillel joined the kibbutz band in playing a medley of the Zionists' favorite tunes. Noticing Bat Sheva's pained expression as she stood to the side watching Ben Zion dance the *hora* with the girls of the kibbutz, the accordion player could readily see that she was in love with the egotistical *shvitzer*. But like all Jews, Hillel believed in the power of miracles. When Ben Zion picked Sonia up in the air and swirled her around in circles which made her dress fly up over her legs, Bat Sheva's face turned the color of beet soup. She ran away across the yard into the low-roofed barn. Hillel stopped playing and followed.

Lugging his accordion, the lame musician stepped quietly into the wooden structure which the kibbutznikim called a *tzreef*. Bat Sheva stood slumped over a haystack, weeping. Hillel reached into his pocket and took out his harmonica. Softly, he started to play. Hearing the music, the girl looked up and sniffled. Hillel smiled as he brought forth a melodious tune filled with hope and longing. The notes reached into her soul, coaxing her out of her gloom. She walked over and sat down beside him.

"Isn't their dancing awful?" she said, glad to have someone to talk to.

"Well, to be truthful, it looks like a lot of fun, but of course, mixed dancing is strictly forbidden."

"Everything is forbidden," she said.

"Not everything," he answered.

"What isn't?"

"Music. Poetry. Love."

Bat Sheva ignored the hints which seasoned his remark.

"It's disgusting the way he plays with her as if she were a doll."

Hillel didn't answer. Bat Sheva kept speaking, as if she were pouring her heart out to one of her sisters.

"I can't imagine what he sees in her. She doesn't have a brain in her head. She's rude and opinionated. And she isn't even that pretty," she said.

"Not as pretty as you."

"Do you think so?" she asked.

"Absolutely. I think you are very special indeed."

Hillel began to play a soft Sabbath tune which told of the love between a husband and wife.

"I wish Ben Zion thought more about me, but he is in love with that girl."

"From what I see, he seems more in love with himself. I suggest you forget him, and find someone more faithful."

"Who?"

"Well, there is me, for example."

Without thinking, Bat Sheva laughed. "You?" she said with a giggle as if it were the most ridiculous thing in the world.

Hillel blushed. "Am I as pitiful as that?"

"Oh no," she said, realizing that she had hurt him. "You are so much older than I am, that's all."

"And I can't dance like Ben Zion, can I?"

"Oh, I didn't mean that at all. Who cares how he dances? You play music like an angel. That's a real gift."

Uncomfortably, she backed away from the minstrel. She was angry at herself for having been so inconsiderate. She didn't know how she could take back the wound which her insensitive laughter had caused.

"I have to be going," she said. "It's my turn to watch the children."

"It's all right," he said. "You don't have to apologize."

In a moment, she vanished, leaving Hillel alone in the barn with the horses. He picked up his accordion, just as he had all of his life. His fingers moved melancholically over the keys, evoking a melody of exile and heartbreak, the lot of the Jews. But then, as if his fingers had a will of their own, they began to dance over the keyboard in a happier tune. Playing as hard as he could, Hillel lifted himself out of his sadness. After all, a Jew was commanded to serve His Maker with joy. Soon his body was swaying, and his lame foot was stomping the ground. While everyone was eating dinner in the dining hall, a lone and lonely accordion player sat in the barn with the animals, pouring out the love in his heart.

A few days later, Hillel said *"L'hitraot"* to Tevye and set off with Shmuelik over the mountains toward Zichron Yaacov, trusting that God, in His kindness, would lead him to the woman he was destined to wed.

Their departure left Tevye saddened, but he didn't have time to brood. Not wanting to be a *shnorrer* dependent on others, he insisted on working alongside the kibbutzniks for as long as he stayed in Shoshana. The back-breaking day started at five in the morning. Though the milkman habitually woke up every morning while the stars were still in the sky, he was not used to the strenuous physical work in the fields. True, milking a cow put a strain on the spine, and lugging containers of milk wasn't easy, but after tilling the rocky soil for hours on end, Tevye understood how the Jews in Egypt must have felt when Pharaoh increased their slave labor.

The first day, in order to show the young settlers that he was no stranger to hard, honest toil, he picked up a pickax and joined in the work of upturning the rocky earth to clear a new field for planting.

"Conquer the work, conquer the land!" Perchik yelled out as the work day began.

The young people labored with unbounded enthusiasm. Singing songs, the pioneers dug up the soil, as if in conquering each new patch of earth, they were performing some joyous religious devotion. In trying to keep up with them, Tevye failed to notice his heavy breathing. Long before noon, with the sun beating down on the nape of his neck, he began to feel dizzy. The ground beneath his feet started swaying as if he were on a boat. Blisters broke out on his fingers and palms, and trickles of blood dripped down the handle of his pick.

"Lunch break!" someone finally called out.

The words echoed in Tevye's ears like a bell. He had worked without respite, refusing to surrender to his thirst and exhaustion, and now that he could relax, a feeling of weakness made his limbs tremble. The pickax dropped out of his hand. He took one step forward and fainted. While the young people walked off for some food and some rest, Tevye lay collapsed in the field. Flies buzzed hungrily around him, but he didn't have the strength to brush them away. He lay on his back, unable to move, blinded by the fiery sun.

When her father didn't return with the others for lunch, Hodel ran out to the field, holding a flask of water in one hand, and her pregnant belly with the other. She found him sitting up dazed in the sun, his *yarmulka* on the ground, his lips parched, blood on his hands, his pickax lying on the soil beside him.

"*Abba,*" she hollered in a fright.

"I'll show them," he mumbled. "I'll show them."

"Look at you."

"I'm fine, don't you see?"

"I see a stubborn old man who doesn't know when to stop. You don't have to be such a hero."

Gently, she let him drink from the flask she had brought from the house, and splashed drops of water over his face.

"The day is still young," he said.

"For you, the day is over," she answered.

"I want to do my share of the work."

"You have done enough work for one day. Tomorrow, you will do more. But not in the fields. I'll have Perchik put you to work with the cows."

"I want to work the land too, like everyone else," he insisted.

"My brave pioneer," Hodel said, wetting her kerchief and moistening his forehead and his dry, sun-cracked lips.

Together, they walked back to the colony of thatched, mud-brick houses. Hodel soaked her father's hands in soapy water to wash off the blood and the dirt. After lunch, with a groan, he pushed himself up from the table, put on his cap, and insisted on returning to work. When Hodel blocked the door with her big, swollen belly, Tevye let out a roar.

"I am still your father," he bellowed.

Obediently, his daughter stepped away from the door. Grabbing a water pouch, Tevye strode outside and headed determinedly back to the fields. Tevye, the son of Reb Schneur Zalman, was nobody's freeloader. Nobody was going to say that he didn't carry his share of the load. Nobody was going to say that a religious Jew didn't work as hard as the Zionists. Not on his account anyway. Arriving back at the field, he waved to his fellow workers and reached down for his pick.

"Easy, easy, old man," a handsome, clean-shaven kibbutznik advised.

The girl working beside him laughed as Tevye swung the pickax over his head and drove it into the stony soil. The pick hit a rock. The handle reverberated in his hands, painfully reopening his blisters. Seeing Tevye wince, the kibbutznik held out a spade.

"Let's swap tools for a while," he said. "I enjoy working with a pick, and with your weight, the shoveling will go easier."

Without arguing, Tevye switched tools. He stuck the spade into the ground and pressed his boot on the rim of its blade. The spade broke through the crusty topsoil. With a flick of his wrists, Tevye flipped the shovelful over, revealing a richer, darker soil below. The kibbutznik was right. Using the weight of his body to break up the earth, Tevye was able to relieve some of the strain on his hands. Working at a more relaxed pace, he upturned a long stretch of field and started back in the opposite direction. What was the hurry, he thought? It was a big country, and after all, the Almighty had made him a man, not an ox. What they didn't finish today, they would finish tomorrow. As the famous Baal Shem Tov had taught, in serving the L-rd, the main thing was to be happy.

"Want to learn a new song?" he asked the young workers around him. They all gladly said yes.

"It's a *mitzvah* to be happy," he sang. "It's a *mitzvah* to be always happy."

Tevye repeated the simple tune a few times until his fellow workers joined in. Soon, everyone was working to the rhythm of the song. Maybe, Tevye thought, there was a hidden reason why God had brought him to this encampment of secular Jews. Maybe he could teach them some *Yiddishkeit*. Surely, he thought, without a connection to Torah, all of their love for the Land would one day turn sour. How long would a man break his back, struggling to coax life out of a desolate wasteland for socialist dreams?

That night, Tevye slept like a baby. Not even the rapacious mosquitoes disturbed him. If the night guard hadn't pounded on the door of his adobe-brick hut in the morning, Tevye would gladly have slept until noon.

Though it was summertime, the nights in the Galilee mountains were cool, and the kibbutzniks took advantage of the pre-dawn breezes to put several hours of work behind them before the sun rose in the sky. When the workers paused for a drink of tea, Tevye took out his *tefillin* and prayer shawl, and prayed.

The long work day finished, Tevye could barely drag his legs back to the dining hall. Nevertheless, after dinner, he forced himself to follow the kibbutzniks to the schoolroom where a two-hour class in Hebrew was taught. More often than not, he fell asleep in his chair at the back of the room. After a few classes, the teacher got used to raising her voice over the sound of Tevye's snoring. Bat Sheva and Hava sat beside him in class, nudging him awake whenever he started to slumber. What could he do? Didn't they say, when in Rome, do as the Romans do? Now that he was in Israel, he had to learn to be a *Sabra*, and that meant speaking Hebrew. True, Hebrew was a serious, holy language, lacking the spicy words and curses which made Yiddish such a rich, tasty soup. But as the Zionists asserted, Yiddish was an heirloom of the exile, the language of the *shtetl*, a jumble of foreign expressions and tongues.

"Did Moses speak Yiddish?" Ben Zion asked Tevye during one of their frequent discussions. "Did King David? Did Rabbi Akiva?" No they had not, Tevye conceded. So, at the end of the day, though he was exhausted and dreaming of bed, Tevye would squint at the new Hebrew words on the blackboard. Sometimes he felt that the classes at night were as punishing as his labor during the day. Instead of a pickax and shovel, he was using a pencil and eraser to overturn the rocks in his brain. As the Elders had taught – when you write on a new sheet of paper, the ink is absorbed; but if you write on an old sheet, the ink drips off the page. The grammar which his daughters grasped after repeating one or two times, Tevye had to hear time and again. Fortunately, he could already read Hebrew, and he already knew the Bible and Mishna, so he didn't have to start out from the first letter, *alef.*

"Don't be discouraged," Ben Zion told him one evening. "Rabbi Akiva was forty years old when he began to learn how to read."

"True, but Rabbi Akiva was Rabbi Akiva, and I am Tevye, the milkman turned farmer."

"Before he was Rabbi Akiva, he was just Akiva the shepherd, was he not?"

"I suppose that he was," Tevye admitted.

"Be patient, old man. You will catch on like everyone else."

"*Haleviy,*" Tevye sighed, relying on a timeworn Yiddish expression. "I hope you are right."

Not only was the milkman from Anatevka learning a new

profession and struggling to speak Hebrew, Ben Zion decided it
was time for Tevye to begin using his Hebrew name.

"Tuvia," he called him.

"Tevye," the milkman insisted.

"Tevye is Yiddish. You're Tuvia now."

Tevye wasn't convinced. True, God had changed Abram's
name to Abraham when He brought him to the Land of Israel. As
the Sages taught – change of name, change of fortune. And, after
all was said and done, his Hebrew name truly was Tuvia the son
of Schneur Zalman. Tuvia meant "the goodness of the Lord." But
just like you can't change a horse's name in the middle of a
journey, Tevye stayed Tevye, just like Golda would have wanted.

When he finally reached his bed after a day of hard work,
Tevye would fall into a cavernous slumber, still dressed in his
clothes. Often, he dreamt of sword-yielding Cossacks and sea
storms, but one enchanted evening, he dreamt that his Golda was
hanging up the day's wash on the Shoshana kibbutz.

"Ahh, Golda, Golda," he sighed. "The Almighty was right. It is
not good for a man to be alone."

"So get married already," Golda said.

"But I am married," Tevye said, as startled as a man could be.
"I'm married to you."

"You were married to me, but I'm not around anymore."

"Then why are you here, hanging my wash up to dry?"

"Somebody has to do it," she said. "But it's a chore for me to
come down from Heaven to do it for you, so get married already."

Tevye bolted upright in bed. It was a dream which set him to
wonder. But the idea of marrying a woman other than Golda was
so preposterous that Tevye soon put it out of his head.

After her father had fallen to sleep, Bat Sheva would sneak
outside to join the other young people around the nightly campfire.
Poems and short stories were read, songs were sung, and books
were discussed at great length. For the young girl from Anatevka,
the cool summer evenings under the stars opened up exciting new
vistas. The kibbutzniks spoke about writers with reverence, the
way her father spoke about the Sages of Torah. Inflamed with

curiosity, Bat Sheva asked Perchik to lend her some of his books, and he was happy to give her a novel of Tolstoy called *Anna Karenina*. Late into the night, she would stay up reading the breathtaking romance by candlelight until the wax melted down to the table.

Tired with her job of watching the children, Bat Sheva decided to join her father in the fields – at least for a few well-meaning hours. Trying to impress Ben Zion and keep up with the energetic Sonia, who were working together nearby, she overtaxed her strength and collapsed into her father's arms in exhaustion. He carried her to a sycamore tree at the edge of the field and sat her down in its shade.

"Why are you working so hard?" he asked.

"Why are you?"

"We are few in number, and there is a lot of work to do in farming the land," he said.

"Then why shouldn't I work as hard as everyone else, just like you?"

"You are not built for it, that's why."

"I am as strong as all of the other girls," his daughter insisted.

"Oh, so that is the reason," Tevye said, suddenly understanding. "When are you going to stop trying to win that false messiah's attention?"

"I am not trying to win the attention of anyone," she answered in protest.

"He is not the man for you."

"He might be if you and Goliath didn't watch over me like hawks."

"It is the task of a shepherd to guard over his flock," her father answered.

"I am old enough to make my own decisions."

"Yes, very old. Sixteen, seventeen, I forget."

"I am almost eighteen years old."

"A wrinkled old maid, indeed."

Bat Sheva blushed. "Don't you try to rule over my life the way you did with my sisters," she answered.

Tevye paused. He remembered his battles with Tzeitl, Hodel, and Hava. Experience had taught him that curses and threats did not influence head-strong, love-struck daughters. In a huff, Bat Sheva stood up and marched back to work.

Where did the girl's stubbornness come from, Tevye wondered? Obviously from her mother's side of the family. Golda, may her memory be for a blessing, could be as obstinate as a mule. He, on the other hand, followed the advice of the Sages to be like a reed which sways in the wind without breaking.

Bat Sheva bent down to pick up her hoe. Out of the corner of her eye, she saw Ben Zion staring at her with a confident grin. She blushed, angry at herself that he could so easily see into her heart. Raising the tool, she began beating the earth. Once, twice, three times, the metal hit the ground with a clang.

"You are hitting a rock," Ben Zion said, walking over. "Let me help you dig it out with my pick."

"I don't need any help, thank you," she told him.

In response, he flashed her one of his know-it-all grins.

With a mighty swing, she brought her hoe down on Ben Zion's foot. Yelping like a wounded puppy, he hopped on one leg, and fell to the ground on his butt.

"Oh, I'm so sorry," Bat Sheva exclaimed.

At the very same moment, both she and Sonia knelt down beside him. The women stared at each other like two cobras ready to do battle. Ben Zion pulled off his boot and moaned, pained by the blow, but enjoying the attention of the two pretty girls.

"You did that on purpose," Sonia accused.

"I did not," Bat Sheva answered.

"You're jealous, that's all. I see it in your eyes. I see the way you look at us when we dance. Wouldn't the sheltered religious girl just love a man to sweep her around in a circle and give her a kiss?!"

Dropping her hoe, Bat Sheva sprang at her rival. She scratched at Sonia's face with her fingers, but Ben Zion wedged his arms between them and pushed them apart. Now it was their turn to fall on their bottoms. Indignantly, both girls stood up and charged off in opposing directions. Ben Zion laughed. Across the field, Tevye stood glaring at him, clutching his pickax in his hands like a weapon. Seeing Bat Sheva's father, the grin slowly vanished from Ben Zion's face. Not that he was frightened of Tevye, but with his scraggly beard and angry eyes, Tevye looked like some enraged Biblical prophet poised to hurl a lightning bolt down from the sky.

Tevye looked up at Heaven.

"Please God," he said, "let my Hodel give birth to her baby, so that I can take up my journey and rescue my youngest daughter from the hands of this *vilda chaya* of a beast."

That evening, Bat Sheva stayed by herself in the house while everyone went off to the dining hall. She was tired of Ben Zion's confident glances, and the embarrassment they caused her. She had been a fool long enough. Her father was right. It was time she start thinking about a husband and not an imaginary romance. But later in the evening, when she was out walking to cool off her passions, Ben Zion and Sonia galloped by her on their way to guard-duty patrol. The kibbutz girl wore a cartridge belt across her chest, and a rifle was strapped to her back. She bounced gracefully in the saddle. Her long locks of hair spread out in the wind. Bat Sheva's heart sank. How could she ever compete with a creature like that? Compared to the pioneer girl, Tevye's youngest daughter felt like a dinosaur out of the past.

It was exactly the reaction which Ben Zion had planned. Two days later, while Tevye was plowing a field with a team of two horses, Ben Zion surprised Bat Sheva in the barn, where she had been put to work cleaning the stalls.

"I need someone to join me for guard duty," he said. "Want to come?"

He held up a spare rifle. Bat Sheva's hands trembled on the broom she was clutching. Her heart pounded like galloping horses.

"I have never held a rifle," she said.

"I'll teach you."

"I'm not very good at riding a horse."

"You can ride with me. Come on. We'll be back in two hours before the workers finish in the fields."

It was now or never, she thought. Going with him was madness, but she couldn't say no. With a fluttering heart, she leaned her broom against a haystack and followed him out of the barn. The main thing, she thought, was to let him see she was brave. He swung himself onto his horse and held out a hand to lift her up behind him.

"Put your foot on my boot," he said.

A whimper escaped her lips as he grabbed her hand and swung her up behind him onto the horse. She held tightly onto his waist, frightened by the dizzying height of the steed. With a commanding *"Yalla!"* he flicked at the reins, and they rode off in a gallop. Bat Sheva grasped at his clothing as she was bounced up and down on the hard, muscular back of the horse. The earth passed by beneath them at an incredible speed. Wind blew in her face. When she opened her eyes, they were racing over a hill, away from the kibbutz, into a valley she had never seen before. Her heart beat wildly, not as much from the ride as from the feeling that she was doing something terribly sinful. But another voice said, nonsense – what was sinful in riding a horse? The hooves of the animal pounded the earth beneath her. Her body trembled from the jolts of the ride, loosening all of her joints. The sense of freedom was dizzying. As they rode up a hillside, she clung to Ben Zion's back, wondering if he were a man she could trust or a demon?

Finally he stopped by the well where Peter had been wounded. He slid down from the horse and reached up with both hands to help her. Suddenly, she was in his arms, her toes just touching the ground, captive in his embrace. He grinned with his handsomest smile and squeezed her tightly around her waist. When he released her, her legs didn't stop trembling. Her heart kept pounding as if she were still on the horse.

"Have a cool drink," he said.

He stepped over to the well and began pulling on the rope. Soon, a bucket appeared splashing with water.

"I found this spring with Peter," he said. "A few times when we were out riding, we saw gazelles grazing around this oak tree. When we investigated, we found puddles of water and realized that there must be an underground stream here. We started digging and discovered this well."

The water in the bucket was clouded with dirt, but after a few moments, the sediment sank to the bottom. The taste of the water was clean and refreshingly cool. Bat Sheva poured some into her hands and washed the dust of the ride off her face.

"I hope you are not still angry with me about our last meeting in Russia," he said.

Bat Sheva blushed. "Why should I be angry."

"Some women think a kiss is a proposal of marriage."

Bat Sheva kept silent.

"It seems to me a man and woman can love each other like friends without rushing to get married."

Bat Sheva still hadn't stopped trembling. She blushed, imagining that she looked like a frightened little girl.

"Your father warned me not to talk to you, so I have been keeping my distance."

"My father doesn't own me," she said. "I am old enough to live my own life. My sister, Tzeitl, got married to Motel when she was my age, and my mother was even younger when she married my father."

"I don't think that age is the problem. Your father dislikes me because I am not religious."

"Everyone is religious in his own way," she answered.

"That's what I believe."

He smiled at her in a way that made her cheeks even pinker than they were.

"Then we can continue to be friends?" he asked.

"I don't see why not," she replied. Her legs were still quivering, no longer from the ride, but from the strain of trying to appear unflustered and poised.

"Good," he said with a broad, tooth-filled grin. "Come over here, and I will teach you how to shoot your rifle."

Bat Sheva followed him to the other side of the shade tree. The valley spread out before them. Hills surrounded them on all sides. As far as she could see, they were completely alone. He told her to kneel down and handed her a rifle.

"Put the butt on your shoulder. That's right. Now place your left hand on the barrel."

He knelt down beside her and reached over her shoulder to position her hands on the rifle. He was so close to her, she could feel his breath on her cheek. Once again, she started to tremble.

"Hold it steady," he said.

"I can't."

He reached his other arm around her to steady the barrel. Now their cheeks were touching. When she turned her head toward him, she fell into the pool of his piercing blue eyes. Their lips met. The rifle slipped from her hands. He caught it and set it gently down on the ground.

"I waited a long time for that kiss," he said.

"You really did?" she asked, wanting to believe him.

"Yes." He smiled and kissed her again. She knew that their kissing was wrong, but she didn't have the strength to resist.

"Don't move!" a gruff voice commanded.

It was the voice of an Arab. Bat Sheva didn't understand the words, but she knew it was an order. Ben Zion froze in her arms. Slowly he pushed her aside.

"Don't move!" the voice warned.

Bat Sheva saw a pair of sandals and the long, hanging skirt of a Bedouin. He bent down and picked up her rifle.

"Now yours," the voice ordered.

Two other Arabs stood with their rifles aimed at the Jews. In the distance, another Arab stood holding the reins of their horses. The highwaymen had left the horses behind to sneak up on foot.

Ben Zion decided that this was not the time to be brave, especially with the girl at his side. Slowly, he pulled the strap of his rifle over his head.

"Don't worry," he told her.

"Quiet," the Arab shouted.

Ben Zion held out his rifle. The Arab closest to them reached down to take it. Slowly, Ben Zion stood up.

"What do you want from us?" he asked the leader in Hebrew.

"This is our well," the Arab replied in a Hebrew as good as the Jew's.

"I dug this well with my friends," Ben Zion insisted.

"We dug the well first. When we moved away from here, we covered the well up. Now we have come back to pasture our sheep on our land."

"This is our land," Ben Zion protested. "We bought the land from the Turkish government, and we have the deed to prove it."

"My grandparents were here before the Turks," the Arab maintained.

"That doesn't make legal ownership," Ben Zion answered.

"For us it does. We dug this well, grazed our flocks in this valley, and planted the olive trees on the hillsides."

Ben Zion realized he wasn't going to convince the Arabs with arguments, but without his rifle, and with the girl at his side, a fight was out of the question. Guns were pointed at them from all sides.

"We want you to stay away from our water. You and all of the *Moscowbim* with you." Because the settlers came from Russia, the Arabs called them *Moscowbim*.

"And we forbid you to plow up our fields."

"Good neighbors shouldn't quarrel," Ben Zion answered. "If there has been a misunderstanding, I am sure we can clear it up. I suggest we bring this dispute before the Turkish magistrate in Tiberias."

The Turkish magistrate can be bribed, and you have more money than we do."

"You may not recognize his authority, but if you harm us, my comrades will make sure that your leaders are put into prison, and your tribe will be expelled from the region."

Bat Sheva could not tell from the Arab's dark expression whether Ben Zion's threat had made an impression.

"Take their horse!" the leader commanded.

One of the Arabs grabbed the reins of Ben Zion's horse.

"That's robbery!" he said.

"You steal from us, we steal from you."

With a bow, the Arab started to walk backward. When they were a safe distance away, they turned and ran back to their horses. Bat Sheva breathed in relief. The Arabs galloped away up the hillside, pulling Ben Zion's stallion in tow.

"Now what do we do?" Bat Sheva asked.

Ben Zion pondered in silence. "First, we had better drink a lot of water, and then we will start walking back to the kibbutz."

"On foot?" the girl asked.

"If you walked from Anatevka to Palestine, you surely can walk from here to the village."

"I rode most of the way in our wagon," she said.

"If I could summon a carriage for my princess I would. Since that is not possible, I suggest that we walk, unless you prefer to wait here alone while I go and fetch you a wagon."

"No, no," Bat Sheva said with a nervous glance at the desolate landscape. "Of course I'll come with you."

When they had finished drinking, Ben Zion started off across the valley and up the rocky hillside. Suddenly, his passion for Bat Sheva had vanished, and he seemed to forget the ardor which he had displayed a short time before. He strode along, plunged in his own contemplations, as if she weren't even there. Vowing to set off in revenge, he ranted on about the need to form an army and expel the Arabs from the region. Not only had the scoundrels stolen their horse and their rifles, they had nearly killed Peter. If the kibbutz didn't retaliate promptly, the Arabs would believe that the Jews were afraid to strike back.

Bat Sheva listened in silence. Venting his anger, Ben Zion spoke on and on about bringing hundreds of thousands of Jews to Palestine from Diasporas all over the world. He spoke about war and conquering the Turks.

"By blood and fire, the land of Judea fell, and by blood and fire, the land of Judea will rise," he claimed, quoting the fighting creed of the Hebrew *shomrim*.

As he led the way back to Shoshana, he described the day when Jewish labor would transform the deserted wasteland into blossoming gardens and fields. The land of Zion would be not only a physical refuge for all of the Jews, but a cultural refuge as well. A new spiritual renaissance was beginning, proclaiming the rebirth of the Jews, who, instead of being the downtrodden Jews of the ghetto, would be proud and upright Israelis. Hard work and sacrifice were in order, and the willingness to fight for the new Jewish State.

Bat Sheva grew tired of listening. Never once did he speak about her. Never once did he mention the word marriage. Never once did he mention the day when they would build their own family. She realized that their future together, if it existed at all in his dreams, was only a detail in Ben Zion's magnanimous plans for the Jews. He continued on with his lecture, as if forgetting that she were still at his side. When she stopped to rest, he kept right on walking and talking. Finally, he seemed to recall. He stopped and looked around for the girl.

"Bat Sheva," he called. "Bat Sheva?"

She was hiding behind a large boulder. When his calls became urgent, she stood up and stepped into view.

"What are you doing?" he asked.

"I wanted to see if you remembered that I was still with you."

Ben Zion blushed. "Sometimes I get carried away," he admitted. "Though my dreams may sound like wishful thinking, I can envision the future before my eyes as if it were already happening. If only Jews the world over would wake up and rally behind the Zionist banner."

"You don't have to apologize," she said. "I know it means a lot to you."

"To all of us," he said, holding out his hand.

"We had better not," she said. "We are close to the kibbutz, and I wouldn't want Sonia to see."

"Sonia!" he exclaimed in surprise.

"You seem to stick together like glue."

"She's like a sister, that's all."

Bat Sheva wanted to hear how she was different, but Ben Zion didn't add another word. Down the hill, at the entrance to the kibbutz, a figure stood waiting. He stood with his hands on his hips, staring up into the hills.

"It looks like we have been missed," Ben Zion noted.

"It's my father," she said.

"Yes. I recognized the thunderbolts crashing over his head."

"Surely he's worried."

"He probably has the whole kibbutz searching for us."

"What are we going to tell him?"

"The truth," Ben Zion said.

"He will kill me."

"He'll probably want to kill me too. We can be buried in the same grave, like Romeo and Juliet."

"Like who?" Bat Sheva asked.

"You have never heard of Romeo and Juliet?"

"No. Who were they?"

"You really are something special, aren't you?" he said, as if noticing for the first time.

Bat Sheva blushed, though she couldn't tell if he meant it as a compliment, or whether he was simply laughing at her.

"I will tell you the story the next time we meet," he said. "In the meantime, let's tell your father that you went out for a walk and got lost. I happened along and found you."

Bat Sheva agreed. She wasn't sure she could lie to her father, but it was worth a try. When they reached the bottom of the hill, her father squared his shoulders and snorted like a bull preparing to charge. Bat Sheva tried to return his gaze, but she couldn't. His fiery look pierced through her body like horns.

"*Nu?*" was all he said, waiting for his daughter to explain. But before she could speak, he held up a hand.

"On second thought, I don't want to hear. Why add the sin of lying to the dishonor you have shown toward your father?"

Bat Sheva lowered her glance to the ground.

"Go to the house!" he commanded.

"But, *Abba*," Bat Sheva began.

Hearing his daughter address him in Hebrew made Tevye more enraged than he was, reminding him of the dangerous breaches taking place on the kibbutz all around him, cutting him off from the familiar safeguards of the past.

"Go to the house!" he roared at his daughter.

Blushing, the girl hurried along the path toward the tiny dwellings. Tevye turned to Ben Zion. Under his milkman's blue work shirt, his muscles were twitching.

"You remember my warning to keep away from my daughter?"

"Don't jump to conclusions, Reb Tevye," Ben Zion said. "I found her lost in the valley surrounded by Arabs. I had to barter my horse and my rifle in order to save her."

"You are a liar," Tevye accused.

"I am willing to swear by the Five Books of Moses," Ben Zion avowed.

"I won't let you profane the Good Book on my account. Nor will I let you profane the honor of my daughter."

Tevye's eyes were glowing. His hands squeezed closed as if they were already grasping the veins of Ben Zion's neck.

"Let's settle this here and now," he said.

Ben Zion felt confident that he could fend off the aging milkman, but he had second thoughts about standing in the way of a mad stampeding bull.

"I am telling you the truth," he said.

"The children saw you ride off with Bat Sheva this morning," Tevye revealed.

For a moment, Ben Zion was silent. His eyes darted from side to side, like a fox trapped in a barn. Vaguely, he remembered seeing children playing with horseshoes in a yard when he and Bat Sheva had galloped off.

"Please, Tevye, believe me," he tried to explain. "Nothing happened between us. Not even one kiss."

A bellow rumbled in Tevye's chest. He charged forward, hands outstretched, head lowered like a ram. Ben Zion realized that he couldn't rely on his own strength to save him from the upcoming collision. So he dodged to the side and started to run. Like a gazelle frightened away by a gunshot, he bolted away from the onrushing danger. Tevye stumbled a few lunging steps after him, but the agile youth was already prancing away down the road.

"I'll kill you!" Tevye shouted, waving his clenched fist in the air. "If you ever speak a word to my daughter again, I'll rip out your tongue! If you ever dare touch her, I'll cut off your hands!"

The threat echoed across the hillsides. "Your hands! Your hands!"

Tevye panted for breath. Why didn't Hodel give birth already, so that he could flee this modern-day Sodom and Gomorrah? The longer they stayed in Shoshana, who knew what fate awaited his daughter?

Chapter Eighteen

PEACE IN THE MIDDLE EAST

The emergency bell clanged throughout the valley of the Shoshana kibbutz. Workers who were building the first stone edifice on the settlement put down their chisels and masonry tools. Field hands set aside their scythes and their sickles and started back toward the compound of mud and wood dwellings. Within minutes, all of the settlers sat crowded together on the benches in the dining hall. With great indignation, Ben Zion related how the Arabs had ambushed them at the well and stolen his horse and two rifles. He demanded that a small force be organized immediately and set off in retaliation.

"Why didn't you shoot?" someone asked.

"We were outnumbered, and I did not want to endanger the girl," he answered, leaving out the embarrassing details of how the Arabs had snuck up and surprised them.

"You know the rule that a *shomer* is forbidden to go out on guard duty alone. Why did you break it?"

"I was teaching the girl how to shoot."

"I wish he would teach me how to shoot," a plain-looking girl quipped loudly enough for her neighbors to hear. Other girls giggled. Ben Zion's friends broke out in laughter. Since it was Gordon's turn to preside at the general meeting, the gavel was in his hand. He gave it a bang on the table, and the ruckus subsided. Sonia, standing in a corner of the hall, flashed a look of accusation at the faithless Don Juan. Ben Zion smiled. Rogue that he was, he cherished all of the attention.

"No one wants a war," Perchik said. "Let the Arabs have the well. We can always dig another."

Immediately, another clamor broke out in the crowd. Shouts of protest or agreement came from all corners of the hall. Once again, the fierce-looking Gordon wielded his gavel.

"Water can't be found everywhere," a kibbutznik asserted. "Without our wells, what will we do in the event of a drought?"

"What about the stolen horse and the rifles?" another man asked. "Do we give them away too?"

The uproar resumed. This time it took a full minute of gavel banging to restore a semblance of order.

"I volunteer to lead a contingent from the kibbutz to enter into negotiation with the Arabs," Perchik announced. "If nothing can be accomplished in a peaceful manner, then we can think about fighting."

"If we don't respond with a show of force, they will only take advantage of us in the future," Ben Zion warned.

Once again, a vote was taken. This time, Ben Zion's followers were one vote shy of a deadlock. Peter had gone to Tiberias to have a doctor examine an infection in his wounded shoulder.

"That's not fair," Ben Zion protested. "Peter is not here to vote."

"You know the rules of the voting," Gordon responded. "A voter has to be present."

Ben Zion cast a frustrated look over the crowd.

"One minute," a voice called from the doorway. "You didn't count me. I vote with Ben Zion."

It was Bat Sheva.

"She doesn't belong to the kibbutz," Sonia called.

"I want to join," Bat Sheva responded.

Tevye stood up from his seat on a bench in the back of the room and glared at his daughter. She stared defiantly back at him. Ben Zion's frown immediately turned to a grin.

"The vote is even," he said.

"No it isn't!" Tevye bellowed. "I too want to join the kibbutz. And I vote with Perchik!"

It was no easy decision for Perchik. On the one hand, Tevye's vote assured a majority for his non-violent faction, averting the danger of military encounter. On the other hand, if Tevye were actually to reside in Shoshana, that would be the end of Perchik's happy home life with Hodel. But, then again, if Ben Zion's forces won out, Perchik's influence on the kibbutz would be seriously weakened. For Tevye also, siding with his socialist son-in-law was no easy matter, but he was willing to do it to bring about Ben Zion's defeat.

"We have the majority," Perchik claimed, accepting Tevye's vote.

"The decision is final," Gordon announced. "We negotiate with our neighbors."

Another commotion erupted. Everyone had something to say, either about the Arabs, or about the way the kibbutz had accepted new members without a community vote. Bat Sheva glared at her father and strode out of the hall. Tevye started after her, but Perchik walked over and gave him a congratulatory pat on the back.

"I don't know if your decision to join our kibbutz is genuine, but thank you for standing behind me."

"I didn't do it for your sake," Tevye said.

"Then for the cause of peace."

"Not for peace either."

"Well, whatever your reason was, you saved the kibbutz a lot of needless bloodshed. Come with us when we go to meet with the Arabs. You are a businessman. You know how to negotiate. I respect your experience."

"A milkman is not really a businessman," Tevye said modestly, not unaffected by his son-in-law's flattery. "Still, I did have my share of dealings with a wide range of clients who were willing to pay a few extra *kopeks* for my top line of cheeses."

"The tastiest in the region, I remember," Perchik agreed.

Tevye also remembered how the young, university student would gobble down the delicacies which Golda set before him as he prattled on and on about his crazy *farblondzhet* ideas.

"Even back then when you invited me into your home to teach your daughters to read, I recognized your worldliness and wisdom," Perchik said.

That was a joke, Tevye thought with a grumble, recalling that black, tragic day. What *Tisha B'Av* was for the Jewish people as a whole – the day marking the Jerusalem Temple's destruction – the day that Tevye had taken a fancy to Perchik marked the crumbling of the protective wall which Tevye had erected around his family. If Tevye were really so wise, he never would have opened his door to the loquacious Shabbtai Tzvi.

Outside, the dining room, Bat Sheva was nowhere in sight. Neither was Ben Zion. But Tevye did not have the time to set off on a search. Already, Perchik was organizing a negotiating team to meet with the Arabs. Once again, Tevye found himself mounting a horse. Even as they rode out of the gate of the kibbutz, he looked back for a glimpse of his daughter.

True to Tevye's fears, she was in the barn with Ben Zion. He had found her there sitting alone with the milk cows.

"Thank you for trying to help me," he said.

"I don't know why I did it," she answered. "You are really not worth it."

"That's not very nice."

"Well, it's true. The way I was raised, if a man likes a woman, he asks her to marry him without a thousand test kisses. That is the honorable way to behave."

Ben Zion walked around to the other side of a cow, as if to keep it between them.

"This isn't Anatevka," he said.

"Are people so different here?"

"In a way, I suppose they are, yes. We no longer live according to the rules of the past."

"What rules do you live by?" she asked.

"I don't live by rules. I do what my feelings tell me."

"I see. And what do your feelings say about me?"

Ben Zion patted the cow. "I like you very much. But I am not certain that I am ready for marriage."

"Well until you decide, there will be no more kisses, at least not with me."

Turning her back to him, Bat Sheva strode out of the barn. Ben Zion smiled as he watched her march out of the door.

"That was interesting," he mused. The girl had more spunk than he realized. For the first since he had met her, he began to give her some serious thought.

"What do you say, cow?" he asked the beast in the stall. "Should I marry the milkman's daughter?"

Bat Sheva strode away from the barn, secretly hoping to hear Ben Zion call her. She wondered if she really believed in what she was doing, or whether it was the influence of her sister, Hodel, to whom she had gone for advice. After all, Hodel had been in a similar dilemma with Perchik, when she had had to choose between her feelings of love and the ties of the past. Though Perchik and Ben Zion had different political views, they were fish from the very same pond. After Bat Sheva had poured out her heart, her older sister warned her not to succumb to passionate promises and even more passionate stares. After their discussion, Bat Sheva resolved to cling to her honor. But immediately upon leaving the barn, she had second thoughts.

"You idiot," she thought to herself. "Now you have gone and spoiled everything. Now Sonia will have him all to herself. Now he will think you are just a boring, old-fashioned girl from the *shtetl*."

Nonetheless, Bat Sheva had made up her mind. She wasn't going to let him turn her into some little *dreidel* that he could swirl with his finger. She was a person, not a plaything, and she wanted to be treated that way.

The peace delegation spotted the Arab encampment from the top of a ridge a half-hour ride away from Shoshana. A dozen black Bedouin tents were scattered in the valley below. Instead of rising to a point like regular tents, the nomadic dwellings were spread over large rectangular areas. Each tent housed extended families, from grandparents, to uncles, distant cousins, and in-laws, as well as an assortment of animals. Herds of sheep grazed over the hillsides. Shepherds in white *kefiahs* and black headbands lounged in the shade of sycamore trees, letting their dogs chase after stray sheep. In the fields, women squatted over rows of vegetable plantings. Camels rested lazily in the sun on their haunches, munching on patches of weeds. Seeing the Jews approaching, a watchman fired a rifle shot in the air. Arabs hurried out from the shade of their tents to see who was coming. Abramson, Bronsky, Karmelisky, Mendelevitch, and Tevye swung their rifles into a readied posture in front of their chests.

"Not so fast," Perchik said. "We have come to make peace, not to fight."

"I just want to be ready," Abramson said. "Just in case."

As if out of thin air, five riders on horseback came forward to meet them. Four wore the striped gowns and cloaks of tribal soldiers. They were armed with long barreled rifles, and they brandished an assortment of polished daggers and swords in their belts. Their leader sat on a stunning white stallion. He was dressed in the regal headset and robes of a sheik.

Perchik called out, "*Shalom.*"

The sheik responded in Arabic. While Perchik had picked up the rudiments of the language, he felt more comfortable conversing in either Hebrew or Turkish, the official language of Palestine. Tevye sat poised in the saddle, trying to decipher whatever words he could. The sheik did all of the talking for the Arabs. Later, Perchik explained to Tevye what had transpired.

The sheik claimed that the Jews had illegally settled on their ancestral homeland. When Perchik showed him their deed of purchase, the tribe leader stared at it with a stony expression. The Turks, the Arab maintained, had no right to the land, and no right to sell it. Perchik answered that the nations of the world recognized the four-hundred-year rule of the Turks over the region, and that the Shoshana colony's deed to the land would be considered valid in any international court. The sheik wasn't persuaded. The land of the kibbutz, and all of its wells and springs, belonged to his tribe, he maintained.

Within minutes, the Jews were surrounded by fierce-looking tribesmen, dozens of women and children, and the elders of the village. Tevye did not have to count to see that their peace entourage was seriously outnumbered. Sweating from the ride in the sun, he longed for a drink, but he did not want to remove his hand from his weapon. Contrary to tales of Arab hospitality, no one invited them into a tent to relax in the shade and moisten their lips with a little date liquor.

After an intensive discussion, an agreement was reached. The Arabs could keep the disputed well at the edge of the kibbutz. The Jews would fence in the area described in the deed, and the tribe was free to graze their herds everywhere else. As a gesture of goodwill, the Jews would pay the sheik compensative damages, a onetime payment of 500 pounds. In return, the Arabs would sign a document attesting that the settlers of Shoshana were the sole and rightful owners of the acreage. The sheik also promised to return Ben Zion's horse and his rifle.

"There were two rifles," Tevye reminded Perchik in Russian.

"It is best not to embarrass him," Perchik answered.

"Embarrass him?" Tevye said in wonder. "You've given him the well. You've promised him 500 pounds. The only thing you haven't yet surrendered is the harvest."

"Would you prefer war?"

"Five-hundred pounds is more than the kibbutz treasury has in reserve," Bronsky remarked.

"We can borrow from Kibbutz Degania," Perchik said.

"I feel this is something we should vote on," Mendelevitch advised.

"A vote was already taken," Perchik reminded him, "And we won the right to negotiate a settlement."

"I advise that we take a vote between us right now."

Perchik hesitated. Bronsky and Mendelevitch were the treasurers of the kibbutz. It was largely due to their tight-fisted policy that the commune was holding its own. If peace had a price, they could be expected to vote against it, even if the alternative meant bloodshed. Karmelisky was a close friend of Perchik, a vote he could trust. That meant that once again, the issue would be decided by Tevye. Hands went up for and against the agreement.

"Well, Tevye, your vote decides," Perchik said. "What do you say?"

On the one hand, Tevye thought, an Ishmaelite couldn't be trusted. It was a lesson Abraham had learned long ago. Ever since then, history had proven it again and again, wherever Jews had lived under Moslem rulers. On the other hand, the Jews were still a minority in Palestine and had to survive as peacefully as they could until more reinforcements arrived. Then again, only a fool would agree to pay twice for the same piece of land. On the other hand, if Perchik returned to the kibbutz with a signed agreement, it would be a blow to Ben Zion. To Tevye, that was the most important factor of all. Thus, once again, Tevye sided with Hodel's husband.

Victorious, Perchik swung his leg over the back of his horse and slid down to the ground. Smiling, he walked up to the sheik and held out his hand. Ceremoniously, the chieftain lowered himself from his mount and accepted the hand of the Jew.

"On behalf of our kibbutz, I invite you to an evening of song and cultural exchange in Shoshana," Perchik said.

"Perhaps," the sheik answered.

"There is a lot we can learn from each other," Perchik continued.

"Perhaps," the Arab responded.

"Your people have a knowlege of farming, and we have new scientific advancements. Hopefully one day, all fences can come down, and we can live side by side in peaceful co-existence, an example to the world."

"A wonderful dream," the Arab said, with no trace of a smile.

To Tevye, the chief did not seem overly enthused, but as Tevye had to admit, only a fool could become excited over Perchik's crazy *meshugenneh* ideas.

Pleased with their agreement and with the peace he had made, Perchik returned to his horse.

"Maybe we should get something in writing before we leave," Bronsky suggested.

"There isn't a need to force things. These Arabs stand by their word," Perchik assured.

"The Torah says otherwise," Tevye advised.

"Your Bible stories are fantasies," Perchik said. "In these modern times, our task is to reach the heavens without leaving the earth of reality. All men are basically good, Jews and gentiles alike. You just have to treat everyone fairly, and you will be treated fairly in return. No people or religion is better than any other. We are all equal in the eyes of the Creator, and one day we will be a united community of nations without racial hatreds, class inequality, and worker exploitation. How fortunate we are to be the pioneers in this great dream of harnessing the winged horse of utopia with the wagon of pragmatic action and thought."

Perchik's speech was a lot of double-talk to Tevye, but he didn't bother to argue. He knew that debating with his son-in-law was a hopeless affair.

When they arrived back at Shoshana, a Galilee sunset was bathing the kibbutz in a warm golden glow. The stillness of the late afternoon was only interrupted by the sound of Goliath splitting logs, but the whacks of his axe did not spoil the serenity in the air. On the contrary, the sounds of the wood chopping seemed a natural part of the pastoral setting. Before entering the straw-roofed, adobe house where his family was living, Tevye prayed the afternoon prayer in the yard, facing south toward Jerusalem. The tumult of the day melted away, leaving him alone with his Maker. It was a time of reflection, reminding a man that although he was commanded to labor and toil, the success of his endeavors depended on God. When he opened his eyes at the end of the prayer, little Moishe and Hannie stood at his feet.

"Can we go for a ride on your horse?" the little girl asked.

Bat Sheva appeared in the doorway. Tevye stared at her without saying a word. He had not yet decided how to deal with his youngest daughter. She was like a prancing young colt who longed to escape its corral. To tame the streak of wildness in her, a gentle, yet firm grip on her reins was needed.

His grandchildren were waiting for an answer.

"That is a very good idea," Tevye said.

He lifted the two *kinderlach* onto the animal's back, then climbed up beside them.

"Hold on tightly," he said.

Bat Sheva disappeared from the doorway and Hava appeared in her place.

"Be careful, *Abba*," she called.

"Don't worry," Tevye answered. "I used to take you and your sisters for rides."

He clicked his tongue and gave a slight tug on the reins. The horse started off on a slow, easy walk. Goliath appeared with an axe on his shoulder and waved with a melancholy expression. Ever since Tzeitl had died, the happy-go-lucky giant had acted like a different person. He spent most of his days alone, chopping wood. Soon, towering stacks of firewood sprang up alongside the barn. He rarely ate in the dining hall with the settlers, and while he could not be called skinny, his face became almost gaunt. With Tevye at work in the fields every day, the two men barely found time to speak. This coming *Shabbos*, Tevye decided, he would find time to have a heart-to-heart talk with the woodcutter.

Guiding the horse up the hillside, Tevye was glad to have some free time with Tzeitl's children. His long hours in the field kept him away from the house, and by the time he returned home from the evening lesson in Hebrew, Moishe and Hannie were already asleep. When the horse reached the peak of the hill, Tevye set the children down on the ground. In the stillness of the late afternoon, with the day's problems behind him, he paused to remember the true splendor of the Land, the beautiful azure skies, the tranquility of the hillsides, the feeling of rest and eternity which saturated the Biblical landscapes. With joy in their eyes, the children watched the fiery orb of the sun slip below the distant horizon. As the sun sank out of sight, the sky turned an artist's palette of colors.

"*Saba*," the girl asked, using the Hebrew word for grandfather. "Where does the sun go when it sets?" the girl asked.

"To sleep," Tevye answered.

"No, really," Hannie said.

"It keeps on traveling through the sky to shine on different places in the world. Right now, it is shining on your Aunt Baylke in America."

Thinking of her, Tevye plucked a few blades of grass out of the ground. He would put them in an envelope with the letter he was intending to write to his daughter, so that she could see with her very own eyes that the Promised Land was real.

"Why don't the boys in Shoshana have *peyes* like I do?" nine-year-old Moishe asked.

Tevye was taken aback by the question. While he was chagrined by the sacrilegious lifestyle he had found on the kibbutz, his main concern was the harmful influence it was sure to have on Bat Sheva. Now he realized that his grandchildren were being confounded too. If the boy was asking about side-locks, he probably had a dozen other questions and doubts in his head.

"They are not as religious as we are," the grandfather answered.

"They are not religious at all," Hannie corrected. "That's what Shmuelik said when he left."

"They will all be religious one day," Tevye said. "They just haven't learned."

"Why not?" Moishe asked.

"Because their father and mother did not teach them the Torah."

"Why not?" the boy asked again.

"Because no one taught them either."

"They want to live like the gentiles," Hannie said.

No doubt, Tevye thought, she had heard that from Shmuelik also.

"Are all gentiles bad?" Moishe asked.

"No, certainly not. Not all gentiles are bad," Tevye answered. "There are many good gentiles too. The tax collector in Anatevka was a good, honest man, and the blacksmith would remove stones and nails from the hooves of my horse without charging me money. The good Lord has created all of the world's people, and we are commanded to love them all – except for our enemies, of course."

"Everyone is our enemy," Moishe said. "Nobody likes the Jews."

"Sometimes it seems that way," their grandfather agreed.

"Are the Arabs gentiles?" Hannie asked.

"Yes," Tevye answered, realizing that the only non-Jews the children had known were the Caucasian, granite-faced Russians.

"Wasn't Abraham their father too?"

"Yes," Tevye answered.

The children stared at him, waiting for their grandfather to explain. Tevye remembered that he had a great responsibility which he had been ignoring. Work was not the only task in life. A man had the sacred duty to teach his children the Torah, as it said in the *Shema*, *"You shall teach these words diligently to your children."* Now that both Tzeitl and Motel were gone, Tevye had inherited the obligation of passing on the traditions of Sinai to his grandchildren. They gazed up at him with eyes as big as setting suns. Now more than ever, they needed a father. They needed answers to their questions and guidance.

Tevye asked them if they wanted to hear a story. Gladly, the children agreed.

"You know," their grandfather began, "when Abraham was a boy, even younger than you are, he looked into the sky and saw that the sun ruled in the heavens. So he decided to worship the sun. Then, when nighttime came, he saw the sun go down and the moon come up, and he said, 'Surely, I was wrong. The moon rules the heavens.' So he decided to worship the moon. Then, when the moon disappeared in the morning, he realized that even the moon had a master. So he said, 'I will worship the God who rules over both the sun and the moon.'"

The children stared at Tevye with spellbound looks on their faces. How thrilling it was to be outdoors all alone with their grandfather on the high, windy hill. Being close to him, listening to his deep, familiar voice, watching his eyes glow, snuggling into his powerful arms, and inhaling his warm earthy smell, were incredible pleasures for them.

"Little Abraham started to tell everyone he met about the one and only God who ruled over the world. At that time, people believed there were many gods, each one possessing a different power. In fact, Abraham's own father, Terach, was a maker of idols. He had a store where he sold all kinds of wood and stone statues. One day, he put little Abraham in charge of the store when he went out on an errand. As soon as his father was gone, Abraham took a hammer and began smashing all of the idols. Before long all of them lay in pieces on the floor, except for the biggest statue which Abraham left standing. The clever boy placed the hammer in its hand. When his father returned, he stared in horror at all of the broken idols.

"What have you done to my idols?" Terach angrily shouted.

"It wasn't me," Abraham answered. "The big idol broke them all with his hammer."

"That idol can't do anything," his father yelled back. "It is just a lifeless chunk of stone."

"Then why do you worship it?" Abraham asked. His father was tongue-tied. He didn't have an answer.

"There is only one true God," Abraham said. `These silly stone and wooden statues don't have any power at all."

"We know that story," Hannie said when her grandfather had finished.

"Why didn't you tell me?" Tevye asked.

"We wanted to hear it again."

Tevye nodded his head and grinned at his two little treasures. Night had descended and stars sparkled all across the celestial vault.

"You still haven't answered my question," Moishe said.

"What question was that?" Tevye asked.

"If Abraham was the father of the Arabs, why aren't they Jews like we are?"

"Well," Tevye began, "to make a long story short, Abraham was married to Sarah, and they were married for a very long time without having children. So one day, Sarah told him to marry her handmaid, Hagar, who was the daughter of the Pharaoh of Egypt. They had a child named Ishmael. He grew up to be a wild child, a robber and highwayman. When Abraham was a hundred years old, he finally had a son with Sarah. They named the boy Isaac. The descendants of Ishmael are the Arabs, and the descendants of Isaac are the Jews."

"Tell us another story about Abraham," Hannie demanded.

With a groan, Tevye stood up and stretched his tired back. "When you are both in bed," he said. "Now we have to go home."

As they rode silently back to the kibbutz on the horse, Hannie suddenly asked her grandfather a question.

"Why did God take our *Ema* away?"

Tevye had taken enough Hebrew classes to know that *Ema* meant mother.

"So that she could be with *Abba*," her brother answered.

"Will God take us to Heaven too?" the girl asked.

"One day, but not for a very long time," Tevye answered.

"I want to be with *Ema* and *Abba*," Hannie said.

Tevye hugged her and gave her a kiss. "One day we all will be back together," he comforted. "But right now, God wants us down here on earth. We have to settle this Land, just like Abraham did, so that when you two grow up, your children will have a country of their own."

Back in their small cottage, Tevye listened as his grandchildren recited the words of the bedtime *Shema*, the time-honored affirmation of faith, *"Hear O Israel, the Lord our God, the Lord is one."* Then he kissed them goodnight, blew out the candle, and sat quietly in the darkness with them until they had fallen asleep.

Chapter Nineteen

A TRAIL OF TOMATOES

The indefatigable woodchopper, Goliath, provided the posts and slats for the fence which the settlers began erecting around the kibbutz. Ben Zion adamantly opposed the idea, claiming a fence would turn the settlement into a ghetto and curtail any further expansion.

"If the fence is intended to keep our enemies out, I have a better way," Ben Zion declared, holding up his rifle. "And if the fence is intended to keep us inside its borders, we left the ghettos of Europe and Russia behind us. Fences are for frightened people. If we want to build a proud and brave nation, we have to start acting like one."

While even the philosopher, Gordon, said that Ben Zion was right, Perchik insisted on honoring the agreement, arguing that they could purchase additional land when their economic situation improved. To keep Shoshana's end of the bargain, he arranged for a loan from the older, more established Degania kibbutz on the southern shore of the Sea of Galilee. Several days later, the goodwill money was paid to the Arabs.

As it turned out, peace was achieved on another front as well. Miraculously, Tevye did not have to go to war with Bat Sheva. She apologized on her own. She confessed that she loved Ben Zion, but she was not going to run after him like a chicken without a head. Until he was ready to marry her, she did not want to see him again.

"Hodel is right," she said. "Ben Zion is so in love with himself, he doesn't have room in his heart for anyone else."

So that's what caused the turnaround, Tevye thought. Thank the good Lord. Bat Sheva had been speaking with her sister. That was a smart thing to do. As King Solomon said, "Wisdom comes from increased advice." The girl had some intelligence and *sechel* after all. What a pity that Hodel herself had not confided in someone before running off with her own egotistical *shpritzer.*

"He will never have any respect for me if I don't first have respect for myself," Bat Sheva said.

Tevye was pleased to hear his little girl speak with such common sense. If he had uttered the very same words, Bat Sheva would have protested and bolted angrily from the house. In retrospect, Tevye realized that he should have been more patient with his other daughters. With a little more tolerance and trust on his part, they might have been less rebellious.

It seemed that any day now Hodel would have to give birth. Her belly was so swollen, when she walked, she waddled back and forth like a duck. If she sat down in a chair, she needed help getting up. With a feeling of great expectation, Tevye drove his wagon out to the fields for another morning's work. Who could tell? Perhaps his Hodel would give birth to a boy. A year ago in Anatevka, who would have dreamed of celebrating a *brit milah* in the very Land where the covenant of circumcision between God and the Jewish people had been forged?

The day's chore was to harvest the tomatoes which had been planted in a rocky field at an edge of the settlement. Because there was no private ownership on the kibbutz, Tevye's wagon had been appropriated to serve the needs of the community. He had reluctantly agreed, with the stipulation that he be the only driver. And he made it clear to the appropriations committee that if he were to leave the kibbutz, the wagon would depart with him.

As usual, the kibbutzniks riding in his wagon sang happy songs about Zion and about the glory of working the Land. Spirits were especially high in expectation of the harvest ahead. What greater joy for a farmer than gathering the fruits of his labor? Imagine everyone's shock upon reaching the field of tomatoes and finding every vine bare! The tomatoes had already been picked! Not a vegetable remained on a stalk. The shattered fence and fresh wagon tracks leading north toward the Arab camp were clues any blind man could read. During the night, while the Jews of Shoshana were sleeping, the Arabs had come and harvested the entire crop.

After rounding up a troop of armed *shomrim*, the Jews started off in pursuit. Ben Zion rode at the head of the cavalry. Ironically, his soldiers looked as much like Arabs as the Arabs did themselves. If Tevye had been in the middle of a battle, he wouldn't have known in which direction to shoot. The *shomrim* had adopted the white blouses, *kefiah* headdress and head band to show that the Jews were an indigenous part of the Land, and not out-of-place looking Russians. Until the *shomer* groups had been organized, the Arabs had nicknamed the unarmed pioneers "Sons of Death," because their kibbutzim were so vulnerable to attack. More than a few Jewish land surveyors had been found murdered in the hills, and Bedouin highwaymen made traveling a risky affair. At first, to protect themselves, the Zionists had hired Arabs to guard their isolated enclaves, but when pillage and theft became an almost nightly occurrence, the new Jewish immigrants realized that they would have to defend their settlements by themselves.

As if to make the chase after the tomato thieves easier, the culprits had left a trail of discarded, insect-eaten tomatoes which a child could have followed. Driving his wagon over the primitive terrain, Tevye winced every time its wheels hit a bump. Surprisingly, the thieves had not taken their booty to their camp. At a crossroad, the trail of bruised tomatoes continued westward toward the sea. Ben Zion reasoned that the Arabs were taking the harvest straight to the port city of Acco, where the fresh vegetables would command a higher price. At his urging, the Jews kept in hot pursuit. Before long, they caught up with their harvest. Two wagons piled high with tomatoes, and accompanied by a half dozen Arab women on foot, rumbled slowly along the road. Apparently, the women had done the looting while the armed drivers had stood guard. Ben Zion fired a shot in the air, and the kidnapped tomatoes came to a halt. Clearly outnumbered by the rifled *shomrim*, the drivers held up their hands in surrender. The women started screaming in high-pitched, hysterical wails. They pelted the

Jews with tomatoes. Tevye was hit in the head. The barrage ended only when the kibbutzniks retreated out of range, not out of fear, but to salvage their precious crop.

"What do you want with us?" one of the drivers called out.

"We want our tomatoes," Ben Zion answered.

"The tomatoes are ours," the Arab said. "They grew in our fields."

"We had an agreement," Mendelevitch declared. "You promised to keep away from our crops."

The Arab shook his head. "There was never any agreement."

"What?!" the startled kibbutz treasurer asked. "I was there. I witnessed the payment. If you don't believe me, we will go and speak with the sheik."

"The sheik has moved his tribe to the Negev," the Arab informed.

Mendelevitch was speechless. He stared open mouthed at Ben Zion.

"Tell them, Tevye," he muttered. "You were there. Tell them you saw the sheik promise to keep his people away from our fields."

Before Tevye could answer, another barrage of tomatoes came flying through the air like miniature red cannonballs. The Arab women had snuck back within range. Ben Zion fired a shot over the heads of the screaming women, frightening them away. His white blouse was stained crimson with tomato paste as if he had been shot in the heart.

"I should shoot one of them to teach them a lesson," he said. "If only to get even for Peter."

He raised his rifle and aimed at the driver who had done all of the talking.

"Wait," Mendelevitch shouted. "I say we speak to the Turkish *Habok*. He's in charge of this region. Before we act on our own, we should notify the Turkish authorities. It's their job to settle this matter."

The office of the local *Habok* was a good three-hour ride down the mountain at the base of Lake Kinneret.

"It will take us all day," Ben Zion said. "Besides, we have talked long enough. Perchik's peace is a joke. They have stolen our money. They have stolen our harvest. They have stolen our well. What other outrages are we to tolerate before we strike back?"

"We can't just shoot them," another kibbutznik said. "I think Mendelevitch is right. Let the *Habok* or the Turkish magistrate deal with the Arabs."

Surprisingly, Ben Zion's friend, Ari, agreed.

"It sounds like a sensible plan," he said. "I think we should give it a try. What do you say, Tevye?"

To Tevye's way of thinking, if the Turkish officials were anything like the commissioners of the Czar, appealing to them for assistance was a total waste of time. Then again, violating the commandment not to murder was out of the question. Of course, if someone tried to kill you, it was a man's duty to rise up and kill the assailant first. But for the theft of tomatoes, as far as Tevye recalled from his studies, the death penalty didn't apply.

"I suggest that we take their horses and the two wagons with the tomatoes and return to the kibbutz," he said. "That should teach them a lesson."

"Here here," Ari agreed.

Mendelevitch wasn't convinced.

"What's to stop them from going to the *Habok* themselves and claiming we stole their wagons? In the name of the peace initiative which the kibbutz membership voted upon, I insist on handing this matter over to the official authorities."

Once again, Ben Zion's desire for revenge was frustrated. Glum faced, he stood aiming his gun at the Arabs while Mendelevitch galloped off to fetch the Turkish district magistrate. The scene remained frozen that way for ten minutes. Then, fed up with waiting, the Arab women picked up their long skirts and began walking away. Ben Zion's threats and shots in the air didn't faze them. Either they knew he wouldn't shoot them, or they simply didn't care. Even when his bullets exploded the dirt at their feet, they kept walking back to their village.

"They will bring reinforcements," he warned.

"You can't shoot them – they're women," Tevye said.

Frustrated, Ben Zion lowered his rifle. He ordered the Arab drivers to turn the wagons around and head back toward the kibbutz.

"There is no point in waiting here," he said. "If their friends try to come to their rescue, it's better for us to be back at the kibbutz where we can strengthen our forces."

The Turkish *Habok* was the chief of police in the area. The magistrate was above him in power, but the magistrate was more like a governor, in charge of the district in an administrative way. When disputes arose involving the local populace, it was the *Habok's* job to find a solution. Punishments included fines, imprisonment, and expulsion from the country. Occasionally cases were brought to court. Matters of an especially sensitive nature, such as the dealings of Baron Rothschild, were handled directly by the Turkish Military Governor of Palestine, the infamous Jamal Pasha.

The *Habok* in Tiberias had no great love for the Jews. But since Shoshana was isolated in the hills, the kibbutznikim rarely had dealings with him. Once a month, he would arrive at the kibbutz with several soldiers, as if on patrol of the area, to ask if they had any problems. The Jews treated him with a show of respect, since he could order the destruction of buildings which the settlers erected in excess of the quotas designed to keep Zionist expansion to a minimum. Accordingly, the kibbutz council leaders would pour him glasses of wine until a suitable feast could be cooked. Finally, after gulping down all of the food set before him, and receiving some generous gift, he would rise from the dining-hall table and lead his men back to Tiberias.

Accompanied by Mendelevitch and three Turkish soldiers, the *Habok* arrived in Shoshana wearing his official white uniform with shining buttons, polished boots, and a tall red turban on his head. Ben Zion related the story in all of its details, including the wounding of Peter, and the argument over the wells. As Perchik stood silently listening with a serious look on his face, Ben Zion told the *Habok* about the agreement the kibbutz had made with the sheik, and how the Arabs had broken its terms. Before doing anything else, the Turkish official dismounted from his horse and walked to a wagon to squeeze a few red-ripe tomatoes. Polishing a choice sample on the side of his jacket, he opened his mouth and took a big bite.

"This is indeed a very fine tomato," he said. "How much are you asking?"

"For his honor, the *Habok*, I am sure we can reach a fair price," Mendelevitch answered.

The *Habok* turned to the Arabs who were sitting on the ground in the shade of the wagon, their hands tied behind their backs.

"This property belongs to the Jews," he declared. "Their deed to this land is one-hundred percent legal, certified by the Director General of the Imperial Land Office in Constantinople. For your criminal theft of the tomatoes, I am fining you with the loss of your wagons, horses, and rifles, and one of you will have to come back with me to sit out a term in the Tiberias jail."

One of the Arabs starting yelling. Angrily, he jumped to his feet. The *Habok* nodded to his soldiers. They rushed forward and grabbed the prisoner, silencing his shouts with a punch to the stomach and a quickly tied gag.

"Another outburst like that and I will put both of you in prison for attacking an officer of the Turkish Government," the *Habok* threatened.

"There is also the money we paid to the sheik as a gesture of goodwill when we made the agreement," Ben Zion said. "The Arabs insist he took off for the Negev, no doubt with our funds. It seems to me that some additional compensation is in order to cover our loss."

"If he took off for the Negev, there is nothing I can do," the *Habok* replied. "That is not in my jurisdiction. You will have to deal with the matter yourselves, but you should know that the Negev is a very big desert. It may be impossible to find him. I suggest the next time you think about signing an agreement with Arabs, you come see me first before scattering your money to the wind."

Ben Zion glanced at Perchik with an "I told you so" expression.

"But to be sure that these Arabs are telling the truth, I will send one of my men with you to their village to see if the sheik is still there."

The Turkish police chief stepped over to Mendelevitch to exchange a few private words. Mendelevitch listened, nodded his head, then stepped away to confer with Ben Zion and Perchik. Finally, an agreement was reached. The *Habok* saluted and headed back to Tiberias with a wagon load of tomatoes at almost half their market price. His profit from their sale in Tiberias would make him a rich man until the next harvest in the spring. Mendelevitch insisted that the loss of revenue was justified if the bribe would put an end to the kibbutz's quarrel with the Arabs. Besides, the Jews were getting the two wagons and horses, not to mention the rifles. And, last but not least, it paid to have the Turkish official as their friend.

Without untying the hands of the Arab driver whom the *Habok* had left behind, Ben Zion gave him a solid kick in the rear and sent him stumbling on his way back to his village. A group of Jews set off with the Turkish soldier to see what had become of the sheik. But just as the Arabs had said, the sheik was nowhere to be found. The questions of the Turkish soldier only brought silence and blank, expressionless stares from the shepherds who remained in the few remaining tents. An elder smoking a water pipe confirmed that the sheik had gone south to the Negev, but in answer to Perchik's question, where in the Negev, the old shepherd could only respond with a shrug and a cloud of sweet-smelling smoke.

The Turkish soldier said that as far as he was concerned, the case was closed. There was nothing more to be done. Perchik was seething with frustration as they headed back to the kibbutz.

"Don't take it so hard, Perchik," Ben Zion chided. "Anyone can make a mistake. But it does look like Tevye's Bible stories are more accurate than your dreams of fraternity and peace."

Perchik didn't answer. True, his "sons of the desert" had turned out to be a caravan of thieves, but he was loath to abandon his belief in the potential brotherhood of man.

The incident taught Perchik a lesson. Now, when Ben Zion insisted that more men were needed for guard duty, he didn't argue that the manpower was better put to use in the fields. While the *shomrim* reclaimed the well for the Jews, the loss of the harvest, and the loan which had to be repaid, were blows to the young kibbutz. Perchik's star plummeted among the kibbutznikim, and Ben Zion's influence began to be more and more dominant.

For Tevye, life on the kibbutz returned to normal. If it could be called normal to have a grandson born in the Land of Israel! Throughout the labor, Hodel hollered as if the house was on fire, but, thank God, when it was over, both the mother and baby were healthy. It was an event of great celebration, not only for Tevye, but for everyone on the kibbutz. To their way of thinking, the newborn was the cooperative's child, not the exclusive possession of the parents. Thus everyone participated in the joy of the birth.

Tevye couldn't recall the last time he had drank so many "*L'Chaims*," and the child's *brit milah* was still eight days away! Since he was more concerned than anyone else that the *mitzvah* be carried out properly, Tevye volunteered to ride to Tiberias to notify a qualified *mohel*. A circumcision was not a job for any ordinary *klutz* with a knife. It required a delicate, experienced hand. Tevye half-expected Perchik to protest that a *brit milah* was a cruel and primitive rite, but the happy new father didn't express a word of objection. No matter how far a Jew was from observing the Torah, a circumcision was the mark of his heritage, binding him to the holy covenant which Abraham had entered into with God .

Since Tevye was already in Tiberias, he decided to spend the night in the beautiful lakeside city and have a good kosher meal at the home of the town's only Ashkenazic rabbi. In the morning, he prayed in a *minyan*. An enterprising Jew approached him and offered to take him on a visit to the holy gravesites of the great medieval scholar, Maimonides, and the famous Sage of the Talmud, Rabbi Meir Baal HaNess. For a few *piasters*, of course.

Tevye gladly assented. It was only because of great Sages like these that the Torah had survived through the centuries of persecutions, assimilations, and pogroms. If a Jew cut himself off from his past, he had nothing to pass on to the future.

"Oh God," Tevye prayed, bending over their graves. "In the merit of these great Rabbis, and all of the Torah they learned, please bless my new grandson, the son of Hodel and Perchik, and bless Moishe and Hannie, the children of Tzeitl and Motel, and let them grow up to be filled with a love for Your commandments. May they see Your Temple rebuilt in Jerusalem, and may they witness the coming of the *Mashiach*. Amen."

The night before the *brit*, Tevye sat awake studying Torah in Hodel's house to keep away evil spirits. Outside, another sort of guarding was supposed to be taking place – the guarding of the kibbutz. Ben Zion, who was in charge of security, had arranged for Sonia to be his partner for the night. To rest from their rounds along the fence's perimeter, Ben Zion suggested they share a cigarette in the dark tool shed which was located at the edge of the colony.

"Is this where you take Bat Sheva?" Sonia asked as he led her inside.

"Bat Sheva? Who has anything to do with Bat Sheva?" he answered.

Striking a match, he lit the wick of a lantern and hung it over a nail in the wall.

"You can't fool me," Sonia said. "I see the way you look at her."

"It's your imagination. Besides, I would much rather look at you."

"Truthfully?"

"Truthfully."

Not for the first time, he took the girl in his arms and kissed her. Without letting her go, he backed her against the wall of the shed. Tools fell to the ground with a clang. She pretended to put up a struggle, but her protests fell on deaf ears. At first, when he felt the sharp metal blade rip into his back, he thought that Sonia had stabbed him. Then when she screamed, he knew that he had made the same mistake once again. The Arab standing by the door of the shed glared in hatred and fled. Ben Zion heard Arab voices and footsteps running away. He reached for his rifle, but his hands had no strength. Falling forward, he collapsed into her arms.

"Get help," he gasped.

Unable to hold him, she clumsily eased him down to the ground. Blood covered her hands. Terrified, she ran out of the shed. Her screams brought everyone out of their houses. "Ben Zion has been stabbed! Ben Zion has been stabbed!" she called out again and again.

Without closing the book he was studying, Tevye ran out of the house.

"Where is he?" he yelled.

"In the tool shed."

Bat Sheva and Hava appeared in their robes.

"How could it be?" Hava asked.

Bat Sheva stared at Sonia and instantly knew. Her heart sank like a stone cast into a bucket of water. Shuddering, she ran after her father toward the tool shed. Tevye was the first one to reach the wounded Ben Zion. He had crawled out from the shed and collapsed, clutching the earth he revered. A knife handle stuck out of his back. Perchik came running and knelt down beside him. With his last waning strength, Ben Zion gazed up at his comrade and rival.

"Some peace agreement," he said.

Then, invisibly, his soul flew out of his body. The once strong, passion-filled Zionist lay dead. A circle of settlers gathered around them. Bat Sheva pushed through to the front. Seeing the knife in Ben Zion's back, she gasped out in horror.

"Don't look," Tevye said, standing up. Embracing his daughter, he led her away from the crowd.

Perchik yelled to saddle up the horses. Someone shouted for the wagon. Men ran in all directions. The emergency bell clanged. Gently, Tevye handed Bat Sheva over to Hava.

"Take her home," he said.

"Where are you going," Hava asked.

"With the others," Tevye answered.

This time he was ready to fight. So was Perchik. With determination in their eyes, they rode off with all of the armed men they could muster. Carrying torches, they galloped through the darkness like a wave of fire. The rumble of their horses echoed through the hills. Before reaching the Arab village, Perchik raised up his hand, signaling the war party to halt. Half of the group, he commanded, would circle around and attack from the rear. After the lead charge, the others would follow and set fire to the tents with their torches. But when the Jews reached the top of the hill overlooking the valley, there were no tents in sight. The encampment had vanished.

"They've gone," Mendelevitch exclaimed.

Perchik was silent. Torchlight flickered over his grim, clean-shaven jaw.

"Like thieves in the night," Abramson said. "Ben Zion was right."

"My God," Ari said quietly. "Here we are in our own country and still they attack us and kill us."

Tevye was pensively silent.

The following day, a few hours after Ben Zion was laid to rest in the Shoshana cemetery, Hodel's baby boy entered into the covenant of Abraham. Perchik wanted to postpone the circumcision, but Tevye told him that unless a baby was ill, the *brit* had to take place on the eighth day after his birth. The ceremony was solemn, overshadowed by the tragedy of the murder. Draped in a prayer shawl, Tevye, the *sandek*, held the baby in his lap while the *mohel* from Tiberias made the cut of circumcision. Perchik recited the words of the blessing, and his son became a link in a four-thousand-year old chain of tradition.

The *mohel* chanted the traditional verses, "By your blood you shall live. By your blood you shall live."

By the blood of circumcision, a symbol of the bond between the Jewish people and God, the bond which gave the Jews the strength to persevere over all of their enemies and seemingly unending misfortunes.

The baby was named Ben Zion.

Chapter Twenty

ZICHRON YAACOV

With the birth of Hodel's baby, the time had come for Tevye to journey onward. Family was a matter of tantamount importance, but a Jew had an even higher allegiance to God. Had not the Almighty warned that life in the Holy Land must be lived according to the commandments of the Torah? That meant observing the laws of the Sabbath and the holidays, eating kosher food, donning *tallit* and *tefillin*, guarding the treasures of marital purity, and observing all of the six-hundred and thirteen commandments – most of which were flagrantly ignored by the young pioneers on the kibbutz. True, they were good, idealistic souls, risking their lives, and giving up material comforts to build a refuge in Israel for the Jews all over the world. Their dedication to making the barren Land bloom was in itself an act of great religious faith, but, to Tevye's way of thinking, faith in working the Land wasn't enough. Ultimately, a Jew had to live by the Torah. It was enough of a tragedy that his daughter, Hodel, had been led astray by her husband – Tevye now had to think of Moishe and Hannie, who were bound to be influenced by the other children on the kibbutz. And it was wise, Tevye felt, to whisk Bat Sheva away before she fell victim once again to her passions and grow enamored with some other free-spirited hero.

After Ben Zion's funeral, the heartbroken girl plunged into a gloomy silence. Tevye also felt troubled. The cold-blooded killing weighed on his mind like an omen. He wondered what would be with the Arabs. True, in his travels through the country, Arab villages were few and far between. Occasional caravans would pass along the road, and Bedouin shepherds would appear now and then in the landscape. But as picturesque as they were to Perchik,

Tevye had learned that, like snakes in the roadside, their bites could prove fatal.

Driving his wagon along the trail through the mountains toward Zichron Yaacov, where Shmuelik and Hillel were living, Tevye found himself engaged in deep thought. He even imagined that the Baron Rothschild had invited him into his palatial office to discuss the dilemma of establishing a large Jewish population in the midst of hostile neighbors.

"Well, my respected Reb Tevye, how do you propose we deal with the Arab situation?" the Baron asked in his daydream.

Tevye stood by the large globe of the world in the center of the Baron's wood-paneled study. Gently spinning the orb, his fingers slid over continents as he pondered his response. Tevye's footprints, muddied from the barn, had left dark stains in the carpet, but the Baron hadn't seemed to notice. Why should he? With a staff of round-the-clock servants, why should the dirt of an honest, hard-working milkman disturb him?

"I must confess that I am not a political analyst, but only a simple laborer," Tevye responded.

"Even a simple laborer has opinions," the Baron said. "And I respect the opinions of every man."

"My opinions are the teachings of our Sages, and the pearls of wisdom which I have learned from the Torah."

"And what does the Torah say on this matter?" the Baron inquired.

Before Tevye could answer, the famous philanthropist held out a mahogany humidor filled with fragrant cigars. Tevye took one and allowed the Baron to graciously light it.

"The Torah says that the Arabs are to dwell in the lands of the Arabs, and the Jews are to dwell in the Land of the Jews."

"The Torah was written a long time ago. Perhaps political equations have changed."

"The word of the Lord is forever," Tevye answered. "The sons of Ishmael have been blessed with lands of their own. The Land of Israel belongs to the Jews."

"Your faith has strengthened me, Tevye," the Baron said. "Your faith has strengthened me indeed."

Of course, daydreams are daydreams, and life is life. True, Tevye generally had mud on his boots, but if Baron Edmond de Rothschild ever summoned him to a chat, his secretary forgot to deliver the message. In fact, the Baron was not to be found in Zichron Yaacov at all. He ruled over his Palestine colonies from his castles in France. *"Av HaYishuv,"* the settlers called him. "Father of the Settlement." Others called him *"HaNadiv,"* meaning, "The Benefactor," after his beneficent ways. Still others called him less pleasant names. His dignified portrait hung in the JCA office, above the heads of the officials who carried out his commands. Under the dark Homberg hat in the picture was a hawkish profile, patriarchal whiskers, a benevolent smile, and a fur-collared coat. Tevye, who fancied himself a fair judge of character, understood right away that the Baron was a unique individual, deserving great respect. As for the bald-headed Frederick Naborsky, Director of the Jewish Colony Association in Palestine, Tevye was less convinced of the sterling nature of his personality.

"We are not interested in giving handouts to *schnorrers* and beggars," he said at the beginning of their interview in the Company Director's plush office when Tevye arrived in Zichron. "Our settlements are not havens for paupers. We are not settling up *shtetls* of the past, but showplaces of the future, where Jews are to live useful lives. With all due respect to tradition, the final word does not lie with the rabbi, but with the Company. The Baron decides what will be, and we, his executives, are entrusted to enforce his decrees. I presume this is clear?"

His small beady eyes peered over his eyeglasses at Tevye. Tevye nodded his head, just as Shmuelik and Hillel had coached him.

"At the moment, we are in the process of acquiring several new settlement sites. New seed groups will be venturing out to start new colonies when all of the legalities are completed. In the meantime, you and your family can find temporary housing in Zichron."

Again Tevye nodded.

"You will be expected to sign an oath of allegiance to the Company, and to obey all of the conditions stipulated therein, as follows...."

Naborsky adjusted his spectacles on his nose and read from a document.

"I hereby agree to submit myself totally to the orders which the administration shall deem necessary in the name of Monsieur Le Baron in anything which concerns the cultivation of the land, and if any action be taken against me as penalty for any infraction, or for the benefit of the settlement, I have absolutely no right to oppose it...."

Tevye's attention drifted away in the middle of the long recitation. He kept nodding his head, wondering what the difference was between the servitude of the Company, or, *l'havdil*, on the other extreme, the servitude demanded by the Czar. Still, the rulers of the Company were, for the most part, Jews, and the motherland they were to cultivate was Israel, not Russia. What could you do, Tevye thought? Just like an ox had a yoke, so did a poor Jew. Company, shmompany. The real yoke was the yoke of the Lord. Emperors, Caesars, Czars, and Barons came and went, but the Kingdom of God was forever. What did it matter what was written in the document which the Company Director was reading? A Jew's first and only allegiance was to his Maker.

"Is this understood," Naborsky asked.

Again Tevye nodded his head.

"Can you write?"

"Write what?" Tevye asked.

"Your name."

"In Russian, Yiddish, and Hebrew."

"Either one will suffice," the Company official said, holding out the document for Tevye to sign. He pointed to a line at the bottom of the page. Tevye took the quill pen and inscribed his full name in Hebrew – Tevye, the son of Reb Schneur Zalman.

The Zichron Yaacov settlement was the Jewish Colony Association's model *yishuv*. Located along the Mediterranean coastline between the seaports of Acco and Jaffa, it enjoyed well-travelled land routes and mild weather throughout most of the year. Over two hundred families already lived there, in quaint little houses situated along manicured, tree-lined streets. Like in Anatevka, there were cobblers, tailors, blacksmiths, bakers, a milkman, a rabbi, and even a matchmaker, but unlike the *shtetls* and Jewish villages which Tevye had known, most of the Jews in Zichron Yaacov squeezed out their livelihood by farming the land. Workers with caps on their head labored in the fields, using an assortment of reapers and plows. The sweet smell of pressed grapes wafted over the settlement from the winery. The valley of Zichron Yaacov produced barrels and barrels of Rothschild wine which were exported all over the world. Acres and acres of vineyards spread out to the north and south as far as the eye could see. In a good vintage year, the revenue from wine sales filled the colony's coffers, giving the Baron hope that his costly and ambitious Zionist enterprise might one day prove self-sustaining and even a financial success.

If not for the two-story building located in a remote corner of the colony, far away from the houses and workshops, Zichron Yaacov could have passed for a dream come true. The isolated building was the infirmary, serving all of the Jewish settlements in the country. Tevye and his family were sent there for health examinations on the first day of their arrival. Outside was a large frangipani tree with shining red flowers. The ground floor looked like a modern city hospital, with sparkling clean tiles, curtained examining rooms, and shining equipment. But a sign by the stairs, forbidding unauthorized personnel from entering, gave Tevye an uneasy feeling. In answer to his question, a doctor told him that the wards were filled with patients stricken with malaria, typhus fever, cholera, yellow fever, and what he simply termed the plague. Quarantined quarters and limited drugs such as quinine and sulfur were the only remedies the doctors could offer the ill. In a gesture of goodwill, the Baron provided health care and drugs free of charge, to Jews, Turks, and Arabs alike, but the infirmary's staff was ostensibly helpless in combating the scourge of diseases in the plague-ridden land. Tevye was stunned to learn that almost half of the Jewish settlers died from incurable ailments within their first few years in the country. Hillel morosely referred to the building as the "*Chevra Kadesha*," the society in charge of burying the dead.

"Thank you, dear God," Tevye said when the examination was over and he walked out of the building alive. Gratefully, he inhaled the wine-scented air. Rays of the sun warmed his face. His mother, may she rest in peace, had been right. Health, she always maintained, was the Almighty's most precious gift to man. Without a healthy body, a person might just as well be dead. He could have all of the money in the world, but if he had even a little headache, what good were all of his rubles?

"May we never have reason to step foot in there again," he said to his daughters, making sure they answered, "Amen."

Hava had other thoughts. Moved by the suffering of the sick people crowding the wards, she decided that she would volunteer to help in whatever way that she could. Seeing a notice on the infirmary bulletin board which announced the start of a course to train authorized nurses, she immediately inquired how she could register. It was an opportunity to do something useful while she waited for Hevedke to finish his yeshiva studies. Her father adamantly opposed, but she stuck to her decision. How could she only worry about herself when so many people were suffering?

"Let someone else help them," Tevye said.

"I know you really don't mean that, *Abba*," she answered. "After all, aren't you the one who taught me that a person is responsible for every other person, and that a man has to love his neighbor just as much as he loves himself."

Tevye mumbled.

"That's all well and good," he answered. "But the Torah was not talking about working in disease-infested hospitals.

"Someone has to do it," she said.

"Why does it have to be my daughter?"

"It's because I'm your daughter. Being kind to people is the first lesson you taught me."

Tevye clasped his hands in entreaty before her.

"I am proud that my daughter has such a big heart, but please my dear, Hava, I have lost my sweet Shprintza in the prime of her youth, drowned by a heartless suitor and a heartless lake. Another one of my treasures took off to America, and who knows if your father's tear-filled eyes will ever see her again? I have lost my wife, Golda, and your saintly sister, Tzeitl. Is a man made of stone? Is a heart made of granite? It is a wonderful thing to dream of saving the world, but think about your poor, miserable father."

His plea did not move her.

"Think about the man that you love," he urged, desperate to talk her out of her plan.

Hava looked at him quizzically. It was the first time her father had mentioned Hevedke's existence since their parting in Jaffa.

"I think of him all of the time," she said, "and I know that he would approve."

Tevye knew he was beaten. With a sigh, he raised his eyes up to Heaven, as if to say, "You have vanquished me again." At least, he thought, her crazy *meshugas* would only last a very short time, until they were assigned to one of the Baron's new colonies. Hillel and Shmuelik had already arranged a place for Tevye with a group of *Hasidim* who had banded together to start a *frum* religious community. The moment the land purchase was completed, the bearded pioneers would set off with the Company's blessings and aid. In the meantime, Tevye was given a Hebrew dictionary, written by a fellow named Eliezer ben Yehuda, and published by the Baron Edmond himself. On the Company Director's orders, he was enrolled in a Hebrew *ulpan* class to once again wrestle with the intricacies of Hebrew grammar, just like a young boy must struggle with *Rashi's* puzzling and unfamiliar script at the beginning of *Talmud Torah*.

After a meeting with the Zichron foreman, Lishansky, Tevye was given a new occupation. The locals called it "*sabalut*," but to Tevye it was plain and simple "*shlepping*." Twice a week, wagon loads of seeds, grains, dried fruit, and other staples arrived from Jaffa. The produce was stored in warehouses in Zichron Yaacov, apportioned, and shipped out to JCA settlements throughout the northern half of the country. It was Tevye's job to stand by a wagon, bent over like a hunchback, and catch a hundred-pound sack on his back. Then, like a beast of burden, he would carry the load to the warehouse and drop it onto the stacks. After his first day of work, he could barely straighten his spine. He complained to the foreman, begging him to transfer him to the barn and the cows, but the settlement already had two experienced milkmen. Lishansky, who seemed like a fair man to Tevye, promised to find him an occupation which demanded less lifting. When Shmuelik arrived that evening to take Tevye to Hebrew class, he found him lying flat on his back, moaning about his miserable lot.

"You know what the Midrash teaches about Moses?" Shmuelik began.

"I have a feeling you are going to tell me," Tevye said.

"When God refused to let Moses enter the Land of Israel because of a single sin, Moses got down on his knees and begged the Almighty to turn him into an ant if need be – just to enter the Holy Land. He didn't demand to be king, or a leader of the people. So great is the privilege of being in the Land of Israel, Moses pleaded to cross the border even as a bug."

"In other words, I should thank God for turning me into a bug who has to *shlepp* one-hundred-pound sacks on his back from morning till night."

"Moses would have been thrilled."

"We learn from this that Tevye is not Moses."

"Moses was not Moses either at first. When the Almighty first appeared to him at the burning bush, Moses begged Him to send someone else. It was only by arising to the challenge was his greatness revealed. Come on. Get up. We will be late for our class in Hebrew."

Leaning on Shmuelik like a staff, Tevye walked bent over to school, as if he were still lugging a sack of seed on his back. Within a matter of days, he learned how to shift the weight of the sacks to his legs, and the exercise actually helped strengthen his brittle milkman's bones. When Lishansky showed up with an offer to put Tevye to work behind a plow, Tevye had second thoughts. But when he learned that the plow had wheels and a seat, he took up the offer. Once again, Tevye was back to what seemed to be his lot in life, staring at the rump of a horse.

Shmuelik worked in the vineyards. Hillel was a packer of grapes, and Goliath became a maker of barrels. Bat Sheva worked on a sewing machine in a room filled with talkative women. Like a flower which closes its petals at night, she remained in mourning for Ben Zion. She was quiet, moody, and bitter, as if life had betrayed her. Tevye invited Shmuelik to their quarters, ostensibly to teach Moishe the Torah. He secretly hoped that an interest would develop between the scholar and his sullen daughter. While Shmuelik was ready to pursue such a match, Bat Sheva refused to grant him a smile.

For the first time since their arrival in the Promised Land, Tevye and his family sensed that they were establishing roots. Once again, Tevye prayed every day in a *minyan*. Every night before his class in Hebrew, he sat with Moishe and Hannie, told them a bedtime story, sang them a song, and made sure they recited *Shema Yisrael*. He insisted that the children speak to him in Hebrew, and that his daughters address him as *Abba*, not *Tata*. The first opportunity he had, he wrote a letter to Ruchel, describing their wanderings and Tzeitl's tragic death, including Tzeitl's last wish that the children grow up with her sister and Nachman. In closing, he promised to bring them to Rishon LeZion the very first vacation he had.

To Tevye's surprise, he received a reply from Ruchel a mere two weeks later. She wrote that they were very happy, and that Nachman was pleased with his work at the school. The news of Tzeitl's death had upset them deeply, and Ruchel prayed that God would give them the strength to carry on as if Tzeitl were still with them. As for Moishe and Hannie, Nachman had spoken to the colony manager, Dupont, to receive his permission, and he had refused. Adoption was against Company rules. Their friend, Aharon, had also tried to persuade him, but the heartless manager wouldn't be swayed. Ruchel herself had made his ears ring with an outburst of scorn, but his only response was that several other teachers had applied to him for jobs, and that if the children were so important to them, then she and Nachman could leave. Ruchel said she was seriously considering his suggestion. She had discussed her feelings with Nachman, and he was prepared to stand by whatever decision she made. Were there positions for teachers in Zichron Yaacov, she asked? She also inquired about the new Hasidic colony which her father had mentioned. When did he think the settlement would begin, and could he secure them a place on the list? While they were happy in Rishon Le Zion, they had left the Czar behind in Russia, and they were not going to let any Company clerk dictate the terms of their life. Lastly, there was a chance that Ruchel was pregnant.

The thought of being united with his Ruchel boosted Tevye's spirits. It seemed like his fortune might be taking a turn for the better. Who could tell? The Almighty worked in mysterious fashions. One day, He could snap a man's back like a twig, and the next day raise him up to sit at a table with kings. With a little *mazel*, things would work out for the best. Bat Sheva would marry Shmuelik. Hava would forget about Hevedke. Perchik would recognize his misguided path and become a penitent *baal tshuva*. Ruchel and Nachman would join them in building a new settlement. The *Mashiach* would come, and Golda, Tzeitl, Shprintza, Motel, and even Ben Zion would all arise from the dead.

Two weeks later, Tevye received a second letter from Ruchel. She had lost her pregnancy. The very same night in a dream, Tzeitl had appeared to her saying that Moishe and Hannie were waiting. Nachman had told her to go back to sleep. But an hour later, Tzeitl had returned with the very same message. "A dream which is repeated is true," Nachman said. The next morning, they had written a letter to the Baron Rothschild himself. If the Jewish Colony Association was truly Jewish, how could it turn its back on the *mitzvah* of caring for orphans? They would wait for the Baron's answer, Ruchel said, and if it were negative, then Tevye should plan to come to pick them up in his wagon.

Since he was writing a letter to Ruchel, Tevye decided to send a letter to his daughter, Baylke, in America. He did not know where she was, but his wife, Golda, may her memory be for a blessing, had a cousin in Chicago. Tevye had saved his address between the pages of his battered and yellowing Psalm book.

"Who knows?" Golda had said in her pragmatic manner. "Maybe you will need his address one day. We were never the closest of cousins, but family is family."

When Baylke set off for New York with her good-for-nothing husband, Tevye had given her the Chicago address and told her to write to their cousin to let him know where she was living. Not that his beautiful, headstrong daughter ever took his advice, but in a strange land like America, she might long for some family to remind her of home. Reb Heshie Mendel was his name, cousin of the same Menachem Mendel who had swindled Tevye out of the only savings he had ever managed to amass in his life. Tevye sent him a note, asking him to please forward the letter to Baylke if he knew where she was. Before sealing the envelope, he stuck a few blades of grass inside with the prayer that the blessing and holiness of *Eretz Yisrael* would bring good fortune into her life.

The new Hasidic colony was to be named Morasha, which meant inheritance in Hebrew. Two things in the Bible were called *Morasha* – the Torah, and the Land of Israel. These two foundations went hand in hand, as it said, "*Therefore you shall keep all of the commandments which I command you this day, that you may be strong, and go in and possess the Land which I give you as a Morasha, a land flowing with milk and honey.*"

Apparently, bureaucratic problems in Constantinople were holding up the purchase of the land which the JCA had offered to buy from the Turkish government. While many kibbutzim had been started in deserted regions by buying tracts of land from Arabs whose claims of ownership were based on the principle of squatters' rights, the Baron was meticulous in acquiring legal permission through all of the authorized channels. In the meantime, the small group of fifteen *Chabad Hasidim* met every week to draw up plans for the colony. They had been sent to *Eretz Yisrael* by their *Rebbe* to join in the great *mitzvah* of settling the Land.

One morning, Tevye joined the band of bearded Jews on a reconnoitering mission to the site, a half-day journey southeast of Zichron Yaacov. The land which the Company had chosen lay along the ridge of a mountain which rose over the coastal plain. When they reached the area, broad, rolling vistas stretched out before them, making their dreams of establishing a new colony a reality. Tevye fell to his knees and scooped up a handful of earth. Hillel opened a bottle of wine. Everyone drank a happy *L'Chaim*. Only Goliath sensed that something was missing. Among the novice settlers, he was the only Jew who had earned his livelihood outdoors in the wilds. Tevye was a milkman. Hillel, a musician. Shmuelik, a scholar. Reb Lazer, a tailor. Munsho, a blacksmith. Reb Shilo, a carpenter. Pincus, a storekeeper. Reb Shragi, a scribe. Yankele was a butcher and a *mohel*. And Chaim Lev, the Galitzianer from Poland, who had joined the group of Hasids, was a handyman and fixer. Only the big lumberjack knew how to read the layout of the land, and the first thing he noticed, or rather didn't notice, was water. Standing on a knoll overlooking the imaginary orchards before them, he noticed that there wasn't a brook in sight.

"Where is the water?" he asked.

Everyone turned toward Mr. LeClerc, the dapperly dressed, redheaded Company official assigned to oversee the founding of Morasha.

"That's the one drawback," he said. "There is an underground spring on the property, but it is a short distance away."

"How far?" Tevye asked.

"Not far at all," LeClerc said, not giving a definite answer.

"Let's go see it," Shmuelik suggested.

"We should be heading back," LeClerc advised, "in order to get back to Zichron Yaacov before nightfall."

"Where exactly is this spring?" Yankele, the butcher asked, taking a threatening step forward.

Like many butchers and *mohels*, he had been born with a heavy influence of Mars in his zodiac. His *mazel* was a portent of murder and blood. Fortunately, taking the Talmud's advice, Yankele had channeled his powerful passions into becoming a butcher and *mohel*. But he still had a menacing appearance. The JCA clerk stepped instinctively backwards. Munsho, the blacksmith, whose arms were like clubs, walked forward and stood beside the slaughterer. LeClerc turned toward his horse, only to run into Goliath. The three strapping settlers surrounded the Frenchman like towering cedars.

"Show us the spring!" the butcher demanded.

"It's four kilometers from here," LeClerc answered.

"Four kilometers!" Yankele repeated. "That is more than an hour's walk!"

"You can build your houses near the spring," LeClerc responded, becoming red in the face.

"What will that gain?" Goliath asked. "Then our fields will be an hour away."

"This is the land that is available for purchase."

"How are we supposed to irrigate our crops?" the blacksmith asked. "With our spit?"

Normally, the quip would have brought a round of chuckles, but the settlers were in no joking mood.

"There is a plan to build a canal which will connect the spring with the fields," the nervous Company official explained.

"The *Mashiach* will come first," Pincus, the storekeeper, said.

"What about the Arabs?" Tevye asked. "Are there Bedouin tribes in the area?"

"The closest Arab village is a few hours away. They have absolutely no claim to the land. That is one of the reasons why the Company has chosen this site."

"Land without water is like a forest without trees," Goliath, the lumberjack, said.

"And like a pen with no ink," the scribe added.

"And a chair with no legs," the fixer said.

"Or a cow with no udder," Tevye chimed in.

"When it is your money, you can buy whatever piece of property you like," the *pakid*-clerk of the Baron answered. "In the meantime, since the Company is the only one undertaking the financial obligation, we decide where new settlements will be built."

"Anything to save a franc, is that it?" Reb Shilo said.

"Believe me," LeClerc replied, "if the Baron's main concern was money, he could find a lot more profitable enterprises than squandering his millions in this godforsaken land."

"A godforsaken land? *Chas v'shalom*," Tevye said angrily. "How can you say such a thing?"

Until then, Tevye had imagined that LeClerc was a Jew, but now he realized that a neatly-trimmed beard and a derby hat did not make a person a rabbi. Instinctively, he glanced up to Heaven. How long were gentiles to rule over his life?

"No one promised you that building a new settlement would be easy," LeClerc declared.

That was true, Tevye thought. Even their forefather, Isaac, had encountered problems with the Philistines over water and wells. In the same way that the Patriarchs had trusted in God, the builders of Morasha would have to put their faith in God too.

Until the awaited date arrived when the *Hasidim* could set out to plant their first seeds on the Morasha site, Tevye plowed acres of furrows in the fields of Zichron Yaacov. In the evenings, he forced his weary brain to learn conversational Hebrew. During the six months which passed waiting for the land purchase to clear, Hava received a certificate of nursing. Tevye shuddered every time she set off to the infirmary, and he studied the color of her cheeks every time she came home. She spoke with great satisfaction about patients who recovered, and though she never mentioned the dead, Mendelson, the tombstone maker, was kept constantly busy. And there were weeks on end when Reb Guttmacher, the undertaker, was called out from his quarters each day to prepare a body for burial.

"I was worried about leaving Russia," he confided to Tevye. "At least with all of the pogroms and *tzuris*, I had a good livelihood there. But, to my great dismay, there is more business here."

When an outbreak of typhoid fever swept through the country, claiming victims in every *yishuv*, Reb Guttmacher raised his hands up to Heaven and said, "*Dai*. It's enough."

One day, he seized a hold of Tevye's sleeve and pulled him aside.

"Tevye," he said. "I am tired of digging holes for the dead. In the time I have left in this world, with whatever strength I still have, I want to dig holes for the living. Take me with you to this new settlement you are starting. Put me to work in the fields. Give me a shovel and let me plant trees. If it's a canal you need, I can do the work of three men. Please, I need to feel a part of the future, not only the past."

Thus the undertaker joined the group of Hasidic pioneers.

For weeks on end, wagon loads of sick people arrived at the infirmary. Hava often had to work day and night. When the plague reached its zenith, the hospital staff was quarantined in tents and separated from the rest of the colony. Tevye dreaded seeing Reb Guttmacher the undertaker, fearing that one day he would be the harbinger of bad news, God forbid, regarding his daughter, Hava. Other nurses perished, but in God's mercy, Hava was spared.

In the midst of the epidemic, a letter arrived from Ruchel. The Baron had written them a sincere apology. He was outraged by the callous disregard for the welfare of the children which the Director of Rishon LeZion had displayed. The Baron personally asked their forgiveness on behalf of the Company. Dupont was instructed to rescind his refusal, and the orphans were to be welcomed as full-fledged members of the Rishon community. A personal check of 5,000 francs was included in the letter to cover whatever expenses the family might have in raising the children. To Ruchel and Nachman, it was a fortune of money.

True to the Baron's promise, Dupont came to the house and apologized for having misunderstood the Company policy. The children, he said, were free to join the colony. So now, Ruchel wrote, there was nothing to prevent Tevye from bringing Moishe and Hannie to Rishon.

When the next wagon train of wine barrels was sent off to Jaffa for export, Tevye set his wagon in the rear of the caravan. He packed the children's few belongings and hoisted them up into the seat beside him. Goliath rode with them to fulfill his graveside promise to Tzeitl. With tears in their eyes, Bat Sheva and Hava hugged Moishe and Hannie good-bye. Hava walked alongside the wagon, not letting go.

"You promise me you will go to see Hevedke?" she asked her father imploringly.

Tevye only grumbled.

"Promise me," she begged.

"If I can," he said, refusing to make a commitment.

"Please, *Abba*, please."

Tevye stared down at her eyes, the same eyes as her mother. They reached out and tugged at his heart.

"We shall see," he said.

Bat Sheva cried. The departure of the children was particularly heartbreaking for Tevye's youngest daughter. For months, Bat Sheva had been like a mother to them, feeding them, dressing them, washing their clothes, teaching them to read, and telling them bedtime stories. Though she could never replace their mother, she gave them all of the love she could give. The volcano of emotions which she had harbored for Ben Zion found an outlet in her care of the children. A new feeling of mature responsibility had begun to guide her actions. But now that Moishe and Hannie were leaving, she felt a hole in her heart once again. A feeling of blame seized her. After all, if she had been married, the children could have stayed in her care. Was that the meaning of Hillel's look when he turned to stare at her as the wagon rolled away down the road? Is that what Shmuelik was thinking when he passed her by without glancing up from his book, as she walked sullenly back to the house? They were both good, honest men. Why was she afraid of them both? Why had she run after a man who hadn't loved her, and run away from others who did? In the suddenly quiet, empty house, she felt lost and alone.

Chapter Twenty-One

THE REUNION

The journey from Zichron Yaacov to Jaffa took almost three days. For Tevye, it was a chance to see another part of the Land of Israel, the sandy, swamp-infested coastline bordering the Mediterranean Sea. Most of the landscape was barren, with only an occasional settlement along the way. The colonies of Hadera, Kfar Saba, and Petach Tikvah were like oases where the Jews could find a prayer *minyan* and stock up on supplies. Otherwise, the land lay in abandonment and ruin. Toward the end of the third day, the movement of ships out to sea told them that they were nearing the busy port city of Jaffa. In the distance, they could see the hill overlooking the harbor and the tower of the citadel which had been built during the Crusades. At the outskirts of the city, a new village consisting of rows of wooden houses and tents was being constructed on the beach. Someone said it was called Tel Aviv.

"Are they Jews?" Tevye asked.

"Free thinkers," one of the winery workers said in a deprecatory tone.

"Free-thinking Jews," Lishansky, the Zichron work foreman added, out of respect for all pioneers.

"You can't be free thinking and still be a Jew," the religious wine worker said.

"You can't be a Jew without being free thinking," Lishansky corrected, enjoying a little intellectual debate to pass the monotony of the journey.

"A Jew is obligated to do what God instructs him to do," Tevye argued.

"That may be true," Lishansky agreed. "But that in itself is the greatest freedom."

The clang and pounding of hammering punctuated their talmudic discussion. Stone buildings and wooden frames were being erected along a dirt roadway, which was to become Tel Aviv's main thoroughfare, Dizengoff Street. Within a short time, they reached the clustered dwellings of Jaffa, passed Rabbi Kook's neighborhood, and continued on to the Rothschild wine warehouse. Tired from the journey, Tevye decided to spend the night sleeping between the rows of barrels. For a wine connoisseur like Tevye, he couldn't have found a better hotel. The mosquitoes were merciless, but after purchasing a wholesale bottle of a vintage red brew, he managed to drift off to sleep. In the morning, Tevye and Goliath said so long to their comrades and kept heading south with the children. As they left the port city, a few settlers from Rishon hopped on the back of the wagon with bundles of food and supplies.

"Thank the Almighty," Tevye said, "for sending us angels to help guide us on our way."

"We are only simple Jews," one of them answered.

"Can there be such a thing?" Tevye asked, in a philosophical mood. "Aren't we all sons of the King?"

Moishe climbed into the front seat of the wagon and leaned sleepily against his grandfather. The mosquitoes in the warehouse had kept the boy awake all through the night. Not wanting to be left alone in the rear of the wagon with the strangers, Hannie followed after her brother and rested against Goliath's secure, sturdy frame. Soon they had left the bustling port city behind.

Arriving in Rishon LeZion after sunset, they found Ruchel and Nachman at home in their small wooden cottage. How ecstatic the young couple was to see them! Since their wedding, it was the first time that family had come for a visit. While Ruchel hurried to set freshly baked cakes on the table, Tevye and Goliath carried the sleeping children to a corner where a spare bed was waiting.

"I have ordered another bed from the carpentry shop," Nachman said, beaming with the happiness of a man who had found his niche in life. He even looked a little rounder around the belly, in praise of Ruchel's cooking.

"Sit, *Abba*, sit," he said to Tevye, motioning him to a chair. "You must be tired from the long journey. Please, by all means, take some cake. *Ess, ess.* Eat. Honor our house with a blessing over the food that God has so graciously given us."

The guests sat down at the small table to eat. The sweet, creamy pastry was just what Tevye longed for after the long dusty trail. A picture of the past flashed in his eyes as he remembered his wife, Golda, and the delicious cakes she always had waiting when he trudged home from work.

"Just like your mother used to make," he said. "May her memory be for a blessing."

"She taught me," Ruchel reminded him.

"A good thing for me," Nachman said. "You should know, Reb Tevye, that your daughter has opened a business. In honor of the Sabbath, she bakes the most delicious pastries and cakes, and sells them to our neighbors."

"As they say, like mother like daughter," Tevye replied. "Wasn't I known all over Russia as the milkman with the very finest cheese pastries?"

Their conversation extended late into the night. Tevye told them about their time in Shoshana, and their situation in Zichron Yaacov, and the happy young couple described their new life. Sliding an envelope out from beneath the tablecloth, Ruchel proudly showed her father the letter which the Baron had sent. The money he had sent for the children, she said, was safely locked away in the colony vault.

After an appetizing *forshbite* of pastries and a sip of some wine, Ruchel set plates of fresh, homegrown vegetables before them. Tevye's eyelids began to feel heavy. After the meal, he lied down on a mat beside the children and fell into a deep, dream-filled sleep. Sometimes a person remembers his dreams, and other times he doesn't, but the dreams he recalls often have meaning, if he separates the chaff from the wheat. In the middle of the night, Tevye found himself swimming in the ocean with whales.

Suddenly, one of the mammals opened its jaws and swallowed up him up with his wagon. Terrified, he landed with a thud in the creature's foul-smelling belly. Around him were piles of skeletons. To Tevye's surprise, he recognized their faces – Lazar Wolf, the butcher; Ephraim, the matchmaker; Jeremiah, the fishmonger; and his other friends from Anatevka. Everyone was there except Golda.

Tevye awoke in a sweat. The children slept peacefully. The door to the bedroom was closed. In the darkness, his hand scraped along the floor until he found the *yarmulkah* which had slipped off of his head.

"May the dream be for a blessing," he said.

Quietly, he slipped out of the house. Goliath was snoring under the wagon.

"May your dreams be more pleasant than mine," he whispered as he set off down the path toward the cemetery. How could he leave Rishon in the morning without first paying a visit to Golda? Passing a small garden in the yard of a house, he stopped and gazed at the flowers. How could he go to the grave of his wife without something in hand? Quickly, he looked left and right to see if someone were watching. As he reached out to break off a rose, his hand paused like a bee hovering over a petal before stealing its pollen. True, they weren't wildly growing flowers, but was it a sin to pick flowers for the *mitzvah* of honoring the dead? Isn't that what flowers were for? Tevye would actually be doing the owner of the garden a favor by doing a good deed with his roses. Still, to ease a guilty conscience, after snapping off a twig, he stuck a Turkish mark over a thorny branch to pay for the petty larceny.

"Okay?" he asked, looking up at the sky when he had concluded the transaction. Stem and flower in hand, he set off for the grave. It was an hour before sunrise, and the first rays of light were beginning to appear in the sky. He remembered the way to the cemetery along the path of tall eucalyptus trees. Gently, he set the modest bouquet on the simple slab of stone which marked the earthly abode of his wife.

"You won't mind me sitting down beside you, my sweet Golda," he said. "If I stand I will feel like I have to deliver a sermon, when the reason I have come is to be close to my dear wife."

Leaning his cheek against the tombstone, Tevye remembered the voyage to Israel and the extraordinary ordeal it had been to *shlepp* her coffin along. He recalled, with a shudder, how he had almost lost her, and how God, in his compassion, had commanded the waves of the ocean to return her to him. Then, with a sob, he remembered their sweet Tzeitl. It wasn't like Tevye to cry, but in a cemetery, he didn't have to worry that someone would notice.

"You're right," he said, as if his wife were sitting beside him. "It isn't my fault that Tzeitl wouldn't go to the hospital. No doubt, she is better off where she is up in Heaven than down here on this mosquito-filled planet called Earth. If you weren't already in *Gan Eden*, I might worry, but I know you will look out for her the way you looked out for all of us. Oh, how we miss you, dear Golda."

Once again, sleep overcame the road-weary settler. Without knowing it, he fell on his side alongside her grave.

"Good night, my sweet Tevye," his wife said.

Soon, his snores sounded over the cemetery. Imagine the surprise of a worker on the way to the fields when he heard Tevye's trumpeting and discovered a corpse lying above ground by a grave.

"Are you all right?" the husky voice asked.

Tevye sat up, blinking the sleep from his eyes. "Is it morning already?" he asked.

"The sun's in the sky."

"I must have fallen asleep here."

"I just wanted to make sure you weren't dead," the man said.

"Some days I feel that I am," Tevye answered.

"You should live until you are a 120 years old," the field worker responded, coining the age-old expression.

Tevye grumbled. That meant another seventy years of aggravation and toil. He stood up and brushed the dirt off his clothes. With a heavy heart, he headed back to colony. The day's task was one of the hardest he ever had to face – saying good-bye to the children. Already, he missed his little *kinderlach*. Hadn't he been like a father to them? Ever since Motel had died, Tevye had been the dominant man in their lives. He was more than their grandfather. But Tevye knew that the children needed a real home which only a husband and wife could provide. And, as their mother had wanted, with Ruchel and Nachman, they would grow up in a house filled with Torah.

When he returned to the house, the look in the children's eyes pierced Tevye's heart. He had been careful to hide from them the real reason for the visit, so when Ruchel had innocently told them that morning, they had received a grave shock. Ruchel might have been their aunt, but Tevye was, in their eyes, their father. How could they live without him? His presence was as vital to their existence as air. When he entered the house, they rushed at him passionately and grabbed a hold of his legs.

"I'm staying with you," Moishe said, clinging to his grandfather's pants.

"So am I," Hannie said.

Tevye bent down on one knee. "You can't, my sweet children," he said. "You need to be raised by a mother and father, not by a broken-down horse."

"You aren't a horse," Hannie said.

"If I had another two legs I would be," her grandfather answered.

"I'll run away," Moishe threatened.

"So will I," Hannie agreed.

Tevye looked up at his daughter. This wasn't going to be easy. He sensed that the situation demanded a tenderness that he didn't have. He knew how to milk cows without hurting them, but children were a far more delicate matter. When Ruchel stepped forward, Moishe and Hannie retreated behind their grandfather's back.

"Your aunt Ruchel loves you both very much," Tevye said.

"So does Uncle Nachman," Ruchel assured.

"We hardly even know him," Moishe said.

"We'll get to know each other," Nachman promised, looking up from the tome he was studying.

"Nachman is one of the best storytellers in the world," Tevye said.

"Who cares?" Moishe said.

"Who cares?" Hannie echoed.

"Your mother's last wish was that you grow up with your Aunt Ruchel and Uncle Nachman," Tevye informed them.

"He isn't our uncle," Moishe said.

"Yes he is," Hannie told him. "They're married."

"Who cares if they are married," Moishe responded. "I'm staying with *Saba*."

"You can't," Tevye said. "And that's final."

He stood up and tore the children away from his legs. The time had come to be decisive. To lay down the law. He had to let the children know there was no chance of returning with him to Zichron Yaacov.

Moishe and Hannie glared at him, hurt and betrayed.

"What about Goliath?" the little girl asked.

The big lumberjack stood by the door with tears in his eyes.

"Maybe I can stay on for a while," he said. "Until the children are used to the change."

"Maybe we can find you a place here in Rishon," Nachman added. He turned to the children. "Would that make you happy?"

"No," Moishe said. Sobbing, he stared at his grandfather. "You just want to be rid of us," he accused. "Nobody wants us. Just like *Abba* and *Ema* left us, you are leaving us too. I wish I were dead like they are."

Crying, he ran for the door but Goliath caught him by the shirt.

"Let me go," Moishe screamed, taking a bite out of the giant's big paw.

Goliath let go with a whelp and let the boy free. Hannie ran out of the house after her brother. Together, they took off toward the fields.

"Let them go," Nachman said. "They'll come back when they get tired."

"They are little children. They could get lost," Ruchel protested.

"They won't go far," Nachman assured.

"How do you know? Since when are you an expert on children? God forbid they wander into the swamps."

"She's right," Tevye said.

"Maybe you should go back to Zichron Yaacov now," Nachman suggested. "We'll find them and bring them back to the house. If you have already left, it might be easier for the children to realize they don't have a choice."

"I can't leave until I know that they are safe," Tevye answered.

Outside the house, the adults split up in different directions. Shouting out the names of the children, Nachman hurried toward the swamps, a short distance from the settlement. The settlers had long ago drained the malaria-infested waters which had surrounded the colony, but there were still patches of swampland close by. Goliath ran toward the fields to search for them. Ruchel headed for the orchards, and Tevye was to look along the main road leading to Jaffa. Passing the barn and inhaling the aroma of horses and cows, he stopped and decided to take a quick look inside. If he were a runaway child, the first place he would hide was the barn. Sure enough, almost as soon as he entered, Hannie jumped up from behind a hay stack and started to flee. Tevye darted after her, but the sheep pen was dirty with sheep dung and Tevye slipped in the muck. Luckily, he landed just clear of the droppings, but by the time he sat up, the girl had already scampered out the barn door. Moishe tried to jump over his grandfather, but Tevye grabbed onto a leg. The boy hollered and scrambled away. Quickly, he climbed up a ladder to the hay loft. Tevye raced up the ladder after him, but the fiesty little *vance* squirmed away. Bravely, he leapt down onto the haystack below. Holding his pounding heart, Tevye climbed back down the ladder.

Outside the barn, he could see the children running toward the gate of the colony. Hurrying back to Ruchel's house, he climbed into his wagon and urged his horse to take up the chase. The wagon clamored through the *yishuv*, drawing curious glances. Outside the gate, he caught up with the fleeing children.

"Wooo!" he called, halting his horse.

He jumped down from the wagon, and with a great sustained effort, he ran after Moishe and scooped him up under his right arm, then ran after Hannie and lifted her off of her feet with his left. With his heart beating like galloping horses, and his lungs screaming for breath, he hoisted them up into the wagon. Pinning them down under his legs, he turned his horse around and headed back toward the colony.

"You don't love us," Moishe accused.

"Of course I do," he told them. "Even more than I love my wagon and horse."

"You just say that, but you don't mean it. Otherwise you wouldn't give us away."

"I'm doing what your mother wanted, may she rest in heavenly peace. You may not like it now, but one day you both will be glad that you grew up with Ruchel and Nachman."

When they arrived back at the house, the children ran into the bedroom and slammed the door shut in their grandfather's face. He had to sit down and rest. His pounding heart told him that Tzeitl was right. The children needed a young father and mother, not an old, weary mule like their grandfather. He heard their sobs from the other side of the door, but didn't have the courage to face them, so he waited outside on the porch until Ruchel came home.

"Thank God," she said when he told her that the children were safe in the house.

"I think Nachman is right," Tevye said. "It is better if I leave right away. In a few days the children will get over the change. It may be hard for them to understand now, but one day they will realize that everything God does is for the best. After all, He is the Master of the World, not us."

"Sometimes, it is hard for me to understand everything He does," Ruchel confided.

Ever since her father had arrived, neither of them had

mentioned the pregnancy which had not come to fruition. If Tevye could see an unspoken sadness in his daughter's eyes, neither of them wanted to bring the matter up now.

"Whether we understand or not, we have to believe," Tevye said. "That's what faith is about."

He bent down and kissed his daughter's forehead. Wanting to feel more of his love, she gave him a hug.

"Oh, *Abba*, I've missed you so much," she said.

"I have missed you also, my daughter. As the Sages teach, 'More than the baby calf wants to suck, the mother cow wants to give milk.'"

Tevye climbed up into his wagon. Once again, he headed for the gate of the colony. Ruchel stood watching as the wagon rolled over the dirt road leading away from the house. To her surprise, Moishe and Hannie raced by her, running after the wagon.

"*Saba*!" they yelled. "*Zeide*! Don't leave us!"

Ruchel ran after the children. Returning from the swamps, Nachman saw his wife scampering away from the house. Goliath, on his way back from the fields, saw Nachman race off after Ruchel. He too joined in the chase. Outside the settlement gate, Tevye heard the calls of the children behind him. Tugging on the reins of the wagon, he ordered his horse to once again halt on the road.

"Take us with you," Moishe pleaded, latching on to the wagon. "We want to come with you. We don't want to grow up with anyone else."

They climbed into the wagon and hugged him, unwilling to let go. Puffing, Ruchel caught up to her father. Nachman ran up beside her. Within moments, Goliath arrived on the scene. The picture told the story. Moishe and Hannie refused to let go of their grandfather. Sobbing, they snuggled under his arms like terrified ducklings. Tevye glanced at his daughter with a shrug.

"What can I do?" his expression seemed to say.

Ruchel looked at her husband. Though they had only been married a very short time, they could read each other's thoughts. It was a question they had debated dozens of times. To stay in

Rishon where Nachman was happy with his teaching, or to join up with the rest of the family? For Ruchel, the decision rested with Nachman. True, she wanted to be with her father and sisters, and she wanted with all of her heart to raise Tzeitl's children, but not if it went against the will of her husband. As her father would say, "Wasn't it written, '*And thy desire shall be to thy husband, and he shall rule over thee*'?"

Nachman took her aside.

"The children want to be with their grandfather," he said to his wife.

"Yes," Ruchel answered.

"It seems to be what they need. They've suffered enough loss in their lifetimes. First a father, then a mother, and now their grandfather too? It could shatter their faith in the Almighty completely."

"What should we do?" Ruchel asked.

"We should go with them," Nachman answered. "Just like we decided before we received the Baron's letter. That way we can raise the children like Tzeitl wanted, and they can be near their grandfather too."

Ruchel hugged him with happiness. "Oh Nachman, I love you," she said. "But what about you? What about your teaching position?"

"Wherever we go there will be a need for teachers of Torah. Rishon LeZion will have no trouble finding someone to take my place, whereas there is a special *mitzvah* to look after orphans."

"Are you sure?" Ruchel asked.

"Yes, I'm sure."

Tevye looked on in suspense.

"What's all the whispering?" he asked.

"We have decided to leave Rishon and come with you," Nachman answered. "Right now, the children need their grandfather more than anyone else in the world."

A wide smile filled Tevye's face.

"Do you hear that children?" he said. "We are all going back to Zichron Yaacov together!"

The children cheered. They jumped happily all over their

grandfather. Goliath beamed at the wonderful news. He loved Nachman like a brother, and the thought that everyone would be together gave him such a feeling of joy, he felt that he could lift up the wagon with everyone in it.

"Everyone hopped in the wagon," Tevye called.

Happily, they all climbed aboard. With a tug on the reins, Tevye turned back once again toward the house, this time to load Ruchel's and Nachman's belongings onto the wagon for the trip back to Zichron Yaacov.

Chapter Twenty-Two

A VISIT TO THE YESHIVA

Not only was Tevye's family going to be together, they were going to be rich! The Baron's gift of 5000 francs would make them the new aristocrats of Palestine. But Tevye's daydreaming didn't last long. When he heard that Nachman was planning on returning the money, Tevye nearly fell out of the wagon.

"I won't allow it!" he said, dizzy from the shock.

"The Baron gave the money to us on the premise that we would raise up the children in Rishon," Nachman explained. "In the Talmud, it is called a *Mekach Ta'ut*, meaning that the money was given on the basis of false information."

"Don't quote the Talmud to me," Tevye stormed. "The money was given for the children, and as their guardian, I am in charge of their interests."

Ruchel looked at her husband. "The Baron didn't stipulate in his letter that we couldn't move to another *yishuv*," she said.

"It was obvious that the adoption was to take place in Rishon, and not somewhere else," the young rabbi insisted.

"Why don't we write him and ask him before we give up the money?" Ruchel suggested.

"Why tell him at all?" Tevye said. "I am not a scholar in Talmud, but the money is in your pocket. If the Baron has a claim, then he is the one who has to prove it."

"I want to be fair to the Baron," Nachman answered.

"With all of his billions, a man like the Baron doesn't even remember that he wrote out a check. To him, 5000 francs is a tip. But think what the money will mean to the children."

Nachman fell silent. It was true that the money was a blessing to the orphans, but honesty was a foundation of Torah. Especially in matters of money, where greed and temptation could make a crooked line seem straight, a man had to be cautious.

" God performs a miracle, and you want to tell Him no thank you," Tevye said. "Don't be such a big righteous *tzaddik*."

"All right," Nachman said. "We will hold onto the money for now. But in Jaffa, we will go and ask Rabbi Kook. Whatever he advises, we'll do."

Tevye grumbled. He didn't like putting the decision in someone else's hands, but what could he do? The money had been sent to Nachman and Ruchel, not to him. The main thing was getting the money out of the Company safe. With the money in hand, at least for the time being, his family would be rich. And maybe Rabbi Kook would have compassion on the plight of the children.

The whole argument turned out to be pointless. When the colony Director, Dupont, heard that Nachman and Ruchel were leaving Rishon, he refused to open the safe and give them the funds. Either they stayed in Rishon with the children, and the money would be theirs, or the money would be sent back to France.

Tevye felt like picking up the little Dupont and strangling him until he opened the safe. But he remembered that his assistants had guns.

"If that's the case, I suggest the children stay here until we hear from the Baron himself," Tevye said. "We can telegram him for an immediate answer."

But Nachman's mind was already made up. The happiness of the children was the most important thing, and they wanted to be with their grandfather. Money was secondary. With or without the Baron's assistance, God would provide for their needs. So, trusting in the Holy One Blessed Be He, Nachman made the decision to set off without the money in hand.

All the way to Jaffa, Tevye brooded over the loss of the gift. It was a glaring injustice, he said. Dupont should be hanged! Who was he to decide for the Baron? Tevye was even prepared to journey to Paris to appeal to the Benefactor himself.

Nachman reminded Tevye that it was decreed on *Rosh HaShana* everything that would befall a man in the coming year. If the money was truly destined On High for the children, it would get to them, no matter how much Dupont protested. Tevye knew that, but still, a man was commanded to do whatever he could down on earth before relying on assistance from Heaven.

Arriving in Jaffa, they traveled straight to the house of Rabbi Kook. Once again, the Rabbi's kindly wife led them into his study. Once again, Tevye was amazed by the aura of holiness which seemed to surround his saintly figure and suffuse the whole room. Rabbi Kook's eyes shone with both a mystical light, and a kind, compassionate smile. He listened as Nachman explained the dilemma. Tevye waited anxiously for his answer.

"While it is true that the money is legally yours," the Rabbi decreed, "to be clear of any possible doubt, it is, as you suggest, a prudent idea to write the Baron himself and hear what he has to say."

Tevye frowned, but he didn't dare refute the Rabbi's advice. There was nothing to do except pray that the Baron would stand by his benevolent gesture.

"As to your decision to leave Rishon LeZion, you should not harbor any doubts," the Rabbi said to Nachman as if sensing the uncertainty in his heart. "Thank God, Rishon LeZion is an established community, and another teacher of Torah can surely be found. But what you and your family are doing, venturing forth to build a new settlement, this is an act of supreme importance. The person who most sacrifices himself for the rebuilding of our Land will receive the most bountiful blessing in Heaven."

Nachman blushed and lowered his head. Then, Rabbi Kook turned a profoundly serious glance at Tevye. Instinctively, the milkman looked around to see if the Rabbi were gazing at someone more important behind him. But there was no one else in the study. The words of the Rabbi were addressed directly to him.

"Until all of our scattered brethren come to settle in our uniquely Holy Land, each of us has to demand all that he can of himself. We must always remember, that the Land of Israel is only acquired through trial and suffering. However, the Almighty does not test a man with more difficulties than he can bear. On the contrary, He gives us the strength and the courage to persevere. If we encounter problems, tragedies, and setbacks, it does not mean that the path we have chosen is wrong, but rather that the Almighty, in His great love, is providing us with a test to strengthen our faith. When we cling to Him with love and with joy, even in difficult times, like our Forefathers did in the past, we rise up in His service to the holiest levels which a person can reach. And this closeness to God is a greater gift and blessing than all of the comfort and wealth in the world."

Tevye nodded. His palms moistened with sweat. Was he made out of glass that the Rabbi could see all of his inner doubts and fears? He remembered Golda's words, "Be strong, my husband, be strong." All he could think about was getting out of the room before the scholar's searing gaze transformed him into a pile of ashes. Then, a kind smile flashed over the Rabbi's face, putting the milkman at ease.

"Your family is depending on you to be strong, Reb Tevye, and to show them that our allegiance to God and our holy traditions will forever be a beacon to light up whatever temporary darknesses that life sets in our path."

Tevye turned the conversation to Hevedke. Rabbi Kook reported that he was learning day and night in a small yeshiva nearby, and his progress was truly astounding. Hearing this, Tevye was not overjoyed. In his heart of hearts, he harbored the hope that rigorous discipline of Talmudic studies would prove too much for the Russian poet's mettle. Rabbi Kook said that the secret to life lay in a man's will, and that Hevedke was driven by a passionate desire to overcome the barriers which lay in the path of every soul who sets forth to climb up the ladder of holiness.

"A passionate desire for my daughter," Tevye thought, still unconvinced of Hevedke's sincerity in becoming a Jew.

While Nachman lingered to converse with the Rabbi, one of the Rabbi's disciples escorted Tevye from the house to the yeshiva where Hevedke was learning. Standing in the doorway of the *Beit*

Midrash study hall, it wasn't hard to pick out the blond Russian from the other dark-haired students. Sitting with his back facing Tevye, Hevedke's head and broad shoulders towered over the lot. Bobbing back and forth like a Jew *davening* in prayer, he listened in fervent concentration as the scholar across from him explained a polemic of Talmudic law. Hevedke's study partner made a movement with his hand and his thumb, as if he were scooping up some insight from the pages of the large volume of *Gemara* which lay on the table between them. He glanced up at Tevye just long enough to cause Hevedke to turn and look up at the visitor. Seeing Hava's father, the young Russian leaped up with a bright happy grin.

"Tevye!" he boomed.

All of the students looked up. The clamor of their learning turned to a hush. Hevedke rushed over to Tevye, grasped him in a bear hug, and lifted him off of his feet. "Tevye," he said. "Reb Tevye!"

When Hevedke returned him back to the floor, Tevye stared into a strange, unfamiliar face. Hevedke's smooth, angular jaw was now bearded. A *yarmulka* covered his head. But the very great difference lay in his eyes. Tevye couldn't explain it, but they were not the same eyes he remembered. A beautiful light shone within them, as if a candle had been lit from inside. The face of Hevedke, the Russian, had vanished. Confronting Tevye was the face of a Jew.

"How is Hava?" he asked. "You must tell me, please. I am dying to know."

The other students continued to stare at them.

"Come outside," Hevedke said. "We are interrupting their studies. How long are you here for? Is Hava with you? Is everything all right?"

Tevye assured him that everyone, thank God, was fine. For the moment, they were living in Zichron Yaacov. Hava had completed a course in nursing and was now working in the infirmary.

"Did Hava ask you to give me a message?" he asked. The youth spoke with such genuine hope that Tevye himself was disarmed.

"She asked me to send you her greetings."

Hevedke beamed as if Tevye had handed him a bagful of rubles. His eyes shone with delight.

"You can tell her that I am enjoying my studies more than I have enjoyed anything else in my life."

A forced, crooked smile formed on Tevye's lips. "*Oy vay*," he thought. "He likes learning Torah!"

"Better yet," Hevedke said. "I will write her a letter. How I have longed to know where you were living. You have another few minutes, I trust, my kindly Reb Tevye?"

Kindly Reb Tevye? After all the trials which Tevye had forced this daughter-robber to bear, he addressed him as "kindly" Reb Tevye? When had Tevye ever been kind to him? Either Hevedke was still a glib talker, or else a miraculous transformation was indeed taking place inside the youth's soul.

Hevedke hurried back into the study hall of the yeshiva and grabbed a piece of paper. Excitedly, he sat down and started to write. He scribbled at a furious pace, looking up now and then to make sure that Tevye was still waiting. The other students in the room kept on with their studies. The vibrant sound of debate filled the air. Study partners, or *hevrutas*, as Tevye remembered they were called from his days in Talmud Torah, sat facing one another, entangled in lively *Halachic* discourse.

When it seemed that Hevedke was never going to finish the long *Megilla* he had started to write, Tevye sat down at a table. Absently, he flipped open the book of Psalms before him, and placed his finger on some random verse, knowing that the Lord's Providence watched over every movement in the world, from the movement of clouds in the sky to the path of a leaf falling to earth. His fingernail landed on a verse from the *Hallel* prayer: "*He raises up the poor out of the dust, and lifts the needy out of the ash heap; to sit him with the nobles, with the nobles of his people.*"

Tevye looked around at the study hall. These impoverished students of Torah, who labored day and night to master the intricacies of the Biblical texts, these were the true Jewish nobles. The Torah scholars were the true barons and guardians of *Am*

Yisrael, the nation of Israel. It was they who had kept the nation intact for thousands of years. Foreign armies and rulers had swept over the Holy Land, boasting of their might and their glory. The pages of history were filled with their sound and their fury. Each succeeding conqueror had declared the final defeat of the Jews. And yet, long after these emperors and empires had collapsed, long after their temples and palaces had all turned to rubble, the Jews had returned to their homeland. The Jews had survived because of these very same scholars who had clung, through persecution and plague, to the sacred code of law which God had given to their forefathers thousands of years before.

Embarrassed that the letter writing had taken so long, Hevedke blushed and handed the folded papers to Tevye.

"Give Hava my best," he said with a shy, hopeful smile.

"Keep up with your studies," Tevye answered.

"I intend to, don't worry."

Tevye nodded. If stubbornness were one of the traits of a Jew, then Hevedke deserved a diploma. No doubt he would be another Rabbi Akiva.

"That wouldn't be the end of the world," Tevye thought to himself. Rabbi Akiva had stayed away from his wife for twenty-four years in order to sit and learn Torah. So should it be with Hevedke.

The two men shook hands on the street, and Hevedke returned to the yeshiva.

For Hevedke, an incredible transformation was truly taking place. It was as if he had discovered a completely new world. A world where all darkness and confusion had vanished, where there were only horizons and horizons of light. In the yeshiva, for the first time in his life, he had discovered a true connection to God. To a God who was mysteriously working behind the curtain of history to fulfill the promise He had made to the Jews to bring them back from the four corners of the world to the Land of Israel.

Many nights, Hevedke fell asleep in the study hall, draped over his opened books. Though his thoughts often wandered to Hava, he didn't want to leave the yeshiva's hallowed walls. He didn't want to be far from the shelves of holy volumes, even though they were written in a language which he was still struggling to understand. Suddenly, the world outside seemed like a figment of the imagination, a passing fancy, a deceiving charade, something which could only distract him from the learning that he loved and from the worlds he had discovered in the pages of the Talmudic writings. To the poet who had read all of the works of Tolstoy, Gorki, Hugo, Voltaire, Shelley, Shakespeare, and Keats; who had championed the philosophies of Aristotle, Plato and Locke; and who had clung in blind faith to the Christian gospels, a true revolution was occurring. Like candles held up to the sun, all of the luminance he had once found in the classics disappeared in the blazing light of God's Torah. A new, incredible the truth became clear. *"Hear O Israel, the Lord our God, the Lord is one."*

Probing thinker that Hevedke was, his spiritual journey was not without clarifications and questions. But the rabbis he learned with always had answers, gleaned from the Sages of the past. The traditions of learning had been passed down generation after generation ever since the giving of the Torah on Sinai. What Hevedke's keen mind found particularly striking was that, unlike the origins of other religions, the revelation at Sinai had been an historical event, witnessed by two million people, and accepted as fact by all of the world. Both Christianity and Islam had constructed their doctrines upon the foundations of the Jewish religion. Every other philosophy, religion, political movement, or creed originated with man. But Judaism was different. The Torah had been given by God. It was God's own plan for all of existence. And the nation He had chosen to elevate the world out of its darkness was Israel. The very nation which all of the world hounded and attempted to destroy!

The discovery was so profoundly moving, it overwhelmed all of the young man's thoughts and all of his waking moments. It entered into his dreams. As his learning progressed, his mind dwelt less and less upon Hava. He still loved her with all of his being for having led him to the real purpose of living, yet that love was now shared by his passionate yearning for God. Now that he had discovered his Creator in the pages of the Talmud, Hevedke longed to be purged in His great healing light. Profoundly ashamed for his beliefs of the past, he cried out to God for forgiveness. He filled up notebooks with poems declaring his love for his Maker. He prayed for hours on end, begging God to come into his life and to open his eyes to the teachings of Torah. But, at first, God didn't answer. Crestfallen and ready to give up the yeshiva, he had visited Rabbi Kook's house filled with despair.

"God has already answered your prayers," the wise Rabbi said. "Look around you. Just open your eyes. Where are you? You are learning the Torah in a yeshiva in the Holy Land. God has opened the door to His palace. If you are saddened because you want to enter the royal chambers immediately, and that door seems closed, that does not mean that God is not with you. He simply knows you aren't yet ready. One needs patience, great faith, and diligent study. The learning of Torah takes many years, and a man must be willing to surrender himself to it completely before God unlocks the doors to its innermost chambers and secrets."

Gazing at the holy Rabbi and seeing in his eyes the wisdom of thousands of years, Hevedke felt foolish for acting like a child who impatiently wants a new toy, now, and doesn't want to wait. The Torah came through toil. The Torah came through sacrifice. Simple belief was not enough. All of life had to be a sanctified, conscious striving to become closer to God. A religious Jew had to be holy in all of his endeavors, with every breath of his life, from morning till night. With everything he ate, everything he said, everything he did, a Jew had to be conscious of God and abide by the laws of the Torah. And all of this had to be learned through detailed, painstaking study. For the free-thinking poet, this meant bowing to a wisdom greater than his. It meant putting all of his previous arrogance and theories aside and relying on the teachers who could guide him through oceans of unchartered waters. It meant learning a new language and a whole new way of being. It meant severing himself from his past and building a new future. Once his youthful heart came to understand that this was the whole secret of life, to discover God and to cling to His ways, he was possessed with a passion that even his great love for Hava couldn't match. It was the most joyous, wondrous, frightening, challenging, light-filled journey which Hevedke had ever embarked on.

Somewhere, someday, at the end of the voyage, he knew that Hava was waiting, and that gave him courage and faith. Even if it took him years, like Rabbi Akiva, Hevedke was willing to dedicate all of himself to this holy, spiritual mission.

Chapter Twenty-Three

A NEW KIND OF JEW

All of Tevye's life, it seemed like he was always saying good-bye. Back in the old country, what now seemed like lifetimes ago, his Hodel had left him for Perchik. Then Hava had run off with her gentile, and Shprintza had drowned. Then the heart and soul of his being, his devoted wife, Golda, had departed for a more eternal world. His beautiful Baylke had left for America. Then the family had been chased out of Anatevka to set off like gypsies without country or home. When Tzeitl had died, a candle in his soul had been extinguished, but the need to take care of her children had made him stand strong. True, he had the joy of being united with Ruchel, but Tevye wasn't convinced that his troubles were over. So, with one eye on his daily chores, and one eye raised toward the sky, Tevye waited for the next blow to fall. And so it was, when the time came to leave Zichron Yaacov for the new settlement site, Tevye had to say good-bye once again – this time to Hava who was staying on as a nurse in the hospital's malaria clinic. She had made up her mind. None of his arguments had an effect.

"May the Lord protect you and keep you," he said, laying his hands on her head and blessing her with the prayer which Jewish fathers had blessed their children for thousands of years. He hugged her and gave her a kiss, then once again climbed up into his wagon, just as he had been doing all of his life.

Fifteen pioneer families plus children were journeying off to establish the new Morasha community. Ruchel and Nachman. Hillel, Shmuelik, and Goliath. A near *minyan* of nine Hasidic families from Lubavitch. A family of Yemenite Jews. Tevye. And Reb Guttmacher, the undertaker, who repeated his motto to whomever he met, "I've dug enough holes for the dead. Now I want to dig holes for the living."

"To life!" Tevye agreed as their caravan left the Zichron road to venture east across the flatlands which led to the mountainous spine of the country. *"L'Chaim!"*

"L'Chaim!" the *Hasidim* exclaimed. Instantly a bottle of vodka was afloat in the air, passing from hand to hand until all of the pioneers had made a toast on the success of their enterprise. Not wanting to be left out, Elisha, the dark-skinned Yemenite, took a swig of the harsh-tasting brew. Choking, he spit the vodka out on the ground.

Tevye laughed. "We'll make a Jew out of you yet," he said.

The others joined in with his good-natured laughter. Hillel gave the small, exotic-looking Jew a whack on the back.

"You'll get used to it, don't worry," he said.

"You can keep it," the Yemenite responded. "I have something better."

He reached out a hand and one of his grown sons handed him a bottle.

"What is it?" Hillel asked.

"Arak."

"What's Arak?" the Russian Jew asked.

The Yemenite passed him the homemade brandy, distilled from the fruit of the etrog and herbs. Hillel raised it to his nose and inhaled a deep scent of licorice.

"If it tastes as good as it smells, I'll buy a few bottles," he said.

Throwing his head back, he took a big gulp. Suddenly, it was his turn to choke. Beneath the liquor's sweetness was the kick of a mule. Hillel bent over coughing. Now it was Elisha's turn to slap Hillel on the back. Soon both bottles were being passed through the air. Urged on by the Hasids, everyone, including the Yemenite, began singing a lively *Baruch Haba* welcome to *Mashiach*.

"Baruch Haba, Baruch Haba,
Melech HaMashiach.
Baruch Haba, Baruch Haba,
Melech HaMashiach.

Ay yay yay, Melech HaMashiach,
Ay yay yay, Baruch Haba,
Ay yay yay, Melech HaMashiach,
Ay yay yay, Baruch Haba."

When the long-gowned, long-sidelocked, prayer-shawl enswathed Yemenite had first arrived in Zichron Yaacov, the Russian Jews had found it difficult to believe that this golden-skinned apparition could be a Jew. The first time Tevye saw him, he mistook him for an Arab. But an Arab with *tzitzit* and *peyes*? The sight was a puzzle. When Elisha joined them in prayer, this seemed even stranger. Everyone knew that only a Jew could be included in an official prayer *minyan* of ten. Still more bewildering, the Yemenite spoke Hebrew more fluently than all of them. True, the melodious wailing which ushered from his lips was a Hebrew which Tevye had never heard, but it was the language of his forefathers nonetheless.

"You are really a Jew?" Tevye asked in surprise.

The man nodded yes. He looked at Tevye from head to foot. "Are you?"

"Am I a Jew?" Tevye bellowed.

"You don't look like a Jew," the Yemenite said.

Tevye's back stiffened. "My mother and father were Jews, and their mother and father were Jews, and their mother and father before them, all of the way back to Abraham," Tevye declared.

"So were mine," the man answered, standing in a pose of defiance, but smiling at Tevye with his eyes. "All of the way back to Abraham. We must be related."

"Nonsense," Tevye said. "Your skin is as brown as clay."

"Did you think that Abraham wore a *shtreimel* hat and spoke Yiddish?"

"Of course not. But he certainly wasn't black."

"There is a tradition which teaches that when God gave the Torah on Sinai amidst thunder and fire, the people who loved God the most ran forward to get as close as they could, and their skin was burned by the flames. These were the Yemenite Jews. Others, frightened by the fire and thunder, ran away to the edge of the camp. These became Ashkenazic Jews. In punishment, when the exile came, God sent these Jews far away from His Land to the cold northern countries of Russia and Europe. The Jews whose skin was darkened because they rushed to be close to the mountain, were exiled close by, in neighboring lands, in reward. Like my people, the Yemenite Jews."

"A *boobeh-miseh* fairytale of a story if I ever heard one!" Tevye declared.

The exotic-looking Jew smiled a warm happy smile. His eyes, black as coal, seemed to glow. Graciously, he invited Tevye to join him in his quarters for a drink. That's how their friendship began. Surprisingly, he led Tevye to one of the settlement's chicken coops. Upon their arrival at Zichron Yaacov, the Yemenite family had been assigned to live with the chickens. With a wife and eleven children, the arrangement made for cramped living, but the happy-eyed Jew hadn't complained. The coop had a roof, and the family wasn't bothered at all by the smell of the fowls. During the day, the chickens didn't stop squawking, but having been blessed with their own brood of children, Elisha and his wife were no strangers to noise. Fortunately, during the night, in harmony with the Almighty's plan for Creation, the chickens slept peacefully until the first signs of morning – when it was time to get up to go to work in the fields.

Though Elisha was the same age as Tevye, he looked twenty years younger. So did his wife. If not for the white kerchief she wore swirled on her head, Tevye would have mistaken her for one of his daughters. Her color was more golden red than her husband's, and she had the same dark glowing eyes. As if times had never changed, she wore the tribal robe which Yemenite women had been wearing for ages. For the length of Tevye's visit in their chicken coop of a home, she never uttered a word. Most of the time, she stayed out of view behind the curtains which they used as a room divider at the far end of the coop. Occasionally, she would appear to see if their plate of grapes needed refilling, or else she would send one of her strikingly beautiful daughters. Like Tevye's wife, Golda, she served generous portions, but whereas Golda was quick to add her opinion to every discussion, Elisha's wife let her husband do all of the talking.

Their eldest children were a little older than Tevye's, while their youngest was still crawling on the floor. All had the same gem-like Yemenite eyes. The hue of their skin was the color of rich golden earth. The boys had side locks down to their shoulders, and the long black hair of the girls hung down their backs like the manes of Arabian stallions.

Over a glass of Arak, and the happy, thankful smile which never left his face, Elisha told Tevye his life story. Like every other place on the globe where the wandering Jews had settled, there had been good times and there had been bad times in Yemen. For several generations, Jews had been left to live in peace, but like in Russia, things eventually had taken a turn for the worse. The Yemenite Jews were third-class citizens, hounded by Moslem terror, victims of beatings and theft. Their complaints to the ruling Turks fell on deaf ears. The only work they could find was invariably outside of the city, and highwaymen made the roadways a peril. All of his life, Elisha had heard magical stories about *Eretz Yisrael*, about the gigantic oranges and figs which a man could barely lift with two hands, and about the Yemenites who had become wealthy farmers and businessmen there. When Moslems began killing Jews, instead of merely praying in the direction of Zion three times a day, Elisha had decided to embark on the long and hazardous journey.

Before continuing his narrative, Elisha once again filled Tevye's glass to the brim, as if to fortify him for the saga he was about to relate. Tevye listened intently. Chickens scurried around them and occasionally flew onto the table, but the two men ignored them. With a broom, one of Elisha's children kept sweeping them away from the "salon."

With eighty fellow villagers, Elisha's family had set forth with all of their meager belongings. Uncles, aunts, cousins, and parents accompanied them for miles before waving tearful good-byes. Children and grandparents who had trouble walking, rode on the few camels they had. Everyone else traveled on foot. After three days, they reached the great desert and began a punishing trek. Their mornings would begin an hour before sunrise, when they would set off in cool of the dawn. Hours later, when the sun rose over their heads in the sky, they would seek rest from its pitiless heat, crowding together in whatever shade they could find. Scorched by the sun and desert wind, the men had to strip off their undergarments. The desert water was bitter, barely quenching their thirst. For meals, the women baked *malawach*, a thin, wafer-like pancake of bread. All through the day, flies clung to their faces, no matter how much they were swatted away. In the late afternoon, when the sun's fury lessened, they once again set forth over the endless landscape of dunes. In the evening, they would walk until they came upon a village, where they would buy whatever staples they lacked. More often than not, hostile tribesmen sought to rob them, but four of the Jews had guns, and one blast from a rifle was enough to scare marauders away.

One night, they were surrounded by a company of Moslem soldiers. When the soldiers attacked, the Jews pulled out their swords. Elisha's oldest son, Ariel, opened fire with his rifle. Immediately, the soldiers panicked and fled. But the victory was short-lasting. In the next village they came to, more soldiers were waiting. The Jews were arrested as traitors and held under guard for a week until the decision arrived from the capital to release them. Elisha called it a miracle.

"Thank the good Lord," Tevye said, pushing his empty glass forward.

"Amen," Elisha responded. "In the merit of our righteous forefathers who remained faithful to our holy Torah for thousands of years in the face of oppression and danger, God saves us again and again."

"To our forefathers," Tevye said, holding up his replenished glass. The two men toasted and Elisha continued his tale.

Weeks later, after having marched on foot over two-thousand kilometers, the Yemenites reached the coast. Some fainted at the sight of the water. A grandfather collapsed in the water and drowned. To escape the sun and the heat, they gathered sticks and cloth and made primitive shelters on the beach. They were told that the steamer traveling to Palestine passed by once in six months. They could wait or take sailboats to Aden, but Jews were forbidden to enter Aden with arms. So they sold their rifles and swords, even their slaughtering knives. For weeks they ate fruit and fish. Then, while waiting for the boat to arrive, a company of soldiers on horseback appeared on the seashore and charged at them while they were unarmed. The only defense they had were the weapons of their forefathers – the blasts of their shofars and their prayers. Elisha stood with his long, curving ram's horn and sent three militant blasts through the air. "*Tekiah! Tekiah! Tekiah!*" Other shofars sounded around him. Thinking that the Jews were calling evil spirits, the soldiers turned and retreated. The Moslems, Elisha explained, were superstitious people, and they feared that the Jews could bring down thunderbolts from Heaven.

In the meantime, a sailor came running with the news that a boat was waiting out in the harbor. Walking in water up to their chests, they reached the small rowboats which ferried passengers out to the ship. With a cheer, the Jews climbed on board.

Tevye raised his empty glass once again with a broad, cheerful smile. But this time, Elisha did not extend the bottle. His eyes squinted with seriousness as he went on with his story. Their joy, he said, was short-lived as storm clouds rushed toward them and enveloped the ship in turbulent waters. Crowded together, with rain pouring down on their heads, and a howling wind piercing their bones, the terrified Jews roped themselves together so that the waves crashing down over the boat would not wash them away. They begged the Almighty to save them. A week passed without a glimpse of the sun. When Elisha's pregnant wife went into labor, the other women sat in a circle around her, screening the men from the birth. Not a peep passed her lips as her eleventh child was born. But before Elisha's friends could wish him a *mazal tov*, a mast snapped like a twig, and a sail flew away over the ocean. Waves splashed on board. Planks shattered and seawater poured through the breaches. Three children were washed overboard. No one could save them. Working heroically, the crew managed to anchor the ship close to the shore, where hasty repairs were made. Elisha paused in his story to bend down to the floor and pick up the toddler who was crawling under the table. Fittingly, he had named the boy, Yonah, after the prophet who had been saved from a stormy and turbulent sea.

Tevye was breathless. His own journey to Israel had been no simple hike, but Elisha's tale was astounding. Once again, the Yemenite filled up their glasses and took up his adventure, spinning his tale with the deftness of Tevye's acquaintance, the famous writer, Sholom Aleichem. Continuing in the morning, the boat reached Aden by noon, but the Moslems refused to let them disembark. When night came, Elisha's eldest son, Ariel, snuck down the ladder and swam into shore. In the morning, he made his way to the market and found a rich Jew who was able to arrange permission for the Yemenites to land. On the dock, they were detained by police and herded into an empty warehouse. After waiting two weeks, they boarded a French boat which was loaded with lumber and heading for *Eretz Yisrael*. Nine days later, they finally reached Jaffa. Their prayers and dreams had come true. Falling on their hands and their knees, they kissed the holy soil.

But that was only the beginning of their journey, Elisha said with a smile. He poured Tevye another drink of the aromatic liquor. In Jaffa, the Yemenite said, it had been impossible to find decent work. Unlike the success stories which they had heard, the Jews immigrating from Yemen were paid the lowest wages. If that wasn't humiliating enough, Yemenites, who managed to find work in the fields, were terrorized by Arab laborers who felt threatened by the meager pay the "black" Jews received. The Yemenites could all recite the Torah by heart, but their spoken Hebrew was basic, preventing them from working in their trades. Furthermore, the Ashkenazic pronunciation which dominated the new Jewish pioneer communities didn't sound to them like Hebrew at all. To survive, Elisha found himself learning Yiddish from his boss at the Rothschild warehouse where he worked at "*sabalut*," lugging barrels of wine to the port. Elisha insisted that he wasn't complaining. He was merely relating the conditions which his family had met upon reaching the Promised Land. Abraham, he said, had journeyed to the Land of Israel when there were no Jews at all in the country. A famine awaited him instead. Even though God had promised that the country would be an eternal gift to him and his children, he had to beg the people of Hebron to sell him a burial site for his wife. The wells which he and his son Isaac had dug were filled in again and again by the Philistines. The trials of the Patriarchs had been endless, he said, so who was he to complain?

After several glasses of the powerful liquor, Tevye had come to love the happy little Jew who lived in a chicken coop of a house. But not complain? That was asking too much of a man. After all, complaining was a part of being Jewish. How could a Jew not complain? How else, in his miserable existence, was he to find any pleasure? Other luxuries cost money, while complaining was free. Not that Tevye ever doubted the goodness of the Master of the World, *chas v'sholem*. To Tevye, complaining was no worse than snoring. But he let Elisha finish telling his story and conquered his urge to debate.

It was Baron Rothschild who had tried to integrate the poor immigrants from Yemen into the settlement colonies. They proved to be excellent workers, far surpassing the Russians. Exceedingly humble, and accustomed to the Mediterranean heat, the Yemenites were willing to do all of the menial work which the Ashkenazic Jews disdained. Rather than hiring Arab workers, the Baron felt that he could bolster the cause of Jewish labor by employing the lower paid Yemenites. But a caste system developed, and when the Yemenite Jews at Zichron were segregated into their own tent village on the outskirts of the *moshav*, Elisha decided to volunteer to become a founding member of Morasha. There, he believed, a fairer, more utopian community could be established with equal rights for every Jew, no matter the shade of his skin.

Elisha smiled, concluding his saga. The bottle of Arak stood empty on the table.

"Carmel," he called.

The curtain behind him rustled and one of his pretty, golden-skinned daughters appeared. She kept her eyes lowered modestly toward the ground as Elisha held out his hand, motioning her to come forward. Barefooted, she stepped gracefully next to her father and let him embrace her around her waist.

"We need some more refreshments for our guest," the master of the chicken coop said.

The girl reached down for the empty plate of fruit and the bottle, but when she turned to leave, her father continued to hold her.

"This is my oldest daughter, Carmel," he said, introducing the young woman to Tevye. "Carmel, this is our new neighbor, Tevye."

Tevye didn't know whether the dizziness he felt in his head came from the liquor, or from the glow in her eyes when she glanced at him with her dark, exotic expression.

"Truthfully," Elisha said, "in deciding to join the Morasha group, my main concern was my daughters. We Yemenites have kept our community pure for thousands of years, and all of you are from Russia. Who are my daughters going to marry?"

Tevye glanced away from the young woman in order to gain his composure.

"With God's help," Elisha said, "the colony will grow, and more Yemenites will follow. That's what we are hoping. Isn't that right, my sweet daughter?"

With a blush, the young women slipped away from her father. Her long skirt rustled and she hurried back behind the curtain.

"You too have daughters?" Elisha said.

"Yes," Tevye answered.

Could it be he was drunk on only half a bottle of liquor? True, he wasn't used to the licorice-tasting Arak, but it surely was no stronger than good Russian vodka. Behind the curtain, he heard an exchange of whispers that he couldn't make out. When the curtain was drawn back again, instead of the girl, Elisha's wife reappeared, carrying a plate of cakes and another bottle of Arak.

The Yemenite smiled as he uncorked the new bottle.

"In the manner of you Russian Jews, let's make a toast. May God help us find good husbands for our daughters."

"Could it be?" Tevye wondered as Elisha filled up his glass. "No, no, it couldn't. It was absurd. It was ridiculous. Dark eyes or not, the girl was the age of his daughter!"

Chapter Twenty-Four

MORASHA

The Jewish Colony Association had chosen the mountainous location not for its suitability as farmland, but because of its price. When more and more Jews began immigrating to Palestine, the Turkish government began doubling and tripling the cost of the land until parcels were often ten times more expensive than farmland in Europe. The Baron had learned that supporting a settlement through its first struggling years was a certain financial disaster. Having to pour relief funds down never-ending holes, he strove to keep his initial investment to a minimum. While the theory was sound, Morasha was a perfect example of the problems inherent in absentee ownership. True, the vast stretch of property sat on the strategic ledge of mountains which ran down the spine of the country. But if the Jews chose to live near the only spring of underground water, they would have to trek two hours to work every day to reach the cultivatable fields. Likewise, if they built their homes near the fields, then their water supply would be an impossible distance away. But that was their problem, not the Baron's. "Some big *metsia*," Elisha had said during a scouting trip to the site. It was one of the Yiddish expressions he had learned in the winery. The Yemenite had taken the words out of Tevye's mouth - the tract of land was no big bargain. Once again on their second scouting visit, all of the settlers had protested, but Mr. LeClerc, the Company manager who was in charge of the project, told them to take it or leave it. What did he care? After a few years with the Company in Palestine, the unctuous gentile would return to Paris and a secure job in one of the Baron's banks. He had come to Palestine, not for ideological reasons, but for the promise of advancement in the Rothschild empire after his two-year indenture. Unlike the Frenchman, the settlers were committing themselves for a lifetime. They were ready to sacrifice for the *mitzvah* of building the land, but *shlepping* two hours to work, or to fetch a barrel of water, that was a proposition doomed from the start.

"Surely there are other areas more suited for settlements," Shilo, the carpenter, had argued, when a caravan of camels had dragged lumber out to the site in preparation for the approaching encampment.

"The Company has made its decision," the redheaded LeClerc declared.

"Then let the Baron live here," Hillel remarked.

"All of you Jews want to live like the Baron," the Frenchman answered in disdain.

"We don't have to live like the Baron," Tevye said. "Give me a wagon and a horse and I'm happy. But the Lord created man with a brain, and He expects him to live with some intelligent *sechel*. We are not Bedouins that we can live without water."

"Our agronomists have determined that this acreage comprises some of the best farmland in the country," the manager asserted.

"That may be so, but if we have to travel two hours to work, and another two hours to return, so that four hours a day of work time will be wasted on traveling instead of plowing and planting, then it sounds like the Baron has been given some lousy advice on what to do with his money."

"Therefore," LeClerc said. "The main camp will be built in the middle of the property, equidistant from both the fields and the water. Thus, you will only need to travel one hour each way."

Tevye had sighed. Could it be that the Almighty had brought him to the Land of Israel to take orders from this pompous Frenchman? But what choice did they have? To go back to Russia? That was out of the question. America? Who knew what troubles would be waiting him there? If a Jew was hounded by troubles and *tzuris* in Israel, in the place he belonged, he could be certain to find even more heartache in a foreign country.

At least, with hard work, the parcel of land would become their very own. A man had to look optimistically toward the future and trust that everything would turn out for the best. Nothing was built in a day. As Nachman reminded them, the Torah itself starts with the words, *"In the beginning...."*

"God could have created the world all at once," he said, "all complete at the start, but the story of Creation spans seven days to teach that a man has to have patience. Great undertakings take time. Hasn't the settlement Company promised to build us a canal to bring the water to our homes and our fields? *Savlanut*, as they say in Hebrew. Patience is the secret to our success."

Invigorated by the spirit of freedom which swept over the windy mountain terrain, Shmuelik agreed.

"All of us knew that this adventure wouldn't be easy," he said. "Yet, we all volunteered. Isn't it better that we break our backs, and not leave the hard work to our children? Did Abraham, our forefather, demand to live in a castle? No. He was happy to live in a tent."

Hearing this rallying speech, Tevye was surprised at the young scholar, as if some other person were speaking. These were the passionate words of a Perchik or a Ben Zion, not of a lad who had spent most of his life learning in a backwoods, Russian yeshiva. When had Shmuelik become such a Herzl? But the spirit of their mission, of the Land, and of the pioneers themselves, even seized Tevye. As the first tent stakes were hammered into the ground, he found himself one of the settlement's leaders. In addition to being put in charge of the livestock and stables, he was appointed chief of defense. Tevye, the general! After all, he knew how to ride a horse, and he had learned how to shoot. God forbid that the Jews of Morasha would ever have to fight, but if they were attacked, they had to be ready. How could Tevye refuse the trust which his comrades were placing in him? As the Sages had taught, "In a place where there isn't a man, be a man." Immediately, he appointed Elisha's eldest sons, Ariel and Yigal, to be his lieutenants. They would be in charge of guard duty and training, while Tevye would provide the overall army strategy and command. As far as the embarrassing incident with Elisha's daughter, Tevye blamed his infatuation on the dizzying liquor and put the matter out of his mind.

The first month, the women and children remained behind in Zichron Yaacov, while the men set up the compound. Goliath and Reb Shilo, the carpenter, cut wood for fencing and for the walls of the barn. Reb Guttmacher, the undertaker; Munsho, the blacksmith; and Hillel, the musician, started digging the canal which would bring the spring water down from the mountain to the more fertile plateaus. When Hillel's blistered hands prevented him from playing his accordion at the nightly campfire, he was replaced by Ariel and Yigal, and assigned lighter work looking after the animals. Chaim Lev, the fixer, made furniture, while Shragi, the scribe; Yankele, the butcher; Pincus, the storekeeper; and Elisha went to work clearing the rocky soil for seeding. Lazer, the tailor, was set to work repairing the second-hand tents which the Company had provided. By virtue of a unanimous settlement vote, Nachman and Shmuelik were to set up a Beit Midrash, where their job was to sit and learn Torah all morning. In Russia, the *Rebbe* had told his *Hasidim* that wherever they went, they were to make sure that a yeshiva was the cornerstone of their community. In the afternoon, the two scholars worked alongside the others outdoors, and in the evening, Nachman led a class in the writings of the famous *Baal HaTanya*, Rabbi Shneur Zalman of Liady. He explained the Kabbalistic mysteries in simple metaphors which the settlers could grasp, but exhausted from their day-long labor, his students would often fall off their benches and sleep at his feet. On the Sabbath, two settlers would be left to guard the Morasha site, while the others returned to Zichron to be with their families. Though the land had been purchased in accordance with all of the Turkish mandate laws, one could never be sure when nomadic Arabs would appear to contest the settlers' claims to the property.

The task before them was staggering. Like shipwrecked sailors thrown onto a desert island without means or resources, they literally had to dig with their hands when there were not enough shovels for everyone. But they all set to the work like true pioneers, determined to prove that they could conquer the land before the land conquered them. Every morning, Tevye got down on his hands and knees and kissed the holy soil.

"You are going to be kind to us today, aren't you, my beloved?" he whispered, addressing the earth as if it could hear. "Your children have come home, so you can put your thistles and thorns away, and open your arms to embrace us. Believe me, we have suffered enough in our exile. May bygones be bygones, and let's start again anew just like a bride and a groom."

"Talking to yourself?" Reb Guttmacher asked, passing by with the shovel that never left his hand.

"I was just saying good morning to our sweet Morasha soil."

"Take the advice of someone who has worked outdoors all his life, if you are going to work in the fields, you should wear a hat with a brim. The sun can make a man crazy."

Tevye stood up and brushed the dirt off his pants. "Sometimes I think we are all a little crazy."

"Yes, I know. As Dr. Weizmann is supposed to have said, `You don't have to be crazy to be a Zionist, but it helps.'"

"You have to admit, it is better to be a poor farmer in one's own land than a rich businessman in someone else's."

"Do you really believe that?" the undertaker asked.

Tevye smiled. "I'm trying to," he said.

At Tevye's age, working in the hot sun all the day was no simple matter, but he was determined to carry his share of the burden. The undertaker assisted him, teaching him some of the tricks of the trade, how to best hold a spade and upturn the hard soil without straining his back, but the hours took their toll. Until an outer layer of callous grew over his soft milkman's hands, his palms would blister and bleed. Sometimes, the pain was so great, the shovel would slip from his grip, but immediately, he would lift up the tool and set back to work. The younger settlers like Ariel and Yigal encouraged the older settlers along, singing songs and shoveling in time to their music. And in the evening, to bolster their spirits, Nachman extolled the great virtues of being in the Holy Land, where every shovelful of earth brought them closer to God.

"You are right," Tevye agreed. "We certainly are getting closer to God, because this back-breaking toil is killing us."

Every morning, the farmers rose before dawn to make the long trek to the fields. Work on the canal was temporarily postponed so that the shovelers could join in the task of clearing a road for their wagons. Lunch consisted of sour bread, sardines, and cucumbers bought from the Arabs who lived in the neighboring hills. For a generous fee, the Arabs gave them permission to draw water from a well on their property. Water was retrieved by dropping a bucket and rope into a hole ten meters deep. Usually, it took several efforts before they succeeded in filling the bucket, and by then the water was murky with mud. With the unsightly black water, they boiled a tea of sorts which was hardly refreshing. It wasn't unusual for a worker to pass the night with a fever and a vomiting attack of green bile. But the next morning, everyone was back to work, driven by the call of their mission. When the colony's roots were established, a team of agricultural specialists sent by the Company to instruct the new settlers in planting techniques and fertilization arrived in Morasha. The JCA also provided each settler with a team of two horses, a harness, a cart, a plow, seed for 150 dunams, one cow, a chicken coop, five chickens, animal fodder, a food allowance for one year, and fifty francs for sundries. Mattocks, picks, shovels, sickles, and scythes were not on the company list, so the pioneers had to share the few tools they had until an emergency requisition order arrived after a long, four-month wait. While many needed items were missing from each shipment, the relief wagons were always met with a great celebration, as if the *Mashiach* himself had come. LeClerc frowned on their demands, as if the expenses came out of his pocket. Finally, desperately needed equipment arrived. There were eight new mattocks, four shovels, two scythes, a saw, an axe, a hammer and nails, three buckets, four pairs of suspenders, four floppy sun hats, one rifle, four blankets, some writing paper, and a dog. Important as the supplies were to the settlers, it was the feeling that they weren't alone – that other Jews stood behind them, including the Baron and all of his wealth.

That, along with their faith in God, gave them the strength to keep going.

The cherished tools were carried into the shed they had built and stored away in a corner like a treasure. The long, rectangular structure was their first wooden dwelling, thanks to the skilled handiwork of Shilo, Chaim Lev, and Goliath. According to Turkish law, only animal stables, called *"chans"* were allowed wooden roofs. All other Jewish dwellings had to be left roofless, or covered with canvas, straw mats, branches, or removable slats. Petitions could be submitted for permanent roofing, but applications often lingered for months on the desks of Turkish officials in Caesarea until a large enough bribe could be paid. Like Noah in his ark, the settlers slept with their animals in the *chan*, and all of their community meetings were held in the presence of their horses and cows.

Their first attempt to build houses was interrupted when Turkish officials arrived and ordered the roofs-in-progress demolished. LeClerc had not secured the necessary permits, and without a permit, the settlers couldn't build roofs. However, if a structure had already been constructed, and if its roof was already in place, then the Turkish inspectors needed a court order to raze the building – and if a case got to court, the judge could be bribed with the traditional *baksheesh*. Because of the building infraction, their applications for permanent permits were rejected.

Needless to say, LeClerc's ineptitude, or lack of concern, didn't win him the respect of the settlers. Like the Turks, he was seen as an enemy who couldn't be trusted. When he deigned to spend a night in the settlement, he slept in his spacious tent, while the Jews slept in the barn. For two weeks, work in the fields was suspended. Goliath and Hillel took off with a wagon and returned from Zichron Yaacov laden with reinforcements and lumber. Tevye positioned four guards in the corners of the colony to give early warning in the event the inspectors returned. Working around the clock, the Jews put up two barns and eight one-room cottages. The next time the Turkish officials visited, the roofs were all finished and sitting in place. The date for a court hearing was set. In the meantime, LeClerc applied to the Turkish Magistrate for the necessary permits. With the Baron's intercession, the appropriate papers were signed. Fittingly, the permits and a letter from the Baron arrived on *Tisha B'Av*, the day the ancient Jerusalem Temple had been destroyed. Wasn't it written that the sadness of the Jews would turn into joy, that their tears would turn into singing and laughter, and that the day of destruction would turn into a day of rebirth? With hard work and patience, it was all coming true.

And that wasn't all. The letter from the Baron was personally addressed to Nachman. The "Benefactor" congratulated him on becoming a founder of a new Rothschild colony in Israel, and he wrote that the 5000 franc gift for the children was being transferred to Zichron Yaacov for the family's convenience! The Baron appreciated Nachman's honesty and concern, and wanted to assure him that the money was meant for the children, no matter where they lived, so long as they stayed in the Land of Israel.

When houses had been erected, the Morasha pioneers sent for their families. Once the women and children arrived, lives became more normal. Like the light which had filled the tents of the Matriarchs, Sarah, Rebecca, Leah, and Rachel, from one Sabbath to the next, a woman in the house brought a man a special blessing. But it was a blessing that Tevye was not privileged to share. Because of the shortage of houses, married couples were given first preference. Naturally, LeClerc, was given a cottage, even though his wife lived in Paris, and he himself spent more time in Zichron Yaacov and Jaffa than in the new colony of Morasha. Nachum and Ruchel insisted that Tevye share their tiny cottage with them, but Tevye refused. He didn't want to intrude on the newlyweds. Little Moishe and Hannie slept in their one room as it was, so Tevye remained in the barn with the rest of the bachelors and cows.

"*Oy vay*," he thought. That's the way it goes. You work all of your life, you raise seven daughters, you live with a woman twenty-five years, and then you are left out in the barn to sleep with the beasts. Every man had his *mazel*. If the barn was to be Tevye's, so be it. His Golda had been an angel. So who was he to complain? Twenty-five years with an angel was reward enough for one lifetime. Not that it had always been easy to live with an angel, but even in her angriest moments, Golda never made her husband sleep in the barn.

It wasn't that Tevye felt lonely. He had other men to talk to, and, like in the past, he still enjoyed a good conversation with a horse or a cow, but neither a man nor a beast was a woman, and a mattress of hay could never take the place of a bed.

"Why don't you marry again?" Hillel asked him during one of their frequent late evening walks.

It was one of those magical nights that are so unique to the Holy Land, when you feel like you can reach out and touch thousands of stars. It was during these tranquil nocturnal strolls, or during his secluded night hours of guard duty, that Tevye most felt the full wonder of life. Under the vastness of the heavens, when the labors of the day gave way to peaceful contemplation of night, a man could feel his smallness in the universe, and experience the greatness of his Creator.

"Marry again?" Tevye asked. "What for?"

"A wife is better than a cow, is she not?"

"That depends on the woman, and the cow," Tevye answered. "Fortunately, I was married to an angel. No woman could ever replace her."

"The Torah says that it is not good for a man to live alone," Hillel reminded.

"So why don't you marry?" Tevye asked.

"What woman wants a lame minstrel like me?" Hillel said with a sigh.

"What woman wants a broken down horse of a milkman like me?"

"You're still as strong as an ox," the musician said.

"An ox with one foot in the grave," Tevye tiredly answered.

"In this world, we all have one foot in the grave."

"Comfort me with your music instead of your speeches," Tevye said. "Besides, if I were to marry, my angel Golda would haunt me the rest of my life. Do you think she wants a strange woman sharing my bed? I'd rather sleep with the cows than awaken the wrath of my Golda."

Hillel took up a tune on his harmonica, and the two bachelors walked on accompanied by the lonely chords of his song.

Weeks passed. Spurred on by the challenge of transforming the rugged terrain into fertile orchards and vineyards, the Jews of Morasha kept to their mission with a passionate fervor. As Tevye guided his team of horses and plow along the long furrows which would one day sprout bushels of corn, he thought of his children and grandchildren. Everything he was doing, he was doing for them. And for Golda. Often he would talk to her out loud, to take his mind off of the pains in his back. He didn't remember his Golda speaking about the Land of Israel, but in his imagination, he built it into her dream. This is what she would have wanted for her children. Her voice rang in his ears, encouraging him, helping him to hold the plow in line, helping him to believe that the seeds he was planting would truly grow into corn stalks and wheat. With her great faith in him, nothing could break him, nor dampen the spirit of optimism which he put into all of his labor.

Not that everything was all roses. Almost nightly, there were discussions about abandoning the area to search out a better irrigated site, but the settlers decided to stay with the hope that their work would be blessed from Above. Whenever LeClerc visited the new settlement to see what progress had been made, all of the settlers crowded around him with a chorus of demands and complaints. They were short of manpower, short of horses, and short of tools. They had been promised 150 square dunams of land apiece, but had received only seventy-five. Shipments of meat which were supposed to be sent from Zichron Yaacov rarely arrived, and their stock of medicine and bandages was depleted. Finally, the distance they had to travel to their fields, day after day, was a punishment that was taking a toll on everyone, including their mules and their horses. LeClerc made notes in a pad and promised to pass on the information to the appropriate officials in Paris.

"Paris?!" Tevye exclaimed. "We're the ones living here. We

know what we need. What do our problems have to do with some clerk sitting on his *tochis* in Paris?"

"I sympathize with your plight," the dapper dresser told them. "I sincerely do. And so does the Company. For this reason, I have brought a team of experts to assist in the great task before you."

With him were an agronomist, a botanist, an engineer, and a mechanic whose job it was to study the area and make a report to the central office detailing how Morasha could be built into a money-making project. For the moment, Tevye's anger abated. Though he didn't know what an agronomist did, he was impressed by the professionalism of the contingent. None of the settlers understood French, so no one knew what the experts were saying, but they certainly gave out an impression that they knew about farming. They spent a full day exploring the site, taking measurements with some sort of surveying instrument Tevye had never see, making notes, testing the soil and water, and even taking some pictures with a camera they had brought in their wagon. At the end of the day, the settlers were handed a list of crops to plant. Seeds of mulberry, fenugreek, lentils, sorghum, sesame, maize, tobacco, sunflowers, and almonds were to be shipped out immediately, though, of course, they didn't arrive until the planting season was over.

A short time afterward, a "welcoming committee" of Arabs came on a peace mission. Their caped and caftaned leaders were called *Muktar* Abdul Abdulla and *Muktar* Muchmad Mohammed. They said that they represented the villages in the area, and that they had come to make a treaty with the Jews. Elisha, the Yemenite, spoke Arabic fluently, and he served as translator and spokesman for the Morasha pioneers. He said that a *Muktar* was the chief of a village, like the sheik of a bedouin tribe. Tables were set up outside and refreshments were served to the guests. *Muktar* Abdulla said that they recognized the right of the Jews to settle the country, saying that it was written in their holy Koran that the Jews would return to the Land of Canaan one day, and that Allah had promised the Land to the children of Jacob. They wanted to make peace, to work together, and develop the region. The *Muktar* said he held legal claim to a large tract of land on the other side of the mountain, which was far superior to the Morasha site, and he was willing to sell it to the Jews. The land could house thousands of families, he said, and its water supply was abundant. Furthermore, he confided over a second glass of vodka, the Arabs wanted to unite with the Jews to throw out the Turks. They had 300 trained soldiers ready for battle, but the Jews would have to supply them with guns. When they conquered the Turks, they said, the Jews could have *Eretz Yisrael* with all of its Biblical borders, while the Arabs would take the lands which Allah had given to Ishmael.

Tevye ordered his daughters to gather the food which was set aside for the Sabbath and to prepare a festive banquet. Hadn't Abraham welcomed all travelers into his tent, even idol worshippers with dirt on their feet? After all, didn't the Jews and the Arabs share the same ancestral father, Abraham? Furthermore, the Arabs had come with an offer of peace, and *shalom*, the rabbis taught, was the foundation of the world.

"How can you trust them?" Bat Sheva asked. "Remember what they did to Ben Zion."

"May his soul rest in peace," Tevye said.

True, Arabs had murdered Ben Zion, but maybe the tribes in the region were different. They certainly acted sincere.

"Obviously, these Arabs are more religious," he said. "And though I don't understand what they are saying, your father, Tevye, has done business in the far corners of the world, and he knows when a man can be trusted. So hurry and prepare us a feast for our neighbors."

"What about food for *Shabbos*?" Yankele asked, reluctant to slaughter a chicken for a weekday repast.

"God won't let us go hungry on the Sabbath," Tevye assured him.

Bottles of wine and Arak appeared, and the Arabs and Jews sat down for a meal. True, the Arab soldiers escorting the chiefs kept their rifles strapped over their chests, and Goliath never wandered far from his ax, but a spirit of brotherhood surrounded the occasion.

Fortunately, LeClerc was absent, away on one of his frequent trips to Jaffa, where he was rumored to have a mistress. The *Muktar*s, Tevye noticed, religiously abstained from liquor. For entertainment, two of the Arab horsemen demonstrated their skill with their swords, slicing melons in half at full gallop, and Hillel played his accordion. Inspired by the liquor and the prospects of acquiring a better piece of land, Tevye balanced a bottle of vodka on his head and taught *Muktar* Abdulla, how to dance like a Hasidic Jew. By the end of the banquet, Tevye had made a new friend. The *Muktar* bowed low and invited the settlers of Morasha to visit his village for a tour of the property which his tribe was offering to sell. A date was arranged, and the Arabs rode off. Immediately, Nachman wrote a letter to the Baron regarding the available land, promising to forward more details as soon as they inspected the site and determined its price. But a reply from Paris was never received. When LeClerc was told about the visit of the Arabs and the proposition they had made, he wrote his own letter to Paris, advising the Baron against further land acquisitions in the region, at least until the Morasha experiment proved that the area was conducive to increased Jewish settlement.

"For the moment," he wrote, "the stamina and mettle of these religious Jews is an unknown commodity which only time will disclose. If their complaining can be turned into constructive hard work, then the Morasha project might deserve greater manpower and investment. But for the present, further Company outlay and development in the region is to be strongly discouraged."

Chapter Twenty-Five

TEVYE CURES THE MUKTAR'S DAUGHTER

On the arranged date, the Jews set out to survey the land which their Arab neighbors wanted to sell. The *Muktar* Abdulla graciously sent them a guide who showed them the way through the mountains to his village. Traveling on horseback, the journey up and down the hillsides and valleys took them two hours, but a bird could have spanned the same distance in minutes. While LeClerc was adamantly against the meeting, calling it an excuse to take off from work, the Morasha settlers went all the same, having reached the conclusion that the Morasha colony desperately needed to find a new site. The topography of their present location was simply not suited for farming. If the parcel which the Arabs were selling had more potential than Morasha, than the settlers would advise the Baron to buy it. They hoped that by appealing to the Baron directly, they could circumvent his parsimonious clerk.

In the meantime, the Morasha pioneers had made another important decision. After days of debate, the community forum had voted to hire Arab laborers to work with them in the fields. Nachman and Shmuelik were against the plan for ideological reasons. It was important, they claimed, to build a Jewish work force, and to rely solely on Jewish labor. Tevye was more pragmatic. The settlers were shorthanded, the work was never ending, and they needed to make as much progress as they could before the winter began. Also, if there were Arabs to work in the fields, the Jews would be free to erect more houses. In the end, Tevye's supporters won out.

The Arab village was modest in size, consisting of a few dozen mud dwellings, surrounding a centralized mosque. Children walked barefoot and scavenged through mounds of garbage. Many were skeleton thin, and yellow pus dripped from their eyes. Dogs lounged lifelessly in the shade, their tongues hanging out of their mouths, their ribs clearly visible in their emaciated chests. Chickens ran around everywhere. Dangling from a pole was the head of a camel. Flies swarmed around the blood which was still dripping from the cut where the neck had been severed from the animal's body.

"Camel is an Arab delicacy," Elisha told Tevye.

"They eat it?" Tevye asked, his eyes wide in surprise.

"Not only do they eat it – they'll expect you to eat it too."

The *Muktar* rushed forward and greeted them warmly, falling on his knees and bowing. His hand moved ceremoniously from his heart to his lips in gestures of loyalty and devotion. For what seemed a full minute, the Jews faced the Arabs and bowed in exchanges of mutual honor. How different this tribe was from the Arabs who had murdered Ben Zion, Tevye thought. Still bowing, the chief inviting the Jews into his house, where a feast was laid out before them. Noticing their worried glances, the *Muktar* assured them that in preparing the food, he had been careful to respect the dietary laws of the Jews. All of the salads, vegetables, and fruits could be eaten, and the main course was to be a Mediterranean couscous with raisins and nuts. The *Muktar's* daughters poured tea from gleaming brass pots, and a water pipe filled with aromatic herbs was passed around for all to imbibe. Nachman refrained from eating the Arab pita, but Tevye and Elisha washed their hands and made a *HaMotzei* blessing on the bread, not wanting to offend their host who insisted they eat. Watching the Yemenite break off pieces of pita and scoop up the heavily oiled techina and humous, Tevye followed suit, as if he had been eating oriental salads for years. To his surprise, he found himself taking seconds of the pasty, exotic spreads. Nonetheless, as more colorful dishes and salads were spread out before them, Tevye kept an eye out for the other half of the camel which they had seen hanging outside.

The *Muktar* poured the Jews glasses of a tasty date liqueur which Elisha called *Yaish*.

"*L'Chaim*," the chief toasted, allowing himself a small sip.

"*L'Chaim*," the Jews responded.

After the satiating meal, the *Muktar* Abdul Abdulla showed the Jews his land deed and led them on a tour of the parcel of land which he wanted to sell, a short ride away from the village. The site was situated upon a plateau, with breathtaking views to all sides. Underground wells were plentiful, and, in the past, much of the land had been cultivated, obviating the need to carve fields out of the rocky soil. Hillsides had been planted with olive trees, and terraced for vineyards.

"All we would have to do is build houses," Tevye said after they had circled the property.

One did not have to be an expert in farming to see that the plateau was ideally suited for crops. Also, the view which the site commanded overlooking the surrounding valleys had obvious strategic advantages. Furthermore, the *Muktar* assured them, as long as they were his neighbors, he would protect them and keep other, less friendly tribes away.

The hearty feast, the beauty of the region, and the Arab's sincerity combined to convince the Jews. But to everyone's surprise, Elisha shook his head, no. As far as he was concerned the site was out of the question. The altitude of the plateau would make for brutal winters. Plus, the site was in the middle of nowhere, a long six-hour journey from Zichron Yaacov, and a two to three day excursion to Jerusalem, Jaffa, or Tiberias.

"Who needs to be close to Jaffa?" Tevye asked.

Elisha walked over to his friend and took him a few steps to the side.

"If we seem too eager, the cost of the land will be four times the price. Abdulla may be a decent man, but he's still an Arab. He'll flash a big, sincere smile and let us pay ten times what the property is really worth. You've seen his village. They need the money even more than we need the land. I grew up with the Moslems, so leave the bargaining to me."

Sure enough, the *Muktar* wanted the equivalent of fifty francs per dunam, almost five times the amount which the Baron had paid for the Morasha site. When Elisha told the Arab that the price was outrageous, a look of insult spread over his face, and he angrily walked away. The Yemenite winked at his friends and motioned with his head for them to follow him as he walked to his horse. Seeing that the Jews were getting ready to leave, the *Muktar* turned around and told them to wait. He had reconsidered the matter. Because he liked them so much and wanted them as neighbors, he would subtract five francs per dunam off of the price. Elisha mounted his horse. The other Jews did the same.

"Twenty francs per dunam," the Yemenite said.

"Twenty francs!" the Arab exclaimed. "For a choice piece of land like this? Where else in Palestine can you find such excellent land?"

The *Muktar* bent down and scooped up a handful of brown soil. He continued his sales pitch, listing all of the land's many praises. More than that – the land was an inheritance from his father. How could he let it go for so much less than its value?

"Thirty francs per dunam," Elisha said with the face of a card player.

"Get down from your horses and we will talk," Abdulla said.

"Why get down when we will only have to mount once again?" the Yemenite answered. "We are poor farmers with barely enough food for our families. Even if we were to sell the land we own now, we wouldn't have enough money to meet the price you are asking."

The Arab nodded his head.

"I understand," he answered. "We are also poor people. The land is our only wealth. I cannot give it away for less than its worth."

Solemnly, he walked to his horse and mounted.

"Of course, we can still be friends," he said.

"Absolutely," Elisha agreed.

"You have an open invitation to visit our village."

"And you and your people are welcome in Morasha," the Yemenite said.

Elisha raised his hand in a wave and wished the Arab *shalom*.

He yanked the reins of his horse and started to ride away. The other Jews followed. After some moments, the *Muktar* called for them to wait and galloped alongside them.

"Give me thirty-five francs per dunam, and the land is yours."

"Thirty," Elisha answered. "And only if our main Company office in Paris agrees to the price.

"Company?" the Arab inquired. "What company? I thought you were farming the land on your own."

Elisha explained that any transaction for land would have to be approved by the Jewish Colony Association which was headed by the Baron Edmond de Rothschild in Paris. When Abdulla heard the name of the Baron, rubles shone in his eyes. He started to yell. Soon both he and Elisha were shouting. Their hands flew in the air like roosters fighting over the same cob of corn.

"Thirty-five!"

"Thirty!"

"Thirty-five!"

"Thirty!"

"Thirty-five!"

"Thirty!"

Finally, after the Jews made a pretense of riding off once again, the *Muktar* gave in and agreed to lower the price.

On the way back to the village, as the Arabs led the way, Tevye congratulated Elisha on having bargained twenty francs per dunam off of the sale.

"If he agreed to thirty," the Yemenite answered, "you can be sure that it's worth fifteen."

"So why did you agree to pay thirty?"

"Who agreed? I said it was dependent on the Baron. The next time we talk, I'll say that the Baron refuses to pay more than ten. That way we'll settle on twenty."

"What makes you so sure?" Tevye asked. "Maybe in the meantime, the Arabs will sell the land to some other buyer."

"Do you really think people are waiting on line? In this country, who else but a Jew would buy farmland on the top of a mountain in the middle of nowhere?"

"Then why even pay twenty?" Tevye wanted to know.

"Because the *Muktar* can't sell the land for what it really is worth and then go back to being the chief of his people. We have to pay him a little extra to guard his pride."

When they returned to the Arab village, the *Muktar* had a parting request. Several of his goats were sick, and perhaps one of the settlers could offer a cure, for as everyone knew, the Jews knew the secrets of the universe. Instinctively, the settlers looked at Tevye. If anyone knew about goats, it was bound to be a milkman.

"I'm not an animal doctor," he said.

The chief wouldn't take no for an answer. The disease was spreading, and it threatened to infect all of the animals of the tribe. He led them to the outskirts of the village, where the Arabs grazed their herds. The sick goats lay listlessly on the ground. Tevye bent down to examine one of the inert creatures. He opened its mouths to look at its gums and its tongue, then raised up an eyelid to check the white of its eye. Finally, Tevye lifted its stiff, lowered tail for a glimpse of its bottom. The diarrhea Tevye saw in the area confirmed his suspicions. He stood up and brushed his hands on his pants.

"It is probably worms," he said. "Try chopping up garlic into very small pieces, mix it with something sweet like red wine and apples, and feed it to the goats for three days. If it's worms, the garlic should kill them, and if not, then *Allah* will help."

The Arab raised his hands to the sky.

"Certainly Allah will help," he agreed. "He will help through his messengers, the Jews, who he has brought back to the Holy Land."

Bowing graciously, the *Muktar* wished them *"Salaam."* Before they departed, he promised to send them the laborers they needed to work in their fields. Making sure their water pouches were full, and that their saddle bags were bursting with fruit, he sent them on their way with the guide who had brought them to the village.

Immediately upon their return to Morasha, Nachman wrote

another letter to the Baron, describing in detail the property they had found.

Several days later, a dozen Arab workers showed up just as Abdul Abdulla had promised. They brought with them a special gift for Tevye, an exquisitely embroidered caftan fit for a king. The present was a token of thanks for having cured the disease of the goats. The garlic had worked. Tevye had saved the village. News of the incident spread to the neighboring Arab tribes, and Arabs began to show up in Morasha with sick animals in tow. Each time the milkman protested, but the Arabs would wave their hands no, insisting that only "the *Muktar* Tevye" could cure them.

At first, the Arab workers, or "*Fellahim*," as they were locally known, proved a godsend to the struggling new colony. They worked like mules, performing the most difficult tasks without any complaints. Heat didn't seem to faze them, and like camels, they could go without water from morning till night. Often their knowledge of the land and their farming experience saved the Jews from planting in areas which were hostile to delicate crops. When LeClerc insisted that the settlers follow the instructions of the Paris agronomists, the settlers revolted and listened to the Arabs instead. While the Jews had to pay the hired laborers out of their personal yearly allowance, the investment allowed the development of the colony to proceed at a much swifter pace. Work on the canal continued, and the Jews constructed more dwellings to prepare for the approaching winter. It was as if a great weight had been removed from their shoulders. The extra manpower boosted the morale of the colony in such a remarkable way that for the first time, settlers began talking about the future of Morasha. Plans for a *mikvah* were drawn, and a shed was erected near the well to house the ritual bath, so that the women of the settlement wouldn't have to make the long journey to Zichron Yaacov in order to abide by the Torah laws which governed marital relations.

Nachman and Shmuelik remained firm in their opposition to the new Arab workers. Not only were they against the arrangement for ideological reasons, the settlers had to pay for the workers themselves, out of their fugal allowance, and most of the Jews had to borrow the money, at interest, from the Jewish Colony Association. Because borrowing at interest from Jews was a practice forbidden by the Torah, Nachman warned that no benefit or blessing could possibly come from such an affair. A Jew was enjoined to loan money out of kindness, and not to make money from the plight of a fellow Jew. Nachman complained bitterly to LeClerc, but the unctuous clerk shrugged his shoulders, saying that interest on loans was Company policy to insure that the settlers would not become freeloaders living on the Baron's unending charity. Tevye had heard that there were affluent Turks in Jerusalem who lent money to Jews, and he suggested borrowing money from them. True, their interest rate was much higher than the Baron's, but at least the settlers wouldn't be breaking a commandment. If, God willing, the harvest was good, the settlers would have enough money to pay back the Turks, without ever having to transgress the Torah.

"And if the harvest, God forbid, isn't good?" Hillel asked.

"Why shouldn't the harvest be good?" Tevye answered. "With our hard work and the Lord's blessing, of course the crops will be good. Surely, the same God who divided the Red Sea can supply the Jews of Morasha with a good crop of carrots, potatoes, cucumbers, and beets."

A vote was taken in a general meeting, and to Nachman's satisfaction, it was decided that if loans charging interest had to be transacted, they would be made only with Turkish merchants or banks. However, when Nachman called for another vote regarding the hiring of Arab workers, he and Shmuelik remained the only dissenters.

Often, Tevye would look up from his plowing to find himself surrounded by the swarthy, barefooted laborers. Since Tevye was the head of settlement security, he decided to place a *shomer* on guard, not only at night, but all through the day as well, to give the impression that the Jews were constantly on the alert. While he trusted the *Muktar* and his workers, he had lived long enough to have learned that any man can succumb to temptation. Sure enough, though the Arabs did their work in a diligent, well-behaved manner, already in the second week of their employment, the settlers discovered that a mattock was missing. Then a scythe disappeared. When Elisha's healthiest goat was stolen, Tevye sent off an angry letter to the *Muktar*. The very next day, the goat was returned, with apologies and the promise that the stealing would stop.

One day, the *Muktar* himself galloped into the Morasha colony. Sobbing, he fell into Tevye's arms. His eldest daughter was dying. The girl, he said, was ill with some mysterious disease which only Tevye could cure. Tevye protested, insisting he wasn't a doctor. Abandoning all ceremony and stature, the Arab leader fell to the ground, grabbed Tevye's shoes, and begged him to return with him to his village. A physician had examined the girl, and all of his remedies had failed. Her condition was weakening. Only the wisdom of the Jews could save her. He would pay Tevye money, give him cattle and land, whatever Tevye demanded. Finally, at Elisha's prodding, Tevye consented. The relieved Arab prostrated himself on the ground and cried out effusive praise to Allah.

"Hurry, hurry," he urged. "Every moment matters."

"This is madness," Tevye said to Elisha as they saddled their horses.

"If the girl recovers, he's liable to send us workers for free," the Yemenite answered.

"And if she dies?"

"It's hard to say. In Yemen, if a caliph thought a doctor had made a mistake, he would cut off his hands."

Tevye's fingers froze on the horn of his saddle. He glanced at his friend to see if he was joking, but Elisha's expression didn't change.

Just to make sure that he returned in one piece, Tevye brought Ariel and Yigal along as his bodyguards. They rode in a sprint, driving their mounts to keep up with the galloping *Muktar*. The villagers who were gathered around the chief's house made way for the Jews to enter. The high-pitched wailing of grief-stricken women filled the crowded bedroom. Bowing, they hastened outside when Tevye arrived. The room was dark and suffocating. Immediately, Elisha ordered that a hole be made in the mud wall to let in fresh air and light. Axes quickly appeared, and a window was punched through the wall. One look at the feverish girl told Tevye the problem. Her face had turned yellow. Eyes black as the night looked up at him imploringly, as if he were her only hope. She seemed to be the same age as his daughters.

The girl's father stared anxiously at Tevye.

"You can examine her alone if you like," he said. "We can leave the room."

"I don't have to examine her," Tevye answered. "I think she has hepatitis."

Elisha translated the ailment as "the yellow disease."

"Can she be cured?" the *Muktar* asked.

Tevye didn't know what to tell him. In Russia, when hepatitis struck, some people lived and others were carried out of their houses in burial sheets. The only treatment he knew, he remembered from his grandfather's house. But he wasn't at all certain that it would work on an Arab. It was a secret the Jews had kept to themselves. If a plague of yellow fever hit the gentiles, the Jews went about their own business, without saying a word, in fear that if the cure didn't work, the gentiles would attack them for witchcraft.

"Allah is great," Tevye said.

"Yes, Allah is great," the father concurred. "But what can we mortals do?"

"I can only suggest a possible remedy, but I cannot promise the *Muktar* that the treatment will work. Take a young dove and placed it on the girl's stomach," Tevye advised. "If Allah decrees, the fever will pass from your daughter into the bird. The dove will die, and your daughter will live."

Inspired with hope, the father rushed out of the bedroom, ordering that a dove be immediately brought to the house. The girl looked up at Tevye with her dark Mediterranean eyes and said a soft thank you. Abdulla yelled that refreshments be served, and in minutes a banquet of fruit was laid out in the salon before

Tevye and Elisha. Within minutes, a young man rushed into the house holding a dove in his hands. The worried father took it from him and held it out to the doctor, but Tevye modestly declined.

"Your wife can do it," he said.

"Wife!" Abdulla called. Immediately, four women appeared. The *Muktar* handed the dove to one of them, gave her instructions, and they all followed her into the bedroom. "*Gevalt*," Tevye thought. "The old goat has four wives!"

Elisha smiled, reading Tevye's mind.

"Thank God that I'm not a *Muktar*," Tevye said quietly as Abdulla followed the women into the bedroom. His Golda, may her memory be blessed, had been the treasure of his life. But four Goldas? Even if he had had four houses and a Golda in every house, that was a blessing he was thankful to have been spared. After delivering milk from morning till night, what man had the strength to placate four women at home?

The house became tensely silent. The Arabs filling the room stared at the Jewish visitors. Minutes passed. Suddenly, a cheer sounded from the bedroom. The sick girl's mother returned to the room with a dead dove in her hands. She had placed the bird on her daughter's belly, and within minutes, the bird had turned limp and died. The patient was peacefully sleeping.

A happy Abdulla returned to the room. Tevye stood up and said the death of the bird was a positive sign. For the time being, there was nothing more he could do. If the girl didn't improve by morning, they could repeat the procedure again, but two doves were the limit. The grateful father insisted on sending Tevye home with a wagon load of produce, but Tevye refused. If the girl recovered, that would be his payment. Before letting the Jews start on their way, the *Muktar* begged Tevye to pray for his daughter.

"Allah answers the prayers of the Jews," he said.

What choice did Tevye have? The Arabs were their neighbors. The *Muktar*, in a way, was his friend. There was nothing in the Bible which forbade a Jew from praying for the health of a gentile. On the contrary, Abraham prayed for the Philistine king, Avimelech, and the king and his wife were healed. And the liturgy of *Rosh HaShana*, one of the holiest days of the year, was filled with prayers for all of mankind. So Tevye prayed, "May the Almighty heal the *Muktar*'s daughter."

Ten days later, the Abdul Abdulla showed up once again in Morasha. This time his daughter was with him. Like a princess, she rode in a wagon, swathed in a shawl and a veil which covered her cheeks. Flowers, the color of a sunset, were braided into her hair like a crown. Tevye was working in his garden when the *Muktar* rushed up and embraced him. His daughter had miraculously recovered. His friend Tevye had saved her from death. The very same day that Tevye had come to their village, the sick girl had stood on her feet. The next day, her color had returned to her face.

"See for yourself," the happy *Muktar* said, pointing at his daughter.

With the veil hiding the lower half of her face, it was hard to tell how she was feeling. But the look of deep gratitude in her black, flashing eyes told Tevye that she had recovered.

The *Muktar* barked at his daughter, obviously commanding her to lower the veil for the doctor. When her fingers pushed the silk strands away, Tevye understood why Abdulla was so passionately concerned about his eldest daughter. She was, by all standards, a beauty.

"I can never repay you enough," the chief said. "But to show you my gratitude, I want to give you my daughter in marriage. She will convert to your religion. She will learn to speak Hebrew. I promise you, she will be an obedient wife."

Tevye was dumbfounded. For one of the few times in his life, he couldn't find words.

The Arab held out his hand for his daughter to come down from the wagon. A slender golden leg appeared from the folds of her sari-like gown as she stepped down to the ground. Flustered, Tevye glanced away at his garden.

"Isn't she beautiful?" the *Muktar* asked, proudly displaying the girl, as if she were a horse in the market.

Gracefully, like a snake in the grass, the girl moved forward in her long flowing dress. She was young, yes, but a woman all the same. Long black hair cascaded over her shoulders. Embarrassed, Tevye couldn't find words.

"Please," Abdulla said. "Take her. She's yours."

With the *Muktar* grabbing his arm, it was impossible for Tevye not to gaze at the girl. But even if a flood of raging waters were to smash the dam inside him, he would never, never give in. Some things were unthinkable. Some things could never be condoned. How could he ever face God? And how could he ever look at his daughters? What would become of all he had taught them if he himself were to be conquered by the wild beating in his heart? No, he would rather spend his life in the barn with the horses and cows than take some strange Delilah for a wife.

"Save me, dear Golda, save me," he thought, clinging to her memory with all of his might.

"I will give you a rich dowry with land and with horses when you take her," the Arab chief promised. "The marriage will be like a peace treaty between our two peoples."

Tevye shook his head. No, no, it never could be. But he couldn't find the right words to answer.

"Isn't it written in your Bible that a man should not live alone? Allah heard your prayers and brought my girl back to life. Now she is yours forever."

Tevye shook his head. He glanced at the girl, and her eyes flashed a look of unabashed gratitude, so bold and direct that Tevye felt as if a bomb had gone off in his head. He looked down at the ground, but even the mere sight of her sandaled foot made him shudder.

"Golda, save me," he prayed.

Just then, Shmuelik called out his name. He stood in the doorway of the hut which served as the community synagogue. It was time for the afternoon prayer. Apologizing to the *Muktar*, Tevye said he had to hurry and pray before the sun sank in the west. He literally ran away, happier than he had ever been in his life about going to *shul*. The service had already started. Tevye stood there to make up the *minyan* of ten, but neither his mind nor his heart could focus on the words of the prayer. The eyes of the *Muktar*'s daughter haunted him wherever he looked.

"*Gevalt*," he thought. "Please God forgive me for sinful thoughts and get me out of this mess."

At the end of the *Kaddish*, he grabbed Elisha and desperately took him aside.

"You have to help me," he said. "Abdulla is waiting outside. His daughter recovered, and he's so grateful, he's brought her to Morasha to give her to me as a gift."

"As a daughter?"

"As a wife."

"*Mazal tov!*" the Yemenite said.

"What *mazal tov*?" Tevye stammered. "This is the work of the devil. You have got to do something to save me."

Unconsciously, Tevye squeezed his friend's arm until he cried out in pain.

"If you don't want her, tell him no."

"I don't want to injure his pride," Tevye said.

Elisha nodded his head. "That's true. *Muktar*s have killed people for less."

"They are waiting outside," Tevye said.

"Let's go and talk to him."

"You go. I'll stay here. Please. I'll do anything. Just get me out of this hell."

"All right," the Yemenite agreed. "You stay here and have a drink. There's some wine in the cabinet. You look like you need it. I will see what I can do."

Tevye found the bottle. He himself had put it there, so that a proper *"L'Chaim"* could be made on every happy occasion. With trembling fingers, he pulled out the cork and drank straight from the bottle without looking for a glass. But the wine only fueled the fires inside him. Outside the doorway, he could see Elisha talking heatedly with the Arab. "Please God," he prayed. "In the name of the Torah; in the name of our Forefathers, Abraham, Isaac, and Jacob; in the name of my father, and his father before him; in the name of the Covenant of the *Brit* which I bear on my flesh; in the name of Your never-ending mercy, please spare me from the fires of *Gehenna*, and let me return to my simple life in peace."

Looking up, Tevye saw the Arab girl in the door of the synagogue. Not knowing if it were truly her or a demon, he threw himself at the ark where the sacred scroll of the Torah was housed. Wildly, he opened its doors.

"Rise up, O Lord, and vanquish the enemies of Your people!" he called.

When he looked back to the door, the apparition was gone. Elisha appeared in its place. Distressed at the paleness of Tevye's face, he shut the doors of the ark and sat his friend down in a chair.

"The matter has been settled," he said.

"Settled?" Tevye asked. "What does that mean?"

"It means that Abdulla is taking his daughter home and giving you time to make up your mind."

"Make up my mind about what?"

"About whether you want to marry his daughter or mine."

"Marry your daughter?" Tevye asked.

"I had to tell him something," the Yemenite said. "How else could I say that you were not interested and yet not hurt his feelings? So I told him that you were already engaged to my daughter."

"Engaged to your daughter. Yes!" Tevye said with a breath of relief. "That was a wise thing to say. Elisha, my friend, you are a genius."

"At first that didn't bother Abdulla in the least. He said you could marry them both. Just like the great King Solomon had harems of women, so should his friend, Tevye."

"That was King Solomon, while I am only Tevye, the milkman turned farmer."

"That's what I told him. Kings were kings, and farmers have dung on their shoes."

"Truthfully spoken."

"Now there is only one problem," the Yemenite said.

"What problem is that?" Tevye asked.

"If you don't marry my daughter, he will surely come back."

Tevye looked at his friend to see if he was kidding, but the dark face and eyes were unflinchingly earnest.

"Marry your daughter!" Tevye exclaimed. "You must be joking?"

"Does a father joke about marrying off his daughters?"

"Certainly not," Tevye said.

With seven daughters of his own, Tevye knew from experience that the matter was one of the most serious things in the world. Suddenly, he felt surrounded by demons wherever he looked. Not that there was something wrong with Elisha's daughters. One was more beautiful than the next.

"What about my age? I could be a father to your daughters," Tevye protested.

"Experience in life is a great treasure," the Yemenite said. "Besides, it's time my eldest got married."

Once again, Tevye started to sweat. What had happened to his constellations in heaven that his fortune was being spun round and round like a wheel. He had lived a full life already. He was a grandfather several times over. Who had the strength for more new beginnings? And Golda. How could he ever face his Golda? When they met in up in Heaven, how could he ever explain? Not only that, if he were to marry again, and if he got to *Gan Eden*, which one of his wives would be his? If there were such things as pots and pans in Paradise, Golda would be waiting with one in her hand to give him a crack on his head.

"Elisha," Tevye appealed. "You are a reasonable man. To whom are you speaking? To a grandfather. To a man past his prime. To a man who has one foot in the grave. Be fair to your daughter.

"Nonsense. You are as strong as a man half your age."

"And if I were to marry one of your daughters, just between the two of us, how long do you think that my strength would last?"

Elisha slapped his knees in resignation.

"Very well," he said, standing up. "Don't marry my daughter. Marry the *Muktar*'s daughter instead."

"Gevalt!" Tevye said. "Who said I want to marry at all?"

"So live the rest of your life with your cows," the Yemenite answered.

Elisha walked out of the synagogue, leaving Tevye alone in deep thought. He had been minding his own business, tending to the bushes in his garden, and he had ended up insulting both the Arab and the Jew. What did the Lord want from him? To take a new wife? At this stage in his life? Could it be?

He took another drink of wine, returned the cork to the near-empty bottle, and walked to Ruchela's house, longing for a touch of reality. As usual, the children were happy to see him. He sat down on the floor with them and played a game of building sticks as his daughter talked to him from the kitchen. She spoke while she was cooking, but Tevye didn't hear what she said. Images of the Arab girl and Elisha's oldest daughter flashed before his eyes. He remembered the evening when Elisha had introduced him to Carmel and the feelings which her look had aroused even then. Clumsily, he knocked over the tower which the children were building. Moishe and Hannie complained.

"Abba," Ruchel called. *"Abba?"*

"What?" Tevye said.

"Why didn't you answer?"

"Answer what?"

"I asked you what kind of soup you wanted ten times already."

"I didn't hear," Tevye responded.

He stood up and said he had to go. He looked at his daughter. Could he marry a girl a few years older than she was? But, then again, hadn't Lazer, the butcher, been twice Tzeitl's age when Tevye had agreed to a match? And hadn't he been prepared to give one of his daughters to Hillel? Marriages between older men and young women were not so unusual. It wasn't the end of the world. No one yelled scandal. Certainly none of the Hasidic Jews in Morasha would think to raise an eyebrow.

Ruchel was staring at him. "Are you all right, *Abba*?" she asked.

When Tevye looked at her, he saw her mother's features. Would Golda understand? Would his daughters? Of course, he still loved their mother dearly. But yes, he was also a man. True, when Golda had died, he had buried that part of himself with her, but suddenly it had been resurrected. Was that his fault? Was he to blame? Was he truly expected to live out his life in the barn with the mules?

He left Ruchel's house and paced back and forth outside the barn for hours. When he tried to sleep, he couldn't. Every snort of a horse or squawk of a chicken disturbed him. When he shut his eyes, the Arab girl was waiting with a smile. It was the Satan, he was certain, coming to test him. To chase the evil beguiler away, he said *"Shema Yisrael."* But when Tevye closed his eyes again, the Arab girl was back, beckoning him with her gleaming black eyes, and circling around him exotically, in a spellbinding dance.

Tevye leaped up and ran out of the barn. With a roar, he dunked his head in the water trough. When he emerged, his *yarmulka* was floating on the waves. He ran his fingers through his hair and slapped at his face. Then, as if pursued by a devil, he hurried back to the barn, saddled his horse, and rode away into the night. Like a madman, he urged the steed over the mountainside, whacking its rump and jabbing his boots in its belly until its hooves were pounding the earth. Horse and rider raced down the hillside and galloped wildly through the valley. Crazily, he thought of riding to the ocean and jumping into its waves to drown the devil which clung to his back. He thought of riding all the way to Rishon LeZion to fall on Golda's grave and beg forgiveness for his thoughts. He rode on and on until he was lost. Strange mountains loomed up around him. Spurring his horse, he continued his flight. Finally, in exhaustion, he collapsed forward, clutching the horse's neck. Before long, he was snoring. The beast waited patiently, then realizing that its master was sleeping, it started to walk leisurely back home. An hour later, it had found its way back to the barn where the odyssey had begun. Snorting, the horse shook its body, and threw Tevye off into the trough of cool mountain water. The milkman awoke with a gasp. Dripping wet, he climbed out of the trough. Nobody else was in sight.

"Thank God," he said, breathing deeply.

For the moment, the demon had fled.

Chapter Twenty-Six

TEVYE TAKES A WIFE

Both of Elisha's two grown daughters were golden-skinned, beautiful, devoutly religious, and nearly half Tevye's age. The eldest daughter, Carmel, was naturally the first choice of the parents, but Elisha told Tevye he could marry whomever he picked. Embarrassed by the whole distressing business, and wanting the matter to be concluded as discreetly as possible, Tevye told him that Carmel would be fine.

Tevye had never been a man to pay much attention to women, except for his wife, Golda, of course, but now and then on the settlement, he had noticed that Elisha's eldest daughter far surpassed all of the other young women, not only in beauty, but also in the industrious way that she worked. Whether it was in the dining tent, the chicken coop, or the fields, she seemed to do twice as much work as the others. Now that a match was in the making, Tevye helped himself to a few extra looks. Being a man with a great lust for life and a healthy appreciation of the Almighty's Creation, he could not help but notice how truly pretty she was. But her youth made him feel so uneasy, he wanted to forget the whole crazy scheme. As if to make sure, he snuck into Ruchel's house and searched for a mirror. A long time had passed since he had seen his reflection, and now when he stared into her looking glass, he could only shake his head sadly at the old bearded goat that stared back. True, he had not turned grey completely, but white hairs were beginning to sprout in his beard and along the sides of his head like patches of weeds. Catching him with the mirror, Ruchela teased him for being so vain. She said that the "silver" in his hair lent him an air of nobility and wisdom. Laughing, she told him to stop worrying about getting old.

But it was not only his age which bothered Tevye. Suddenly, he noticed that his belly had grown rounder and softer, his teeth had yellowed and chipped, and his back ached so painfully that some mornings he had to summon all of his strength to get out of bed.

"It's all in your mind," Ruchel said. "Besides, Carmel is a woman already with a mind of her own."

To make certain that Carmel was not being forced into the marriage, Tevye sent his daughter on a mission to speak to the bride. He wanted her to know what a broken-down husband she was getting. Tevye himself was too embarrassed to go. Since the day he had agreed to the marriage and shaken hands with the father, Tevye had hardly spoken a word to the young girl herself. For one thing, she was shy, and whenever she glanced at him with her dark, sparkling eyes, Tevye was flabbergasted completely. Suddenly, Tevye, the orator, had nothing to say. Whenever he was next to her, he became as tongue-tied as Moses had been when he had discovered the burning bush.

Ruchel came back with a glowing report. Carmel was all smiles, the happiest girl in the world. For months, she had been casting secret glances at Tevye, her father's best friend. If her father thought highly of him, that was enough for Carmel. The difference in their ages didn't bother her at all. On the contrary, she told Ruchel that Tevye's great wisdom would help them build a proper Jewish house. What bothered Carmel the most, Ruchel said, was her own insecurity in being so young. After all, Tevye hardly ever said a word to her, certainly because he was so learned and worldly, and she was so naive and unschooled.

"What did you answer?" Tevye asked.

"I said that while it was true that you ranked with the likes of *Rashi* and the *Rambam*, you also enjoyed talking to horses and cows, and that she shouldn't let your big beard make her think you were as old as Methusalah."

Tevye nodded. It was good that a wife should feel some awe for her husband. True, Golda hadn't. But she had lived with Tevye for twenty-five years and seen him in his weakest moments, like

when he had let her cousin Menachem Mendel squander all of
their savings on stocks. He realized that Elisha's daughter saw him
as a philosopher, a statesman, a pioneer builder. It was important,
therefore, that he remain bigger than life in her eyes, and not let
her find out that he was really an ordinary *nebick* like everyone else.

Bat Sheva was happy for Tevye too. Unbeknownst to her
father, she had been seeing a lot of Ariel, Elisha's oldest son. She
had arranged to work with him in the fields and even joined him
for guard duty at night. He was as handsome and idealistic as Ben
Zion had been, yet humble and unassuming. To attract him, Bat
Sheva found herself behaving more modestly and religiously than
she ever had in the past. Never once did he touch her or kiss her,
even when she pretended that she didn't know how to shoot a
rifle and asked him to teach her. She did her best not to flirt in a
manner which would scare him away. How strange fortune was,
Bat Sheva thought. If her father and Carmel were to marry, and if
she and Ariel were to wed, Carmel would be not only her
sister-in-law, but her stepmother as well.

Once Tevye's children consented, there was only one obstacle
in the way. Golda. But here too, like in every other question of
life, the code of the Torah was clear. Nachman showed Tevye the
law in the *Shulchan Aruch*. Opening the large volume, he let Tevye
read. If a man's wife were to die, God forbid, as soon as the period
of mourning had ended, he was to marry again. A man was a man,
and he had been created to live with a woman, as it said in the
Bible, *"Be fruitful and multiply."* That was God's will. The Jews had
to populate the Holy Land's borders. They needed farmers,
teachers, builders, rabbis, and soldiers. *"Be fruitful and multiply,"* was
a *mitzvah*. The Jews had a country to build!

Tell that to Golda. She wasn't just a memory that Tevye could
forget. She inhabited his every thought and breath, just as she had
when she was living. She had remained his faithful partner, in
death as in life. How could he abandon her now? How could he
expect her to turn the other way when he brought a strange exotic
woman into his house? He tried to explain to her, to cajole her,
apologize to her, and, patiently, he tried to assure her that he loved

her now more than ever, and that he would never let his new wife take her place in his heart.

"But my Golda," he pleaded, as the day of the wedding approached, "a man needs a women in the house. Have mercy. Is your Tevye an angel that you expect him to share his life with a farm animal forever?"

But all of his entreaties did him no good. The week before the wedding, he hardly slept a wink. Closing his eyes, he immediately saw his wife, Golda, standing at the entrance to the barn with a butcher's cleaver in her hand.

"Is this my reward?" she would say. "After cleaning your dirty clothes and underwear for twenty-five years, you bring a Yemenite princess into my house? A young girl. A child the age of my daughters? Is this scandal my thanks? Is this humiliation to be my destiny in heaven? Is my soul to fly between heaven and hell without rest? Is this why you brought me to Israel? To witness your betrayal firsthand? To die a thousand new deaths each time you embrace this stranger?"

More than once, Tevye woke up in a sweat. On the day of the wedding, desperate to quiet her screams, he went to sit in the blacksmith's shed, and held his head near the clang of the anvil to exorcise the curses he heard. But the ringing of the hammer only made his anguish worse. Finally, unable to stand up to his wife, he searched for Elisha in his field. Finding him, Tevye fell to his knees.

"I'm calling off the wedding," he said.

"Stand on your feet like a man!" the little Yemenite commanded.

Flustered, Tevye stood up. He remembered that when Tzeitl had refused to go through with the match he had made with Lazar Wolf, in order to convince Golda that the marriage would bring only disaster, Tevye had invented a dream. Once again, with Elisha, he would use the same scheme.

"For the sake of your daughter," Tevye said.

"What are you babbling about?" the Yemenite asked.

"A dream," Tevye said in wild excitement. "A dream. The same dream came to me every night for a week – a sign that it's true. My wife, Golda, you never met her. She came to me with a warning."

"Tevye, your wife Golda is dead."

"Dead? My wife Golda? You must be mistaken."

"Didn't you tell me you buried her in Rishon LeZion?"

"I thought that I did. But it must have been somebody else. My wife Golda returns every night. You don't know her. What a revengeful woman she is. What a temper. Her jealousy reaches the sky. Believe me, she is planning to kill your daughter. Each night she appears with her knife. One day when I will be out in the fields, she will suddenly appear and slice your daughter to pieces."

"Tevye, have you been drinking?" the bride's father asked.

"Not a drop," Tevye answered, raising his hand in an oath.

"Then you surely have fever."

"I am as healthy and coherent as a person can be. For your own sake, I'm warning you. The wedding must be canceled. If you truly love your daughter, then save her."

Elisha stared at his friend. Something really was the matter. Tevye's hairs stuck out wildly from his *kippah* as if he had been truly frightened by a ghost. Indeed, a wise expression taught, "When there is a wedding, expect the Satan to arrive with the guests." To prevent two souls from uniting in holy matrimony, the forces of evil exert all of their power to interfere.

"What about Abdul Abdulla?" Elisha asked.

"What about him?" Tevye responded.

"When he hears that you haven't married my daughter, he will insist you marry his. And if you don't, he will bring all of his soldiers, with all of the surrounding Arab villages, to war against us. He vowed to me, just as you and I are standing here now, that if you bring disgrace upon him and his daughter, he will slaughter all of the Jews in the region."

"Slaughter all of the Jews?" Tevye asked.

"Those were his words. Believe me. I grew up among Arabs. When their pride is offended, they become savage beasts. I am sorry, Tevye, but to save all of our women and children, you will have to marry my daughter."

What was Tevye to do? Certainly, it was better to have Golda curse him forever, rather than endanger all of the Jews. Elisha put a hand on his shoulder.

"Come my good friend," he said. "Let's go to the synagogue together. I remember, before my own wedding, my father-in-law took me with him to the synagogue to learn. He said that in a place where there is a Torah scroll and learning, demons weren't allowed to enter. We will sit and study together just as God commanded Moses at Sinai. Time passes and a man comes to forget the many laws which govern a husband's life with his wife. It's time for a review. You will see that the blessing of learning Torah will turn all of your worries to joy. If your Golda truly loves you, which I am sure she does, do you really think she wants you to spend the rest of your life in the barn? On the contrary, I assure you, of all of the guests at the wedding, your Golda will be the most pleased."

Tevye let the Yemenite lead him to the synagogue. How strange, he thought. This man, his very own age, was going to be his father-in-law, and Tevye, who already had grandchildren, was going to be his son.

As it turned out, Elisha was right. Golda was the happiest guest at the wedding. She stood at Tevye's side under the canopied *chuppah*, beaming with pride, like a mother at the marriage of her son. Later, Hodel, who had arrived from Shoshana to be with her family for the wedding, confided to her father that she had noticed her too. Golda was even dressed for the occasion, wearing the same white gown which she had knitted for the wedding of Tzeitl and Motel. Her beauty was only surpassed by the bride's. Carmel was adorned in the traditional Yemenite wedding gown and towering flower headset. Seeing how Golda smiled at her, Tevye let out a breath of relief. A grin spread across his serious expression, as wide as the crossing which God had made in the Red Sea for the Jews. Nachman recited the *Ketubah* wedding contract out loud and chanted the nuptial blessings. The bride blushed, Tevye stepped on the traditional glass, Hillel played on his accordion, *"If I not set Jerusalem above my greatest joy,"* and, miracle of miracles, Tevye, the milkman from Anatevka, had a stunning new Yemenite wife.

The *Muktar* Abdulla was the first guest to step forward to greet him.

"Mazal tov," said the Arab. "Since you have chosen not to marry my daughter, then I am giving her to one of your sons."

For the first time in his life, Tevye was happy that he never had boys. Elisha embraced him and welcomed him to the family. Then Nachman, Shmuelik, Hillel, and Goliath, all shook his hand. Ruchel, Bat Sheva, Hava, and Hodel stood on line, waiting for hugs. Finally, Tevye lifted up Moishe and Hannie and gave them a kiss. The *Hasidim* clasped their hands together and started to dance. Tevye winked at his young wife and joined them. Snapping his fingers and holding his arms in the air, Tevye, the son of Schneur Zalman, forgot that he was nearly fifty-years old. He forgot his back hurt in the morning. He forgot all of his worries and doubts. He now had a wife at his side, a helpmate, and friend. A blessing of completeness returned to his heart. Since Golda had died, his life had felt empty. Now he felt whole. Miraculously, with his bride at his side, he felt that his life was beginning anew. Reb Guttmacher, the undertaker, balanced a bottle of wine on his head and stepped forward to entertain the groom and his guests. Tevye grabbed the bottle and shouted a joyous *"L'Chaim!"*

Thus, the Morasha settlement had its first wedding. And for the first time in months, Tevye didn't have to sleep in the barn. The newlyweds were given their own little cottage. As he blew out their candle, Tevye suddenly had a whimsical thought about his old friend, Sholom Aleichem. How amazed the writer would be if he knew what had become of his milkman!

Chapter Twenty-Seven

HODEL LEAVES PERCHIK

Overnight, Tevye's new cottage became a warm, *haimisher* home. In reality, the hastily built structure was merely a hut with a roof, but in the eyes of the newlyweds, it was a royal abode. The morning after the wedding, as if in a dream, the aroma of freshly baked bread awakened the groom. With a feeling of wonder, Tevye watched his beautiful wife prepare him a breakfast of goat's cheese, olives, and the traditional Yemenite bread, *malawach*.

"You missed the morning *minyan*," she said.

"That's to be expected," Tevye answered with a smile. "After all, I am a new *chatan*." Indeed, he felt like a groom.

"Are you happy?" she asked.

"Very," he answered. "I am the happiest man in the world."

Carmel blushed and went back to the tiny brick oven in the corner of the hut which served as a kitchen. Tevye pulled a curtain along the cord which divided the sleeping area from the salon. He dressed and stepped outside to wash his hands and his face in a basin of water. Nachman and Shmuelik were learning in the synagogue when Tevye stepped in to pray. They stood up and shook Tevye's hand and wished him more *mazal tovs*."

"May your own wedding be soon," Tevye said to Shmuelik.

"From your lips to God's ears," the bachelor responded.

"Why didn't you wake me to pray with the others?" Tevye asked as he donned his *tefillin*.

"A *chatan* is a king for the first year of his marriage," Nachman answered. "And a king deserves his rest. So we decided to go ahead without you."

"Some king," Tevye answered. "There is work to be done."

"A one-day vacation won't kill you. Take it easy. Go on a long walk with your wife. Don't worry. Your work will be waiting for you."

Tevye grumbled. It was true, he needed a rest. He felt like a ragged *shmatte*. With all of the tumult leading up to the wedding, his mind was as drained as his body. But, thank God, the demon had fled. Blessed with new insight, he realized that even that madness and the crazy scheme of the *Muktar* had been sent by the Lord, to rescue him from the barn and bring him to wed. Praise be the work of the Lord.

After *davening*, he returned to the house. With a shy, nervous blush, Carmel set his breakfast before him as if she were serving a king. Silently, she poured him a hot cup of tea. Before he had finished eating, she had already swept the floor. Then, without stopping for a moment, she hung a yellow curtain in the window and spread an embroidered quilt on their bed. Tevye had to rise up his feet as she unrolled the hand-woven rug which the *Muktar* had given them for a present. Not to sit idle and stare, Tevye unpacked the candlesticks he had brought from Anatevka and set them on the dresser which Reb Shilo had made. Originally, the candlesticks had belonged to his mother. When Tevye had married, she had given them to Golda.

"Every Sabbath evening, my wife, Golda, would light the Sabbath candles and say a special prayer, recalling my father and mother," Tevye told his new wife.

"I will recall them also," Carmel said softly.

Alongside the candlesticks, Tevye placed his Bible and the six volumes of Mishna which Nachman and Ruchel had given to the newlyweds as a gift. To help bring the blessing of Torah into Tevye's new house, Reb Guttmacher had volunteered to come over every evening to study with the *"chatan"* as he liked to call Tevye. And, amazingly, Tevye felt like a groom. For the first time in ages, he looked forward to the mornings, as if he had a new lease on life. After all, would God have given him such a tender young ewe if his own end was near? Overnight, he felt strong and invincible, as he had as a youth. The Lord God of Israel was with him, filling him with a confidence and joy that he wanted to share with the world.

He even accomplished twice as much work in the field. Miraculously, his back stopped aching, and instead of crashing to sleep on the floor of the barn immediately after the evening prayers, the whole first week of the wedding, he and his bride feasted and celebrated with friends hours into the night. His joy was so great, he failed to notice that behind his Hodel's smile was a deeply troubled heart. All through the week, she was silent, not wanting to spoil her father's great joy. Of course, when Carmel's brother, Yigal, had come to Shoshana to fetch her to the wedding, she had been astonished and pleased with the news. But it was hard to wear a smile when her own marriage was falling apart.

Not until Tevye was driving her back to Shoshana in his wagon did he remember that in addition to being a newlywed husband, he was still a father too. Suddenly, as they were riding along the bumpy road to the north, Hodel broke down like a baby and cried. The reason that Perchik hadn't come to the wedding was not only because of the fast-approaching winter, and the work which had to be done, but because of their terrible fights.

Tevye tugged on the reins of his horse and brought the wagon to a halt. Weeping, his daughter fell into his arms. Ever since the family's visit and Tzeitl's untimely death, her relationship with her husband had soured. Hodel decided that she wanted their house to have a more Jewish feeling. When her baby was born, and she had started to think of his future, her conviction had become more and more vocal. In reaction, her husband had turned into a monster. Judaism, he claimed, was a primitive relic which had to be buried if the Jews of today wanted to build a modern socialist state. The obsession with family, Perchik said, had to be replaced by a selfless devotion to the kibbutz. Their child was to be raised, not at home by his mother and father, but in the children's nursery. Perchik even wanted to pass a law in the kibbutz forbidding husbands and wives from living together. Married life, he claimed, was "erotic selfishness." To him, a home was "a petty bourgeois cell." A child was not private property, but a "commodity of the collective." Somehow, Hodel managed to live with his gibberish, but when he took the child out of her arms and carried him out of the door to the nursery, she realized she had married a golem without any feelings. Hodel had been so enraged, she refused to let her husband back in the house. Either he came back with the baby, or not come back at all. Once again, to Tevye's chagrin, his daughter broke down and wept. Their argument had even come to blows.

"He struck you?" Tevye asked.

Hodel's weeping answered his question.

"If he learns that I've told you, he will kill me," she cried.

"So the pacifist is really a wife beater," Tevye said, feeling his blood boil.

"I don't want to live in Shoshana," Hodel confessed. "I want to be with my family."

"You will, my princess, you will," Tevye assured her. "We'll go and get the child, and you will never have to see your heretic husband again."

"Oh, *Abba*," Hodel said. "Forgive me for spoiling the joy of your marriage."

"Nonsense," said Tevye. "The hoopla is finished and life must go on. How much joy can a poor man withstand? Isn't it written, *'In pain you shall give birth to your children?'* You are my child, are you not? Does a man turn his back on his family? Before anything else I am your father. And I want my grandson to be raised as a Jew."

"I'm sorry, *Abba*," Hodel wept. "If I had listened to you years ago, this would never have happened."

"Cursed be the day that I brought that free thinker into my house," Tevye said. "But what man today is a prophet? By falling down, a child learns to walk. This too will turn out for the best. As Joseph said to his brothers, *'Fret not for God has brought all of this to pass.'* Wasn't it your good-for-nothing husband who brought you to Israel? If you hadn't come first, we never would have followed. So you see, good things can come out of bad."

During the long journey, they had plenty of time to plan how to kidnap the child. They decided that the best time to arrive was in the morning, just after Perchik left for the fields. While Hodel favored giving her husband one last chance to reconsider the consequences of his stubbornness, Tevye was afraid that Perchik might sweet-talk his daughter into staying, and even swear to mend his ways. To Tevye, it was better to sneak into Shoshana after Perchik had gone off to work, pack Hodel's belongings, take the baby, and head back to Morasha before the scoundrel found out. A divorce could be arranged later. The important thing at the moment was to rescue the child.

"Isn't that like stealing?" Hodel asked.

"Certainly not," her father answered. "You are the child's mother."

"It just doesn't seem right not telling Perchik. Maybe if he sees that I am serious, his feelings will change."

"He doesn't have feelings. Only slogans and high-winded theories."

"Maybe if you spoke to him," Hodel said.

"What for?"

"Maybe you can persuade him."

"Will he agree to keep the Sabbath?" Tevye asked.

"No," his daughter admitted. "I don't think so."

"Will he send the boy to learn Torah?"

"Probably not."

"Will he teach him how to put on *tefillin?*"

"You know he doesn't believe in those things. But it isn't his fault. No one taught him when he was a child."

"That doesn't mean that his ignorance has to be passed down to your son. Do you want the boy to grow up as if he belongs to a nation which has no tradition or past?"

"Of course not."

"Then this is the only way," Tevye said. "If he loves you so much that he can't be without you, then he'll know where to find you. But if you raise up your son amongst pig eaters, then he will become a *chazzer fresser* too."

At first, Tevye's strategy worked according to plan. Reaching the road to Shoshana in the evening, they camped along the roadside in order to get an early start in the morning. When the sun had risen over the mountains, they continued on to the kibbutz. In the distance, they could see workers at labor in the fields. While Tevye kept guard outside of the empty house, Hodel quickly packed her things into a suitcase. At the nursery, she kept the conversation short by explaining that she wanted to show her baby to her father, who was waiting outside. They were all in the wagon making their escape back toward the road, when Perchik came galloping up on a horse.

"Greetings," he said with a smile. "And a hearty *mazal tov* to the groom! When I heard you were here, I came rushing. But where are you off to in such a big hurry?"

Hodel didn't answer. Her face had turned white. She looked at her husband and clutched the bundled child in her arms. Immediately from her expression, Perchik understood.

"I am taking my daughter and my grandson away from here," Tevye declared.

"Is that so?" Perchik asked. "And who the hell are you?"

"The fool who brought a godless knave into his house to steal away his daughter."

"So now you are stealing her back?"

"When the great Rabbi Hillel once saw a dead man floating on a river, he called, 'Just as you have drowned others, now someone has drowned you.'"

"Don't quote to me your foolish sayings, old man," Perchik said. He reached down and pulled his rifle out of its sheath.

"Perchik!" Hodel screamed.

"You shut up" he answered.

"Don't blame my father. I want to go with him," she said.

"He's brainwashed you with all of his mumbo-jumbo."

"He hasn't brainwashed me at all. What normal mother doesn't want to bring up her child herself?"

"That's bourgeois sentimentality," he said. "Women have to be free to work in the fields."

"A Jewish woman belongs in the home," Tevye said.

"The Dark Ages are over, old man."

"Get out of our way," Tevye threatened.

"Hodel, get down from the wagon," Perchik ordered.

"Not unless you agree to raise up the boy the way I want him to be raised."

"He will be raised like every other child in this kibbutz, in the way which will most benefit the collective."

"I don't care about your collective!" Hodel yelled. "I am a person with feelings, not some kind of new farming machine."

"Then you can go with your father. But the boy stays here with me."

Husband and wife stared at each other with eyes flashing fire.

"Never," Hodel said. "The boy comes with me."

Trembling, Perchik pulled back the hammer on the rifle.

"Are you as brave without a gun in your hand?" Tevye asked.

Perchik was shaking. Carefully, he set the hammer of the rifle back into place and set it back in its sheath. Then he swung down from his horse.

"Come see for yourself," he challenged.

Tevye set down the reins of the wagon.

"*Abba*, don't," Hodel pleaded.

But Tevye was determined. He had waited a long time for a chance to wipe the smug grin off of his son-in-law's face. While it was a very grave sin to hit a fellow Jew, Perchik was an exception. Didn't it say in the Passover Seder that the fourth son, the scoffer, was to be given a smash in his teeth? With a smile, Tevye stripped off his jacket. Perchik was equally pleased. For him it was a chance to knock the *yarmulka* off his father-in-law's thick, empty skull. Thrusting one leg forward, he raised both his fists in a statuesque stance.

"Be careful, father," Hodel warned. "Perchik learned boxing at the university."

"University *shmurniversity*," Tevye said. "I'll teach him a lesson he will never forget."

"Come on then, old man," Perchik called. You might have robbed your wife's cradle, but I won't let you rob mine."

Angered, Tevye lunged forward with the first punch of the fight. Deftly, Perchik dodged to the side. Stumbling from the momentum, Tevye tumbled to the ground. Perchik chuckled as the older man rose and brushed the dust off his clothes.

"Go home, grandpa, before it's too late," Perchik teased.

"If you touch him, I'll never speak to you again," Hodel warned.

"If you thought I would let you take away my son, you were wrong," he answered.

Again Tevye lunged. This time, Perchik stepped aside while delivering a blow. The punch caught Tevye in the forehead, and he fell once again to the ground with a groan.

"Stop now, dirty old man, and go home to your black, *cushy* wife," Perchik told him.

Tevye stood up and growled. "You dog!" he said and spit. His temple was bleeding. He took a threatening step toward Perchik, but the younger man shot out a fist before Tevye could get his feet planted. The jab was stiff and stinging. Tevye's beard helped soften the blow, but before he could defend himself, another jab landed painfully on his nose. Blood splattered over his clothes.

"Perchik stop!" Hodel pleaded.

Her plea went ignored. Perchik was having too good a time. His next punch was a surprise uppercut to Tevye's belly. The milkman doubled over with a nauseated groan. Perchik merely had to give him a push to topple him onto the ground. Tevye lay moaning.

"*Nu*, Tevye?" Perchik jeered. "Where's your God now?"

Hodel climbed down from the wagon and hurried over to her father, holding her baby with one arm and lifting Tevye with the other. Mocking a milkman was one thing, but mocking the Lord was another. With the fury of a bear, Tevye pushed her away. Perchik was still laughing. With a roar that rang out to Heaven, Tevye grabbed Perchik's shoulders and gave him a powerful butt with his head. Then he booted him square in the groin with his knee. The socialist's mouth opened wide, but for once in his life, he had nothing to say. He doubled over in agony. Before he could straighten back up, Tevye lifted him in the air and hoisted him over his head as if he were a sack of potatoes. Taking a few strides forward, Tevye threw him over the fence of the pigpen. Squealing, the hogs scattered as Perchik landed with a splash in their muck. He lay flat on his back without moving. Hodel instinctively started toward him, but her father held out a hand to stop her.

"Leave him. That's where he belongs."

"Maybe he's hurt."

"You decide," Tevye said. "Either you come with me now, or you spend the rest of your life with this swine you call a husband."

Tevye picked up his jacket from the ground and climbed up into his wagon. He wiped his bleeding nose with his sleeve and lifted the reins. Hodel stared at her husband. A pig came over and licked at his face. His hands and legs twitched. Regaining consciousness, he squirmed in the mud. Tevye drew the wagon alongside her.

"If he ever matures and becomes a *mensch*, he'll know where to find you," Tevye said.

Hodel knew that her father was right. Maybe this would teach Perchik a lesson. Of course she still loved him, but she wanted to bring up her baby in the way she thought best, and she could never do that in Shoshana. Reaching out, she took her father's outstretched hand. Tevye helped her up into the wagon beside him. Then he flicked the reins and pointed his horse toward the gate.

"That's the end of that demon," he said.

Hodel glanced back for a last look at her husband. Wobbling, he stood up, but his feet slipped in the muck. Once again, Perchik fell back into the mud with the pigs.

Chapter Twenty-Eight

WAITING FOR THE BARON

When word arrived that Baron Edmond Rothschild was coming for a visit, with none other than the famous Dr. Chaim Weizmann, the colony turned into a frantic beehive of activity. Since the death of Theodor Herzl, Weizmann had become one of the driving forces behind the Zionist movement in Europe. The Russian-born chemist had become a leader of the World Zionist Congress, and his diplomatic skill, erudition, personal magnetism, and dedication to the Zionist cause had won the respect of political leaders throughout the world. The rumor of the pending visit was started by the driver of the monthly supply wagon on one of his trips out of Zichron Yaacov. He said that the Baron and Weizmann were due to arrive in Palestine for an inspection of all of the settlements, and that the Morasha region was being considered as the next major development area of both the *Keren Keyemet*, Jewish National Fund, and the Jewish Colony Association. That meant a possible investment of millions and millions of francs to turn the quiet village of Morasha into a bustling agricultural center. The billionaire philanthropist and the charismatic political leader were known to be friends, and if they were impressed by what they saw on their visit, it was almost certain that the Baron would spread money like fertiLazer throughout the hillsides of Morasha.

In the excitement, no one bothered to ask how the driver of the monthly supply wagon was privileged to such exclusive information. As the news spread from settler to settler, the dream of transforming the struggling yishuv into a model metropolis seemed absolutely assured. Someone said that the scientific-minded Weizmann planned to build a university on the crest of the Morasha hillside. Another said the area was slated to be turned into a modern industrial park. It was even rumored that the Baron Rothschild was thinking of Morasha as the site of a new summer mansion.

Hearing these wild fantasies, Tevye scoffed.

"A *boobe-miseh* if I ever heard one," he said. "And I suppose that the *Mashiach* is on his way too."

His reference was to the Jewish messiah, whom the Jews had expected for two thousand years. Faithful to the promises of the Prophets and Sages, the Jews waited for his coming every day. The *Hasidim* were especially on alert for his arrival. If nightfall came without a sign of his appearance, they took solace that certainly the *Mashiach* would come the very next day to usher in the awaited age of salvation. It was a dream Tevye had fostered every day of his life. He believed it with all of his soul. If only the Jews would return to their Maker in repentance, surely the scion of King David would come to rescue the downtrodden nation.

Tevye was far more skeptical regarding the coming of Baron Rothschild. But when the Company manager, LeClerc, arrived with the very same news, Tevye also caught the fast-spreading fever. His imagination proved as fertile as his neighbors. Not only would Morasha become the Paris of the Middle East, Tevye could very well become one of the wealthiest men in the region. Stranger things had happened in life. Hadn't Joseph, the simple shepherd boy, become ruler of the mighty land of Egypt? Every schoolboy knew the story. And what was the secret of Joseph's success? His dreams!

LeClerc assembled the settlers together outside of the barn as the sun sank over the distant ocean. The historic visit, he said, was just three days away. Because of political developments in Europe, the entourage had embarked sooner than planned. After brief stops in Rishon Le Zion and Zichron Yaacov, the Baron and the Doctor of Chemistry were arriving in Morasha to scout the site themselves to determine if the expansive, virgin region could be transformed into a center of Jewish immigration for the hundreds of thousands of Jews whose lives were being threatened by the worsening persecutions in Russia.

Needless to say, LeClerc continued, it was imperative that the Morasha colony and its settlers put on their finest appearance. To this end, a shipment was due to arrive the next day with building supplies, paint, flowers and plants, new clothes for the settlers, and enough food to prepare a banquet for a king.

Everyone spoke out at once with suggestions of what should be done to insure the success of the visit, and of course, quite a few of the settlers took the opportunity to yell out complaints.

"Why are building materials only coming now to put on a show for the Baron, when we have been living like animals for months?!" Shilo, the carpenter, shouted.

"He's right," Munsho, the blacksmith, called out. "And while you are handing out presents, you can add a new anvil to the list!"

Shmuelik raised his hand politely. He had requested books for the synagogue's library, but his letters had never been answered.

"How are we going to cook all of the food?" the storekeeper's wife wanted to know. "We hardly have any pots?"

"If pots and pans didn't arrive today, they will be arriving tomorrow, along with silverware, glasses, plates, tablecloths, and cloth napkins," LeClerc responded.

"What is a tablecloth?" Hillel cynically asked.

The settlers laughed.

"What is a table?" the tailor, Lazer, added.

The laughter increased. Lazer wasn't exaggerating. Their spartan lifestyle was so impoverished that many of life's necessities were missing.

"You know what a table is," Reb Shragi joked. "A plank with four legs."

"Like my cows," Tevye said.

Everyone enjoyed the good humor. Except the tight-lipped, straight-faced Company manager. The gentile LeClerc shouted for order. Time was being wasted. They could joke after preparations had been completed. He was in charge of the visit, and if it were to be a success, people would have to listen to his orders and set to work on their tasks.

"Your futures are at stake," he reminded them in a rebuking tone, as if he were scolding children.

"He means his future," Hillel whispered to his neighbors.

"And it is my job and responsibiity to see that the honorabIe Baron de Rothschild is welcomed in the fashion which he deserves."

Tevye stood up. "He's right. This is a serious matter, and we don't have much time. I volunteer to welcome our guests on behalf of the colony and to deliver a welcoming speech."

"There won't be time for speeches," LeClerc answered. "In addition to Dr. Weizmann, the Baron will be traveling with a team of land surveyors, investors, and agronomists. He is coming here on a work mission, not a political campaign."

"Surely at lunch, there will be time for some welcoming words," Tevye said.

"The Baron and his entourage will eat in a special tent which will be arriving tomorrow. You will all be expected to continue on with your tasks after their initial tour of the colony. We want to show them that the pioneers of Morasha have come here to develop the land, not to picnic and drink wine in the middle of the day."

Once again, a commotion broke out. Tevye helped LeClerc quiet the crowd. He was sure that he would find an opportunity to exchange a few words with the Benefactor and the Zionist leader. Now, the important thing was to get ready for the imminent visit.

"Our prayers have been answered," Tevye told his wife later that evening. "Our salvation is on the way."

Everyone shared his excitement. Everyone felt that the Redemption was near. Tevye, like many of the settlers, was so filled with joy, he was unable to sleep. Joining a few of the fellows in the barn, there was drinking and dancing late into the night. In the morning, LeClerc did not have to command the Morasha settlers to work. With a burst of great industry, everyone set to the task of making their small village spotless. The barns were all cleaned. The horses were bathed and brushed till they shone. Stacks of hay were neatly piled. Logs were arranged in precise columns. Yards were tidied and houses were scrubbed. When the supply wagon arrived from Zichron Yaacov, Goliath and Shilo unloaded the lumber and set to work making a distinguished-looking gateway at the entrance to the *yishuv*. Others set to work painting fences, while others erected the sprawling tent where the great banquet would be held. Four dozen new rose bushes were planted in the Morasha gardens. In preparation for the visit, women washed their Sabbath dresses and hung them in the sun to dry. In the evening, the men tried on the new white shirts and khaki slacks which had arrived with the supply wagon. In the evening, Tevye started to compose a welcoming speech. No one had appointed him to make an address, but he reasoned that it would make a greater historic impression if a Jewish representative of the settlement welcolmed the guests, and not the gentile manager.

The industrious pace continued all the next day. While there were pressing chores to be done in the fields, everything was set aside in order to turn the tiny settlement into a showplace. Women excitedly prepared the morrow's royal luncheon, and children rehearsed Zionist songs so that the "Morasha Choir" could entertain the visitors. In the afternoon, when LeClerc gathered all of the settlers together to stage a practice welcoming ceremony, an argument broke out between Tevye and Pincus, regarding which one of the two men would deliver the welcoming speech. Both held up handwritten pages which they had already penned. Munsho, the blacksmith, had to step between them to prevent them from coming to blows. Finally, LeClerc announced that he, and he alone, would speak on behalf of the settlers.

"That's ridiculous," Pincus protested. "You aren't even a Jew! What right do you have to decide things for us?"

LeClerc's face took on the bright red color of his hair. "You are all ungrateful scoundrels," the Frenchman retorted. "If I hadn't arranged for the Baron's visit, he never would have deigned to step foot in this miserable wretch of a hole. If I hadn't made a big fuss in Zichron, none of these supplies would have come. You have me, and me alone, to thank for everything you have. If I don't receive the respect I deserve, I will call the visit off now. Is that understood?"

The settlers grumbled. Slowly, while LeClerc waited, they regrouped in their welcoming formation and stood quietly in line. What choice did they have? Though LeClerc himself personally hadn't given them anything, the Company had, and he was their go-between. So, for the time being, until they could survive on their own, they had to obey his commands. Nonetheless, that evening a group of the men got together to write out a long list of complaints which they intended to hand to the Baron, including the demand that LeClerc be immediately replaced.

Tevye slipped his speech into his pocket, where he could easily find it the next day, whether he received LeClerc's permission or not. He was so certain that he would personally meet the legendary Baron, he stood before his wife's mirror and carefully trimmed his beard. The goateed philanthropist was known for his immaculate appearance, and Tevye wanted him to feel like he was conversing with an equally distinguished man.

In the morning, everyone hurried excitedly about making final preparations. A welcoming party of riders was organized and sent out to meet the Baron's contingent and escort them to the *yishuv*. Hillel rode along on the wagon with his accordion to give the Zionist leaders the musical fanfare they deserved. Shmuelik took the Torah scroll out of the ark and carried it to the impressive new gateway of the colony, where he stood holding it in anticipation of the Baron's arrival, as if he were waiting to greet a king. Girls with flower wreaths in their hair stood on the road all through the hot sunny morning, holding baskets filled with flowers which they intended to throw on the visitors, until Guttmacher's wife had the sense to gather them into the shade. Younger children soon became restless with standing on line and returned to their usual games.

Tevye and Nachman walked to the mountaintop lookout to

catch the first glimpse of the Baron and the statesman whom God had chosen to plead the Jewish people's plight before the world's dukes, prime ministers, presidents, emperors, archbishops, and kings. For hours, they stared to the east, waiting for the entourage to appear in the valley below. The sun rose higher in the sky until it was a blinding orb over their heads. LeClerc wasn't sure of the time of arrival, so the settlers had guessed around noon. But when the arc of the sun reached its zenith and began to plunge toward the sea, Nachman said that they had obviously judged incorrectly. As the Mishna said, "The sons of kings awaken three hours into the day." That meant that the aristocrats would not arrive before three. And who could predict the time of his coming for sure? They were, after all, on a scouting tour of the land, and perhaps they had planned other stops on the way.

It was decided that Nachman would go back to the colony and bring Tevye some water and food. For the first time since morning, Tevye sat down. Remembering his speech, he removed the crumpled papers from his back pocket and started to rehearse once again. In the banquet tent, flies and bees were swarming around the buffet table and the lavish assortment of delicacies which the women had prepared. With nervous impatience, LeClerc ran around the tables, shouting at the insects and swatting them away from the food. When Nachman entered the tent and innocently asked the Company manager what time the Baron was due to arrive, the meticulously dressed Frenchman exploded.

"When he gets here!" he yelled. "Why does someone have to ask me every five minutes?"

"He had better get here quickly," the butcher's wife chided, "before the flies eat all of the food."

LeClerc growled as he lunged at a battalion of ants which were advancing along the table and attacking a hill of creamy potatoes. Falling off balance, he tripped over a chair onto the ground. The women turned away and tried to suppress their giggles. Nachman smiled and retreated from the tent. Embarrassed, the Company manager rose to his feet. Brushing the dirt off of his neatly-starched suit and vest, he strode outside, ordering the women to cover up the food, as if they were to blame for the invasion of insects.

Nachman brought Tevye a pouch of water and a nourishing snack, and left him alone on the hilltop to continue his vigil. Instead of wasting more time on the mountain, Nachman announced that he was going to the synagogue to study Torah. Before long, LeClerc joined Tevye on the hillside. His head twitched nervously, as if his cravat were strangling him. With growing impatience, he paced up and down the mountain ridge, peering through a spyglass at the valley below.

"Are you sure they are coming today?" Tevye asked.

"Of course, I am sure," the tyrannical clerk tensely replied. Compulsively, he brushed at his suit jacket, as if to straighten out wrinkles, though it seemed perfectly laundered to Tevye.

"The day is almost over," Tevye noted, looking up at the afternoon sun.

LeClere paced to the other side of the ridge.

"It seems to me that you should let one of the settlers address the Baron on behalf of the *yishuv*," Tevye said.

"Is that all you can think about?"

"It seems to me the proper thing to do."

"As long as I am the Company manager, I will decide what is the proper thing to do."

"You might have a revolt on you hands." Tevye warned.

"Is that a threat?" LeClere asked with increasing irritation. Tevye didn't have tune to answer. Far down the mountain side, a wagon appeared on the trail. Spotting it, Tevye froze, then gave out a shout.

"They're coming!" he yelled. "They're coming!"

Ecstatic, he threw his cap in the air. Beside himself with happiness, he grabbed onto LeClerc's shoulders and spun him around in a whirl. Laughing, he ran off to fetch his cap, which had landed in a bush of wild berries. LeClerc peered through his spyglass down the mountain.

"*Merde!*" he exclaimed in French, almost spitting out the word.

"What's the matter?" Tevye asked.

"The wagon you saw. It's Hillel with Pincus and the scribe."

"Where's the Baron Rothschild?"

"I don't know. They're alone."

"Give me that thing," Tevye said.

He reached out and grabbed the spyglass away from LeClerc. Sure enough, it was the Morasha welcoming wagon. No other wagon, nor carriage, nor horse was in sight.

"*Merde!*" the Frenchman repeated.

Tevye didn't have to ask what it meant. The gentile pronounced the word the very same way that a Jew would say *drek*.

"I'm going back to the colony to meet them and find out what happened," the Company manager declared.

He was so upset, he forgot to take his spyglass. Tevye turned and looked back down the mountain. The only thing accompanying the wagon was dust. Hillel was sprawled out in the rear, his head on his accordion, sleeping.

"Hmmm," Tevye snorted. Obviously, the Baron had been delayed on the way. After all, surveys took time, and he had probably stopped to measure some new tract of land. Also, one could never rule out bandits and highwaymen. Bedouins may have attacked the entourage, forcing them to turn back. Once again, Tevye sat down to wait. He had waited all day. He would wait a little more. After all, a Jew was used to waiting. Another day in *galut*. Another year in exile. Another lifetime waiting for salvation to come. Waiting and hoping, that was the fate of a Jew. Who knew? If the Baron didn't show up, maybe the *Mashiach* would come in his place. Tevye had faith.

Across the hills of Ephraim and the plains of the Sharon, the sun sank like a dream into the ocean. Tevye stood up to pray. Gradually, darkness enveloped the mountain. Tevye crumpled his speech into his pocket. Tomorrow was another day. Perhaps, tomorrow the Baron would come.

Chapter Twenty—Nine

THE PLAGUE

Needless to say, the Baron Rothschild never showed up. For the time being, Hodel and her baby, Ben Zion, moved into Ruchel's cottage. The newcomers shared the curtained-off corner with Bat Sheva, Moishe, and Hannei. Goliath went to work cutting planks in order to add on another room to the house. Tevye told Nachman that he hoped the arrangement would be temporary. He confessed that he had a secret plan to interest Shmuelik in his daughter, Hodel. Of course, as long as Hodel was still Perchik's wife, remarrying was out of the question, but if her rotten husband didn't show up in a hurry with a promise to repent in his ways, Tevye was determined to demand a divorce.

Nachman didn't complain about the overcrowded cottage, nor about the hard work, nor about having had to give up his job as a teacher. Even when his soft scholar's hand turned calloused with blisters, he didn't regret his decision to leave Rishon Le Zion for the remote and windy Morasha hillside.

"Blisters of redemption," he called them.

"My *tzaddik* of a son-in-law," Tevye called him.

While Tevye's faith was as deep as any man's, he wasn't ashamed to complain now and again about injustices he saw in the world, especially when they were directed against him. But Nachman would never dream of such an irreverence. He turned everything into a *mitzvah* in the supreme commandment to settle the Holy Land. Guarding the *yishuv* in the middle of the night was a *mitzvah*. Walking two hours for a bucket of water was a *mitzvah*. And the back-breaking work in the fields was a *mitzvah* too. Why should his overcrowded cottage disturb him? Often, he let his sister-in-law, Hodel, sleep in his very own bed! He preferred sleeping outside under the stars just like his great forefather, Jacob.

Even when Nachman had to give up his morning learning to labor in the fields alongside the Arabs when a settler was sick, he didn't complain. How else were the Jewish People to be redeemed from exile in foreign places if not through the strenuous work of rebuilding their own land? The Almighty was ready to do His part, but they had to do theirs. The Jews had to prove that they wanted the Land of Israel more than anything else in the world. A long time ago, their ancestors had abused the privilege of living in the land of milk and honey, and so, in punishment, God had taken it away and scattered them amongst the gentiles. Now that the Almighty was leading them back to the land of their forefathers, the Jews had to prove that they had learned their lesson.

As Shmuelik said, "What was better? Suffering in exile for whatever crumbs a Jew could gather, or suffering for your own dearly loved soil?"

During his first year in the Holy Land, Tevye was more of a pragmatist. True, he had lived like a dog all of his life in Russia, but not every Jew lived off crumbs. The Baron Rothschild, for instance, with all of his billions, could hardly be said to be suffering.

"How do you know what headaches he has?" Shmuelik asked. "Haven't our Sages taught us, 'The more possessions, the more worries; the more money, the more thieves?'"

"That's true," Tevye admitted. "But all the same, I would be willing to change places with the Baron and worry about his railroads and yachts, while he sits here and tends to my cows."

"Not me," Shmuelik answered. "I would much rather have a wagon and mule in the Land of Israel than all of the railroads in France."

The wonderful thing was that Shmuelik truly believed what he said. His optimism was a pillar of strength not only to Tevye, but to everyone in the settlement. If anyone had a personal problem, they would seek out Shmuelik's advice, even though he was still a young man, If it were a matter of Jewish law, Nachman, the more serious scholar, was the person to ask. But if you needed someone to listen, then the good-natured Shmuelik was the address. And when people weren't coming to him, he was going to them, always seeking to help others and to lend a neighborly hand.

His greatest joy was his garden. To Shmuelik, overturning the soil in his garden with a hoe was a religious act just like putting on *tefillin*. Every new blossom, every new flower, every first fruit was a cause of great celebration. Didn't the Talmud say that when the mountains of Israel give forth their fruits in abundance, then the promised redemption was near? This was the long-awaited redemption itself, in his very own garden! The prophecy of his forefathers was unfolding before his eyes! His cucumbers and carrots were proof!

When Shmuelik worked in the garden, he sang. As if in reward for his love for the soil, every seed he planted seemed to grow with a magical touch. When his first melon sprouted and ripened, he took it around in his arms like a baby to show everyone his great pride and joy.

"*Mazal tov*," Tevye said. "Is it a girl or a boy?"

The New Year holidays arrived and work temporarily came to a standstill. The Jews of Morasha set down their hoes and their plows to remember that all of their success depended, not on their own work and strength, but on the kindness and mercy of God. Certainly a man had to toil, but the bounty of his harvest depended on Heaven.

On *Rosh HaShanah*, Tevye was given the honor of blowing the shofar. If the Satan was lurking anywhere near their village, the warlike blasts of his ram's horn surely drove him away. After the *Yom Kippur* fast, everyone set to work building *succot*. In many cases, the flimsy huts were almost as strong as the tiny cottages they lived in. The important thing was that this year they were building their holiday booths in *Eretz Yisrael*! No longer did they have to erect the temporary dwellings at the back of their houses, in the fear that the *goyim* would come tear them down. More incredible than that, the branches they used for the roofs of their *succot* were not merely branches pulled off any available tree, but rather the long, elegant branches of date palms from Jericho, which they had bought from the Arabs. And to make sure that the festival of the harvest would be filled with God's blessing, Nachman made sure that they received a shipment of the finest four species available: shining yellow *etrogim*, splendid *hadas* stems, *lulav* palm branches, and long, green *aravot* leaves, all freshly harvested at Rishon Le Zion and approved by Rabbi Avraham Yitzchak HaCohen Kook. Everyone, even the women, joyfully rushed to the wagon which brought them to Morasha. With excitement in their eyes, the men opened the crates as if there were treasure inside. Occasionally in Anatevka, the four species never arrived and the holiday passed joylessly, since without an *etrog* fruit and *lulav*, the Jews could not perform the festival's cherished commandments. One year, Tevye had spent a fortune of money to buy an *etrog* in Yehupetz. It was the only *etrog* in Anatevka that *Succot*. Every day of the week-long holiday, except for the Sabbath, of course, all of the Jews in the village stood in a long line outside of his house waiting for a turn to hold the sweet-smelling fruit in their hands. But here, in *Eretz Yisrael*, there were *etrogim* for everyone. Gasps of pleasure surrounded the wagon as each bright pear-shaped *etrog* was held up for inspection. The *lulavim* were equally beautiful, all as long and straight as swords. Each *hadas* twig had the characteristic three-fold leaf of the myrtle, and the willow fronds glistened with a deep green color which showed no signs of wilting in the heat.

When the holiday passed, the settlers left their *succah* huts standing to serve as extra rooms. Then, as if in direct response to the supplications for rain, which the Jews began reciting at the end of the holiday, the first rains of winter began to fall. In Russia, rain had poured down in buckets all year long, summer, autumn, winter, and spring, but in Israel, rain only fell in the winter season. On cold, rainy nights, the children who had moved into the *succot* had to return to sleep inside of the houses. Crude stoves were fashioned for all of the cottages, and Goliath made sure that a huge stock of wood had been stored in the barn. But the fierce cold of the winter was a surprise to all of them, and their stoves proved no match against the winds which blew through all of the cracks of the hastily carpentered houses.

Unfortunately for the settlers, the winter was one of the harshest in years. While the Russian Jews were used to below freezing temperatures and months after months of snow, in Russia they had had warmer clothing and houses which kept out the cold. When the winds and rains began, the pioneers of Morasha were caught unprepared. Most of the *succot* fell down in the gusts which blew over the mountain. The straw-matted roof of Tevye's cottage began to sag over the dining-room table and finally caved in. Because permanent building permits had not yet been granted for recent construction, many of the cottages in the colony had been erected with temporary, *succah*-like roofing. When other roofs began to cave in, an emergency meeting was held and the decision was taken to build roofs which would last.

Working frantically around the clock, the settlers managed to fortify their dwellings before the next rains swept over the Morasha mountainside. Though everyone had expected difficulties in building the new settlement, the hardships never ended. Wandering into the barn one *Shabbat* to make sure that the animals had been fed, Tevye found one of his cows lying lifelessly on its side with its tongue hanging out of its mouth. Years before, Tevye had seen the very same symptoms during an epidemic that had broken out in a neighboring Russian village.

Quickly, Tevye ran to call Nachman. If the sickness spread, it could wipe out all of their livestock. Tevye wanted to remove the infected animal from the barn and bury it immediately, but he remembered that certain Sabbath laws forbade moving objects from place to place, and digging was strictly forbidden. Word spread through the colony, and all of the men who were not taking a Sabbath snooze hurried to the barn to hear the rabbinic discussion. Nachman explained that the fence which the settlers had erected around the perimeter of the colony served as an *eruv* which united the private houses and public yards into one large private domain. This allowed them to move the cow from the barn without violating the law against carrying from one domain to the next. The trail in the dirt which would result from dragging the beast along the ground resembled plowing, which was also forbidden on the Sabbath, but since the marks in the dirt were only the unnecessary by-product of the action, and not their real goal, which was burying the cow, then this too would he permitted. The same principle applied to the digging.

"If we were to dig because we needed dirt," Nachman said, using his thumb for emphasis, as if digging out an answer from the air, "this would be forbidden. But if our goal is the hole. then in an emergency, this could be sanctioned, even though digging resembles field work which certainly isn't in the spirit of the rest which is commanded on Sabbath."

"In that case, we can dig the hole, but we can't use the dirt from the hole to cover the cow afterward," Hillel said.

Tevye was getting impatient. With all due respect to their Talmudic discussion, with every passing moment, the cattle blight might spread.

"Doesn't it say that a Jew shouldn't he overly righteous?" he asked. "If an epidemic breaks out, we can lose all of our live stock."

"There are certain leniencies which can be taken if a great loss is at stake," Nachman answered. "But it seems to me that there is an additional problem here."

Everyone waited to hear the solution to the puzzle as if it were a suspense-filled mystery.

"At the commencement of the Sabbath, the cow was living. Now it is dead. In effect, it is something entirely new - no longer a cow, but a carcass. Thus it has the status of *muksah*, something which can't even be touched."

"Like an egg which is laid on the *Shabbos*," Reb Guttmacher added.

"Precisely," Naehman said. "Because the egg, or in our case, the carcass, was not in existence at the start of the day, it remains forbidden all *Shabbos* long."

"*B'kitzor*," Tevye said. "To make a long story short, we're pickled."

"I'm afraid so," Nachman said. "The carcass has to stay were it is."

"I was wondering," Shmuelik hesitantly began, not wanting to give the impression that he was contradicting his more-learned friend.

"By all means," Nachman encouraged.

"If there is the slightest danger that the disease may spread to the residents of the colony, then perhaps it is a matter of *pekuach nefesh*, which would permit us to violate the Sabbath in order to save lives."

"That's an excellent point," Nachman answered. "But that requires a more expert opinion than mine. Tevye, is there a danger that people can be contaminated from the cattle disease?"

Everyone looked at the famed veterinarian.

"People don't get hoof and mouth disease, but they can be struck by cholera. A lot of epidemics have been known to start in barns."

"God forbid," the undertaker added.

"In that case," Nachman concluded, "It is a *mitzvah* to remove the carcass from the barn and to bury it immediately!"

Thus the animal's carcass was buried, but the incident left Tevye with premonitions regarding the future. One night, a week later, as Tevye trekked through the rain on his midnight rounds, he stumbled over another dead cow.

The very next evening, a cold stinging wind howled over the naked hillside. The night was so black, Tevye could hardly see. To distinguish friend from foe, he had ordered that lanterns be carried by any Jew who left his house after dark. The security committee had adopted this safety precaution after Hillel had taken a wild shot at Reb Pincus. The storekeeper had wandered away from his house late one evening to take care of his private needs in the outhouse. Thinking the dark form might be a prowler, Hillel panicked and fired. Fortunately for Pincus, the accordion player was a terrible shot.

Suddenly, just as Tevye was thinking how vulnerable the *yishuv* was to the elements, to invisible epidemics, and enemy attack, a bolt of lightning lit up the sky. In the brilliant white flash, Tevye saw two figures running away from the barn, carrying what looked like two sheep in their arms. A third figure appeared, cried out, and collapsed by the door of the barn.

"I've been stabbed! I've been stabbed," the minstrel's familiar voice called out.

A crash of thunder echoed through the heavens. Darkness returned to the mountainside. Tevye fired a shot in the air to alert the *yishuv*, and ran after the thieves. With the next crackle of lightning, Tevye spotted the prowlers and fired. The lead Arab tripped and his partner tumbled to the ground over him. Bleating, the two sheep ran free. By the time Tevye reached the site, one of the Arabs had fled. The other was limping as he scampered away. Tevye took off like a stallion. Breathing heavily, he managed to catch up with the thief. Shoving the Arab hard on the back, he toppled him down to the ground. Tevye stood over him, aiming his rifle at his head until reinforcements arrived. The Jews dragged the trembling Arab off to the barn, where Hillel sat slumped in the doorway. His hand glowed a bright shade of red. His shoulder was bleeding. But in the light of their lanterns, his wound appeared worse than it was.

The Jews tied the thief up to a post in the barn. When he refused to tell them to what tribe he belonged, Elisha continued the investigation in a more persuasive manner. The important thing, he said, was not to leave marks. In Yemen, Moslems would beat up the Jews in a similar fashion. That way, the Jews couldn't prove to the authorities that they had been beaten.

The thief, it turned out, was from *Muktar* Mohammed's village. Tevye wanted to complain personally to his friend, Mustafa, but the other settlers said that Tevye had complained in the past, and the stealing had continued even though the *Muktar* had assured them that it would stop.

"Either your friend doesn't know what his tribesmen are up to, or he really doesn't care," Elisha said. A vote was taken, and it was decided to report the incident to the Turkish authorities. Luckily,

Hillel had only been wounded. But the next time, Elisha warned, a Jew might he killed.

None other than Jamal Pasha himself, the Turkish military governor of Palestine, arrived in Morasha to investigate the case. Normally, criminal matters were the jurisdiction of the local *haboks*, but Pasha liked to rule over his fiefdom with an iron hand. He was famous for his hatred of the Jews, for his midnight round-ups of immigrants, for unfounded arrests and expulsions. Prisoners reported how Pasha himself had beaten them with whips.

He sat straight-backed in the saddle of his steed as the Jews stood beneath him, telling their story. He wore a military helmet, and his black eyes and black handlebar moustache gave him a menacing appearance. Tevye couldn't help but recall the last time he had stared up at an officer mounted on a horse – when the Russian district police commissioner, Nemerov, had ordered the Jews out of Anatevka. Horsebacked soldiers flanked Jamal Pasha on all sides, their hands never far from their swords. The complaint which the settlers had filed against the Arabs presented an opportunity for Pasha to see what Baron Rothschild's Jews were doing in Morasha. When Elisha finished recounting the incident and a long list of other thefts, the military governor nodded and spurred his horse into a gait. His soldiers followed in line as he toured the small colony, stopping now and again to stare at the houses. As the entourage made a sweep of the village, Tevye experienced a chilling deja-vu. The color of the uniforms was different, but it was a scene he remembered from Russia.

Pasha circled back to the Jews who were waiting by the barn. Tevye could see his wife and his daughters in the doorways of their houses, anxious to see what would happen. Pasha barked sharp commands to his soldiers. Then he ordered the Jews to untie the thief. They had no authority to imprison an Arab, he said, even if he had been caught stealing their sheep.

"He didn't just steel a sheep. He stuck a knife in my arm," Hillel protested.

"He will be tried by the Turkish military court," Pasha

declared. "To prevent further robbery, I command you to hire Arabs to guard the colony at the same wages you pay to Jews."

"Arab guards!' Tevye exclaimed. "That's absurd!"

"It's standard policy," Pasha answered.

"We ourselves don't get paid wages for guard duty," Guttmacher protested. "It's part of our work obligation."

"Then the Arab guards will be paid the accepted wage for guard duty according to the local *habok's* decision."

"Isn't that like letting foxes guard chickens," Hillel whispered to Tevye.

"Lastly," the military governor continued. "These houses have permanent roofs. I am not aware that the Turkish Housing Authority has issued permits for housing on this site. All permanent roofs, excluding animal shelters, will have to come down. Immediately."

A protest went up from the Jews. What did he mean? Certainly, there was a permit. The JCA had filed all of the papers, and the Baron's personal assistants had made all of the required payments in Caesaria. Surely the military governor, his highness, had made a mistake.

"I am not aware of having seen any such documents," Jamal Pasha responded. "If you do not dismantle the roofing, my soldiers will."

"But it's winter," Tevye declared. "How will we live?"

"That, I am afraid, is your problem. The Turkish government did not invite you to Palestine. You came on your own. Presently, government policy is to turn shiploads of Jews away from the country before disembarkment. In all probability, if I were to check your personal papers, many of you would undoubtedly end up in jail."

This last remark silenced the opposition. Tevye was not at all certain that his black-market permit was really official. And Elisha's large family didn't have permits at all. Everyone had heard of the sneak raids on Jewish settlements, when Turkish soldiers would evacuate Jews from their dwellings, line them up, and demand to be shown the official immigrant *"tezkerah"* card. Any

Jew who didn't have one was immediately arrested, and only a heavy bribe could save him from being deported. As usual, LeClerc, the Company manager, was away on "company business." If anyone had a copy of the proper building permits, it would be him. Disgusted, Tevye spit. Hadn't he warned his comrades not to complain about the theft to the Turkish authorities? Jew haters were Jew haters, no matter what color uniforms they wore.

"Give us a week to bring you the documents," Nachman said. "Our colony manager is away on business. Surely he can produce them."

"The law is the law," the ruthless Turk answered.

With a flick of the white gloves he carried, he gave a sign to his soldiers. While several stayed on their horses to keep an eye on the Jews, a dozen dismounted and spread out through the village. They raided house after house, pushing out the women and children, throwing furniture out the front door, and knocking down the roofs from inside. Blood rushed to Tevye's head. Guarded by the soldiers, he stood paralyzed with the rest of the settlers, watching the methodical destruction of their homes. Only the stable, barns, toolshed, and chicken coop were spared. Everything else, the synagogue and all of the houses, were stripped of their roofs.

After Pasha and his soldiers had ridden off with the thief, the Jews wandered in a daze around their village, wondering where they would find the stamina to withstand this new ordeal.

As usual, it was Shmuelik who cheered them.

"Why the long faces?" he asked. "At least our houses still have four walls. Didn't our ancestors live in simple huts and booths when they were brought out of Egypt? God looked after them then, and He will look after us now."

"It didn't rain in the wilderness," Reb Guttmacher noted.

"And the Clouds of Glory hovered over their heads to shelter them by day and by night," Reb Lazer added.

"I suggest we postpone this Biblical discussion and begin rebuilding the roofs," Tevye said. "If we can't use lumber, than we'll use branches instead. Shmuelik is right about one thing. Complaining won't keep us dry."

And so, the work began collecting branches, broken pieces of lumber, and anything else that could provide them with temporary shelter. Elisha's son, Ariel, rode off to Zichron Yaacov to dispatch an emergency message to the JCA offices in Paris. It was obvious to Tevye and the rest of his friends that in addition to making life miserable for the Jews, Jamal Pasha was hoping to he paid off by the Baron. In the meantime, rain started to fall.

At first, the rain began as a trickle, but soon, ominous clouds appeared in the distance, making their way inland from the sea. Before they were able to repair their houses, the deluge began. Nachman immediately ran to rescue the *Sefer Torah*. Clutching the sacred scroll in his arms, he raced for the toolshed. The sky echoed with thunder. Not since the great Flood had rain poured down with such fury. While the men continued to work, the women and children ran for shelter in the stable and barns, the only stuctures that had viable roofs. Here, on the Morasha hillside, the story of Noah's ark was being relived. People and beasts crowded together to weather out the storm. Women and young children sat down on the earth with the sheep and the goats; the older children squeezed into the coops housing the chickens; and the men collapsed in exhaustion onto the straw in the stalls of the barns. Just months after his wedding, Tevye was back with his cow.

All night long, rain thundered down on the roofs of the barns, which the Turks called *"chans."* Who knew what test God had in store for them? Normally, Hillel would have tried to cheer everyone up with a song, but his accordion had been soaked in the first angry downpour and his arm still ached from his wound. One-handed, he held his harmonica to his lips and played a soulful tune. Even the ever-optimistic Nachman was too exhausted to speak. He had worked with all his might to save whatever he could in the house, dragging their furniture, bedding, and clothes into a shed, and now his muscles cried out for sleep. Soon, all that could be heard from the men's barn was a chorus of snoring and coughing, and an occasional moo. Tevye remembered to leave the door open a crack to make sure the air didn't stagnate. If the germs which had killed the two cows were still on the loose in the stables, Tevye didn't dare think what would become of his family and friends.

In the middle of the night, their slumber was ended. Reb Guttmacher's twelve-year-old daughter came searching for her father. At first, because of the rain, the undertaker didn't notice the tears streaming down her face. Then she fell into his arms crying.

"What is it," he asked.

"*Ema*," she said, unable to finish the sentence.

"What about *Ema*?" he asked.

The girl couldn't answer. She stammered and finally spewed out the words.

"*Ema* is dead."

Guttmacher felt a sledgehammer fall on the back of his head. His wife had gone to sleep with a fever, then suddenly her breathing had stopped. The undertaker wailed. Embracing his daughter, he rocked back and forth, as if he were praying. The girl's tears rolled over his cheeks. Stoically, he stood up and braced himself for the job ahead. True, he was no stranger to death. He had been trained to bury people. He had been surrounded by death all of his married life. But to bury the woman he loved, that was a fate too harsh to bear. It was true that his wife had been a frail woman, exhausted by the long journey to Israel, and weakened by an asthma which had tortured her all through the summer, but the undertaker had never dreamed she would leave him without even a word of good-bye. Shocked, he let his daughter lead him from the barn. The other settlers followed in a silent and gloomy procession. Some of them grabbed shovels and trudged off in the rain to the deserted hillside which the undertaker had set aside for a cemetery upon his arrival in Morasha. Guttmacher went to the barn where the women were sheltered. The body had to be prepared for burial according to Jewish law, and he and Nachman were the only men on the *yishuv* who had learned how to do it.

The women made way as they entered. There was a look of

fear in their eyes. Mothers tried to rock their weeping children to sleep. Goliath lifted the lifeless body and carried it outside. Guttmacher directed him toward the tool shed and instructed him to set his wife down on the worktable out back. He wanted the purifying rain to wash her.

A short time later, he lifted a sheet up over her face. A group of men lifted the plank which she lay on. In the pouring rainfall, the procession set off along the hillside toward the gasoline-lit lanterns which marked the open gravesite. All of the adults in the settlement turned out for the funeral. Water streamed down the hillside. Footing was treacherous. The men carrying the corpse often slipped beneath their burden. When they tired, other volunteers took ahold of the plank. Slowly, the procession made its way to the grave. A strong wind caused the flame off the lanterns to flicker, sending fingers of light into the freshly dug pit. With a sob, the undertaker climbed down into the grave, just as he had done for so many strangers. Then he reached out his hands to receive his wife's body. Gently, he lowered her into the grave, making sure that she rested comfortably in her final abode. His children stood around the graveside, weeping. Loads of damp, heavy earth were tossed over the body. Guttmacher's daughters cried out with each chilling scrape of the shovels. Finally, Nachman intoned the traditional memorial prayer, and *Reb* Guttmacher recited *Kaddish*. For a long while, the family stood around the grave, indifferent to the weather, as if it weren't pouring at all. Following the light of their lanterns, the other settlers silently made their way back down the hill to the barns. The relentless rain continued to fall.

When morning came, Shmuelik didn't have the strength to rise and pray with the *minyan*. His face was pale and his eyes had lost all of their color.

"Don't tell Nachman," he said.

Tevye hurried to bring him some water but the young scholar had already sunk back into a feverish sleep. Not knowing what else to do, Tevye covered Shmuelik's shivering body with his blanket.

"Everything will turn out for the best," Tevye said to assure him.

Kneeling beside him, Tevye placed his hand on Shmuelik's head and said a quiet blessing. Rain continued to batter the roof. With a sigh, Tevye put on his *tallit* prayer shawl and *tefillin* and hurried to join the *minyan* which had already started in a corner of the barn. If day in and day out, a Jew's prayer could become dulled with routine, today's supplications echoed through the rafters. Pigeons fluttered nervously over their roosts, frightened by the cries and heartfelt lamentations.

The praying halted when the barn door swung open. Tevye's Bat Sheva rushed in from the rain. Her wet hair was flattened down to the sides of her head. Even before she spoke, everyone could tell from the fright in her eyes that she was the harbinger of something distressing. This time it was Guttmacher's daughter. She was delirious with fever. Everyone stared at the undertaker as if he had the mark of Cain inscribed on his forehead. Wearing his phylacteries and prayer shawl, he hurried to the barn where the women had slept with the sheep. His daughter gazed at him blankly, without recognizing him in the least. She called for her mother and asked for her doll.

"When will we get to *Eretz Yisrael*"? she inquired.

Elisha said that the fever looked like cholera. If it was being spread by the animals, then all of the women who had slept in the barn might be infected. Until they could find out for sure, he said it was safer for the women to return to their houses, even if it meant getting drenched in the rain. In Yemen, he had seen whole villages wiped out by the plague.

A depression fell over the colony. There was no local doctor to turn to, and no medicines to combat the disease. Other settlers began complaining of a weakness in their limbs. Some had sharp pains in their stomachs. Settlers started moving back to their open-roofed houses, seeking shelter in corners which they were able to close off from the rain. Blankets were draped over tables and children were huddled below. At least the air was breathable in the houses, not like the foul-smelling air in the barns. Still there were those who stayed with the animals rather than exposing themselves to the rain and the cold.

By noon, Shmuelik had taken a turn for the worse. He opened his eyes and looked up at Tevye with a sad smile. "Where is Nachman?" he asked.

"Here I am," Nachman answered. "Right here by your side."

Shmuelik moved his head toward his friend's familiar voice and managed a smile. He reached out his hand. Nachrnan took it and gave it a squeeze.

"What's happening with me?" Shmuelik asked.

"You are going to be fine," Nachman said. "You are just a little down from the weather and tired, that's all."

Tevye turned away with the pretext of fetching some water, but in truth, it was hard for him to see the life seeping out of this beautiful young man whom he had come to love like a son. Nachman also could barely hold back his tears. He loved his friend like a brother. They had grown up together, played together, and learned the Hebrew *alef-bet* together in *heder*. Later, when they were older, they had studied in yeshiva together every day. Shmuelik was a part of Nachman, almost as much as his wife.

Tevye handed Nachman a glass of water. Raising Shmuelik's head, Nachman tilted the liquid toward the pale trembling lips and told his friend to sip. Then he gently rubbed water over Shmuelik's hot sweating forehead.

"I saw your father in a dream," Shmuelik said. "I was waiting at the gateway to Heaven, holding out his hand, but my time hadn't come. I had to come back here to tell you not to I worry. 'Don't let the troubles in this world dismay you,' your father said. 'The real world is waiting. And the reward here is great.'"

Shmuelik gasped and his eyelids closed. Whispering the prayer, *"Shema Yisrael. . . Hear O Israel, the Lord is our God, the Lord is One,"* he seemed to drift peacefully into a coma. Tevye and Nachman slumped over as if a great weight had been placed on their backs. What would they do without Shmuelik? Who would bolster their spirits? Who would remind them that God was always with them, in their joys, and in their sorrows as well?

Tevye stood up and staggered out of the barn. Looking up at the cloudy black sky, he raised his hands to Heaven, as if to ask why. All he received in response was a slap of wind and rain. Across the way, the door of his house opened, and his wife, Carmel, appeared. Trudging through the mud, he entered the crowded cottage. Using broken planks and branches, Goliath had succeeded in roofing most of the house. In a corner, water dripped from the ceiling like a forest cascade, but it was better than being outside in the downpour. Goliath had even succeeded in lighting the stove. The house was by no means warm, but by gathering around the fire, the chill was considerably lessened. Before Tevye spoke, the women in the house sensed that the Angel of Death had claimed someone else. Exhausted, Tevye collapsed into a chair and glanced at his wife and his daughters.

"Who is it now?" Ruchel asked.

"Shmuelik," Tevye said.

Lifting her shawl over her head, Ruchel ran out of the door into the rain. She found her husband quietly sobbing over his best friend's body.

"Oh, Nachman, my love," she said, laying her hand on his shoulder.

"Go back to the house," Nachman told Ruchel. "I have to help here with the burial."

Ruchel nodded. Eyes filled with tears, she walked back out of the barn. Shmuelik had been more than a friend. He had been a part of the family. Every Sabbath, he had joined them for meals. Every evening, he had sat at their table with her husband, learning Torah by candlelight late into the night. And how happy he had been at their wedding! How he had danced!

Once again a funeral procession made its way through the rain to the Morasha cemetery. Nachman delivered a eulogy for his friend. All of the time, gusts of rain battered the hillside.

After the burial, it was decided that a wagon would take the sick to the infirmary in Zichron Yaacov for treatment. Besides Guttmacher's delirious daughter, two of the blacksmith's children were lifted onto the wagon. Tevye was chosen to drive, and

Goliath volunteered to go with him. With a foreboding feeling, Tevye said good-bye to his wife and his daughters. Carmel followed him out to the wagon.

"I will be back by evening tomorrow," he told her. "If the good Lord wills."

"May God be with you," she said.

Goliath sat in the back of the wagon with the children, holding a blanket over their heads like a tent. The blacksmith's wife rode with them. Tevye flicked the reins of the wagon, but the horse didn't budge. With a snort, it turned its head toward Tevye as if to ask if he truly intended to set off into the brunt of the storm.

"This isn't the time for arguments," Tevye told him, flicking the reins once again.

Still the horse wouldn't budge. Tevye climbed down from the wagon and walked over to the beast.

"You are right," Tevye told him. "Only a madman would set off on a journey in a hurricane like this, but people are sick."

The horse only snorted.

"You are right," Tevye said. "People are people, and horses are horses, so what business is it of yours? Well, it so happens that horses have been known to drop dead from the plague, so if we don't get some help, you may never have to pull a wagon again. And if that isn't reason enough, there's this."

He reached into his pocket and pulled out some sugar. The horse lapped it up gratefully. Once again, Tevye climbed into the wagon and gave the reins an authoritative flick. This time, the creature started off. Back in Anatevka, driving his wagon through rainstorms and blizzards, Tevye had come to understand the difference between a man and an animal. A man would do *meshuganah* things because he was crazy, or in pursuit of some higher ideal, but a animal had a more basic down-to-earth sense and had to be bribed.

As Tevye's good friend, Sholom Aleichem, would say, "To make matters short," Tevye drove slowly because of the treacherous footing. Floodwater splashed down the mountain. The trail had turned into mud. After several hours, they reached the stream which ran down from the highlands to the low coastal plain. Because of the deluge, its banks were overflowing. Overnight, the gentle stream had turned into a raging, whitecapped river. Without a bridge, there was no way they could cross with a wagon load of children. If a wheel were to shatter or get stuck in the mud, the children could drown. Standing on the bank of the torrent, Tevye and Goliath worked out a plan. First they carried their passengers across the rushing rapids. Then Goliath ripped off the upper planks of the wagon's rail. Stretching them across the narrowest neck of the stream, he formed a makeshift bridge. The giant walked back into the water and guided the nervous horse into the current. Tevye aligned the wheels of the wagon with the planks of the bridge. Miraculously, the wagon rolled over the boards without tumbling into the water.

Night had already fallen by the time they arrived in Zichron Yaacov. Here too, the streets of the moshav had all turned to mud. Thankfully, the children were still alive when they reached the infirmary, but it was clear to everyone that their fate was in God's hands alone. Hava was one of the nurses on duty. Tevye described the situation in the mountains, and told her that he wanted to return to Morasha immediately with a doctor and medicine. After making sure that the children received beds in the quarantine section of the hospital, and that a doctor had arrived, Hava brought her father and Goliath hot drinks. Then she set off to find a doctor who was willing to travel with them that evening. Without a moment's hesitation, the director of the hospital himself, Dr. Schwartz, volunteered. He ordered that the wagon be loaded with medicine. Hava, he said, would join them.

Since both Tevye and Goliath were chilled and exhausted, it was decided to spend the night in Zichron and to set off at dawn. Elisha's son, Ariel, met up with them also. The Company director had received a telegram from the main Paris office stating that a mistake had been made - all of Morasha's building permits were in order. Copies were being sent out immediately to Jamal Pasha. The JCA directors apologized for the inconvenience, and demanded that LeClerc be in touch with the office in Paris immediately.

Tevye spit.

"Is that what I am supposed to tell Guttmacher and Shmuelik? That there has been some mistake? That the Company apologizes for the inconvenience? Let a plague fall on the Company instead!"

"*Abba*" Hava said. "It isn't the fault of the Company. Without their help, we wouldn't be able to build anything at all."

"Then let the Baron and all of his directors come here themselves and sleep with us in the barns."

A blanket of clouds made the morning almost as dark as the night. Lightning lit up their way as they traversed the coastal plains towards the mountains of the Shomron. When they reached the raging stream, they had no choice but to abandon the wagon. The makeshift bridge had vanished, swept away by the floods. Unhitching the horse, they waded through the turbulent water, holding the bags of medicine high in the air to keep them from getting wet. Hava rode on the horse with her father, and the doctor doubled up with Ariel. Goliath as usual volunteered to set out behind them on foot.

Journeying all morning long in the rain, they reached the Morasha encampment in the mid-afternoon, several hours ahead of Goliath. Since their departure, one of Chaim Lev's children had died, and all of the boy's brothers and sisters were sick.

The doctor confirmed that the invisible enemy was cholera. He advised the settlers to abandon the colony, at least until the winter was over. He said that the medicine which he had brought might be of some help, but once a person had become infected, there was no guaranteed cure.

Before evening, the rains and strong winds abated. The storm clouds passed away to the south. For the first time in days, the sun appeared in the sky before it set in the west, blazing with an angry red glow. Darkness returned to the mountain. The settlers held an emergency meeting to vote on the doctor's decree. Everyone was given an opportunity to speak. Hillel maintained that since they had already talked about moving the *yishuv* to a better location, there was no sense in staying, especially when lives were being threatened every day. Reb Shragi was afraid that if they moved because of the plague, news would spread throughout Russia, and potential new immigrants would be discouraged from coming on *aliyah*.

"They will claim that the Land of Israel devours its inhabitants, just as the Spies claimed in the wilderness, when they gave their false report," he maintained.

Others asserted that saving life was the most supreme value, and that it was better to evacuate the settlement than fall prey to the epidemic. Nachman agreed. Halachically, according to Torah law, that was the proper course to take. Tevye waited to hear all sides of the argument before expressing his opinion.

"If we move from here because of disease," Guttmacher said, "we will have to move from the next place because of Arab marauders, and from the next place because of the Turks, and from the next place because of the mosquitoes, until we will be back on a boat to Russia, and then where will we go?'

Others assented.

"It is better to die here and be a symbol of bravery, than to set an example of cowardice," Munsho, the rugged blacksmith exclaimed.

"Abandoning an area because of sickness is an action of wisdom and prudence, not cowardice," the doctor injected.

"Doesn't it say in the Torah that the commandments were given to live by them, not to die by them?" Hillel added.

Surprisingly, Goliath spoke up.

"I grew up with Shmuelik," he said. "He was like a brother to me. If he were alive, I think he would have decided to stay. But he would have said that everyone should be free to do what he wishes."

"Goliath is right," Reb Lazer said. "This is not something to decide by a vote. Everyone should be free to follow his conscience."

"I second the motion," Tevye said.

"Agreed," a chorus of voices called out.

In the morning, the doctor left with a wagon load of toddlers. Chaim Lev and his wife lifted their sick children into their wagon, along with all their belongings, and set off with the doctor. Hillel limped out from the barn, carrying his accordion and a suitcase. With an embarrassed expression, he set them on the fixer's wagon and climbed on board. His accordion let out a flat note as if it were sighing. Tevye was truly sorry to see his friend leave. Without any hard feelings, he stepped forward to shake Hillel's hand.

"May the Lord be with you," he said.

"May the Lord be with you as well," Hillel answered.

"We will all miss your music."

Hillel smiled, remembering their many nights together when Tevye was still a bachelor.

"If I were healthy to begin with, maybe I'd stay. But what good is a lame accordion player on a mountain farm anyway?"

Tevye grabbed Hillel's side locks and kissed him on the face.

"*L'hitraot,*" Tevye said, waving goodbye to his comrade. "May the Lord bring us together again soon."

The wagons of Pincus and Lazer joined in the caravan. Friends waved to each other as if saying final good-byes. The settlers of Morasha watched the wagons head down the trail until they were out of sight. Every man's face seemed to share the same dark concern, the same worry and doubt, as if they were being foolish for staying.

Tevye's turn in the sick wagon seemed right around the bend. Exhausted from the back and forth journey to Zichron, and from a shortage of sleep, he went to bed with a headache. Two hours later, he awoke in a sweat. A heaviness weighed down his limbs. His teeth chattered. Extra blankets didn't help warm him. Thinking his end was at hand, he called for his wife. She knelt down beside him and wiped his face with a towel. His daughters gathered about. Hava, the nurse, knelt beside him. "What an angel," he thought. He wanted to tell them all how much he loved them, but his head spun in circles, making him too dizzy to speak. Once again, sleep overcame him. A fever broke out on his forehead. While his family crowded around as if keeping guard,

Tevye struggled with nightmares. He yelled deliriously out at an enemy. His children stood trembling, certain that their father was wrestling with death.

"*Abba*, be strong," Hava called out.

"*Saba*, don't die," Moishe pleaded.

Then, with a gasp, Tevye woke up. His eyes opened wide. Summoning all of his strength, he raised himself onto his elbows.

"Bury me beside your mother," he said in a dry, rasping voice.

Then he sank back on his pillow, whispered a final "*Shema Yisrael*," and closed his eyes, prepared to meet his Maker. But his head continued to hammer, his thoughts continued to think, and his daughters' weeping wouldn't give him rest. After a long, dramatic moment, he reopened one eye. His loved ones hovered above him, holding their breaths. Tevye sighed. Escaping from this world wasn't to be his good fortune. Apparently, the Almighty had more tests in store for him before granted him respite from his trials on earth.

Hava took her father's hand and felt for his pulse. 'Thank God," she said. "His heart is as strong as a lion's."

Tevye looked at his wife.

"Don't worry," she said. "You probably just caught a chill."

Comforted by her words and her smile, Tevye fell back to sleep. Carmel stayed awake all night to watch him. Occasionally, she would change the wet cloth on his forehead to keep his fever down. When he opened his eyes in the morning, her face was the first thing he saw.

"What time is it?" he asked.

"The sun is just rising," she said.

"I have to go pray."

"Do you feel strong enough?" she asked.

"That's what gives me strength," Tevye answered.

Hearing his words, Tevye realized his response was the kind of thing that Shmuelik would say. Now that the youth was gone, Tevye would require a double dose of faith to make up for the loss.

Still somewhat dizzy, he sat up from the mat on the floor. He had taken it upon himself to say the mourner's *Kaddish* for Shmuelik, and he could only recite the prayer if he prayed in a minyan with nine other men. Thank God, his fever had passed like the rain. Feeling as if he had been given a renewed gift of life, he headed for the roofless *beit haknesset*, carrying his *tefillin* and *tallit* under his arm. Things which he had taken for granted just yesterday seemed like a miracle now. What a blessing it was to be able to walk, to be able to breath, and to be able to see!

With a heart filled with gladness, he sang out the morning prayers. The Torah scroll was brought back to the synagogue from the toolshed, where it had been housed during the rains. Within a short time, there was almost a *minyan*. Yankele, Munsho, Shilo, Reb Shragi, Elisha, Ariel, Yigal, Nachman, and Tevye. Only Goliath was missing. Nachman had tried to wake him, but the big lumberjack said he felt sick.

Tevye guessed that it was just a passing fever, a one day bout with the Satan, like the chills he had suffered the previous night. After all, what damage could germs do to such a mountain of a man? When he finished his prayers, he went to the barn to visit the sick Alexander, the name Tevye used in the blessing of health for the ill. As he entered the door, his knees turned to soup. Goliath lay sprawled on the ground in the center of the barn. His prayer shawl lay near him. Chickens hopped over his body. Cows bellowed and mooed. With a shout, Tevye shooed away the fowl and knelt down beside the faithful giant. He raised the lifeless head and stared into the now vacant eyes.

"My God, my God," Tevye whispered, recalling a verse from the Torah. *"How the mighty of Israel have fallen."*

Chapter Thirty

WATERS OF EDEN

What was a man, Tevye thought, that one moment he could be so filled with power and seemingly invincible force, and the next moment a motionless pile of flesh? He knew that the body on the ground wasn't the real Goliath, but only the oversized suit which his giant soul had worn during his wanderings on earth. The real Goliath was on his way to Heaven and a world where size was measured in good deeds and Torah, not in physical power and strength. That's what the Rabbis taught, and who was Tevye to disagree? The mysteries and secrets of life were beyond his understanding, but he was certain that the lifeless imposter before him wasn't Goliath. His faithful companion couldn't be gone. The Divine energy called life didn't just disappear. Goliath simply had slipped out of his bulky lumberjack's costume to journey to a less cumbersome world.

"Blessed be the true Judge," a voice said.

It was Nachman.

"When will it end?" Tevye asked.

Nachman could only shake his head as he gazed down at his lifelong friend.

"I told him not to sleep in the barn. Like always, he worried about everyone else without thinking about himself."

Nachman turned away and held on to Tevye.

"He was like a brother and father to me."

Tevye let his son-in-law silently weep in his arms. He remembered how the giant had watched over Nachman, like a mother hen guarding its chick.

"He's in a better world now," Tevye observed.

Nachman nodded, wiping the tears from his eyes. "I know," he said. "I know. But he was such a good friend."

Tevye himself felt like crying, but he had to stay strong for the boy. Death had robbed him of his best friends from the past, and he needed someone to remind him that for a Jew, life always had a happier future. That was the steadfast belief which had kept his People going for the last two thousand years, throughout endless persecutions and wanderings.

"Everything God does is always for the best, even if we can't understand," Tevye told him. "Do you remember on the boat to

Israel, when they turned us away from landing, you had to remind me that everything turns out for our good?"

"I remember," Nachman replied.

"Someday, when we gaze down from Heaven, we will understand these great secrets. But right now, you had better call Guttmacher," Tevye said.

Nachman nodded. He walked out of the barn to fetch the undertaker, leaving Tevye alone with the toppled Goliath. "Alexander, the son of Rivka," Tevye said, saying a prayer for the departed man's soul. Tevye bent down and closed Goliath's eyes. When he stood up, a rooster leaped onto the dead man's chest and perched there like a vulture. Tevye shouted and kicked at the bird. Squawking, it flew into the air. Angrily, Tevye raced around the barn, scaring the chickens away. For Nachman's sake, he had spoken strengthening words of faith. But alone with the very great loss, he succumbed to the more mortal feelings of anger and pain.

"Is this fair?" he called out toward the roof of the barn. "What did Goliath ever do to hurt a flea in his life? Is this the end he deserves - to drop dead amongst the cows and the chickens?!"

The roof didn't answer. Neither did the animals. They were silent, hushed by Tevye's outburst.

"You won't break us!" Tevye shouted, raising a fist. "You won't break us!"

A few pigeons flew out from the rafters.

"If Your judgment has to fall on someone, then leave the others alone. Let it all fall on me!"

Sighing, Tevye lowered his arm. He bent down and grabbed Goliath's boots, thinking to drag the corpse out of the disease-ridden barn. As he gave the great hulk a tug, he heard a vertebra pop out of place in his spine. Tevye cried out in pain. Bent over double, he staggered to the door of the barn, shuffling his feet on the ground like a hunchback. Leaning against the barn wall, he looked up at Heaven and groaned.

"Okay," he said, clutching his aching back. "You win. I shouldn't have opened my big mouth."

Some fighter he was. Within seconds of having yelled out in complaint, his spine already felt broken and he hardly could walk.

Goliath was too heavy to be carried out to the cemetery, so his body was wheeled out in a cart. The work of preparing the double-sized grave took more than an hour. The diggers were exhausted by the time the funeral procession arrived. Once again, the somber, all too familiar *El Maleh Rachamim* prayer, echoed over the hills. Since the deceased had no relatives in Israel, Nachman recited the mourner's *Kaddish*. When the ceremony was over, Nachman lingered at the grave. Tevye walked back to the colony, leaning on a cane to east the pain in his lower back. Yankele, the butcher, approached him with a stern look on his face.

"Do you still think we can hold down the fort?" he asked the bent-over milkman.

"Am I a prophet that you ask me such questions?" Tevye responded.

"With your cane, you do look a little like Moses."

"I feel more like Methusalah," Tevye said.

"Goliath did the work of five men together. How can we manage without him?"

Tevye didn't know. Either his once indefatigable faith was running low, or he was simply exhausted. He spent the rest of the day on his back like a dead man. By late afternoon, thanks to God's never-ending kindness, his vertebra had moved back into place, and he could stand up on his own without the help of his cane. A contingent of soldiers arrived from the Central Turkish Military Authority in Caesaria. They carried a letter signed by Jamal Pasha saying that all Morasha building permits were all in order, and that the settlers were allowed to construct permanent roofs. After reading the letter, Tevye threw it on the ground.

"If I ever see that devil Pasha again, as the Almighty is my witness, I will I kill him with these very hands," he vowed.

"*Abba*," Hava said, "Didn't you teach us that it is forbidden to make a vow in God's Name."

"He caused the deaths of Goliath and Shmuelik, not to mention the others. Jamal Pasha is the murderer, not the plague."

"Even so."

"The Pashas of the world have bossed us around long enough. This is our land, and I'm not taking anymore of their orders."

Tevye stalked off to his house, but like a soldier in battle, he wasn't given a long time to rest. In the middle of the night, Nachman came with the news that Moishe, Tzeitl's little Moishe, had fallen ill. The boy had woken up, screaming from a nightmare. Tevye rushed to the house and felt the boy's burning forehead. When the energetic tot said he felt too weak to stand, Tevye decided not to wait for sunrise to set off for Zichron Yaacov. He hitched up a wagon and lifted the sweating and listless child inside. Hava and Bat Sheva went with him. They sat in the back of the wagon, holding the boy in their laps.

When they reached the stream rushing down from the mountains, they had to make a detour. In the breaking dawn light, Tevye could make out a group of wagon tracks heading north along the path of the stream. Understanding that they were the tracks left in the mud by the wagons which had left the Morasha, Tevye decided to follow them. Sure enough, after a half-hour's ride, they came to a natural crossing where the raging stream ran underground. Two hours later, they reached Zichron Yaacov. When they finally arrived at the infirmary, the boy's body was still burning with fever. Tevye carried him inside in his arms. Hava rushed forward and spoke with a nurse.

"Where should I put him?" Tevye asked.

Quickly, Hava led him down the corridor and out a back door. In the field behind the hospital, a good distance away, a large tent had been erected. All of the sick Morasha settlers were quarantined inside. Guttmacher's daughter had died, along with another one of Chaim Lev's children.

Tevye carried Moishe into the tent and set him down on an empty cot. The sick people in the other beds all appeared gaunt, as if they were wasting away. Chaim Lev was curled into a ball, grasping his stomach.

"Isn't there something that can help them?" Bat Sheva asked.

"Prayer," the nurse said. "We try to make them comfortable, but there is really nothing we can do. All of the medicines we have tried haven't had any effect."

"That's impossible," Tevye said. "There must be some way to cure them."

Neither Hava nor the nurse had an answer. Tevye stepped over to Chaim Lev, the fixer, and put a hand on his feverish head. In his delirium, he didn't even notice that Tevye was there.

A young doctor arrived and asked Tevye to wait outside the tent.

"He's my father," Hava said. "The grandfather of the boy."

"I'm sorry," the doctor replied. "He'll have to wait outside. You also," he said to Bat Sheva.

"I held him all of the way here in the wagon," she protested. "If the boy has the plague, then I have it too."

"Not necessarily," the doctor answered. "Some people seem to have natural immunities."

Tevye didn't want to waste time by arguing, so he left the doctor alone to examine the boy. He stood outside the tent with his eyes closed, praying. Over and over again, he asked the Almighty to heal the boy. He prayed for the health of all of the settlers. A few minutes later, the doctor appeared. Tevye stared at him anxiously.

"I'm afraid the boy has the cholera too. We will try to bleed him, but it hasn't helped the others. I'll ask Dr. Schwartz to look at him just to be sure."

"Bleed him?" Tevye asked. The idea sounded awful. Didn't the Torah teach that a person's lifeforce was contained in his blood?

"That's the standard procedure," the doctor said.

"Won't that just weaken him?"

The young doctor shrugged.

"I won't allow it!" Tevye emphatically shouted. "I won't allow it. Do you hear?"

"Very well," the doctor said. "We really only do it when we don't know what other action to take."

A great weariness overtook Tevye. Hava came out of the tent and told them to go to the workers' dining hall where they could get some food. In the meantime, she would watch over Moishe.

Tevye and Bat Sheva were riding back to the center of the moshav when a bearded Jew ran up to the wagon.

"Are you Tevye?" he called.

"That's right," the milkman answered. "And who are you?"

"Just a simple Jew," the man said.

"Just a simple Jew?" Tevye answered. "Can there be such a thing? Every Jew is a son of the King."

The man held up a finger to his lips. "Shhh," he whispered. "I prefer to keep that a secret. I like a quiet life. If people were to find out that I have a special connection to the King, they'd pester me day and night with all kinds of requests."

"Isn't it our duty to help others in need?"

"The King has many sons. Let them worry about the problems of the world."

"Tell me, how did you know my name?" Tevye asked.

"I had a dream last night that you would be coming, and so far you are the only stranger I've seen."

"May your dream be a good omen."

"I have a message for you."

"My ears are ringing," Tevye said.

"You are to immerse the sick boy in the holy *mikvah* in Safed. There, God will answer your prayers."

Safed was the name of the renowned holy city where great

Jewish mystics had lived. The "*Ari,*" Rabbi Yitzchak Luria, was the most famous of all. Much of the Kabbalah had been based on his teachings. There was a legend that anyone who immersed himself in the running, mountain-spring water of his legendary *mikvah* would be miraculously blessed in the waters which flowed from the Garden of Eden.

"Oh, father, you don't really believe in such nonsense?" Bat Sheva chided.

"Quiet," he ordered, turning back to man in the road. "What else did you see in your dream?" Tevye asked.

"Not a thing," the Jew confessed. "The young fellow who appeared in the dream took off in a very big hurry."

"What was his name?"

"That's right," said the stranger. "He told me to tell you his name."

He paused theatrically, as if to heighten Tevye's suspense. "*Nu?*" Tevye asked.

"He called himself Shmuelik."

Tevye felt chills run up and down his body.

The man waved a hand and continued on his way, wishing the boy a complete recovery. Tevye watched him disappear behind one of the nearby houses.

"It's nothing but superstition," Bat Sheva said. "Shmuelik is dead."

"The righteous don't die," Tevye told her. "Their souls go on living."

With an urgent command to the horse, Tevye turned the wagon around in the road. Within minutes, they were back at the infirmary.

"You are not really thinking of taking Moishe to Safed?" Hava asked in disbelief when her father related the story.

"I certainly am," Tevye said.

"He doesn't have the strength for the journey."

"You heard the doctor. There is nothing that medical treatments can do for him here, except maybe bleed him to death, God forbid."

Nothing that Hava could say could dissuade him. She knew that arguing with her father was useless. Tevye was convinced that the dream had been a message from Heaven, and that the mysterious Jew was no other than the famed prophet of Biblical times, Eliahu *HaNavi*, who traveled from city to city, helping Jews the world over.

"Maybe father has the fever," Bat Sheva whispered to Hava as Tevye carried Moishe out of the quarantine tent to the wagon.

"Guard your tongue," Hava told her. "Who knows? Maybe the dream will come true. Anyway, father is right. There is nothing we can do here. Maybe fresh air will do Moishe more good than lying in a tent filled with germs."

It seemed like craziness to Bat Sheva, but she couldn't let her father travel alone with no one to look after the boy. Hava had to stay at the hospital. So she decided to go along on the journey to Safed.

Hava supplied them with enough water, cheeses, black bread, and fruits to last for a week. She even packed along a bottle of vodka which she found in one of the infirmary's cabinets.

"Now that's a good daughter," Tevye said.

To reach Safed, they first had to travel north to Haifa, and then follow a long winding road high up into the Galilee mountains. The journey took them three days. Moishe slept most of way. Occasionally, he opened his eyes, but he had nothing to say. He lived off sips of water and tiny nibbles of cheese. Bat Sheva sang to him and told him stories, but much of the time, she wasn't sure that he heard.

While Tevye had never studied Kabbalah, he had learned a few things here and there about the secrets of Torah. The influence of the Hasidic movement had spread throughout Russia, and mystics passing through Anatevka had often dined at his house, sharing with Tevye secrets revealed in the *Tanya* and *Zohar*. For a simple Jew like Tevye, the concepts had made his head spin. What good did it do knowing the secrets of Creation when you had to go back to milking your cows? The Kabbalists described the immersion in a *mikvah* as a mystical return to the womb. The person emerging from the ritual pool was like someone reborn. If he had sinned and repented, he could now be forgiven because he was like a new being. Though Tevye decided that the esoteric teachings weren't for him, he had a steadfast belief in everything which the Sages had written. And among the great Kabbalists, the *Ari*, may his memory be for a blessing, was the top of the line. If he had left a special healing blessing in his *mikvah*, then Tevye was convinced that the boy would be healed.

The city of Safed was literally up in the clouds. As they ascended the mountain, gusts of wind swirled around them, blowing flakes of snow in their faces. The entrance to the city was guarded by a wall of fog and mist, as if only the privileged could enter. For several long moments, their horse disappeared in the vapor in front of them. Then the curtain of fog seemed to part, revealing a mystical enclave which seemed to hover in the sky on a platform of clouds high above the earth.

Reaching the city was like entering another world. For one thing, Tevye did not see anyone who wasn't Jewish. Ever since the time of the Second Temple, for nearly two-thousand years, Jews had lived in the ancient, mountain refuge. The roadway had never been smoothed, as if no one cared about physical comfort. Buildings were interspersed with crumbling ruins. A series of devastating earthquakes had left rubble everywhere. A legend claimed that the disasters had happened because of the awesome power of the Kabbalists' prayers. The houses still standing were built out of large blocks of stone. The Jews who passed by on the roadside had long, untrimmed beards and burning mystical eyes. They darted swiftly down narrow alleyways, their eyes on the ground, their thoughts up in Heaven. Most of them lived on charity sent by Jews overseas. They spent their days fasting, engrossed in study and fervent prayer. When Tevye asked the way to the famous *mikvah*, they all pointed in a direction away from the town, down the sloping hillside.

The steepness of the descent was frightening. Tevye's horse balked. At the outskirts of the old, picturesque village, the road ended and the wagon ride came to a halt. Tevye took the towels which Hava had packed with the food, and an extra blanket to make sure that Moishe didnt catch cold. A narrow dirt path led down to the ancient mountainside cemetery of Safed. Many of the tombstones were cracked. Though the earthquakes had made ruins of the city, the cemetery itself has been spared. A group of Hasidim stood reading Psalms around the gravesite where the *Ari* was buried. Day and night, supplicants prayed at the grave of the famous Kabbalist. Candles burned on the monument. A short distance away was the grave of Rabbi Yosef Caro, author of the *Shulchan Aruch*, the codified volumes of Jewish Law. Further down the hill was the tomb of the Prophet Hosea, and the cave where the martyred Hannah was buried with her eight slaughtered sons.

A serene, holy stillness hung over the hillside. Even Bat Sheva, who was normally skeptic, could sense the mystical pull of the site. She walked beside her father, not saying a word. Moishe opened his eyes and stared at the cemetery. Only God knew what the small boy was thinking.

"That must be the *mikvah*," Tevye said, pointing to the mouth of a cave, where a *Hasid* was standing.

"I'll wait for you here," Bat Sheva said.

"There's a woman in the cemetery," her father said, "Go pray by her side."

Embarrassed, Bat Sheva hesitated. She stood awed, feeling that all of the holy Rabbis were gazing at her from their graves. She was filled with shame, as if her lapses in keeping the Torah made her unworthy to pray in so sacred a place.

Carrying the boy in his arms, Tevye descended toward the cave. Its entrance was a narrow archway of rock. Inside, candles burning on a ledge lit the darkness. The walls were all solid stone, as if the cave had been carved out of a gigantic boulder. Deeper into the cave, an underground stream flowed into a small natural pool. The shadowy figure of the *Hasid* appeared behind them. Without questioning Tevye, he wished the boy a speedy recovery and asked if he could help. Tevye let him hold Moishe as he quickly undressed. The cold rocky floor sent chills through his body. In the flicker of the candlelight, the boy's big eyes stared questioningly up at his grandfather.

"Don't worry, my *tateleh*," Tevye said. "You are going to get better, I promise."

He stripped the boy bare and scooped him up in his arms. Careful not to slip on the wet, rocky slate, Tevye inched toward the *mikvah*. He knew the mountain water was bound to be cold, but when his foot descended the first stone step into the pool, he felt as if he had submerged it into an ice-covered pond. Why prolong the agony, he thought? With a gasp, he rushed forward and leaped into the freezing pool. He carried Moishe down with him under the water, then let him go for the briefest of moments so that the boy would be completely immersed in the pool. Then with a shivering roar, he burst out of the water and lunged for the steps. The *Hasid* reached down and swept the boy into a towel. Tevye's teeth chattered as he hoisted himself back up to the floor of the cave. They dried and dressed the boy quickly, then bundled him up in the blanket which his grandfather had brought. The *Hasid* said that Tevye could bring the boy to the yeshiva up the hill, to warm him by the stove. Tevye readily accepted the offer. Quickly, so that Moishe wouldn't catch a cold, he followed the black-garbed Jew up the steep path. Outside the yeshiva, the *Hasid* stopped in a narrow alley and knocked on a door. An old, kerchiefed woman appeared. After a moment's explanation, Bat Sheva was invited inside while her father took Moishe into the wooden building which housed the yeshiva.

The study hall was filled with *Hasidim* dressed in the long black frocks and fur hats common to the pious Jews of Anatevka. Many wore prayer shawls and *tefillin*. For a moment, Tevye felt like he had stepped into a yeshiva in Russia. Talmudic volumes, their covers torn from use, filled the shelves along the walls. An elaborately carved ark, the *aron hakodesh*, holding the Torah, stood in the south of the study hall so that prayers would be directed toward Jerusalem. The *Hasid* sat Tevye and Moishe in chairs by a large metal stove. The heat from its fire rose around them, removing the chill from their bones. Within a minute, cups of hot tea were brought to the visitors.

Tevye watched in happy wonder as Moishe took the cup in his hands. The youth sipped at the warm, fragrant brew and smiled.

"Drink my child," Tevye told him, amazed at the improvement he saw.

Every second, the boy seemed to get stronger. For the first time in days, color returned to his cheeks. A plate of biscuits and small pastries was set before them.

"*Es*," Tevye said, handing the boy a sweet-smelling cake. "Eat some cake.

Moishe ate the tasty morsel with relish. Joyfully, his grandfather held out another.

"I want to go pray," Moishe said.

They were the first words the child had spoken in days.

"Eat another piece of cake."

"Later," Moishe said, standing up.

"Are you sure you have the strength?" his grandfather asked.

"*Hashem* will give me the strength," the boy said.

To Tevye's surprise, the boy didn't stand up to pray in the yeshiva. He walked to the door and hurried outside. Like a deer, Moishe ran down the hillside path which led to the cemetery. Tevye watched in amazement. Chills shook his body, not from the cold, but from the miracle he was witnessing. As if the boy had lived in the city of Safed for a lifetime, he ran straight to the grave of the holy *Ari*. Praying, his little body swayed back and forth like the Hasidic Jews beside him. Tevye looked up to the sky and said thank you. With joy in his heart, he walked down the dirt path to join his grandson in prayer at the grave of the holy *Tzaddik*. To the beleaguered milkman, it was a sign that God was still with him.

Chapter Thirty-One

HEVEDKE THE JEW

Almost at the same time that Tevye was immersing little Moishe in the mystical *mikvah* in Safed, Hevedke Galagan was immersing himself in a *mikvah* in Jaffa as part of his conversion to Judaism. Afterward, a special *brit milah* circumcision was performed, and the blond Russian youth entered into the covenant between God and the Jewish People. His new Hebrew name was Yitzhak ben Avraham, a name chosen for its Biblical significance, and for its similarity to the name of the Chief Rabbi of Jaffa, HaRav Avraham Yitzchak HaCohen Kook, who the new Issac so greatly admired.

Issac's studies had progressed remarkably quickly. He learned to speak Hebrew more fluently than Tevye, and with much less of a Russian accent. In addition, he had learned to read Aramaic and had already completed one tractate of the Talmud. Naturally, having only just started, he was behind everyone else, but with his characteristic long strides, he labored diligently to catch up. Jokingly, his friends called him Akiva, after the famous uneducated shepherd who had matured after decades of study into Israel's greatest teacher of Torah.

Now and again, Issac had taken time from his busy learning schedule to write Hava a letter, but, true to his promise, he had not seen her in over a year. That had been the terms of his bargain with Tevye, and he had been stringent about keeping his end of the deal. But now, finally, the time had come to make their marriage kosher.

"If she will still have me," he thought.

True, now he was Jewish, and that was a mountain out of the way, but he was no longer the same glib, outspoken poet who had mezmerized her in the sleepy village of Anatevka. The Torah had changed him. Discovering the unending depths of its wisdom, his own eclectic understandings had been exposed as superficial and false. All other religions were the inventions of man, whilst the Torah was given to the Jewish People by God. His former religious views and his vilification of Judaism filled the depths of his being with shame. When he realized how the New Testament had turned mankind away from the pure faith of the Torah, he understood why Tevye had banned his daughter from the house for having eloped with a stranger to their faith.

His day and night learning of the Talmud, and the thick volumes of Jewish law, had taught him that truth was more than platitudes. God's will for man extended to every facet of life, to every thought and deed. Believing in a faraway deity wasn't enough. A servant of God had to obey all of the orders of the King. But Hevedke didn't look on the Torah's commandments as an obligation or yoke. He embraced them with indescribable joy.

Recognizing the grandeur of his Creator, Hevedke's boyhood bravado became a thing of the past. The yeshiva was like a fiery kiln, searing his pride, refining his coarse edges, and making him humble. Even his posture had changed. Instead of his once tall, upright swagger, the new Issac walked slightly bent over, with his head toward the ground, in constant awe of his Maker.

In a way, when Hava finally saw him after over a year, it was like meeting an entirely new person. From his letters, she knew that he was engrossed in his studies, but she never dreamed that it would cause such a change in his bearing. If he had not written her that he was coming to Zichron Yaaeov to marry her, she would not have recognized him when she saw him on the street. For one thing, he wore a hat. Not a fur *shtreimel* like Rabbi Kook, nor the cap of kibbutz worker, but a black fedora from Italy, like the hats worn by Jewish businessmen in Europe. Instead of his high Russian boots, he wore shoes, and instead of his casual suede jacket, he wore a simple black overcoat. But the biggest changes were his spectacles and his beard. Together they hid his youthful good looks. Long evenings of candlelight study, squinting at the flamelike Hebrew letters, had made eyeglasses a must. Though he needed them only for reading, he wore them the first time they met. And his reddish blond beard covered his cheekbones completely, taking away his Slavic appearance, and making him look like a Jew.

The change wasn't only on the outside. Instead of the conceited confidence which Hava remembered, there was a quietness and calmness to him now. Instead of speaking first, he waited for others to voice their opinions. Instead of staring at her boldly, he turned his eyes modestly away toward the ground. And the new Issac's Hebrew was a wonder. Unlike her own clumsy accent, his Hebrew came out like a song.

Ever since she had received Issac's letter, Hava had been in a daze. The day he was due to arrive, she took the afternoon off from her work. She dressed up in her prettiest outfit, but after meeting him, she soon realized that if her beauty had attracted him before, now he was interested in something much deeper. Curiously, she sensed that he was far more religious than she was. While she wore her Jewishness naturally, like a comfortable robe, he seemed to work at it with all of his might. In a way, his newfound religious fervor seemed like a barrier that got in the way. He listened intently to everything she said. He earnestly wanted to hear everything that had happened to her and her family. But something was missing. When she spoke of the tragedies, his head shook with sorrow, and when she related the joys, his face shone in a smile, but the love which had flowed between them so naturally now seemed to be much more guarded and formal. It didn't show in anything he said. Nor in any facial expression. With a woman's sensitivity, she felt a barrier between them instead of a bond. But this, Hava hoped, was only a matter of time. After all, for more than a year, he had been living with nothing but books and long beards. Of course he behaved like a rabbi. Surely with time, his newfound modesty would thaw, and he would return to being the man who had swept her off her feet.

As they talked, they strolled around Zichron Moshe, wandering through the fields, the orchards, the pastures, and vineyards. Hava pointed out the winery, the barrel factory, the duck pond, and infirmary. She had written him about her job as a nurse, but she still had a lot of stories to tell. Behind the hospital building, Hava stopped and motioned toward the small village of tents in the distance where her father and sisters were living. On orders from the JCA office in Paris, the Morasha colony had been abandoned until the epidemic had passed. Their family, along with the rest of the Morasha settlers, had been quarantined for the past several weeks in the tent colony to make sure that no one had contacted the fatal disease. Doctors in Paris had decreed that the Morasha carriers could jeopardize the health of entire Jewish community in the country. But, thank God, ever since Tevye had returned from the *mikvah* in Safed, no other deaths had occurred.

"Can't I even wish them *shalom?*" Issac asked.

"I'm sorry," Hava answered. "We have strict orders that only the hospital staff is allowed to make visits."

"How long do they have to be there?'

"Not much longer I hope."

"They could catch pneumonia in those tents," Issac said in concern.

"God forbid," Hava replied.

"Yes, of course," Issac corrected himself. "God forbid."

As they stared out at the tents, Hava gently reached over and took a hold of Issac's hand. Awkwardly, he pulled it away.

"No one can see us," she said.

"It isn't allowed," he answered.

"We were once-upon-a-time married, you know."

"You know that marriage doesn't count."

"Hevedke," she said with a blush, "I want a husband, not a rabbi."

The tall, bearded man averted her gaze.

"We have waited this long, we can wait a little longer," he answered. "And please call me Issac. I hate the name Hevedke."

"I'm sorry, Issac," she told him. "I promise I will."

They agreed to get married as soon as her father was allowed to leave quarantine. When the sun began to set, Issac hurried off to the synagogue to join the afternoon prayers. Filled with excitement, Hava ran out to the tents behind the infirmary to tell her family the news. But to her surprise, her father was missing.

"How long can you expect *Abba* to stay cooped up like a chicken?" Bat Sheva asked.

"Where did he go?" Hava asked.

"To Morasha."

"To Morasha? Is he crazy? Does he want to get sick?"

"God forbid," another voice said. It was the tailor's wife. In the confines of the tent, she could not help fom overhearing the conversation.

"Of course," Hava said. "God forbid. But why did he go back to Morasha?"

Tevye had ridden off to Morasha with Elisha to make sure the guard they had left there was doing his job. He wasn't. They found him lying in a puddle of blood with a bullet in his back. Shocked, they stared in silent wonder at the destruction they saw all around them. All of the houses had been burned down to the ground. All of the livestock and tools had been stolen. The vegetables and flowers in Shmuelik's beloved garden lay trampled and uprooted. The Torah ark was smashed into pieces. Luckily, the settlers had taken the sacred scroll with them when they had left. Tevye and Elisha gazed at the devastation. The settlement of Morasha had vanished, as if the earth had swallowed it up.

"At least," Tevye said, "There is one consolation."

"What is that?" the Yemenite asked.

"They stole the animals too."

His friend looked at him with a puzzled expression.

"The animals were diseased," Tevye said. "Hopefully, the murderers and thieves will be too."

Hava's wedding was held on a chilly, moonlit evening in the Hebrew month of *Shevat*. Festive torchlights were lit in one of the orchards where the ceremony was to be held. The *chuppah* was ready and waiting. Everyone in the settlement turned out to welcome Rabbi Kook, who had journeyed all the way from Jaffa to officiate at the marriage. Crowned by a fur *shtreimel* which accentuated his regal appearance, the heralded Chief Rabbi took the time to exchange a greeting with each and every guest. As much as the settlers loved Rabbi Kook, he loved them for their devotion to building the land. More than that - he loved them simply because they were Jews. And had they been gentiles, he would have loved them just the same. Everyone whom God had created, Rabbi Kook loved. Once, he had confided to Nachman, that even people who fell into sin were deserving of love. Certainly not for the evil they did, but for whatever small good, because they too had been formed in God's image.

How ironic life could be, Tevye thought! The scandal that had been his greatest shame was now the cause of his greatest honor. Taking his daughter's hand, he led her to the wedding canopy, accompanied by the distinguished Rabbi. What an honor of honors it was for Tevye to stand beside the revered Rabbi Kook as he chanted the blessing over the wine and read out the formal wedding *Ketubah* agreement. The traditional wedding glass was broken, recalling the destruction of Jerusalem and how the joy of the bride and the groom couldn't be complete until the Holy City was restored. With a cheer from the crowd, Issac became Hava's one-hundred-percent kosher husband.

The festive wedding meal was held in the Zichron Yaacov community hall. Wine was plentiful, and the dancing was joyous. Tevye was in exceptionally high spirits, fulfilling, with great gusto, the *mitzvah* of rejoicing with the newlyweds. Hillel played his accordion alongside a clarinet player and a *Hasid* with a fiddle. The wedding guests danced and danced. A group of Russian Jews balanced bottles of wine on their heads, entertaining the *chatan* and *kallah*. Not to be upstaged, Elisha's sons Ariel and Yehuda folded up newspapers into cones, lighted them with matches, and balanced the flaming torches on the tips of their noses - an act which drew enthusiastic applause from the crowd.

The groom hugged Tevye and called him father. Laughing, Tevye dragged Hava's husband over to meet the Yemenite side of the family. If Tevye was Issac's father, that made Elisha a grandfather of sorts to the groom! Could better proof be found that the Almighty was gathering His exiled children from the four corners of the earth? In the joy of the great celebration, all of the winter's sorrow was gladly put aside, as King Solomon had said, there was "a time to weep, and a time to laugh; a time to mourn, and a time to dance." There was enough sadness and tragedy in the life of a Jew. When an occasion of happiness fell out from the sky, a man had to seize it.

Only Hodel felt left out of the *simcha*. Ever since she had run away from Perchik, she hadn't heard a word from her stubborn mule of a husband. But she was happy for her sister just the same.

Three weeks later, Bat Sheva married Elisha's son, Ariel. Thus Ariel became not only Tevye's brother-in-law, but his son-in-law as well. The wedding was more modest in size, but lovely all the same. Ariel's sisters insisted on dressing Bat Sheva in the traditional Yemenite wedding gown and decorative head dress which Tevye's wife, Carmel, had worn at her wedding. Tevye stood up during the festive dinner and held up a glass and a vintage bottle of wine. *"Shecheyanu, v'keeymanu, v'higeyanu l'hazman hazeh!"* he called out, thanking the Lord for having kept him alive to see this great day. Finally, all of his daughters were married! He could imagine his Golda *kvelling* with joy in Heaven. True, he still had to figure out a way to get rid of Hodel's communist pig farmer, but, with patience, that happy day would arrive as well.

The string of weddings had a healing effect on the Morasha settlers. It was even rumored that the matchmaker had arranged a *shidduch* for Reb Guttmacher, with a rich widow who lived in Rechovot.

"Didn't King Solomon say that there is a time for every thing?" Tevye reminded his friend, the undertaker, when he came to pour out his heart and his feelings of guilt. "A time to die and a time to live?"

"Is it right," the undertaker asked, "that I should remarry when the worms are still eating my wife?"

"Of course it is right," Tevye answered. "Didn't I remarry? And I am glad that I did."

Not only was Tevye glad - he was flabbergasted. His Carmel, God bless her, was pregnant!

"Stop acting so surprised," Elisha told him on that dizzying day when his wife had informed him.

"Whoever thought?" Tevye stammered.

"Did you forget what it leads to?"

"At my age?"

Elisha's eyes twinkled. "Yemenite women are fertile," he said. "Families with ten children are small."

"Ten children?" Tevye exclaimed.

"My grandmother raised eighteen."

"*Rachmonis,*" Tevye moaned. "May the Lord have mercy."

Elisha quoted a few verses of Psalms. "*Happy is the man who eats from the labor of his hands. Thy wife shall be like a fruitful vine inside thy house; thy children like olive plants around thy table.*"

What was meant to be, would be, Tevye thought. And what wasn't meant to be, wouldn't. For instance, Morasha. After Arab marauders had burnt it to the ground, it seemed that establishing a settlement on that site just hadn't been a part of the Almighty's great Divine plan. The houses which the Morasha settlers had built had been razed. The saplings they had planted had been pulled out of the earth. The fields they had sown had been trampled by horses. As it says, "*Unless the Lord builds the house, those who labor to build it, labor in vain.*" What could a man do against the judgment of God? The great ledger in the sky had been opened, the Hand had written, and the sentence had been decreed. The ways of the Lord were a mystery. The task of a man was to lower his head in submission and say, "*Baruch Hashem,*" thanking God over misfortune, just as he thanked God when events turned out for the good.

Who knew, Tevye thought? Maybe if they had remained in Morasha, the plague would have killed them all. Maybe, its deadly microbes were still lingering over the mountain side. Maybe by having the Arabs destroy the colony, God had really saved the Jews from a far graver fate.

Meanwhile, the tent village behind the infirmary had become

their temporary home, even after the quarantine had been lifted. Until the Jewish Colony Association purchased a new tract of land, Tevye and his comrades were staying in Zichron Moshe. A vote had been taken, and the settlers had decided that when the epidemic was over, they would refuse to rebuild Morasha. They were tired of saying the mourner's *Kaddish*. If Baron Rothschild didn't like it, he could go and and rebuild the ruins of Morasha himself.

Like Abraham and Sarah before them, Tevye and his bride set up their home in a tent. Tevye became a *shlepper* of wine barrels, hauling them from the Zichron warehouse to the wagons that transported them to Jaffa. And, like fruitful vines, while he was at work, his family expanded and grew. The orphans, Moishe and Little Sarah, came to love Ruchel and Nachman just like a real mother and father. Not only was Tevye's wife, Carmel, pregnant, Ruchel was too. A radiant smile shone on her face whatever she was doing. Bat Sheva was as happy as could be as a homemaker. Hodel lived in a tent with unmarried young women, and Hava returned to her room in the infirmary dorm.

At first, the newlywed, Hava, was stunned when Issac informed her that he wanted to return to his studies in Jaffa.

"I am just beginning to embark on the real learning of Torah," he said with an earnest glow in his eyes. "Up till now, I've been like a child studying the alphabet, learning to read and to write. If I hope to truly progress, I have to study for years. Don't you understand, my Havila? I want to feel like a Jew, not only on the outside by growing a beard and wearing a hat, but in the depths of my very being. There are hundreds of books on the shelves of the yeshiva, and I have barely opened a few."

Realizing how important his learning was to him, Hava didn't have the heart to protest. He said that in Jaffa, near the yeshiva, they could rent a room in someone's house. At first that seemed all right with Hava, but as days passed, she began to realize that her work as a nurse in the infirmary was as important to her as Torah learning was to him. Why should she sit alone in a room all the day, waiting for her husband to come home, when she could really help people, and even save lives! Though notices were posted all around the colony, offering free training for nurses, not every young woman was willing to work in a building filled with yellow fever and plagues. As it was, the infirmary at Zichron Yaacov was sorely understaffed. Hava's energy and selfless devotion had made her one of its most counted-on workers. How could she leave?

After long discussions between them, they came to a joint conclusion. For the Zionist cause to succeed, it needed men learned in Torah, and women who were willing to sacrifice and work, not only at home, but wherever the ocassion demanded. Issac would continue to study in Jaffa. Hava would continue to work at the hospital. They would get together for Shabbos, whether in Zichron or Jaffa, whenever they could.

Firm in their resolve, they entered Tevye's tent like soldiers reporting before their commanding officer. After they had finished their speeches, Tevye looked incredulously from one to the other. Is this why Hevedke had followed after his daughter all over the world? To leave her for a bunch of yeshiva boys and books? Was this why Hava had torn out her father's heart in seeking his acceptance of a stranger - to live like a widow in a cholera ward, surrounded with sickness and death? Tevye smashed his fist on the barrel which served as a table.

"No!" he roared. "I won't allow it! This isn't love - it's madness! To hell with Zionism and your crazy *meshuganah* dreams. A husband is commanded to live with his wife!"

"What about Rabbi Akiva?" answered Hava. "Didn't he leave his wife, Rachel, to study Torah for twelve years without ever once coming home for a visit?"

"And when he finally went home and reached the window of his house," Hevedke added, "he overheard her say to a friend that she would be happy if he were to keep studying, so he went straight back to the yeshiva for another twelve years without even saying hello."

"Don't quote me Rabbi Akiva!" Tevye shouted. "What do you have in common with a scholar like Rabbi Akiva?"

Tevye raised a hand as if to give the new convert a blow on the head, but Hava reached up and grabbed her father's arm before it could fall.

Embarrassed at Tevye's behavior, the saintly Issac lowered his glance.

"*Abba*, be fair," Hava pleaded. "Once upon a time you were angry at Issac for not being Jewish. Now you are angry at him for being too much of a Jew. Isn't studying Torah the greatest *mitzvah* of all?"

Tevye grumbled. He dropped his raised hand to his side. He looked at the red-bearded scholar who stood humbly before him. Was this really the braggart Hevedke, or was the scoundrel acting out a role in some Chekov play? Tevye didn't know what to think. Yes, studying the Torah was the greatest *mitzvah* there was. But building the land was also a supremely holy deed. Why should this one sit and learn all day long, when others slaved like mules, breaking their backs from morning until night in the fields? On the other hand, Tevye reasoned, if nobody learned, how would the scholarly traditions be guarded? Who would teach the future generations? Who would make sure that the *menorah* of Torah kept burning?

But just as important to Tevye, the father, was the ultimate question - if this Chaim Yankel of a son-in-law were to study full time in Jaffa, who would look after Tevye's daughter?

"A husband belongs with his wife!" Tevye decreed.

There was silence in the tent. The newlyweds exchanged worried glances.

"I am proud of Issac's decision," Hava insisted. "I want him to study. And I can look after myself. If I were with him in Jaffa, I would only take his mind away from his learning."

"I know I am an old man who is losing his senses," Tevye said, "but tell me one thing. Why did you bother to marry?!"

"Because we love each other," Issac answered. "As King Solomon said, '*The greatest floodwaters cannot quench love.*'"

"Now he's quoting King Solomon!" Tevye responded.

"The arrangement won't be forever," Issac assured. "And I will come to visit as often as I can."

"We only came to inform you, not to ask your permission," Hava said with a peppery tone to her voice. Tevye was speechless. Not to ask his permission? He stared at his strong-willed daughter. That was the Havila he remembered. She hadn't listened to him in the past, why should she now? The two young people loved each other, that was certain. What could he do? At least Hevedke was taking off to study in a yeshiva, and not, God forbid, to become a priest in some church. A Jewish father could be thankful for that.

Chapter Thirty-Two

A LETTER FROM AMERICA

One late afternoon when Tevye returned to his tent after a back-breaking day in the winery, a letter was waiting from Baylke. Sure enough, she had been in touch with Golda's distant cousin in Chicago, and he had forwarded Tevye's letter to her in New York. She had been thrilled to hear from her family, and hoped that more letters were in the mail. She wrote that the news of their safe arrival in Palestine had quieted a nagging fear in her heart that perhaps, like so many others, they had been caught in the bloody persecutions in Russia. She was happy for them, but when she read about her big sister's death, she had fallen into a week-long depression. The blades of grass from the Land of Israel which her father had stuffed into the envelope had brought tears to her eyes. She reported that neighbors came by their flat throughout the day to see the holy blades and to hold them in their hands. Though the letter had taken months to arrive, Baylke said that the grass had remained a deep shade of green.

"A miracle!" a friend of hers had exclaimed in the sweater factory where she worked.

Baylke wrote that they were doing wonderfully. At first, they had shared a flat with another family, but now they had their own large apartment. Her husband, Pedhotzer, had found work in a bank, and it hadn't taken long before the management had recognized his outstanding business savvy and talents. He was now a manager in the loan department, and as soon as he mastered English Baylke was sure that he would be promoted to an even higher position. Of course, his goal was to start a business of his own, and his work at the bank was only temporary in order to learn the ins-and-outs of American enterprise.

America, she confirmed, was truly a land of gold and fortune. Though dollars didn't grow on trees, with hard work a man could become a millionaire. They had met people who had arrived in New York with nothing, and who now owned Manhattan hotels, theaters, dress factories, and jewelry stores on Fifth Avenue. It wouldn't be long, she wrote, until they had a luxurious apartment of their own, but in the meantime, they had an extra room in their Essex Street flat, and she wanted her family to come.

The city of New York, Baylke wrote, was like a dream. Its buildings reached up to heaven. Kings and queens walked the streets. Cafes, restaurants, and nightclubs never closed. Stores were filled with treasures from all over the world. Everyone could own his own automobile. And a Jew didn't have to live in a ghetto. He could be an American, like everyone else.

"That's the end of the Jews in America," Tevye said wryly.

"It sounds wonderful to me," Bat Sheva argued. "Why does a Jew always have to be different? If we were like everyone else, the gentiles would stop hating us."

"The gentiles will stop hating us when men will walk on the moon," her father responded.

"That's ridiculous," Bat Sheva answered. "Men will never walk on the moon."

"Neither will the *goyim* stop hating us."

"Then again," Tevye thought out loud, the very next day, as he was *shlepping* barrels of wine on his back like a donkey, "where is it written that Tevye has to be a poor *shlemiel* all of his life. If I had a million dollars like all of the Jews in New York, I could study, give charity, and do a long list of good deeds. I could become a great man like the Baron himself! After all, if the Almighty wanted a man to work like a mule all his life, He would have graced him with another two legs."

Tevye carried the barrel on his shoulder from the warehouse to a wagon outside. With a groan, he let the great weight slide off his neck and roll onto the planks of the wagon. Walking back to the warehouse, he could barely stand straight. Why bother? He would only have to stoop over again to lift another barrel onto his back. But if he were in New York, there he could be a wealthy importer of wines, or the owner of a fancy restaurant, or the manager of one of his son-in-law's hotels. True, Pedhotzer was a swine of a person, but for the sake of the family, Tevye could pretend to get along. He would move in with his daughter until he could get started on his own. With a little luck and hard work, it wouldn't be long before Tevye could afford a mansion like everyone else.

The sweet reverie was interrupted by a whack on his back as another *shlepper* of barrels crashed into him.

"Look where you are going!" Tevye called out.

"Who told you to fall asleep on the job?" the other worker retorted.

That's what a man got for day-dreaming. A whack on the back. His mansion would just have to wait. Right now, there was more important work to be done in Palestine. After all, Tevye wasn't a fool. He could read between the lines of his daughter's letter. If things were so good in America, why did she have to work in a factory? And even if Padhatzur were to make himself millions and buy a palace for his wife, the last person in the world his highness would want to find on his doorstep was Tevye, with his barnyard stink and dung on his shoes. Baylke's pompous husband had humiliated Tevye enough for one lifetime, thank you very much. Tevye was staying right where he was in the Holy Land. With all of its trials, at least it was the land of the Jews. America would just have to get along with one less *Yid*. Tevye was needed far more in the Promised Land.

Tevye trudged on with his barrel. What had Rabbi Kook said? That every man had to do the work of one thousand? Every day, Jewish settlers were abandoning the country in despair, heading back to Russia and Europe, as if they had forgotten why they had left. Chaim Lev, who had lost two of his daughters in the plague, fled from Zichron Yaacov without being able to look Tevye in the eye. What could the goodhearted fellow do? His wife wanted to return to the old country, pogroms and all, to save her remaining children. Nothing which the repairman could say could convince her. And others, like Pincus, the storekeeper, set off for the "Promised Land" of America. If Tevye, and others like him, didn't stay to build a Jewish homeland in Palestine, where would the Jews of the world find shelter from the never-ending fury of Esau and his bloodthirsty offspring?

It wasn't long before another letter for Tevye arrived, this time from his daughter, Hodel. Before sneaking off from Zichron Yaacov, she handed the envelope to her sister, Hava, to deliver to their father. Hodel hadn't had the courage to face him. She wrote that she loved being with the family, but Perchik was still her husband, and the father of her child. If he were too stubborn to come and fetch her, then she would follow after him, just like it said in the Bible, *"Thy desire shall be to thy husband, and he shall rule over you."* Hodel said that she was giving Perchik one last chance. Their child was still a baby, unable to tell the difference between the Sabbath and any other day of the week, so for the while, his education in Torah could wait. The important thing for Hodel was to try and save her marriage. She asked for her father's forgiveness, and promised to write. So once again, just like she had in the past, Hodel journeyed off after her free-thinking husband.

It was Nachman who told Tevye about a place called *"Olat HaShachar."* On a visit to Jaffa, he had heard from a new immigrant that a group of religious Jews from Russia were starting a new *yishuv* along the coast, a few hours south of Zichron Yaacov. They belonged to the religious Zionist movement, "Lovers of Zion," which had been founded many years before by the famous Rabbi Shmuel Mohaliver. With the help of the *Keren Keyemet* organization, these *"Chovevei Tzion,"* as they called themselves, had purchased a large tract of land for thirty-thousand francs, and they were looking for more Jews to join them. The land, Nachman reported, was an ideal stretch of rich, black soil, just waiting to he cultivated.

The news came as a ray of hope for the disgruntled Morasha settlers. After their refusal to return to the ill-fated colony, their request for a new tract of land was ignored. They were given the most menial jobs at Zichron and made to live in tents. The Company was certain that a cooling-off period would put an end to their rebellion, but the punitive treatment only further embittered the Morasha settlers against the dictatorial landlords. To their way of thinking, the Company's policies were an obstacle to settling the land, not an aid. The settlers wanted freedom from foreign rulers, but Tevye and his friends found themselves being ruled by tyrannical officials and a portrait on the wall of the Baron who gave orders to the settlers from France. Lacking their own resources and funds, the would-be farmers had no choice. They either signed an oath of allegiance to the Baron or starved. But hearing about the new, religious colony, the Morasha settlers decided that they no longer had to be slaves to the Company. To hell with "The Benefactor" they thought, not realizing that the money which the "Lovers of Zion" were using to buy and develop the new Olat HaShachar location had come in large measure from the ever-gracious donation of the very same *Nediv*, the Baron Edmond de Rothschild.

In Hebrew, the expression *"Olat HaShachar"* meant "dawn." As they set out on their new adventure, Nachman explained to his fellow pioneers that the Talmud describes the redemption of Israel using the very same term. Salvation, the Rabbis taught, comes in slow, gradual stages, like a dawning new day. After the darkness of exile, slowly, slowly, the light of salvation begins to appear on the nation. At first, small, scattered groups of Jews return to Zion. Fields are plowed. Houses are built. Fruit once again grows on the stark, barren hillsides. Little by little, more Jews arrive and more homes are built, until one day, as if miraculously, a new country is born.

"Spoken like Rabbi Kook," Tevye approvingly said.

"Yes," the young scholar admitted with blush. "I have heard Rabbi Kook describe our revival in the Land of Israel in this very light."

"Nothing good comes easy," the scribe, Shragi, said.

"Not only that," Nachman added. "Just as the darkest part of the night comes just before the dawn, so too, we can expect to see more difficult times before experiencing the fruits of our labor."

"The birthpains of *Mashiach*," Guttmacher noted, referring to the long-awaited messiah.

"If you ask me," Tevye said, "the bad times are over. We suffered enough labor pains in Morasha, may its memory be erased from our minds. Good times lay ahead."

"From your mouth to God's ears," Munsho replied.

"We have had enough darkness," Tevye declared. "As the Almighty Himself said, *'Let there be light.'*"

Hillel popped a cork out of a bottle of wine.

"L'Chaim!" he called.

Everyone responded, *"L'Chaim!"*

As it turned out, Nachman's warning was right. As they reached the new settlement, a rank, musky smell of foul, stagnant water hung heavily in the air. The acres and acres of supposedly rich black soil was nothing but swamp. Sand dunes and swamp. Sand dunes and swamp, as far as the eye could see.

Chapter Thirty-Three

THE SETTLERS DRAW LOTS

Tevye and the former Morasha settlers became the new pioneers of Olat HaShachar. It soon became clear that the only thing poetic about the new colony was its melodious name. The swamps smelled like rotten eggs and sulphur. Scorpions, spiders, and snakes crawled over its sands. Mosquitoes swarmed in the air like demons.

"Isn't it a blessing?" Shimon asked, waving his hand out over the vista below.

Miles of sand dunes and swamp land stretched out before them as Tevye, Nachman, and the overweight leader of the "Lovers of Zion" brigade stood on the crest of a hill overlooking the coastline terrain. A village of tents had been erected between the dunes to house the new pioneers.

"This is a blessing?" Tevye asked.

"Of course, it's a blessing," Shimon enthusiastically responded, as if his eyes saw orchards and groves filled with fruit. "Our own plot of land in *Eretz Yisrael*! What could be a greater blessing than this?"

"You call this land?" Tevye asked. "This is nothing but desert and swamp."

"I am surprised at you, Tevye. You look far wiser than your words. I see in your eyes that you have the heart of a believer. Is it too much for God to turn what you see into gardens and vineyards? To quote from the Scriptures: '*Is the Lord's hand too short?*'"

"The Lord can do whatever He pleases. The question is, can we?"

"If we can't, then nobody can. This is the land that God gave us. Surely, if we set to the task with trust in our Maker, our Rock shall not fail us."

"With God's help, we can turn these swamps into cities," Tevye's son-in-law said.

"I think both of you are dreamers!" Tevye answered. "A Jew is called upon to have faith, but suicide is forbidden."

Tevye's skepticism seemed to puncture their bubble. Even the energetic Shimon was momentarily quiet.

"How many of your men have already been lost?" Tevye asked.

"Three," Shimon admitted. "But their lives won't be in vain. We'll dry up this swamp, you'll see. We have waited two thousand years to return to our heritage, and we are not going to let some bothersome mosquitoes stop us."

Tevye gazed at the young settlement leader. In a way, he reminded Tevye of Ben Zion. He spoke with the same fervor and had the same happy gleam in his eyes. The only difference was that Shimon had a beard, and while Ben Zion had relied upon his own strength and cleverness, Shimon relied upon God's. His faith was as big as his bulk. What Goliath had been blessed with in height, Shimon had been blessed with in width. But it was the muscle of a bull, not fat, proving he was no stranger to work.

"You actually expect us to go into that quicksand to dry it up?" Tevye asked.

"How else?" Shimon responded.

"It's like sacrificing humans to Molech," Tevye observed.

"It's a job that has to be done," Shimon answered.

"Rishon Le Zion was once all swamp land too," Nachman noted. "With hard work and God's help, we will succeed in transforming this wasteland into a paradise for all Jews."

"Both of you are crazy," Tevye said.

Not only Shimon and Nachman were crazy. It turned out that all of the "Lovers of Zion" had their heads in the clouds. Not that they were mystics in the traditional sense of the word. Tevye didn't see any of them walking around with the holy *Zohar*, but they all had a towering, supernatural faith in their mission.

Nachman tried to explain their great passion. Unlike popular legend, he said, the Zionist movement had not started with Theodor Herzl, but with the great rabbi, the *Gaon* of Vilna, more than a hundred years earlier. Possessed with a prophetic spirit, the renowned scholar had urged his students to make the long, dangerous journey to *Eretz Yisrael* With tears in his eyes, he warned that only in Zion would the Jews find a refuge from the horrible persecution which was destined to befall thcm in Russia and Europe. Faithful to their teacher's command, his students had been the first Jewish pioneers to have reached the shores of Palestine during the first wave of immigration, or *aliyah*. Other great rabbis took up the call of the *Gaon* in rallying the Jews to wake up from their Diaspora slumber. The time had come to fulfill the words of their prayers and the longings of generations to return to the land of Zion and Jerusalem. Rabbis Guttmacher and Kalisher founded the "Lovers of Zion." In fact, Nachman insisted, it was another great spiritual leader, Rabbi Shmuel Mohaliver, who inspired Baron Edmond Rothschild to support the Zionist cause. Naturally, as the movement spread, Jews from all walks of life became enthused with the dream of building a homeland in Zion, free from the oppression that had hounded them for nearly two-thousand years of wandering in foreign lands. For some, like Herzl, the new Jewish State would solve the "Jewish problem" by providing a political refuge for the Jews. For others, like Perchik and other disillusioned Marxists, it was a chance to build a new social utopia. And for the followers of the Vilna *Gaon* and the "Lovers of Zion," the Jewish national revival in *Eretz Yisrael* was all of those goals, but also something much greater. The re-establishment of the Jewish nation in Israel was to be the harbinger for the Kingdom of God in the world, ushering in a time of universal blessing and peace.

"*Meshuggeners*" Tevye called the crazy bunch.

He believed in God as strongly as anyone. But to walk knee deep into a malaria-infested swamp, that was sheer madness. He had come to the Land of Israel to be reunited with his daughter, not to build Heavenly Kingdoms. Certainly, at the Anatevka crossroads, the dream of stepping foot in Jerusalem had given him an extra push. But to grab hold of a bucket and stick his hands into a hellish *Gehenna* of mosquitoes, that was out of the question.

"Didn't Abraham survive a fiery furnace?" Shimon asked.

"I am not Abraham," Tevye answered.

"Didn't Joseph survive a pit filled with spiders and scorpions?"

"I am not Joseph."

"Didn't Daniel survive being thrown into a den of lions?"

"I am not Daniel either. I am Tevye, the milkman. And I want to stay Tevye, the milkman."

"God has decreed otherwise," Shimon said, as if he had some inside information that Tevye lacked. "Tevye, the milkman, is no longer to be Tevye, the milkman. He is to be Tevye, the pioneer. Tevye, the builder. Tevye, the drainer of swamps. One day, legends will be written about you."

"You've got the wrong man, I'm afraid."

"You will go down in history," Shimon declared.

"I don't want to go down in history. On the contrary. For the moment, I would like to stay on my feet as long as I can so I can watch my new child be born, grow up, and get married."

"If our forefather Abraham had thought only of himself and his family when God commanded him to sacrifice Issac, where would the Jews be today?"

"Here we go again with Abraham," Tevye groaned.

"My respected elder and friend," Shimon said with a patient smile. "You should know - men don't make history; history makes men. Each one of us has to be like a thousand. We have been chosen to resurrect our nation from the graveyards of Russia and Europe, and with God's help, we shall succeed."

Rabbi Kook's words again, Tevye thought with dismay. He felt like the girl in the story which Perchik had told to his daughters - "Alice in Wonderland" - surrounded by a bunch of Mad Hatters. By chance, he had followed the path of the Zionists at the Anatevka crossroad, and, suddenly had fallen into a drama of unfolding Biblical history!

As if he were dreaming, Tevye found himself standing in a line with the other Morasha settlers. Shimon passed a hat filled with pieces of paper from one pioneer to the next. On each piece of paper a number was written. Each settler drew a number out of the hat to determine the order that he or she would work in the swamps. Teams of three worked together. Taking a deep breath, Tevye pulled out a slip of paper. Like a revolver about to explode, the hat passed from hand to hand. When the lots had been drawn, Tevye unfolded his slip. He had drawn number five. Yankele was number one. Ari was number two. Bat Sheva had drawn number three. They would be the first new team into the swamp. Their job was to fill up buckets of murky water and pass them to Guttmacher, who would be stationed up on the bank. He, in turn, would pass the buckets to Tevye, and he on to number six, Reb Shilo's oldest daughter, and on down the line until the deadly swamp water was dumped into a pit in the sand. There, in the hot sun, the water would evaporate, and the larvae of the mosquitoes would be buried in the earth. Other settlers were put to work as diggers, working on the canal-like ditch which was to drain the swamp water into the sea, nearly a kilometer away.

"Give me your number, and you take mine," Tevye told his youngest daughter when the nerve-wracking drawing was finished.

"I can't," she said. "You heard the rules. We are not allowed to switch places with anyone else."

Tevye was taken aback. When had his little one become such a saint? The answer was clear. From the time she had married Ariel. The Yemenite youth was as righteous and brave as they came, always volunteering to do whatever had to be done, without any thought or concern for himself. Since her wedding, Tevye's wild, unpredictable daughter had become a model, obedient wife. As if overnight, Ariel's idealism and faith had become a part of her being. Just as her husband would walk unflinchingly into the swamp, she would unflinchingly follow.

"Maybe it isn't too late to return to Morasha," Guttmacher told Tevye on their first day of the job.

The undertaker stood on the bank of the swamp and reached out to grab a bucket splashing with rancid black water from Bat

Sheva's hands. Like all of the other workers in the swamp, she wore high rubber boots and long sleeves. But before long, she was drenched head to toe with the foul-smelling water.

"For what?" Tevye asked, reaching out to take the bucket from the undertaker.

"Haven't you had enough of the plague?"

The swamp water splashed over Tevye's hands as he passed the bucket on down the line.

"Is this any better, I ask you?"

"God will protect us," Guttmacher said.

"One place is filled with the plague. The next place is a haven for malaria. What is person to do?"

"Pray," Guttmacher told him.

Tevye reached out for the next bucket and passed it along to Reb Shilo's oldest daughter. A mosquito landed on his forehead and took a hungry bite. With a slap, Tevye killed it and stared at the splatch of blood on his hand.

"Dear God," Tevye said aloud, gazing up at the sky. "First, You almost killed us in a snowstorm. Then Cossacks nearly cut us in half with their swords. Then, You almost drowned us in the ocean, and when that didn't work, You almost killed us with thirst. You took Tzeitl in Your mercy. When Arab marauders didn't murder us all, You nearly finished us off with a plague. I ask You, haven't we suffered enough? Must we also be eaten alive by mosquitoes?"

Guttmacher slapped at his neck. "Devils," he said. "That's what they are. Little devils."

"You know," Tevye said, taking another bucket from his friend, "when we left Anatevka, our Rabbi said that we shouldn't go with the Zionists to Palestine. Maybe he was right."

"Maybe he was wrong," his friend countered. "For example, our Rabbi told us to go."

"Wouldn't it be wonderful if one day all of the rabbis got together and decided the very same thing?"

"If that ever happened, the *Mashiach* would come for sure."

In the middle of the swamp, waist deep in the water, Yankele

was furiously swatting a cloud of mosquitoes. Apparently, in the
middle of filling up buckets, he had stepped on a nest. With a
scream, he made his way through the muck and climbed out of
the swamp. Frantic to escape the angry mosquitoes, he threw
himself on the ground and rolled over and over in the sand. When
he stood up, he looked like a ghost. His body was trembling.

"I can't take it," he said.

"Take a rest," Guttmacher advised.

"I can't go back there," the distraught butcher exclaimed.

"Sure you can. Because if you don't, I'll have to."

Guttmacher stepped back into place and swung another bucket
toward Tevye. In the swamp, Bat Sheva and Ariel kept working.
They looked at each other and smiled. The buzzing mosquitoes
didn't seem to disturb them, as if they were in a cloud by
themselves. Tevye was amazed at his daughter. All of her life, the
girl had never been much of a worker. And if a spirit of
self-sacrifice had been Golda's emblem, their youngest child had
grown up with an opposite nature. But suddenly, the girl had
become an industrious pioneer, scooping up bucket after bucket
without a word of complaint.

"I quit," Yankele proclaimed, brushing the sand from his
clothes. "I can't take this anymore. You people can be heroes if
you want to. I'm going to America."

"What do you think you are going to find in America?" Tevye
asked.

"Swimming pools, for one thing, not swamps. I read your
daughter's letter. She didn't say one word about mosquitoes, nor
about Arabs, nor about plagues."

"My daughter, God bless her, doesn't always see things for
what they really are. For instance, I would rather stay here with
the snakes and mosquitoes and work in this swamp than live with
her miserable husband who treats me with scorn because I work
in a barn."

"*B'vakasha,*" Yankele said. "By all means. You can have my
place in line. Be my guest."

Yanking off his boots, the butcher threw them to the ground and strode away from the swamp.

"Hey, where are you going?!" the undertaker called out. The butcher didn't turn back. Tevye set down the bucket he held in his hands. Everyone watched as Yankele strode off. For a few moments, they all asked themselves the same question - why not walk off with him? In truth, that was the sensible thing to do. If life was only lived for the moment, for the happiness and fruits of today, then Yankele, the butcher, was right. But if life was something greater, something with a future, and a past, than there was a reason to stay and continue to work - so that the swamp today would turn into a field tomorrow. Fields of apples, and oranges, and corn for their children. So that the struggles and sacrifices of their parents and grandparents, and their great grandparents before them, wouldn't have been in vain.

"*Yalla,*" Ariel called, using a popular local expression. "There's work to be done!"

"Ariel's right," Tevye assented. "We have a country to build."

He gazed at Reb Guttmacher, his friend. With Yankele's desertion, the undertaker became number three. It was his turn to descend into the swamp. Already, he had lost his wife and a daughter. His eyes filled with hesitation.

"What's wrong with building America?" he asked.

Tevye didn't have an easy answer for the man who had already given so much.

"Let the Americans build America," Ariel told him.

He scooped up a bucket of swamp water and handed it to Bat Sheva. Bat Sheva turned toward the bank and held out the bucket, but there was no one to take it. Tevye and Guttmacher stared at one another, waiting for the other to make a move first. When Tevye took a step forward, Guttmacher held out his hand.

"It's my turn," he said.

Solemnly, he bent down to the ground and picked up the high rubber boots which Yankele had thrown away in the sand.

Chapter Thirty-Four

FEAR NO EVIL

When the festival of *Pesach* arrived, all work on the new settlement came to a halt in order to get ready for the Passover holiday. Tents had to be searched for *chametz*, and *matzot* had to be baked. As Tevye confided to Guttmacher, at least one thing about their new life in Olat HaShachar was easier than it had been in Russia.

"What's that?" the undertaker asked.

"Searching for *chametz*."

Guttmacher laughed. It was true. Their tents hardly had any furniture. Within minutes, all pieces of leaven and bread crumbs could be swept from the house. There were no sofas to move, no cabinets and dressers to clean, nor kitchens to scrub. But just the same, since the Master of the Universe had commanded them to remove all traces of leaven from the house during the seven day Passover holiday, they searched diligently just as Jews had been doing since the exodus from Egypt three-thousand years before. Tevye got down on his knees with a candle and feather to peer under the folds of the tent for crumbs. And sure enough, his love for the *mitzvah* was quickly rewarded. He didn't find any traces of cake or bread, but he did find two curly-tailed scorpions whose sting was known to be deadly.

When it came to baking the *matzot*, the industrious scene could have passed for Anatevka. A special oven for baking the thin unleavened bread was made out of brick. Water from a nearby well had been stored overnight so that it would be cool at the time of the kneading, to be sure that the flour wouldn't leaven. When the baking began, the men pounded the flour paste on top of tables and kneaded it without stopping until each batch of dough was ready. Once the flour and water were mixed, and the dough was flattened and slid into the oven, if more than eighteen minutes had passed, it had to be burned or fed to the animals before the holiday, in fear that it had already leavened. Nachman was given the honor of separating the priest's due, or *challah*, a *mitzvah* which was done only in *Eretz Yisrael*. Tevye, who was in charge of the kneading, made sure his workers kept shouting out, *"L'shem matzat mitzvah—for the sake of the commandment of matzah."* By the middle of the frantic baking, everyone was sweating. The workers burst out in a spontaneous song.

"Just as God gathered us out from Egypt, he will gather us from the four corners of the earth!"

Surely, a Turkish passerby would have thought the Jews were crazy. What normal man became so ecstatic about baking such poor-looking bread? No outsider could ever understand the great secret of their joy. The joy of doing God's will. The joy in knowing that the words which they were singing were sure to come true.

Shimon wanted the pioneer *chalutzim* to keep working during the intermediate days of the seven-day holiday. He maintained the commandment of settling the Land of Israel took precedence the prohibition of working on *Chol HaMoed*, the intermediary days of the holiday, if the work was vital to the success of the *yishuv*. Of course, this ruling brought groans from the settlers, who were tired of the swamps, the ditch digging, and the planting of eucalyptus trees. *Pesach* was *Pesach*. In Russia, they hadn't worked during the seven-day holiday. Why should they here? Nachman was prepared to side with Shimon, reasoning that the work of draining the swamps could save lives, and this justified working on the festival.

"Going into the swamps is what kills people," Tevye argued, "not staying out of them."

While his point was well-taken, it wasn't completely correct. Dozens of settlers had fallen victim to yellow fever and malaria without actually descending into the swamps. Since the Morasha settlers had arrived, the swamps had claimed two further victims among the "Lovers of Zion." A father and son who were working in the fields near the marshes at the other side of the settlement had come down with the fever and died. The disease-carrying mosquitoes could fly wherever they wished, making the whole vicinity a hazard. But since the overwhelming majority of settlers were in favor of rest, a vacation from work was declared. The mosquitoes could wait. Passover was the festival of freedom, and people were happy for a chance to forget about the dangerous labor of draining the swamps.

On the third day of the holiday, Hillel suggested that they go to the beach for a swim. Nachman frowned at the idea. Swimming wasn't exactly in the spirit of the exaltedly holy holiday, and the Rabbis had warned against treating the sanctity of the festival lightly. But his explanation was met with boos, and an outing was organized. Since there weren't enough horses to go around, Tevye rode on a mule. He had given his own horse and wagon to Bat Sheva and Ariel as a wedding present. Moishe and Hannei rode in a mule-driven cart with Elisha's younger children. Taking along *matzot*, fruits, water, and bottles of vodka and wine, the picnickers headed off to the ocean a short distance away. Relaxing on the beach was, in Tevye's words, a life-giving *"machiah."* Sitting on the shore with his butt in the sand and his feet in the cool frothing waves, the swamp-drainer felt new life seep through his body. The sky was clear blue with puffs of white clouds. A refreshing breeze blew in from the ocean. The water shone with a purity, as if it flowed out of the Garden of Eden. This, Tevye thought, was freedom. He lifted a bottle of vodka to his lips and took a generous swallow. He was accustomed every morning after praying to down a shot glass of vodka with quinine before heading off to work in the swamps, but the holiday was the cause for a little extra celebration. Munsho passed Tevye a bottle of wine, and the pioneer milkman made a healthy *"L'Chaim!"* Before long, his head was dizzy from the sunshine and spirits. Hilled played his accordion. The children splashed in the waves. One last time, Tevye made sure that Ariel was watching them, then he laid back in the sand and drifted off to sleep. A wave washed over him, splashing his face. Startled, he sat up and looked around in a daze. The children were frolicking happily in the water under Ariel's watchful care. Satisfied that he could steal a few winks, Tevye trudged up the beach and lay down against the gentle curve of a dune. Soo he was fast asleep.

When he woke up, the sun was setting. It stared at him like a huge red, hungover eye, then sank slowly into the ocean with a radiant glow. He held his hand to his head and winced. A clanging in his brain rang from ear to ear like a blacksmith's anvil. He recalled Ariel trying to wake him, and answering that he would follow right along. But apparently he had fallen back to sleep. Gazing around, Tevye noted that the beach was deserted. His mule stood tied to the trunk of a palm tree. Tevye braced a hand on the sand to get up, but an overwhelming weakness swept over him as if he had been hit by a gigantic wave. His limbs refused to obey him. Helplessly, he swooned backward onto the sand. With a sigh, he stared up at the darkening heavens, wondering what the Master of the Universe had in store for him now. Then he closed his cumbersome eyelids. In a moment, the sound of his snoring echoed over the shore. The mule clapped a hoof in the sand and brayed, as if to remind its master that nightfall was fast approaching.

When Tevye woke up it was already nighttime. He had no way of knowing the hour. Clouds had gathered over the coastline, blocking the moon's light. The sand dunes looked foreboding, like giants curled up in sleep. The black, tempestuous ocean roared with a steady growl. At least, Tevye's weakness had left him. Once again, his mucles responded to his commands. He had mixed too much vodka and wine, that was all.

"Why didn't you wake me?" he said to the mule, untying its rope from the tree.

Unlike Bilaam's ass, the mule didn't answer. But that didn't stop Tevye from talking. On the contrary, a companion who quietly listened was a man's truest friend. And in the unfamiliar darkness, talking to the dumb creature made Tevye feel less alone.

Not that he was afraid to journey at night. Hadn't he ridden his horse through the black forests of Russian on his way home from peddling his cheeses? But then, he had known the paths in the forest like the prayers in his faded and page-torn *siddur*. The road home to Olat HaShachar was a much greater mystery. In fact, in the darkness, Tevye didn't know the way back home at all.

"Don't worry," he assured the mule as he mounted onto its back. "All we have to do is head east away from the ocean. In no time at all we'll be home. You can put your trust in old Tevye."

The creature moved off in a mule's slow, steady pace. When it reached the summit of the sand dune bordering the beach, Tevye stopped for a look around, but in the darkness, he couldn't see any paths or tracks in the sand.

"Surely at the top of the next sand dune, we'll find our way," he said, more to assure himself than the mule.

In his heart, he felt a faint twinge of worry. It was true that the settlement was only a kilometer or two away, but somewhere up ahead lay the swamp.

The mule made its way down the sand dune and obediently climbed the next hill. The roar of the ocean receded in the distance. At least that was a sign that they were on the right course. Once again, at the summit, Tevye paused for a look, but the landscape seemed even blacker. The moon, which was always full on the first day of the Passover holiday, was shrouded in a thick blanket of clouds.

"It looks like it is going to rain," Tevye noted.

The mule did not seem to care. Patiently, it waited for a kick in the side and started off down the sandy descent. When they reached level ground, the beast decided to halt on its own. Tevye clicked his tongue several times and flicked at the rope, but the creature stood frozen. In the stillness, Tevye got a whiff of the swamp. Inhaling its musty, stagnant stench, he squinted into the darkness ahead of them, but he couldn't make out a thing.

"Good boy," he said. "You're not as dumb as you seem. Now let's see if we can find the path to the colony. You know where it is. Lead the way."

Tevye held the rope loosely and gave the animal a kick. He knew there was a trail because they had traveled over it that morning. It was the path the settlers would take when they met the supply boats from Jaffa. The mule had often made the short journey to pick up shipments of lumber and food. Surely, if Tevye was light on the reins, the creature would find the way home by itself.

At the top of the next sand dune, the mule once again jerked to a stop. Tevye gave it a kick, but it stood firm like a rock. Peering forward, Tevye discovered the reason. They were poised at the edge of a cliff! One additional step forward and they would have plunged into the chasm below. Earthquakes along the coast had left fissures and craters, and the caverns were treacherously deep.

"Woooo," Tevye said.

The milkman gave a cautious tug on the rope. Obediently, the mule responded. It took a few careful steps backward, then turned around on the spot and retraced its path down the slope. When they once again reached the edge of the swamp, Tevye guided the beast to the right. Surely, the road lay in that direction.

A minute had not transpired when the mule halted abruptly again. Its body shivered below Tevye as if it, like Bilaam's ass, had seen the Angel of Death standing before it, grasping an upraised sword. The mule reared up its head and brayed. Tevye sat frozen. The smell of the swamp filled his nostrils. Frogs croaked. To his right, a shadowy creature leaped through the darkness and splashed noisily into the water. An alligator, Tevye thought, not sure if there were alligators in this part of the world. Or a bobcat. Or more probably, a wild, man-eating boar.

"*Oy vay,*" Tevye thought. Either he would fall off a cliff, drown in the swamp, or be eaten by some wild creature. He heard a voice in his head remind him of a famous quote from the Talmud: "It isn't the bite of the snake which kills, but a man's very own sin." Tevye trembled. Why had he gone to the beach and gotten drunk like an ignorant peasant? Why had he treated the sanctity of the Festival so lightly? Surely, he was being punished for that. If he had stayed in his tent, studying Torah, he never would have gotten lost in the swamp. Why hadn't he listened to Nachman?

In a situation like this, what could a Jew do but pray?

"Though I walk through a valley of death, I shall fear no evil, for Thou art with me," he recited, recalling the Psalm of Kind David by heart.

Insistently, Tevye gave the mule a kick. It stepped forward uncertainly, as if treading on treacherous ground. With a mind of its own, it refused to continue.

"Don't be such a stubborn ass!" Tevye shouted, kicking its abdomen again. He flicked at the rein, urging it forward. The recalcitrant creature advanced a few short paces until it lurched forward. Its forelegs sank in the swamp. Tevye felt water splash into his shoes. With a growl, another invisible animal dived into the reeds up ahead.

"Eeeoooh!" Tevye yelled in alarm.

"Eeeaaah!" brayed the mule.

Fiercely, with all of his strength, Tevye jerked the reins to the left. The mule staggered forward and stopped.

"Yaaahh!" Tevye shouted, commanding the mule to respond.

"Yaaahh! Tevye screamed, booting the mule in its belly.

"Yaaahh!" Tevye bellowed, tugging the reins.

But the mule would not budge.

Angered, Tevye batted the mule on the head.

"*Habayta*, you jackass!" Tevye yelled out in Hebrew, urging the animal home. "*Habayta!*"

With a bellow, the frightened creature stumbled unsteadily forward. Once again its forelegs sank into the mud, this time up to its knees. The animal froze, its head slanting down toward the swamp, its rump in the air, as if it were a stallion trying to throw off a rider. Tevye grasped at the mule's neck, bracing himself with all of his might so that he didn't tumble forward into the water.

"CARMEL!" Tevye screamed. "ELISHA! NACHMAN! SOMEBODY SAVE ME!"

His shouts were answered by silence and the ominous buzz of mosquitoes.

"CARMEL!" he yelled, calling out for his wife. "ELISHA! NACHMAN! COME HELP!"

Certainly, someone was near. Certainly, his calls would be

heard. The colony was only a short distance away, and certainly when Tevye was late in returning, a search party had already been sent out to find him.

But what if his shouts were heard by Arabs, not Jews? What if his yelling brought Bedouins? It wouldn't be the first time that an Arab killed a Jew for his mule.

Tevye shut up. The buzzing of the mosquitoes grew louder. When one landed on his face, he gave it a slap, but the movement upset his already precarious balance. His legs squeezed the mule tightly as they both tilted dangerously towards the water.

"Oh Golda," he whispered. "Don't be angry with me. Get me out of this mess and I'll leave my new wife.'

Again, a wild boar splashed into the swamp. Alarmed, Tevye tugged at the reins, pulling the mule backward. The animal made a great effort and staggered to unglue himself from the muck. But this time, his hind legs sank into the swamp. With a shudder, it stood rigid, unable or unwilling to budge.

"SOMEBODY HELP ME!" Tevye screamed.

His cry echoed over the swamp. Tevye looked up at the sky. The thick wall of clouds was beginning to scatter. The moon peeked through the umbrage as if to see who was causing all of the commotion below. For the first time, Tevye could see the reeds and bulrushes around him. In front of them was swamp. Behind them was swamp. All around them were bulrushes and reeds. Beneath him, Tevye felt the mule sink down another inch into the mud.

"*Gevalt*," he mumbled. "It's quicksand."

The mule turned its head to look back at Tevye, as if to say, "*Shmuck*, why did you make me go forward?"

Tevye frowned. His legs dangled in the warm, musty water. Once again, he felt the heavy animal sink into the soupy floor of the swamp. He cried out again in the night, but the echo of his cry was swallowed up by the darkness. No one could hear him. And one wrong movement could topple him off the back of the mule to a lonely and ignominious finish. Until the whole swamp was drained, nobody would ever find him.

Tevye sat frozen, like a statue of some general on a horse. Terrified, he allowed himself just the slightest of movements, a lift of an eye up to Heaven.

"Dear God," he began, "If You get me out of this mess, I promise to give up drinking. Have mercy, my King, have mercy. Is a man to blame for a small taste of vodka? Is getting a little *shikor*, a reason to drown a man in a swamp? Perhaps if I were a priest who served in the Temple, but I am only a poor milkman with less brains than this mule."

Dark clouds once again covered the moon, as if sealing up the window to Heaven.

"If You are angry at me, please let me know why, and I will be glad to repent," Tevye passionately pleaded. "If it is because I complain now and then, from now on I will keep my mouth tightly sealed. If it is because my mind wanders now and again in the middle of my prayers, I promise to pray like King David. If it is because I spoke *loshon hora* against Golda's cousin, Menachen Mendel, if I ever see the thief again, I'll get down on my knees and kiss his shoes."

The wall of clouds remained impervious to Tevye's entreaties. Mosquitoes landed on his face. Afraid to lift his hands from the nape of the mule, he let them bite him at will. A deep, sorrowful bellow sounded from the beast. Once again, it sunk another inch into the quicksand.

"Did I ever miss saying *Shema Yisrael?*" Tevye asked, in growing desperation. "Did I ever lift a finger on *Shabbos?* Did another man's ruble ever find its way into my pocket in an unlawlul way?"

Tormented by the bites of mosquitoes, Tevye bent over to squash them against the neck of the mule. Once again, the shift of weight caused the animal's front legs to sink deeper into the abyss.

"The Lord is my shepherd," Tevye whispered, continuing on with the Psalm. If his own merit wasn't sufficient to bring forth a miracle, out of God's love for King David, surely the All-Merciful would answer his prayer. *"I shall not want. He makest me to lie down*

in green pastures. He leadest me beside the still waters. He restores my soul."

Tevye paused. Where was it written that drowning in quicksand was restoring the soul? But this wasn't the time to begin arguing with God.

"I am a worthless old milkman, I know," he continued. "But I have little Moishe and Hannei to care for, and an unborn child on the way. Why punish them? Why leave them without a father? Does leading a man in righteousness mean leading him into a swamp? *'Though I walk through the valley of death, I will fear no evil, for Thou art with me.'* So, if You are listening, please send me Your rod and Your staff."

In the distance, Tevye could vaguely hear the roar of the sea. A great weariness overcame him. The mosquitoes were stinging him with a fury, but if he leaped off the mule, where would he be? Who would ever find him? Thinking back on his life, and on his long list of sorrows, he realized how truly precious life was! What a wondrous gift! How good it was to live, even in a hot, airless tent with scorpions and spiders! Why hadn't he been grateful for every single moment of his time in the Holy Land?

"Please God," he prayed. "Please let me live. For the sake of Abraham, Issac, and Jacob. For the sake of Moses and Aaron. For the sake of Joshua and Samuel. For the sake of Kings David and Solomon. For the sake of all of the Prophets and all the great Rabbis. For the sake of Your mercy and kindness. For the sake of Jerusalem and Your Holy Land. Get me out of this swamp and I will drain it myself empty handed. I'll plow up the wilderness and plant field after field with seeds. Just give me another chance to be a better man than I've been."

When the mule sank down to its neck, Tevye broke out in a sweat. His own legs were completely covered with water. If he got off the mule, he would drown. If he tried to walk, he would be trapped in the mud. Only by staying put where he was on the animal's back could he hope to keep his own head above water. Maybe the mule would stop sinking. Maybe morning would come. Maybe someone would see them.

Seconds crept by like minutes. Minutes like hours. An hour passed as slowly as a lifetime of days. Tevye kept praying. He kept clinging to hope. He reminded himself of the teaching of the Sages - even if a sword rested on the nape of a man's neck, it was forbidden to cave in to despair. Millimeter after millimeter, the mule sank into the quicksand. Water reached Tevye's waist. With tears in his eyes, the words of King David's Psalms poured out from his soul. They were the only lifeline that could save him.

"I will lift up my eyes to the hills, from whence comes my help. My help comes from the Lord, who made the heaven and the earth. The sun will not harm you by day, nor the moon by night....The Guardian of Israel neither slumbers nor sleeps." Tevye prayed for what seemed like hours. When the body of the mule disappeared, and only its neck stuck out from the swamp, it turned to stare mournfully at Tevye. Its large, frightened eyes looked at its rider imploringly, as if to say, "Why don't you get off of my back?"

"What can I do, my good friend?" Tevye replied. "If I climb off your back, I'll end up like you."

The head of the mule began to sink in the water.

"I know, it doesn't seem fair," Tevye lamented. "After all, you have four legs, and I only have two. If saving a life was decided on the basis of that, I should be the one to sacrifice my meager existence for you."

Soon only the creature's eyes and ears could be seen over the shroud of black water

"You should know," Tevye said in words meant to comfort the both of them, "that dying in the Holy Land is a great privilege. Everyone buried in its soil goes straight up to heaven. All of his sins are forgiven, just as if he brought a sacrifice on the sacred Temple altar. So be happy, my friend. You go down, not in disgrace, but in triumph."

The animal's head disappeared underwater. As if in concern for its master, the mule met its fate without panic, without even a shudder. A great love for the creature welled up in Tevye's heart.

"Forgive me, my friend," he said in farewell.

Slowly, the animal's ears vanished from view. A few bubbles

broke the surface of the swamp, and then a deathly silence seized the night. The silence of buzzing mosquitoes.

Miraculously, the mule didn't topple over into the swamp. Embalmed in the quicksand, it stood rigidly upright, as if still protecting its rider. Tevye continued to squeeze the animal's ribs with his legs. Swamp water reached up to his chest. Its stench made him gasp for a breath of fresh air. But he was afraid to inhale too deeply, in fear of losing his tenuous balance. Centimeter by centimeter, he felt himself sinking into his grave. Minutes passed. Before long, only his head stuck out of the water. Trembling, his hands clutched onto the ears of the invisible mule in the damp tomb below him.

"HELP ME!!!" Tevye screamed at the top of his lungs. His cry echoed over the swamp.

"HELP MEEEEEE!" he heard himself call.

His body teetered over the water. So precarious was his perch on the mummified mule, if another mosquito were to have landed on his ear, it would have toppled him over into the merciless abyss.

"Please God," he beseeched with all of his heart. "HEEEEEELLLP MEEEEE!!!!"

"TEVYE!" he heard a voice call.

Behind him, not far away, he saw two swinging lanterns.

"TEVYE!"

It was Carmel!

"I'M HERE!" he called. "IN THE SWAMP!"

"Keep talking!" a man yelled. It was Munsho. "That way we can see where you are."

"HURRY!" the drowning man hollered. "I'm sinking in quicksand!"

"Hurry!" he heard his wife urge.

"I don't see him," Munsho answered.

"There he is!" Ariel shouted, pointing at the head sticking out of the water, a dozen meters away.

"I see him!" Munsho called.

"Grab the rope!" Ariel yelled.

Swamp water wet Tevye's beard. He wanted to turn his head

to see his rescuers behind him, but he was afraid to budge. How could he grab a rope? If he raised his hands from the ears of the mule, he was finished.

"Grab the rope, Tevye!" Carmel called as the loop of a lasso landed on the surface of the water a desperate lunge away.

As the taste of the swamp water splashed over his lips, the drowning man realized that he had no other choice but to make a dive for the slender strip of twine.

"Now, Tevye, now!" Ariel shouted.

Tevye lunged. His hands snatched at the rope, but he felt only water. Floundering wildly, he tried vainly to swim. His legs kicked and paddled below him. One foot landed on the back of the mule, and he used the brief footing to push himself up from the deep. His mouth filled with the stench of the swamp. Choking, he started to sink in the water, but his ineffectual strokes were enough to keep him afloat until Ariel could reach him. Quickly, the robust young man threw the loop over Tevye's shoulder. Clutching the rope with one hand, and his father-in-law with the other, he held Tevye's head out of the swamp.

"Hayaaaa!" Munsho hollered, whacking his horse on the rump. The blacksmith had tied the end of the rope to the saddle. The strong, muscular Jew tugged along with the beast. Together, they managed to pull Tevye and Ariel out of the quicksand.

"Tevye, Tevye," Carmel cried as her hero lay sprawled on dry land.

Tevye choked, spitting out the eggs of a few thousand mosquitoes. An hour later, he was safe and secure back at home. Bundled in a blanket and wearing dry clothes, he sipped at a hot cup of tea. Ariel, Munsho, Guttmacher, Elisha, Hillel, Nachman, his daughters, and Carmel stood gathered around him. How good and pleasant it was to be alive, Tevye thought. How good it was to sit with one's family and friends. How good it was to have a God who answered when you called out to Him from the depths of your heart. How cozy his tent seemed. How blessed he was with such a brave and caring wife.

"To life!" Hillel said, holding up a bottle of vodka.

"To the mule!" Munsho added.

"Which one?" Elisha asked.

"To the mule who is no longer with us."

Everyone smiled. True to his vow to give up hard liquor, Tevye raised up his cup of warm tea.

"To the mule," he answered. "May his memory be for a blessing!"

Chapter Thirty-Five

A THOUSAND TEVYES

The day after Tevye's rescue, he stayed in bed with a chill. His face and his hands were so swollen with mosquito bites, he barely looked like himself. Feeling too queasy to eat, he sipped on tea and quinine. As if expecting the worst, visitors stopped by all the day long to pay their respects. Carmel stood guard by her husband, making sure the guests didn't linger too long and weaken his strength. Several times, he dozed off to sleep but awoke in a sweat, gasping from the same terrifying image — the head of the heroic mule sticking out of the swamp. Fearing that the creature would appear everytime he closed his eyes, Tevye preferred not to sleep. The following evening, he mustered enough strength to sit down with guests for a holiday meal. It was the last day of Passover, and Tevye filled up his silver goblet for the traditional *Kiddush*. True, he had vowed to give up drinking, but *Kiddush* couldn't be called drinking. The blessing over the wine was a *mitzvah*, and he certainly hadn't vowed to give up any *mitzvah*! With relish, he gulped down the sweet, pungent wine.

Thankfully, his chill went away. The malaria which everyone feared, never developed. After all, what sense did it make to save a man from the swamp, just to have him drop dead in his tent? No, you could be sure that God had some greater destiny in store for old Tevye.

When the holiday ended, Tevye joined the other settlers back at work in the swamp. With a new fearlessness, he reached out for the buckets of swamp water. If his night in the bog hadn't killed him, his work during the day wouldn't either. After all, he had received enough bites to be immune from malaria for life.

The work of draining the insect-filled swamps progressed with a frustrating slowness. But as weeks went by, the settlers could see that they were winning the battle. Little by little, the water marks on the reeds sticking out of the swamp began to descend. Slowly, slowly, the water level receded. Bucket after bucket passed from hand to hand in a constant rhythmic motion. Thousands and thousands of buckets were dumped into pits in the sand. Wagons arrived filled with tall eucalyptus trees, which cost the colony as much money as they had paid to buy the land. Planted in the swamps, their roots sucked up water like hoses.

Teams of diggers toiled day and night on the canal which was to drain swamp water off to the sea. Pipes were laid in the ditches, and the stagnant, deadly, marsh water began to trickle and flow.

Just when victory seemed within reach and a spirit of hope filled their labor, tragedy struck. Tevye was passing a bucket to Esther, the carpenter's eldest daughter, when he saw Guttmacher swoon in the middle of the swamp and fall limply into the water. Quickly, Ariel grabbed him and pulled him out of the marsh to the shore. The undertaker was shivering. His eyes were red, his face yellow with fever.

"Let's get him into a wagon, quickly!" Tevye called.

Immediately, Ariel ran for his wagon. Tevye bent down and grasped his friend's hand. Though it was the middle of the day, with the sun high in the sky, the undertaker's body was shaking. Bat Sheva handed a canteen to her father. He raised it to Guttmacher's lips, but he was too ill to drink. The water spilled over his mouth.

"Where's my wife? Where's my wife?" the sick man deliriously asked.

Tevye trembled, recalling the black, stormy day when they had buried Guttmacher's wife. Sand flew into the air as Ariel arrived with the wagon. By nightfall, Tevye reasoned, they could be in Zichron Yaacov. Though only a small number of the infirmary's patients walked out alive, there was always a chance. The workers helped Ariel lift Guttmacher onto the wagon. For a moment, his eyes seemed to clear. He clung onto Tevye's sleeve.

"Tevye, why bother?" he asked. "Bury me here."

"You're not going to die," Tevye answered. "You can't. You're the only undertaker we have."

Guttmacher smiled. Then his eyes closed and he drifted off to sleep. A half hour into the journey, he regained consciousness. He gazed up at Tevye and said, "I have a brother who lives in Minsk. He can take care of my children."

His eyes closed once again. Tevye held him in his lap. An hour later, he was dead. For a long while, Tevye and Ariel rode on in silence. Finally, Ariel brought the wagon to a halt.

"Where are we going to bury him?" Ariel asked.

Tevye glanced around at the road, as if to gage where they were.

"We are still about three hours from Zichron," Ariel said. "It makes more sense to go back to Olat HaShachar."

"Yes," Tevye said. "I suppose that it does. But you would think that a man who spent his life burying people would be granted a more respectable burying place than a swamp."

"It won't always be a swamp," Ariel said. "He gave his life for that."

"I suppose," Tevye answered, squinting off toward the distant mountains. His thoughts drifted away. Holding on to the reins of the wagon, Ariel stared at his father-in-law, waiting for a decision.

"What are you thinking, *Abba*?" he asked when Tevye continued to gaze off into space.

"I was thinking that he probably would want to be buried alongside his wife."

"In Morasha?"

"Yes," Tevye answered.

"It's almost a day's journey away."

"Yes, that's true. But he'll have a long time to rest after he gets there."

"Yes," Ariel reflected. "I suppose that he will."

The Yemenite fell silent. His wife's father had a well-meaning heart, but sometimes Ashkenazic Jews could be crazy. In *Eretz Yisrael*, what difference did it make where a man was buried? The whole land was holy. Wherever they buried him, his soul would go straight up to Heaven. Guttmacher would meet his wife there.

"I think that is what he would have wanted," Tevye said.

Ariel didn't argue. He flicked at the reins. "You knew him better than anyone."

Before making the ascent into the mountains, Tevye insisted on stopping at Zichron Yaacov to prepare the body for burial in the proper ritual manner. He dragged Ariel into the local undertaker's workroom to learn how to do the procedure. They watched as the undertaker administered the purifying bathing and carefully unloosened all of the corpse's joints.

"What was his occupation?" the undertaker asked.

"The same as yours," Tevye answered.

The Jew looked up in surprise.

"Why didn't you tell me?" he asked.

"What difference does it make?"

"It's a matter of professional courtesy," the undertaker answered. "You know how it is. People die here like flies. With all the epidemics we've suffered this year, I'm kept busy day and night. You try to do your best with everyone, but sometimes, I don't have to tell you. When I have the honor to work on a fellow undertaker, I like to do an extra special job. I mean he deserves it, am I right?"

Tevye nodded. "As the Rabbis say - the way you treat people is the way you get treated in return."

When the body was ready, they wrapped it securely in a sheet and lifted it back onto the wagon. Hava was waiting outside. Upon their arrival, Tevye had sent a youth to the infirmary to fetch her. The father washed his hands in the basin by the door of the undertaker's workroom and kissed his daughter on the cheek.

"What will become of his children?" she asked, remembering Guttmacher's remaining young son and a daughter.

"They have an uncle in Russia. In the meantime, they can move in with me."

"Why don't you spend the night in Zichron Yaacov and set out in the morning?" Hava suggested.

"Out of respect for the dead, the sooner he is buried, the sooner his soul will find rest."

Tevye led his daughter a few steps down the path, where he could speak about more personal matters.

"When was the last time you saw your husband?" he asked.

"He was here for a *Shabbos* two months ago."

"Two months ago?" Tevye queried.

"He's very involved with his studies. But in another two weeks, I have a vacation. I will be joining him in Jaffa for three days."

"That's what you call a marriage - to see your husband for one or two days every few months?"

"He's happy," Hava answered. "So I'm happy too."

Tevye frowned. He wanted to tell his daughter how foolish she was, but remembering the dead man in the wagon, he resisted the temptation to begin a lengthy discussion.

"Come to Olat HaShachar if you can," Tevye said, walking back to the wagon. "We would all love to see you."

Hava promised that she would try to come for a visit. Giving her father a kiss, she waved goodbye, and the men set off in the wagon.

"Involved in his studies?" Tevye wondered, riding away with Guttmacher's corpse. "What man could be so involved with his studies to ignore his young wife right after their marriage? Not only that, but Hevedke, or Issac, as he called himself now, had been separated from Hava for over a year. Like a mad, panting dog, he had followed her across half of the world, and now he was content to see her every few months? Something smelled fishy. As the Rabbis taught - a man is a man, and not an angel. At the first opportunity, Tevye made up his mind to investigate. If that smooth-talking imposter had some other woman in Jaffa, Tevye would make sure he boarded the first steamship leaving for Russia.

In the middle of the night, they reached the ghost town on the dark Morasha hillside. Their Arab neighbors had not only razed the houses and barns, they had also smashed gravestones and desecrated the small Jewish cemetery. Tevye gazed at the scene in despair.

"It's good that we came," Ariel said. "There is other work to do here besides burying Guttmacher. In Yemen, the Moslems would desecrate our cemeteries all of the time."

Late the next evening, Tevye and Ariel returned to Olat HaShachar. Long before they could see the colony of tents, the stink of the swamps filled their nostrils. An ocean breeze wafted the nauseating stench into their faces, reminding Tevye that come morning, he was to take Guttmacher's place in the swamp. Tevye was exhausted, but he felt he had made the right decision. The undertaker was now resting peacefully beside the graves of his wife and his daughter.

The ordeal was over for Guttmacher, but for his children, it was just getting underway. Tevye had to tell them the heartbreaking news. The milkman had already decided to take care of the orphans if they wanted to stay in Palestine. There was room in his tent. They were both nearing the age of *bar mitzvah* - they were old enough to decide for themselves. Why return to Russia? What future was waiting for them there? In any event, God would provide for their needs. As far as Tevye was concerned, they could even share some of the money which the Baron had given to Moishe and Hannei.

Arriving at the colony, Tevye trudged off to his tent. He would tell the children in the morning. Now he needed to sleep. But surprisingly, his wife was not home. Where could she be at this hour of the night? Stepping outside, he saw a group of dark figures down the path leading toward Bat Sheva's tent. Coming closer, he made out his wife, Carmel, standing with her father and one of her sisters. They didn't have to say a word for Tevye to sense that bad news awaited. Their usually smiling expressions were as somber as the night. Inside the tent, Ariel sat by the bed, holding Bat Sheva's limp hand. In the dim candlelight, Tevye could see beads of sweat on her forehead. He stood frozen, unable to believe the sight confronting his eyes. His other daughter, Ruchel, stood up from a chair when her father appeared. Ariel turned and looked up at Tevye. The hollow gaze in his eyes made the older man tremble.

"How is she'?" Tevye asked.

Ariel shook his head. "Come see for yourself."

Tevye stepped closer and gazed down at his daughter, his beautiful, beautiful daughter. All of the rosiness was gone from her cheeks. All of the life was drained from her features. In the flickering candlelight, she looked like she had already been claimed by some other world.

"She has been sleeping all day," Carmel said, taking her place beside her crestfallen husband. "Yesterday, after lunchbreak, she said she felt too weak to return to the swamp. We found her in bed with a fever. She managed to sip a little quinine, but then she passed out. We've tried to wake her, but she doesn't seem to hear."

Tevye stiffened. His eyes flashed with anger. He straightened his shoulders and took a deep breath.

"Is this why You spared me from sinking in the swamp?" he thought. "To witness the death of my daughter?"

Wildly, he stared at his wife.

"Is it?!" he said. "IS IT?!" he asked even louder.

Not understanding what he was saying, Carmel reached out for his hand, but he brushed it away. Eyes burning with pain, he charged out of the tent.

"IS THIS WHY YOU SPARED ME?!" he yelled up to the sky. "SO I COULD WITNESS THE DEATH OF MY DAUGHTER?!"

The star-studded heavens sparkled in all of their unfathomable wonder. Who was he, Tevye, the milkman, that the Almighty Creator of heaven and earth should single him out from all of the universe? What did God want from him? Was he Job that he could suffer such torture? What was the use of complaining? The Master of the World filled the universe, and he was just a speck down on earth. The Lord gives, he remembered. And the Lord takes away.

"Please God," he said quietly. "Take me, but don't take my daughter."

He felt a hand on his shoulder. Elisha stood beside him.

"Let's go for a walk," his good friend said.

"My daughter," Tevye answered.

"There's nothing to do now but pray."

He gave Tevye a tug and led him away from the tent.

"You have to be strong, Tevye," he said. "Everyone here looks up to you as a leader. We need you to set an example."

"My daughter," Tevye said again in a whisper.

"I know," Elisha answered. "Today is your turn. Tomorrow, God forbid, someone else's. We have to be strong for our children.'

He led him to the tent that served as their synagogue. Nachman sat inside, in front of the holy ark, reading from a book of Psalms. He stood up when Tevye entered. There was nothing to say. Tevye looked at him blankly, then sat down on a bench. Absently, he opened the prayer book before him. He stared down at its pages through the tears in his eyes. Elisha set a hand on his shoulder. Tevye looked up at his face, at the face of a people who had survived oppression and plague for thousands of years with an unbreakable faith. Quietly, Tevye looked down at the prayer book and began reading the comforting words of King David.

Bat Sheva died before sunrise. For the first time in his life, Tevye refused to do what the laws of the Torah commanded. After the funeral, he refused to sit *shiva* for his daughter. He refused to sit and mourn. What good would mourning do for a week? Grabbing a bucket, he strode off to the swamp. His work would be his memorial to his daughter. Enough people had died. The insatiable swamp had to he drained.

The other settlers watched him in silence. Feeling his friend's anguish, Elisha grabbed a bucket and walked off after Tevye toward the swamp. Without saying a word, Shimon, Yigal, Hillel, and Munsho grabbed buckets. Even people who didn't have to work in the swamps set off to join Tevye, who set to work with an incredible fierceness. Like a man driven with rage, he attacked the swamp with his bucket, as if beating a foe with a club. Buckets after buckets of water flew through the air onto the bank of the swamp. Elisha organized the settlers into a chain and buckets were passed hand to hand at a furious pace. Tevye stood knee-deep in the muck, working like a machine, putting all of his pain into the task of destroying the monster *moloch* which had claimed Bat Sheva's life. For hours, he worked without rest.

"Don't give up! Don't despair!" he told himself over and over.

Settlers far younger than Tevye found it impossible to keep up with his pace. When his muscles ached with exhaustion, he growled and continued to fill up his bucket. He worked with the might of one thousand men, ready to drain the swamp single-handed. When it came time for lunch, Tevye rolled up his sleeves and kept working. Alone, he carried his splashing bucket to the bank of the swamp and went back for more.

"Don't give up, Tevye!" the voice echoed in his brain like a song. "Don't give up! Don't despair!"

The sun blazed high in the sun. Dizzy with exhaustion, he remembered Rabbi Kook's words, "Each Jew has to be like a thousand."

An illumination, as bright as the sun, filled all of his being. All of the suffering and all of the trials were coming to transform Tevye, the milkman, into Tevye, the pioneer builder.

When his arms were too tired to lift up the bucket, he felt someone come to his aid. Goliath stood by his side, in a pool of dazzling sunshine, helping him lift the bucket out of the swamp. Goliath, as alive and real as could be.

"Don't give up, Tevye! Don't despair!" he urged.

Squinting into the swamp water's brilliant reflections, Tevye saw that Goliath wasn't alone. Shmuelik, stood beside him, his hands outstretched, waiting to grab a bucket! He took the bucket from Tevye and passed it to Guttmacher! The undertaker passed the bucket to Bat Sheva! With a smile, Tevye's daughter handed the bucket to Guttmacher's wife! And Guttmacher's wife passed the bucket to Golda! They were all there beside him, working in the swamp. And they weren't alone. Hundreds worked with them. Turning around in astonishment, Tevye saw his oldest daughter, Tzeitl, and Motel, the tailor! He saw his mother and father! He saw faces from Anatevka whom he had known as a boy! He saw Jews from all ages, from countries all over the world! He saw the *Baal Shem Tov* and the *Gaon of Vilna*! He saw Rabbi Akiva

and Bar Kochva! He saw Judah the Maccabee and King David
working side by side, hurling waterfalls of refuse out of the swamp.
Encouraged, Tevye set back to work. He wasn't one single man,
but an army. Elisha, and Ariel, and Yigal, and Nachman, and Hillel,
and Munsho, and Shilo, and Shimon, and Reb Shragi, the scribe,
all joined in the task of draining the swamp. Together with Tevye,
and with all of the Jews of the past, they filled their buckets again
and again, transforming a curse into a blessing, and bringing new
life to their cherished Promised Land. For all the Jews of the
future.

Chapter Thirty-Six

TEVYE THE BUILDER

As weeks passed, Tevye felt more and more invincible. An inner transformation was taking place which he himself couldn't explain, as if a new soul had entered his body. He felt like he was not only Tevye, but someone much greater, as if the spirits of Goliath and Shmuelik, Bat Sheva and Golda, Tzeitl and Guttmacher, along with the heroes of history, had all become a part of his being. The strength of generations impelled him forward in his tasks. He was tireless in his labor. In addition to draining the swamps, he dug ditches throughout the night. When a wave of hot desert winds made work in the swamps too dangerous, he plowed fields and planted, sawed wooden planks and hammered the foundations of buildings. Unable to sleep more than a few hours a night, he did double shifts of guard duty, chased away snooping Arabs, and greeted the sunrise, wrapped in *tallit* and *teffilin*. Instead of mourning, he worked and he built. On the Sabbath, he rested, just as God had commanded. But come *Motzei Shabbos*, with the appearance of the first three stars in the sky, Tevye rushed back to his labor.

Busy with the endless work on the settlement, Tevye fought off moments of doubt and philosophical reflections. He knew that thinking too much could get a man into trouble. Why the Almighty did what He did was something no human could grasp. Nothing could be gained by complaining. It was God's world to run things the way He saw fit. It was a mortal man's duty to accept his fate in contentment and song. As Nachman always reminded them, that was man's task and trial on earth, to trust in the Lord, in good times and bad, whether we understood God's mysteries or not.

Which isn't to say that Tevye turned into a saint. Many times he was angry. And often, there was more fury than joy in his work. And he was still wont to turn a questioning eye up to Heaven, and occasionally, even to sneer. But, for the most part, he kept his lips sealed. If anything, he shared a private battle with God. Like a boxer dizzy with blows, he was determined not to fall down. And if he fell down, he was determined to get back on his feet. He wouldn't be beaten. His faith wouldn't die. His body could ache and become food for mosquitoes, but his soul couldn't be touched by a swamp. Where once he had been cautious, now he didn't feel any fear. Tevye wasn't worried about meeting the Angel of Death. "Come and take me!" he roared.

Like the Jewish People, he would live on forever. Tevye's revenge was his work. He became an example for everyone. Summer arrived, bringing along hot, sandy winds from the desert. There were days a man couldn't open his eyes without being blinded. While the settlers sought shelter in their tents, Tevye stood in the swamp, his eyes tightly closed, scooping buckets of water out of the swamp. The heat was scorching. There were no cool drinks to quench the nagging thirst, no ice, no shade, no air to breath in the oppressively humid lowlands. Even the ocean was warm. And nights were so still, no relief from the merciless desert *sharav* could be found, even by sleeping outside of their airless tents.

Still, work in the swamp continued. If not by the settlers, by the fiery rays of the sun. As if the Lord was pitching in some help of His own, the swamps began to evaporate and dry. By late August, the canal to the sea approached completion. Only a pipe-length section remained. When that last piece was set into place, the remaining swamp water would be drained off into the ocean. Only one small obstacle stood in the way. The pipe had to be laid in the most dangerous part of the swamp, where the mosquitoes had built their main encampment. Whoever connected together the last two sections was sure to be eaten alive. Descending into the nest of mosquitoes meant almost certain death. A general meeting was called which everyone had to attend. Lots were to be drawn to determine the unlucky hero.

"Unless someone wants to volunteer," Shimon, the settlement leader, called out.

Eyes darted back and forth to see if someone would step forward. Without hesitation, Tevye raised up his hand.

"I volunteer," he said.

"You know what it means?" Shimon asked.

"It means we'll finally be rid of the cursed mosquitoes."

"That's the hope," Shimon answered. "But it may also mean the end of our fearless worker, Tevye."

"If the demons haven't killed me yet, they won't kill me now," Tevye asserted. "But I'll only do it on one condition."

"What condition is that?" Shragi asked.

"On the condition that when I go into the swamp, everyone in the settlement will stand on top of the highest sand dune and pray until I come out."

The condition was unanimously accepted. Everyone stepped forward to shake Tevye's hand. Tomorrow he might be a dead man, but for now he was everyone's hero.

That night, before going to bed, Carmel spent more time than usual combing her hair. By the candlelight, her husband was cleaning his shoes.

"Why do you bother?" she asked.

"I really don't know,' he confessed, "Every morning they just get filled up with mud once again."

"Are you sure about tomorrow?' she asked.

"Somebody has to do it," he said.

"Why does it have to be my husband?"

Tevye glanced up at his wife. In the darkness of the tent, her beauty was golden. He had noticed the same thing with Golda. Whenever she was pregnant, she seemed to glow with a joyful inner light.

"For one thing, I am older than everyone else."

"A man is as old as he feels."

"Then I am twice as old as everyone else."

She set down her brush and came over to the bed where he was sitting.

"You do so much work already," she said. "Do you have to do this too?"

He gazed into the fathomless pools of her eyes.

"Ah oh," he said, as if her coquetish look was as dangerous as the depths of the swamp.

Blushing, she sat down beside him.

"Carmel, I need my strength for tomorrow."

She put her hands on his shoulders and bent forward to kiss him.

"On top of everything," he thought.

But what could he do? A man was commanded to make his wife happy. That was a *mitzvah* too.

The very next day, all of the settlers gathered on the summit of the sand dune which overlooked the area's biggest swamp. Eyes filled with apprehension and suspense as Tevye descended into the marsh, dragging a long pipe behind him. The pipe was the last link in the canal which would carry the swamp water away to the ocean. Tevye had to set it in place and fasten the ring which would connect the last two pieces together. Already, as if sensing a battle, a squadron of mosquitoes rose up to greet him as he waded into the water. He waved at them with an arm, but his swattings were useless. Up on the sand dune, the settlers gasped as a cloud of mosquitoes surrounded Tevye and nearly hid him from view. On the hill where the women had gathered, Carmel turned away. Nachman opened his Psalm book and motioned for the others to follow. Swaying in his prayer shawl at the peak of the sand dune, the pious scholar chanted out a verse of King David's Psalms.

"Out of the depths I cry to Thee, O Lord.

Lord, hear my voice...."

The settlers, men, women, and children, all joined in, echoing his words, raising their voices to Heaven.

"Out of the depths I cry to Thee, O Lord.

Lord, hear my voice...."

Once again, Nachman recited a verse and the others repeated his cry for salvation and mercy.

Tevye tried to pray too, but when he opened his mouth,

mosquitoes rushed in, biting his gums and his tongue. Spitting them out, he continued the prayer in his heart.

"Though I walk through a valley of death, I will fear no evil, for Thou art with me..."

As he stepped on the main nest of mosquitoes, swarms of insects buzzed furiously around him. They stung him on his hands, on his ears, on his nose, on his eyelids. They bit through his clothes and flew into his pants and his shirt. Growling, he slipped the ring over a pipe and pulled the two pipes together, determined to slay the beast once and for all. Far away, he heard the prayful cries of the settlers, like the shouts of a city under siege. As he twisted the ring over the pipes, he heard the blast of shofars. Elisha, Ariel, and Hillel stood on the hillside, blowing ram's horns like trumpets with all of their might, to petition God's aid. Carmel ran down from the sand dune, unable to look at the black cloud engulfing her husband. Only when the settlers cheered did she have the courage to stop and venture a gaze. The mosquitoes were flying away into the air. Tevye had fastened the pipes into place!

Staggering, he flailed his way out of the marsh. Blinded by the mosquitoes and their bites, he flung himself onto shore. Choking and crawling on all fours, he scurried away from the bank. Standing, he ran blindly forward, but the cloud of mosquitoes stayed with him. They bit him ferociously, over every inch of his flesh. Screaming, he flung himself to the ground and rolled over and over in the sand. Settlers ran over and swatted the mosquitoes away. Hands slapped Tevye on the head and the back. Munsho pulled him to his feet. A horse and wagon clattered to his rescue.

Elisha yelled out, "To the ocean!"

Hands lifted Tevye up into the wagon. Carmel raced over. Seeing her husband, she gasped.

"My God," someone said. "He's all swollen!"

"He looks like he's been eaten alive!"

Carmel climbed up into the wagon. She reached out to take Tevye's hand. But it wasn't a hand anymore. It looked like a chunk of red meat. His face was puffed-up, two times its normal size. His eyelids bulged like a frogs. His nose was incredibly swollen.

Ariel whipped the horse, and the wagon bounced off toward the ocean. Tevye still couldn't see. He couldn't open his eyes. He opened his mouth, but his tongue couldn't speak. It had enlarged to the size of a cow's.

"You will be all right, my darling," Carmel said. "You did it! You succeeded! You're a hero!"

Tevye didn't feel like a hero. On the contrary, he felt like a *shmuck*. All he could say was "Ahhhh," as if a doctor had put an examining stick in his mouth.

The settlers ran after the wagon. Other raced forward on horseback. It was only a kilometer and a half to the ocean, and everyone was in jubilant spirits. Their work on the canal was completed! They had triumphed over the monster! They had battled nature and won. Mosquitoes would no longer make a nightmare of life, and the dreaded fever would no longer visit their tents.

Reaching the sea, Ariel and Yigal lifted Tevye and carried him to the water. Stumbling under his weight, all three of them fell into the ocean at once. The water revived Tevye immediately, but his arms and his legs couldn't move. He managed to unglue his eyelids and squint. Ariel held onto his head, and Yigal had hold of his shoes. His body floated on the waves like a goatskin inflated with water. Elisha pulled off Tevye's clothes so that the salt water could bathe him completely. Out of modesty, he left on his undershorts, in consideration for the women who were arriving on the beach. Slowly, the tormenting itching was soothed. A sensation returned to Tevye's fingers and toes. He opened his mouth and whispered, "Water."

Quickly, a canteen was fetched. Elisha poured a few drops onto Tevye's tongue.

"Do you want quinine?" he asked.

Tevye shook his head no. Ariel guided him back to the shallows. His body floated on the incoming waves like a whale washed onto shore. Other settlers splashed happily into the ocean. Suddenly, cries of joy and celebration came from the beach.

"Water!" Shimon screamed. "Swamp water! It's coming out of the pipe!"

Everyone ran over. Sure enough, up the beach, a trickle of black water was dripping out of a pipe onto the sand. Settlers cheered and started to dance. Men embraced and swung each other around. Woman danced in a circle, a modest distance away. Children happily ran into the ocean to bob up and down in the waves.

"Let's let him see what he's done," Elisha said to his son.

They lifted Tevye and set him on his feet in the ocean so that he too could have a glimpse of the miracle. Pushing them away, he staggered up the beach. The sight of Tevye in his underwear brought shouts and giggles from the women. Embarrassed, they scurried away down the beach.

Tevye staggered up to the pipe which jutted out from the beach embankment. Already, a small pool of swamp water had formed at its mouth. A trickle began to run in a riverlet through the sand toward the ocean. Before long, the swamp would be drained. In its place, a field would be plowed. Seeds would be planted. In time, the land would give forth its fruits. Because of the sacrifice of the pioneer settlers.

"Congratulations, Tevye," Shimon said. "You've dried up the swamp. Your bravery has saved many lives. On behalf of the whole settlement, I thank you."

Smiling, Shimon extended his hand, but Tevye's was like a swollen red ball. It was only then that Tevye realized that he was practically naked.

"Where are my clothes?" he asked.

Quickly, hearing the laughter of the women and children, he ran back down the beach to hide in the waves of the ocean.

Chapter Thirty-Seven

A SON AT LAST!

"I think it's coming," Carmel said.

Tevye opened his eyes. As far as he could tell, it was the middle of the night.

"What's coming?" he sleepily asked.

"The baby."

"Go back to sleep," he said, rolling over onto his side. Tevye was no great scholar, but he was knowledgeable about two things in life — cows and babies. After all, he had fathered seven daughters. And with Golda, it was always the same hysterical false alarms until the real moment arrived. Tevye knew from experience that the birth of the baby could he hours away. Even days.

"Tevye. . .Tevye," Carmel called in the dark.

Tevye grumbled. The next moment he was snoring.

"Tevye," Carmel called urgently, poking her husband in the back. "Are you ready to be the midwife?"

Tevye stirred and sat up in bed.

"Midwife? What midwife?"

"I need a midwife, Tevye. I'm having the baby."

"You're having the baby?" Tevye asked, still groggy from sleep. He reached over to the table, found the matches, and lit a candle. On the other side of the tent, Guttmacher's two children were sleeping. Carmel's eyes were wide with a mixture of fear and wonder. Her forehead was sweating.

"You have contractions?" he asked.

She shook her head yes.

"For how long?"

"For hours," she said, biting her lip as another painful contraction seized a hold of her hips.

"Why didn't you wake me?" he asked.

"I tried to. Three times."

Tevye attempted to think clearly. If that were the case, his wife was liable to give birth to the baby right then and there in his lap. Wasn't it written that the Hebrew women in Egypt gave birth in a lively fashion before the midwives would arrive? Maybe his Yemenite wife was like them. He stood up and thought about what he should do. In Anatevka, he would go and get Shendel, the midwife. But who knew where Shendel was now?

"Whom should I call?" he asked his wife as he hurriedly pulled on his trousers.

"My mother," she answered.

"Your mother is a midwife?"

"All Yemenite women are midwives."

"All of them?"

"Well, maybe not all of them, but most of them. Will you please hurry and call her before the baby comes out!"

"My shoes," he said. "Where are my shoes?"

"Outside the tent," his wife answered. Her back arched in pain and she let out a long anguished sigh. She clutched the bed with both hands and whimpered. Sweat shone on her forehead.

"Hurry!" she whispered. "But first check your shoes for scorpions."

"What a saint," Tevye thought. His wife worried about him, even when she was in the middle of labor. Quickly, Tevye hurried out of the tent. He didn't bother to put on his shoes. He ran straight to the tent of Elisha.

To make a long story short, as the great writer, Sholom Aleicheim, would say, Carmel gave birth to a boy! When the moaning and groaning were over, Tevye had been blessed with a son! After seven daughters, a male child was born to Tevye, the son of Schneur Zalman! In the middle of the night, the whole settlement turned out to wish the proud father *mazal tovs* and *L'chaims*! While Carmel embraced her precious baby in the tent, Tevye danced outside. Everyone shared his great joy. Hillel was so happy, he played his accordion, stamped his feet, and blew into his harmonica, all at the very same time. Liquor and refreshments arrived as if by magic. Everyone joined in the party.

In the middle of the dancing, Tevye felt he had to make sure that this happiness wasn't a dream. He simply couldn't believe his good fortune. After so much hardship and sorrow, how could there be such great joy? He hurried to his tent and demanded to see the baby. The crowd of women made way. Pushing the cloth diaper aside, the father took a glimpse to be certain. There was no doubt about it. The good Lord had blessed Tevye with a boy! Holding his newborn son triumphantly up in one hand like a freshly baked loaf of *challah*, Tevye carried the bundle toward the door of the tent.

"Where are you going?!" Carmel asked.

"To show off our baby," Tevye answered.

"Is he crazy?" one of the women asked.

"Father," Ruchel protested. "You can't!"

But nothing was going to stop Tevye. He had waited for this moment for a lifetime - almost as long as Abraham had waited for his cherished son, Issac. When the crowd saw Tevye holding the child aloft in the air, a new wave of *simcha* filled everyone's heart. The settlers formed a circle around Tevye and everyone danced. At the door of their tent, Carmel's eyes filled with tears. She thanked God in her heart for being the one to have brought Tevye such gladness.

Eight days later, everyone in the settlement once again gathered for the *brit*. Tevye ran around nervously, like a chicken without a head, making sure that everything was ready for the circumcision. With trembling hands, he put on his prayer shawl and *tefillin*. Then, like a protective mother hen, he watched every move which Yisroel, the ritual slaughterer, made as he removed the baby's diaper.

"Don't worry, Tevye. It isn't my first circumcision," the combination *shochet*, butcher, and *mohel* assured him.

"Just remember, it isn't a flank of mutton."

"Maybe you would prefer to do it yourself," Yisroel suggested as Tevye continued to breathe down his neck.

The nervous father backed off. The way his hands were trembling, the last thing in the world he wanted to hold was the glistening knife.

Upon Yisroel's instructions, Tevye set his son gently on the lap of the *sandak*, Elisha, who was also draped in a prayer shawl, in accord with the great honor of his role. Tevye's voice cracked as he recited the emotional blessings, thanking God for bringing his son into the covenant of Abraham, and for having allowed Tevye to experience this long-dreamed-for day. Nachman recited the blessing over the wine and formally announced the child's name - Tzvi Schneur Zalman ben Tevye. The mother and father had decided to name the boy Tzvi after the Land of Israel which was called *Eretz HaTzvi*, the land of the deer. And they gave him the name Schneur Zalman after Tevye's father, may his memory be for a blessing. Everyone present shared the same uplifting feeling that, with all the hardships, the Jewish People live on!

Upon the birth of his son, the anger that Tevye had felt after Bat Sheva's death transformed into a feeling of joy. If his frenzied labor had been fueled by an unresolved fury, Tevye was now propelled forward by a feeling of gratitude and great blessing. If he had worked with the strength of one thousand men after the death of Bat Sheva, now he worked with the strength of two thousand, one thousand to carry on the dreams of the past, and one thousand to build the world of the future. His baby boy had entered into the covenant between God and the Jewish People, making him an inheritor of the Land of Israel, and Tevye wanted to turn the desolate land into a Garden of Eden so that his son would grow up to harvest the fruit from the seeds which his father had planted.

When the marshes were dry, the Baron Rothschild was persuaded to advance the budding *yishuv* a large sum of money. Tools were purchased, fields were plowed, wheat and fruit trees were planted. Lumber arrived from Jaffa in wagons and boats. Houses, barns, worksheds, and fences were built. As if overnight, a synagogue appeared on a hill. Tevye lent a hand in all of the labor, whether it was clearing rocks from a road, leveling a sand dune, or pitching hay into a loft. Work was the key to the future. Work was the path of success. Work was the way a man could serve God, *Rebbono Shel Olam*, in the great endeavor of rebuilding the land.

Tevye no longer complained. He no longer felt bitter. His trust in God was complete. The Lord had taken loved ones away, and the Lord had given new ones to nurture and love. The dark cloud that was hanging over his life had been blown out to sea. The future was filled with sunshine and light. It was a time of happiness, a time of hope, a time to plant, a time to build, a time to take long walks with his wife, cradling his baby boy in his arms. Miraculously, he no longer felt like an old, broken-down man. He felt young!

It was a time when everything seemed to prosper around him. Little Moishe and Hannei grew bigger each day. Nachman taught in the *Talmud Torah*. Passing by the synagogue, one could hear the singsong verses of Bible being recited by the high-pitched voices of the children. Ruchel opened a kindergarten, though she didn't know how long she could run it alone. She was pregnant, thank God, and as the months passed, and her belly grew bigger, she found herself exhausted by mid-morning.

The arrival of Hodel solved the problem. One day, she showed up in *Olat HaShachar* with her child. With her head bowed in shame, she told her father that she was divorced. Upon her return to Shoshana, she had found her husband, Perchik, living with the girl called Libby. He had taken the strumpet into their house, at first as a house maid, he said. But they had been living together ever since Hodel had left, in defiance of everything holy.

"I'll kill him," Tevye exclaimed.

"It's all right," Hodel answered. "I've left him. We arranged for a divorce with the rabbinical court in Tiberias."

"You have a *get*?" her father asked.

Hodel showed her father the official writ of divorce.

"What a *shandah*! What a scandal!" Tevye thought. Who ever heard of a Jewish husband and wife getting a divorce? In all of Anatevka, he couldn't think of one case. With such a black stain, who would ever agree to marry his daughter? Then again, Tevye thought, it was better than going back to her swine of a husband.

Tearfully, Hodel explained how she had lived months and months in Tiberias until a proper divorce was granted. Perchik had wished her good riddance and told her that he never wanted to see either her or their child again. Angrily, Hodel had vowed that he wouldn't.

"You have done the right thing," Tevye said. "Here, you can be sure that your child will be raised like a Jew."

"Oh, *Abba*, it was so awful," she cried, weeping in his arms like a baby.

Tevye hugged her. When she stopped sobbing, he wiped her tears away.

"Why didn't you send word to me sooner?" he asked.

"I've been so ashamed."

"It isn't the end of the world."

"I loved Perchik so much. My heart was so broken. I suppose it still is. He was everything to me."

"You made a mistake, that's all."

"I felt so betrayed."

Tevye nodded his head. He didn't want to say, "I told you." How could he? He himself was to blame. Hadn't he invited the free-thinking Perchik into his house to teach his daughters about the wonders of the world? Well, now, thanks to her father, she knew.

In the meantime, to cover up the scandal, Tevye told his friends that his daughter, Hodel had come for a visit. She started to help Ruchel in her kindergarten, and the sisters got along fine. But the unpleasant matter left Tevye pensive. Not only about Hodel's uncertain future, but about his other daughter, Hava. Could it be that her husband, the convert, was deceiving her also? What was he doing alone in Jaffa, separated weeks on end from his wife?

The suspicion harped at Tevye for days, like a mosquito that won't go away. Finally, he decided to find out the truth for himself. Taking the day off from work, he awoke before dawn, mounted a horse, and rode off toward Jaffa. He reached the city by mid-afternoon. Stopping by the Yemenite market which bordered the Jewish neighborhood, Tevye bought himself a long flowing caftan and turban. He had decided that for his intrigue to work, he would have to wear a disguise. That way he could spy on Hevedke without being recognized. He slipped the white robe over his clothes and let the salesman adjust the turban in the proper fashion on his head. The salesman held up a mirror, and his customer nodded in approval. Straightening his shoulders and holding his head high, Tevye rather fancied the regal image he made. He looked like an Arab sheik with a bushy Jewish beard, or he could have passed for a holy Jew from Morocco. The salesman praised Tevye's new wardrobe and offered to sell him a sword and string of gleaming trinkets, but Tevye refused. He paid the persistent merchant and led his horse through the market, feeling like a newly crowned prince. He walked leisurely, as if he had all the time in the world. Nobly, he bowed his head to passersby, and enjoyed the deep bows he received in return, as if he were really a man of importance. Remembering the location of the yeshiva, he walked up to the side window and glanced in. Immediately, Hevedke's, or Issac's, blond hair and red-pepper beard caught his attention. He was engaged in a fervent discussion, arguing a point of Talmudic law with a study partner, just as he had been when Tevye had visited the yeshiva over a year before.

   For more than an hour, Tevye stood outside the yeshiva watching the learning. When the time came for the afternoon prayer, he faced in the direction of Jerusalem like the students inside the building and started to pray in the alleyway. Spotting a Jew swaying back and forth in prayer outside of the building, Hevedke rushed outside to invite him into the study hall.

   "You're a Jew?" Hevedke asked.

   Keeping his head down, Tevye silently nodded.

   "Come inside and join us."

   Tevye shook his head no.

   "Come in. Please. By all means," the gracious student insisted.

   Again Tevye shook his head no. He glanced up to Heaven and

moved his lips in silent prayer, as if to remind the yeshiva student that it was forbidden to speak in the middle of the silent *Amidah* prayer. Even if a snake were to coil around a Jew's feet, it was forbidden to interrupt the holy supplication.

Unless the snake was poisonous, of course. Hevedke, or rather Issac, had learned the law. Nodding his head, he put his feel together and began to pray beside Tevye. When they had finished, and the *shaliach tzibor* inside the yeshiva began to repeat the prayer aloud for the congregation, the kindhearted student once again invited Tevye to Join them inside.

Waving a hand, Tevye shook his head no. He didn't want to speak and betray his thick Russian accent. A piece of his turban unraveled, and he nervously stuck it back into place.

"I can take you to a Sephardi synagogue if you prefer," Hevedke offered, thinking that was the reason why the oriental Jew didn't want to enter the Ashkenazic yeshiva.

Lowering his head, Tevye waved no again. As he was mounting his horse, a hand grabbed his garment.

"Can't you speak?" Hevedke inquired.

Tevye shook his head no. He made a slicing motion with his thumb just under his beard.

"Oh, no. You're throat has been cut?" his son-in-law asked in alarm.

Tevye answered with a nod.

"By the Arabs?"

Tevye shook his head no.

"By the Turks?"

Tevye nodded.

"Devils. May they be chased from our Land. Wait here," the saintly youth said. "I'll bring you a glass of water."

When Hevedke ran off, Tevye mounted his horse. But just then, as he was planning to bolt, a Bedouin shepherd led a flock of bleating sheep into the alleyway. Tevye tugged on the reins of his horse to turn it around, but the sheep swarmed all around them, pinning the horse where it stood. Nervously, the creature reared up on its hind legs with a neigh. Taken by surprise, Tevye tumbled backwards out of the saddle. Sheep bleated and scattered as the horse's rider crashed down on their backs. Luckily for Tevye, his fall was absorbed by the animals. But before the alley had cleared, a stampede of hooves battered his bones. Their scratches drew blood from his face. As Hevedke ran back to the alley, Tevye quickly adjusted his fallen and disheveled turban.

"Are you all right?" his son-in-law asked.

Holding the cloth head-covering in place, Tevye nodded.

"You're bleeding. Let me help you. You can come to my place and rest. I have a room down the street."

Hevedke put his arm under Tevye's and helped him up to his feet. A sharp pain in the back made Tevye groan. He could hardly stand straight. His old milkman's spine had been knocked out of place.

"Can you walk?" Hevedke asked.

Tevye took a careful step forward and froze. The nerves in his back screamed out in protest. His boot remained implanted in the sheep dung in the alley.

"Don't worry," his son-in-law said. "I'll carry you. It isn't far to my room."

"Put me down," Tevye wanted to yell, but he couldn't without revealing his sham. Hevedke bent down and, with a grunt, lifted his crippled father-in-law on his back. Calling inside the yeshiva, he yelled for someone to tie up the horse in the alley.

What could Tevye do? He was paralyzed. He had to continue the luckless charade. The minute Hevedke left him alone, he would flee from the city.

"This is what I get for having suspected a fellow Jew of committing adultery," he thought. Didn't the Torah command a Jew to judge others in a favorable light? More than that. A Jew was to be especially kind to a convert. As it says, *"For you were strangers in the land of Egypt."* And this was no ordinary convert. Hevedke was truly a *tzaddik*, as moral and straight as a plowshare's furrow. Tevye was no skinny chicken, yet Hevedke carried him on his back all of the way down the street and up a flight of stairs to his room in an old boarding house.

"You can rest here," Hevedke said. "My wife will take care of you. She's a nurse."

He pushed open a door with a shove. Across the small room, Hava sat at a table folding clothes. She stood up as her husband barged in, carrying the stranger on his back. With a grunt, Hevedke dropped Tevye onto the bed. He rolled onto his side so that his daughter couldn't get a look at his face.

"He fell off a horse," Hevedke said. "I'll run and fetch a doctor."

"Who is he?" Hava asked.

"I don't know. A traveler from out of town. He can't speak. The Turks slit his throat."

"How awful," Hava said.

Tevye heard the door close and the sound of Hevedke's footsteps hurrying away down the stairs. Reaching around to his back, he grabbed onto his traitorous disc and gave it a shove back into place. Almost immediately, his pain went away.

'I'll bring you some water," Hava said.

"Don't bother," he answered.

Hava was already pouring water from a pitcher when he spoke. The voice was strangely familiar. Surprised, she looked up at the turbaned stranger as he sat up on the bed. Their eyes briefly met.

"*Abba!*" she exclaimed. "What are you doing here?"

Tevye held up a finger to his mouth. "Not so loud," he said.

"Why are you dressed like an Arab?" his daughter asked in confusion.

"I bought a costume for Purim."

"Purim is two months away."

"How often do I get into the city?"

"Why did you tell Issac that a Turk slit your throat?" she asked.

"I never told him anything of the kind. He jumped to conclusions."

"But why all the secrecy?" she asked.

"I wanted to surprise you."

"Well you certainly have. But why did you make Issac rush off for a doctor?"

"Well, I did fall off my horse. That much is true. But I am feeling much better. Anyway, I can't explain matters now. I have to get going. There is a lot of work waiting for me back at the colony."

"You just got here!" Hava protested.

"Yes, but now that I see that everything is all right with you two, I have to set back on my journey. By the way, what are you doing here?"

"I took a three-day vacation from the hospital."

"I'm glad," Tevye said.

He stepped forward and kissed his daughter on the cheek.

"Be sure to come visit us soon," he added as he hurrily walked to the door.

"*Abba*, wait!" she called, running after him. "This doesn't make sense. Where are you going? What should I tell Issac?"

Tevye stopped on the stairs. "Don't say it was me. Tell him I got up and left. Let him think he did a good deed for a stranger."

"*Abba*, I don't understand," Hava called.

But Tevye didn't answer. He rushed down the stairs. He didn't want to be around when Hevedke returned. His mission was accomplished. His heart was at rest. His daughter had truly found herself a genuine Rabbi Akiva.

Chapter Thirty-Eight

A LOVE SONG FOR HODEL

Months passed. Yankele and his family boarded a freighter and headed back to Russia. Guttmacher's brother either never received, or didn't bother to answer the letter Tevye had written to him, so Guttmacher's two orphaned children became permanent fixtures in Tevye's home. Another addition to the family also arrived. Ruchel and Nachman had a baby - a princess of a girl whom they named Sarah Tzeitl.

Buildings continued to sprout up in the Olat HaShachar colony. The dry beds of the swamp land were plowed. Crops were planted, wheat, barley, maize, and rye. Looking out from the hilltop synagogue, fields and vegetable gardens decorated the landscape like a colorful patchwork quilt. Wagon loads of water melons, tomatoes, cucumbers, squash, cabbage, beets, and onions were shipped off to the Jaffa market. Citrus trees were planted, but the religious law of *orlah*, one of the agricultural laws which God had commanded the Jews to obey in the Holy Land, forbade the settlers from eating the fruit for the first three years of its growth. Laws requiring that gleanings and the corner of fields be left for the poor were also strictly observed, as well as the rules governing mixed plantings and tithes. Nachman, who had spent several days in Jaffa studying the agricultural laws with Rabbi Kook, was appointed to oversee their enforcement on the *yishuv*.

As if it were another law of the land, Arab marauders made periodic raids on the colony, stealing whatever they could lift or uproot. When two bulls were stolen, the settlers began chaining the legs of their livestock at night, but the measure didn't foil the Arabs. Instead of leading the bulls away, they chopped them up with machetes and hauled them away in pieces. Once again, the

Jews complained to the local Turkish officials, but nothing was done to apprehend the offenders. Past experience had taught Tevye that only a decisive response by the Jews would discourage the Arabs from further encroachments. His motion to organize an ambush was accepted. For a week, the Jews hid at night in the small forest of eucalyptus trees which had been planted to dry up the swamp. On the sixth night, a group of armed Arabs snuck out of the sand dunes bordering the colony. Silently, they darted through the darkness toward the barn. With a roar, Tevye rose to his feet and charged forward. Like a platoon following its commander, the other Jews raced out from their hiding places. Their shouts startled the Arabs. Only four of the settlers had rifles, but the roar of their gunfire terrified the thieves. Dropping their weapons, they ran to their horses and fled. Though none of the marauders had been wounded, the Arabs learned a lesson. Half a year passed without a further incident of trespassing or theft.

For the time being, life was a pleasure. A long stretch of spectacular weather arrived. Work progressed in leaps and bounds. At the end of the day, Tevye collapsed into bed in happy exhaustion. He felt that his sins, as well as the sins of the land, had been granted atonement. New life sprouted up everywhere. In his heart, in his house, and in the once desolate fields. Like the fruit of the sabra cactus which grew wild in the hills, the land was thorny and hard on the outside, but sweet and juicy within. As if overnight, wherever the eye looked, instead of swamp and sand, blossoming gardens and orchards covered the landscape.

"*Blee ayin hara,*" his wife Cannel said.

Anytime Tevye would praise their good fortune, his wife would whisper, "*Blee ayin hara,*" hoping that the evil eye would not cast its glance on them. It was an expression she had learned from her father. In this world, a man could never be certain what lay ahead. He could never take credit for his achievement and success, believing that his own wisdom and strength had brought him his good fortune. Everything was a blessing from God, and a man had to keep his head humbly bowed and always give thanks to his Maker.

At least for the moment, Tevye's heart was at peace. As the Rabbis said, why should a man look out for a storm on a clear, sunny day? Or maybe Tevye had said that. Sometimes he couldn't remember which words of wisdom the Rabbis had written, and which expressions he had coined on his own. Be that as it may, the only small worry that Tevye had was his unmarried daughter.

Ever since her divorce from Perchik, his poor daughter, Hodel, had become the opposite of her usually happy and spontaneous self.

"Why the sad face all of the time?" Tevye asked her. "You should be happy. Thank God that you are finished with that scoundrel."

But Hodel was not consoled. After all, Perchik had been her whole life. As an impetuous teenager, she had run away from home to marry the man of her dreams. She had torn herself from her family, and from all of their ways. She had followed after him to Siberia, and then, when he had become bitter with the revolutionary cause, she had followed dutifully after him to the Land of Israel. She had trusted in him and shared all of his visions. And now, their great balloon ride had come to a tragic crash. He had introduced her to Dostoyevsky and Tolstoy, to Shakespeare, Voltaire, and Abraham Lincoln, but what good did it do her now? She was alone. She was abandoned. She was betrayed. The rib she had shared with her husband had cracked. A part of her was missing. Bringing up their child kept her busy, but a child wasn't a husband. A child wasn't a man.

Tevye found it difficult to talk to his daughter. He didn't understand her deeper emotions. To his way of thinking, she was depressed because of the shame. After all, in Anatevka, a divorce was unheard of. If a man and woman didn't get along, they learned to live with each other for the good of their children. The stigma was so great that a matchmaker wouldn't even consider arranging a match for person whose parents had divorced. Nonetheless, Tevye told his daughter, if a divorce meant getting rid of an unbeliever like Perchik, it wasn't such a terrible thing. In fact, it was a great *mitzvah*.

"You don't understand me at all," she told him sadly. "'Unfortunately, you never have."

"That ended their conversation. Perhaps, it was true, Tevye thought. After all, Hodel belonged to a generation which was far different from his. Young minds were full of questions. Simple answers weren't enough. Tevye's simple faith was scoffed at. The wisdom of the Sages, all of their insights, and all of their pearls, were looked at as primitive prattle. For the young generation, the existence of God had to be proved! In short, sons and daughters grew up with minds of their own, and parents no longer knew how to answer their bewildering questions.

Strangely, Tevye didn't have the same problem at all with his wife. Though she was almost the same age as Hodel, she understood Tevye completely. Sometimes Tevye felt that Carmel had slipped into his beloved Golda's soul, may her memory be for a blessing. True, his young wife was from Yemen, and Jews had lived a sheltered life there. The thought of disagreeing with her husband and challenging his ways never entered her mind. Peace was achieved by giving in to the man of the house. And besides, she truly respected her husband's life experience and wisdom.

But in Anatevka, living side-by-side with the gentiles, how could a father protect his children from the modern world and the heretical culture it bred? It was no wonder that one generation didn't get along with the next. Outside of the ghetto, the world changed every day. Now there were automobiles, airplanes, and telephones. The eternal truths stayed the same, but in an age of cameras and fast-moving pictures, who was interested in dusty, worn volumes of Talmud? So, instead of getting into a quarrel with his daughter, Tevye sent his wife to find out what was the matter.

"She needs a new husband," Carmel said after spending a long evening with Hodel.

Tevye's wife didn't know who were Spinoza, Mendelssohn, or Karl Marx, but she knew that Hodel needed a man.

"Did she mention anyone in particular?" Tevye asked.

"No. She's still too hurt about Perchik to be thinking about getting married again."

"Do you have any suggestions?"

"You know her better than I do," Tevye's wife answered.

"She's fiery, and stubborn, and is filled with all kinds of highfalutin ideas. I remember that she always liked music, that is, before she learned how to read."

Carmel was silent. Tevye loved her for that. She knew when to speak up, and when to leave matters to him.

"You know, that isn't a bad idea" Tevye said.

"Who?" Carmel asked.

"Hillel."

Tevye's wife thought and nodded her head.

"Unless you think he's too old for her," Tevye added with a grin.

His wife smiled back. The great difference in their ages was a joyful joke between them.

"Do you want me to suggest it to her?" Carmel asked.

"No, no," Tevye said. "That would end it before it began. If she thinks that it's something I've planned, she'll say no just for spite. She may have learned a big lesson about husbands, but if I know my daughter, she still has a stubborn, willful streak. So we have to proceed with caution."

Tevye grabbed a bottle of wine, and without waiting another minute, he set off to the barracks where the bachelors all slept. The musician was leading a symphony of snoring. Tevye sat on his bed and poked at his friend until he woke up with a startled expression.

"What's the matter?" he asked.

"It isn't good for a man to be alone," Tevye said.

"You've woken me in the middle of the night to tell me that?" Hillel asked.

"It's time you got married."

Hillel wiped the sleep from his eyes. "With whom?"

Whispering, Tevye related his plan. The lovelorn musician agreed with a big grin at once. As if concluding a transaction, the father of the bride handed the bottle of wine to the groom.

"*L'Chaim,*" Tevye said.

"*L'Chaim,*" Hillel answered. Singing the blessing in the traditional wedding tune, he raised the bottle to his mouth and drank. Then he handed the bottle to Tevye.

"I can't," Tevye said. "When I was sinking in the swamp, I made a vow to give up drinking."

"This isn't drinking. It's a toast."

"A vow is a vow," Tevye said. "But if my daughter agrees to marry you, I will speak to a rabbi before the wedding to see if I can take a sip or two to celebrate such a great *simcha.*"

The very next day, outside the packing house of the colony where Hodel worked packing vegetables into the sacks and crates which were sent to the market, a man started singing a love song behind her. It was Hillel. He had been "transferred" from the fields to the packing house to help speed the packing.

Though other unmarried women worked alongside her, with a woman's intuition, Hodel felt that Hillel's ballads were being aimed in her direction. By their smiles, the other women seemed to sense it too. As his love songs continued, Hodel felt herself blushing.

Without looking at Hillel, she fastened the lid on a crate of tomatoes and carried it toward one of the wagons. Yentel, the wife of the butcher, walked over beside her.

"Running away from a love song?" she asked.

"Nonsense," Hodel answered.

He certainly isn't singing to me. I'm married, and so are Minnie and Ruth."

"So?"

"And the other girls are too young to get married."

"A minstrel doesn't need a reason to sing," Hodel answered.

"Perhaps not. But Hillel has been long-faced for months. All of a sudden, you show up, and he turns into a nightingale."

Again, Hodel blushed. Walking back to her heap of tomatoes, she caught Hillel's eye. He stared at her with an unabashedly friendly smile, the kind of a smile which a religious man doesn't give to a woman unless he has serious intentions. With a polite, if frigid, reaction, Hodel set back to her work.

"Can I marry Hillel, the minstrel?" she thought. He was the age of her father! And lame! Not that lameness was a sin, but it certainly wasn't an attractive quality in a man. "Why does a man have to be attractive?" a voice inside her asked. Her husband, Perchik, had been attractive and where had it gotten her? It turned out that he loved himself more than he had loved her. What did good looks matter if a man was a rogue inside? And in this world, in one way or another, wasn't everyone lame? No one was perfect, except the Creator, so who was she to look askance at the shortcomings of Hillel or anyone else?

The sweetly sung song courted her ears. Though the lyrics metaphorically spoke of the love between a man and a woman, she knew it was a song about a Jew's love for God.

"Love, *shmov*," she heard her mother's voice say. "What does love have to do with marriage? A man and a woman are brought together to bring children into the world. They live in the same house to raise up a family. What does love have to do with anything? Cooking, and cleaning, and scrubbing, and folding, and putting up with a man's moanings and tantrums, that's love."

Immersed in her thoughts, Hodel began putting tomatoes into a potato sack. Yentel smiled and gave Hodel a wink as Hillel limped by, lugging a load of tomatoes over to the wagon.

"You're not a spring chicken anymore yourself," the older woman whispered, as if reading Hodel's thoughts.

"Oh stop it," Hodel protested.

It was ridiculous. How could she marry a man her father's age?

Just as her mind asked the question, a wagon rode over and stopped a short distance away from the packing house. A mountain of tomatoes had arrived, waiting to be crated and shipped. Tevye was driving. Carmel sat beside him, holding their baby. The boy was big enough now to take along into the fields. While his mother picked tomatoes, little Tzvi Schneur Zalman rested nearby in the shade of an improvised lean-to. With a big, happy grin, Tevye got down from the wagon. He held out his hand and helped Carmel climb down with the child. How happy they seemed, Hodel thought. And though her father was much older than his wife was, they looked like a match made in Heaven.

"More of the Lord's tomatoes," Tevye cheerfully said to the packers. "The bounty of the land. Nurtured by hard work and God's blessing. Sun-ripened tomatoes, harvested out of the remains of a swamp. Treat them gently, dear ladies, for the vegetables I set before you are not plain tomatoes - they are miracles! Yesterday, they were ravenous mosquitoes, and today, instead of them eating people, people are about to eat them!"

Everyone laughed. Tevye's happiness was infectious.

"How's my big tomato?" he asked, pinching Hodel's cheek. Indeed, the way she blushed, there was a resemblance. Strolling off with his wife and child, Tevye stopped to say *shalom* to his good friend, the musician. Her father liked Hillel, she knew, and her father was a good judge of men, except, of course, in the case of Menachem Mendel, who had conned her father out of the family's modest savings. If her father liked a man, it meant he was honest. And being a musician, Hillel's mind certainly wasn't closed down to art, literature, and creative inquiry, like so many other religious Jews. The beauty of his singing revealed that his soul, like hers, needed unfettered horizons. Yet, at the very same time, he was unquestionably God fearing. As the man of the house, he was sure to pass on the Jewish traditions which had become important to Hodel ever since Tzeitl's death.

The next evening after dinner, someone knocked on the door of the cottage where Hodel lived with her child and four other young, single women. It was Hillel. Gallantly, he took off his cap and bowed.

"Sorry to disturb you," he said. "But a wagon load of tomatoes has just arrived from the fields and workers are needed to pack them."

"Now? In the evening?" Hodel asked.

"The fresher they are, the better price they will command in the market," he answered. "When the harvest time comes, you can't tell tomatoes to wait. A wagon is leaving for Jaffa tonight."

"I'll get my shawl," Hodel said with a blush.

Hillel waited outside. They walked to the packing house without speaking. He whistled happily, as if to draw attention away from his limp, which really wasn't so bad, Hodel decided. At the packing house, a wagon piled high with tomatoes had been left unattended, waiting to be unloaded and packed for shipping, but no other workers were present.

"Where are the others?" Hodel asked.

"I don't know," Hillel said.

"Who sent you to fetch me?"

"Shimon," Hillel answered, making up a tiny little lie for the sake of keeping peace between Tevye and his daughter. For in truth, the wagon load of tomatoes had been Tevye's idea, and if she found out, she would be furious with her father for interfering in her life.

"Who else is coming?" Hodel asked.

"I don't know."

"Without other helpers, this will take us all night."

"I suppose that it will, but I don't have anything else on my schedule this evening. Do you."

"Yes," Hodel answered, though she really had nothing at all to do once her child went off to bed.

Hillel started pulling tomatoes out of the wagon. They were big, hard, and red - sure to bring a good price at the market.

"Do you ever get lonely?" he asked.

"Lonely?" she repeated, embarrassed by the question.

"Yes, lonely."

"Well, I have a child to take care of, and my work."

"Yes, I know. But an adult person cannot really talk with a child, and certainly not with tomatoes."

"I can talk to my sisters and friends," Hodel said.

"Yes, I suppose so. I have no family here in the Holy Land, and the friends that I came with died in the plague, except for Nachman, but he's busy with his studies and teaching. Before your father got married, we used to live together in the barn, and I used to talk for hours on end with him about everything under the sun.

But, of course, I can't blame him for wanting to get married, can you?"

Hodel was silent. She tried to concentrate on her work, but she felt that something was happening beyond her control. "Can you?" he asked once again.

"Can I what?"

"Blame your father for marrying again? As the Bible says, '*It is not good for a man to live alone.*'"

"Who am I to disagree with the Bible?"

"Don't they seem happy together? It's a match made in Heaven. Even though, on the surface, you might never think it possible. I mean she's from Yemen and he's a Russian Jew. And of course, their ages are very far apart."

"My father is young at heart."

"I feel young at heart too," Hillel answered. "Look."

He picked up three tomatoes and started to whistle. It was a familiar tune about being constantly happy. At the same time, he juggled the three tomatoes in the air. His hands moved so fast, Hodel could hardly follow their speed.

"Don't bruise them," she said. "Nobody buys bruised tomatoes."

One by one, Hillel caught them and held them out for her inspection. Not a blemish could be found.

"Playing the accordion makes one's fingers very nimble. Here, have a look."

Hillel playfully held out his hands and wiggled his fingers. Thinking he was going to touch her, Hodel gasped and pulled away.

"Don't worry," Hillel said, grinning. "I wasn't going to touch you. After all, this isn't Paris."

Hodel blushed. The lantern-light picked up the reddish glow of the tomatoes and cast it over her cheeks.

"You have been to Paris?" she asked.

"No, but I have read several classics of Hugo which unfold in the enchanted courtyards of the city."

"You have read Victor Hugo?" Hodel asked in surprise.

"Why certainly. Do I look like an ostrich that has his head in the ground? I love literature as much as I love music. In fact, other than the Bible, I think that *The Hunchback of Notre Dame* is my favorite book. Have you read it?"

"Yes, I have," Hodel confessed. It was one of the books Perchik had given to her, to show her how the peasant class must be freed.

"Quasimodo is my favorite character," Hillel said. "You can understand how a lame musician like myself could identify with a hunchbacked bell ringer. Tell me, do you think that Esmeralda came to recognize the inner beauty of his soul?"

"Yes, I'm sure that she did," Hodel answered. "I'm sure that she realized that he was someone entirely different inside."

"I found the end especially poignant. When the Hunchback and Esmeralda are discovered buried together in a grave. Of course in Judaism it's unthinkable, but I felt that Hugo found the perfect metaphor to reveal that in the real world of souls, beyond the fleeting imprisonment of our bodies, they were truly a match made in Heaven."

"Yes," Hodel said, swept away by Hillel's discourse. Looking at him, his faced seemed to change. For the first time since she had met him, she glanced deeply into his eyes, discovering the gentle, passionate, deeply-sincere man inside. His gaze struck a chord in her heart, more powerful than words. For a long moment, all barriers seemed to collapse. In the very same moment, they both understood that they were two lonely people, brought together on account of something more than tomatoes. When the moment began to linger too long, they both glanced away.

"Of course," Hillel said, bringing them back to safer ground, "I feel that the Bible and our own Jewish literature should command the most honored place in the home, but I see no reason why serious artistic works can't be given a respected place also. Naturally, books have to be screened by parents for any heretical ideas that could lead children astray, but I believe that Judaism isn't a fragile glass structure which can't withstand novel ideas, whatever their source."

"Yes," Hodel said, feeling weak in her knees.

She was spellbound to have found such sensitivity in a face adorned by dangling sidelocks and a beard. But it was truly a beautiful face, filled with gentleness, happiness, and wisdom.

That night, after packing a few thousand tomatoes, Hodel collapsed into bed. Her eyes stared up at the roof of the tent which she shared with some younger girls. Even though she was exhausted, she couldn't fall asleep. Not because of the heat, nor the crowing of roosters who forgot that they were supposed to keep still until morning. She couldn't get to sleep because of a dizzying feeling she had. When she closed her eyes, she saw her sister, Tzeitl, smiling. If Tzeitl approved, it meant that Hodel had found the right man.

She woke up after dawn, dressed in her clothes. Her little boy, Ben Zion, was still fast asleep. Quickly, she rushed to the cottage of her father. He was still wearing his prayer shawl and *tefillin*. Seeing his daughter, he finished his devotions.

"I woke up too late for the *minyan*," he said, explaining why he was *davening* at home, and not in the *shul*.

"I have something to tell you," Hodel said, taking an extra breath for courage.

Tevye glanced over at his wife with an innocent expression.

So early in the morning?" he said, lifting the small black *tefillin* box off of his head. "Is everything all right?"

"Everything is fine, *Abba*, finally."

"Finally?" Tevye asked. "What can that mean?"

"It means I have news."

"Good news, I hope. Otherwise, it would be better if I first ate my breakfast. Then we can get on with your riddles."

"I think I want to marry Hillel," she announced.

"Hillel!" he roared. Theatrically, he spun around as if in great surprise. With his mouth hanging open, he fell into a chair, still draped in his *tallit*. Carmel turned her back so that Hodel wouldn't see her laughter.

"Hillel, the accordion player?" Tevye asked.

"That's right," Hodel answered. "Do we know any other?"

"He's almost twice your age!" her father protested.

"So? What's wrong with that? Look at you and Carmel."

Like a born actor, Tevye looked over at his wife and back at his daughter. A flabbergast expression filled his whole face.

That's true," he said. "And we are certainly happy, *blee ayin hara*. But tell me. When did all of this happen?"

"Well, it hasn't happened yet. I mean, he hasn't proposed. But I know that he will if I give him a sign. Only I wanted to ask your opinion."

"My opinion?" Tevye said, standing up in wonder. "You have come to ask your father's opinion? Can this really be Hodel that I see before me? My little girl, Hodel? When did you ever ask my opinion before?"

"I'm not the same little girl that I was in Anatevka. I've learned a few lessons. Other things are important to me now."

Tevye removed the *tefillin* which was still on his head. Lovingly, he gave the small, black box a kiss. Inside was parchment penned with the words of the *Shema Yisrael* prayer.

"Bless the Lord Who has kept me alive to see this day," Tevye said.

"Well?" Hodel asked.

"Well what?"

"Is Hillel a good choice?"

Dramatically, Tevye paused. He put his fist to his chin as if thinking. Then he nodded his head. "Yes, he's a good choice. He's a good, honest man. He'll make a good, faithful husband. And a wonderful father to your children, may you be blessed with many more."

Hodel rushed into his arms.

"Oh, *Abba*," she said. "I'm so glad."

Hodel and Hillel were married two weeks later. If Hillel was lame, no one would have known it from the way that he danced at the wedding. His feet never seemed to touch the ground.

And, of course, the bride's father was in fine form himself, hugging all of his friends, and dancing up a storm. For just this one occasion, Nachman said that Tevye could drink a glass of wine, since Hillel had given his new father-in-law the honor of reciting the marriage blessing of *"boreh pree hagefen,"* thanking God for having created the fruit of the vine.

Seemingly a lifetime ago, Tevye had stood at the Russian railway station saying a tearful goodbye to his daughter. Today, embracing her under the nuptial *chuppah,* he felt like he was once again saying hello.

Chapter Thirty-Nine

WINDS OF WAR

Word arrived that boatloads of new Jewish immigrants from Russia were arriving in Jaffa. Rumors spread that a wave of bloody pogroms were causing thousands of Jews to flee from their homes. Every settler was anxious to learn which villages had been attacked. Everyone had friends and relatives in Russia, and, of course, all of the settlers were worried about their fate. Not only was the Czar's empire in turmoil, all of Europe was quaking in the throes of a cataclysmic war. As if overnight, enlightened, "civilized" Germany had become a raging, bloodthirsty beast. At least for the moment, the remote Turkish province of Palestine was far away from the conflict.

More often than not, the Turkish authorities refused to grant permission to allow the boatloads of immigrants to disembark. Many Jews had to sail back to Russia or Italy. Others journeyed on to Egypt. The fortunate and the brave either swam, or were secretly ferried ashore along the desolate Mediterranean coastline. Among the Jews who received legal papers, and among those who didn't, a trickle found their way to Olat HaShachar.

With all of the building on the settlement, and with the success of their first two harvests, a decision had to be made. To keep up with the rate of development and expansion, more workers were needed. If the pioneers of Olat HaShachar truly wanted to conquer the land, they first had to conquer the workload. Presently there were not enough hands. Acres and acres of farmable land lay untouched. Sand dunes waited to be leveled and turned into vineyards. Barren wasteland waited to be transformed into pastures. The possibilities for growth were endless, but many more workers were needed.

One afternoon, a group of thirty young Jews marched into the colony. None had beards, and many didn't even wear caps. Their backpacks were filled with apples, bread, blankets, and coconut oil, which some used for cooking and others for protecting their skin in the sun. They were led by a distinguished gentleman named Dr. Arthur Ruppin. He explained that the new immigrants had all joined his workers' union, which he fittingly called "The Workers of Zion." The goal of the movement was to unite all of the Jewish labor in Palestine, secure favorable terms for the workers, and thus make the Jews of the land independent, without having to depend on Arab labor to survive. Ruppin told Shimon, Tevye, Elisha, and a crowd of curious settlers, that the worker's union was willing to hire out the laborers to the colony for minimal wages and board.

While the veteran pioneers gathered around the new immigrants to learn what was happening in Russia, Shimon took Tevye and a small group of other settlement leaders aside.

"This is a godsend," Shimon said. "We've been desperate for workers for months."

"Now we can get rid of the Arabs we hired to work in the fields," Elisha added.

"Hiring these Jews will surely cost us much more," Baruch said. He was Shimon's right-hand man, in charge of the administration of the colony.

"Not according to this Ruppin," Shimon answered.

"It's too good to be true," Tevye said.

The others all turned to him.

"What do you mean?" Shimon said.

"I thank the good Lord for every Jew who steps foot in the Land of Israel. But, I am sorry to say, I don't see any rabbis among them."

"Tevye's right," Shragi agreed. "Do we want so many free-thinkers living in Olat HaShachar? They nearly outnumber us."

"They will only be hired workers," Shimon answered. "They won't have a say in how we run the *yishuv*, nor a vote in our general assemblies."

"Even if they don't have a vote, their presence is sure to be a dangerous influence," Tevye said. "I've raised seven daughters, and I know the pitfalls of exposing young minds to their godless ideas. Thank the good Lord, all of my daughters are married, but there are others who could be courting disaster."

The others were momentarily silent. Elisha realized the reality of the problem. He still had three unmarried daughters and half a *minyan* of young, impressionable sons. Everyone turned toward Nachman.

"First we have to look at the new arrivals as our beloved Jewish brothers," he said. "Their desire to join us in rebuilding our land is a wonderful thing. By being here, they will be exposed to the treasures of Judaism and the beauty of the Torah. As the great Sage, Hillel, taught us - we should be like the disciples of Aharon, loving our brethren and bringing them closer to Torah. At the same time, we have to be careful to put a guarding fence around our sacred beliefs, as Reb Tevye has rightly observed."

Shimon decided the proper thing to do was to call a general meeting so that everyone could express their opinion. One thing was clear - the colony needed more workers. Reluctantly, they had hired Arabs to work in the fields during harvest time and planting. Besides the disappearance of animals and tools which always occurred when Arab workers were hired, there was always a feeling that security-wise, it was dangerous to have outside workers overly familiar with the day-to-day workings of the colony. So that now, when Jews showed up demanding the right to work, how could the settlers of Olat HaShachar turn them away?

When all of the men in the colony had finished voicing their views, Shimon proposed that the workers be given a six-month trial. A vote was taken and the proposal passed by an overwhelming margin. In fact, only Tevye and Eliahu dissented. A formal contract with Ruppin was signed, and the workers were given quarters in a half-empty barn, where they were invited to sleep on the ground. In the morning, they were given tea and chunks of black bread. Singing a medley of Russian tunes, the happy new immigrants set off to work.

When the Arab workers arrived, Shimon met them and told them that their labor was no longer needed. Clearly displeased, they hung around for several hours with scowls on their faces before stalking off into the dunes.

The new immigrants set to their tasks with a passion, wanting to prove that they could provide the colony with invaluable help. Their spirits never seemed to tire, spurred on by their dreams of rebuilding Zion, and by the Histadrut's goal of conquering the work market for the Jews.

The first problem occurred on the Sabbath. While the settlers of Olat HaShachar were praying, a boy came into the synagogue and reported that the new immigrants were working with their tools in the fields! With their white prayer shawls billowing behind them in the wind, everyone ran out of the synagogue, as if a fire was raging in one of the barns.

"Stop! Stop!" everyone screamed as they ran to halt the unheard of desecration of the holy Sabbath.

The workers were startled at the sight. When they were told to immediately cast down their tools, a fiery argument broke out.

They had come to Olat HaShachar to work. They wanted to work on the Sabbath just like any other day of the week. They wanted to keep building the land, and they wanted to be paid for each day of their labor.

"Our work isn't bothering anyone. What do you care?" one of the workers asked.

Shimon tried to explain the prohibition of working on the Sabbath, but talking about the Bible to the Zionists was like trying to convince a child to eat a food he doesn't like. His entreaties fell on deaf ears. As long as the workers lacked respect for the laws of the Torah, to them one day was the same as the next.

Under the threat that the workers would leave Olat HaShachar to work in a non-religious kibbutz, it was decided after the Sabbath was over to pay them double for the work they did on Friday, so that they too would welcome the Sabbath's rest.

"In effect," Tevye said, "they are getting paid not to work on the Sabbath. I say we get rid of them now."

Once again, his advice was ignored. Everyone could see the benefit which the extra manpower would bring to the colony. And with harvest-time coming, there was an overabundance of work to be done in the fields.

It turned out that Dr. Ruppin had only come with the workers to negotiate their contract. After he left, a tall, quick-witted youth proclaimed himself manager of the group. It was his job, he said, to secure better conditions for his comrades and to guard them from being exploited. Instead of living with the cows in the barn, he demanded a barracks just for the workers. And the barracks had to have beds.

"The better we sleep, the better we work," Zeev, the young, union leader, announced.

Though Tevye naturally liked people, and though he tried his best to judge others in a positive light, the self-assured youth made him wary. He reminded Tevye of Ben Zion and Perchik. All of them were filled with avalanches of good intention; all of them abounded with idealism and spirit; all of them could make a man dizzy with slogans and speeches, but where did all of their glib talk and charisma lead? To a breakdown of tradition. Not only that, Tevye warned his friend Elisha to keep an eye on his unmarried daughters.

Just as Tevye had prophesied, it wasn't easy to restrict the workers and their foreign ideas to the barn. After their first few weeks in the colony, the newcomers began to mingle with the families on the *yishuv*. Only naturally, the new immigrants were invited to join in Sabbath meals. Nachman said it would bring the workers closer to a yearning for Judaism. For the most part, they had grown up in Russia in families who had strayed from the fold. They had never had an opportunity to discover the Sabbath's great inner beauty. True to Nachman's hopes, a few of the workers developed a sincere interest in learning more about Torah. But, just as Tevye had predicted, the interaction went in both directions.

Munsho, the blacksmith, was the first to feel the experiment's painful sting. One day, his teenage daughter was missing. A search of the fields and the barracks revealed that one of the workers was missing as well. It turned out they had gone to the beach "for a walk." Munsho kept the girl in the house for two weeks as a lesson and gave the worker a no-nonsense punch in the nose. Then Shragi, the scribe, found his son smoking cigarettes which he had bought from one of the workers. And in the house of Shilo, the carpenter, a volume of plays by a writer named Henrick Ibsen was found under the eldest girl's pillow.

When Guttmacher's boy, Dovid, walked into Tevye's house holding the writings of Spinoza in his arms, Tevye exploded. Just a few months before, he had accompanied the lad up to the Torah to recite his bar mitzvah portion and to become a full-fledged adult, responsible to observe all of the teachings of Moses. Proudly, like a father, Tevye had guided the orphaned child to love the Torah and its commandments. This was the least he could do for his good friend, the undertaker, may his final rest be in peace. As long as Guttmacher's brother failed to answer the letters which Tevye sent, Tevye was still the boy's guardian, and he was damned if he would allow heretical poison to enter the young lad's head. Grabbing Dovid by the collar, Tevye dragged him into the fields to point out the culprit who had given him the poisonous writings. Angrily, Tevye tossed the book in the dirt.

"If you ever lend a book to one of the children again," Tevye warned him, "I'll make you eat it, page after page."

But the greatest danger fell on the house of Elisha. Being one of the wagon drivers who hauled the settlement produce to the market, he was frequently away from his house. In the innocence of his heart, he had invited the union leader, Zeev, to join his family in a Sabbath meal. The youth behaved with respect and decorum, asking about the different customs and ritual blessings, as if he were truly interested in learning about his roots. With an embarrassed smile, he confessed that he had received no Jewish education in his home, nor at the gentile school he had attended in Russia. His questions were insightful and seemingly sincere, with none of the cynical glibness which could be heard in the workers' barracks. The evening meal had been so pleasant for everyone, Elisha invited Zeev back again. A natural friendship seemed to sprout between the guest and Elisha's son, Yigal. During their leisure hours, the two strapping youths could be found invariably together, racing their horses over the sand dunes, or running like stallions along the great white stretch of beach which extended almost uninterrupted all along the country's Mediterranean coastline.

What Elisha didn't notice was the attraction which had developed between the union leader and Moriah, the Yemenite's daughter. At first, it consisted of surreptitious glances, more bold on his part than hers, but Zeev could tell from her blushes that she liked him. From the first time he saw her, he was drawn to her dark, exotic beauty. Without any doubt, she was the most beautiful girl he had ever seen in his life. Even before they ever spoke with one another, he felt an attraction for her which gave him no rest. Eating dinner with her family, he asked questions and nodded politely because he wanted to be invited for other Sabbath meals. He enjoyed Yigal's company, but in the back of his mind, there was always another reason for their friendship - the hope that Yigal would be his conduit to the girl. He knew that if he asked Elisha's permission to meet with his daughter, his invitations would end. Their worlds were simply too different. And if he approached the timid girl directly, he felt she would be frightened away. So without any evil intention, he became the best of friends with her brother.

One day when Elisha had driven the wagon off to Jaffa, Zeev suggested to Yigal that they take Moriah along on a picnic. Yigal wasn't surprised in the least. He sensed that his friend harbored secret feelings for his sister. Why not, he thought? What harm could come of it? It would be good for his sister to get out of the house.

They walked through the undulating sand dunes toward the beach. As usual, Zeev did most of the talking. He had become Yigal's tutor, teaching him about literature, world history, and modern political thought. For Yigal, his friendship with Zeev opened exciting new worlds. Growing up in a tiny village in backward Yemen, he had received no formal education at all. He could recite the whole Torah by heart, but he had never learned how to read, and he had absolutely no knowledge about secular subjects. So he was happy that he had found a friend like Zeev who could lead him out of his intellectual darkness. Moriah also found it fascinating to listen to Zeev's descriptions of novels and plays. When they arrived at the beach, Moriah sat in the shade of a palm tree, her head turned modestly away as the two youths stripped to their undergarments and sprinted into the water. Moriah was startled at her brother's behavior. Going for a swim was perfectly natural, but undressing in her presence with another man, that was unheard of. She felt like heading home on her own, but she feared that she would get lost, or encounter Bedouins on the way. She didn't want to spoil their fun. They wrestled in the water, and threw one another under the waves, without ever seeming to tire. When they finished, they raced along the beached, then circled back, and began wrestling again in the sand. Modestly, Moriah kept her gaze focused in another direction, but she had glimpsed enough of Zeev's arms and legs to be filled with conflicting emotions.

Finally, the friends slipped on their trousers, and they all sat down for a picnic. Though Zeev didn't speak with her directly, she felt that all of his speeches were meant for her ears. Occasionally, he would throw an endearing smile her way, and a few times he asked her opinion, but she was too tongue-tied to answer and could only say that she didn't know.

By evening time, when they returned to the colony, Zeev was madly in love. As far as he was concerned, the girl didn't have to talk. She didn't have to be intelligent and witty. She was beautiful the way she was. She had an innocence and naturalness he felt he had to possess for his own. There were girls from Russia whom had joined their journey to Palestine, but Moriah outshone them all. She was the dream of Zion itself, magical, golden, and Biblically pure. With the same passion he had to conquer the land, he longed to conquer the girl.

The opportunity presented itself in a roundabout way. Two

months after the workers arrived in Olat HaShachar, Dr. Ruppin, the union's founder, returned to inspect operations. After talking to his workers and hearing their complaints, he took Zeev aside. A new group was heading off to join the work force in Midbara, a non-religious kibbutz on the edge of the Negev, not far from the port city of Gaza. Ruppin wanted Zeev to go along as group leader.

"Leave Olat HaShachar?" he asked.

"That's right," Ruppin said.

"But I'm happy here."

"That's good. A worker should be happy. But you can just as easily be happy somewhere else."

"But our work is only just beginning."

"I'll appoint someone to replace you. Things seem to be well organized here. Moral is high amongst the workers, and the settlers are satisfied with worker productivity. You've done a commendable job. That's why we need you down south."

"Can I have an hour to think about it?" Zeev asked.

"I suppose an hour won't hurt. But, remember, you are a soldier of the union. What matters is the general good. If we want to build a worker state in this country, we have to be willing to make personal sacrifices."

Zeev nodded at Ruppin's speech, believing every word. In different circumstances, he would have said the same thing himself. As a rule, personal matters shouldn't interfere with the needs of the collective. But how could he leave Moriah?

Quickly, he rushed to meet Yigal, who was working on the construction of a silo. Pulling him aside, he told him that the union had appointed him to be the leader of a new group setting off for a kibbutz in the south. He wanted Yigal to join him. He said that they shared the same goals, and that they were brothers at heart. More than that, Zeev confessed that he was in love with Moriah, and that he wanted to make her his wife as soon as he could. He knew that their father wouldn't let her marry an unreligious man like himself, so he had kept his love secret. Now, before he left for the Negev, Zeev wanted Yigal to tell his sister how much he loved her. If she had the courage to follow him to Midbara, they would be married there. But he warned him - if their father learned of their plans, he would surely interfere. So if Moriah wanted Zeev for a husband, she would have to sneak away on her own.

Dutiful friend that he was, Yigal told his sister everything Zeev had said. Blushing, the innocent girl was too stunned to react. Mingled with the excitement she felt was a fear of her father. A fear of what he would say. A fear of what he would do. A fear of hurting her parents. A fear of the passions swirling within her. And a fear to strike out on her own.

Yigal told her that he was going to Midbara with Zeev. He would be there if she came. She wouldn't be alone without family, he assured her.

"You don't have to decide right away."

"Why?" she asked. "Why are you going?"

Yigal reflected before he answered the question.

"I want to be on my own," he responded. "I want to be free. I want to decide for myself how I want to live my life, without having the past decide for me."

His words struck a chord in her heart.

"In Yemen, all of the Jews were religious," he said. "I never knew there was any other way to be. But here, in *Eretz Yisrael*, there are Jews who don't follow the Torah. Zeev says that there are millions of them all over the world. Maybe their way is right. Look at our family. We never even learned how to read a book or write. Just because father says that Joshua blew a *shofar* and the walls of Jericho fell down, that doesn't mean that it's true. I have to find out for myself."

If Moriah had been uncertain, her brother's eloquence cast out the doubt from her heart. Her eyes were shining.

"Tell him I'll join him," she said.

"I'll come back for you in thirty days. We'll meet at dawn at the southern entrance to the colony. If I am not there, I will come the same time the next day. Take along whatever you need, but don't tell anyone. We'll send word to father after you've left."

Yigal said good-bye to his sister and hurried off to look for his father. He found him outside the packing house, lifting sacks of produce into his wagon. Yigal helped throw a few heavy sacks of potatoes onto the load, then turned to break the news to his father.

"I have something to tell you, *Abba*."

Elisha looked at him with a kind, loving smile.

I have decided to leave the *yishuv*."

His father's expression didn't change. He stared at his son with a smile, absorbing the words.

"A new group of workers is going off to join a kibbutz in the south, and I want to go with them. I want some time to be on my own."

His father nodded. "Are you going alone?"

"No. I'll be going with Zeev."

"With Zeev," his father repeated. His wise eyes narrowed in understanding. "What kind of kibbutz is it?"

"A worker's kibbutz."

"What kind of workers?"

"Good, hard-working Jews."

"Do these good, hard-working Jews keep the Torah?"

"I don't know. I didn't ask."

His father wiped the sweat off of his gleaming, golden brow. The lines in his forehead stuck out like the furrows of a field.

"And if I refuse to give my permission?"

"I am going to go anyway," Yigal answered. "I'm old enough to decide my future on my own."

It was the first time in Yigal's life that he had challenged the ways of his father, and he could feel his knees tremble.

"Is this your idea, or your friend's?"

His father's eyes seemed to peer into his soul. For a moment, Yigal couldn't find words to answer.

"Are you sure they are our kind of people?" Elisha asked.

"Look at you," the youth said. "We are the only Yemenites on this settlement. You get along with the settlers from Russia, why shouldn't I?"

"Yes, that's true. But this settlement is religious. All of our neighbors are God-fearing Jews. That's the main thing. Our family has been religious for four thousand years. Will you be the first link to break in the chain because of some modern ideas?"

Yigal trembled. This was precisely the yoke he wanted to throw off his back. He wanted to feel free, to experience life for himself, without always having to haul a wagon load of history behind him.

"Don't worry, *Abba*. I know what I am doing."

Elisha nodded, but he didn't seem convinced. His son waited for a hug good-bye, but instead, his father turned away and picked up a sack of potatoes.

Later that night, Tevye poured his friend a comforting glass of vodka. He kept a bottle in the house for occasions like these, even though he himself no longer imbibed.

"Do I have to drink alone in my sorrow?" the Yemenite asked.

"A vow is a vow," Tevye answered with a shrug.

Elisha recited a blessing and drank. His face twisted into a snarl as the harsh Ashkenazic beverage flowed down his throat.

"You shouldn't be disheartened," Tevye said. "With God's help, it will turn out for the best. Didn't my daughter, Hodel, run off with a free thinker? And today she is married to Hillel. And things with my Hava started out even worse. But today, her Hevedke is a Talmudic scholar. Your son will find his way home, don't you worry."

"Tell me what I did wrong?" Elisha wondered.

Carmel couldn't bear seeing her father's chagrin. She put a shawl on her shoulders and quietly slipped out of the house to see how her mother was reacting to Yigal's departure.

"It's the new generation," Tevye said. "What can you do? When they get to be teenagers, they start going crazy."

"My son's head is filled with questions and doubts."

"My girls were the same."

"Why don't they come to us for the answers?"

"Eventually, they do. When they find out that life is different than the romances in all of their head-spinning books."

"You warned me," Elisha said.

"A man has to learn for himself. When you invited the devil into your house, you thought you were doing a good deed."

"You're my friend. I should have listened to you."

"We are a stubborn people. That's why God loves us. Who else in the world would have remained faithful to Him after all we've been through?"

Elisha shook his head back and forth.

"How can it be that for thousands of years in Yemen, we lived faithful to all of our traditions, and here in our Biblical homeland, my son is lured away by a Jew who never learned a sentence of Torah?"

Tevye nodded, sharing his friend's deep perplexity. Absently, his hand grasped the vodka bottle. The question demanded a drink. He tilted the bottle to pour a glass for himself, but remembering his vow, he set it back down on the table.

"He'll return," Tevye assured him.

Elisha managed a smile. But when his daughter, Moriah, disappeared one month later, his heart felt like it had been wrenched from his chest. She hadn't even wished him good-bye. She hadn't said a word to him, nor to her mother, nor to any of her brothers or sisters. The only thing she had left behind was a letter from Zeev, which Elisha gave to his friend Tevye to read.

"I apologize that I could not meet with you in person," the letter began, "to ask your daughter's hand in marriage, but I felt that you would not give us your blessing, and that you would try to interfere, so we decided to be married on our own. We love one another and are doing what will make us the happiest. I respect you, your family, and your daughter with the utmost regard, and I assure you that I shall do everything in my power to be a good husband, to provide for Moriah, and to put her happiness above that of my own. We will be living in a kibbutz called Midbara, five kilometers northeast of Gaza. While the kibbutz is not religious, Moriah is welcome to keep whatever customs she likes. We hope that you will visit us soon. Yigal sends you his greetings and his love, and he asks me to assure you that he is happy with his work, with his new friends on the kibbutz, and with the workers' union. May our dreams for our own Jewish statehood be quickly realized,

and may the winds of war sweeping through Europe bring an end
to the rule of the Turks in our land."

The letter came as a shock to Elisha. He collapsed down in a
chair in Tevye's house. His daughter, Carmel, hurried to warm up
some soothing herb tea.

"At least she wasn't kidnapped," Tevye said, trying to cheer
his friend's spirits.

"Wasn't she?" he asked.

"I mean by an Arab or Turk, God forbid."

"Yes," Elisha answered softly. "I suppose there is some
consolation in that."

"Gaza is not so far away. The journey, I think, can be made in
two days."

"Have you been there?" Elisha asked.

"No. But I've heard the workers talk about it."

"What's down there?"

"Desert. Date trees. A few Bedouin tribes. A small city of
Turkish soldiers, Arabs, and Jews, and a port that doesn't seem to
be used. There's an old synagogue there, some say from the time
that King David conquered the region. I think the railroad which
goes from Jaffa to Cairo stops there."

"Why didn't she tell me?" Elisha asked with a mixture of
wonder and hurt.

No one could offer an answer. Instead, Carmel set a cup of hot
nanna mint tea before him.

"I am beginning to be sorry that I ever stepped foot in this
land," the Yemenite said.

"Oh, *Abba*, don't say that," Carmel protested.

"Everyone has his tests," Tevye added. "You once said so
yourself."

Elisha looked up at his friend. He remembered the death of
Tevye's daughter, Bat Sheva. He remembered walking with Tevye
to the synagogue and telling him that he had to be strong. He
remembered repeating the very same words to eldest son, Ariel,
who had married Bat Sheva just a short time before. Yes, he
decided. He too had to be strong. He still had eight children at

home to look after, thank God. And, in the merit of their forefathers, Yigal and Moriah might still find their way back to the fold.

"What did he write about war?" Elisha asked to take his mind off the subject.

"He said there were winds of war sweeping Europe."

"What does that mean?" the Yemenite asked.

Tevye gazed back down at the letter. "I'm not really sure. Maybe the conflict is spreading. Let's hope that the Germans attack Russia and wipe out the Czar and his soldiers, may they be cursed to a thousand lifetimes in hell."

"What did he say about Palestine?"

"He seems to think that Turkish rule over Palestine may be overthrown too."

"By who?"

"I don't know. He doesn't say."

Elisha said he would try to find out on his next trip to Jaffa. Once again, Tevye had comforted him in his gloom. But Elisha's personal hardship was only a warning that was destined to spread. The very next Sabbath, the peaceful Friday night meal of the settlers was interrupted by loud raucous music. Everyone rushed out of their houses. Music on *Shabbos*? It was absolutely forbidden. Nonetheless, the merry strains of an accordion and fiddle shattered the serenity of the sacred Sabbath night.

That wasn't all. Tevye stopped short in his tracks as he ran toward the worker's barracks. Not only was there music. There was dancing. But not the kind of dancing familiar to the Jews of Olat HaShachar. This dancing was with men and women together! To the beat of the music, they whirled around and around, holding hands and singing, as if they were purposefully mocking the sanctity of the day. Out of nowhere, three musicians and a wagon load of women had arrived to boost worker moral. The settlers of Olat HaShachar stood in speechless wonder. It was impossible to tell who yelled out first, Tevye, Shimon, Munsho, or Shilo. Simultaneously, they charged forward, raising threatening hands. The young girls screamed. The dancing immediately halted. The powerful blacksmith grabbed the accordion and hurled it through the air. It landed with a protesting, out-of-tune clang. Shimon snatched the fiddle and snapped it in half. Only the clarinet player managed to escape with his instrument intact.

Enraged workers started pushing the settlers away. Arguments erupted. Soon everyone was shoving somebody else. In the free-for-all, the holiness of the Sabbath was forgotten.

The girls who had come from a nearby kibbutz fled to their wagon to keep away from the fight. Here and there a punch was exchanged, but most of the brawl was just pushing. The workers were furious. What right did the settlers have to interfere in their party? It was their day of vacation - they could do what they wanted. They didn't bother the settlers; why should the settlers bother them? There was no law in the country against music and dancing. If the settlers wanted to be religious, that was their business, but they couldn't tell the workers how to live.

The settlers argued that they were in charge of the colony. If the workers didn't want to respect the laws of the Torah, they could gather their belongings and leave. What they did in the barracks was their business, but a public infringement of *Shabbos* screamed out to Heaven. And mixed dancing! That was the gateway to unthinkable sins!

"I demand that they leave our settlement now," Shragi angrily shouted. "What will protect us in this land if not our observance of the Torah?"

"Our strength will protect us, and our weapons, and our spirit!" one of the workers retorted.

Suddenly, a group of settlers charged at the wagon. The workers rushed to rescue the terrified girls. More pushing and shoving erupted. One worker gave Tevye a push, while another crouched down behind him on all fours. Tevye toppled backwards and landed on the tail of his spine. The fall left him moaning. In the noisy melee, the driver of the wagon made a hasty getaway. Women from the colony shouted out curses, as if they were chasing the devil away. Gradually, the quarrel subsided, and the settlers returned to the cold Sabbath food on their tables.

By the end of the Sabbath, Tevye's traitorous vertebra had slipped back into place and he felt well enough to attend the emergency general meeting. After a heated debate, it was decided that the hired workers would have to agree to conditions if they wanted to be employed by the colony. First and foremost, no violation of the Sabbath would be tolerated. Secondly, the rules of the holidays and the kosher laws would have to be observed. Thirdly, workers were forbidden to hand out propaganda or literature in any form whatsoever. And there would be no public gatherings without the consent of the settlement board. Any worker who refused to sign his assent to the rules would not be employed. Only Shimon and Nachman objected to the strictness of the edict. Shimon warned that it would destroy the spirit of their work force, and Nachman warned that the compulsory laws could cause a dangerous division among the two camps. Just as God was One, the Jews should be one, not divided into hostile parties and factions.

When the ultimatum was delivered, the workers reacted with anger. Was Palestine a free country, or were they back in Czarist Russia? Adamantly, they all refused to sign. In the name of the Workers' Union of Zion, they refused to give in to managerial demands.

"We'll break the bosses of Olat HaShachar," they sang, "And then we will break the bosses of the Baron."

In defiance, they tied the red flag of the union on the roof of the barracks. When the settlers went off to work in the morning, the workers barricaded themselves in their fort. Battle lines were drawn, and neither side would budge. In response to the strike, the settler's stopped supplying the workers with food. The winds of war which were spreading all over the world had reached Olat HaShachar too.

All through the week, the workers continued their strike. They emerged from the barracks only to fetch pails of fresh water and to take care of their needs. The evening before the Sabbath, a relief wagon arrived from the union, smuggling in food. Ruppin demanded that the settlers retract their demands, but the settlement committee refused. Another week passed in protest. Elisha and Tevye demanded that the workers be thrown out of the colony, but Shimon refused. They were in the Land of Israel, not Russia. How could Jews in the Jewish homeland throw other Jews out of their homes?

"You call these rebels Jews?!" the usually soft-spoken Shragi shouted. "They're heretics, not Jews!"

It was Nachman who quieted his outburst.

"They may not believe everything we do," he said, "but they are Jews all the same. And it is our duty to love them. Not through condemnation will we win them over to Torah, but by patiently bringing them near."

As always with the Jews, the settlers of Olat HaShachar woke up too late to the disaster which was brewing in their midst. Even the self-controlled Ariel was drawn into the blaze of fraternal strife. Discovering one of the workers drawing water from the well, he proceeded to give him a thrashing. Perhaps he was venting his father's frustrations over the fate of Moriah and Yigal. Perhaps when he was hitting the worker, he was really hitting Zeev. Whatever the reason, the senseless hatred between brothers, which had destroyed the foundations of the ancient Jerusalem Temple, was about to bring a curse down on Olat HaShachar too.

Tevye was out in the fields when he saw it. At first, he couldn't believe his eyes. When he looked up from his harvesting, it seemed like a cloud. A great black cloud spanning the horizon as far as the eye could see. A strange and ominous cloud filled with movement and life. Tevye wiped the sweat from his eyes, and with a shake of his head, he stared once again at the vision.

"No, it can't be," he said to himself as the frightening darkness surged forward.

Like a punishment out of Heaven, the cloud spread over the colony, turning daytime to night.

"No, no, it can't be," Tevye whispered.

But it was.

Not a cloud. But locusts! Swarms and swarms and swarms of locusts!

Chapter Forty

LOCUSTS

Two thousand years before, the armies of Rome had conquered Jerusalem and razed the holy Jerusalem Temple. The Rabbis taught that Rome was not the cause of the Kingdom of Israel's downfall, but rather the hatred which prevailed at the time between the Jews themselves. The House of Israel was divided within, and this is what brought about the nation's destruction by a foreign conqueror.

At first, Tevye stood paralyzed. The low flying cloud approached with menacing swiftness. All over the colony, field workers were shielding their faces from a dry, stinging wind. A gusty *hamsin* was not an unusual thing, but a desert wind had never been followed by the ominously descending black cloud. The Arab workers who had been hired since the start of the strike threw down their tools.

"*Jarad! Jarad!*" they hollered, running away in fear.

More clouds appeared, one following the other like battalions. A gust of wind blew a dozen locusts directly at Tevye's face. He swatted at them and watched them fall to the ground. Suddenly, the dense cloud swooped down upon him. Futilely, he tried to shield the corn stalks with his body, but his efforts were hopeless. Hundreds and thousands of locusts rained down on the field. They battered Tevye all over his body. Wings flapped in his face. There was nothing that he could do. Falling down on his knees, Tevye clutched his head in his arms and prayed.

Long minutes passed. When the roar of the storm abated, Tevye looked up. Locusts blanketed all of the corn. The ears were invisible. The stalks had turned into columns of the Heaven-sent demons. The corn field had turned into a forest of locusts.

All over the settlement, the scene was the same. Locusts covered the wheat fields, the orchards, the vineyards, and the vegetable gardens. Stalk after stalk, vine after vine, branch after branch, were enveloped with the plague. The shocked settlers were still inspecting the scope of the damage when yet another hot wind blew out of the east and a second black cloud swept over the plain. Defenseless against the great swarms, the Jews ran for shelter inside of their houses and tents. The roar of the locusts sounded over their rooftops like the thunder of heavenly chariots.

Locusts crawled under doorways and battered against tightly closed shutters. With brooms, hysterical women beat at the creatures which fell down from the cracks in their roofs.

By late afternoon, the prisoners could once again venture forth from their houses. The evil wind had vanished, but the army of locusts remained on the crops. Tevye had never seen anything like it. The nearest thing to his memory was a late Russian frost. With sunken expressions, the settlers weighed the devastation. A year's work was doomed. Tevye's own tomato patch had disappeared under the heaps of insects in his garden. There were so many of them, he could hear them munching away. When he kicked them off a vine, others quickly took their place. Stunned by the nightmare, he cast a glance up to Heaven. This new plague was worse than the mosquitoes and swamps.

"Are we made out of iron that You test us like this?" he asked, raising his hands to the sky. "Is it fair to send millions of locusts against a handful of men? Why? Tell me why?"

"It's a punishment from God," Carmel said, standing beside him, holding their son in her arms.

"Yes," Tevye said. "We don't always behave like we should. But if He wanted us to be angels, He should have created us with wings.

Elisha blew on a *shofar*, summoning the settlers together. After leading the afternoon prayer, Nachman stood before the congregation with a Bible in his hand. Even the striking workers were present, feeling an equal sense of tragedy and loss.

"When a disaster falls upon the community, we are all called upon to examine our deeds," he exhorted. "All of the feuding, the curses, the words spoken in anger and hatred between brothers, this is the cause of this terrible plague. Listen to the words of the Prophet...."

Not a man in the room made a rustle. Everyone sat in the synagogue and listened intently as Nachman read from the Book. Outside the door, the woman crowded together to hear.

"Hear this, you old men, and give ear all of you inhabitants of the land. Has such a thing transpired in your days, or even in the days of your fathers? That which the cutting locust has left, the swarming locust has eaten. And that which the swarming locust has left, the hopping locust has devoured. Awake drunkards and weep. Howl all you drinkers of wine, because the sweet wine is cut off from your mouth.... Be ashamed, O you farmers. Wail, O you vine growers over the wheat and the barley, because the harvest of the field is perished."

The assembly was silent. The voice of the Prophet seemed to echo through the synagogue like a condemnation from the past.

"Sanctify a fast!" Nachman read. *"Call a solemn assembly! Gather the elders and all of the inhabitants of the land into the house of the Lord your God, and cry out to the Lord!"*

"We have to make peace with the workers!" a settler stood up and shouted.

Other voices assented. Settlers turned toward the non-religious laborers in conciliation and friendship. Everyone shook hands. A fast day was called for the morrow. In the morning, as dawn rose, the locusts still clung to the crops. The corn fields had been wiped out completely. Ears sagged like empty sacks. Here and there, kernels littered the earth. Stalks, like wounded soldiers, wilted lifelessly toward the ground. Not a tomato was left in Tevye's garden.

Predictably, the Arab laborers didn't show up. Instead, the striking union returned to the fields. For the first time in a month, the Jews set off together. But no one knew what to do. If they left the locusts alone, the voracious insects would wipe out the crops. But when the settlers tried to beat them away, they flew into other orchards and fields. Most dangerous of all, Elisha told them, was the chance that the locusts might begin to lay eggs. He had seen storms of locusts in Yemen, and they had always left starvation and ruin in their wake. The only thing that could save them, he said, was a wind that would blow the ravenous grasshoppers into the sea.

Like the sands on the seashore, there were so many locusts, they could never be numbered. The settlers decided to try to shovel them into wheelbarrows and beat them with brooms, but the strategy proved hopeless. The enemy was simply too numerous. True to Elisha's warning, the locusts hopped away onto other stalks. The women of the settlement followed after the men, carrying shovels and sacks. As the men whacked at the locusts, knocking them to the ground, the women scooped them into the folds of the burlap. Not every woman's stomach was strong enough for the job, and gradually their ranks began to dwindle. But as soon as the settlers cleared one row of stalks, more locusts would fly through the air to replace them. The settlers and workers were finally united at work, but the peace they had made proved fruitless against their common enemy. When they tried to harvest whatever crops they could salvage, locusts swarmed in their faces. Defeated, the workers returned to their barracks, and the settlers retreated to their homes.

The afternoon brought another dry wind and cloud after cloud of locusts. Darkness fell over the colony. Gloom fell over everyone's heart. Not a furrow or field was spared in the onslaught. The following morning, a feeling of despair hung over the whole yishuv. Not knowing what else to do, a strategy suggested by Elisha was put into action. Settlers emerged from their kitchens carrying all of the pots and pans they could gather. Like a marching band, they walked along the rows of their crops, clanging the utensils together, making a thunderous noise. Startled by the racket, the locusts flew into the air. All morning long, the settlers chased after the demons, pots and pans crashing like cymbals. Determined to win, the Jews chased the unwanted invaders from field to field until they flew off in a cloud further south. With cheers of success, the settlers returned to their fields. But the joy of their victory didn't last. The damage was almost total. Most of the season was lost. Only the melon crop was spared, and the carrots, turnips, and potatoes which had been in the ground. But at least they had gotten rid of the enemy.

Or so they thought until they took a closer look at the earth and discovered thousands and thousands of eggs!

That night, Tevye slept restlessly. The clamor of the pots and the pans continued to ring in his head. He dreamed of bondage in Egypt and the plagues God had sent to humble Pharaoh.

"Let my people go!" Tevye yelled out in his sleep.

The locust storm lasted a week. After a long, solemn Sabbath, the troublesome eggs had to be gathered. Myriads upon myriads remained in the fields. Workers and settlers alike got down on their hands and knees to pick them out of the soil. Like the pioneers had done in clearing the swamps, ditches were dug and the eggs were dumped inside. After pouring arsenic into the pits, the locust graveyards were sealed. The Jews all prayed that the clean-up would put an end to the enemy, but, as Elisha pointed out, if neighboring settlements didn't take the same precautions, a new invasion was sure to erupt. Messengers galloped off to coordinate the campaign with the other Jewish colonies along the coast, but no one was certain that Bedouin villages would agree to join in the battle against the eggs to prevent them from hatching. When the cleanup was finished, the settlers set to work plowing and planting, as if they were starting anew. Besides the loss of their produce, the poisons used in destroying the eggs cost large sums of money. And five cows were lost when they lapped up a trough-full of groats which had been inadvertently sprinkled with the arsenic used in destroying the eggs.

Shimon was crushed. Here, they had almost proven that a colony could survive without the massive bureaucratic machine of the Baron, and then, as if overnight, the locusts had wiped out their gains.

"It isn't as bad as all that," Tevye said, trying to cheer him. "After all, in the beginning we started out with nothing at all. This time, we are starting out with houses, and barns, plus dry, workable farmland, and fields that have already been plowed."

For all of Tevye's optimism, the always energetic Shimon was a crestfallen man when he rode off to Zichron Yaacov to put in a request for emergency JCA aid.

Once again, Tevye returned to work in the fields.

"Don't despair," he said to himself over and over until the famous Talmudic teaching turned into a song. "Even if a sword is poised to slit a man's neck, it is forbidden to fall into despair."

As he walked along scattering seeds into a dry sandy wind, he glanced up at the horizon. At first, he thought that the advancing black cloud was rain. Then he reasoned that it must be a dust storm. But as he stood shielding his eyes from the increasing gusts, his fears were soon proven true. Once again, coming out of the north, locusts flew out of the sky like flashes of angry lightening. A vast cloud spread over the colony as if covering the face of the earth. Like in the days of the Flood, the sun disappeared in the face of God's wrath. Locusts hopped, jumped, and flew over everything. Wings slashed at Tevye's face like daggers. Within minutes, whatever vegetation remained in the fields was totally consumed.

Holding his arms over his head, Tevye staggered through unending swarms toward the shelter of his house. Animals cried out in panic as settlers herded them toward the barns.

"How much, O Lord?" he asked. "How much suffering does a man have to bear to prove his devotion to You?"

When he barged open the door to his house, tears were streaming down Carmel's face. She had been in the field with Moishe and Hannei when the new storm appeared in the sky. Before they could return to the house, the locusts engulfed them. Carmel had lost a hold of the children. They were still wandering somewhere outside in the tempest.

"Where were you?!" Tevye demanded.

"We had just reached the orange grove," she answered.

In an instant, Tevye was out of the house. Locusts smashed at his face. He couldn't see two steps ahead of him. Looking down at his shoes, he forged his way through the storm in the direction of the orange grove. Locusts battered him fiercely, darting into his eyes and catching a hold of his beard. Blindly, he staggered forward, shouting out the names of the children. When he reached the orange grove, he heard Moishe calling. The grove was no longer a grove, but a cemetery of leafless trees. Calling to one another, Tevye made his way toward the boy's voice. Hannei was sobbing hysterically. Her brother lay over her, protecting her from the hurricane of ravaging insects.

"It's all right," Tevye said, snatching her up in his arms.

Her face was bleeding from scratches, but otherwise she seemed all right.

"Can you run?" he asked Moishe.

"Sure," the boy said.

"Grab a hold of my pants," Tevye told him.

Carrying the girl, Tevye headed back toward the house. Moishe ran alongside him. Once, he slipped, but Tevye held him up by the collar. Battered and bleeding, they made it safely back to the house. With a groan of relief, Tevye collapsed into a chair. His little son, Tzvi, looked up from the floor. Seeing his bloodied father, the child started to holler and cry.

"Wash the blood off of your face," Carmel told her husband as she rocked Hannei back and forth in her arms. "You're frightening the child."

"Thank God the baby wasn't outside in the fields with you," Tevye replied. "The locusts might have carried him away."

Tevye wasn't joking. In the first plague of locusts, four lambs and a dog had disappeared. Whether they had run off, or been eaten by the locusts, nobody knew. This time, after another week-long invasion, three goats were missing. When God's wrath abated, the settlers once again took up their pots and their pans and started chasing the locusts off of their devastated property. Once again, the settlers and the union workers got down on their knees to search for the eggs left behind. Ditches were dug and more arsenic was shipped in from Jaffa.

A feeling of hopelessness pervaded the settlement. At night,

Tevye had nightmares of slugs hatching into locusts and bursting through the floor of his house. Sleep became a terror. In his weakness, he started drinking vodka again. At an emergency meeting, when Shilo suggested they abandon the area for some other part of the country, at first Tevye remained silent along with everyone else. Then he said no. One place was just like the rest. The Master of the Universe had many messengers, whether they be mosquitoes, marauders, locusts, or wars.

"Since I have stepped foot in Zion," he said. "I have buried two daughters and a half-dozen friends. I have been shot at by Arabs, stricken with fever, nearly drowned in a swamp, and now I've watched hordes of locusts wipe out our crops. If things can get worse, I don't know how. Therefore I vote that we stay."

One after another, the other settlers agreed. Almost immediately, their perseverance was rewarded. Shimson returned with the news that the Baron Rothschild was giving them a loan - nothing astronomical, but enough to get the colony back on its feet.

The work of burying the locust eggs continued. Ditches were dug day and night. Everyone anxiously waited for the two-week gestation to end. If the eggs hatched, no one knew if the strength could be found to withstand another assault of the insatiable grasshoppers.

Blessedly, the devils didn't come back to life. The harsh decree ended. No more black clouds appeared in the sky. But the settlers of Olat HaShachar could only tremble in awe as they gazed out at their fields. The locusts had transformed their property back into a desolate wasteland.

A few days later, the union workers abandoned the stricken *yishuv*. Once again, the settlers faced the task of rebuilding alone. A horticulturalist employed by the Baron visited the settlement and advised them to let their fields lay fallow for a year. Tevye received the news as if he had been hit on the head with a hammer. Not work for a year? It was out of the question. How would the settlers survive? Rallying the others, he said he was going back to his farming, even if he had to plow and plant his field all alone.

No one responded. No one agreed. Even Nachman and Shirnon were silent.

"Are we going to let a bunch of grasshoppers defeat us?" Tevye asked. "Is that all the mettle we have?"

"Why break our backs working if the Baron is willing to pay us to sit and do nothing?" Shragi wanted to know.

"Because we came here to work," Tevye said. "And not to take handouts like beggars."

Alone, he strode off to the barn to fetch a mule and a plow. Shilo hurried to catch up to him.

"Where are you going?" he asked Tevye.

"Back to work. What about you?"

"I've decided to go to America," the carpenter confessed.

Tevye stopped by the barn. He looked at his good friend sadly. "America?" he asked.

"Yes. America. I'm fed up with this hell."

"What do you think you will find in America?"

"I don't know. But at least it won't be locusts and swamps."

"Locusts come in many sizes, and swamps come in many shapes," Tevye said cryptically.

Whatever Tevye was implying, Shilo didn't catch on.

"If you were smart, you'd leave this place too before the next disaster strikes."

"If I were smart," Tevye answered. "I would have been a rich man like the Baron, and not such a penniless fool."

"With a smile, he left Shilo standing outside the barn. The mules looked up at him in surprise as he entered. They hadn't worked in two weeks. Immediately, they brayed out in unison, letting him know they were hungry. Looking around, he spotted a sack of carrots which had miraculously escaped being devoured by locusts. He fed a handful to each beast and chomped on one himself. Selecting a mule from the pack, Tevye gave it a slap on its rump.

"Brains before beauty," he said, following the brute out the barn door.

Elisha met Tevye on his way to the field.

"Tevye," he cautioned. "If you plow up your field, you may uncover one of the ditches we dug."

"So I'll start a new field," Tevye answered. "There's plenty of land. This mule here has strength in its back, even if I don't."

He harnessed the creature and hooked it up to the plow.

"Anyway," Tevye added. "The worst is over now."

Instinctively, both men looked up at the horizon. The sky was blue and clear. A man had to believe with all of his heart that the Lord would bless his endeavor. For the moment, thank God, there was no sign of locusts. That in itself was a blessing.

Strapping the harness of the plow over his shoulders, Tevye headed back to the fields.

Chapter Forty-One

WAR

After a year of prayer, and hard, back-breaking work on the soil, patches of greenery reappeared in the fields of Olat HaShachar. Fruit trees budded. Tomatoes sprouted once again on their vines. God's anger seemed to have passed, leaving the settlers with a new hope for the future. Even Shilo was filled with a revitalized spirit. As it turned out, his eyes never feasted on the money-paved streets of New York. His *Rebbe* had answered his letter asking for permission to go to America with the command that he stay in *Eretz Yisrael*, where with patience, everything would work out for the best. With the *Rebbe's* encouragement, the carpenter set back to work with a renewed belief in his mission of rebuilding the Holy Land.

While their life wasn't easy, Tevye strove to be content with his lot. As the Sages taught, the truly rich man was the man who was happy with what he had. Tevye was naturally optimistic by nature, and it was important to be a beacon of faith for the morale of the community. True, there was a long list of things to complain about, but who had the strength? After a long day of labor, Tevye would eat and gladly collapse into bed. On the Sabbath, he studied a little Torah with Guttmacher's son. But his greatest pleasure came from his son. The golden-skinned toddler could walk and even put simple sentences together. He spoke Hebrew, the language which his father and mother spoke in the house. With an indescribable pleasure, worth more than all of the wealth in the world, Tevye taught his son the words of the *Shema Yisrael* prayer. When Shragi asked Tevye why he didn't teach the boy Yiddish, Tevye answered that Yiddish belonged to the past. Their future was in the mountains and plains of *Eretz Yisrael,* and not any longer in the confines of a ghetto.

The east winds which had brought the locusts were replaced by winds from a different direction. Each time a wagon arrived from Jaffa, settlers ran to meet it to hear the latest news about the war which was raging in Europe. At the beginning of the bloody conflagration, the battle between Germany, Russia, England, and France didn't affect the small Jewish colony in Palestine, but when Turkey became an ally of the German Kaiser, things began to change. At first, many of the settlers wanted Germany to win and crush the Czar's army, to punish the Russians for their oppression of the Jews. But when the Turk's secret pact with the Germans was revealed, the Jews sided with the British, hoping that England's forces in Egypt would roust the Turks and expel them from *Eretz Yisrael.*

One Friday afternoon, Hava and Isaac arrived in Olat HaShachar for a family reunion. Hava was pregnant with a child, and her Talmudic husband was pregnant with news. The former Hevedke had changed so completely that he bore no resemblance to the Russian poet of the past. His beard was longer than Tevye's. He wore glasses, and covered his barbered blond hair with a hat. His baggy black jacket hid his muscular build, and he no longer held himself straight, but rather stooped in a humble pose which made him seem much smaller than he was.

With shining eyes and great excitement, he spoke at the evening meal, telling them everything he had heard about the war, and about Rabbi Kook's visit to Europe. Hodel and Hillel, along with Ruchel with Nachman, joined them for the meal, and of course, Nachman listened intently to every word which Isaac related about the revered Rabbi Kook. For Tevye, it was a supreme Sabbath joy to have his family together. Like the cluster of glowing Sabbath candles which his wife and daughters had lit, a radiance shone on his face.

"Before the war broke out," Isaac related, "the *Agudat Yisrael* organization in Germany invited Rabbi Kook to come to Berlin to participate in a rabbinical congress against the Zionist movement.

Agudah represents the German ultra-orthodox who are adamantly opposed to the secularists. They believed that by having Rabbi Kook at their assembly, they could deal a blow to the Zionists who had been trying to win world approval for the creation of a Jewish State in Palestine. At first, the *Rav* couldn't decide whether to attend the congress or not. He said it was extremely painful for him to leave the Holy Land's shores, but he felt he might be able to influence the *Agudah* rabbis to moderate their opposition to the Zionist cause. Finally, his doctor recommended that a few weeks' stay in a Swiss sanatorium might be beneficial to the *Rebbetzin's* ailing health, so the *Rav* agreed to make the journey for the sake of his wife. When the war broke out, the congress was canceled, and the *Rav* was stranded in Switzerland with no way of returning to Jaffa. Apparently, all passenger ships have been refitted and turned into ships of war."

"What is he doing in Switzerland?" Nachman inquired.

"He is writing, I'm told. An important congregation in London has invited him to be their rabbi while he is in Europe, but he has not yet decided. In a letter to the yeshiva, he wrote that he still hopes that he can find some way to return to the Holy Land."

Inevitably, the effects of the war reached Palestine too. For one thing, there was no *aliyah*. To the Turks, the Jews asking entry from Russian were citizens of an enemy state. New Jewish immigrants ceased to arrive. As the war spread and spread, a steamship or freighter wasn't to be seen in Jaffa's harbor. In a short time, staples like flour, sugar, and rice all disappeared from the market. People started storing up food. Export trade stopped. Loans stopped arriving for the settlements. The Baron's Jewish Colony Association was headquartered in France, and France was at war with the Germans, and the Turks, who were allied with the Germans, were reluctant to grant special favors to the benefactor of the Jews. Without funds to sustain them, the settlements became imperiled, and *yeshivot* in Jerusalem had to close.

In the third year of the war, the Turkish military government of Palestine started a countrywide draft. Tevye was spared because of his age. Nachman was deferred because he was the colony's rabbi. Hillel was rejected because of his leg. But others, who couldn't afford to bribe their way out, were taken away to be turned into soldiers in the Ottoman army. Shimon, the settlement leader, went into hiding. The Turkish soldiers searched the stables and barn, but they didn't think to lift up the floor of the tool shed where the bulky Shimon was hiding in a secret cellar the settlers had dug. Not to leave empty-handed, the Turks confiscated the tools that they found and conscripted them into the war effort.

In short, the colony work force was crippled. A month later, more armed Turkish soldiers arrived and took away clothing and food. On their next visit, they took horses, wagons, camels, and mules. When harvest time came, soldiers confiscated half of the produce. Heavy taxes were levied, and only by bribing a Turkish captain was the colony left with some food.

Word came that the Jews of Jerusalem were starving. The community of rabbis and scholars in the holy city depended on charity from abroad, and when the country's foreign banks closed, their survival was threatened. Soup and bread kitchens were opened, but dozens of poor people starved to death every month. Only through the great kindness of the American Consul, a righteous gentile named Glazebrook, were the Jews of Jerusalem saved. Until the United States entered the war against Germany, he continued dispensing the charity which he received from America, even though the Turks kept a close watch on everything he did.

Miraculously, just before all postal service was suspended to Palestine, a letter arrived from America. It was from Baylke. Months had gone by without a letter from the family in Israel, and she was worried. She had started to light candles on Friday night, and when she ushered in the Sabbath, she prayed for their welfare with all of her heart. There were rumors, she said, that America would have to enter the war to fight against the Germans. In the meantime, she and her husband were fine. Padhatzur had won several promotions, and his stock investments had paid a handsome return. She was sending five-hundred dollars to the family through the American Consulate in Jerusalem, and she wanted her father to receive it himself. It was all the money she had managed to save.

To Tevye and his family, five-hundred dollars was a fortune. The money which the Baron had given for Moishe and Hannei had long ago been loaned to the treasury of the settlement to help it get back on its feet. So Baylke's letter came like a gift out of Heaven. Immediately, Tevye set off to Jerusalem on foot. The colony had no wagon to spare, not even a mule. Luckily, the good Lord was with him. A carriage carrying JCA officials from Zichron Yaacov to Jaffa stopped on the way. When they learned that Tevye was the father of the infirmary nurse, they graciously made room in the carriage. Brushing the dust off of his clothes, Tevye climbed into the crowded, but comfortable compartment. After politely refusing a flask of brandy and a cigarette from a shiny silver case, he answered their questions about the effect of the war on Olat HaShachar. Then Tevye listened as the Company officials confidentially discussed the state of the JCA.

To make a long story short, the Baron was in a pickle. On the one hand, he had to display allegiance to the Turkish government in Palestine, and on the other hand, he had to continue to take care of the Jews. His chief agent, Kalorisky, had traveled to Istanbul and Damascus to appeal to Turkish leaders that Jewish settlers be freed from serving in the army so that they could continue the farming which kept the country alive. Whether out of rudeness, or to display their power, the Turks had delayed giving an answer. In the meantime, Jamal Pasha, the Turkish Military General of Palestine, was trying to destroy the entire Jewish enterprise. He had ordered all Jewish schools, factories, and hospitals closed. Jews were forbidden to bear weapons and to leave their houses at night. Letters could not be sealed, and writing in Hebrew and Yiddish was banned. The Zionist Bank had been closed. Jewish land had been confiscated, and heavy taxation was driving Jewish colonies into bankruptcy. Leaders of the Jewish community had been arrested without trial, and Jews refusing to become Ottoman citizens had been uprooted from their homes and deported. Dozens of others had fled on their own. To make matters worse, typhus fever and cholera were sweeping through the stricken community, claiming dozens of victims each month.

Tevye listened in silence. After all, he was a simple farmer, a pawn in the great drama of history. When the flask of brandy was passed around once again, this time Tevye accepted the offer. Not to take a real drink, but just for a sip to wet his parched tongue. Surely by taking a tiny little sip, he wasn't breaking his vow.

Either influenced by the liquor, or because they felt they could trust Hava's father, the men began to discuss what sounded to Tevye like military secrets. To pass the time on the road, one official after the next disclosed what he knew about the Jewish underground movement which was spying against the Turks. Putting the sometimes incomplete pieces together, Tevye sat silently and listened to the riveting story.

One of the keys to the Mediterranean was the Suez Canal, which was controlled by the British. In the spring of 1915, after a Turkish attack on the Canal had been repulsed, a small group of Jews decided to secretly approach the British and offer their aid in conquering the Land of Israel. Aharon Aaronson was the name of their leader. A renowned scientist in Palestine, he had many high connections in the Turkish Military Government. At the beginning of Jamal Pasha's oppressions, he came to the conclusion that the Jews had no future under Turkish rule and organized an underground cell to fight against them. The spy ring was called *"Nili,"* an abbreviation of the Biblical verse, *"Netzach Yisrael Lo Yishaker,"* meaning that the Eternal One of Israel would not lie by abandoning His promise to stand by the Jews.

Along with Aaronson, the leaders of the group were Aharon's brother, Alexander Aaronson; their sister, Sarah; and Avshalom Feinberg. Though the men in the carriage spoke about them with a mixture of admiration and scorn, it was obvious that the JCA leadership in France was against them, fearing that their activities, if discovered, would bring reprisals from the Turks. Aharon Aaronson was considered a renegade and an individualist capable of taking irresponsible risks in convincing Jewish soldiers who were serving in the Turkish army to spy for the British. They were to report on all Turkish troop movements, installations, and plans. As special advisor to Jamal Pasha on the persistent locust problem, Aaronson himself had access to valuable information. *Nili's* goal, one of the travelers disclosed, was to facilitate a surprise British invasion by landing forces on the coast. Tevye couldn't help but glance at the flask of brandy which the Company official was clutching in his hand. Hearing all of these secrets, he longed for a fortifying drink. He even thought about yelling for the driver of the carriage to stop and let him out before he heard anymore. What if he were arrested and interrogated? Would he be able to withstand torture and not give these secrets away? Not to mention being thrown into prison as an enemy of the Turkish regime!

Frustrated with problems in relaying information by boat to the British in Egypt, Avshalom Feinberg was captured trying to cross the border to Egypt himself. He was accused of spying, but Aharon Aaronson interceded and succeeded in arranging for his release. Be that as it may, Feinberg was discovered murdered, apparently by Bedouins working for the Turks.

With a groan, Tevye moved his legs to a different position. In the cramped compartment, his back was beginning to ache from the bumps of the journey. Once again, the bald-headed official with the flask offered him a drink.

"Just a sip," Tevye said. He twisted off the cap and took a long greedy sniff of the brandy. If he couldn't fill up his belly, at least he could fill up his lungs.

The spy ring, Tevye learned, consisted of no more than eighty men. They used boats to smuggle supplies to the Jewish settlements along the coast, and to transfer information from the port of Gaza to British encampments in the Sinai. Now, with the arrest and murder of Avshalom Feinberg, the JCA officials were worried that the Turks would crackdown on the Jews.

True to their fears, when the carriage arrived in Jaffa, the Jews were in an uproar. Soldiers on horseback stampeded through the Jewish market, hauling down canopies, smashing tables and booths, and upturning merchandise all over the road. A rider clubbed a Jew on the head.

It was a scene Tevye remembered from Russia. An official in the carriage shouted for the driver to flee, but Tevye jumped out to be with his endangered brothers. Finding the bleeding Jew in the road, Tevye dragged him to safety. The man's eyes were frightened, but thankfully, his arm had deflected the blow to his head. When he grew calmer, Tevye asked what was happening. That morning, he said, Jamal Pasha's soldiers had rounded up hundreds of Russian Jews. Men and women had been beaten, families had been split up, and sword-wielding soldiers had herded Jews off to the dock. Anyone who didn't have a valid immigrant permit, and anyone refusing to sign an oath of allegiance to the Turks, was loaded onto a boat and shipped off to Alexandria. The wounded Jew had hid from the soldiers on the roof of a building. His wife, thank God, had signed the paper. But he was still worried. If the British won the war, she could be put into prison for being loyal to the Turks.

Down the road, Turkish soldiers continued to ransack the Jewish market. Produce was scattered all over the street. Booths were destroyed. When there remained nothing left to overturn, the cavalry of hoodlums grouped around their commander. Tevye recognized him at once from the way he sat straight-backed in his saddle. It was Jamal Pasha, the same black-eyed dog who had ordered the destruction of the cottages which Tevye and his friends had built in Morasha.

Tevye spit in the dirt. "Murderer," he whispered, recalling his oath of revenge.

Pasha shouted out an order to his troops. The horsemen reared their mounts, and the soldiers galloped off down the road. Burning with anger, Tevye ran into the street. He wanted to drag Pasha down from his horse, and give the devil a thrashing, but he was surrounded by a wall of his soldiers. The horses thundered by. Tevye stood in the cloud of their dust, his hands clutching at air. The moment the soldiers could no longer be seen, Jews started appearing from every direction. Merchants ran to their booths to salvage whatever they could. Seeing a small bearded Jew trying to drag a large crate, Tevye hurried over to give him a hand. To

Tevye's amazement, he recognized the man's face. It was Eliahu, the Jew who had helped them escape from Odessa!

"Eliahu!" he shouted, embracing the startled fellow in a bear hug.

"Mercy," the small man cried. "I need my arms intact to feed my family."

"Remember me?" Tevye asked.

"I am sorry to say that I do. It was a black day in Odessa when you left. The same curse that has befallen us today, fell upon us then. Then the butchers were Russian. Today, they are the Turks. The names and countries change, but their hatred remains the same."

"I heard you were arrested."

"Not for the first time, and probably not for the last. Officials I knew arranged for my release from the Odessa prison, at the expense of most of my savings. As you can see, I've gone down from being a respectable shipping agent to a miserable *shlepper.*"

"Thank God you are alive," Tevye said. "The oversized fellow who threw that Russian policeman into the harbor was killed in a plague of cholera."

"May the good Lord have mercy on all those who have left us, and on all who remain, and may He send the plague on our enemies, for as the wise Sage, Rashi, teaches, the enemies of the Jews are the enemies of God."

"Amen," Tevye responded.

As if for old time's sake, Eliahu arranged for Tevye to ride to Jerusalem in a wagon carrying emergency food to the city. Knowing he was going to receive the money which Baylke had sent from America, Tevye invited his friend along, so that he could more properly reward him. But Eliahu refused, saying that he had to look after his family and put their *fatumult,* topsey-turvy life in order. As a gesture, Tevye gave him the small amount of money he had left after paying the driver of the wagon. After all, Tevye reasoned, it was his fault that Eliahu was forced to bail himself out of the Odessa prison.

Though it was an exceedingly bleak time for the Jews in the

Land of Israel, Tevye felt an indescribable thrill on his wagon ride to Jerusalem. Riding up the mountainous ascent to the holy city, Tevye had the feeling he was ascending to the palace of the King. Who ever thought that the dream of Jerusalem could ever come true? As they journeyed up the slow winding ascent from the coastal lowlands to the mountains of Yehuda, Tevye felt a spiritual elevation as well. Tevye, the milkman from Anatevka, was going up to Jerusalem. The dream of his father, and his grandfather, and his great-grandfather before them was now only hours away.

How could it be, you ask? How could it be that a city which Tevye had never seen could occupy such a powerful place in his heart? For a Jew, the answer was simple. For two thousand years, three times a day, Jews prayed to return to their city. After every meal, after every piece of bread, and every piece of cake, they prayed for Jerusalem's welfare. No matter where a Jew lived, the city of Jerusalem was to be the center of his life. It was the place where the Pascal lamb was to be eaten on the Passover holiday, and where first fruits were brought on the Festival of *Shavuot*. There, by the pool of Shiloach, joyous water celebrations were held on the holiday of *Sukkos*. It was the site of the ancient Temple, the *Beis HaMikdash*, may it soon be rebuilt. It was the place where the Sanhedrin declared the new months, and where the High Priest atoned for the nation on *Yom Kippur*. There, the miracle of Hanukah had occurred when the Maccabees had won their great victory over the Greeks. For Jews all over the world, each day started with the hope – perhaps this was the day when God would rescue them from their exile in foreign lands and bring them back to Jerusalem.

Yes, the journey up the mountain was tiring. Yes, his bones ached and his body cried out for rest. But a singing in his heart made all of the pains disappear.

Finally, miles and miles from Anatevka, after what seemed like a two thousand year journey in itself, the wagon approached Jerusalem. Billowing white clouds floated just over Tevye's head, as if crowning the city. Rays of sunlight slanted down from the sky, bathing the Biblical hillsides in a soft, golden glow. Suddenly, the city came into view, spreading out before the wagon a plateau surrounded by hills. The city's holiness extended out to greet a traveler even before he entered its walls. Protruding over the massive, Old City walls were Ottoman towers, ramparts, minarets, and a golden-domed mosque. Inside the fortress-like citadel were clusters of dwellings, constructed from sand-colored stone. Gone were the palaces of King David. Gone were the magnificent stables of Solomon. Gone were the Temple, the Sanhedrin, and the throngs filling the streets for the Festivals. Gone were the Altar, the Menorah, and the Holy of Holies, along with the Ark with the Tablets of Law. Alas, as the Prophet Jeremiah lamented, *"Is this the city that men call the perfection of beauty, the joy of the whole earth?"*

As the wagon approached the Jewish Quarter of the city inside the Damascus Gate, starving Jews in tattered garments ran forward to meet it. Men, women, and children, with gaunt, yellow faces and emaciated frames, clambered around the emergency shipment of food. Officials of the Jewish community pushed their way to the wagon, shoving the poor masses away. Tevye was aghast. The proud remnant of Jerusalem had been turned into paupers. The guardians of the Holy City, who labored day and night over the Torah, had been compelled to go begging. Women lay swooning in the street. Children wandered through the alleyways in sackcloth. Dogs prowled through the deserted market like foxes, looking for morsels of food.

Nonetheless, standing in Jerusalem, Tevye experienced an incredible sensation of awe. The milkman reached up to make sure that his cap was planted securely on his head, just as he would have done if he were entering a king's palace. The windmill built by Moses Montefiore stood like a sentry, guarding the city. The ancient cemetery on the Mount of Olives, where the resurrection of the dead would begin, shone with an unearthly white light on Jerusalem's eastern hillside. Outside the towering Damascus Gate, locals engaged in commerce with formally dressed Europeans who looked out of place in the timeworn setting. A Turkish policeman ordered Tevye to disembark from the wagon and proceed into the walled city on foot. A Jew who reminded Tevye of the little Eliahu said he would guard their wagon and possessions for a meager ten kopeks. Tevye walked on, mystically pulled into the labyrinth of alleys, as if his feet had a will of their own, as if he had passed in this direction before. Merchants called out to him to stop and examine their wares. Water carriers approached at every corner, offering drinks from the inflated animal skins on their backs. Suddenly, Jews were everywhere. Most were pious, with long beards, sidelocks, and black coats and hats, the color of mourning which Jews had worn for centuries to commemorate the destruction of Jerusalem. Other Jews, with dark Mediterranean complexions, wore long white robes and round furry hats. Nachman had said that the Jews of Jerusalem were scholars who devoted themselves to learning and prayer. They weren't in Jerusalem because of Theodore Herzl, or the writings of Echad HaAm. Their forefathers had lived in the holy city for centuries. They were its protectors and keepers.

With long anxious steps, Tevye proceeded along the narrowing foot paths into a shadowy Arab *casbah*. When he emerged from an archway, it was as if he were back in the *shtetl*, surrounded by Jews of all kinds. There were Jewish shops and Jewish smells, and doorways that had *mezuzahs* cemented into the walls. Cats walked confidently through the alleyways as if they had the right of way. Tevye noticed a donkey-drawn cart inscribed with bold, Hebrew-lettering, spelling *CHALAV*. The cart belonged to the Jerusalem milkman. On any other occasion, Tevye would have greeted the man and stopped to exchange a few words of professional gossip, but now he was on a mission. He felt a force like a magnet pulling him toward the Wall.

The Wall. The *Kotel*. That was how it was known to Jews all over the world. The Western Wall of the ancient Temple courtyard. The Wailing Wall, where Jews had poured out their tears for nearly two-thousand years. Tevye hurried through a maze of tiny alleys, around buildings and shacks, and there it was, suddenly towering over his head. The *Kotel*. The dream of a lifetime, pulsating with a holiness you could reach out and touch. Its massive stones had withstood every siege and assault, every battering-ram and fire, every attempt by the nations of the world to erase every last trace of the city's Jewish history. Goose-bumps broke out all over Tevye's flesh. In this world of earthly existence, standing at the *Kotel* was the closest a man could ever come to God.

Turkish soldiers stood at the entrance to the alley leading to the *Kotel*. They stopped Tevye and demanded to see his papers. He stood obediently waiting, controlling the anger he felt toward the arrogant heathens who behaved with such self importance. They were the trespassers, not he. They were the ones who should be showing their papers. Palestine was his homeland, not theirs.

Returning the permit to Tevye, the soldier let it purposely drop to the ground. He laughed as Tevye bent down to pick it up. Containing his anger, Tevye walked away and approached the sacred Wall. His fingers gripped its great boulders. His cheek pressed against the cool stones. This place was the ladder to Heaven. The gateway of prayer. God's Presence hovered over the Wall for all people and nations to bask in its light. Even though only a small part of the Wall could be seen, its size told of the grandeur of the Temple which the Romans had long ago razed. Turks and Arabs had defiantly built houses against its holy stones, hiding its full length from view. Civilization after civilization had fallen at its feet, burying its deep foundations. Yet even along its narrow, uncovered span, the light which shone off its boulders was blinding. Behind it was Mount Moriah, the site of the ancient Temple, where Abraham had had been tested with the sacrifice of Isaac. Hundreds of thousands of Jews had given their lives defending the Temple against Babylonian, Persian, Greek, and Roman conquest. Jewish women had hurled themselves from its ramparts, rather than be captured by the enemy. For these reasons, Jews cried when their hands touched the Wall.

Tevye's head became dizzy. Words of prayer spilled out from his heart.

"My God and God of my fathers. Who am I to be standing before You in this sacred place? Who is Tevye, the son of Reb Schneur Zalman, that You have brought him here to Your holy dwelling? You know my sins and my temptations, my complainings and *kvetchings*. My life is an open book before You. Only through Your mercy and kindness can I open my mouth to speak, for what great difference is there between Tevye and his horse? King of the Universe, please bless all of my family. Bless my Golda in Heaven, and don't let her be angry at me for having remarried, as You Yourself have commanded a man to do. Bless all of the Jews of Anatevka, wherever they may be. May the Czar, and all of the Czars after him, meet the punishment they deserve. Look upon the disgrace of Your people and have mercy upon us. Drive out the wicked Turks from Your holy habitation, and bring all of Your children safely home to Your Land. Please don't forget us forever. Renew our days as of old."

When Tevye reached the American Consulate, a long line was waiting to enter the building. Jews pushed and shoved, trying to inch forward toward the door. Widows with children, *kibbutznikim*, rabbis, workers, *Hasidim*, Ashkenazim, Sephardim, new immigrants, and Jerusalemites whose families had lived in the city for ten generations, all crowded together. A *Hasid* came out of the building with a smile as if the *Mashiach* had arrived. To Tevye's surprise, the man took off his *shtreimel* hat and overcoat and handed them to a simply dressed worker. Instead of the round, furry head covering, he placed a ragged blue cap on his head. Quickly, the worker put on the other man's outfit.

"What are they doing?" Tevye asked the man next to him in line.

"Sometimes more money is handed out to the ultra-religious. They have all kinds of charity organizations in America for *schnorring*. Some people lie and say they belong to one of their groups."

Tevye learned that Glazebrook, the American Consul, had been keeping the Jews in the city alive. The elderly, gentile professor was a personal friend of President Wilson. He had asked for an appointment in Jerusalem because he loved the Land of Israel, and he wanted to help the Jews, whom he called the "Children of the Bible." After paper currency became valueless with the outbreak of the war, he would travel to Jaffa himself to receive the gold coins which arrived on boats from America. The coins were kept in a big safe in his office, and he distributed them to the needy.

"Why do the Turks allow him to continue to help the Jews?" Tevye asked his new acquaintance in line.

"That's a good question. I will tell you the answer. The rabbis of Jerusalem agreed to distribute a sizable portion of the charitable funds to the poor among the Turkish residents of the city. Since it comes to a lot of money, the Turks allow American ships carrying gold to enter the port in Jaffa. In other words, the Turks let him continue, but it's not out of their love for the Jews."

Little by little, the line inched forward, and Tevye finally stood under the red, white, and blue flag which hung over the door of the Consulate. After another few minutes, he was escorted into the lobby by an American soldier who motioned him to wait in the hallway.

"Maybe you know my daughter, Baylke?" Tevye asked. "She lives in New York."

The blond cadet looked at him blankly.

"You don't speak Russian, I guess," Tevye said. "What about Hebrew or Yiddish?"

"English," the soldier answered.

Tevye shrugged. The only word he knew in English was "dollar." Suddenly, at the end of the hallway, a group of Jews started screaming. Their hands waved excitedly through the air, as if they were throwing punches. A lean, spectacled gentleman appeared from the office behind them. He wore a three-piece suit, and a watch chain dangled from the pocket of his vest. With a dignified air, he escorted the shouting Jews along the corridor. Naturally, they were arguing about how to divide up the money they just had received. Their shouting continued all the way to the door. The stately Professor Glazebrook accompanied them down the hallway until he stood by Tevye.

"It is easier to raise one million dollars in America," he said, "than it is to distribute one thousand in *Eretz Yisrael.*"

Tevye was struck by the American's use of the original Hebrew name for the Land of Israel. *Eretz Yisrael* was the name used by Jews to express their great love and longing for their Biblical homeland, whereas the Roman-coined "Palestine" was for foreigners. Obviously, this kindhearted gentile felt deeply attached to the land. Courteously, he invited Tevye into his office. Two American soldiers stood by the door. The large room was filled with books, a presidential-sized desk, stately chairs, an American flag, and photographs framed on the wall. The famous iron safe stood in a corner. "Please have a seat," the Consul said in Hebrew.

Tevye sat down and glanced at the thick, leather-bound Bible on the Professor's orderly desk.

"I read a chapter of the Bible every morning," he said. "It gives me my strength for the day. Today I read the inspiring words of the prophet Ezekiel, guaranteeing that the outcast Jews would one day return to their land. How lucky we are to be living at this time in history when God's word is unfolding in front of our eyes."

His speech reminded Tevye of the lessons of Rabbi Kook.

"If your honor doesn't object to my saying - these days, the lucky person is the person who doesn't have to wait two hours on line."

"Yes, I apologize about that, but when has it ever been easy to be a Jew?"

Tevye nodded as if the man across the desk were Jewish himself, the way he sympathized with the children of the Bible.

"I would very much like to chat further with you, but as you mentioned, the line is long, and I really don't like to keep people waiting. Please tell me, what is your name and where are you from?"

"Tevye from Olat HaShachar."

"Ah, Tevye," the Consul said with a smile. "I have been waiting for you."

He stood up and walked toward the safe.

"I have nothing but respect for you pioneer builders of the land."

"The land is building us more than we are building it," Tevye philosophically answered.

"Very well said," the Professor responded.

He opened the safe, and after a brief search, he pulled out an envelope.

"This is a letter," he said. "In addition, your name is on my list to receive five hundred dollars in gold. Is that correct?"

"That's what my daughter wrote me."

"You have your papers with you, I presume."

"Certainly," Tevye said.

He handed the Consul his immigrant papers and received the letter in return. Inside the envelope was a large newspaper clipping, folded several times over. The first thing which caught Tevye's eye was a photograph of Padhatzur. Scanning over the Yiddish text quickly, Tevye understood that the article was about his son-in-law's success in the banking world of New York.

"Good news I trust," the Consul said, handing back Tevye's papers.

"Yes. Thank the good Lord."

With another warm smile, the Professor counted out five gold coins and set them in Tevye's hand.

"If you would like to change them into smaller coins, there is a currency exchange on the other side of the lobby. The black market rate may be higher on the street, I really don't know, and it isn't my job to offer financial advice, especially when it is against the law of our good friends, the Turks."

"May their rule be erased from the land," Tevye said.

"Precisely," Glazebrook agreed. "But, as I am sure you understand, there are certain things my position doesn't allow me to say."

"Thank you," Tevye said. He reached out and grasped the Consul's hand. "May the Lord bless you for helping us."

"My work is blessing enough. I feel very privileged to have been chosen for this great and holy task."

The Professor escorted Tevye back to the door and bowed in a respectful farewell. The Jewish farmer bowed back.

"If I can help you in the future, please let me know," the kind Consul added.

With his hand on the money in the pocket of his pants, Tevye made his way back to the door. Soldiers escorted him to the lobby as another Jew was led toward the Consul's office. Not wanting to chance being swindled in the black market, Tevye exchanged three of his gold coins in the building before venturing out to the street. Though evening was approaching, the line extended all of the way down the block. As Tevye passed, people rushed forward to ask him for money, as if he were the Baron Rothschild himself. True, a Jew was commanded to give a tenth of his earnings to charity, but charity began at home. Tevye had to take care of his daughters, plus Moishe and Hannei, and Guttmacher's two children, not to mention his own little boy. And his friends on the settlement needed money as well. Hurrying along, he brushed away the outstretched hands.

"The Lord have mercy," he thought. "May the British army soon come and chase the cursed Turks from the Land."

Suddenly, two men stepped forward and grabbed Tevye by the arms.

"Come with us," one said in an urgent whisper. His hand held Tevye's arm like a vise.

"What do you want from me?" Tevye asked in alarm. The men pushed him forward.

"We won't hurt you, don't worry."

Quickly, they herded Tevye into an alley.

"Thieves!" Tevye screamed out.

One of the assailants covered Tevye's mouth with his hand. The other shoved Tevye up against a wall.

"We aren't thieves," the larger man said.

If Tevye thought of fleeing, the sight of a revolver changed his mind.

"Have you ever heard of *Nili?* one asked

"No," Tevye answered.

"Never?"

"Never," Tevye said, sweating.

"Tell us the truth, grandfather. We're on your side."

Tevye shook his head no. The man holding the gun slipped it back into his jacket.

"We're with *Nili*," he said.

Tevye stared at them. He tried to keep a blank expression on his face, as if he didn't know what they were talking about.

"One of the passengers in the carriage you took to Jaffa told us about you. You told him you were on your way to Jerusalem to pick up some money."

"Me and my big mouth," Tevye thought. Golda had been right - if he hadn't bragged to her cousin, Menachem Mendel, about the money the rich ladies of Boiberik had given him for rescuing them in the woods, he would still have been a rich man today.

"We need money to continue the struggle against the Turks."

"I am a poor man," Tevye said.

"We are all poor men. The Turks have kept us that way. Now is our chance to topple their government and expel them from the Land."

One way or the other, God collects His tithes, Tevye thought. If he hadn't been so tight-fisted when he turned all of the beggars outside the Consulate away, these two rogues would never have been sent in his path. True, their cause was just, but how could he become a benefactor of *Nili?* He could be hanged by the Turks for collaborating with spies!

"Whatever you can afford will help our joint cause. Other people are risking their lives."

Tevye stared at their sincere eyes and their tense, serious expressions. When the Jews were at war, it was an obligation for every Jew to join in the battle. Tevye was too old to fight, but he could at least stand behind people younger and braver than himself. Was there a greater *mitzvah* than defending one's land against enemies? Hadn't Joshua, and King David, and Judah the Maccabee been soldiers? It wasn't enough to settle the Land of Israel and farm it, the Jews had to re-conquer it too.

Tevye reached his hand into his pocket and took out a gold coin.

"May God help you," he said, handing it over.

"You mean to say, may God help us. This is everyone's fight."

"Yes," Tevye said. "May God help us vanquish our enemies."

Both of the men doffed the tips of their caps, then scurried surreptitiously away down the alley. Fortunately, the way back to Olat HaShachar passed without further adventure. Two days later, Tevye thanked the good Lord as the roof of the hilltop synagogue appeared in the distance. Tired from jolting wagon rides, and a long six-hour walk at the end of his journey, Tevye was happy to be home. Jingling the coins in his pocket, he hurried toward his cottage, eager to recount the events of the journey with Carmel. Though the day was still young, the colony's fields were deserted of workers. A scarecrow in the tomato patch was cracked and bent over. Dozens of birds hopped between the vines, having an undisturbed picnic. Hollering, Tevye charged forward, frightening them away. The crows circled in the air and flocked down on the nearby blackberry patch. Tevye roared out a curse and charged the scavengers again. Hearing her husband, Carmel hurried out of the house, holding little Tzvi's hand. The boy broke away from his mother and ran along the path.

"*Abba, Abba!*" he called.

A big, hand-knitted *kippah* covered his head, and little *tzitzit* dangled down from under his shirt. Tevye scooped up the boy in his arms.

"Where is everyone?" Tevye asked his wife when she reached them.

"They're gone. My father, Munsho, Shilo. The Turks took them away to build roads in the south. Only Nachman, Hillel, and Shragi remain, along with the older Lovers of Zion."

"What about Shimon?"

"He disappeared."

"With his wife?"

"No. She's still here. But she hasn't heard a word from him since he left."

For all intents and purposes, the settlement was doomed. Tevye did his best to take the place of the draftees, and perform as many tasks as he could, but he could never keep up with the work. He milked the cows and looked after the chickens; he plowed new fields and planted new crops; he climbed up ladders to repair roofs and lofts; he picked clusters of grapes and taught the children to stomp them into grape juice and wine; he drove the wagon to neighboring settlements to gather vital supplies; and he put in a few hours of guard duty at night. The Turks had confiscated their rifles, so all Tevye had to defend the settlement from prowlers were his prayers and a rusted old pistol. Shragi continued to instruct the children in Mishna, while Nachman gave up his learning to work in the fields. Hillel became a chopper of wood, but because lumber was scarce, the Jews had to use the dung of their camels for fuel. The older children shared in the agricultural labor, but throughout most of the year, the brunt of the work fell on Tevye, Nachman, the older pioneers, and on those who had hid from the Turks. Carmel, Ruchel, and Hodel worked day and night in the fields, in the gardens, in the stables, and in their homes. On the Sabbath, there was barely a *minyan* of men to make up a service. After the Torah reading, Tevye added a prayer of his own that the British would soon rout the Turks and chase them out of the land.

Their petitions for JCA aid were rejected. Every settlement was suffering, and Olat HaShachar was considered a breakaway colony. Reinforcements finally arrived when the Jews of Tel Aviv and Jaffa were forced to abandon their homes. The Turks claimed that the evacuation order was meant to protect the Jews from a British invasion, but it was really another stage Jamal Pasha's goal of destroying the Jewish community in Palestine. Most of the refugees headed for the northern cities of Tiberias and Safed, and others were leaving the country for Syria, but Tevye managed to persuade a few religious families to take up residence in Olat HaShachar. One pious Jew, an acquaintance of Hevedke, reported that Tevye's son-in-law had moved to Hebron to continue his studies when the yeshiva in Jaffa had closed. Immediately, the new families joined in the work. Then, to everyone's joy, Ariel returned from the army with a dozen other young men from the colony. The JCA had succeeded in persuading the Turks to release Jewish soldiers from duty so that they could return to their agricultural work in the fields, not for the sake of the Jews, but to save the impoverished, starving country. With the supply of new manpower, Olat HaShachar was saved.

Chapter Forty-Two

TEVYE THE SPY

One night, several hours after Tevye had fallen asleep, he was awoken by an insistent pounding on the door. Lighting his bedside lantern, he hurried to see who was there.

"Who is it?" he asked, straightening the *yarmulka* on his head.

"Shimon," a harried voice whispered. "Open the door."

Quickly, Tevye slid the door latch aside. A gaunt, much leaner Shimon pushed his way into the house as if someone were chasing him. He was dressed in a Turkish army uniform. His beard had been trimmed. He stared at Tevye with gleaming eyes. Carmel tiptoed off behind the curtain where the children were sleeping.

"Lock the door," Shimon ordered.

He stood in the middle of the room, holding a rifle. A backpack was slung over his shoulder. His breathing came heavily, as if he had been running.

"Sit down," Tevye said.

"There isn't time."

Tevye didn't argue. He waited for the young settlement leader to talk.

"The Turkish army is searching for me. For the past year, I have been spying for *Nili*. I enlisted in the army so that I could have access to military secrets. Two weeks ago, one of our leaders was arrested. When he was tortured, he confessed everything he knew. Sarah Aaronson has committed suicide. Yosef Lishansky and others are on the run. Aaron Aaronson has gone underground. My name is also on the list. I came here to give my wife some money. Look after her, Tevye. Station guards to watch the settlement day and night. At the first sign of soldiers, any Jew who was in the Turkish army should flee. Let them dig caves to hide in. They should even sleep outside of their homes. Jamal Pasha, may his name he erased, has declared all Jews to be traitors. He wants to expel us all from the land. His soldiers have been raiding settlements, rounding up innocent people, just to break the resistance."

Shimon reached into his trousers and pulled out a gun.

"Take these," he said, handing both of his weapons to Tevye.

"What about you?" Tevye asked.

"I am going to Europe to arouse world opinion against this bloodthirsty regime. There's a boat waiting for me off the coast."

Shimon stepped forward and gave Tevye a hug.

"So long, comrade. May God be with us."

Then, as suddenly as he had arrived, Shimon was gone. Carmel pushed the curtain aside and stared at her husband.

"What are you going to do with those?" she asked, looking at the weapons.

"I'll hide them in the hayloft."

A moment later, gunshots sounded outside. Horses thundered through the colony. Quickly, Tevye glanced around the house, searching for a hiding place for the guns.

"Give them to me," Carmel said.

She took them and hurried to the kitchen. She pulled up the rug and the board covering the hole in the ground where she kept pots of food warm on Sabbath. Tevye hurried outside. Soldiers rode through the village, shouting out orders in German and Turkish.

"He got away!" a voice shouted.

"Go after him," the German commander ordered. "Take two of your men. The others are to get everybody out from the houses."

Knowing Yiddish, Tevye was able to understand the commands. With precision training, the German troops forced the frightened Jews out from their homes. Turkish soldiers searched through the houses. Settlers were beaten and made to stand in a line. Children screamed. Clutching her son in her arms, Carmel was shoved into a group with the women.

"Who lives in this house?" a soldier called out from Tevye's doorway.

For a moment, Tevye was silent. Then he stepped out of the line.

"I do," he said.

"Arrest him!" the soldier called out. "He's a spy! We found an army rifle in his house!"

Another soldier came out of the house, holding Shimon's rifle and gun. He strode over to the helmeted commander and held them up for his inspection.

"Arrest the traitor!" the German barked

A soldier grabbed Tevye and hurled him down to the ground.

"I'm not a spy!" Tevye protested.

The soldier kicked him in the back with his boot. Hillel jumped forward. Immediately, a soldier seized him from behind.

"Arrest that one too!" the commander ordered.

"He's lame, sir," the soldier responded.

"I don't care if he doesn't have legs. He's a Jew. For all I care, he can crawl on his belly to prison."

Ariel stood poised, ready to come to the aid of his friends. The few rifles the colony had were hidden under the tool shed. But he knew his chances were slim. He would have to fight off eight soldiers, not counting the handful that had ridden off toward the coast.

In a short time, all of the settlers had been rounded up in the yard of the colony. The commander rode his horse along the line, picking Jews out at random.

"You will be taken to prison and brought to trial as spies," he declared.

He jerked the reins of his horse and spurred it over towards the women.

"Who is the wife of Shimon Karmensky?" he asked.

After a long hesitation, Shimon's wife stepped forward. Her two young children clung to her night robe.

The commander swung down from his horse. He pulled a

riding crop out from his belt and slapped it sharply in his palm. His black leather boots crunched over the gravel.

"Was your husband here tonight?" he shouted.

When the woman didn't answer, the German struck one of her children on the neck with his crop.

"Yes, yes," she cried out, bending over her screaming young girl.

Tevye tried to rush forward, but a soldier dealt him a blow with a whip. Other Jews surged at the soldiers. The commander fired a pistol shot over their heads. Frightened by the warning, the settlers backed off.

"Tie up the prisoners!" the commander shouted. Then he turned back to Shimon's sobbing wife.

"What did he want?" he demanded.

"He gave me some money," she answered.

"Where is it?"

"Here."

She reached into her robe pocket and held out the money.

"Take it from her," the German commanded one of his soldiers, as if he didn't want to touch the hand of a Jew.

"What else did he want?"

"Nothing."

"WHAT ELSE DID HE SAY?"

"Nothing, your honor."

"DON'T LIE TO ME!" the monster yelled.

Shimon's wife trembled.

"You will all be punished for this!" the commander threatened. "Take her and her little rodents away! They are to be expelled from the country for treason."

Other women were afraid to protest, lest the decree fall on them as well. Soldiers pushed Shimon's wife and her children away from the yard. The prisoners were tied up together. Until dawn, they sat under guard. With the first morning light, a group of Bedouins rode into the colony, dragging a prisoner in tow. It was Shimon. His hands were tied up, and his captors pulled him along by a rope.

The commander of the soldiers would not have been happier if he had been offered a prize. Gladly, he agreed to pay the ransom which the Arabs demanded. After all, it was money he had stolen from the Jews.

"Well, well, look who we have found," he called out. "If it isn't Simon the spy. Too bad that your wife isn't here to greet you, but she is on her way to Egypt by now."

Shimon tugged on the rope, but soldiers surrounded him.

"Tie him up with the others," the commander ordered.

"What have they done?" Shimon demanded. "They are all innocent."

"We shall see. As you know, we have ways to make prisoners talk."

"Let them go!" Shimon shouted.

A soldier struck him with the butt of a gun. The once robust Jew crumbled like a sack to the ground. An hour later, the prisoners were led out of the colony. At least, Tevye thought, in Anatevka, he had the dignity to leave in a wagon. Here, in his homeland, he was being expelled from his village, tied hand and foot. Sadly, he took a long last look at his wife and his son. Would he ever see them again, he wondered? Would the good Lord grant him that blessing? As Hillel gazed good-bye at Hodel, he started to sing.

"No singing!" a guard yelled, dealing the minstrel a blow.

Hodel buried her face in her hands. Ruchel held her sister protectively and led her away.

"Why doesn't God help us?" Hodel asked.

"Don't worry," her sister comforted her. "He surely will."

Stumbling and tripping over the ropes which tied their legs together, the prisoners trekked off in the sand. At first they were despondent and silent, but then, being Jews, they started to speak.

"How does it feel to be harnessed and whipped like a mule?" Hillel asked Tevye.

The former milkman groaned. "Surely, it's my punishment for having whipped my devoted horse when he was too tired to make his way through the snow."

"It could be worse," another prisoner remarked.

"How so?" Tevye asked.

"They could have gagged us too. That's the worst punishment there is for a Jew."

"Yes, I suppose that's true," Tevye answered. "Though, you know, with my hands tied up, its very hard to talk as it is."

"Quiet!" a guard barked. His riding crop landed with a crack on Tevye's neck. "There is to be absolutely no speaking!"

So it was most of the journey. A few words here and there, and a whack on the back of the neck. Like slaves marched off to Babylon, the Jews trudged on, hanging their heads in silence. The only words the soldiers allowed were the monotonously droned, "right, left, right, left," which the prisoners chanted in unison to keep their steps in rhythm so they wouldn't trip over the ropes which tied their ankles together. Like dominoes, when one fell down, the others fell down too. Dust covered their bodies. Their cries for water were ignored. Instead, they were beaten and spit at by the soldiers. Prisoners fainted in the heat and had to be dragged by their comrades. Before the end of the day, blood oozed out of the rope burns on Tevye's ankles and wrists. Come evening, new guards were waiting on the roadside to replace their tired companions. The march continued into the night. The prisoners were given no rest, no time for prayer, no food. The only respite they had was a rare sip of water and the pleasure of cursing the soldiers in Yiddish. When their legs refused to carry them further, the guards pushed them into a ditch by the roadside where they slept in a tangled heap.

In the middle of the night, Tevye opened his eyes and stared up at the sparkling heavens. His comrades snored loudly around him. He tried to rise, but legs and bodies pinned him down where he lay.

"Guard," he called out. "I have to pee."

"So pee," the Turk answered. "What do you want from me?"

"Untie me, so that I can do my business in peace."

"Do your business where you are. Do you think you are in a hotel?"

Tevye sighed. Was he an animal that he had to relieve himself in his pants? His body shivered in the cool evening wind. Biting down on his lip, he tried to think about something else, to take his mind off his predicament. He remembered the article which his Baylke had sent him from a Yiddish newspaper in New York. Once again, her husband had become a rich man. Padhatzur, the banker. Padhatzur, the stock *maven*. Padhatzur, the theater owner. Padhatzur, the proprietor of fancy hotels. For his daughter's sake, Tevye was pleased. His Baylke deserved the best that life had to offer. True, her husband was a pompous ass of a man, but who was Tevye to question how the Almighty handed out fortunes. Some people got to pee in golden toilets, and others in their pants.

The prisoners continued their trek in the morning. Once again, new guards appeared to replace the old. With guffaws of laughter, they beat and spit at the Jews, as if they were enjoying a game. Most of the day, the soldiers led the "spies," as they called them, through valleys and fields, a good distance away from the road, so their cruel treatment of the Jews wouldn't attract attention. The guards forced the prisoners to crawl up hills on their hands and their knees, and they shoved them along the descents until they tumbled down the steep, rocky inclines like balls. Once again, the day passed with no food and only small sips of water. Tevye was filled with such rage, he would have ripped the savages apart with his hands if he could have broken through the knots in his shackles.

By evening, they reached the Turkish prison in Lod. Finally, the ropes were unfastened, but before they could express their relief, they were thrown into a pitch black dungeon. A heavy metal door clanged shut behind them. In the dark, a chorus of shouts echoed out around them as they tripped over prisoners who sat on the floor. Queries rang out in a *mishmosh* of languages. Tevye crawled over bodies until he found a vacant corner. He couldn't see a thing. An odor of feces and urine pervaded the cave. It was like he had been cast into hell.

"Are you Jewish?" he asked his invisible neighbor.

"Unfortunately," came the reply.

"Where is the bathroom?"

"You're in it."

"I don't believe it," Tevye said.

"What were you expecting? A suite for a king?"

"A little human decency, that's all."

"Amongst the Turks? Hell will freeze over first."

"How long have you been here?" Tevye inquired.

"Eight days. Nine. I don't remember."

"What were you arrested for?"

"I don't know. Every time I ask them, they give me another day in this *gehennah*."

Tevye sank into silence. The other new prisoners were all busy talking, trying to learn as much as they could about the ins and outs of the prison. Arab, French, and English voices yelled at the Jews to shut up. They were disturbing everyone's sleep. A guard banged on the dungeon door. Soon, all that could be heard was the buzzing of mosquitoes and flies.

"It doesn't pay to make the guards angry," Tevye's neighbor whispered. "If they put you in solitary confinement, there isn't even room to stand up. Save your strength and get whatever sleep you can. Keep your hands in your pockets so the rats won't eat your fingers. Tomorrow, if you are one of the lucky ones, they'll give you something to eat and let you walk in the yard. The food isn't kosher, so I just eat the fruit and the rice. We can thank God for that. So you see, the Almighty hasn't abandoned us completely."

True, Tevye thought. Why give up hope? Hadn't the Biblical Joseph risen to grandeur after having been dumped and forgotten in a prison? Who could unravel the mysteries of the Almighty? Hadn't He rescued Abraham from the fiery furnace, and Daniel from the lion's den? Not that Tevye could measure up to their righteous deeds, but getting him out of this miserable dungeon wouldn't have to be such a great miracle. After all, he was innocent. Just as God had helped his father's namesake, the famous rabbi, the *Baal HaTanya*, get out of prison in Russia, God would help Tevye, the son of Schneur Zalman, get out of prison in Lod.

In the morning, Tevye woke up to find himself surrounded by a motley assortment of political prisoners and thieves. There was hardly room in the dungeon cave to stand up. Noah's ark could not have been more overcrowded. Inching their way past other prisoners, the new arrivals squeezed into a corner where the Jews were gathered into a self-fashioned ghetto. The metal door opened and loaves of black bread were tossed inside, along with a large jug of water. The prisoners who hadn't leaked in their pants during the night, took care of their needs over a grated hole by a wall. A small window up by the ceiling let in a few rays of light. Not only didn't the Jews have their *tefillin* and prayer shawls, the stench of the place made *davening* impossible. When breakfast was finished, the dungeon door opened, and Shimon was summoned outside.

A short while later, his screams could be heard echoing down the corridors of the dungeon. They came at intervals, wild, animal-like cries which chilled Tevye's body. Other longtime prisoners continued on with their card games, as if they didn't hear anything at all. But Tevye was aghast. Finally, he couldn't stand the wails any longer. He shoved his way to the door of the dungeon and screamed at the top of his lungs.

"STOP IT! STOP IT! STOP TORTURING HIM!" Tevye shouted, pounding the thick metal door with his fists.

"Save your strength," his friend from the previous night advised him. "There is nothing you can do. Just pretend you don't hear it."

"Pretend I don't hear it?" Tevye responded.

"You don't have a choice. Anyway, after a while it stops."

"He's right," another prisoner said. "The bastards make sure we can hear it in order to break our resistance. They want us to confess whether we did something illegal or not."

"It's monstrous," Tevye said. "They treat us like animals."

"What else is new?" another gaunt figure injected. The look in his eyes said that he too had been tortured. "The only way it will change is when we are the jail keepers and the Turks are the ones who have to sit in this dungeon."

Tevye knew he was right. Finally, all of the speeches of Ben Zion and Perchik, Rabbi Kook, Zeev from the worker's union, and Shimon, clicked into place. Each had their own style, but their message had one thing in common. The Jewish people had to be free. They had to have their own land. It took a trip to the dungeon for Tevye to realize that only when the Land of Israel was theirs could a Jew hold his head high and live like a normal human being.

Shimon's shouts ceased. An eerie silence remained. A feeling of tension gripped the prisoners in the dungeon as they waited for Shimon's return. When he wasn't brought back, even the most hardened criminals fell into a sullen depression. Finally, the cell door swung open.

"The Jew, Tevye!" the guard shouted.

Tevye approached the door of the dungeon with a dry gulp in his throat. His hands were fastened together, and soldiers pushed him along a long prison corridor. Momentarily, they stopped at an open cell door. Glancing inside, Tevye saw Shimon's body hanging limply from the ceiling. A shudder swept through Tevye's limbs. Shimon hung strangled by a noose, his neck broken, bruises covering his face and his arms, his feet dangling off the ground.

The soldiers shoved Tevye forward. They pushed him into a room. The prison magistrate sat at a desk. He wore the uniform of a high-ranking soldier. A man dressed in a smart business suit sat a short distance away. The guards who had escorted Tevye from the dungeon remained at the door.

"Sit down," the magistrate said.

Tevye sat down in the chair on the other side of the desk.

"This is Mr. Barnaby, your lawyer," the magistrate said.

Tevye glanced over at the cold, gentile face. "I'll get more help from the devil," he thought.

The magistrate opened a file.

"At the beginning of this year, you took a carriage ride to Jaffa with a Jew named Novisky of the Jewish Colony Association, is that right?" he began.

Tevye paused before answering. His attorney was staring down at a pad in his lap. The magistrate tapped a ringed finger on the desk, waiting for a reply.

"I didn't take a carriage ride, as your honor infers," Tevye answered. "I was walking along the road and the carriage stopped to give me a lift."

"Is it your experience that carriages carrying Jewish Colony Association officials stop to give poor farmers like you a ride? Of course not," he said without giving Tevye a chance to respond. "The rendezvous was obviously planned."

"That isn't true," Tevye said, facing the lawyer. Dutifully, as if for appearances sake, the well-dressed attorney wrote in his pad.

"And isn't it true you spoke about secret underground plans to assist the British in invading Turkish-ruled Palestine?"

"I was only a passenger. I didn't pay attention to the conversation. Most of the time I slept."

"Are you pretending not to have known that Novisky was a top *Nili* agent?"

"I don't even know which of the men was Novisky. I had never met them before, and I have never met them since."

"That's a standard operating procedure between spies," the magistrate told the lawyer.

Tevye tried to concentrate on the discussion, but an image of Shimon dangling from the ceiling kept distracting his mind.

"And isn't it furthermore true that in Jerusalem, just a day or two later, you transferred money from Novisky to another *Nili* agent?"

"I may have given charity. A Jew is commanded to give alms."

"You didn't know he was a spy?" his lawyer asked.

"Certainly not," Tevye answered, lying for the sake of his family.

"I should inform you that he told us all about your meeting," the magistrate disclosed.

Tevye didn't answer. Strangely, he wasn't afraid. Maybe

because he was tired. Maybe because he was mad. Maybe because he had been treated worse than a dog, and that they couldn't do anything worse than kill him, and that had to be better than going back to the dungeon.

"Tell me," the magistrate asked. "If you didn't get money from Novisky, where does a poor Jewish farmer have the funds to be such a gracious giver of charity."

"I received money from my daughter in America and that is the reason I went to Jerusalem. You can confirm that I am not lying by asking at the American consulate."

"I am afraid we can't do that," the lawyer remarked. "When the United States entered the war on the side of the British, the consul and his staff were forced to flee from the country."

"They weren't forced to flee - they were legally expelled," the magistrate corrected. "But that is not relevant to our discussion. What interests me the most is how you managed to have in your house an arsenal of weapons?"

"I believe only a rifle and a pistol were found. They were used in the defense of our settlement."

"Defense against whom?"

"Marauders."

"A likely story," the magistrate said to the lawyer. "I suppose that all Jewish settlers have rifles issued by the Turkish army."

"I bought the rifle in the market in Jaffa. I don't know to whom it originally belonged."

"To your friend, the spy, Shimon Kaminsky, perhaps?"

"If he was a spy, I didn't know."

"He was hung as a spy and a traitor. We have his confession. Furthermore, he admitted that he gave you his guns."

"I'd like to see his confession," Tevye said to the lawyer, not believing that Shimon, even under the most horrible torture, would have incriminated a fellow Jew.

"It's his right," the lawyer reminded the magistrate.

"A prisoner's confession is a secret matter of state."

"If this is a trial, the defendant has the right to see the evidence against him, the lawyer countered.

"This isn't a trial. It is an investigation," the magistrate declared. "And in an investigation, when lawyers aren't present, we have ways of making prisoners tell the truth."

Then, as if he were frustrated, he stood up from his desk.

"That's all for now," he concluded. "Think things over in your cell for a while, and we shall meet once again."

The guards stepped over to Tevye as he stood up from his chair. The lawyer followed Tevye out of the room.

"One minute," he said to the soldiers. "I want a few words with my client alone."

Obediently, the soldiers walked a few paces away.

"If the magistrate demands a trial, I will request conducting it in Damascus. You will have a better chance there."

"What do you care?" Tevye asked. For a second, he gazed deeply into the other man's eyes.

"I believe that you're innocent," he said. "My powers are limited, but there are certain things I can do."

Tevye nodded his head. He wanted to say thank you, but the words wouldn't come out. Down the corridor, in the open cell, Shimon was still hanging by a rope for other prisoners to see.

"Why didn't my friend have a lawyer?" Tevye asked.

"He did. I was his lawyer. Maybe that is why I want to help you."

Impatiently, the soldiers stepped over and gave Tevye a push. Back in the dungeon, he sank down to the floor by the door. Hillel pushed his way through the overcrowded cell to ask his friend a battery of questions.

"What did they ask you? What did they do to you? Did you see Shimon?" he asked.

"They hung Shimon," Tevye answered.

"They hung him?" Hillel repeated with a gulp.

"Yes," Tevye said. "May his murderers be avenged."

A short time later, Hillel's name was called out with the other Olat HaShachar settlers. They were being released. Only Tevye had to remain in the dungeon.

"Tell my wife that I'm fine," Tevye said to his son-in-law and friend. "And if anything happens to me, look after my boy."

Hillel nodded. For a moment, he couldn't find words.

"Don't worry," he finally answered. "We'll get you out of here. I promise."

"You and the *Mashiach*," Tevye answered. "May his coming be soon."

"Remember," Hillel said. "Even if a sword is resting on a man's neck, it's forbidden for him to despair."

Tevye nodded. Hillel was right. "I can't give up now," he told himself. He had a family to care for, and a volcanic rage in his heart to revenge Shimon's murder. It wasn't enough anymore for a Jew to be just a good husband and father. If a Jew wanted freedom, he had to be willing to fight.

After his friends embraced him and wished him goodbye, there were still other Jews in the dungeon to keep Tevye company. Tevye could find solace in that - until that luxury was taken away from him also. Once again, the iron door opened and his name was called out. This time he was led to a low door down the corridor which resembled the door of an oven.

"The magistrate wants you to think a little more about your answers," a guard said with a smile.

Grabbing Tevye's shoulder, he forced him to his knees.

"Inside, you piece of Jewish filth!" he commanded. "Now!"

A boot kicked Tevye hard in the rear. Crawling on all fours like a rat, Tevye lowered his head and entered the dark hole. The compartment was no more than the length of a body. A crack of air space under the door was the only ventilation. When he tried to stand up, he hit his head on the ceiling. A prisoner could either stand doubled over, sit, or lie curled like a dog. The cell was pitch black and reeking of urine.

"It could be worse," Tevye said, though there was no one to listen. "I could be dead, and as they say, there's no way to do *mitzvahs* and good deeds in the grave. True, this hole is no bigger than a coffin, but at least I'm still breathing. A man can thank God for that."

After some hours, a thirst seized his throat. His mouth was parched and dry. He yelled out for water, but his cries were ignored. Why had he broken his vow not to drink hard liquor? The sips of vodka he had snuck were undoubtedly the very same sips denied to him now.

Having nothing better to do, Tevye started singing. He sang a Yiddish tune, then a Psalm, then he switched into a medley of whistling. A guard yelled at him to be quiet, but Tevye ignored him. What more could they do to him? True, there was physical torture, but he preferred not to think about that. Hadn't Rabbi Akiva sanctified God's Name as the Romans flayed at his flesh with hot iron combs? As his soul left his body, the noble Sage cried out, *"Shema Yisrael,"* clinging to his faith in God. So Tevye kept singing. His jailers could imprison his body, but not his spirit and soul.

Thankfully, he knew a lot of songs. Hours passed in solitary confinement. A rat crawled over his legs and he smashed at it with his shoes.

"Don't despair, Tevye," he said. "Don't give up. Don't let them break your spirit. Be a *mensch*. Be a man. Remember what Hillel said. Even if a sword is poised on your neck, don't lose faith. Everything that God does is good. One day the *Mashiach* will come, or the British, or somebody else, and God will take His revenge on the Turks for the oppression of His people.

A clanging on the tile door woke him. He couldn't tell how long he had slept. The cell door opened, and a guard ordered him to exit. He crawled out backwards on his hands and knees.

"Stand up!" the guard ordered.

After being in pitch blackness, even the dim light of the prison corridor was blinding. Tevye braced a hand on the floor, but he could hardly move. His back felt rigid. His spine had locked into place.

"Stand up you swine!" the guard shouted, kicking his prisoner in the kidneys.

Groaning, Tevye raised himself to his feet. He stood bent over like a hunchback. Out of the corner of his eye, he saw that there

were two soldiers guarding him. With a supreme effort, he might
have been able to overcome one, but the second would have shot
him for sure. He would just have to be patient and wait for his
chance to escape. Once again, his hands were fastened, and he was
dragged along the corridor like a cow.

"Where are you taking me?" he asked.

"To the opera, where else?" one of the soldiers quipped.

His comrade laughed. They led Tevye past the magistrate's
office and up a flight of winding stone stairs. To his amazement,
they dragged him outside. His back straightened, as if from the
fresh air which filled up his lungs. A crowd of other prisoners was
standing in the yard. The guards shoved Tevye forward. Another
Jew caught him, preventing him from falling on his face.

"Where are they taking us?" Tevye asked.

"To Syria," the prisoner answered." "For trial."

"Why to Syria?"

"To have an excuse to ship us out of the country."

"We'll come back," Tevye said. "Just as God led the children
of Israel out of bondage in Egypt and brought them back to the
Land of Israel, we shall return here too."

For the first time in days, he felt like a human being again.
True, his hands were still tied and he needed a bath, but compared
to his state in the solitary cell, he was free. In his gratefulness, he
remembered that there was even a blessing for being set free from
prison. He pronounced the words loudly for everyone to hear.

"What's your hurry?" another Jew asked. "We are not out of
the lion's den yet."

"God is with us," Tevye assured him.

"Sure he is," a cynic observed. "He sent this squad of Turkish
soldiers to protect us, don't you see?"

To make a long story short, the prisoners were marched off to
the train station and loaded like livestock into a windowless train
car. Once again, doors slammed shut behind them. With no food
or water, they sat in blackness, waiting hours for the ride to begin.
Prisoners fainted in the stifling heat. Tevye grew discouraged.
They had simply changed one hell for another. Every bone in his

body seemed to ache. Finally, the train's whistle blew. Beneath them, the floor rumbled and wheels moved along the tracks. But hardly a trickle of air entered the tightly-sealed cabin. It wasn't long before Tevye felt nauseous. The jolts of the journey knocked everyone off balance. Prisoners lay piled upon one another like bundles of hay. There was no place to move. After hours of traveling, someone broke out in a sweat.

"He's got the fever!" a voice cried out in the dark.

Prisoners panicked. Hands and feet banged on the walls of the car.

"We'll all drop dead in this grave," someone said.

"Be calm!" someone else shouted. "Panic won't help. At the snail's rate that this train is traveling, we could be locked in this compartment for days."

That information only heightened the claustrophobia in the car. A heavy, foul-smelling body fell over Tevye. The man had fainted. Gasping, Tevye felt a sharp pain seize his heart.

"*Oy vay,*" he groaned, feeling his end to be near. He stared up at the ceiling of the train car. "At least, dear God, grant me a more noble end than being squashed to death by a Jew in this hell."

The pain in his chest spread through all of his body. He felt like his lungs would explode.

"Well, at least there's a *minyan* here to say *Kaddish* over me," he thought as his soul began to soar out of his body. Suddenly, the brakes of the train let out a painful groan. Screeching like the wheels on the tracks, Tevye's soul returned to his body. He realized that he was still breathing. The train whistle blared. A horn blasted out a panicked warning. The roar of the brakes filled the cabin. Underneath the floorboard, the steel of the wheels grinded to a spark-filled halt on the tracks.

Outside, up ahead of the train's locomotive, a herd of bleating sheep were crossing the tracks. Arab shepherds on horseback were trying to urge the animals out of the way. The engineer of the train stuck his head out of the door to yell at the shepherds. But he never finished his curse. A hand reached out and grabbed him, and hurled him out of the car. The startled engineer landed with a thud and rolled clown the embankment alongside the tracks. The Turkish soldier who was riding in the locomotive beside him never had a chance to fire a shot. A red-bandannaed Arab on horseback shot him as he raised up his gun. Other Arabs rode along the passenger cabins, shooting at the soldiers on board. Guards were tossed to the ground. Others threw down their rifles and surrendered. The latch of the prisoner cabin was opened and the door slid aside. Tevye raised up his head, but the sunlight was blinding. Squinting, he made out an Arab rider on horseback.

"*Yalla!*" their rescuer shouted in Hebrew. "Everyone out of the train!"

Feeling air fill his lungs and a renewed burst of life, Tevye squeezed away from the prisoner who had fainted over his chest. He sat up and stared out of the cabin. Blinking, he made out a *kefiah*, a bullet belt, and the white gown of a Bedouin tribesman. The Arab had a thin moustache and strangely familiar eyes. To Tevye's surprise, he realized that their savior wasn't an Arab at all. It was Perchik, his former son-in-law!

"Tevye!" he called out in recognition.

"Perchik!" Tevye exclaimed.

Tevye was actually happy to see him! He may have been a no-good adulterer in the past, but today he had saved Tevye's life.

May the Lord bless you and guard over you," Tevye declared.

"I don't need your Lord's blessings," Perchik characteristically responded. "If I knew that you were one of the prisoners. I wouldn't have ordered my men to ambush the train."

Tevye smiled. His son-in-law hadn't changed. Toward the front of the train, other Hebrew-speaking shepherds rounded up the Turkish soldiers at gunpoint and sat them, hands in the air, on the ground. All of their Arabs saviors were Jews.

Perchik called to some men to come help the prisoners down from the train car. Obviously, he was their leader. Then he rode back along the tracks to give orders. The captured Turks were paraded off into the woods. Other Jews searched through the train. The sheep were cleared from the tracks, and the liberated prisoners were gathered into the shade of a nearby olive grove. A wagon was driven up to the locomotive and sticks of dynamite were planted under its wheels. Within minutes, a gigantic explosion rocked the earth. The locomotive burst into pieces. One-by-one, the cars of the train toppled over and fell off of the tracks. As a cloud of smoke and dust settled over the area, Tevye cheered with the rest of the prisoners. Lo and behold! A little shepherd boy had toppled Goliath! The Philistines had fallen, and the star of David was on the rise!

Chapter Forty-Three

THE HEBREW BRIGADE

As always, Perchik's eyes shone when he spoke. By the light of a campfire, he explained the events which had led up to the successful assault on the train. His new wife, Libby, handed Tevye a cup of hot coffee. She wore a bullet belt across her chest and a kerchief tied round her neck like the other fighters in Perchik's troop.

"Like they have been doing to every Jewish settlement, the Turks have nearly wiped out Shoshana," Perchik told Tevye. "We simply couldn't go on with their taxes, their thievery, and their raids. Like always, our people were divided in how to react. The *HaShomer* group, to which I belonged, fostered a policy of acquiescence to the Turkish demands. They were adamantly opposed to *Nili*, fearing reprisals against the kibbutz. They wanted to continue on with the work of settling the land without being drawn into the war. Surprising as it may seem to you, I spoke out against their neutralist stand. We all aspire toward peace, but first the Jews have to have their own State. If the Turks rule over us, they can always raid our settlements whenever they please. Just like in Russia."

Tevye nodded. A change had transpired in Perchik. He spoke more like the bellicose Ben Zion than the pacifist he used to be. Unabashed, Libby sat with the men, a rifle resting across her lap. The other freed prisoners listened in silence.

"Yosef Lishansky from Zichron Yaacov was a top *Nili* spy. When he was arrested by the Turks, he confessed, and to get even with *HaShomer*, he incriminated the movement for planning a revolt against the Turkish regime. In a raid on Shoshana, a lot of my friends were arrested. Luckily, I escaped. We received an emergency message that a train out of Lod would be carrying prisoners to Syria. That's why we set up the ambush. But instead of finding my comrades, we found you."

"God works in many strange ways," Tevye said, thinking that it was probably Hillel who had sent out the emergency rescue call.

"What does God have to do with this?" Libby retorted. "We were the ones who blew up the train. If not for us, you would have been out of the country by now on the way to face a Turkish firing squad."

Tevye smiled at the young woman. If Perchik had grown wiser with years, his wife certainly hadn't. But Tevye didn't want to get into a religious debate. If a person came with serious questions and a sincere desire to learn about faith, that was one thing, but to convince a person who wasn't ready to listen, that was like smashing one's head into a wall.

"I remember Lishansky," Tevye said, "from the time when I was in Zichron. He is a compassionate, dedicated man."

"If he was, he isn't anymore," Perchik said. "The Turks hung him in Damascus."

"Blessed be the true Judge," Tevye said. "If not for the grace of God and your bravery, we all might have shared the same fate."

Libby asked Tevye what he had done to have been imprisoned with the others. Briefly, Tevye told her the story.

"How is my son?" Perchik asked.

"Fine, thank God," Tevye answered. "He's a strong little lad."

"And Hodel?"

She's living with us on the *yishuv* in Olat HaShachar."

"Has she remarried?" Perchik asked.

"Are you still interested?" Libby wanted to know.

"Yes," Perchik said. "She shared a part of my life. She's the mother of one of my children. I wish her the best."

"Well," said his new wife in a huff, "I will let you two reminisce by yourselves over the good old days in Anatevka."

The fiery young woman stood up and walked off with her rifle. Perchik laughed good-naturedly.

"Hodel has married the accordion player, Hillel," Tevye informed him.

Perchik absorbed the news and nodded. *"Mazal tov,"* he said. "I am glad. Of course I was angry with Hodel at first, but personal disappointments pale in the enormity of the problems and challenges we face as a nation."

"I agree," Tevye said.

"Then perhaps you would like to join us. We are recruiting soldiers for a Hebrew Brigade."

"A Hebrew Brigade?" Tevye asked.

"That's right. It's time we had an army of our own."

In the light of the fire, Tevye's eyes seemed to glow. Those were words that he wanted to hear. The image of Shimon flashed through his mind. The passionate idealist would have rushed to volunteer.

"I am not so young anymore," Tevye said. "But I can ride a horse and shoot. I would be proud to be a part of your army."

"Our army," Perchik corrected.

The younger man held out his hand. Tevye grasped it firmly. It was a pact for the future, and a truce over the past. The two men had had their differences, and their quarrels had even come to blows, but now they were united by something much greater than their own private lives. They were bonded together by the most noble cause, the struggle of a people for its land.

Immediately, several prisoners volunteered to join the armed struggle. Others, in the morning, set off for their homes. The remainder headed for the country's borders, to follow after their families who had already been expelled. As for Tevye, he wanted to see his family before setting off to war. Perchik agreed to accompany him to Olat HaShachar in order to see his son. Insulted, Libby mounted her horse and rode off toward Shoshana, where she was to wait for further orders.

On the way, Perchik explained that the Hebrew Brigade was still in its diapers. The ambush of the train was their first major military action, and it was certain to bring a new wave of persecution by the Turks. He, and people whom he didn't want to name, had been traveling from settlement to settlement to sign up recruits. In many places, they had found fear, despair, and the same helpless attitude which characterized the Jews in Russia and Europe, but here and there, they had found a valorous soul prepared to fight for his freedom. A secret meeting of over two hundred people had been held near Tel Aviv. There, they had decided that a fighting force would be formed to participate in the liberation of the land from the Turks. The brigade would be Jewish, open to Jews from all over the world. Only Hebrew would be spoken, and they would carry the new Jewish flag with the Star of David emblem. Training had already started on the outskirts of Jerusalem, and they were waiting to hear from British forces in Egypt how they could play a part in the long-awaited allied advance into Palestine.

Perchik warned that Turkish soldiers might be in the area searching for Tevye and the ambushers of the train, so before riding into Olat HaShachar they changed into the garb of Arab herdsmen. Perchik's soldiers camped a distance away in the sand dunes. After sunset, Tevye led the way into the colony. Ariel was on watch duty. Sighting the Arabs, he fired a warning shot in the air. Tevye called to him, and his wife's brother galloped over to meet them. Hearing the gunshot, settlers gathered in the main yard of the colony to learn what had happened. Carmel ran forward to embrace her husband when she heard who the visitors were. Tevye's son jumped into his arms.

"Look, *Ema*, *Abba* is an Arab!" he said.

Everyone laughed except Hodel. Her smile turned to stone when she recognized the man accompanying her father.

"Shalom, Hodel," Perchik said, removing his *kefiah*. "How is Ben Zion?"

For a moment, she couldn't find words. She glanced at her father for an explanation, but he was happily embracing his son. Hillel hurried over to hug Tevye and welcome him home. Seeing Perchik, he kept his distance while his wife's former husband spoke with her.

"He's fine," she said, still shocked by Perchik's sudden appearance.

"Can I see him?" he asked.

"He's sleeping."

"I've come a long way."

Hodel stared at her former husband, the man who had swept her out of her home in Anatevka with a promise of transforming the world. She was happy with her new husband, Hillel, but facing Perchik, she felt an old dizziness swirl in her head.

Seeing them together, Tevye strode over and put his arm around Perchik.

"Here's the hero who saved me!" he heartily said. "A *landsman* from the old country. General Perchik by name. What are you waiting for? Come, I have something to show you."

He began to lead Perchik away. With his other arm, he pulled Hillel close to him.

"I'll explain in a minute," he said. "In the meantime, call everyone to a general meeting in an hour. Then bring Ruchel and Nachman to my house. And you and Hodel, of course."

Tevye gave Hillel a gentle push and sent him on his mission. Then he led Perchik to the house of his daughter. The child was sleeping inside. Perchik stood gazing at the boy with a fatherly smile. Tevye sat on the bed and gently shook the boy's shoulders until he woke up.

"Ben Zion, wake up. Wake up. Look who's here."

The lad sat up in bed and grinned ear to ear when he saw his grandfather.

"*Saba!*" he greeted. "You're back!"

"Of course I'm back. How could I stay away from my grandson so long? But look who I brought with me. Your *Abba*."

The boy stared at the man who had become a stranger to him. A look of confusion spread over his face. Perchik set down his rifle and lifted the Arab caftan off his head. Smiling at the child, he held out his hands. Tevye gave the hesitant child a nudge.

"Your *Abba* is a brave Jewish soldier. He is fighting against our enemies in the war. That's why he can't be with you more often."

Ben Zion grinned. "*Abba*!" he exclaimed. "I knew you didn't forget me."

The boy jumped out of bed and ran to his father. He jumped into Perchik's outstretched arms.

"Forget you? How could I forget you? I love you so very much."

Happily, the boy clung to his father. Tears welled in Perchik's eyes. Tevye also felt misty. There were many great treasures and dreams in the world, but nothing could compare to embracing one's son. It was reassuring to know that even a communist like Perchik had a human heart too.

"You don't have a *kippah* on your head, *Abba*," the boy noted at once.

"That's right," Perchik said, feeling his skull. "I was wearing a *kefiah* instead."

"Why are you dressed like Arabs?"

"So Turkish soldiers don't know that we're Jews," Tevye explained.

Letting father and son be alone, Tevye withdrew from the house. Who could tell? Tevye hadn't been able to make a *Yid* out of Perchik. Maybe the little boy would.

Ariel stood on guard outside of the house.

"Since the arrests, people here have been afraid to talk with one another," he said. "Everyone thinks that their neighbor may be a spy for the Turks, and that they could be arrested for speaking with him. The Turks made raids on Zichron Yaacov and Rishon LeZion. Dozens have been jailed. Wives and children have been sent out of the country. Work on the settlements has stopped. The Jewish neighborhoods of Jaffa are like ghost towns. Jamal Pasha has promised that if the British conquer the land, there will be no Jews in the country to greet them. If we don't do something now, the whole Jewish settlement here will be ruined."

"Find someone to replace you on guard duty, and come to my house," Tevye said.

The family was waiting when Tevye arrived. Moishe and Hannei jumped out from behind the door in an ambush. With

Tzvi's help, they wrestled him down to the floor. The aroma of hot food filled Tevye's nostrils. It seemed like he hadn't eaten a real meal for weeks. After playing with the children, he sat down at the table.

"This is a meal of thanksgiving," he proclaimed, "Thanksgiving to God for saving me from danger and for bringing me back to my family."

Everyone listened in silence as Tevye related his prison adventure and rescue. When Perchik arrived with his son, Tevye stood up and brought him to the table where Carmel had already set out a plate for the guest. Hillel and Hodel stepped away to the rear of the room. Tevye called for some vodka, but because of the war situation, there wasn't a bottle to be found, so the men had to settle for wine. Except for Tevye. True to his vow, he contented himself with a whiff and passed the bottle over to Nachman.

"We have another reason to celebrate," the young rabbi declared. "Have you heard the good news?"

"Good news?" Tevye inquired.

"The English Parliament in London is debating a resolution which states that the Land of Israel belongs to the Jews!"

"Can it be?" Tevye wondered.

He looked at Perchik to see his reaction, but his expression was uncharacteristically noncommittal.

"If it passes the Parliament, we can thank Rabbi Kook," Nachman claimed.

"Rabbi Kook?" Tevye asked, not understanding what the connection could be between the renowned Rabbi of Jaffa and the British House of Lords.

With his usual enthusiasm, Nachman proceeded to explain. After having been stranded in Europe at the outbreak of the war, Rabbi Kook accepted an offer to preside temporarily over an orthodox congregation in London. Because he had been born in Russia, he was allowed to enter England as an ally. Thus when the issue of Palestine arose in the Parliament, British legislators turned to Rabbi Kook to learn how religious Jews felt about Zionism and the growing demands for a Jewish State. Dr. Chaim

Weizmann was leading the political struggle. He had found a sympathetic ear in the British Foreign Secretary, Lord Balfour. A lover of the Bible, Balfour called the Jews, "the people of the Book."

"Not only did God arranged for Rabbi Kook to be in England at this crucial time," Nachman said with shining eyes, "but listen to this...."

In one of the great "coincidences" of history, all arranged by the incognito orchestration of God, the very same Dr. Weizmann, a noted chemist by trade, had provided the British army with a new way of making ammunition, by producing a synthetic cordite to replace the acetone which had been imported from Germany before the war. When the Minister of Ammunition, David Lord George, asked him how the Government of England could express its gratitude, the Zionist leader had said, "If you win the war, give Palestine to the Jews." The righteous gentile had readily agreed, but when it came time to convince his associates, he met heated opposition, especially amongst the assimilated Jews of Parliament who maintained that claims of Jewish nationality and a Jewish homeland had nothing to do with the Jewish religion. They insisted that the Jews of England were Englishmen, and opposed the idea of a Jewish national homeland. After a month-long debate, a letter from Rabbi Kook strongly supporting the Zionist platform was read. The land of the Bible and the people of the Bible were indivisible, he claimed. The nations of the world had perpetuated a horrible injustice by ousting the Children of Israel from their land, and they must atone for their enormous sin, Rabbi Kook wrote, by assisting the Jews to return to their homeland.

After Rabbi Kook's letter was read, the Speaker of the Parliament stood up and asked, "Whose viewpoint should we rely upon for the true religious aspect of this issue? Upon Lord Montague and the Jewish assimilationists among us, or upon the revered Rabbi Kook?"

"*Nu?*" Tevye asked, expressing the question in everyone's mind. "What happened?"

"I don't know," Nachman answered. "To the best of my knowledge, the matter has not reached a vote."

"The English have other things to worry about, more pressing than the Jewish problem," Perchik commented.

"It's a promising development, you have to admit," Tevye answered.

"What's most important," Perchik began, "is not what the Parliament of England decides, but what we Jews do here in Israel. First, this war has to be won. Right now, the Turks are in charge here, not the British. We have to do what we can to bring their rule to an end."

Everyone in the room turned their attention to Perchik.

"I have other reasons for coming here besides visiting my son," he continued. "A Hebrew fighting brigade has being organized to fight against the Turks. Several divisions have already been training with the British in Egypt. Since we are already in the country, we can do things that a foreign force can't. I have received information that General Allenby is considering a blitz campaign from the south, but he needs our forces to open the doors for him. Tevye has already agreed to join us, and I am looking for other volunteers."

All eyes focused on Tevye. Especially Carmel's. Tevye averted her gaze. A woman's look could be dangerous, and he didn't want to be dissuaded from joining the fight.

"You can count me in," Ariel said.

"Me too," Hillel added.

Both Perchik and Tevye glanced skeptically at the lame musician.

"If you can't use me as a fighter, I can entertain the troops," he said, reading their thoughts.

"I am also ready to join," Nachman asserted.

His desire to volunteer did not stem from pressure to be like everyone else, but out of a true yearning to play an active part in the struggle. When it came to the great *mitzvah* of conquering the Land of Israel, no able-bodied man was free to run away from the battle.

"I am sure there are many other settlers who will also volunteer," Tevye said. "I have already called for a general meeting."

"These matters are best approached one on one," Perchik advised. "I suggest you make a list of the most suitable candidates and speak to them privately in their homes."

Perchik and Tevye agreed that they would rendezvous in a week in the Motza Valley on the outskirts of Jerusalem. Then Perchik led his son outside. Hillel nodded at his wife that it was all right for her to follow them.

"Your *Abba* has to leave you to go fight in the war," Perchik told the boy.

"Are you a soldier. *Abba?*" the child asked.

"Yes, Ben Zion, a Jewish soldier."

"I want to be a soldier too."

"I hope you won't have to be. That's why I am going to fight. So that you can grow up in peace."

Hodel came over and stood a short distance away. Ben Zion ran over to his mother.

"*Abba's* a soldier," he said.

"I know. You should be a very proud boy. Now say good night to your father and hurry into the house. And don't forget to say *Shema Yisrael.*"

"I said it already," the child protested.

"Say it again."

She kissed him and sent him off on his way. He stopped and reached up to give Perchik a kiss.

"Good night, *Abba*," he said.

"Good night, son."

Perchik kissed the boy a final goodbye. Then Ben Zion stuck his thumb in his mouth and walked sleepily off to the house.

"He's like little man already," Perchik observed.

"Yes," Hodel answered.

"Well, I see that you've found what you wanted."

"Yes, I suppose that I have."

"Are you happy?"

"Yes, I am. And what about you?"

"It is hard to be happy in these troubled times. But if you mean with my wife, yes, we get along fine. She is also a soldier in our fighting brigade."

"Do you have any children?"

"Twins. Two little girls."

"*Mazal tov*," Hodel said. "Are they soldiers too?"

"Not yet," Perchik answered with a smile.

"Do you have to take Hillel?" she asked.

"He volunteered."

"How can he help? You know that he's lame."

"Like he said – his music can help boost the morale of the troops."

"For the sake of your son, don't take him."

"For the sake of my son, we need every man we can get. Hillel is a grown man. He's free to do what he wants. But I must say, I am surprised that these *dosim* are so quick to volunteer."

"Religious people aren't cowards," she answered. "In fact, they are more idealistic and brave than you could ever imagine."

"Maybe your father will make a kosher Jew out of me yet."

"Look out for him, Perchik."

"Don't worry. Your father doesn't need me. He's already got someone keeping an eye out on him."

Hodel looked at him questioningly. Perchik pointed up to the sky.

"He'll watch over your father."

"May He watch over you also."

"I can watch over myself," Perchik said.

With those last parting words, Perchik mounted his horse and started to gallop away. He had mellowed a bit, Hodel thought, but the stubbornness in his heart hadn't changed. Inside her house, Ben Zion was sleeping. The stick which he used as a rifle lay on the mattress beside him. Hodel pulled a blanket up to his chin. Now that she had seen Perchik again, she could see the resemblance the boy bore to his father.

Hillel appeared in the doorway.

"Don't rush off to become a soldier just because everyone else is," she said.

"Do you want me to stay behind with the women?"

"I didn't mean it that way."

"I want to fight too."

"Who will be left to work here in the settlement?" she asked.

"You. Your sister. Tevye's wife. The rest of the women. If we truly want this to be our country, there's no other choice."

Similar discussions were being held in houses all over the colony. After all, what wife enjoys having her husband go off to war? In line with Hodel's reasoning, many of the men decided to remain at home to keep working in the fields. It was true that to be independent you needed an army, but it was also true that the army's soldiers needed to eat. Farmers were a vital part of the battle.

After visiting his neighbors, Tevye had recruited two other men. For the next two days, he rested to let his body regain its strength after the nightmare of his arrest. He scrubbed every inch of his flesh, from his dirt-ridden feet to the lice which he found in his hair. The following morning, he set off to find Elisha and Munsho, who were working on a military supply road connecting Gaza and Beer Sheva. Carmel hardly spoke. When her husband had made up his mind, she had learned not to interfere. She was happy to hold him in her arms and give him as much love as she could before he left on his journey. Who knew when she would she him again?

In Nachman's house, the scene was less tranquil. Ruchel stood glaring at her husband as he packed some holy books into his pouch.

"Why don't you take this one?" she asked. She picked up a book and threw it at him. "And this one?"

Nachman dived to catch the holy texts. Kissing the prayer book which had landed on the floor, he stared at his angry wife.

"The prayer books you kiss. Me you leave alone with the kids."

"Ruchel, what's the matter with you?" he asked in astonishment.

"You are a rabbi, not a soldier."

"A rabbi can also be a soldier," he answered.

"Don't tell me about Moses and Rabbi Akiva! I don't want to hear about all of the heroes of our Biblical past! Can't you see that I'm frightened and that I don't want to be left alone?"

"You have to have faith."

"I want a husband, not faith."

"Ruchel, you don't know what you are saying."

He set down the books in his hands and walked toward his wife. She took a step backward with a look that said stop. Nachman froze in his tracks, remembering that it was the time of the month that a Jewish husband and wife were forbidden to touch. That certainly didn't make his saying goodbye any easier.

Their little daughter reached up from the floor and tugged at her mother's ankle-length skirt.

"Think of your father," she said. "What would he say if he knew you were going off to be a soldier?"

"After what the Russians did to our village, my father would be the first to agree."

"Other men are staying on the settlement to work."

"That's why I am not needed."

"What about all of your students?"

"A month vacation from school won't ruin them."

"Who will teach them Torah?"

"Shragi. I've already spoken with him."

"And how am I to manage alone?"

"The same way that Hodel and Carmel will manage."

Ruchel realized she couldn't convince him. There was a knock on the door. It was Tevye. Immediately, he sensed the mood of tension in the room.

"Are you ready?" he asked.

Nachman nodded. He returned to the table and squeezed his *tefillin* and *tallit* into his pouch with his books. Outside in the yard, the Olat HaShachar recruits were waiting in the wagon which Tevye had given as a wedding present to Ariel and his daughter, Bat Sheva, may her memory he for a blessing. It too was being enlisted in the Hebrew Brigade, in the first Jewish military inscription to have occurred in the world in nearly two thousand years.

Carmel, Hodel, and Ruchel stood together in the yard as the men waved goodbye. Tevye gave Tzvi a last kiss and handed him to his wife. Shragi, the scribe, walked up to the wagon as Tevye picked up the reins.

"Don't conquer them all," he quipped with a smile. "Leave a little something for the *Mashiach* to do."

"We've been waiting for the *Mashiach* long enough," Tevye answered. "It's time we did a little of his work on our own."

"He's probably waiting for us in Jerusalem," another settler added. "To join in the Hebrew Brigade."

"Who knows?" Hillel said. "He may turn out to be General Allenby."

"If the *Mashiach* is General Allenhy," Nachman quipped, "then I'll eat my hat."

Everyone laughed. Hillel started to play a lively tune on his harmonica, and the unlikely group of soldiers rode off into the night to face the unpredictable fortunes of war.

Chapter Forty-Four

TEVYE THE SOLDIER

If on the outside, Tevye maintained a cavalier, song-filled demeanor, his heart and soul were filled with a sense of mission. As the words of the *Shema* teach a Jew, *"And you shall love the Lord your God with all of your heart, with all of your soul, and with all of your might,"* which means loving God completely, even if you have to give up your life. Rabbi Akiva had done it in defiance of the Romans, and Tevye was prepared to risk his life in defiance of the Turks. After all, a man without his own land was no better than a slug in the ground, not knowing when it was going to be uprooted by the next shovel-load of earth. No matter how good a citizen a Jew tried to be, soon or later, he would be treated to a boot in the rear, a club on the head, or worse. The only solution was for the people of Israel to have their own land, as the Almighty had decreed long ago.

But, on the other hand, Tevye was no foolish youth. He understood the damage which a bullet could do. So, to make sure that angels would guard him on his way, he brought his wagon-load of fighters to Rishon Le Zion, to enlist more recruits, and to ask for his wife Golda's help.

The war had turned the Baron's premiere settlement into a ghost town. Many settlers had set sail for Europe. Others had been expelled by Jamal Pasha, or drafted by force into the Turkish army. A breakout of cholera had been the last blow. Starvation gripped the settlement. Fields lay in ruins, as if the curse of the past still hovered over the land.

Telling his comrades to look for recruits, Tevye set off alone to the cemetery. Eucalyptus trees, twice as tall as Tevye remembered from his first visit years before, towered along the deserted path. While growth was generally considered a blessing, the rows upon rows of new tombstones in the Rishon Le Zion graveyard were a sobering sight. The return of the Jews to Israel was a miracle all right, but it was a miracle which had come through blood, sweat, and many tears.

"May the memory of all of them be for a blessing," Tevye said, standing at the edge of the crowded cemetary.

It took him a while to find Golda's grave. He thought he remembered, but with all of the new tombstones, he was confused. Finally he spotted the modest stone slab engraved with her name. Weeds grew all over the plot. Brokenhearted, Tevye bent down on his knees and started to yank them up by their roots.

"Don't be angry with me, my sweet Golda," he said. "Don't be angry that I haven't come to visit until now."

"Look who is here!" he heard her say, in a cynical high-pitched voice. "The war hero! The awaited *Mashiach*! My big *pisher* of a milkman!"

Tevye straightened, backing away from her scorn.

"Ahhh, Golda, that isn't fair. After all, I haven't been on vacation."

"Who wants to hear your excuses? You think I have time? *Nu?* What have you come for? Talk."

Tevye had forgotten what a general his Golda could be.

"Well, my darling, as you see, I am a soldier...."

Tevye heard his wife laugh.

"Whoever heard of a Jewish soldier?" she asked.

"What about King David?" he began to debate.

"Don't start in with King David," the voice of his Golda barked in his head. "What's between you and King David?"

"You mean you won't put in a good word for me?"

"A good word with who?"

"You know who I mean."

"Do you think I'm a witch? Is that how you think of your wife?"

"*Chas v'shalom.* I just thought that perhaps you could intercede on behalf of your beloved husband."

"Am I Esther, the queen, that I have influence on the King?"

"I thought...."

"Go to Hebron and ask Abraham, Issac, and Jacob. I am only the wife of a milkman whose snores were so loud that not even the cows in the barn could get a decent night's sleep."

The sweet voice in Tevye's ears stopped ringing, as if someone had hung up a telephone. Tevye stood up and brushed off the dirt on his pants. He had heard his Golda's voice as if she had been standing right there, but there was no other soul in the graveyard.

Hebron, Tevye thought. The home of the Patriarchs. The second holiest place in the world, where the forefathers of the Jewish people were buried in the Cave of the Machpelah, along with their wives, the Matriarchs, Sarah, Rebbeca, and Leah. His Golda had come up with an excellent idea. Just like Joshua and Calev ben Yefuna had prayed at the Cave of the Patriarchs before they set out to conquer the Promised Land from the Canaanites, Tevye would go there to ask for courage and Divine assistance too. And at the same time, he could visit Hevedke.

Back at the Rishon Le Zion meeting hall, Tevye's old friend, Aharon, was the only recruit the would-be soldiers could find. For safety, he had already sent his wife to Alexandria, and he had nothing better to do. While he didn't have a rifle, he had a few dozen counterfeit immigration cards which the local scribe and printing press had produced. For someone like Tevye, who was wanted by the Turks as an escaped prisoner and spy, his new identity card and alias, Misha Yolansky, was a godsend as valuable as a gun.

To make a long journey short, the fighters of the Hebrew Brigade set off down the coast in search of their comrades from Olat HaShachar. Jews fleeing from Gaza passed them on the way, heading for cities up north. A few adventurous souls jumped onto the crowded wagon when they heard about the new Jewish army. As they approached the desert wilderness of the Negev, bands of Turkish deserters could be seen. While the Turks had repulsed the first British attack on Gaza, Aharon said it was a sign that General Allenby's troops were advancing in the Sinai.

Fortune seemed to be smiling on their bold enterprise, for their information proved accurate. They found Elisha and their friends from Olat HaShachar swinging pickaxes on the road to Beer Sheva. The soldiers who were supposed to be guarding them were asleep in the shade of their wagon. Observing the scene from afar, Tevye told his comrades to be quiet. Standing up in the wagon, he held a hushing finger up to his mouth and waved at Elisha to come over. Laying down his work tool, the Yemenite silently signaled to the others and rushed over to the wagon. His son, Ariel, was the first out of the wagon to greet him. Tevye jumped down to the road and the two friends embraced. Soon, all of the Jews were embracing.

"What are you doing here?" Elisha inquired.

"We've come to take you away," Tevye replied.

"And where do you propose to take us?" Shilo, the carpenter asked.

"To join the Israeli army - the new Hebrew Brigade."

"Hebrew Brigade?" Munsho asked. "What's that?"

"You are looking at it," Tevye answered. "We and several other divisions already attached to the British."

"Who are we fighting against?" Shilo asked.

"The Turks," Hillel answered. "I see our first two prisoners right now."

Everyone looked down the road at the sleeping soldiers.

"Why haven't you run away from this bondage?" Tevye inquired.

"At least we get a few *piasters* at the end of the month," Elisha explained. "That's more than we could make in Olat HaShachar".

"How are our families?" the big blacksmith, Munsho, wanted to know.

"Everyone is fine," Tevye assured them. "We will tell you on the way. Are you with us? Yes or no?"

"You can count me in," Shilo said.

"Me too," Elisha added.

Everyone looked to the blacksmith. His big smile was all that they needed to see.

"There is only one problem," Aharon said. "There is no more room in the wagon."

Everyone's glance turned back down the road toward the empty wagon and the two sleeping guards.

"Thou shall not steal," Shilo said.

"That is in peacetime," Nachman said. "Appropriating an enemy wagon for the Hebrew Brigade is a *mitzvah* in this holy war."

With the Rabbi's permission, the Jews of Olat HaShachar ran down the road to the wagon. Quickly, they threw in their tools and the rifles they stripped off the soldiers. When the Turks woke up and jumped to their feet, Munsho grabbed them from behind by their hair.

"So long, fellahs, *l'hitraot*," he said, cracking their two skulls together.

The soldiers collapsed in a heap.

"Take their uniforms!" Aharon commanded. "They may come in handy."

The next stop was Hebron. By now the Hebrew Brigade was a convoy. But nobody stopped them. Why should they? With two Turkish soldiers driving the lead wagon, it seemed like a perfectly ordinary work gang of Jews. Unless you remembered that most Turkish soldiers didn't have long beards like Aharon and Tevye, who were as pleased as could be in their brass-buttoned uniforms and red turbans.

By the end of the day, the wagon train arrived in Hebron, where the shepherd boy, David, had first become king. Slowly, the wagons descended the long winding road into the ancient city. Its steep, rocky hillsides were like impenetrable walls keeping modern civilization away. Earth and stone houses stood in clusters the slopes of the deep valley. Eyes peered out of doorways at the caravan of strangers. Merchants passed by them on donkeys laden with produce and wares. Cripples hobbled along the narrow streets. The residents looked as ancient as the city itself, as if they had been living in Hebron for thousands of years. Strangely, Tevye didn't see any Turks in the streets. Only Arabs and Jews. They seemed to live peacefully together, as if Ishmael and Isaac had found a way to live side-by-side in the exalted shadow of Abraham, their father, whose burial tomb towered over the city.

At sunset, an inspiring stillness hung over the Tomb of the Patriarchs. The massive stone walls of the building, quarried during Solomon's reign, rose over the tall palms trees which were situated in the very same yard that Abraham had purchased from Efron, the Hittite, four thousand years before. The minaret that the Ottomans had added onto the huge, ancient edifice looked out over the *casbah* of Hebron from the top of the towering parapet. The tomb was bigger than any monument that Tevye had ever seen. No wonder Hebron was called the city of the giants. Just as real giants had lived there in Biblical times, giants lay buried in the ancient sepulcher even now - the giant forefathers of the Jewish people, Abraham, Isaac, and Jacob. It was their giant righteousness and merit which had guarded over the Children of Israel down to that very day. Of their saintly wives, only Rachel was missing. She had been buried in Beit Lechem on the way to Efrat, to guard over her children during their wanderings away from the land.

Tevye's brigade hurried up the rocky path leading to the tomb's towering stone archway. They prayed in the Hall of Isaac in a stone-floored, Islamic-style rotunda which was also used as a mosque by the Arabs. Tevye felt his prayers fly from his lips and soar up a ladder toward Heaven. It was a mystical feeling so powerful that all other thoughts and concerns disappeared. In the presence of his forefathers, his soul was uplifted to the heights of pure awe and devotion. Nachman too was swept up by an emotion he had never experienced before in his life. When the *Mincha* prayer was finished, Tevye was moved to offer a prayer of his own by the mausoleum marking the site of Abraham's grave, which was actually hidden several underground caverns below the rotunda.

"Dear Lord, in the merit of our fathers, Abraham, Isaac, and Jacob, may we succeed in our mission to overcome those who oppress us in our very own land," he chanted aloud. "In the name of the eternal covenant which You forged with them here in

Hebron, grant us victory over our enemies, and plant us firmly in our homeland, just as You promised our holy forefathers, that all of the world may know that the word of the Lord stands forever."

Everyone answered, "Amen."

They found Hevedke at his yeshiva, studying with a small group of pious-looking Jews. A light shone in his eyes as if he had discovered the secrets of the universe. His face was gaunt, the face of an ascetic who had been engaging in rigorous, devotional fasts. He glanced up at the visitors without excitement or surprise, as if he knew they were coming. A peaceful joy spread over his face.

"Tevye," he said. "May your coming be a blessing."

He hugged his father-in-law and warmly greeted the others.

"I hope you haven't come to arrest me," he said, with a look at Tevye's uniform.

"It's just a disguise," Tevye assured him.

"How is Hava?" he asked.

"I have no news to tell you," Tevye answered. "I have not heard from Zichron Yaacov for months."

"This war is a terrible thing," Hevedke responded. "But the hand of God is in everything, and He is sure to bring a great light out of this darkness."

"Amen," Tevye said.

"You look like men on a mission," the scholar observed. "But we have all night to talk. Right now, it is time for the evening prayers."

He offered Tevye the honor of leading the congregation, but Tevye humbly declined. Nachman was chosen in his stead. Once again, Tevye felt that the prayers which he had been reciting from his childhood suddenly took on an inspired life of their own. In the holy atmosphere of the Hebron yeshiva, where Jews learned day and night, each benediction became a plea for mercy before God, whose Presence was overwhelmingly near.

When the evening prayer was concluded, Hevedke-turned-Isaac invited the visitors to share a modest supper of goat's cheese and bread. Like everywhere else in the country, the war had brought hard times to Hebron, where Jews had lived continuously

since Biblical times. Among the one thousand Jews who lived in
the city at the start of the war, only half remained. The Hadassah
Clinic still dispensed free health care to Jews, Turks, and Arabs
alike, even though many of the Jewish doctors had been drafted
into the Turkish army. The *yeshivot* in the city, including the
Lubavitch Yeshiva in the two-storied dwelling, Beit Schneerson,
still remained open, though contributions from the Diaspora had
been reduced to a trickle. Isaac told them that for the past several
years, Jewish merchants, tailors, and craftsmen had lived alongside
the Arab population in peace. When Turkish soldiers had pulled
out of the city to go off to the front, a group of Arabs took it upon
themselves to guard the Jewish Quarter so that no misfortune
would befall the Jews, who were responsible for the increased
prosperity and improved health care in the poverty-stricken
enclave.

When Tevye related to his son-in-law why they had come, the
young scholar said he would join them at once.

"Are you sure?" Tevye asked.

"I learned how to shoot back in Russia. We often went hunting
for ducks. I'm sure I'll remember."

"What about your studies?" Tevye asked.

"Being that you are all far more learned than I am, I don't have
to remind you of the teaching of our Sages that study is not the
main thing, but practice. Joshua never ceased from studying Torah
in Moses's tent, but when enemies threatened the nation, he
rushed out to take part in the fight. And didn't Abraham himself
enlist all of his students in battle to rescue his cousin, Lot, from
enemy hands? Besides, if a scholar like Nachman is with you, there
can be no question that it is a very great *mitzvah* to join the
Hebrew Brigade."

Thus, the next morning, after wishing a final farewell to the
Patriarchs, Tevye's inspired troops headed north through the
mountains of Judea toward the hills of Jerusalem. The yeshiva
made a contribution to the war effort, a Torah scroll which Isaac
embraced in his arms as he rode in the wagon. Just as the Ark of
the Covenant containing the Two Tablets of Law had led the

Children of Israel into battle against the armies of Canaan, a *Sefer Torah* was to be at the head of this Jewish army too.

Though Tevye and his comrades were all simple Jews, each and every man was seized by the historical destiny of the mission. Looking back at the road behind them, Tevye imagined he could see the soldiers of Bar Kochva, risen from the battleground of Betar, rush out of the hillsides to join them. Thousands of years earlier, the Matriarch Rachel had wept in her grave as Jews driven out of the land by the Romans had passed by her tomb. Now, as the wagons carrying the soldiers of the Hebrew Brigade reached the holy site in Bethlehem, Nachman quoted the comforting words of the Prophet, *"Thus says the Lord, keep thy voice from weeping, and thy eyes from tears; for thy endeavors on behalf of thy children shall be rewarded, says the Lord; and they shall come back again from the land of the enemy. And there is hope for thy future, says the Lord, and thy children shall return again to their own borders."*

True to his word, Perchik was waiting for them with a gathering of over one hundred soldiers on the outskirts of Jerusalem. They were camped in the valley of Motza, on the other side of a steep embankment which hid the cluster of tents from the road. Smoke from camp fires rose in the air. Men dressed in undershirts and suspenders relaxed in the shade of their tents. Tevye noticed women among them. Perchik strode forward to greet them.

"Bring the wagons around to the end of the camp. We've got a tent for you waiting. I figured you religious would want to be together."

"How do you like that?" Hillel quipped. "There is already a ghetto in the Hebrew Brigade."

The *kibbutzniks*, who were already installed in the camp, watched in curiosity as the pious Jews passed by in the wagons. Several pointed their fingers and laughed. Isaac proudly gripped the sacred Torah. Munsho rolled up his sleeve and flexed a hefty bicep to show them they were ready for battle. A smart aleck doing sit-ups paused to whistle and give them a mocking salute.

"They will be sure to test us to see if we've got what it takes," Shilo observed.

Before anyone could answer, a shout turned their heads.

"*Abba*! *Abba*! It's me!"

Elisha was startled to hear the voice of his son. Behind them, Yigal ran toward the wagons. Tevye yanked on the reins. The youth hopped onto the wagon and gave his father a hug.

"How I've missed you," he said.

Elisha stared with stern eyes at the boy who had been stricken with wanderlust and who had run off with his Zionist friend from the worker's union. The Yemenite gazed at his son's uncovered head and raised a hand in the air as if to give him a slap in the face. But then he broke into a smile and embraced him.

"Moriah and Zeev are here too," the youth said. Elisha glanced back and spotted his daughter standing in the entrance to a tent with the sweet-talking rogue who had stolen her away from the family.

"How's *Ema*," Yigal asked.

"Come visit and find out for yourself," his brother, Ariel said, giving him the whack on the head which their father had only threatened.

"I will. As soon as the war is over. I promise."

Tevye called out a soft "*Yalla*" to his horse. With the communication that had developed between them over the years, he didn't have to say anything more. With a tug, the beast pulled the wagon. Like a husband and wife, they had come to understand one another. Even after Tevye had given the horse to Ariel and Bat Sheva for a wedding gift, Tevye had continued to drive the wagon and care for the horse in the stable. After a hard day of work, brushing its flanks and combing its mane soothed Tevye as much as it calmed the horse. It was a lifelong habit Tevye was unable to break. Plus, a horse could be trusted to keep secrets when a man confessed feelings of weakness that he didn't want to share with his wife.

The wagons rolled on toward the end of the camp, but before Tevye's horse could establish a gait, a strange foreign yell pierced the air. A rope sailed down out of the sky and a lasso circled over Tevye's torso.

"Yaahoo!" the raucous voice hollered in English. "I've lassoed myself a real authentic Jew!"

The rope yanked tightly, pinning Tevye's arms down to his sides. Behind him, an unshaven cowboy in a white cowboy hat reared up on a horse as he pulled on the lasso.

"I got me a Moses!" he exclaimed.

When his horse's forelegs landed back on the earth, the cowboy bit the cork off the top of a bottle and spit it out on the ground.

"*L'Chaim!*" he called, raising the bottle aloft in his hand. Then, holding his head back, he poured the liquor down his throat without spilling a drop. When the bottle was empty, he tossed it high into the air. Just as the bottle reached the peak of its climb and started to fall, the cowboy drew a pistol out of his holster and fired. The bottle shattered into pieces in the air.

"Yaahoo!" the stranger yelled. Then he galloped to the wagon and jumped off his horse.

"Thank the good Lord," he exclaimed. "Finally these starving eyeballs can set their gaze on some genuine Old Testament Jews! I've come all of the way from Dodge City to help the Children of Israel drive the Turkish Apaches out of this land, and up until you fellas came along, the only Hebrews I've found is this penny-arcade cavalry of clean-shaven choirboys."

Jumping up onto the wagon, he grabbed Tevye's beard and gave it a tug.

"Shiiit!" he exclaimed. "I'll be damned if it ain't the real thing."

Tevye growled and squirmed to squeeze out from the grip of the lasso. Excited, the cowboy took off his Stetson and threw it high into the air. With practiced swiftness, his six-shooter once again appeared in his hand. Without seeming to look at the target, he fired. The bullet hit the hat and set it spinning even higher. Another gunshot roared out, and again the hat leaped through the air as if it were being pulled by a string.

"What the hell is going on?!" a voice behind them yelled out in English. "Do you want to bring the whole Turkish army upon us?"

The voice had a thick Russian accent. It belonged to a small, pipsqueak of a Jew with a serious expression, a cropped-off moustache, and a tight-fitting army uniform which had a Star of David stitched on its sleeve.

"Let the damn Indians come!" the American answered. "I'm ready to die defending the right of you people to live in this land. I've fought my share of Comanchees, Blackfeet, and Sioux, but this is the most righteous fight of them all."

"Get this rope off of me!" Tevye yelled.

Laughing, Elisha lifted the lasso over his friend's head.

"No offense, rabbi," the drunken cowboy said, sitting down on the seat beside Tevye.

"Get these men into uniforms," the little colonel barked out at Perchik.

Behind him, another soldier appeared, carrying a riding crop which he flicked against the khaki trousers of his British officer's uniform. Frameless spectacles were miraculously balanced on a distinctly Jewish nose.

"Who are the officers?" Hillel asked.

"The smaller one is David Ben Gurion," Perchik explained. "And the one in the British uniform is Zeev Jabotinsky. They are the founders of the Hebrew Brigade."

"Time is wasting!" Ben Gurion called out impatiently. "We have to make soldiers out of these men."

"Yes, sir," Perchik responded with a salute.

"For such a little *pisher*, he certainly acts like a big *k'nocker*," Tevye observed.

The cowboy stood up in the wagon.

"Wagons ho!" he called out, pointing the way onward. Munsho grabbed his shoulder and shoved him back down on the seat.

"Who is he?" Tevye asked.

"Nobody knows," Perchik answered. "He calls himself Cassidy. He says he was a marshal, bounty hunter, and Indian fighter in America."

The cowboy grinned, not understanding a word of their Hebrew. Truly, he had the grizzly look of a man who had fought many battles. Though he was boisterous and robust, the wrinkles in his forehead and the red in his eyes told the story of a fighter past his prime. Two of his front teeth were missing, unquestionably from chomping the corks out of whiskey bottles.

"What is he doing here?" Tevye asked.

"He claims his father was a minister who taught him to love the Jews. He calls us the real Christians. When he heard there was a war on in Palestine, he says he set out to volunteer on the first steamship he could find."

"I thought this was a Jewish army," Tevye said.

"He claims all Christians are Jews."

"He's crazy," Shilo said.

"Who needs him here?" Munsho asked. "Maybe he's really a spy."

"Until one of you can shoot better than he can, he's welcome to stay and join in the fight," Perchik said.

Not only did the cowboy, Cassidy, stay, he moved his holster and saddle bags into the tent of the religious Jews from Olat HaShachar. Feeling immediately at home, he spread out a blanket, sat on the ground, and pulled off his boots.

Once the settlers had unrolled their bedding, Yigal dragged his father toward the flap of the tent.

"Come with me to see Moriah and Zeev," he urged.

Elisha resisted. "My daughter can come here, if she still remembers that she has a father," he answered.

The words sounded familiar to Tevye. He recalled the anguish he and his Golda had suffered when their love-stricken daughters had run off with their Romeos. It didn't seem to matter if a father came from Russia or Yemen, the new generation was crazy with modern ideas. It wasn't enough that Jewish girls ran away from home with non-religious boys, now they insisted on wearing pants and being soldiers! What would be next, Tevye wondered?

It wasn't long before Zeev appeared in the tent. Elisha stared at him, uncertain how to react. He still didn't know what to make of this strange breed of Jew who turned his back on the Torah, but was willing to risk his life in defense of his land. After all, could something be more religious than that?

"*Shalom,*" the youth said.

He was wearing the long sleeved, high-collared, white blouse which the Jewish *shomerim* wore. Perhaps in deference to Elisha, he had put a hunter's hat on his head. A bullet belt and the strap of his rifle crisscrossed his chest.

"It's good to see you, Elisha," he said. "Moriah is waiting outside."

The settlers stared over at Elisha to see what he would do. Everyone knew of the story. But before he could react, Perchik entered the tent and pushed Zeev aside.

"Everyone out of the tent on the double," he ordered. "It's time to learn how to be soldiers. Dinner will be served after sunset. In the meantime, everyone is to line up in a neat row outside."

Cassidy leaped to his feet. He didn't understand the language, but he knew enough about cavalries and posses to understand the command.

"If it means setting off after heathens and infidels, I'm ready," he said. "You've got to slaughter them, it's as simple as that. That's what we did in America, and that's what you've got to do here."

Tevye asked Perchik to translate. His former son-in-law had been a devotee of enough intellectual circles at the university in St. Petersburg to have picked up some basic English.

"He says that we have to kill all the Turks, like the Americans killed all the Indians."

"There very well may be something to that," Tevye agreed.

"Not only the Turks," Cassidy added. "The A-rabs too. They're ornery critters. If you don't get rid of them now, you'll only have trouble with them later. I say we chase them both out of the country in one tidy little sweep."

Tevye waited for a translation. When Perchik relayed the cowboy's advice, Tevye nodded.

"For a gentile, he's not stupid," he remarked.

"The gentiles were also created in God's image," Nachman

reminded them. "They may not possess Torah, but they have wisdom," he observed, quoting a Talmudic expression.

Hevedke stood up. He didn't choose to speak. As the great Rabbi Shimon ben Gamliel had said, "All of my life, I have grown up amongst Sages, and I have never found anything so beneficial to a man as silence."

Watching Cassidy buckle his holster, Hevedke thanked God for having led him to discover the Torah. Truly, his transformation from the person he had been in Russia, to the person he was now, had been a miracle. For not so very long ago, he had been as cocky and filled with himself as the American cowboy.

Outside the tent, a troop was riding off with Jabotinsky and the diminutive Ben Gurion in the lead. A blue and white flag adorned with the Star of David blew in the wind as the cavalry made its way up the hill which guarded the valley. Perchik said they were heading for the Sinai to rendezvous with divisions of the Hebrew Brigade which had been training in Alexandria alongside the British army.

"The Turks have expelled both of them from the country,' Perchik explained. "They snuck back from Egypt to lead our new recruits into battle."

"Where are we supposed to fight?" Hillel asked.

"It hasn't been decided," Perchik replied. "When it is, I'll inform you."

For the moment, Elisha didn't have a chance to speak to his daughter. Outside the tent, she gazed at him with tender, penitent eyes, as if seeking his forgiveness. He knew that he would be reconciled in the end, but in the right place and occasion. Now it was time to behave like a soldier and join the others in line.

Perchik waited until all of the settlers stood silently at attention. Cassidy found a place at the end of the line near Hevedke, who also knew some rudimentary English.

"Cassidy," Perchik called. "You don't belong here. You're attached to troop number two."

"I request a transfer, sir," the cowboy answered, taking a step out of line. "I want to fight with the Jews."

"We are all Jews," Perchik answered.

"Yes, sir, I know that. I'm a Jew too, just like Jesus."

Smiling, he looked down the line of bearded Jews. They stood at attention, as stoic as wooden Indians. Spitting out a stream of tobacco juice from the wad he was chewing in his jaw, the cowboy stepped back into line.

"What's that flag?" Shilo asked, staring up the hill at the troop heading out to the front.

"The new flag of Israel," Perchik told him.

"It looks like a *tallit*," Tevye remarked.

"Why don't we fly one in the camp?" Shilo asked.

"It's against Turkish law," Perchik informed them.

"So why are they doing it?"

"They're going off to war," Perchik answered. "And you are just starting your training."

While most Jewish troops were being trained in Egypt under the command of the British Colonel Patterson, the settlers of Olat HaShachar were to receive their training in the Motza Valley, and in the Judean Mountains, a short journey away. They would be issued uniforms, Perchik explained, but they shouldn't be disappointed if there weren't enough to go around for every soldier. He said they had supplies of British war rations and meat, so they wouldn't go hungry.

"British meat isn't kosher," Aharon protested. "We want our own kosher meat."

Others settlers agreed. Cassidy asked Hevedke why everyone was agitated. Hearing the explanation, he nodded his head.

"Hell yes," the cowboy assented. "Whoever heard of a Jewish army without kosher meat?"

"Whoever heard of a Jewish army?" Tevye asked.

The others laughed.

Perchik called the soldiers to order. He appointed Aharon to be in charge of the troop kitchen. There were deer in the mountains. If they shot one, Perchik said, they could cook up a feast.

"You can't shoot an animal and then eat it," Nachman explained. "It has to be slaughtered in the proper ritual fashion."

"So catch a deer if you can," Perchik responded. "Maybe Cassidy can lasso you one."

Everyone laughed.

"What's all the fuss?" the bounty hunter asked when he understood the problem. "I'll go off tonight and rustle us some cattle from the Indians."

"We are forbidden to eat stolen cattle," Hevedke responded.

"Shiiit!" the American said, sending a glob of spit arcing through the air. "You can't eat this. You can't eat that. No wonder you drove Moses out of his cotton-picking mind."

Losing his own patience, Perchik scolded them for their breaches of discipline. Being in the Jewish army, he said, was as holy as being in a synagogue. When the commander spoke, he didn't want to hear a whisper from anyone. Lives were at stake, and they had only two weeks to become a professional fighting brigade.

"Why only two weeks?" Aharon asked.

"When the time is right, I will tell you," Perchik cryptically answered. "In the meantime, I am assigning Tevye to be in charge of your unit. If you have any complaints, go to him. He'll discuss them with me. Right now, I want everyone down on the ground. Twenty-five push-ups. On the double. Now!"

With a mixture of groans, the settlers got down on the ground. When everyone had finished, Perchik had them run five laps around the camp. Tevye was puffing when he brought up the tail of the race.

"Twenty-five sit-ups!" the commander shouted.

"*Rachmanus*," Tevye groaned. "Have mercy."

"Come on, Tevye," Perchik teased. "Show us what a real Jew is made of."

Tevye growled and gritted his teeth. After twenty sit-ups, he collapsed on his back in exhaustion.

"Another five laps around the camp!" Perchik ordered.

Moaning, the old-timers set off after the much younger Ariel, Hevedke, and Nachman. Tevye lay on his back, staring up at the sky. His heart pounded. His lungs heaved up and down. Perchik's shadow fell over him.

"If you can't keep up with the others, Grandpa, I'll have no choice but to send you back home."

Tevye rolled onto his side and pushed himself to his feet. Perchik was smiling the same cocky grin he had worn when the two men had squared off for a fist fight in Shoshana when Tevye had come to take Hodel's baby. So that was it, Tevye thought. Perchik still wanted revenge. Well, he wouldn't get it. Call it pride, or call it stubbornness, Tevye wasn't about to give up. He would wipe the grin off the clean-shaven face, if not with blows, then by proving that he could be as good a soldier as anyone else.

By the time Tevye finished the last lap of the camp, the sun was beginning to set. The others were in the supply tent, trying on uniforms. Munsho stood as stiff as a scarecrow in a shirt which was several sizes too small. Everyone except Cassidy was issued a rifle and bullets. The cowboy was content with the firearms he had brought from back home. True to Perchik's warning, when Tevye's turn came, all of the military clothing was gone.

That night, the soldiers went to bed early. Only Elisha stayed up to go for a stroll with Moriah. As Tevye said, "A daughter is a daughter." Was it her fault that she had fallen in love with a man who had received no education in Torah? If Elisha rejected her now, would it help? Would it bring her and her husband closer to him or to God? Besides, it wasn't the Yemenite's nature to carry a grudge. Somehow, he told himself, with patience and love, it would all turn out for the best. The children would return to the way of their fathers, and the fathers would come to understand the needs of their children. If Elisha was too simple a man to explain the great beauty of tradition to them, then Elijah the Prophet would come and reunite the estranged generations in peace.

Tevye opened his eyes when his friend tiptoed quietly back into the tent and lay down beside him.

"How did it go?" he asked.

"She is a good child," Elisha answered. "So is Yigal. In Yemen, they never saw anything outside of our tiny village. All the Jews were religious. Here, I'm afraid, the world is far more complicated and confusing."

"On the outside," Tevye said. "On the inside, things haven't changed so much. As King Solomon said, 'There is nothing new under the sun.'"

"Children don't understand that. They see a big, exciting world, and they want to experience it all."

"They'll come back. Like my Hodel. You'll see."

Soon, their snores joined the symphony of tired soldiers around them. If he hadn't known better, the guard outside would have thought that a pack of wild animals were caged inside the tent. In the morning, the training continued. Each man was taken for a gallop on a horse to measure his skill as a rider. Firing practice began in the middle of the day. They were taught how to shoot standing, crouching, and lying prone on the ground. Cassidy refused to join them. He could only hit a target, he said, if it moved. When the sun began to sink in the west, Perchik ordered the new recruits back to the camp where they were scheduled to have a tug-of-rope war with the kibbutzniks of troop number two. After a long, back-and-forth struggle, the younger men dragged Tevye and his friends across the dividing line. But that evening, Munsho, the blacksmith, restored the honor of the religious settlers by crashing hand after hand to the table in an arm-wrestling contest. Just as he pinned the last challenger, a rider appeared at the crest of the hillside, waving something white in his hand. Raising a bugle to his lips, he blew out a calling. Soldiers stood up and hurried forward to meet him as he galloped down the slope into the camp.

"Allenby's forces have opened canon fire on Gaza!" the out-of-breath rider declared.

Hearing the news, everyone cheered. Tevye and Perchik embraced. Elisha hugged his two sons. Joyfully, he shook Zeev's outstretched hand. Nachman and Hevedke prayed a short thank you to God and added a plea for success. And Cassidy hollered a wild rodeo cheer and once again threw his hat into the air and shot it full of holes.

"Wait," the messenger called, holding up the newspaper in his hand. "That isn't all. The British camel division has entered Beer Sheva in a surprise sneak attack. The city has been liberated from the Turks!"

Another cheer went up from the Hebrew Brigade.

"And listen to this from the British Foreign Minister," the rider exclaimed, dropping down from his horse. As everyone crowded around him, he read from the journal:

"From the British Foreign Office. The second day of November, 1917. Dear Lord Rothschild, I have much pleasure in conveying to you on behalf of His Majesty's Government, the following declaration of sympathy with Jewish Zionist aspirations which has been submitted to, and approved by, the Cabinet...."

Another cheer sounded from the troops. Gunshots rang out in celebration. Perchik yelled for silence.

Once again the messenger held up the newspaper and read:

"His Majesty's Government views with favor the establishment in Palestine of a national home for the Jewish people, and will...."

He wasn't allowed to continue. Joyful cheers rang out through the camp. The newspaper was snatched from his hand. Jews, religious and non-religious, jumped up and down. Men and women embraced.

"They are going to grant us our own Jewish State!" someone shouted.

Aharon grabbed Tevye by his collar and gave him a jovial hug.

"Our homeland is ours!" he cried. "Our homeland is ours!"

Spontaneously, the Jews started dancing. Only Perchik remained unenthused. He grabbed the crumpled gazette and read over the letter. It was signed by Arthur James Balfour, the British Foreign Minister.

"Colonel Perchik, why are you looking so serious?" Tevye asked. "Come join in the dancing!"

"I am afraid everyone's joy is unfounded."

"What are you talking about?" Tevye asked. "Your dream has come true! The British are going to give us our homeland back."

"Don't be naive, Tevye. History teaches us otherwise. Once

the British conquer the land, they won't be so eager to give it up to the Jews. You'll see. After we get rid of the Turks, we will have to get rid of General Allenby too."

"One war at a time," Tevye answered. "Right now, it's a time for rejoicing."

As the circle of dancers swirled around and around, Tevye reached out a hand. Munsho grabbed him and pulled him into the whirl. For the soldiers of Olat HaShachar, it seemed like the Mashiach was on the way. Hillel played his harmonica and a soldier ran out of his tent carrying a fiddle. The settlers danced in one circle, and the *kibbutznikim* danced a *hora* in another, the men and the women together. The supply sergeant rushed out of the supply tent, waving a Jewish flag on a pole. Soon all of the women soldiers were running through the camp, holding flags over their heads like capes. As they danced, the blue and white colors flapped in the wind as prettily as miniature skies.

Perchik remained deep in thought. With a serious expression, he grabbed the messenger and strode off with him toward his tent. As the happy soldiers continued to dance, the harbinger of good tidings reached into his mail pouch and handed Perchik a confidential dispatch. The training of the new recruits had to be accelerated. Troops two and three were needed in action. A dangerous, clandestine mission had to set out by the end of the week, and British Military Headquarters in Egypt was counting on the soldiers of the Hebrew Brigade.

Chapter Forty-Five

HANUKAH

Torchlight shone on the faces of the soldiers of the Hebrew Brigade as they stood listening to Joseph Trumpeldor explain the mission before them. The tall, imposing figure was one of the founders of the tiny Jewish army. In Russia, fighting in the Russian-Japanese War, he had lost an arm in combat, and a sleeve of his jacket hung loosely down by his side. An early pioneer of Kibbutz Degania, he had been deported from Palestine at the outbreak of the war for his alleged loyalty to Russia. Now, he had snuck back into the country to organize troops. Information had been received at British Headquarters that the Turkish army was planning a counter invasion. Divisions had left Damascus and they were on their way to Palestine. It was the task of the Hebrew Brigade to stop their advance by blowing up the Jordan River bridges which the new Turkish units would have to cross to come to the aid of the beleaguered forces in Palestine. Additionally, in order to cripple the firepower of the Turks, the main ammunition installment in Jericho was targeted to be destroyed. The top secret missions were dangerous, Trumpeldor said, since the fort and bridges were constantly under guard. However, working to their advantage was the weapon of surprise, and the fact that no one knew that a fighting brigade was already stationed at the outskirts of Jerusalem, a night's march away from the city of Jericho and the Jordan River Valley.

When Trumpeldor's briefing was finished, he asked for volunteers. Immediately, all of the soldiers stepped forward. Not a man, nor a woman, remained behind.

"I'm glad," Trumpeldor said. "And proud of you all. It is a great thing to die for one's homeland."

"It's even better to live for it," Tevye noted.

The joke shattered the deadly seriousness of the hour. When Trumpeldor smiled, the other soldiers all laughed.

"Your troop commanders will decide who goes out on the mission. For now, to officially sum up your training, I want to present each one of you with the blue and white armband of the Hebrew Brigade, and with a Bible, which is the eternal deed to our land. As the L-rd said to Joshua, '*Be strong and filled with great courage for you are to lead this people to inherit the land which I swore to their fathers to give them.*'"

It was a moving moment for everyone, a sense of history spanning thousands of years. A flag proudly shone in the torchlight, representing the dreams of Jews all over the world. A stirring drum roll was played. Tevye stood at attention and proudly returned the one-armed commander's salute. Then Trumpeldor shook Tevye's hand firmly and held out a Bible. Tevye's hand trembled as he reached out for the Book.

"Be strong and of great courage," he heard a voice inside him repeat.

The eyes of even the toughest kibbutzniks moistened when Trumpeldor handed out the Bibles and shook each soldier's hand. On Perchik's cue, Hillel raised his harmonica to his lips and began to play the song, "*Hatikva*," which had become the Zionist national anthem. Trumpledor led the singing, but it was Nachman's cantorial voice which rang out with the most heartfelt rendition of all.

Later, when the ceremony had finished, Perchik gathered his soldiers into their tent and detailed the plan of the mission, Elisha, Munsho, Shilo, Nachman, and Hevedke would be joining Troop Two for the clandestine attack on the bridges. When they reached the mountain range overlooking the Jordan Valley, they would separate into three teams. Under the cover of nightfall, each team would make its way to its target. Perchik warned them that they might have to crawl on their bellies for great distances to avoid being seen. Each man would also be carrying charges of dynamite in his backpack. The plan was to surprise the guards at the bridges and overcome them stealthily without drawing gunfire, which would alert Turkish troops in the area and imperil the mission. Troop Two had been trained in the use of explosives, and their soldiers would wire the bridges. The settlers of Olat HaShachar would take up positions on both banks of the river and keep watch while the dynamite teams did their work. When the bridges had been detonated, each team was to return to the same rendezvous point in the mountains. Perchik said that the mission was physically demanding and dangerous, and that he would understand if someone wanted to be transferred to a different assignment. He waited for the men to decide, but no one requested a transfer. Looks of determination and resolve gripped all of their faces.

The attack on the ammunition fortress, Perchik explained, demanded different tactics and different skills. He himself would be leading the assault with Tevye, Ariel, and Cassidy. Since, out of all of the soldiers, Tevye had the most experience with wagons and horses, he had been selected to drive the vehicle which would blow up the fort. The wagon would be loaded with explosives which the Brigade had smuggled by sea from British headquarters in Egypt. To avoid detection along the road to Jericho, the team would take the far more difficult path through the mountains and down the infrequently traveled slopes of Wadi Kelt. The treacherous, cliff-side path had been abandoned for years and was now used only by shepherds. Because of the dangerous footing, they would travel with mules and not horses. When they reached the plateau overlooking the plains of Jericho, the wagon would be positioned and released in direct line to the fortress which was situated, Perchik said, at the foot of the sloping plateau.

"If it is all the same to you, I would prefer to have my horse lead the wagon instead of a mule," Tevye said.

"The trail is all rocks," Perchik said.

"My horse is no stranger to rocks," Tevye answered. "The main thing is that we know one another. A man can take risks for all kinds of reasons, but an animal is much more cautious. If you expect a mule to carry dynamite along mountain ledges and cliffs, he had better know his driver. Mules have wills of their own. If he doesn't like what he's doing, he can sit down in the middle of the road, and all of the dynamite in the world won't move him."

"Your point sounds reasonable," Perchik said. "I will discuss it with the commanders of Troop Number Two."

The next day, final preparations were made. Tevye carefully checked out the brakes of the wagon and its wheels. He had Shilo repair a broken spoke, and asked Munsho to grease all of the axles, and to make sure that his horse's horseshoes were tightly fastened for the journey ahead. For precaution's sake, he removed a wheel from his own wagon to take along as a spare. Then he helped Ariel and Cassidy carry the heavy cases of dynamite from the ammunition tent to the wagon.

In the middle of their work, a soldier lit a cigarette and casually tossed the match into the air toward the wagonload of explosives. Tevye's shout alerted Ariel who dove to snatch the tiny torch in mid-flight. But his hand closed shut on air, and the match landed on one of the crates of gunpowder. Tevye threw himself to the ground, but nothing occurred. The flame, thank God, had gone out. Some thanked the wind. But Tevye knew differently. At the last second, the puff of an unseen angel had snuffed out the danger. Wasn't it written in the story of Jacob that angels watched over the camps of the Jews? Still, Tevye was shaken. If miracles were needed before they even began on the mission, who knew what dangers they would meet on the way? Even Tevye's horse needed reassurance. Smelling the gunpowder, the animal snorted nervously as Tevye hooked him up to the wagon.

"Easy boy," Tevye urged, calmly stroking its neck. "We are off to do a big *mitzvah*, which is sure to earn you a great reward."

The horse shook his head and snorted, as if to say, "*Mitzvahs* are for Jews, not for horses."

"You are right," Tevye agreed. "If the wagon blows up while we are in it, at least I will go to Heaven a hero. You want to know what's in this adventure for you."

The horse nodded yes in agreement and beat its front hoof on the ground. Tevye reached into his pocket and pulled out a few lumps of sugar. The horse lapped them up.

"There's more where that came from," Tevye whispered in its ear.

"*Haleviy,*" Tevye thought to himself. "If only I knew how to speak to people the way I do to horses, I could be a Trumpledor or a Weizmann myself."

That was the key to effective communication - to speak to the listener in the language he understood. What good would it have done to talk to the horse about the exalted value of martyrdom and the reincarnation of souls? Tevye himself didn't know what reincarnation was, and, like his horse, he was in no great hurry to learn.

A large piece of canvas was spread over the wagon's cargo to hide the explosives and protect them from the burning rays of the sun. In the early afternoon, the mission left camp in order to reach the Judean mountains by nightfall. Hillel stood playing the song "*Am Yisrael Chai*" as the soldiers marched off. Elisha rode in the lead group of riders with his son, Yigal, Moriah, and the flag-bearer, Zeev. The kibbutzniks that Perchik had brought from Shoshana formed the corps which would blow up the second bridge. And Nachman, Hevedke, Munsho, and Shilo set forth with the soldiers who had been chosen to blow up the largest and most heavily guarded Jordan River crossing.

When the demolition teams were a safe distance away, Tevye called to his horse, and the wagon filled with dynamite rolled out of camp. Ahead of them rode a soldier named Gal, who had scouted out the trails winding through the canyons of Wadi Kelt. Perchik sat at Tevye's side, his rifle in his lap. Ariel and Cassidy rode behind them on mules to guard the wagon from the rear. At the edge of the camp, Hillel and Aharon kept waving. Perchik had decided to leave them behind. A few soldiers were needed to keep watch over their tents and supplies. With his organizational skills, Aharon had become the camp sergeant, and a lame harmonica player would only slow down the mission. God-willing, if the soldiers returned in safety, Hillel would have the honor to greet them with a joyful medley of victory songs.

In the voluminous writings on the First World War, historians have dedicated scant paragraphs to the contributions of the fighting force called the Hebrew Brigade, and the details of the Jordan Valley mission have never been told. But scholars of Jewish history know that the brave expedition which set out from the small encampment in Motza paved the way for Britain's conquest of Palestine. Reaching the heights of Mount Scopus, the Hebrew cavalry began the long descent toward the Dead Sea. Traveling along the Jericho road, they made their way through the mountainous wilderness. Rocks jolted the wagon, rattling the cases of dynamite under the canvas. Tevye sweated more out of apprehension than from the scorching rays of the sun. The horse pulled the heavy load reluctantly, as if it weren't pleased with the task. Before long, Tevye and Perchik lost sight of the faster moving forces. Bedouins in primitive encampments gazed indifferently at the soldiers as they passed. Before sunset, Gal led them off the main road onto a trail which led north into the mountains. An hour after nightfall, they reached Wadi Kelt and a winding descent toward a mountainside monastery. The desert moon shone brightly to illuminate their way, but there was no road to follow. True, a trail had been carved out by generations of shepherds and herds of sheep, but it wasn't even a path. On a ridge overlooking the canyon below, Tevye's horse came to a halt.

"Wait up!" Perchik called to the scout up ahead.

Tevye stood up in the wagon and peered down the cliff-side into the darkness below.

"What's the matter?" Perchik asked.

"There's no road," Tevye said.

"Straight ahead," Perchik insisted.

"I may be aging, but I am not blind. I have driven thousands and thousands of miles through blizzards and the blackness of night, and I know a road when I see one."

"Follow the scout."

"The scout is on horseback and this is a broad wagon."

"I told you that we needed a mule for the journey."

"We have a mule. Me. For agreeing to this crazy scheme. The problem isn't the horse, it's the wagon. It's too wide for a trail like this."

"We have no other choice."

Tevye stared at the mule-headed Perchik. He remembered how stubborn he could he."

"What's the matter?" Ariel asked, riding up beside them.

"We've come to the end of the road," Tevye answered.

Suddenly, Cassidy let out a yodel. His shout echoed again and again through the canyon.

"Tell that idiot to stop it!" Tevye told Perchik. "He'll frighten the horse."

"I'll drive the wagon if you want," Ariel said. "I think we can make it."

Tevye straightened his back. He peered once again down the mountain. Gal reappeared on his horse and asked what was holding them up.

"The trail," Perchik said. "It's too narrow."

"It widens just around the bend," the scout said.

All eyes were focused on the onetime milkman.

"We will have to ride with the brakes down the mountain. The load is so heavy, with even the smallest momentum, the wagon could roll out of control."

"We'll go slowly, don't worry," Gal reassured.

"Even if I agree, it doesn't mean that my horse will."

"If it doesn't," Perchik said, "then you, Tevye, will go down in history as the man who prevented the Jewish people from re-conquering our land."

Tevye's eyes narrowed. His brow became wrinkled in thought.

"Do you want to be remembered as Tevye, the milkman, or as Tevye, the hero of the Hebrew Brigade?"

Tevye frowned. Years before, the Lord had brought him to a similar crossroad, at the outskirts of Anatevka, on the way to America or to the Holy Land. Then, he had chosen the more uncharted path.

"Where is your faith, Tevye?" Perchik asked.

Tevye stared at his daughter's ex-husband. Wouldn't he have the last laugh if his faith proved greater than Tevye's? Grumbling, Tevye climbed down from the wagon. He walked to his horse, reached into his pocket, and fed him a bribe of some sugar. Then, for good measure, he swallowed a handful of the sweet crystals himself. Fortified, he walked back to the wagon and climbed back inside. Without looking at Perchik, he picked up the reins.

"*Yalla*," he called to his horse.

Obediently, the creature took a careful step forward and began the descent. Gal rode on ahead.

"You work the brakes," Tevye told Perchik. Gently, he eased the horse down the slope. He could feel the weight of the wagon behind them. Slowly, a step at a time, the wagon inched forward. True to his word, the scout was waiting for them, a dozen yards ahead on a much wider ledge.

"If you ask me, the Romans made this trail for their wagons two-thousand years ago during their siege on Jerusalem," Perchik said. "Now, we are using it to take back what is rightfully ours. Isn't history ironic?"

Tevye didn't have time for philosophy. He was praying that the wheels of the wagon wouldn't break under the strain of the bumps and the cumbersome load. The ledge gave way to another treacherous curve around the face of the canyon, and this time Tevye had to get down and lead the horse by his reins. He himself was afraid to gaze down the sheer drop of the cliff. Instead, he gazed back at his horse. Gal grabbed his arm and led him and the horse and the wagon around the bend to a welcomed stretch of sure footing.

"Just another half kilometer and we'll reach the plateau," he assured Tevye, whose legs were trembling as much as the horse's. "After that, there is a gradual slope leading to the ridge overlooking the valley."

At the same time that the wagon was making its laborious way down the Wadi Kelt canyon, the demolition teams were progressing toward the Jordan River at a much faster pace. At least until they reached Jericho. The world's oldest city had become an enclave of Turkish soldiers. Just as the walled city had guarded the land of Canaan from invasion in the time of Moses and Joshua, its broad surrounding valley still controlled the eastern gateway to the country and the road which stretched from Damascus to Jerusalem. To protect this vital trade and military route, the Ottomans had surrounded the area with forts. Turkish soldiers were stationed in the ramparts overlooking the valley, but because British troops were still far to the south, no one suspected that a secret force of Jews would stage a daring nighttime attack. Nonetheless, to be sure that the guards wouldn't see them, the soldiers of the Hebrew Brigade crawled for hours through the sand until they had bypassed the watchtowers and walls of the city. Like crocodiles, they made their way toward the river. Dynamite on their backs, faces and hands covered with sand, they crawled on their bellies until their arms and legs ached. But no one complained. Elisha, Yigal, Moriah, and Zeev were united in the joy of their mission. Munsho and Shilo were happy for the chance to take revenge on the Turks. The thoughts of Nachman and Hevedke were filled with prophecies of the past and visions of the Maccabees and the soldiers of Bar Kochva and Rabbi Akiva. It was the beginning of Hanukah, they remembered, and no one had lit the first holiday light.

To make a long evening short, as Sholom Aleichem would say, Tevye and his wagon load of dynamite reached the Jordan Valley plateau as the first signs of daylight spread through the heavens. Down below, at the foot of the sloping descent, the walls of the ammunition fortress shone in the waning moonlight. Silence hung over the sleeping valley. Not a soul was awake. Just the cries of distant roosters reached the weary resistance brigade on the mountain. But to everyone's surprise, a ravine stretched between the fort and the mountain, and only a narrow bridge connected the two. Without saying a word, everyone realized it would be impossible to release the wagon on the slope and expect it to travel straight across the bridge on its own.

"What the hell is this ravine doing here?" Perchik asked.

"I don't know," the scout said. "It isn't marked on my map."

"Weren't you ever here before?"

"Yes. Less than a week ago. But not as far down the mountain as this. Maybe from my vantage point, or with the morning sun in my eyes, I didn't notice the ravine."

"It can't be done," Tevye said. "If we release the wagon on this side of the slope, it will never keep on a course straight enough to cross over the bridge. Someone will have to go with it."

Everyone kept looking at him. Before Tevye could tell them how crazy they were if they expected him to volunteer for the mission, a tremendous explosion shattered the pre-dawn silence. The roar echoed over the broad desert plain. Gal's horse stood up on its hind legs and neighed. Birds squawked and flew out of their mountainside nests.

"That's one of the bridges," Perchik said. "We have to hurry. The blast is bound to wake up the garrison. Come on! We have to move fast!"

Tevye didn't have time to protest. Perchik grabbed the reins out of his hands.

"Forward!" Perchik commanded, but the horse didn't budge.

"Forward!" he yelled.

Perchik picked up the whip and was in the motion of striking the beast when Tevye reached out and seized his arm.

"What's the matter with this animal?" Perchik barked.

"He doesn't know you," Tevye answered.

He took the reins hack from Perchik and gave them a flick.

"*Yalla,*" he called out.

Immediately, the horse started forward.

"Everyone stay on this side of the bridge and keep us covered!" Perchik commanded as the wagon gained speed. Soon the horse was galloping down the slope of the mountain. The crates of dynamite rumbled in the rear.

"When we cross over the bridge, I'll light the fuse," Perchik shouted. "Keep the wagon on course toward the western wall of the fortress, and when I give the command, you jump!"

The wagon raced forward with a dangerous speed. Tevye knew

that if he tried to hold back the horse, or guide it toward the bridge, the slightest pull to one side or the other could topple the wagon. Sometimes, a horse has to trust his driver, and sometimes a driver has to trust his horse. That's what a partnership was. Perhaps the horse sensed the significance of their mission. Perhaps, like the American cowboy, he wanted to help the Jews. Or maybe, it just wanted another handful of sugar. Whatever its reason, it thundered straight toward the bridge. Back up the mountain, Cassidy hollered out a rodeo cheer and waved his bullet-sprayed hat. The hooves of the horse clattered over the bridge. The planks creaked under the wheels of the wagon. Gunshots rang out from the walls of the awakened garrison.

"*Yalla!*" Tevye yelled, striking the reins.

The fortress loomed up before them. The horse continued to race down the slope. A bump jolted Tevye into the air. A wagon wheel screeched as if it was coming loose from its axle. Perchik turned toward the back of the wagon and reached over to light the fuse. More gunshots rang out around them.

"Jump!" Perchik ordered.

Tevye saw Perchik leap into the air and vanish. Gazing back, he got a glimpse of him rolling in the dirt behind the charging wagon. The fortress was less than a hundred meters away, but how could Tevye jump and let his horse be blown to oblivion? True, a horse was a horse, but hadn't the good Lord commanded a Jew to be kind to all creatures? Many were the times when Tevye had been lost in the woods, or trapped in a snowstorm, and his devoted horse had saved him. And hadn't a mule saved his life in the swamp? Could he repay a lifetime of kindness by letting his horse be blown into smithereens? Certainly not.

Hearing more gunshots around him, Tevye stood up and balanced himself on the front plank of the wagon. Then he leaped forward onto the horse. Landing hard on the animal's back, he slipped and hung dangerously down toward the ground, hanging on to the steed with one arm. With a groan, he hauled himself up and collapsed over the animal's neck.

"*Yalla,*" he said as he struggled to loosen the reins and the harness. Gunshots whistled by him. The horse galloped on. With a final last lunge, the harness came free. As Tevye clutched onto its mane, the animal instinctively veered away from the garrison. The wagon thundered on down the slope.

"Let this be my Hanukah candle," Tevye prayed.

Before he could sit up on the horse and see where they were heading, an explosion shook heaven and earth. The horse went down beneath him. Tevye rolled in the sand. Another explosion roared through the valley. Then another. And another. The earth rumbled. Dirt fell down on Tevye like rain. Another blast exploded in his ears. One after another, crates of ammunition exploded in the garrison until Tevye could only hear ringing in his brain. When he looked up, the fortress was gone, as if the earth had opened its mouth and swallowed it. A few soldiers staggered out of the smoke in torn pajamas and uniforms as if they were drunk. Debris was everywhere. Tevye's horse snorted and rose to its feet. Far in the distance, the echo of an explosion reached the valley like an angry blast of wind.

"Another bridge," Tevye reflected.

He stood up dazed and without any strength in his legs. His horse brushed against him, and Tevye managed to pull himself up onto its back. He lay on his belly, holding on to the animal's ribs. The horse carried him off like a dead man. Perchik was waiting back at the bridge. But he wasn't alone. Three Turkish soldiers on horseback were with him, their rifles aimed at his head.

When Tevye's horse halted, its dazed and exhausted rider slid off to the ground. The fall shook him out of his stupor.

"On your feet, Jew!' a soldier commanded.

Looking around, Tevye realized that their Hanukah luck had run out. Slowly, his back aching, he raised himself to his feet.

"I say we kill them," a soldier said.

"We need to question them first," another replied.

"They won't tell us anything."

"After they are tortured, they will."

"Yoohoo," a singsong voice called out.

It was Cassidy. He stepped out from behind a boulder and

smiled, pausing to give the soldiers time to react, so that he would have a moving target to shoot at. As they all turned with their rifles, the cowboy slid out his pistol and fired three shots from the hip. His first round of fire was aimed at their hands. One after another, their weapons splintered into the air. The next volley of shots was aimed at their hearts. Two of the soldiers slumped over dead, but the third had jumped off of his horse before the cowboy could shoot. The Turk grabbed Perchik and put a pistol to his head. Tevye dove forward and landed a punch to his jaw. With an "oomph," the soldier collapsed to the earth.

"Come on!" Perchik yelled, fleeing over the bridge.

Gunshots sounded behind them. Soldiers on horseback galloped forward, shooting as they rode. Ariel fired his rifle from his perch on the slope. A Turkish horseman fell. Cassidy shot two others off their mounts, but in the return fire, Ariel was hit. Tevye ran for the bridge, but his foot banged against a plank and he tripped. Bullets whizzed over his head. The cavalry of Turkish soldiers blasted the plateau with bullets. Outnumbered, the Jews had to flee up the hill. Cassidy, Perchik, and the scout got away. Ariel was mortally wounded. Tevye was captured alive.

Chapter Forty-Six

THE WALLS OF JERICHO

The sun was rising over the mountains on the eastern shore of the Jordan River as enemy soldiers shoved Tevye into the gate of Turkish headquarters in Jericho. The garrison was an old Ottoman fortress, almost four hundred years old. Sand and clay walls towered over a large inner courtyard. Soldiers still ran around in confusion, stunned by the barrage of explosions which had awoken the Turkish army from a deep, peaceful sleep. Trumpets summoned the unprepared forces to war, as if the British army had already invaded the valley. In the middle of the mayhem, a horseman galloped to and fro in the yard, trying to organize his troops. Tevye recognized him immediately. It was the wicked Jamal Pasha, the Turkish military commander of Palestine, whom Tevye had seen twice before. Once in Shoshana when Pasha had ordered their houses destroyed, and once in Jaffa, when the ruthless Turk had led a pogrom through the city, murdering Jews and expelling hundreds of others from the country.

As soldiers pushed Tevye toward the prison, another explosion sounded in the distance, rumbling the walls of the fort. For seconds, everyone paused.

"Bridge number three," Tevye thought.

Seeing the captured prisoner, the agitated military commander galloped over on his horse.

"Who is this?" he demanded to know.

"One of the Jews who blew up the ammunition base."

"Is that so?" Pasha said. His black eyes flashed. Spurring his horse forward, he raised his riding crop and smashed it down on Tevye's head. Tevye deflected the blow with his arm, but its force knocked him off balance. He fell to the ground and glared up at the monster he had vowed to avenge. If he was killed in return, so what? He was fed up with Russian police commissioners, Cossacks, and Turkish commanders. He was fed up with being down in the dirt while his persecutors rode like kings on their horses. Scooping up a handful of sand, he rose to his feet. Before Pasha could whip him again, he hurled the sand in the eyes of the horse. Blinded, the horse reared up with a roar. Wildly, it stood on its rear legs, throwing off its startled rider. Pasha lost his grip on the reins and tumbled backward toward the earth. His spine cracked in half when he landed. Everyone stood frozen as the angry stallion rose up once again in the air. With a blind rage, it crashed its front feet back down on its rider. Just as Pasha had stampeded others, he was stampeded himself. Measure for measure.

For Tevye, it was sweet satisfaction. At least until he felt a club crash down on his neck. Suddenly, the light of the world was extinguished. Once again, he collapsed to the ground. But his time in this world had not yet expired. When he woke up, the serious face of Nachman was the first thing he saw. Next to him, Hevedke gazed down at him with an equally grave expression. Slowly, his eyes were able to focus. Shilo was with them too. His shirt was drenched with blood from the bullet which had put a hole through his arm.

"Are we dead?" Tevye asked.

"We should be so lucky," the carpenter answered.

"God forbid," Nachman said.

Looking around, Tevye realized that they were in some kind of dungeon. The cell was dark, with a lone opening for air high up in the stone wall near the ceiling.

"How long have we been here?" Tevye asked, feeling the painful bruise on the back of his neck.

"A few hours," Nachman replied.

"What happened to you?" Tevye wanted to know.

Hevedke told Tevye the story. Groups one and two had succeeded in reaching the river and wiring the bridges without being seen. As planned, their explosions had gone off only a short time apart, so that the Turks wouldn't have time to react. The third group had to travel further up north, and to avoid a Turkish patrol, they had to wade through the Jordan River. By the time they reached the target, the first two explosions had alerted the Arabs who were guarding the bridge for the Turks. A battle erupted, and the Jews had to fight. In the exchange, Shilo was shot in the arm. Finally, after a brief round of firing, the Arabs had thrown down their rifles and fled. After all, it wasn't their homeland - why should they risk their lives for the Turks? On the way back, Nachman, Hevedke, and Shilo had been captured. As far as they knew, everyone else had made it safely back to the mountains.

Before Tevye could tell about the success of his mission, the heavy wooden door of the cell swung open. Two Turkish soldiers charged inside and grabbed Tevye.

"May the Almighty be with you," Nachman said.

"And with all of you," Tevye replied, as he was dragged to his feet. "If you see my wife and family again, tell them how happy I was that we succeeded in our mission."

Outside the cell, six more soldiers were waiting. Tevye's hands were tied, and after the Turks took turns spitting at him, they shoved him off down the corridor. Finally, a hand pushed him outside to the yard. Squinting in the brilliant noon sunlight, Tevye's gaze focused on a line of soldiers standing at attention, their rifles held by their sides. But a firing squad wasn't going to be the instrument to send him to Heaven. A crueler death had been chosen. Tevye was going to be hung. Across the courtyard, at the end of the procession of soldiers, a hangman marched up the steps of a gallows and reached out for the noose. A drummer standing on line with the soldiers started a long, solemn drum roll.

Tevye gulped. He felt his neck tighten. Life was a sandglass which was turned upside down the moment a man was born. Some people lived twenty years. Some people lived forty. Others reached eighty. When the sand ran out, the adventure was over.

A soldier walked over leading Tevye's horse.

"Get on it!" he ordered.

Tevye held up his tied hands.

"Get on it you filthy Jew!" the soldier barked, giving Tevye a hard kick in the butt.

The prisoner grimaced. Other soldiers snickered. The drum roll continued to play.

"*Gevalt*," Tevye thought. What could he do? After another shove from the soldier, he threw himself over his horse. His foot found the stirrup, and he swung a leg over the saddle. At least he wouldn't die amongst strangers. Not that a horse could say *Kaddish*. But at least Tevye would be sharing his last moments with a friend. With an effort, he sat up in the saddle and looked at the gate of the fort. If he tried to bolt, the line of Turkish sharpshooters would surely make Swiss cheese out of his back. He had to think up a plan. Maybe God would send a thunderbolt out of the sky. Not that He owed Tevye any more miracles. Apparently, Tevye had used up his share. The Lord gives, and the Lord takes away. Blessed be the name of the Lord.

Then again, Tevye thought, as a soldier led the horse under the gallows, why was a man given a mouth if not to call out in prayer? Hadn't Samson, blinded and robbed of his strength, beseeched the Almighty for one last kindness as the Philistines made a laughingstock out of the Jew?

The hangman slipped the noose over Tevye's head. With a menacing grin, he fastened the knot against Tevye's neck. The heavy cord ripped into his skin. A slap on the rear of his horse, and Tevye's life would be history. Who would tell all of the wonders to Sholom Aleichem so that he could finish writing his stories?

A soldier held up a paper and read out the sentence.

"In the name of the Turkish government, this rebellious Jew is to be hung on the gallows for murder, treason, espionage, and waging war against the Ottoman Empire."

Tevye recalled that even in a situation like this, the Talmud had something to say. Even if a sword was poised on a man's neck, it was forbidden to give in to despair. If it were true about a sword, it was certainly true about a hangman's noose also.

"In the name of His Majesty, the King of the Universe," Tevye hoarsely called out, appealing to a Higher Authority for a last-minute reversal. "And in the name of my forefathers, Abraham, Isaac, and Jacob, I beg you, my King, to annul this decree and rescue me from this gallows, just like You rescued Daniel from the den of the lions."

"The prisoner will remain silent!" the commanding soldier shouted. Snapping his boots together, the soldier raised up his sword. The drum roll suddenly ended. A silence as vast as eternity hung over the courtyard.

"*Shema Yisrael....*" Tevye started to say, sensing that the end was at hand.

At first he heard what sounded like a bugle. Then he heard the blare of a trumpet. But when the elongated blast continued to sound over the walls of the fort, he recognized the blast of a *shofar*! Outside the fortress, a ram's horn was blaring, just as in the days of Joshua and the battle of Jericho!

"*Tekeah*! *Teruah*! *Tekeah!*" the *shofar* called out, like on Rosh HaShanah.

All heads turned toward the mountains.

"The British are coming!" a Turkish soldier yelled out. Panicking, he broke out of rank. Suddenly, the shrill sound of a whistle arched through the air.

BOOM!

The first cannonball hit the south wall of the garrison. It landed with a deafening explosion. Soldiers were blown off of the parapet surrounding the fort. Tevye's horse neighed. Its feet jittered nervously.

"Steady, boy, steady," Tevye whispered, swaying dangerously in the saddle, as the noose cut deeper into his neck.

"The British!" another Turk shouted.

Soldiers broke out of line and fled in all directions. They had no way of knowing that it wasn't the British at all, but rather Elisha's *shofar* and the other soldiers of the Hebrew Brigade. After overrunning a Turkish outpost, they had commandeered a cannon in order to rescue their friends. The second cannonball landed square in the middle of the courtyard. Soldiers were thrown in the air into a swirling cloud of sand and dust. Tevye's horse raised its head and snorted, but, miraculously, it didn't bolt. Just like the mule in the swamp, the faithful creature didn't budge. Tevye didn't know if it stood its ground out of kindness, to repay Tevye for having saved its life in the morning, or because God had pinned down its feet, but the horse didn't budge from under the gallows.

Just as it says in the Book of all Books, the *shofar* blasts blew, and the walls came tumbling down. The next cannonball smashed into the wall of the dungeoun, setting the prisoners free. Dust and smoke filled the courtyard. Soldiers ran for their lives. But suddenly, just as Tevye thought that he might once again see his wife, and his son, and his daughters, his fortune ran out. A cannonball crashed in the yard, just meters away from the gallows. The horse neighed in fright and leaped forward.

"*Oy vay,*" Tevye mumbled in chagrin.

When the smoke cleared, he was dangling in the air, his feet a long way off the ground. The noose sliced into his chin. He felt his spine stretch, and his lungs begin to burst. Then, a figure, like an angel, appeared out of the settling cloud. Caped in a white prayer shawl, he sat poised on a white donkey in the gate of the fort. "*Mashiach,*" Tevye thought.

But it was only Cassidy. He took a slug from a bottle of *Arak* and casually took aim with his rifle. A shot rang out. The bullet whizzed by Tevye's ear without even hitting a thread of the rope.

"Shiiit," Cassidy said.

A dry rattle escaped Tevye's throat. His eyes looked like they were going to pop out of their sockets. With his last ounce of strength, he glanced up to Heaven as if to say, "*Nu?* You may have all the time in the world, but have pity on a *shlimazl* of a milkman."

"Damn!" Cassidy said, cocking his rifle and taking aim once again. "Why don't you move!"

An angel must have carried his words across the wide courtyard, because Tevye remembered that the cowboy needed a target in motion. Desperately, he gave a last kick. The rope swayed a fraction. The rifle shot cracked. The bullet hit the knot of the noose and sliced it in half. Like a sack of potatoes, Tevye crashed to the ground.

Nachman, Hevedke, and Shilo rushed over.

"Tevye! Are you all right?" Nachman shouted, pulling the noose off his neck.

Gently, they lifted Tevye into a sitting position. Cassidy galloped over on the donkey and flipped the bottle of liquor to Hevedke.

"*L'Chaim!*" said the cowboy. "Give the man something to drink."

Gasping, Tevye reached for the bottle. He threw his head back and was about to quench a fiery thirst when he remembered his vow not to drink *shnopps*. His hand froze in midair. Liquor splashed over his face. Once again, he looked up at Heaven.

"This time, it's You who deserves a *L'Chaim*," he said.

With the help of his son-in-laws, Tevye stood up on his feet. Reaching back, he threw the bottle high in the air. It arched upward and upward over the last remaining wall of the fort. The Jews watched it soar toward the sky. Before Cassidy could draw out his pistol and shoot it, the bottle vanished before the cowboy's bewildered eyes. A cloud of smoke, in shape of a giant Hand, seemed to reach out from the sky and snatch the bottle away.

A roar of thunder sounded. Perhaps it was another cannon shot. To Tevye, it sounded like a Heavenly "*L'Chaim!*"

Tevye, Nachman, and Hevedke all heard it, but the cowboy was left squinting disbelievingly into the sun, still searching after the bottle, waiting for it to fall back down from the sky so he could shoot it with his upraised pistol.

By the time Elisha and Perchik came running into the fort, all of the Turkish soldiers had fled from the garrison, just as all Turkish soldiers would soon flee from Jerusalem, and from every other stronghold in *Eretz Yisrael*. British soldiers would replace them, and, as Perchik had prophesied, they would cause the Jews in the Promised Land just as much sorrow as the Turks. But with God's help, just as He had stood by the Children of Israel from the beginning of time, the Jews would find the strength to overcome the new conquerors also.

Tevye gave Elisha a hug. Then the Yemenite let out another long, victorious blast of his *shofar*. Overwhelmed with joy and with gratitude that he was still among the living, Tevye turned to Perchik and gave him a hug too. After all, when all was said and done, though Tevye believed one thing and Perchik believed another, deep down in their hearts they were brothers.

"L'CHAIM!" Tevye shouted. "TO LIFE!"

THE END

Glossary

Abba: father

Alef: the first letter of the Hebrew alphabet

Alef bet: the Hebrew alphabet

Aliyah: immigration to Israel; an ascent

Allah: God

Amidah: the central prayer recited three times a day

Am Yisrael: the Nation of Israel

Am Yisrael Chai!: the Nation of Israel lives!

Apikorsim: heretics, non-believers

Apikorsut: heresy

Ashkenazic: a Jew whose descendants lived in the regions of Russia and Europe

Av: the name of a Hebrew month, associated with mourning over the Temple's destruction

Baal hesed: a doer of good deeds

Baal tshuva: a penitent, someone who returns to religious practice

Bar-mitzvah: the time at age thirteen when a Jewish boy becomes obligated to observe the commandments

Baruch haba: an expression of welcome; may your coming be blessing

Baruch Hashem: thank God

Beit HaMikdash: the Jerusalem Temple

Beit Knesset: a synagogue

Blee ayin hara: a wish that the "evil eye" should not bring a curse

Boobeh miseh: a tall tale; a foolish notion

Brit: a covenant; the Covenant between God and the Jewish People; a circumcision

Brit milah: circumcision

B'vakasha: if you please

Challah or challis: Sabbath loaves
Chametz: leavened bread forbidden on Passover
Chassan or chattan: a groom
Chas veshalom: God forbid!
Chevra Kadesha: Jewish burial society
Chol HaMoed: the intermediary days of a week-long Jewish
    holiday
Chulent: a meal of meat, potatoes, and beans eaten on the Sabbath
Chumash: the Five Books of Moses; the Bible
Chuppah: a wedding canopy
Chutzpah: brazenness
Claf: parchment from the hide of a kosher animal
Chalutzim: pioneers
Chan: an animal shed
Daven: to pray
Dai: enough!
Dlatt: a pumpkin
Dos, dosim: an Orthodox Jew
Dunam: a measure of land area, roughly half an acre
Dybbuk: a departed soul which returns to possess a person
Ema: mother
Eretz Yisrael: the Land of Israel
Ess: eat
Farblondjet: mixed up, lost
Farchadat: confused
Fatumult: upside down; disordered
Forshbite: an appetizer
Frum: religiously observant
Frummer menschen: an observant Jew
Frummer Yidden: observant Jews
Galut: exile from the Land of Israel; the Diaspora
Gan Eden: the Garden of Eden; Paradise
Gaon: a genius; the famous Rabbi Eliahu of Vilna, known as
    "HaGra"
Gehenna, gehinom: Hell
Ger: a convert

Get: document of divorce
Gevalt: an exclamation of astonishment or trouble
Golem: a monster in human form
Gonif: a thief
Gottenu: O my God!
Goy, goyim: a gentile, gentiles
Habok: Turkish regional administrator
Habyta: homeward
Haimisher: regular, down-to-earth
Halacha: Jewish law
Haleviy: if only it would be
Hallel: a prayer of praise and thanks to the Almighty
Hamotzei: the blessing over eating bread
Hamsin: a hot, dry desert wind
Hashem: God
Hasid, Hasidim: a righteous Jew; a sect of religious Jews
Hazan: the leader of congregational prayer
Hazzer, hazzerim: swine
Hazzer fresser: a ham eater
Heder: a religious school for young Jewish boys
Hevruta: study partner
Histadrut: workers union
Hora: an Israeli dance
Kaddish: the mourner's prayer
Kallah: bride
Kaporas: an atonement, sometimes said over something lost
Kashered: made kosher according to Jewish law
Kashrut: Jewish dietary laws
Kefiah: Arab bandana
Ketubah: a wedding contract
Kiddush: the Sabbath and holiday blessing recited over wine
Kiddush Hashem: the sanctification of God
Kibbitz: to talk a lot, to gossip
Kibitzer, kibitzing: a gossiper, gossiping
Kibbutznik: member of a communal settlement known as a
    kibbutz

Kinderlach: little children
Kippah: a skullcap
Kittel: a white gown
K'nocker: a big shot
Kohen: a member of the priestly class
Kohen HaGadol: the High Jewish Priest
Kopel: a Russian coin, 1/100 of a ruble
Kosher: religiously permitted; clean
Kotel: the Western Wall, the Wailing Wall in Jerusalem
Kvelling: great pride and enjoyment
Kvetch, kvetching: a complainer, complaints
Jarad: locusts
Landsman: a Jew; more specifically, a Jew from the same country
Lashon hara: speaking derogatorily about someone
L'Chaim!: to life!
Leviim: members of the tribe of Levi who served in the Temple
    and who did not have land of their own
L'havdil: to differentiate; usually between something holy and
    non-holy
L'hitraot: see you again
L'shame matzat mitzvah: the intent to bake matzot for Passover
Maaser: tithes separated from agricultural produce
Machiah: revitalizing, life giving; a great pleasure
Mama: mother
Mamzer: a bastard; a rascal
Manna: the wafer-like bread which was miraculously supplied to
    the Children of Israel in the wilderness
Mashiach: the Jewish savior and messianic king
Matzah: unleavened bread
Mavin: an expert
Mazel: fortune
Mazal tov: congratulations; literally, a good constellation
Mekach ta'ut: a transaction based on false information
Megilla: a scroll; a story; a long involved tale
Melamed: a teacher
Menorah: candelabrum

Mench: a responsible person

Meshugas: craziness

Meshugennah: a crazy person or act

Metsiah: a bargain

Mezuzah: verses of Torah inscribed on parchment and attached to a doorpost

Mikvah: a ritual purifying bath for immersion

Mincha: the afternoon prayer

Minyan: the ten men needed for congregational prayer

Mishegoss: craziness

Mishmash: a mix-up of things

Mitzvah, mitzvot: a religious commandment; a good deed

Mohel: the man who circumcises a baby

Moloch: an idol demanding human sacrifice

Motzei Shabbos: the evening upon the conclusion of the Sabbath

Muksah: an object forbidden to be carried or used on the Sabbath

Muktar: Arab leader

Narrishkeit: nonsense

Nebick: an inconsequential person; a loser

Nediv: benefactor

Nudnik: a bothersome person

Nu?: an impatient expression meaning, "What now?" or "Hurry up," or "Do something already!"

Orlah: the fruit of trees from the first years of their growth

Oy vay!: uh oh! here comes trouble!

Pakid: a clerk

Pekuach nefesh: a matter of saving life; self-sacrifice

Pesach: the holiday of Passover

Peyes: side curls, side locks

Pitseleh: a little thing

Purim: a Jewish holiday when people wear costumes

Rachmonis: an appeal for mercy

Rashi: a famous Bible commentator

Rav: rabbi

Reb: mister

Rebbe: a Hasidic rabbi, usually the head of a Hasidic sect

Rebbetzin: a rabbi's wife

Ribono Shel Olam: the Master of the World

Rosh Hashana: the Jewish New Year

Rugelach: a small pastry

Saba: grandfather

Sabaloot: hauling cargo

Sabra: an Israeli; a cactus thorny on the outside and sweet on the inside

Sandak: the person honored with holding the baby at a circumcision

Savlanut: patience

Schlemiel: a bumbler, a good for nothing

Sechel: intelligence

Seder: the Passover holiday recital and meal

Sefer Torah: Torah scroll

Sephardi: a Jew whose descendents came from Spain or the surrounding Mediterranean and North African countries

Shabbati Tzvi: a false messiah

Shabbos: the Sabbath

Shaliach tzibor: the prayer leader

Shalom: hello, goodbye, and peace

Shalom alechem: a greeting meaning "Peace to you"; also the writer, Shalom Aleichem, author of the original "Tevye the Milkman" stories.

Shanda: a scandal

Shavuos: the holiday commemorating the giving of the Torah on Mount Sinai

Shechyanu: a prayer of thanks for having reached a happy time

Shema: the fundamental Jewish prayer declaring the Oneness of God

Shidduch: a marriage match; a date

Shikor: drunk

Shiva: a seven-day period of mourning

Shlepp: to carry, to lug

Shlimazl: an inept person, a loser

Shmatta: a piece of cloth; a rag; a simple dress; an exhausted condition

Shmo: a dope

Shmuck: a fool

Shnopps: hard liquor

Shnorring: collecting for charity

Shnooze: sleep

Shnoz: nose

Shochat: ritual slaughterer

Shomer: a guard; the name of the first armed Jewish defense organization in Israel.

Shtetl: a Jewish village in Russia and Eastern Europe

Shtreimel: a costly fur hat

Shul: synagogue

Shvitzer: a braggart

Siddur: prayerbook

Simcha: joy

Sukkot, sukkos: the Festival of Booths; also the booths themselves

Talmid chocham: a Torah scholar

Talmud Torah: the study of Torah; a Jewish grade school where Torah is studied

Tanna: a Mishnaic sage

Tateleh: young child

Tata: grandfather

Tefillin: religious phylacteries worn on the arm and head

Tehillim: Psalms

Tisha B'Av: the day on which the ancient Jerusalem Temple was destroyed

Tochis: rear end

Tovel: the immersion in a mikvah

Trumah: a portion of agricultural produce set aside for the priestly class

Tsatske: a plaything, toy

Tzaddik: a very righteous person

Tzitzit: the ritual fringes worn on a four-cornered garment

Tzuris: aggravation, trouble

Ulpan: a class where Hebrew is learned
Vance: an energetic and mischievous child
Vayzmeer: an expression of worry
Vilda chaya: a wild animal
Yaka: the Jewish Colony Association
Yarmulkah: skullcap
Yerushalayim: Jerusalem
Yeshiva bocher: a yeshiva student
Yid: Jew
Yiddishkeit: Judaism, Jewishness
Yishuv: settlement; also use to describe the entire Jewish
    community in the Land of Israel
Yom Kippur: the Day of Atonement
Zaida: grandfather
Zohar: the fundamental treatise of Kabbalah

ABOUT THE AUTHOR

Former Hollywood screenwriter, Tzvi Fishman, was awarded Israel's Ministry of Education prize for Creativity and Jewish Culture for his novel *Tevye in the Promised Land*. Other original and off-beat novels on a wide range of Jewish themes include: *Dad*, *The Discman and the Guru*, *Fallen Angel*, and *Heaven's Door*. He also has co-written four commentaries on the writings of Rabbi Kook with Rabbi David Samson. Other writings appear on his popular blog, "Hollywood to the Holy Land," at www.IsraelNationalNews.com.

Made in the USA
San Bernardino, CA
05 March 2013